'A lovely, fat, c[illegible]ge of a book, packed with suspense and romance . . . A thrilling adventure and a truly epic love story' *The Times*

'The much-anticipated third part of Kate Mosse's Languedoc trilogy is finally here . . . This action-packed epic contains everything we've come to expect – mystery, adventure and long-buried secrets just waiting to be uncovered'

Good Housekeeping

'A breathtaking tale of daring and sacrifice that makes a triumphant finale to Mosse's Languedoc trilogy'

Woman & Home

'Kate Mosse has firmly established herself as the go-to girl for blockbuster time-slip romantic adventure . . . a proper adventure story, engrossing and packed with suspense at every turn of the page' *Metro*

'Mosse has a masterly feel for time and place . . . A remarkable achievement' *Daily Express*

'*Citadel* is a deeply satisfying literary adventure, brimming with all the romance, treachery and cliffhangers . . . steeped in a passion for the region, its history and legends, and that magical shadow world where the two meet' *Observer*

'Thrilling conclusion to her Languedoc Trilogy . . . A mix of Girl's Own adventure and wrenching war history'

Sunday Times

'Mosse's descriptions of the majestic stone ruins of Carcassonne and the idyllic landscape around it shimmer with authenticity' *Independent on Sunday*

'Full of action, roman[illegible]y, so it cracks along at a [illegible]nd easy read' *Emer[illegible]*

By Kate Mosse

Fiction

THE LANGUEDOC TRILOGY

Labyrinth

Sepulchre

Citadel

OTHER FICTION

Eskimo Kissing

Crucifix Lane

The Winter Ghosts

The Mistletoe Bride & Other Haunting Tales

The Taxidermist's Daughter

Non-Fiction

Becoming a Mother

The House: Behind the Scenes at the Royal Opera House, Covent Garden

Chichester Festival Theatre at Fifty

Plays

Syrinx

Endpapers

Dodger

Kate Mosse is the author of three works of non-fiction, three plays and seven novels, including the number one multi-million international bestselling Languedoc Trilogy – *Labyrinth*, *Sepulchre* and *Citadel* which was published to outstanding reviews and sold in more than 40 countries throughout the world in 38 languages. As well as historical fiction, Kate also writes ghost stories including *The Winter Ghosts* - also a number one bestseller - *The Mistletoe Bride & Other Haunting Tales*, confirming her position as one of our most captivating story-tellers. In recognition of her services to literature, Kate was awarded an OBE in the Queen's Birthday Honours List in June 2013. To find out more visit www.katemosse.co.uk

CITADEL

Kate Mosse

An Orion paperback

First published in Great Britain in 2012
by Orion
This paperback edition published in 2014
by Orion Books,
an imprint of The Orion Publishing Group Ltd,
Carmelite House, 50 Victoria Embankment,
London EC4Y 0DZ

An Hachette UK company

3 5 7 9 10 8 6 4 2

A CIP catalogue record for this book is available from the British Library.

ISBN 978-1-4091-5315-3

Typeset by Input Data Services Ltd, Bridgwater, Somerset

Printed and bound in Great Britain by Clays Ltd, St Ives plc

The Orion Publishing Group's policy is to use papers that are natural, renewable and recyclable products and made from wood grown in sustainable forests. The logging and manufacturing processes are expected to conform to the environmental regulations of the country of origin.

www.orionbooks.co.uk

We are, I am, you are
by cowardice or courage
the ones who find our way
back to this scene
carrying a knife, a camera
a book of myths
in which
our names do not appear.

---

from *Diving into the Wreck*
ADRIENNE RICH (1973)

In memory of the two unknown women
murdered at Baudrigues
19 August 1944

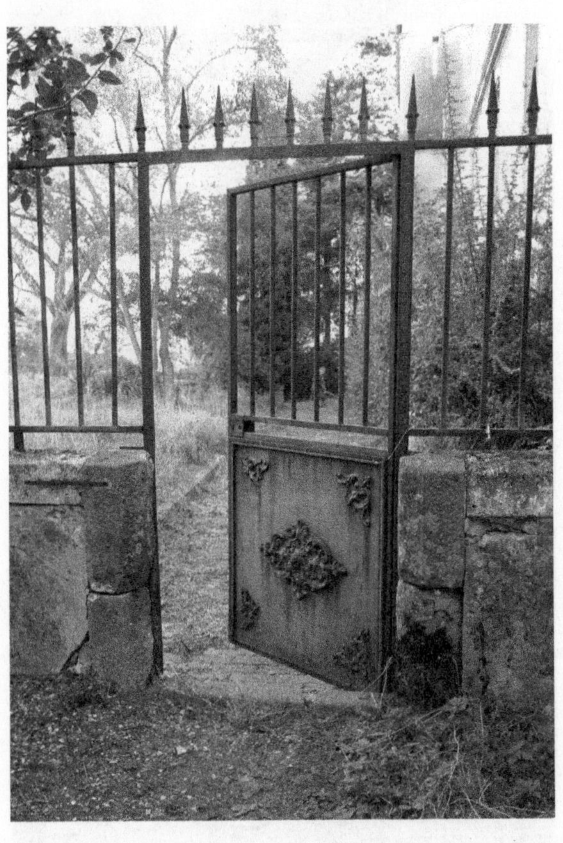

LA VILLE DE CARCASSONNE
A LA MÉMOIRE
DES VICTIMES
DE LA BARBARIE NAZIE
DES ATROCITES NAZIES
TOMBES LE 20 AOUT
CHASSAING
FOURNES
FAGES
JASSIN
JUSTO
GELIS
MAZZER
REY
PRADELLES J.
QUINTIN
VIZCARRA

Note for the 2014 Edition

Citadel is a work of fiction, although the imaginary characters exist against a backdrop of real events. It was inspired by a plaque in the village of Roullens, outside Carcassonne, commemorating the 'Martyrs of Baudrigues', the nineteen prisoners who were executed by fleeing Nazi forces on 19th August 1944, a matter of days before the Languedoc was liberated by its own people. Over time, most of the victims have been identified. There are three commemorative stones at Baudrigues: one apiece for the two leading members of the Aude resistance – Jean Bringer ('Myriel') and Aimé Raymond – and one listing the names of the others who died that day, including two 'unknown women'. Wondering about who they might have been was the starting point for this novel. 2014 is the seventieth anniversary of their deaths. It is to those brave – as yet, still unidentified – women that *Citadel* is dedicated.

Kate Mosse
January 2014

LA VILLE DE CARCASSONNE
A LA MÉMOIRE
DES VICTIMES
DE LA BARBARIE NAZIE
20 AOUT 1944

TOULOUSE
TOLOSA
LE VERNET
LANGU
SEPTIM
River Ariège
FOIX
MONTSÉGUR
Pic de Vicdessos
TARASCON
TARASCO
LOS SERES
SPAIN
HISPANIA

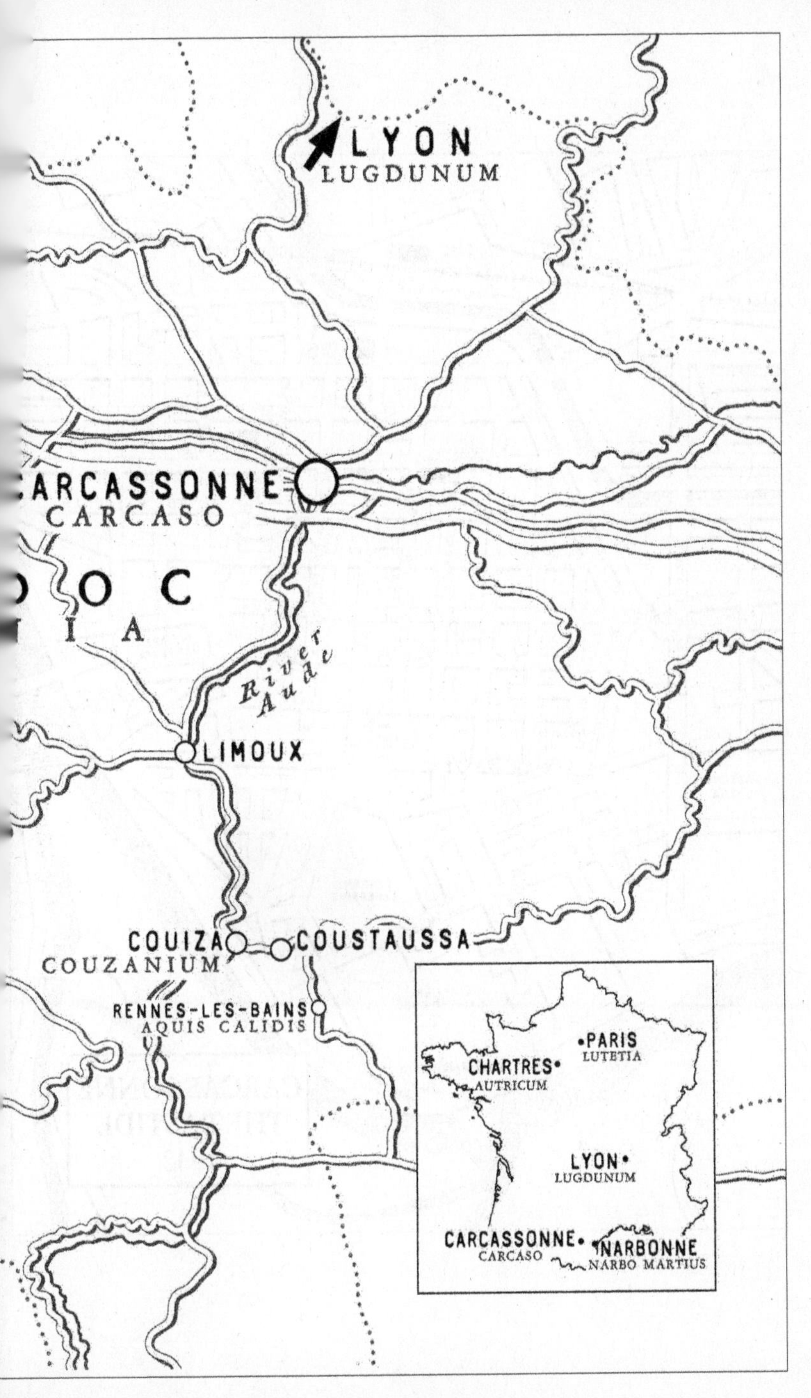
LYON
LUGDUNUM
CARCASSONNE
CARCASO
OC
IA
River Aude
LIMOUX
COUIZA
COUZANIUM
COUSTAUSSA
RENNES-LES-BAINS
AQUIS CALIDIS
PARIS
LUTETIA
CHARTRES
AUTRICUM
LYON
LUGDUNUM
CARCASSONNE
CARCASO
NARBONNE
NARBO MARTIUS

GARE
QUAI RIQUET
PONT MARENGO
CANAL DU MIDI
HÔTEL TERMINUS
BOULEVARD MARÉCHAL PÉTAIN
RUE DU PALAIS
PALAIS DE JUSTICE
CATHÉDRALE SAINT-VINCENT
RUE GEORGES CLEMENCEAU
RUE DE LA PRÉFECTURE
RUE MAZAGRAN
RUE DU MARCHÉ
RUE DU PORT
RUE DE L'AIGLE D'OR
PLACE CARNOT
ALLÉE D'IÉNA
PLACE DAVILLA
RUE DE VERDUN
SQUARE GAMBETTA
RUE DE LA MAIRIE
RUE DES CALQUIÈRES
RUE VOLTAIRE
JARDIN DU CALVAIRE
CATHÉDRALE SAINT-MICHEL
PONT VIEUX
BOULEVARD BARBÈS
CASERNE D'IÉNA
CASERNE LAPERRINE
RUE DU 24 FÉVRIER
CIMETIÈRE SAINT-MICHEL
RIVER AUDE
CAFÉ PAÏCHÉROU
CARCASSONNE
THE BASTIDE
1942

Contents

Principal Characters

THE 'CITADEL' NETWORK

Sandrine Vidal
Marianne Vidal
Lucie Ménard
Liesl Blum
Suzanne Peyre
Geneviève Saint-Loup
Eloise Saint-Loup

IN CARCASSONNE

Raoul Pelletier
Robert Bonnet
Leo Authié
Sylvère Laval
Marieta Barthès
Jeanne Giraud
Max Blum

IN THE HAUTE VALLÉE

Audric Baillard
Achille Pujol
Erik Bauer
Yves Rousset
Guillaume Breillac

PROLOGUE

August 1944

Coustaussa
19 August 1944

She sees the bodies first. On the outskirts of the village, a pair of man's boots and a woman's bare feet, the toes pointing down to the ground like a dancer. The corpses twist slowly round and around in the fierce August sun. The soles of the woman's feet are black, from dirt or swollen in the heat, it's hard to tell at this distance. Around them, flies cluster and swarm, argue, feed.

The woman known as Sophie swallows hard, but she does not flinch and she does not look away, returning to them a kind of dignity stolen by the manner of their death. She can't risk going closer – it might be a trap, it looks like a trap – but from her hiding place in the undergrowth that marks the junction with the old road to Cassaignes, Sophie can see the victims' arms are tied behind their backs with rough farm rope. The man's hands are balled into fists, as if he died fighting. He has blue canvas trousers – a farmer or a refugee, not a partisan. The skirt of the woman's dress lifts lightly in the breeze, a repeat pattern of lilac cornflowers on a pale yellow background. Sophie shields her eyes and follows the line of the rope, up through the dark green leaves of the old holm oak, to the branch that serves as the gibbet. Both victims are hooded, coarse brown hessian sacking, jerked tight by the noose and the drop.

She does not think she knows them, but she says a prayer all the same, to mark the moment of their passing. For the ritual of it, not out of faith. The myth of Christianity means nothing to her. She has witnessed too much to believe in such a God, such beautiful stories.

Every death remembered.

Sophie takes a deep breath, pushing away the thought

that she's too late, that the killing has already started. Crouched, she half runs, half crawls, hidden by the low, long wall that runs along the track down towards the village. She knows there's a gap of fifteen feet, maybe twenty, between the end of the wall and the first outbuildings of the old Andrieu farm. No cover, no shade. If they are waiting, watching from the blackened windows of the house beside the abandoned cemetery, this exposed patch of land is where the bullet will find her.

But there's no sniper, no one. She reaches the last of the *capitelles*, the ancient stone shelters that cluster in the hills to the north of Coustaussa, and slips inside. For some time, they used them to store weapons. Empty now.

From here, Sophie has a clear view of the village below, the magnificent ruins of the castle to the west. She can see that there's blood on the whitewashed wall of the Andrieu house, a starburst of red, like paint splattered from a brush. Two distinct centres, blurred together at the edges, already turning to rust in the harsh afternoon sun. Sophie stiffens, though part of her hopes this means the man and woman were shot first. Hanging is the cruellest death, a slow way to die, degrading, and she's seen this double execution before, once in Quillan, once in Mosset. Punishment and warning, the corpses left to the crows as on a medieval gallows.

Then she notices smudged tracks in the dirt at the base of the wall where bodies were dragged, and tyre marks that head down towards the village, not towards the holm oak, and fears this means two more victims.

At least four dead.

She suspects everyone has been taken to the Place de la Mairie while the soldiers search the farms and houses. Brown shirts or black, their methods are the same. Looking for deserters, for maquisards, for weapons.

For her.

Sophie scans the ground, looking for the glint of metal. If she can identify the casings, she can identify the gun and it might tell her who fired the shots. Gestapo or Milice, even one of her own. But she's too far away and it looks as if the killers have been careful to leave no evidence.

For a moment she allows herself to sit back on her heels in the welcome shade, propped against the *capitelle*. Her heart is turning over, over in her chest, like the engine of an old car reluctant to start. Her arms are a patchwork of scratches and cuts from the gorse and hawthorn of the woods, dry and spiteful sharp after weeks of no rain, and her shirt is torn, revealing suntanned skin and the distinctive scar on her shoulder. The shape of the Cross of Lorraine, Raoul said. She keeps it covered. That mark alone is enough to identify her.

Sophie has cut her hair, taken to wearing slacks but, thin as she is, she still looks like a woman. She glances down at the boots on her feet, men's boots held together with string and stuffed at the heel with newspaper for a less awkward fit, and remembers the cherry-red shoes with the little black heels she wore when she and Raoul danced at Païchérou. She wonders what's happened to them, if they're still in the wardrobe in the house in the rue du Palais or if someone has taken them. Not that it matters. She has no use for such luxuries now.

She doesn't want to remember, but an image slips into her mind of her own upturned face on the corner of the rue Mazagran, two years ago, looking up into the eyes of a boy she knew would love her. Then later that same summer, in her father's study here in Coustaussa, and being told the truth of things.

'And there shall come forth the armies of the air, the spirits of the air.'

Sophie blinks the memories away. She risks another look, peering out from the cover of the *capitelle* down to the cluster of houses and then up to the Camp Grand and the garrigue to the north. Having warned the villagers of the imminent attack, Marianne and Lucie have taken up position to the west, while Suzanne and Liesl will launch the main assault from the ruins of the castle. There's no sign of anyone yet. As for the others promised, she does not know if they will come.

'And the number was ten thousand times ten thousand.'

The beating silence hangs heavy over the waiting land. The air itself seems to vibrate and shimmer and pulse. The heat, the cicadas, the sway of the wild lavender and shock-yellow genet among the thistles, the whispering wind of the Tramontana in the garrigue.

For a moment, Sophie imagines herself back in the safe past. Before she was Sophie. She wraps her arms around her knees, acknowledging how appropriate it is that things should end here, back where it all began. That the girl she was, and the woman she has become, should make their final stand here together, shoulder to shoulder. The story has come full circle.

For it was here, in the narrow streets between the houses and the church and the ruins of the castle, she played *trapette* with the children of the Spanish refugees. It was here, in a green dusk heady with the scent of thyme and purple rosemary, she first kissed a boy. One of the Rousset brothers, fidgety in case his gran'mère should look out the window and catch him. An awkward meeting of teeth is what Sophie remembers. That, and the sense of doing something dark and illicit and adult. She closes her eyes. Yves Rousset, or was it Pierre? She supposes it doesn't matter now. But it is Raoul's face she sees in her mind's eye, not the blunt features of a boy long dead.

Everything is so still, so quiet. Today, the swifts do not swoop and mass and spiral in the endless blue sky. The linnets do not sing. They know what is to come, they sense it too, in the same way, this past week, each of the women has felt the tension in the tips of her fingers, crawling over the surface of her skin.

Eloise was the first to be caught, five days ago, at the Hôtel Moderne et Pigeon in Limoux. Four days later, Geneviève was arrested in Couiza. The details of the *boîte aux lettres*, the fact that Sous-chef Schiffner was there himself, in person, left Sophie in no doubt the network had been betrayed. From that moment, she knew it was only a matter of hours, days at most. The spider's web of connections that led south from Carcassonne to these hills, this river valley of the Salz, these ruins.

She tries not to think about her friends incarcerated in the Caserne Laperrine on the boulevard Barbès, or within the grey walls of the Gestapo headquarters on the route de Toulouse, fearing what they will suffer. She knows how long the nights can be in those dark, confined cells, dreading the pale light of dawn, the rattle of the key in the opening door. She's drowned in choking, black water, submitted to the violent touch of hands on her throat, between her thighs. She's heard the seductive whisper of surrender and knows how hard it is to resist.

Sophie rests her head on her arms. She's so tired, so sick of it. And though she fears what is to come, more than anything now she wants it to be over.

'Come forth the armies of the air.'

A burst of machine-gun fire from the hills, and the answering staccato chatter of an automatic weapon closer to hand. Sophie's thoughts shatter, like fragments of bright glass. Already she's up on her feet, pulling her Walther P38 from her belt, greasy with goose fat to stop the springs jamming. The weight of it in her hand is reassuring, familiar.

Breaking cover, she runs, low and fast, until she's reached the edge of the Sauzède property. Once there were chickens and geese, but the animals are long gone and the door to the enclosure hangs open on a broken hinge.

Sophie vaults the low wall, landing on the remains of straw and uneven earth, then on to the next garden, zigzagging from one square of land to the next. She enters the village from the east, slipping through the unkempt cemetery, its gravestones like rotten teeth loose in the dry land. Crossing the rue de la Condamine, she darts into the tiny alleyway that runs narrow and steep and sheer along the side of the round tower and down, until she has a clear view of the Place de la Mairie.

As she'd suspected, the whole village has been brought there, beneath the burning sun. There is a Feldgendarmerie truck at right angles across the rue de la Mairie and a black Citroën Traction Avant, a Gestapo car, blocking the rue de l'Empereur, penning the villagers in. Women and children are lined up on the west side by the war memorial, the old men to the south of the small square. Sophie allows herself a grim smile. The configuration suggests they expect the attack to come from the hills, which is good. Then she sees a ribbon of red blood and the body of a young man lying on his back on the dusty ground, and her expression hardens. His right hand twitches and jerks, like a marionette on a frayed string, then falls back to his side.

Five dead.

Sophie can't see who's in charge – the line of grey jackets and black boots, the field greens of the ordinary soldiers, blocks her view – but she hears the order, given in French, that nobody else should move. Equipment is scarce, but these men are well armed, unusually so. Grenades at the waist, bandoliers slung over shoulders, glinting in the sun like chain mail, some with M40 sub-machine guns, the majority with Kar-98 semi-automatic rifles.

The hostages are caught between courage and common sense. They want to resist, to act, to do something, anything. But they've been told not to jeopardise the mission,

and besides, they're paralysed by the realit
dered boy on the ground in front of them
mother, his sister – is sobbing.

'*C'est fini?*'

Sophie can't breathe. She is seeing ev
everything, but can no longer take it in.

That voice.

The one person she'd hoped never to see again. The one voice she'd prayed never to hear again.

But you knew he would come. It's what you wanted.

The rattle of a machine gun fired from the ruins of the castle snaps Sophie back to the present. Taken by surprise, one of the soldiers jerks round and returns random fire. He's no more than a boy either. A woman screams and pulls her children to her, trying to shield them. Jacques Cassou, a Pétainist, though a good man at heart, breaks away from the group. Sophie can see what's going to happen, but she's powerless to stop it. She wills him to wait just a moment more, not to draw attention to himself, but panic has taken hold. He tries to run to the safety of the rue de la Condamine, forcing his tired, swollen legs to carry him away from the horror, but he's an easy target. Sophie can only watch as the Schmeissers tear into the old man, the force of the assault spinning him round. His daughter Ernestine, a lumpen, bitter woman, runs forward and tries to catch him. But she is too slow, he is too heavy. Jacques staggers, drops to his knees. The soldiers keep firing. This second hail of bullets brings them both down.

Six dead. Seven.

The world breaks apart. The signal has not been given, but, hearing the guns, Marianne and Lucie launch the first of the smoke-signal canisters from the Camp Grand. It soars over the houses and lands at the edge of the square by the truck, disgorging a stream of green smoke. Another canister pops, then another and another, releasing plumes

..e and pink and orange and yellow into the stifling The soldiers are disorientated, cross-firing into one ..other's positions. They, too, are on edge, Sophie realises. Whatever they've been told about this operation, they know something doesn't add up. It is no ordinary raid.

'Halten Sie! Halten!'

The Kommandant shouts the order to hold fire, then repeats it in French. Discipline is restored immediately, but the hiatus is long enough for the hostages to scatter, as Marianne had told them to do, heading for refuge in the church, in the shaded undergrowth below the chemin de la Fontaine, the cellars of the presbytery.

Sophie does not move.

Now that the square is clear of civilians, Suzanne and Liesl launch the main assault from the ruins of the castle and the deep undergrowth that lines the rue de la Mairie. Bullets rake the ground. A grenade explodes instantly on impact with the war memorial.

Another order from the Kommandant, and the Gestapo unit divides into two. Some target the contingent in the hills, firing indiscriminately as they storm along the rue de la Condamine and out into the garrigue. The remainder turn towards the castle. Through the coloured smoke and the dust, Sophie glimpses the blue berets of the French Milice vanishing into the rue de la Peur and realises, with a sickened heart, that they do not mean to leave any witnesses alive.

She knows that she is outnumbered, at least seven to one, but she has no choice now but to show herself. Besides, she can see him, in plain clothes, standing with his right hand resting on the black bonnet of the car and his Mauser hanging loose in his left. He looks calm, disengaged, as the firefight rages around him.

Sophie drops the hammer on her pistol and steps out into the light.

'Let them go.'

Does she say the words out loud or only in her head? Her voice seems to be coming from a long way away, distorted, a whispering beneath stormy waters.

'It's me you want, not them. Let them go.'

It's not possible that he should hear her, and yet, despite the noise and the shouting and the ack-ack of the machine guns, he does. He hears her and he turns, looking straight to the north-east corner of the Place de la Mairie where she has positioned herself. Those eyes. Is he smiling, she wonders, or does it pain him that it should be ending like this? She can't tell.

Then he says her name. Her real name. The soft music of it hangs suspended in the air between them. Threat or entreaty, she doesn't know, but she feels her resolve weaken.

He says it again and, this time, it sounds bitter, false in his mouth. A betrayal. The spell is broken.

The woman known as Sophie lifts her arm. And shoots.

PART I

The First Summer
July 1942

Codex I

GAUL
THE CARSAC PLAINS
JULY AD 342

The young monk looked across the river and saw the outline of the town ahead on the hill on the far side. A fortified castellum, the low walls sharply defined in the shimmering light of dawn. A crown of stone set on the green plains of Carsac. The slopes surrounding the settlement were abundant, rich, fertile. Row after row of vines, spread out like a peacock's tail. Silver olive trees and heavy purple figs ripening on the bough, almond trees.

In the east, the white sun was rising in a pale blue sky. Arinius drew closer to the water's edge. A low mist floated above the silver surface of the river Atax. To his right, wooded glades of elder and ash. The reed beds shifting, swaying, in the breeze. The distinctive silhouette of angelica, with its hollow-fluted stems standing like soldiers to attention, the leaves as big as his hand. The familiar bell-shaped pink flowers of knitbone. The splash of fish and snakes, water boatmen skimming their silent way across the mirrored surface.

For week after week, one month, two months, the young monk had walked and walked and walked. Following the sweep and flow of the great Rhodanus from Lugdunum, south towards the sea. Rising before matins each day, with the memory of the gentle murmur of his brothers' voices in his head, he voyaged on alone. In the heat of the day, between the hours of sext and nones, sheltering from the sun in the dense green woods or shepherds' huts. In the late afternoon, as the first stirrings of vespers echoed from the chapel in the community, he would rise again and fare forward. The Liturgy of the Hours marking the progress of the days and nights. A slow and steady progress from north to south, from east to west.

Arinius didn't know precisely how long he had been travelling, only that the seasons were changing, spring slipping softly into early summer. The colours of April and May, white blossom and yellow broom and pink phlox, yielding to the gold of June and July. The green vineyards of the Gallia Narbonensis and the sweep of barley in the fields. The driving wind whipping over the austere salt flats and the blue of the gulf of the Sinus Gallicus. That stretch of the journey followed the Via Domitia, the Roman wine route, along roads of tolls and taxes. It had been simple for him to blend in with the merchants and traders heading for Hispania.

Arinius coughed and pulled the grey hooded cloak tight around his narrow frame, though it was far from cold. The cough was worse again, leaving his throat raw. Bunching the material at his neck, he re-pinned his brooch. A bronze fibula, in the shape of a cross, with tiny white enamel oak leaves decorating each of the four arms and a green leaf in the centre. It was the only personal possession Arinius had been unable, unwilling, to give up on entering the community. A gift from his mother, Servilia, the day the soldiers came.

He looked across the Atax to the walls of the town and gave thanks to God for his safe deliverance. He had heard that here, men of all faiths and creeds were given sanctuary. That here, Gnostics and Christians and those who adhered still to the older religions lived side by side. That this was a place of safety and refuge for any and all who would come.

Arinius put his hand to his chest, needing to feel the familiar single loose leaf of papyrus beneath his tunic. He thought of his fellow brothers in Christ, each of them also smuggling a copy of a condemned text away from the community. They had parted company at Massilia, where it was said Mary Magdalene and Joseph of Arimathea had first come ashore to preach the word of God. From there Arinius and his brothers set sail for Smyrna in Asia Minor. From there, one was bound for the Holy City of Jerusalem and the plains of Sephal, another for Memphis, the last for Thebes in Upper Egypt. Arinius would never know if their efforts had been successful, any more than they would hear of his. Each was destined – burdened – to complete his mission alone.

Arinius considered himself an obedient and willing servant of God. He was not a particularly brave man, nor a lettered one, but he had found strength in his conviction that the holy writings should not be destroyed. He could not watch the words of Mary Magdalene and Thomas and Peter and Judas burning. Arinius still remembered the crack of the flames licking the air, red and white and gold, as the precious writings were consigned to the pyre. Papyrus and vellum, the quires and scrolls, the blister of Greek and Hebrew and Coptic turned to black ash. The smell of reed and water and glue and wax filling the stone courtyard of the community in the capital of Gaul that had been his home.

The papyrus shifted beneath his tunic, like a second skin. Arinius did not understand the text; he could not read the Coptic script, and besides, the letters were smudged, cracked. All he understood was that it was said the power contained within the seven verses of this, the shortest of the Codices, was absolute. As great as anything in the ancient writings of Exodus or Enoch, of Daniel or Ezekiel. More significant than all the knowledge contained within the walls of the great libraries of Alexandria and Pergamum.

Arinius had heard some of the lines spoken aloud by a fellow brother, and never forgotten them. An incantation, wonderful words set free within the cool cloisters of the community in Lugdunum. It was an act that had precipitated the Abbot's rage. Considering this Codex to be the most dangerous of all those proscribed books held in the library, he decreed it to be magic, a sorcery, and those who defended it were denounced as heretics. Enemies of the true faith. The novitiate was punished.

But Arinius believed he was carrying the sacred words of God. That his destiny, perhaps his entire purpose on God's earth, was to ensure that the truth contained within the papyrus was not lost. Nothing else mattered.

Now, floating across the still waters to where he stood on the banks of the river Atax, the toll of a bell for lauds. A simple song calling him home. Arinius raised his eyes to the city on the hill and prayed he would find a welcome there. Then he grasped his staff in his right hand, stepped out on to the wooden bridge and walked towards Carcaso.

Chapter 1

CARCASSONNE
JULY 1942

Sandrine jolted awake. Bolt upright, her eyes wide open, her right hand stretched out as if she was trying to grasp something. For a moment she was neither asleep nor awake, as if some part of her had been left behind in the dream. Floating, looking down at herself from a great height, like the stone gargoyles that grimaced at passers-by from the cathédrale Saint-Michel.

A sensation of slipping out of time, falling from one dimension into another through white, endless space. Then running and running, escaping the figures hunting her down. Indistinct outlines of white and red and black, pale green, their faces hidden beneath hoods and shadow and flame. Always the sharp glint of metal where should have been skin. Sandrine couldn't remember who the soldiers were or what they wanted, if indeed she'd ever known, and already the dream was fading. Only the sense of threat, of betrayal, remained. And those emotions, too, were slipping away.

Little by little, the room came back into focus. She was safe in her own bed in the house in the rue du Palais. As her eyes became accustomed to the dark, she could pick out the bureau of bleached mahogany against the wall between the two windows. To the right of her bed, the high-backed couch covered with washed-green Chinese silk and the bamboo plant stand. Opposite, beside the door, the low bookcase, its shelves filled to bursting.

Sandrine wrapped her bare arms around her knees, shivering in the chill of the early morning. She reached for her eiderdown, as if by touching something real she would feel less insubstantial, less transparent, but her fingers found only the cotton of her crumpled sheet. The eiderdown, kicked off in the night, lay on the floor beside the bed.

She couldn't see the hands on the clock on the chest of drawers, but there was something in the quality of the light coming through the gaps in the shutters, the song of the blackbirds in the street outside, that told her it was nearly morning. She didn't have to get up, but she knew she wouldn't go back to sleep now.

Sandrine slipped out of bed and tiptoed across the room in her bare feet, trying to avoid the worst of the creaking floorboards. Her clothes were piled, raggle-taggle, over the arm of the cane-backed chair at the foot of her bed. She wriggled out of her nightdress and dropped it to the floor. Though she was eighteen, Sandrine still looked like the tomboy she had been, a *garçon manqué*. She was all arms and legs, there was nothing soft about her. Her black hair refused to be tamed and she had the deep complexion of a country girl, tanned from days spent out of doors. Powder made no difference. As she threaded her slim arms into the sleeves of her cotton blouse, she noticed a smudge on the inside of the wide round collar where she'd experimented yesterday with her sister's face powder. She rubbed at it with her thumb, but it was stubborn and wouldn't shift.

The skirt was too big, a hand-me-down. Their housekeeper, Marieta, had moved the hook and eye, taking in a good two inches at the waist, so even though it didn't hang quite right, it was wearable. Sandrine liked the feel of the sateen lining against her legs, the way the chequered pattern shifted through squares of red and black and gold when she walked. In any case, everyone wore hand-me-downs these days. The sleeveless pullover was her own, a blowsy burgundy, knitted by Marieta last winter, that half argued with, half suited, her colouring.

Perching on the edge of the chair, Sandrine pulled on her *écossaises*, the precious tartan socks her father had brought back as a gift from Scotland. His last trip, as it turned out. François Vidal had been one of the many Carcassonnais who had gone to fight and never come home. After the months of waiting, seeing no action – the *drôle de guerre*, the phoney war as it had become known – he was killed on 18 May 1940 in the Ardennes, along with most of his unit. A muddle of orders, an ambush, ten men dead.

It had been two years. Although she still missed her father – and her nights were often broken by bad dreams – she and Marianne had learnt to carry on without him. The truth was, much as Sandrine hated to admit it, the outline of his face and his gentle smile were less clear in her mind with each passing month.

In the east, the sun was rising. Light filtered through the patterned glass of the arched window on the stairwell, casting a kaleidoscope of blue and pink and green diamonds on to the rust-red tiles. Sandrine hesitated a moment outside her sister's bedroom. Even though it was her intention to sneak out, she had a sudden urge to check that Marianne was there, safe in her bed.

Sandrine put her hand on the ornate metal door handle and crept in. She tiptoed over to the bed. In the grey half-light, she could just make out her sister's head on the pillow, her brown hair wrapped in complicated knots of paper and rollers. Marianne's face was as beautiful as ever, but there was a spider's web of worry lines around her eyes. Sandrine could just make out her shoes beside the bed. She frowned, wondering where she had been for them to be caked in mud.

'Marianne?' she whispered.

Her sister was five years older. She taught history at the École des Filles on Square Gambetta, but spent much of her free time at the centre run by the Red Cross in the rue de Verdun. Quiet and principled, Marianne had offered her services as a volunteer with the Croix-Rouge after France's surrender in June 1940, when tens of thousands of dispossessed people from the Occupied Zone had fled south to the Languedoc. Then, her work had been to provide food, shelter, blankets for refugees fleeing the advancing Nazi forces. Now, it was monitoring the condition of prisoners being held in Carcassonne's gaol or being sent to internment camps in the mountains.

'Marianne,' whispered Sandrine again. 'I'm going out. I won't be long.'

Her sister murmured and turned over in her bed, but did not wake.

Considering her duty done, Sandrine stole back out of the room and quietly closed the door. Marianne didn't like her going out in the early morning. Even though there was no curfew in the *zone non-occupée* – the *zone nono* as it was known – there were regular patrols and the atmosphere was often jittery. But it was only in the stillness of the early morning, free from the restrictions and tensions and compromises of everyday life, that Sandrine felt herself. She didn't intend to give up these moments of freedom unless she had to.

Until she had to.

Sandrine carried on down through the silently sleeping house, trailing her hand over the warm wood of the banister. Diamonds of coloured light danced at her heels. For an instant, she wondered if other girls, in other times, had felt the same as she did. Confined, caught between childhood and the adult life to come. And in the air around her, the echo of all those stifled hearts, trapped spirits, fluttered and sighed and breathed. So many different lives, passed over centuries in the narrow streets of the medieval Cité or in the Bastide Saint-Louis, whispered and cried out to be heard. Sandrine could not understand them, not yet, though a certain restlessness moved in her blood, her veins.

For the ancient spirit of the Midi, buried in the deep memory of the mountains and hills, in the lakes and the sky, had long ago begun to stir. To speak. The white bones of those sleeping in the cimetière Saint-Michel, in the cimetière Saint-Vincent and in the country graveyards of the Haute Vallée, were beginning to awaken. A shifting, a murmuring through the cities of the dead, words carried on the wind.

War was coming to the South.

Chapter 2

A narrow corridor with high ceilings led directly from the foot of the stairs to the front door. Sandrine sat on the bottom step to lace up her shoes, then went to the hall-stand. Two umbrellas were wedged into the base. Six brass hooks, three on each side of the mirror, held a selection of hats. Sandrine chose a plain maroon beret. Looking in the glass, she held her hair off her forehead and put the hat on, teasing out a few curls. Then she heard the rattle clatter of a pan and the bang of the screen door, and realised Marieta was already up and about. Little chance of getting out unobserved now.

Sandrine walked down the corridor to the back of the house. As little girls, she and Marianne had spent a good deal of time in the kitchen. Her sister loved to cook and was keen to learn. Sandrine was too impatient, did everything in a hurry. Perched up on the draining board beside the porcelain sink in Coustaussa to help strain the cherries for jam in summer when she was three or four. When she was six, being given the mixing bowl and wooden spoon to lick when Marieta baked cakes for the *bataille des gabels* to celebrate the fête de Saint-Nazaire in Carcassonne. At eight, sprinkling flour over the old wooden table while Marieta taught Marianne how to knead the dough for her *pan de blat*, the rustic wheat bread not available in the boulangeries in Couiza.

She paused on the threshold. Marieta grumbled that the kitchen was too small, but it was cool and well stocked and efficient. Metal pots and pans hung from hooks above the fireplace, where a modern gas cooker had been installed.

A deep enamel sink with a large draining board, and a tall dresser so that the plates and cups were easily within reach. High windows filled the entire back wall. Even though it was early, all four were tilted wide open. Bundles of wild rosemary, dried tarragon and sprigs of thyme gathered at Cavayère hung from the wooden rack suspended from the ceiling.

'Marieta,' she said. '*Coucou, c'est moi.*'

Marieta was sitting at the table with her back to the door, breathing heavily. Beneath a wrap-over housecoat, today's a pattern of yellow and pink field flowers, she wore her customary black, cotton rather than wool her only concession to the season. Buttoned up to the neck and at the cuffs, with dark stockings and sabots, the heavy wooden clogs she always wore. Wisps of grey hair were escaping from the bun at the nape of her neck and her chest wheezed, her breath full of dust.

'*Coucou*,' Sandrine said again, putting her hand on the old woman's shoulder.

Marieta jumped. 'Madomaisèla!'

'I'm sorry, I didn't mean to startle you.'

'What are you doing up at this time?'

'Couldn't sleep.'

Marieta looked her up and down, taking in the beret and outdoor shoes.

'You know your sister doesn't like you to go out on your own.'

'I did tell her.'

Marieta raised her eyebrows. 'But did she hear you?'

Sandrine flushed. 'I didn't want to wake her up.'

The housekeeper leant forward and picked a stray piece of crimson wool from Sandrine's skirt.

'And if Madomaisèla Marianne asks where you are?'

'She won't, she was awfully late home last night.' Sandrine paused. 'Do you know where she went?'

Their eyes met. On the wall above the door, the hands of the clock moved round. One tick, two ticks, three.

Marieta was the thread that held the woven life of the household together. Originally from Rennes-les-Bains, she had spent her life in the service of others. Devout and loyal, she had been widowed young, in the Grande Guerre. She had come to help after Madame Vidal had died, unexpectedly, eighteen years before.

She claimed to be content to live in Carcassonne, though Sandrine knew she missed the ancient green forests of her childhood, the quiet village streets of Coustaussa and Rennes-les-Bains. When war had broken out in 1939, Marieta took it in her stride, saying she had survived one war and would survive another. After the telegram informing them of Monsieur Vidal's death, there had been no more talk about her going home.

'Do you?' Sandrine said again.

Marieta pretended she hadn't heard. 'Well, if you are determined to go out, you'd better have something inside you.'

Sandrine sighed. She knew if Marieta didn't want to talk about something, she wouldn't.

'I am hungry,' she admitted.

Marieta lifted the linen cloth on the table, releasing a sweet smell of flour, rosemary and salt, to reveal a freshly baked loaf cooling on a wire tray.

'White bread!'

Marieta cut a slice, then gestured to the blue china dish in the centre of the table.

'And butter,' she said. 'Delivered this morning.'

Without thinking how it might embarrass the older woman, Sandrine threw her arms around her. The familiar scent of lavender water and sulphur lozenges was reassuring, taking her back to a place before the war, before her father's death. To a simpler and easier time.

Marieta stiffened. 'What's the matter? Did you have another bad night?'

'No,' she said. 'At least, I did, but it's not that. It's . . .'

'Well then, sit. Eat,' Marieta said, then spoke in a softer voice. 'It will be all right, you hear? These times will pass. France will be France again. There are enough good men – men of principle, men of the Midi – they won't sell us out. Not like those criminals in Vichy.'

Sandrine looked down at the piece of bread, her appetite suddenly gone.

'But what if it stays like this for ever? Nothing getting better? Always the fear of things getting worse?'

'We will bide our time,' she said. 'Keep our heads down. The Germans will stay north of the line, we stay south. It won't last for ever. Now, finish your breakfast.'

Marieta watched until she'd finished every scrap. Then, before Sandrine could clear up after herself, she was on her feet and carrying the plate over to the sink. Sandrine brushed the crumbs from her skirt and stood up too. She wasn't sure why she felt so out of sorts.

'Is there anything you need in town, Marieta?'

'Not that I can think of.'

'Surely there's something? I want to *do* something.'

'Well,' said Marieta eventually, 'I suppose if you are going that way, I promised this dress pattern to Monsieur Quintilla's wife.' She took an envelope from the drawer. 'I meant to deliver it myself, but it is such a long walk down to the café at Païchérou and . . .'

'It's no trouble.'

'Only if you're going that way.'

'I can.'

'But don't go over the bridge,' Marieta warned. 'Madomaisèla Marianne would say the same. Stay on this side of the river.'

Chapter 3

Sandrine ran down the steep steps to the small courtyard garden at the back of the house. She got her bicycle and pushed it out into the street. The gate rattled shut on its latch behind her.

She felt her mood lift as the air rushed into her lungs. Tilting her face to the morning, she dropped her shoulders and felt the cobwebs blow away. She picked up speed as she crossed the rue du Strasbourg, weaving in and out of the elegant *platanes* that lined the square behind the Palais de Justice, then left into the rue Mazagran.

The ebb and flow of life as it used to be was most evident in the elegant nineteenth-century beauty of this quartier, all grey stone and wrought-iron balustrades, the chalky pinks and blues of the decorative tiles and plaster on the front of the *maisons de maître*. On mornings such as this, when the lilac sky told of another hot day to come and the green underside of the leaves shimmered silver in the light breeze, it was impossible to believe that much of France was under German occupation.

The Bastide had come into being in the mid-thirteenth century, some fifty years after the medieval crusade that had given Carcassonne its bloody notoriety. The vicious wars of religion had turned the inhabitants of the medieval Cité into refugees. Evicted in 1209, with only the clothes they stood up in, after the treacherous murder of their leader and ruler, Viscount Trencavel, it was only in 1276, some years after the last Cathar stronghold had fallen, that the French king gave permission for a new settlement to be established on the left bank of the Aude.

Despite the fact that Sandrine had lived her whole life in the Bastide, she loved the Cité more. And although she felt guilty even for thinking it, a part of her was grateful that, thanks to Maréchal Pétain's collaboration with Berlin, she did not have to witness German soldiers walking through the cobbled streets of old Carcassonne.

The bells of Saint-Michel were ringing the half-hour as she crossed Square Gambetta, then cycled down the rue du Pont Vieux. Then, suddenly there it was – la Cité – on the hill on the far side of the river. The sight of it never failed to take her breath away.

For a moment, Sandrine was tempted to cross the bridge, but mindful of the promise she'd made to Marieta, she instead turned right. This first stretch of the bank, between the Pont Vieux and the weir above Païchérou, was the prettiest. Silver olive trees, fig trees in the gardens of the large houses. Ivy trailed down painted walls and ironwork trellises with vines. Elegant canopies and awnings and white terraces. Bougainvillea, carnations in pots, red and pink and white.

She pedalled along the water's edge, twigs and stones spinning under her wheels, and arrived at the café. Before the war, tea dances were held at Païchérou each Sunday afternoon, the waiters in their white jackets, and long refectory tables laid out in rows. For a moment, grief caught in her throat, an old memory taking her by surprise. Her father had promised to take her for her twenty-first birthday, a promise he would no longer be able to keep.

The gates into the grounds were open. Sandrine propped her bike against the wall, then knocked at the door. She waited, but no one came. She knocked again.

'Madame?'

She went to the window and peered in. It was dark inside. Everything looked closed up. Sandrine was in two minds as to whether to leave the envelope – Marieta was careful about her belongings. In the end, she posted it through the letter box and decided she'd come back later to make sure Madame Quintilla had got it.

Sandrine had intended to go straight home from Païchérou, but she'd heard rumours that refugees had set up a camp on the far side of the river. She was curious to know if it was true.

She cycled towards the weir and the secluded pocket of trees that stood at the bend of the river, just below the cimetière Saint-Michel. A glade of pine and beech, elm and ash. This morning, though, it felt a little too secluded. Sandrine found herself glancing over her shoulder, with a prickling on the back of her neck as if someone was watching her. The flapping of a collared dove, then the slither and splash of a fish in the shallows made her jump.

Sandrine stopped at the water's edge and looked across to the far side of the Aude. She could see nothing unusual at all, nothing different or threatening or out of place. No tents, no gypsy encampment, no shadow city. She wasn't sure if she was disappointed or relieved.

The sky was the colour of forget-me-nots. The bells of Saint-Gimer below the Cité began to ring seven o'clock, the sound floating across the mirrored surface of the water. Minutes later, they were answered by the bells of Saint-Michel and other churches of the Bastide. There had been a time, during the early days of the war, when the bells were silenced. Sandrine had missed them then, the familiar steady marking of each day. Now, though they rang again, she couldn't help hearing a sadness in their voice.

She laid her bike down, then sat on the bank and pulled at the grass with her fingers. Before the war, at about this point in July, they'd be getting ready to leave Carcassonne for their summer house in Coustaussa. Her and Marianne, their father. Marieta fussing and packing three times as much as they needed. Picnics on the banks of the river Salz in the deep shade of the afternoon with her oldest friend, Geneviève. Cycling to Rennes-les-Bains for supper at the Hôtel de la Reine in the evening. Playing 'Docteur Knock' in the kitchen for hour upon hour with the battered old playing cards.

Sandrine leant back against the trunk of the tree and looked at the towers and turrets and spires of the medieval Cité, the walls of the Château Comtal and the distinctive thin outline of the Tour Pinte. Like a finger pointing to heaven. And, between the two Carcassonnes, lay the river. Still and flat and silver.

Like a sea of glass.

‡

Codex II

‡

Gaul
Carcaso
July AD 342

The shimmering waters of the river Atax glinted bright in the early-morning sunlight. The young monk crossed the wooden bridge, then followed the track that led up to the main gates on the eastern side of the fortified town.

Ahead, Arinius could see the walls of Carcaso, not much more than twice his own height perhaps, but wide and solid. They looked strong enough to keep out any invaders. The foundations were large stone blocks, two or three deep, with a layer of mortar on the top. The façade was a mixture of lime and rubble. Spaced at regular intervals were horseshoe-shaped bastions, short squat towers on the northern section of the walls, curved on the outside and flat on the side facing the town.

'A place of refuge,' he said, praying that it would be the case. He was weary and intended to rest in Carcaso for a few days, to gather his strength for the final leg of his journey into the mountains. His throat was sore and his ribs ached from coughing.

Pressing his hand against the dry papyrus beneath his grey habit – an action that was now as natural and unconscious as breathing – Arinius joined the early crowd waiting to gain access to the town. Merchants, farmers from the *faratjals*, the pastures on the plains below the hill, weavers and those with pottery or ceramics to sell.

Even in these uncertain times, this trade route along the coast of Gaul remained one of the busiest. Traders and wine sellers travelling to and from Hispania. Rumours of marauding *bagaudes*, bands of deserting soldiers or barbarians from the East, could not deter the men and women of commerce.

Arinius pulled his hood over his head as he approached the gate, a coin in his hand ready to pay the toll. An old denarius, though he felt sure it would still be accepted. Money bought nothing these days, but silver was silver. His heart began to thump. If the Abbot had put a price on his head, it was at the gates of Carcaso he was likely to be taken. Branded not only a heretic, but also a thief.

'Protect me, Father,' he murmured, making the sign of the cross.

The crowd shuffled forward once more. The wheels rattling on an old cart, struggling over the rough ground. A flock of geese, herded by a scrawny girl with arms like sticks, a dog snapping at the heels of its choleric owner. Another step forward. Just then, a mule kicked its back leg, sending a barrel flying. The wood split and red wine began to leak out, like a seam of blood on the dry earth.

Arinius pushed the image away.

The merchant started shouting and began to remonstrate with the owner of the animal, their words turning the pale morning air blue. Grateful for the diversion, Arinius slipped in front of them and up to the gate. There were two guards on duty. One, a brutish-looking man, was watching the altercation with a greedy glint in his eyes, itching for a fight. The other, a young man with a pockmarked face and a helmet too large for him, looked tired after his night's watch.

'*Salve*,' said Arinius quietly. 'Greetings, friend.'

'Where are you from?'

'Massilia,' Arinius lied, holding out the silver coin. It

was significantly more than required and the boy's eyes widened. He took it, tested it between his teeth, then waved Arinius through.

'*Salve*,' he said with a grin. 'Welcome to Carcaso.'

Chapter 4

CARCASSONNE
JULY 1942

Sandrine was woken by a squeal of tyres on the road as a motorbike took the corner too fast. She blinked up through the quilt of dappled leaves, for a moment not sure where she was. Trapped once more in the same nightmare? Then, the sound of the bells of Saint-Gimer striking the half-hour, and she remembered.

She sat up, picking a twig out of her hair, and looked out across the river. The sun had climbed higher in the cloudless sky. Way upstream, she heard the plash of the water against Monsieur Justo's barge as he pulled hand over hand on the wire. If the ferry was working, it must be past nine o'clock.

Sandrine scrambled to her feet. As she grabbed her beret, something caught her eye ahead of her in the reeds. Something blue, beneath the overhang of the marsh willow. She paused, certain it hadn't been there before. She walked upstream, along the water's edge, moving out of the bright sunlight into the green shadow beneath the tree.

She bent down. It was a man's jacket, snagged half in and half out of the water. Sandrine reached out to get it, but it was caught on the underside of a branch and it took a couple of pulls to get it free. Holding the dripping material away from her, she examined it. The pockets were empty, apart from a heavy silver chain, the sort of thing a man might wear. The catch was broken and initials – AD – had been carved on the underside.

She frowned. It wasn't unusual for things to be jettisoned in the river, old boxes, flotsam, torn sacks from the market gardens upstream. But not clothes, not jewellery. Everything had a price or could be traded for something else. And the Aude was fast at this point; there were no rocks on this side of the river, only reeds and grass and flat riverbank that curved gently, so mostly the current sent its cargo rushing downstream.

Sandrine looked out over the river. Now she noticed there was something else in the water, caught on the ridge of jagged rocks below the weir. Pushing the chain into her pocket, she shielded her gaze with her hand, reluctant to believe the evidence of her own eyes.

It looked like someone trying to swim. One arm stretched out, the white material of the shirt billowing in the current, the other holding on to the rocks.

'Monsieur?' she shouted, hearing the fear in her voice. 'Monsieur, do you need help?'

Her voice sounded thin, not loud enough to carry above the roar of the water over the weir.

'Monsieur!'

Sandrine looked around for help, but the ferry had reached the far bank and was out of earshot. She dropped the jacket on to the grass and ran up towards the road. There was no one about, no sign of the motorbike she'd heard, no one walking past.

'Help, I need help,' she shouted.

There was no answer, no movement, just shadows reflected in the water, a pattern of light and dark. Sandrine ran back to the river, hoping she'd imagined it, but the man was still there, on the rocks beneath the weir, his shirt moving to and fro in the current. It was down to her. There was no choice. There was nobody else.

She removed her shoes and her socks, tucked her skirt into her underwear, then waded out into the water.

'I'm coming, hold on.'

The further she went into the current, the faster the water swirled about her legs, harder and fiercer against her calves, her knees, the backs of her thighs. Deeper, colder. Sandrine struggled not to be knocked off her feet.

'Hold on,' she cried again.

Finally, she was close enough to touch him. A young man, unconscious, dark skin, black brows, long hair. His head lolled to one side. His mouth and nose were out of the water, but his eyes were closed. She wasn't sure if he was breathing or not.

'Monsieur, can you hear me?' she said. 'Take my hand, if you can.'

He didn't respond.

Steeling herself, Sandrine reached out and touched him. Still nothing. She took a deep breath, then manoeuvred herself around so that she could get her hands beneath his armpits. She tried to pull. At first, nothing happened, he was held somehow on the rocks. But then his grip slackened and after a few more heaves, suddenly he came free.

Sandrine lurched and nearly collapsed under the sudden responsibility of his weight, but then the water took over and held him up. Feeling the squelch of mud between her toes, slowly she began to drag him back to the bank. She tried not to look at his pallid skin and lifeless features, his dark hair. She thought he was breathing, hoped he was. Tiny sounds seemed to be coming from his mouth, but she wasn't sure. Every drop of her strength was focused on the task of getting him back to the safety of the shore.

As the water became shallower, he grew heavier in her arms. The last few steps were almost impossible, half dragging, half pulling, until his upper body at least was out of the water. With what little energy she had left, she managed to roll him on to his side before sinking to the ground on the grass beside him.

She took deep breaths, steadied her heart. A few moments later and she forced herself to look at him properly, at his bruised and lifeless face. There were rope burns around his wrists, red marks on his lower arms. Not the sort of marks he could have got from the water. She looked at his feet, seeing the soles were also bruised.

Sandrine swallowed hard. Not drowned. Rather, someone had tied him up, beaten him. She took another deep breath, fighting the panic that was threatening to overwhelm her, trying to work out what might have happened.

Without warning, the man's eyes snapped open. He coughed, began to choke, as if the oxygen had suddenly started to feed into his lungs again. Sandrine leapt back, just as a stream of river water spewed from his mouth. He attempted to sit up, but he had no strength and fell back to the ground.

'Spirits of the air,' he muttered. 'The number was ten thousand times ten thousand ...'

His eyes were staring at her. Pleading, suffering eyes, shot through with despair.

'Don't move,' she said quickly, trying to sound calm. 'I'll get help. You need help.'

'Tell Baillard,' he whispered. '*Trouvez-lui. Dîtes que ...*'

'I'll fetch help,' she said. 'The police, we—'

His hand shot out and grabbed her wrist. Sandrine stifled a scream.

'No police. Can't trust ... no!' he gasped. 'Tell the old man, tell ...'

'A doctor, then,' she said, trying to prise his fingers from her skin. 'You need help, I must fetch someone. You can't—'

'Tell him … it's true. A sea of glass, of fire. Speak and they will come.'

'I don't understand,' she said desperately. 'I don't know what you mean.'

'The spirits of the air …' he whispered, but his voice was fading.

'No, don't give up …'

A terrible rattling in his throat. A gurgling, then a snatching at the air. Every gasp of breath hard fought for.

'Save your strength. Help is on its way,' she lied, glancing up to the road again.

'All true,' he repeated, almost looking as if he was smiling. 'Dame Carcas …'

'It will be all right. Just …'

But he was drifting away, his colour fading from pink to grey to white. Sandrine kept shaking him, trying to keep him with her. Her wet skirt was clinging to the back of her legs as she pushed against his chest, her feet muddied and cut from the stones on the riverbank.

'Hold on,' she said, trying to keep him breathing. 'Help will come soon, hold on.'

Then she felt a prickling on the back of her neck. Someone was there. Someone was standing behind her.

'Thank God,' she started to say, except something felt wrong.

Fear, rather than relief, jabbed her between the ribs. She spun round, but she was too slow. A blinding pain at the side of her head, dazzling white and yellow and red light, then she was falling, falling, her legs buckling under her. The smell of the river and the reeds, rushing up to meet her. A hand on the back of her neck, pushing her face down into the water. The river, framing her face now, lapping into her mouth, her nose, the shimmer of shadow and light on the surface.

For an instant, a whispering. A voice she couldn't identify, a sound heard but not heard. Experienced somewhere beyond language, beyond hearing.

'*Coratge.*' A girl's voice, glistening in the light. Courage.

Then, nothing.

Chapter 5

The Haute Vallée

Audric Baillard stood in a clearing at the edge of a beech wood in the French Pyrenees. Rather than his customary pale suit and panama hat, he was wearing the nondescript clothes of a man of the mountains. Corduroy trousers, an open-necked shirt with a yellow handkerchief at his neck, a wide-brimmed hat. His skin was tanned, the colour of leather, and heavily lined. He was old, but he was strong, and there was a resolve in his eyes that bore witness to the evidence of his years.

Beside him, mopping his brow in the heat, was a smartly dressed man in a black suit and iron-grey trilby, with a fawn trench coat over one arm and a leather valise. At his side, two silent little girls and a thin woman with dead eyes. A little apart stood a young man in country smock and boots. All around, the sounds of the forest. Rabbits, squirrels, wood pigeons calling one to the other.

'Good luck,' said Baillard.

'I can't thank you enough,' the American, Shapiro, replied, pulling an envelope from his pocket. 'I hope this is sufficient …'

Baillard shook his head. 'It is not for me, my friend. It is for your guides, the *passeurs*. It is they who take the risk.'

'Didn't mean to offend you, sir.'

'I am not in the least offended.'

The American hesitated, then put the envelope back in his pocket. 'If you're sure?'

'I am.'

Shapiro glanced at his guide, then lowered his voice so the woman and children couldn't hear.

'But as a businessman, sir, I hope you don't mind me asking what's in it for you?'

'Merely to be of assistance,' Baillard said quietly.

'Though you're taking a chance too?'

Baillard fixed him with his steady, quiet gaze. 'These are difficult times.'

Shapiro's face clouded over. Baillard knew that this man's family, French Jews, had been among the first to be rounded up in Paris. He had come over from America, thinking his money might save them, but in twelve months he had succeeded only in finding his brother's wife and two of her four children. The others had disappeared.

'You cannot blame yourself,' Baillard said softly. 'Because of you, Madame Shapiro and your nieces have a chance. We each do what we can.'

Shapiro fixed him with a look, then he nodded. Something in Baillard's voice persuading him of his sincerity.

'If you're sure,' he said again. He glanced once more at the *passeur*. 'What about this guy, does he speak English?'

'No. Very little French, either.'

Shapiro raised his eyebrows. 'So what am I looking out for? The landmarks, in case we get split up.'

Baillard smiled. 'I am sure you will not, but in any case, the route is simple. Keeping the sun ahead of you, you follow the *draille*, these wide tracks the shepherds and goatherds use. You'll cross several brooks, passing through open meadows as well as sections of woodland. The first lake you come to will be the Étang de Baxouillade. Keep the water on your left. You'll travel through a pine forest and on further, until you reach the banks of the Étang du Laurenti. There, all being well, a second *passeur* will be waiting. He will be accompanied by three others who are making the crossing today. He will take you over the summit of Roc Blanc, ready for the descent to the border with Andorra.'

'This guy's not sticking with me?'

'There are different guides for different sections of the mountain. I cannot say for certain, but I think it likely your second aide will be a Spaniard.'

'That's grand. I have a little Spanish.'

Baillard smiled. 'At the risk of now offending you, monsieur, I would recommend you keep conversation to a minimum. Your accent will give you away.'

'You could be right,' he said amiably, acknowledging the comment with good grace. 'How long do you figure the journey will take, sir? Give or take?'

'With the children, perhaps four hours to the Étang du Laurenti, then another two hours to the summit of Roc Blanc. The descent will be easier.'

The *passeur* cleared his throat. '*Sénher, es ora.*'

Shapiro turned round, then back to Baillard. 'What's that he's saying?'

'That it is time to leave.' Baillard held out his hand. 'The *passeurs* know these paths, this mountain. They know where the risk of being spotted by a patrol is at its highest. Do as they tell you.'

'Here's hoping,' said Shapiro, clasping Baillard's hand and shaking it. 'And if you're ever in New York, you look me up. I mean it.'

Baillard smiled at the American's confidence, hoping it was not misplaced. In the two years he had been helping smuggle people over the Pyrenees – exiles, fugitives, Jews, communists, those without an exit visa – many had ended up imprisoned in gaols in Spain or repatriated to France. Americans in particular did not understand that, in this war, money did not talk.

'*Pas a pas*,' he murmured to himself.

He watched the small party set off along the path. Like so many of the wealthy refugees Baillard had guided to the escape routes, they had brought too much with them. The American was not dressed for the mountains, the children would struggle with their cases and the woman looked defeated, someone who had seen too much to think she could ever be safe again.

Baillard sighed, wished them luck, then turned and retraced his steps to the village of Ax-les-Thermes. The air was fresh and clean, but the sun was hot and would get hotter, and he was tired. He had walked many thousands of miles through these mountains, and he accepted that the time was coming when he would no longer have the strength required for such arduous journeys.

He knew many of the secrets hidden in these hills, yet an explanation for the purpose of it all eluded him. He had published books – on folklore, on the bloody history of the region, about the citadel of Montségur and the caves of the Sabarthès and Lombrives and the mountain peaks of the Vicdessos – but still the truth of his continuing mission remained stubbornly beyond his comprehension.

He took one last look. His charges were specks on the horizon, five diminishing figures walking slowly uphill. He said a prayer for them, then turned and slowly began his descent.

It took Baillard nearly an hour to reach the outskirts of the town. There, he changed back into his usual clothes. He noticed a police car idling at the corner of the road and quietly changed direction. The police did not notice him. Or if they did, they had no interest in an elderly man in a white suit taking the morning air. But he took no chances, no unnecessary risks. It was why he had never been caught, not in this conflict nor in any other war in which he had been called upon to play his part.

He circled the town, walking slowly, with apparent lack of purpose, then came back in through the northern streets and went to the Café des Halles by the bridge, where he was to wait. The local doctor was due to visit a pregnant woman, expecting twins any day now, and had agreed to take him back to Rennes-les-Bains, where he hoped the package from Antoine Déjean would be waiting. Baillard allowed himself a moment of anticipation. If all was well, then there was a chance.

'Come forth the armies of the air,' he murmured.

Old words, ancient words, from a sacred text Baillard believed destroyed more than fifteen hundred years ago.

But what if the rumours were true? If it had survived?

He glanced at his watch. At least three hours to wait, if the doctor came at all. He ordered something to drink and eat. The café only had thin wine and ersatz coffee. No milk, of course. But Baillard didn't require much. He ate a dry biscuit, dipping it into the tepid brown liquid, and sipped the rough mountain rosé.

He had seen many summers such as this, the gold of the sunflowers and the pinks, blues and reds of the mountain flowers fading into wine-coloured autumns as the leaves fell. Harsh winters following on behind, the passage of rain and mist to snow and ice. The endless march of the seasons. So many years, wondering whether each might be his last.

The sun rose higher in the sky. Baillard continued to wait and to watch the road, looking for anything, anyone out of place. There were spies everywhere, undercover rather than in plain view as in the occupied zone, but here all the same. Members of the Kundt Commission, the branch of the Gestapo operating in the *zone non-occupée*; SD and SS of course, but also Deuxième Bureau. Willing partners with the invaders whose aim in time, he had no doubt, was to subjugate all of France.

Baillard took another sip of wine. The uniforms were different in each age, the battle colours under which they marched changing as the centuries marched on. Boots and guns had replaced banners and horses, but the story was the same.

Men with black hearts. With black souls.

Chapter 6

Carcassonne

'A sea of glass …' she murmured, bright in the shimmering.

Sandrine knew it was her own voice she was hearing inside her head, but it seemed to be coming from a long way away. Shapes shifting, fragments of sound. An echo slipping in and out of conscious thought, as if underwater. Or through the clouded gaps between the valleys. She felt the hard metal of the chain in her pocket digging into her hip. She pulled it out, but her fingers didn't seem to work and the necklace slithered to the ground.

'Mademoiselle, can you hear me?'

Now she was aware of her hair being stroked gently off her forehead.

'Mademoiselle?'

A man's voice, sweet, soft, and a scent of sandalwood. So close, she could feel his breath on her skin.

'It's all right,' he said. 'It's all right, you're safe now.'

'Sleep,' she murmured.

'You shouldn't sleep,' he said. 'You must wake up.'

Sandrine felt his hands beneath her shoulders, then the warmth of his skin through his shirt as he held her against him. 'Open your eyes,' he was saying. 'Try to wake up. Open your eyes.'

She felt herself growing heavy in his arms, slipping away again. Then, his lips on hers, the lightest of touches. Breathing life into her. A kiss. Sandrine felt something inside her stir, a shock, a jolt. Then he kissed her again. For a single, unique moment, her eyes fluttered open, but she couldn't seem to see.

'I ...' she murmured, as her eyes closed once more. 'I can't ...'

Now his hand was cupping the back of her neck, cradling her head in his arms.

'Wake up. Please, mademoiselle. Sit up.'

Sandrine was aware of the sound of an engine, a different timbre from the motorcycle she'd heard earlier. Louder, a car coming closer. She felt the man's muscles tense, then she realised she was not in his arms any more. She was being laid back down on the grass, his skin no longer touching hers.

'You'll be all right,' he said.

Sandrine wanted him to stay. Wanted to ask him to stay, but the words wouldn't come. The car was getting closer, the belch of an exhaust.

'I'm sorry,' he said, his voice fading. 'I'm sorry, I can't be found here ... I'm sorry.'

Then he was gone. The air was still, empty. She could feel herself drifting away again. The smell of the riverside giving way to other scents, wild lavender and rosemary, the green and purple of the valleys around Coustaussa. Honeysuckle and the sharp tang of wood smoke in winter. Images now, cold reflections. The old wooden sign on the back road marking the way to the *castillous*, the arms crooked like a broken cross. In town, walking alongside her sister and her father beneath a red and yellow CGT trade union poster, a demonstration, before the war. Everyone singing for peace, for liberty, as they walked past the gardens and white balustrades and the marble angel statue in the centre of the lake in Square Gambetta.

'*Paix*,' Sandrine murmured.

Carcassonne had marched for peace in 1939, but war had

come all the same. In 1940, defeat had come all the same. Their voices had counted for nothing.

'*Patz*,' she murmured again. 'Peace.'

‡

Codex III

‡

GAUL
CARCASO
JULY AD 342

The young monk made his way through the crowds of people filling the narrow streets of the fortified town. Despite the air of trade and commerce, and the brave attempts of everyone to behave as if nothing had changed, Arinius detected a hint of unease, of watchfulness in the air. The same atmosphere that was spreading through all of Gaul since the death of Emperor Constantine. All around him, hands hovering ready to draw a knife from its hilt, eyes darting this way and that.

Arinius knew little of military strategy or the diplomacy of emperors and generals, but from stories overheard in the forum in Lugdunum or told by the merchants he'd met on the Via Domitia, he knew that the history of his country was one of invasion and counter-invasion. From century unto century, the imposition of a new set of values upon the old – defeat, then collaboration, then assimilation. The prehistoric tribes who once lived on the Carsac plains, the Celtic settlers who had come after them, the Volcae Tectosage three centuries before the birth of Christ, the armies of Augustus. Now, it was said, tribes were coming from the East to reclaim what Caesar once had ruled.

Arinius didn't know how well or how often Carcaso had been called upon to defend her walls, but he could see they had been built to withstand siege and invading armies. The horseshoe-shaped watch towers in the northern sections were faced with courses of dressed ashlar and intersected by red brick. On the first floor of each tower, three semi-circular windows were underscored by red-brick arches. The wooden walkway and the battlements, accessed by ladders set against the base of the walls, were guarded by foot soldiers in chain mail and silver helmets, some armed with a *pilum*, a weapon like a javelin, others carrying slings. Some were Roman, but many were clearly from local villages – typical of the *limitanei*, the frontier garrison troops who now protected even these outposts. Arinius wondered for whom these disaffected men on the walls would fight. For the failing Empire? For their neighbours and families? For God? He wondered if even they themselves knew where their loyalties lay.

There were four major streets, forming the shape of a cross within the walls, with other smaller roads connecting different quadrants of the town. Most of the buildings were tiled rather than the bush and thatch still common in the villages of the south. A small central square, a covered forum, was packed with merchants selling spices and herbs, geese and rabbits in wooden cages, wine, woollen tunics and strips of leather to patch broken sandals and belt fastenings. There was hammering from the forge, where a blacksmith worked on a scrawny bay mare.

Arinius saw many different skin colours and different ways of dressing. Some men wore beards, others had bare faces. Higher-born women with braided hair, jewelled and adorned, the daughters and wives of the Roman garrison commanders and men. Others walked freely with their heads uncovered in the older style, pale woollen tunics worn beneath hooded cloaks. It was hard to say who were natives, the original inhabitants of the land, and who the outsiders.

A fit of coughing caught Arinius by surprise. He doubled over, pressing his hand against his chest until the attack had passed, struggling to get his breath. He looked at his palm, saw spots of blood, and a wave of panic washed through him. He had to keep the illness at bay until the Codex was safe. That was all that mattered. Not his life, only that he fulfilled his mission.

He walked slowly on. He needed to rest. Arinius found a tavern opposite the residence of the garrison commander, an imposing two-storey house with red guttered tegulae forming the roof. Outside, the paved street was littered with clay pots, some broken, meat bones, and figs split and oozing rotting purple flesh, but inside the tavern was clean and it offered board and lodging at a reasonable price.

The formalities observed, Arinius drank two cups of wine, ate a handful of almonds and some hard white goat's cheese with honey. Afterwards he lay down on the hard wooden bed. He unpinned his mother's brooch, took off his cloak and used it as a blanket. Then, using his leather bag as a pillow, he folded his hands across his chest and, pressing the Codex close against his skin, Arinius slept.

Chapter 7

CARCASSONNE
JULY 1942

'She's coming round.'

A different voice this time. Another man, formal, educated, northern, not a local accent. Not the boy who had whispered to her, not the boy who had kissed her. The memory faded away. The real world returned, cold and hard and colourless.

'Mademoiselle,' the Parisian said. 'Do you know what happened to you? Can you tell us your name?'

Sandrine was aware of the sharp grass, that she was cold and damp. She tried to sit up, but pain exploded at the base of her skull. She attempted to lift her arm, but she had no strength. The muscles and bones could not be made to work.

Then a woman's voice, sing-song high. 'Actually, I think I know who she is.'

Sandrine managed to open her eyes. A pretty girl in her early twenties, with blue eyes, ultra-thin brows and blonde waved hair the colour of corn, curled off her face. She was wearing an orange and red summer print dress, with big white buttons and trim on the collar and sleeves.

'Aren't you Marianne Vidal's sister?' the girl said.

She nodded, setting her head spinning again.

'Sandrine,' she managed to reply. Her name felt thick in her mouth, like wet cloth.

'Sandrine, that's it. On the tip of my tongue. Thought I recognised you. I'm Lucie, Lucie Ménard. We met once, at the Café Continental I think it was, a while back. We were going on somewhere, can't quite remember where.'

Sandrine recalled the evening well. Marianne had been on the terrace and had waved her over to meet her friends. Lucie had stood out. She looked like an American movie star. Mad about anything to do with Hollywood, according to Marianne.

'You were going to a jazz concert at the Terminus.'

Lucie's face lit up. 'How about you remembering that!' She put her arm around Sandrine's shoulders. 'You look like you took one heck of a knock. How are you feeling?'

'Giddy.' Sandrine put her hand to her head. Something was stinging, raw. Her fingers came away sticky, red. 'What happened?'

'We were hoping you could tell us,' Lucie said.

Sandrine frowned. 'I can't remember.'

'Did you come off your cycle and hit your head?'

'There are tracks down by the water,' the man said.

'Although they're a little too wide for a cycle,' Lucie said. 'More like a motorbike.'

'No,' Sandrine said slowly, struggling to remember. 'No, there was somebody here. He pulled me out of the water.'

'We didn't see anyone,' said Lucie, turning to her companion. 'Did we?'

'No.'

Lucie smiled. 'Sorry, forgot to do the honours. Sandrine, this is my friend Max. Max Blum, Sandrine Vidal.'

'Mademoiselle Vidal,' he said formally.

Sandrine took a proper look at the man standing beside Lucie. Tall and slim, slightly stooped as if he spent his life trying to conceal his height. He wore heavy black-framed glasses, a dark suit and sober tie. With black hair just visible beneath the rim of his hat, he looked rather like a bird of prey.

'Lucky the river's shallow at this point,' Lucie continued, 'given you pitched head first into the water.'

Sandrine looked down at her clothes. Tartan skirt, burgundy jumper, blouse, everything was soaking wet. Dry mud on her feet and ankles. Had she gone into the water? To get the jacket, yes. She had waded in, but only up to her knees. Why was she so wet?

Then she remembered. 'There was someone in the river. A man. He was drowning, at least that's what I thought. I pulled him out. There, by the willow, and . . .' She opened her hand, but there was nothing there now. 'There was a necklace, a chain, in the pocket of the jacket.'

Finally the shock hit her. She felt a rush of heat, then a sour, bilious taste in her throat. Sandrine flung herself forward, doubled over on the grass on her hands and knees and was sick.

She retched until there was nothing left inside her, then sat back on the grass, her arms and hands resting on her knees. She felt hollow, utterly spent, chilled to the bone despite the warmth of the sun on her face.

'You'll feel better now,' Lucie said sympathetically, looking rather green herself.

Sandrine nodded, knowing she would have felt embarrassed if she didn't feel so wretched.

'Any sign of the jacket?' Lucie called to Max, who had discreetly wandered away.

'Not yet.'

'It was caught in the reeds beneath the marsh willow.' Sandrine pointed. 'Down there.'

'I'll keep looking,' he said.

'I dragged him to the bank,' Sandrine continued. 'He was lying there.'

Lucie's eyebrows went up. 'Hang on, didn't you say *he* pulled *you* out of the water?'

'No, that was afterwards. Someone else,' Sandrine said,

realising what a muddle it all sounded. 'Someone else hit me.'

'You're telling me you were attacked?' Lucie said doubtfully.

'Yes.'

'Who by?'

'I don't know.'

Lucie was frowning. 'Someone attacked you, then ran off, leaving you to be pulled out of the water by somebody else? Two different men.'

'Yes,' said Sandrine, though sounding less sure.

'And this second man, he ran off too?'

'Because he heard the car,' Sandrine said. 'I heard it too, the engine. Or the motorbike.' She stopped, suddenly not sure of the order in which things had happened. 'No, a car.' She looked up at Lucie. 'Your car, he heard you coming and—'

'Why would he bolt unless he'd done something wrong?'

'I don't know,' she said. 'I know it sounds ridiculous, but it's what happened, I'm not making it up.'

Lucie smiled. 'Hey, kid, it's not that I think you're making it up, but you did bash your head pretty badly. Bound to be muddled.'

Max came back. 'There's nothing there. I looked all around and in the water. No jacket, nothing resembling the piece of jewellery you described.' He paused. 'No … person.'

'But he must be there. He was hurt, badly hurt. Unconscious, maybe … He wasn't capable of going anywhere.'

Sandrine looked at them. Max's hawk-like face was thoughtful, calm. Lucie was concerned and sympathetic. But it was clear that neither of them believed her.

'I'm not making it up,' she said again. 'He was unconscious, he half woke up, but then someone else came …'

Lucie stood up and straightened her dress. 'Come on, we should take you home,' she said. 'Get you out of those wet clothes.'

Sandrine was sure she hadn't imagined it, she couldn't have. Her aching muscles were testament to that. She looked over to the glade and the willow tree. She hesitated. Had somebody hit her? She had thought so, was sure of it. But was it possible she had slipped? Her fingers stole to her lips. Sandalwood, gentle, his breath soft on her skin where he'd kissed her. She hadn't imagined that.

Lucie's voice cut into her reflections. 'Sandrine?'

She blinked. 'I'm sorry . . . I didn't hear.'

'I said, if we take you home, will there be someone to look after you? Patch you up?'

Sandrine nodded, sending her head spinning again. 'Marieta, our housekeeper.'

Lucie held out her hand and helped Sandrine to her feet. 'In which case, let's get going.' She retrieved Sandrine's things from the edge of the water. 'I like your socks, by the way. Unusual. Really something.'

'Thanks.' She managed a smile. 'My father brought them back for me from Scotland. Just before he was called up. Then, of course . . .'

Lucie's pretty face clouded over. 'Yes, I'm sorry. I heard he didn't make it back.'

'No.' There wasn't anything else she could say. 'What about you?'

'My father's in a POW camp,' Lucie said in a tight voice, 'though we're expecting him to be released any day.'

'That's good news.'

'My mother says she'll be pleased to have him back,' she said sharply. 'So far as I'm concerned, the Germans are welcome to him.'

Sandrine looked at her in surprise. She waited for Lucie to say more, but she didn't.

'Marianne's fiancé's in a camp in Germany,' Sandrine said to fill the silence.

'Thierry, yes.'

'You know him?'

Lucie's smile came back. 'It was me who introduced them.'

'I don't know him awfully well. His cousin, Suzanne, is a friend of Marianne's, but she hadn't been seeing him long when Thierry was called up. He seems nice.'

'He is nice.'

'Marianne got one of those grey cards last October, saying he'd been captured. She's not heard anything since then.'

'That's tough.'

Max caught the end of the conversation. 'What's tough?'

'Not knowing what the future holds,' Lucie said, looking up at him.

'You worry too much, Lulu,' he said softly, touching her cheek.

They climbed into the car. Lucie started the engine and they drove up the hill towards the rue du cimetière Saint-Michel. Sandrine closed her eyes, but immediately vivid images of the events of the morning rushed into her mind – distorted, distressing, confusing – and her lids snapped open again. She tried not to think of the man's face, the desperate touch of his fingers on her arm, the rattling in his throat. What had happened to him? Where was he? Was he still alive?

A shudder went down her spine.

'You all right, kid?' said Lucie, glancing sideways at her.

'A little bit cold.'

'That's the shock kicking in.'

Sandrine forced herself to focus on what she could see through the window of the car. Ordinary, everyday sights. A cat sunning itself on a wall, its black tail twitching back and forth against the white paint like a windscreen wiper. Two terracotta pots, like amphorae, standing either side of a door painted the colour of a bishop's robe. A man's hat lying at the side of the road in the rue du 24 Février.

As they turned into rue du Manège, Sandrine remembered why the name Blum was familiar. There was a Liesl Blum in the class beneath her at school. Max's sister perhaps, or his cousin? A quiet, studious girl, much older than her years, Liesl had been one of several students to arrive in Carcassonne after Paris fell. Now she was one of only two or three Jewish pupils left in the school. Anyone who had the money to get out, to America or to England, had gone.

Lucie turned left into boulevard Barbès. She and Max were discussing the car, a blue Peugeot 202. Lucie was animated, her eyes bright. She seemed to know a lot. Sandrine remembered that the Ménard family owned one of the biggest garages in town.

She leant her head against the glass, trying to decide what to do. Round and around went her thoughts, like wool unravelling from a skein. Unrelated fragments, but creating a pattern of connections all the same. And all the time those strange words echoing in her mind. So vivid, so clear, even though she didn't understand what they meant.

Chapter 8

Raoul didn't stop running until he reached the montée Saint-Michel. Then he slowed to a fast walk, up the steep hill and over into the rue du 24 Février. Only when he drew level with the entrance to the cemetery did he pause. He doubled over, trying to catch his breath in the heat.

'Damn,' he muttered. 'Damn.'

An elderly woman, stooping to fill a watering can inside the gate, looked at him with disapproval.

'*Pardon*,' he apologised.

Raoul waited until she was out of sight, then leant back against the wall in the shade. It had all happened so fast. One minute he was walking along the river, thinking about tomorrow. Then he'd come around the corner and seen the girl half in, half out of the water. Tried to help. Given her the kiss of life. Then the relief of realising she was all right, and he'd kissed her again. He didn't know what had got into him.

'Damn,' he repeated.

When he'd heard the car, his instinct for self-preservation had kicked in. Three years of war and defeat, trusting no one, meant he couldn't hang around and see who it was. That was asking to be caught. These days, apart from doctors and a handful of civil servants, almost nobody but police and members of the administration ran private cars.

Even so, Raoul felt shabby for leaving the girl. He ran his fingers over his hair, realising he'd dropped his hat somewhere en route. It wasn't a great loss, but even so. He looked down. The bottoms of his trousers were wet, but the material was dark and it didn't show.

He pulled the chain from his pocket. The girl had been holding it. A simple silver chain, but Antoine never took it off. Could they have been together? Arranged to meet? She didn't look like a courier, but then of course that was the point.

He looked at his watch. He'd got time for a drink. He needed a drink. Raoul headed for the Place des Armes. There was nowhere to sit at the Café Lapasset – he needed somewhere where he could see what was going on around him – but he found a table at the Grand Café des Négociants with a good view of the square and the Portail des Jacobins on the opposite side of the road. He ordered a glass of red wine and took a cigarette from a crumpled packet, knowing he'd get through his ration before the end of the week if he wasn't careful. A trail of white smoke twisted up into the chattering, jackdaw air.

Raoul borrowed a copy of *La Dépêche* from a man on the next table. A Vichyist publication these days, it was the same stale mix of international and domestic politics, propaganda most of it. Arrests in Narbonne – ten partisans printing and distributing anti-Vichy tracts, of whom four had been shot dead by French police officers. Flash floods in Tarascon, preparations for the Fête de l'Âne at the end of the month in Quillan, taking place for the first time since 1939. A few shreds of loose paper in the middle where ration coupons had been torn out. Weather reports for the beaches at Gruissan and La Nouvelle.

The man got up to leave. Raoul went to give the newspaper back, but he shook his head.

'Keep it. Not worth the paper it's printed on.'

'You're right about that,' Raoul said.

His eye was caught by an article about Maréchal Pétain. The hero of the battle of Verdun – and for two years head of the French government in exile in Vichy – Pétain was still a popular figure in the *zone non-occupée*. To traditionalists, he was a symbol of fortitude and honour, the embodiment of old-fashioned, Catholic French values. They'd even renamed the boulevard Jean-Jaurès after him, though the signs kept being defaced. Supporters of Vichy claimed the '*voie de la collaboration*', as Pétain christened his relationship with the Nazis, was part of a longer-term strategy: that the Maréchal had a plan to save France, if only they were patient. Those like Raoul, who would not accept the status quo and supported Général de Gaulle and his Free French forces, were considered troublemakers.

The article was about how although Jews in the occupied zone were now being forced to wear yellow stars, as in all other conquered territories, Vichy had stepped back from implementing the policy in the *zone libre*. 'Proof' of the government's principled behaviour, the editorial claimed.

Raoul tossed the paper down in disgust, his fingers stained black by the ink. The naïvety of it turned his stomach. Each new edict, each new compromise made him ashamed to be French. Like many men of the South, he was sickened by the wholesale arrests of communists, many of whom he'd fought alongside in 1940, of the internment of those who opposed Vichy and of Jews no longer considered French. Little by little, France was being absorbed into the Greater Reich. Raoul despised what was happening and despised those who, by design or by neglect, were letting it happen. Sins of omission, sins of commission; the same result in the end.

He stood up, tossed a couple of coins on the table, then crossed the boulevard Barbès, unable to stop himself wondering – as he so often did – what his brother would have made of it all. Bruno had been murdered by Franco's fascists in Spain in December 1938, but at least he hadn't lived to see France on her knees. Raoul hoped that he himself had grown into a man his brother would have been proud to know. His heart hardened by his loss, he had fought bravely and honourably against the Nazis. He had killed and seen men die, but had always done his best to protect those he fought alongside. After the defeat and surrender in June 1940, Raoul joined a mountain Resistance network, helping to smuggle refugees and Allied airmen over the border to Spain. Obtaining false papers and travel documents, providing currency and passports for those who had lost the right to stay in France. He thought Bruno would have done the same, had he lived.

Raoul's network had operated for nearly two years before it was betrayed, his comrades arrested and sent to the notorious camp of Le Vernet. Raoul only evaded capture because he was away from base when the police came. With everything gone, no papers and no means of support, he'd been forced to return to the anonymity of his home town of Carcassonne. To his grieving mother treading the boards of their tiny, sombre flat on the Quai Riquet, with only Bruno's ghost for company.

Raoul hated it. He was unsuited for civilian life and missed his brother even more in Carcassonne, in the streets where they'd grown up together. So when, a few months ago, César Sanchez, one of Bruno's former comrades in the International Brigade, had approached him to see if he'd join a group of patriots in Carcassonne, Raoul hadn't hesitated.

He looked up and realised he'd already arrived in Place Carnot. He glanced at his watch again. He was still too early, so he kept walking across the square and into rue Georges Clemenceau. César worked in the print shop attached to the Café des Deux Gares. If he went there first, Raoul would at least have the chance before the meeting to tell César he'd found Antoine's chain at the river.

Chapter 9

'Here we are,' said Lucie, parking at the kerb in front of Sandrine's house.

Max got out and unstrapped the bicycle from the rack. 'Where do you want this?'

'There's a gate into the garden at the back.'

He nodded and disappeared around the corner. Sandrine watched him go.

'Max is nice,' she said.

Lucie's eyes lit up. 'I know, isn't he?' She leant over and opened the door. 'There you go.'

Sandrine didn't move.

'You all right, kid? You need a hand getting inside?'

Sandrine shook her head. 'The thing is, I'm thinking I should go to the police. Report what happened.'

Alarm flashed across Lucie's face. 'That's not a good idea,' she said immediately.

'I know you don't believe me—'

Lucie interrupted. 'It's not that . . .'

'—and I don't blame you,' Sandrine continued. 'But I know what I saw. The police should be told.'

Lucie was frowning. 'I absolutely don't think you should get the police involved. It could be difficult for Max, and,' she hesitated, 'in any case, you're all right. No real harm done.'

'But I was attacked,' Sandrine said, taken aback by Lucie's opposition. 'What if he does it again? Attacks some other girl?'

'You'll never be able to persuade the police that's what happened,' Lucie said. 'You've got no evidence.'

'What about this?' Sandrine said, touching the cut on her head.

'That's not evidence, they'll simply say you took a fall. And … if you report it, it might come out that we were there. That Max was there. The police will have your details. You don't want that, surely? No one wants that.'

'A man is missing,' Sandrine said quietly. 'What about him? His injuries were …' She stopped, picturing the rope marks on his wrists, the bruising, the agony on his face. 'It's the right thing to do.'

'Wait until you've talked it over with Marianne. I'm sure she'll agree with me.'

'But his family might be looking for him. Someone might have reported him gone.'

'At least change your clothes before you do anything,' Lucie said, trying yet another approach. 'You'll catch your death.'

'If I do that, it's even less likely they'll believe me,' she said. 'Look at me. They'll be able to see I'm not making it up.'

'They'll see you came off your bike, that's all,' Lucie said stubbornly.

Finally accepting the girl wasn't going to come round, whatever she said, Sandrine decided the only thing for it was to make her own way to the police station once Lucie and Max had gone. She sat for a moment longer, pretending she was reconsidering, then she sighed.

'Perhaps you're right.'

Lucie's relief was palpable. 'It's the sensible thing, kid,' she said in a rush. 'Best not to get the police involved.'

'I'll hang on for Marianne,' Sandrine said, getting out of the car. 'See what she says.'

Lucie hopped out too and gave her a hug. 'You're sure you'll be all right?'

'Yes. Don't worry.'

'And, really, you know I wouldn't mention it to anyone,' Lucie added. 'Apart from Marianne, of course, but nobody else.'

'I won't,' Sandrine said, walking up the steps to the front door.

'All right?' Lucie said brightly to Max as he reappeared.

'I've left your bike just inside the gate,' he said, giving Sandrine a slight, formal bow. 'It was a pleasure to meet you, Mademoiselle Vidal, despite the circumstances.'

'You too. Thank you. You've both been so kind.'

Sandrine watched as Max got into the front seat beside Lucie and they pulled off. As soon as the car had rounded the corner, she ran back down the steps and walked quickly towards the Bastide and the police station.

A few minutes later, Sandrine was standing looking up at the Commissariat of the Police Nationale. In her whole life she had never had cause to go into the elegant white building. Her father had brought her up to trust authority, but that was then. Before the war, before France was cut in two, before the occupation of the north. Given the things the police were obliged to do now – arrests, raids, the implementation of new laws – perhaps Lucie's caution was justified.

At that moment, the door to the police station flew open and two officers appeared on the top step. They looked at Sandrine, then said something to one another and laughed as they walked down. She blushed, made self-conscious by their scrutiny, but it gave her the impetus she needed to go on in.

She ran up the steps. When she got to the top, she turned. The officers were there on the pavement, staring at her. Sandrine turned her back on them, pushed open the door and went inside.

The station smelt of disinfectant and tobacco and sweat. A woman with smudged eye make-up and a bruised face was sitting sobbing on the long bench that ran beneath the window. At the far end, an elderly man reeking of alcohol and muttering, a down-and-out. A copy of the front page of *L'Echo de Carcassonne* with a grainy photograph of Maréchal Pétain was stuck to the wall, beside a black and white public information poster advising citizens to be on the lookout for fifth columnists. There was also a noticeboard covered with mugshots of men sought by the police. Reward posters, wanted posters, they all looked villainous. Less than human.

A dark-haired officer with silver buttons, black tie and flashing on his shoulder came down the corridor and gently touched the woman on the arm.

'We'll keep him in until he's slept it off,' he said. 'Let's be getting you home.'

The woman nodded, then slowly got to her feet. Clasping her handbag to her like a shield, she allowed herself to be led out. Sandrine smiled at her, but the woman's head was bowed and she didn't respond.

When they'd gone, Sandrine approached the counter.

'Excuse me,' she said.

The desk clerk on duty ignored her, just continued to flick through the papers in front of him.

'*S'il vous plaît*,' she said, more loudly this time.

He still took no notice. Irritated, Sandrine leant forward and sharply tapped on the bell. The drunk in the corner began to laugh.

'Jump to it,' he shouted. 'Girl wants you. Come to see you,' he slurred. 'Pining for you, she is. Your girl, is she? Bit young—'

'Enough of that,' the clerk shouted, 'or I'll have you back in that cell.'

He did at least look at her then, raising his eyebrows as he took in her dishevelled clothes.

'Well?'

Sandrine met his gaze. 'I've come to report a crime.'

Chapter 10

Raoul watched the side door into the Café des Deux Gares from the Jardin des Plantes, checking there was nothing out of the ordinary. No sign that the premises were being watched, no unusual activity. A few down-and-outs were sitting on the stone steps surrounding the bust of Omer Sarraut, with their rough cigarettes and dark, sharp eyes. The bronze around the fountain was long gone, melted down for metal during the war.

Once he was certain it was safe, Raoul walked quickly across the road and into the narrow alley that ran alongside the café. He knocked on the door, three sharp taps, pause; three sharp taps, pause; then another three sharp taps. He glanced uneasily down the alley, then in the opposite direction, as he waited for the sound of footsteps behind the door.

'*Oui?*'

'It's me.'

The rattle of the chain and the key being turned in the lock, then César opened up.

'What are you doing here?'

'Wanted to catch you before the meeting.'

'Come in, I'm not quite finished,' César said, pulling him inside and shutting the door. 'Five minutes.'

Raoul followed César down a set of steps to the basement. César flicked on a dim red ceiling lamp, then closed the door.

The darkroom was well stocked, a legacy from the days before the war when the pressmen had developed their pictures here to wire to the Parisian papers. There were bottles of developing fluid, clearly labelled, an enlarger and a dryer for prints. Pegged to the wire above the wooden counter Raoul saw a row of black and white photographs of the camps at Argelès and Collioure. He recognised the coastline, swampland, the air black with mosquitoes. After France's surrender in June 1940, Raoul had spent several weeks travelling between the camps in Collioure, Saint-Cyprien, Rivesaltes, Argelès, helping Bruno's former comrades in the International Brigade. The photos triggered many painful, broken memories.

'How did you get hold of these?' he said quietly.

'Smuggled out by the Croix-Rouge women,' César replied.

'Brave of them.'

César nodded. 'Yes.'

The photographs had obviously been taken illegally – the angles were odd, the definition blurred and out of focus – but the story they told was clear. Emaciated women and men, children, standing behind barbed-wire fences, staring out at the camera. Raoul looked along the line of prints, his eye drawn by a smaller photograph showing the sign that hung at the entrance to the camp at Argelès: CAMP DE CONCENTRATION D'ARGELÈS.

His eyes hardened. 'You know the worst of it? That it's French soldiers policing these camps. Doing Hitler's work for him. That's the truth of Vichy's "*voie de collaboration*".'

César nodded as he tidied the bench. 'I'll print the tracts tonight,' he said. 'Machines are too noisy now, too many people around.'

'These are excellent, César.'

He shrugged. 'Best I could do. Make people realise what's going on, not that most of them care.'

'Some do,' said Raoul.

'You've heard the latest? For every Nazi killed by the Resistance in Paris, they're executing ten Frenchmen.'

'I heard a hundred.'

César shook his head. 'And yet everyone walks around with their eyes shut, grateful to be in the so-called "free" zone. People still think things could be worse.'

Raoul put his hand on César's shoulder. 'That's why we're trying to change their minds. Make them understand. Your tracts, the papers we put out, these photographs, all of it makes a difference.'

César gave a long, deep sigh. 'I wonder . . .'

'Attitudes are changing,' Raoul said, with more confidence than he felt. 'People are starting to realise. More people are starting to support us.'

For a moment they were silent. Then César flicked off the light. 'You go first,' he said. 'I'll come out the front. See you in the rue de l'Aigle d'Or.'

It was only as Raoul crossed boulevard Antoine Marty that he remembered he hadn't told César about Antoine's necklace. He kicked himself. The sight of the photographs had sent everything else out of his mind, brought back the familiar tightness in his chest when he thought about Bruno and how he'd died. In any case, César was in an odd mood – uncommunicative, morose.

With any luck, Antoine would be at the meeting and he could give the chain back and it would turn out he'd been making something out of nothing. Raoul doubled back and crossed the rue de Verdun. He didn't want to think about the alternative.

Chapter 11

Raoul watched César enter the building next to the Café Lagarde in the rue de l'Aigle d'Or. He waited a couple of seconds, then followed and gave the password.

'*Per lo Miègjorn*.' For the Midi.

He was admitted into a dark hallway, where César was waiting for him.

'Any trouble?'

Raoul shook his head. 'Nothing. You?'

'All quiet.'

They went up the narrow stairs in single file, towards an apartment on the first floor. Voices were muffled, just audible. César knocked – four slow raps – then opened the door.

Raoul followed him in and found himself in a dingy kitchen. The air was thick with tobacco smoke, stale food and blocked drains.

'Sanchez,' said the man leaning over a map on the table. 'We were about to give up on you.'

César shrugged. 'You were the one who wanted photographs on the flyers, Coursan.'

Raoul glanced at César, surprised by his tone, but his face gave nothing away.

'You must be Pelletier,' Coursan said, offering his hand. 'And this is Robert Bonnet, and his brother Gaston.'

Raoul nodded at the two men sitting at the square table in the middle of the room. Robert was large and amiable-looking, with a handlebar moustache. Gaston was short, with mean, small eyes. The glass ashtray between them was filled with spent matches and cigarette papers. An empty jug of water and a half-full bottle of Pastis stood on the counter behind them.

Raoul looked at Coursan, trying to get the measure of the man. He was quite short, no more than five foot seven or eight, but with a commanding physical presence all the same. Clear eyes, balanced features, with five or six days' stubble and a moustache. He wore the same ordinary, nondescript blue trousers and open-necked shirt as the rest of them, though there was something of the bureaucrat about him.

Raoul didn't know where Coursan had served during the war, or what he'd done since the defeat. All he knew was that he'd set up this particular unit of *résistants*. One of the newest of the local groups, according to César, formed partly in reaction to the collaborationist organisations that were operating openly in Carcassonne: the PPF, the SOL, Collaboration, the Jeunes Doriotistes and the LVF were the biggest, but there were others.

'What have we missed?' said César, with the same spike of belligerence.

Raoul couldn't tell whether Coursan was ignoring the edge in César's voice, or was too preoccupied to notice it. Either way, his expression gave nothing away.

'I've been running through the plans for tomorrow,' he said.

'Let's get on with it then, shall we?'

Now Raoul did see a flash of anger in Coursan's eyes, but his voice remained neutral.

'We'll be stationed here,' he said, pointing at the plan of the town, 'here and here. Our comrades from "24 Février" will be coming from the opposite direction, from boulevard Marcou.' He tapped the map. 'According to the wireless, our colleagues from "Libération" will base themselves by the Grand Café du Nord.' He looked at César. 'Is everything all right with the leaflets?'

'Yes.'

Coursan's eyes narrowed. 'Are they printed?'

'They will be,' he said curtly.

Coursan held César's gaze, but didn't question him further.

'The word is,' he continued, 'that the SOL intends to disrupt the demonstration. Drafting in reinforcements from Narbonne and Limoux. Our job is to make sure they don't.'

'How many are we expecting?' Raoul asked.

'No way of knowing.'

'There were thousands at that demonstration in Place Davilla,' Robert said, his bushy moustache wagging up and down as he talked. 'Day of National Mourning, that's what they called it.'

Raoul nodded. 'But that was two years ago. Demonstrations weren't illegal then.'

'True. People are more scared now. Too scared to stand up and be counted these days.'

Raoul turned to Coursan. 'The police must be aware something's planned. Isn't it strange they're not trying to stop it?'

'Getting cold feet, Pelletier?' said Gaston.

'Just assessing the situation.'

'Not having second thoughts?'

'Not at all,' Raoul said quickly. 'I'm just saying that if the authorities think they have more to gain by letting it go ahead than by preventing it, should we be worried?'

Gaston poured himself another drink, slopping Pastis over the table. 'Don't know what—'

Coursan held up his hand. 'Let Pelletier finish.'

'They want to prove that Carcassonne isn't Paris,' he said, warming to his theme. 'But it's also a good way to get us all in one place. The leaders of Resistance groups, partisans, together at the same time.'

'You think there'll be arrests?' Robert said.

Raoul was amazed he was even asking. He glanced at César to gauge his reaction, but his friend's hands were laced behind his neck and he was staring up at the ceiling.

'I'm certain there will be trouble,' Coursan said, 'but it's a risk we have to take. Does anyone disagree?'

No one spoke.

Coursan returned his attention to the map. Raoul loosened his collar. It was very hot, airless. In the corner, the tap continued to drip, drip. Every now and again the pipes gurgled, as if someone was running a bath elsewhere in the building, then the plumbing sighed and settled down again.

'Where's Antoine?' Robert said. 'Isn't he coming?'

Raoul felt a kick in his stomach. Immediately, his hand went to his pocket, found the cold metal.

'Another one with cold feet,' Gaston was saying.

César glared at him. 'He'll be here.'

'I'm sorry,' Raoul said, not sure what he was actually apologising for. He put the chain on the table. 'I don't know if it's important, but I found this. I think it's Antoine's.'

Straight away, there was a shift in the atmosphere. A sharpening of attention. César leant forward and snatched up the silver necklace.

'Where did you get it?' he demanded.

'Down by the river, this morning. Near Païchérou.'

'Did you see Antoine there?'

'No. I'd have said if I had.'

Raoul was aware of Coursan's eyes fixed on him. 'Something the size of this and you just happened to notice it, Pelletier?' he said lightly.

'No,' he said, then stopped, wondering how to explain. 'That's to say, there was a girl …'

Gaston bayed with laughter.

Raoul ignored him. 'There was a girl – don't know who

she was – who had got into trouble. Come off her bike, tipped forward into the water.' He shrugged. 'She was holding the chain.'

'And what time did you say this was?' Coursan asked.

'Ten o'clock, give or take.'

'So you saw the necklace. Took it.' He paused. 'Why was that?'

'I don't know really,' Raoul replied, feeling wrong-footed. 'I suppose because it looked like Antoine's.' He shrugged. 'I didn't really think about it.'

'Did the girl explain why she had it?'

'She was unconscious. Then I heard a car, and since she was all right – and obviously I didn't want to get caught up in anything – I left.'

'A real *chevalier*,' muttered Gaston. 'Gallant.'

'You'd have done the same, Bonnet,' Raoul said. 'Common sense.'

Gaston swallowed a belch, then poured himself another drink. Robert frowned at his brother and sat back heavily in his creaking chair.

'You're sure the girl didn't say anything?' Coursan said. His voice was casual, though Raoul sensed the keen interest behind his words.

'Not really, nothing that made sense. Nothing about Antoine.' He felt the tension tighten another notch. He looked at everyone's faces, seeing nothing unusual, nothing different in any expression, but he was regretting bringing it up all the same. 'Look, I don't know where Antoine is, but I'm sure the girl just happened to be there. Bad luck, good luck, however you want to look at it. She saw the chain, picked it up, end of story.'

'Except for the fact the girl was half drowned,' said César. 'Except for the fact Antoine should be here, and isn't.' He turned on Coursan. 'And Laval isn't here either, come to that. Where is he, Coursan?'

'He'll be here.'

Downstairs, the door to the street slammed. Everybody stopped talking, listening to the footsteps coming up the stairs. The door swung open. Raoul sighed, realising he'd been holding his breath.

It wasn't Antoine.

'Christ, Laval,' muttered Gaston. 'Give us all a heart attack.'

Raoul hadn't previously met Coursan's second-in-command, Sylvère Laval, though he recognised him from César's description. He had the look of a musician, black trousers and shirt, hair slicked back. His eyes were sharp with smoke and drink and late nights. Like Coursan, he had five or six days' growth on his chin.

Laval nodded at Coursan, then sat down beside Gaston.

'We have – might have – a problem,' Coursan said. 'Déjean's not shown up and Pelletier has been telling us how he fished a girl out of the river earlier this morning. She was holding Déjean's chain.'

Raoul saw a look pass between the two men. Again he glanced at César, but he was still examining the necklace and didn't meet his eye.

'Why was Pelletier at the river?' Laval asked.

'On my way here,' Raoul replied, irritated to be talked about as if he wasn't in the room.

César stood up. 'I'm going to check Antoine's flat, see if he's there.'

'Sit down, Sanchez,' Coursan said mildly.

'He's probably in bed nursing a hangover,' said Gaston.

'He's not a drinker.'

'Everyone's a drinker,' said Gaston, swallowing another belch.

'I'm not sitting here doing nothing,' César said, 'when Antoine might be in trouble.'

'Sit down,' Coursan repeated.

He didn't raise his voice, but the authority in it was clear all the same. To Raoul's surprise, César did what he was told. Robert poured a glass of Pastis and pushed it across the table to him. César added water and downed it in one.

'Did the girl say anything?' Laval asked Coursan.

'As I said,' Raoul replied, 'she was unconscious. She didn't do or say anything.'

Laval was looking at Raoul, but still addressing himself to Coursan.

'What do you want to do?'

Coursan drummed his fingers on the table for a moment. 'If Antoine's been arrested, we need to know. It could affect things tomorrow. César, why not check his apartment? If he's there, leave a message in the usual way, behind the bar in the café downstairs.'

'And if not?'

'Our priority is tomorrow.'

'Right,' said Gaston, giving a mock salute.

'Is everyone clear about what they're doing?'

Raoul and Robert nodded. César didn't respond.

'Laval?'

'Yes.'

'In which case,' Coursan continued, 'meet at the Café Saillan at eight tomorrow morning.' He looked at César. 'You'll bring the leaflets there?'

César still didn't answer.

'Sanchez?' snapped Laval.

César stared at him, then gave a sharp nod and stood up.

'I always deliver what I promise.' He swept his tobacco and matches from the table and walked out of the room.

Raoul looked at Coursan, then at Laval, but their faces gave nothing away. Gaston and Robert were already getting up.

'Good luck tomorrow, gentlemen,' Coursan said mildly. 'A word before you go, Laval.'

Raoul followed the Bonnets out. On the landing, he paused just long enough to hear Coursan's voice.

'What the hell happened?'

The door was slammed shut. Raoul pressed his ear against the wood, but couldn't hear anything other than muffled voices. After a moment or two, he followed the others down the stairs and out into the street.

Chapter 12

The rue de l'Aigle d'Or was crowded now. Women queuing, women shopping, talking. Three little girls were playing hopscotch on a chalk pattern drawn on the pavement, and a gaggle of teenage boys, all spots and hungry eyes, were admiring a silver motorbike parked outside the café.

Raoul lifted his hand to shield his eyes from the sun, then saw César was waiting for him at the junction with the rue du Port.

'I'm sorry,' he said. 'I meant to tell you about the chain before the meeting. It's why I came to the print shop, but then I saw the photographs and it went out of my mind.' Raoul took a breath. 'It might not even be his,' he continued, still feeling the need to apologise. 'There must be hundreds like it in Carcassonne.'

'It is his,' César said. 'Antoine scraped his initials on the catch with his knife. I checked. They were there.'

For a moment, both men were silent. The white smoke from their cigarettes spiralled up into the hot lunchtime air.

'No reason to think he's been arrested,' Raoul commented.

César paused, then sighed. 'Last week he told me he was going to Tarascon for a few days, but he should have been back by now.'

'Why Tarascon?'

'His parents live there, but . . .'

'That's all he said?'

César shrugged. 'You know how it is.'

Raoul nodded. Tell nobody anything. Trust no one, not even closest friends and family. What they didn't know, they couldn't speak of.

'But that chain of his,' César continued quietly, 'I never saw him without it on.'

Raoul glanced at him, trying to work out what was going on in César's head. He'd been in an odd mood from the beginning of the meeting, even before he knew Antoine was missing. Might be missing.

'Do you want me to come with you to the apartment?'

César tossed the stub of his cigarette to the pavement and ground it under his heel, then shook his head. 'That's why I waited. It's getting on for lunchtime. I thought if you go to the flat, that leaves me free to try the bars, the café in the rue du Port where Antoine usually goes. I know his friends. They'll talk to me.'

'Fine. Where's he live?'

'Building on the corner of rue Emile Zola and the allée d'Iéna. First floor.'

'All right.'

'I'll be in the Café des Deux Gares about nine, if you find anything out. If you don't, in the Saillan tomorrow.'

'You think you're being watched?'

He shrugged again. 'Not worth taking the risk.'

César started to move off. Raoul put his hand out to stop him.

'Is everything all right?' he asked. 'Aside from this business with Antoine.'

'What do you mean?'

'You know what I mean,' Raoul said steadily. 'You're on edge. Then, in the meeting, there seemed to be something going on between you and Coursan.'

He said nothing.

'César?'

Sanchez hesitated. 'I don't like the way he puts himself above us.'

Raoul frowned. 'Coursan set the group up, it's natural he takes charge. You told me he was a patriot, working to preserve the traditions and alliances of the Languedoc. The Occitan spirit of tolerance, that's how you put it. You certainly thought enough of him to recruit me. And Antoine.'

'Things change,' César said brusquely.

'What kind of things, that's what I'm asking.'

'Nothing worth mentioning.'

Raoul bit back his impatience. 'Well, how do you know Coursan? You must have known something about him to join the unit in the first place.'

'By reputation. People spoke highly of him. Acquitted himself well in the war. Did a lot with the early Resistance in Toulouse.'

'But you'd never met him in person?'

'No.'

Raoul thought for a moment. 'What does he do for a living?'

'Not sure.'

'César, if there's a problem, if you're having doubts – something specific – you've got to tell me.'

'Let's just say he's not the man I thought he was.'

'That's not good enough.'

'All right. I've started to ask myself what's in it for Coursan. What does he really want?'

'Same as us, presumably – to fight the Occupation. Defeat Vichy.'

'I'm not so sure.'

'What then, money? Is that what you think?'

Sanchez didn't answer.

'César?' he prompted again.

'All I'm saying is the man I heard so much about and the man I see in front of me don't match up.'

Suddenly, the antagonism seemed to go out of César and his mood changed. He leant over and rested his hand on Raoul's shoulder.

'Look, forget I said anything. Coursan and I don't see eye to eye, so what?' He shrugged. 'After tomorrow, it won't matter. It's Antoine we've got to worry about.' Then, before Raoul could ask any more questions, he turned and was walking away into the crowds in Place Carnot.

Raoul stood and watched him go, confused by the whole conversation. He thought back to the grievances and conflicts he'd known in groups he'd been involved with in the past. Tempers were always frayed, worse the night before a mission or when they were about to take a new group of refugees across the mountains. Was that César's problem? Just nerves about tomorrow's action, fuelled by his concerns for Antoine, or something more?

Still mulling things over in his mind, he headed towards the allée d'Iéna. The fact César no longer liked Coursan wasn't a problem. No one chose one's comrades on the basis of liking or disliking. Raoul himself hadn't liked everyone in the Banyuls network by any means. But he had trusted them. That was essential.

He cast his mind back to what his brother had written about Sanchez. That he was hot-headed, liable to fly off the handle and to bear a grudge. Something of a lone wolf. But also that his instincts were sound. That he was a good judge of character.

'*Per lo Miègjorn*,' Raoul muttered.

Brave words, fighting words. Spoken by the medieval hero of the Cité, Raymond-Roger Trencavel, to rally the men of the Midi against the northern crusaders in 1209. When Raoul had given the password earlier, it had sounded like a call to arms.

But now? Now, he wasn't so sure.

Chapter 13

Sandrine glanced up at the clock again. She'd been sitting on the hard bench beneath the window for almost an hour. She was thirsty and uncomfortable and only her reluctance to give the supercilious desk clerk the satisfaction of watching her give up kept her there.

The police station was busy, people coming and going. Officers carrying buff folders or box files. Bursts of noise, then silence. Doors opening, closing, a sense of activity and anticipation. The same dark-haired officer she'd seen when she arrived came back into the reception area.

He raised his eyebrows in surprise. 'Still here, mademoiselle?'

'I don't suppose you've any idea how much longer before someone might be free to see me?'

He stopped. 'Your guess is as good as mine. Everyone's got the wind up. Telegrams coming in all night. The girls in the exchange say the telephones haven't stopped.'

'Has something happened?'

He lowered his voice. 'There's a rumour there's going to be a demonstration tomorrow. In support of de Gaulle.'

Their eyes met, and for a moment Sandrine saw the man behind the uniform. She smiled. He smiled back, then the official shutters came down once more.

Sandrine watched him continue on down the corridor, open a door on the right-hand side, and then he was gone.

She approached the desk clerk. 'May I have some writing paper?'

'What?'

'Writing paper,' she repeated, as if talking to a child. 'And a pen. If it's not too much trouble.'

He stared at her, but then leant under the desk, produced a few sheets of lined notepaper and a pencil, and passed them over without a word.

Sandrine went back to the bench. So long as she was here, she might as well make use of the time. Balancing the notepaper on her lap, she wrote the date.

Lundi, le 13 juillet 1942.

She underlined it once, then again.

Déclaration de Mlle Vidal Sandrine.

'This is my true and freely given testament.'

She put the end of the pencil in her mouth, thought for a moment longer, then began to write.

Chapter 14

THE HAUTE VALLÉE

'Tell me.'

Antoine screamed again. He didn't know where he was, he knew nothing. Nothing except the pain. The iron bar came down again, again on the back of his neck and he felt his broken bones jump. His arms were shackled and tied round the back of the chair. Blood congealed around the cuffs, rings of red and broken skin on his wrists. His right hand was swollen purple, his fingernails torn where he'd tried to get across the weir. How long ago was that? One hour, more, less? A day? He no longer knew.

'Where is it? Where is the key?'

It had been Sunday. He remembered Sunday. Thinking about seeing his parents, heading back to his apartment ready to make the journey south. That was when they'd got him. Walking past the river. The catch on his chain had broken, he remembered that. Putting it in his pocket. So hot, even though it was early. He remembered the black Renault Primaquatre coming slowly down the road from the cimetière Saint-Michel, and pulling up. A man, well dressed, foreign, asking for directions to the Cité.

Then, nothing.

At first, in the cellar, the questions and the blows, the tightening of the rope on his wrists. Then they stopped. Left him alone for a long time, he didn't know how long, day and night blurring one into the other. They were waiting for someone, for instructions, though Antoine didn't know it then. Waiting for this man, he realised now.

It was morning when he escaped. Pretended to be unconscious, so they left him unguarded. Managed to climb out of the broken window and snapped the padlock on the gate. But he was too weak to get far and although he made it down to Païchérou, down to the river, on to the rocks, he hadn't the strength. He'd slipped, fainted. The water pressing into his mouth, his nose.

He tried to remember. There'd been a girl, hadn't there? Pulled him out of the water. It hadn't mattered, anyway. They'd come after him, brought him back here. Now, again, the drip, drip of the cellar, the bare earth under his feet.

'*Komm*. If you tell me, this will stop.'

With each word, another strike with the iron bar, cutting through the silent air, the steady breathing of his captors within it, the marks on his broken body telling the story of every blow he'd received.

'He's passed out. Hurry.'

Antoine hoped they were talking about him, welcoming the thought that he would not have to feel any more. But a sponge was thrust into his mouth. The sour, sharp vinegar made him gag. His cracked lips recoiled in protest and he tried to twist free, but hands on his shoulders held him firm. He smelt blood and wondered if it was his own or if someone else had sat on this chair before him. Then water running over his head, his shoulders, down into his lap, shocking him into speech.

'I don't know . . .'

Antoine didn't know if that was true. Hours ago, days, between the kicks and punches and the burns from the cigarettes, the smell of the singed hairs on his arms and the hiss of skin, he'd forgotten what the man wanted. None of it made sense. He didn't know where he was. He didn't know what he had already said.

'Antoine,' said the man, drawing the vowels out so

softly. 'Your friend died, you remember? You had a telegram, yes? Cast your mind back. To March 1939, remember? We found Rahn in the snow, the mountains of the Wilder Kaiser. Nothing you say can harm him now. He's at peace. We have his diaries, all his notes, letters. He worked for us, didn't you know that? We know that if he had left anything behind – the key – it would have been in your safe keeping, yes? The key?'

Antoine knew they were lying. If they had everything, then why were they asking him questions? He didn't understand anything. The old man would know. He tried again to shake his head, but his bones, his muscles, nothing worked any more. Words were coming back to him, fragments of memory.

'*D-Die-Dietrich*,' he said. If he kept saying this, they would believe that there was a key, that they were looking for a key, then the secret would be kept from them at least.

'The skeleton key, yes?'

Antoine felt the man's breath, eager, suddenly on his face. Saw the death's-head brooch on his lapel. Otto Rahn had worn one too. He'd written to tell him he had joined them, then nothing more until just before the end. Life became too dark after that.

'Rahn gave you a key to look after?' The man's voice was closer still. 'Where is it now, Antoine? What's it for?'

His friends hadn't liked Otto, but there was something about him that made you listen to his stories. Beautiful stories, clever, words taking flight. Antoine never dreamt there was any truth in them.

The old man had told him to be careful. Antoine should have listened, but he'd thought he'd outwitted them. In a way he had, though the cost was too high.

'All true ...'

The man's voice, sharp again, impatient. 'What's that you say?'

Antoine was slipping away, like a boat coming loose of its moorings, a gentle letting go. Remembering the words written on the map. He hoped the girl was all right. Kind … she was gentle. She had tried to help. He didn't know his torturer. Hadn't seen his face, only a grey suit and the pink, waxy skin on his left arm when he rolled up his shirt-sleeves, as if he'd been burnt. The Cathars had been given to the fire, hadn't they? The good men, Otto had called them.

The old man knew all about them.

'*Gottesfreunde*,' Antoine whispered. 'Forgotten.'

As he said it, he realised that was true. A few months of friendship, ten years ago, eleven. Otto Rahn, a young German from Michelstadt, travelling with a Swiss friend. Antoine just out of university and with time on his hands. A chance meeting in a café, the pleasure of discovering a shared interest in the same things, treasure and local legends, an initiation into the mythology of the mountains. As 1931 tipped over into 1932, they had read and talked and smoked late into the night, going climbing in the day when the weather permitted, up to the summit of the Pic de Soularac, to the ruins of Montségur and Coustaussa, or down into the belly of the caves of Niaux and Lombrives. Brotherhood – the Fahneneid, the blood oath of the German warrior of legend – it was innocent, harmless. Otto was naïve certainly, but he didn't think like those maniacs. He was flattered when they invited him to join them, proud of his black uniform. Later, he had become disillusioned, wanted to get out, but by then it was too late.

Ten years ago, more. Antoine had been young and understood nothing. A classics student, Latin and Greek, idealistic. He had never killed a man then. Never seen a man die. If Rahn had lived, the two of them would have been on opposite sides. Ten years. It had been one of those interludes in a life starting out. Antoine didn't understand.

Otto had died more than three years ago. Before all the madness started. So why were these men here now?

'*Sprich.*' Speak.

Antoine heard the anger in the man's voice and flinched from it.

'Forgotten,' he said again, feeling the tug of sweet black sleep.

This time the blow caught him across the face. Antoine heard his nose crack, the splinter of it, then felt the blood, warm and wet, coating his dry lips, but there was no pain. Tears, of relief, slipped from his tired eyes.

'We're losing him,' someone else was shouting, a voice thick with violence and cigarettes. An ugly voice.

Antoine was almost free now, floating above the torture cellar and the pain and the sheer pointlessness of it all. They couldn't reach him. Rough hands, cold water, dragging a broken body to its feet, he was beyond them.

'Get the doctor in here,' the man ordered. '*Allez, vite.*'

Antoine realised he was smiling. The sound of running feet, the door being thrown open, the rustle of the doctor in his bag. Needles, light, a sharp prick, so many people pulling him this way, that.

He died ten minutes later, without revealing anything more about his friend Rahn. Without telling them anything about what he had found or what he knew. And without letting the name of Audric Baillard pass his lips.

Chapter 15

CARCASSONNE

Sandrine carried on writing, writing until her arm ached and she'd set down everything she could remember. Finally, she was done. She leant back against the hard wooden bench and flexed her right hand. She looked up at the desk clerk, determined that he should notice she was still there.

He'd gone. The desk was unmanned. This was her chance. If he refused to let her pass, she'd go and find someone herself. Sandrine stood up, her sense of grievance at being kept waiting pushing her into action.

Shoving the sheets of paper into her pocket, she walked quickly away from the reception, in the direction everyone else had been going all morning, and sneaked through the door on the right.

The atmosphere away from the public space was immediately different. She was in a long and featureless corridor. White tiles on the floor, no windows, just strip lighting all the way along. The walls were painted a clinical washed green and no posters or pictures or notices broke the monotony. On either side, heavy studded doors of reinforced steel.

Sandrine hesitated, but then made herself go on. There was a door at the end of the passage with a card on it – COMMISSAIRE DE POLICE – slotted into a wooden holder. She could hear voices inside. She lifted her hand and knocked sharply before she had time to change her mind.

She heard footsteps on the far side of the door, then the

sound of the handle turning, and the same young officer appeared.

'How did you get in here? This is a restricted area.'

'I didn't realise.'

'What the hell's going on?' shouted a voice from inside the room.

Sandrine sidestepped the officer and darted into the room.

'Commissaire, I'm sorry, but I couldn't see what else to do. I've been waiting for hours.'

A senior officer was sitting behind a wide mahogany desk on which a map with small wooden markers was spread out. Behind him was a phalanx of gunmetal-grey filing cabinets, each with several drawers and handwritten white labels set into the handles.

'What in the name of God is going on?' He turned on the young officer. 'Ramond, get her out of here.'

'Mademoiselle,' the young man said, 'official personnel only allowed. You must leave.'

'I want to report a crime,' she said.

'Mademoiselle ...'

'I was attacked this morning,' she said, struggling to keep her voice steady. 'I thought the police – you – would want to know of a crime committed in Carcassonne.'

'For the last time, Officer Ramond, get her out of here!'

She felt the young officer's hand in the small of her back, propelling her towards the door.

'You are supposed to protect us,' she said furiously, then spun on her heel and walked out.

The moment she was back in the corridor, her legs started to shake. Sandrine felt sick, with anger or nerves she wasn't sure. She heard the door open and close, then the sound of footsteps behind her as the young officer caught up with her.

'That wasn't very sensible,' he said.

Sandrine pulled a face. 'I know. I'm sorry, I didn't mean to get you into trouble.'

He gave a brief, sweet smile. 'It's all right. I'm used to it.'

He led her to a bench, sat down and took out his notebook. 'Why don't you tell me what happened?'

Sandrine took a deep breath, then launched into her story. 'I was at Païchérou this morning and there was a man in the water – I thought he was drowning, but there were rope marks on his wrists and ... I think his family, someone, should know – but when I—'

The officer held up his hand. 'Wait, hold on a moment,' he said. 'Let's start with your name.'

'Vidal,' she replied. 'Sandrine Sophie Vidal.'

'And your address?'

'Rue du Palais.'

Chapter 16

Raoul found rue Emile Zola easily enough and Antoine's building on the corner. Six individual apartments, each with their own bell. He pressed, then stood back on the pavement and looked up. The shutters were open, but there was no sign of life. He pressed the bell again, a little harder and for a little longer, then once more stepped back and waited. The first-floor window remained closed. Finally, he rang the concierge's bell instead. A few moments later, a thin woman dressed in black, with a sour expression and sharp eyes, answered the door.

'I'm looking for Antoine Déjean,' he said. 'Have you seen him?'

'He was here earlier.'

Raoul's interest quickened. 'What time was that?'

'Can't remember,' she said, meeting his gaze.

Raoul slipped a coin into her hand.

'Seven, seven fifteen.'

'Did you actually see him?' He got out another couple of francs.

'No,' the concierge admitted. 'But I heard him moving about up there. Who else would it be, that time in the morning?'

Raoul thought for a moment. 'The thing is, I left something with him that I need to collect. Any chance you could . . .'

She stared at him for a moment, then put the coins in the pocket of her housecoat, went into her office, took a bunch of keys from a hook.

'Ten minutes,' she said.

Raoul followed her up to the first floor. She unlocked the door to let him in. Stale, unused air rushed out. A scent of sour tobacco, vanilla, newsprint hot in the sun beating in through the windows.

'Ten minutes,' she repeated.

There was a small lobby, leading into a large room which overlooked the allée d'Iéna, with a fold-out bed in the corner and a kitchenette with a sink and a single gas ring. A few tins of food and two apples, bruised and mouldy, in a china bowl. A narrow corridor led off the lobby to a WC and small bath at the back.

Antoine's newspapers were stacked corner to corner on a desk, with a few banned pamphlets too. Two low armchairs were set at perfect right angles to the window, facing into the room, all oddly neat and tidy. Raoul got a book down from the shelves, put it back, not sure what he was looking for. Evidence of where Antoine had been at the weekend? Evidence of where he was now?

He looked out of the window on to the allée d'Iéna. He saw a travelling salesman arriving at the Hôtel des Voyageurs and two of the green police cars used for transporting prisoners – *paniers à salade* as they were known. They were heading towards the compound of the infantry barracks at the far end of the road.

It didn't take long to search Antoine's small flat. Raoul was loath to leave, just in case he came back. If it had actually been Antoine the concierge had heard. He smoked his last but one cigarette. At two o'clock, he gave up. He scribbled a note asking Antoine to get in touch, then made a quick detour to answer a call of nature before leaving. The tiny WC smelt sour, the water stagnant.

Raoul buttoned his trousers, reached over and opened the skylight window to air the room, then pulled the thin chain. Nothing happened. The water in the cistern above his head churned and gulped, but didn't flush. He tried again, jerking down hard on the chain.

He tried once more, not sure why it bothered him so much that the toilet was blocked, only that it did. He balanced on the seat, feet either side of the bowl, but he couldn't see inside the cistern. Under the kitchen sink he found an old-fashioned wooden plunger with a rust-coloured rubber head. He climbed back up and poked blind at the blockage with the handle, jabbing it down into the cistern, trying not to let the water slop over the sides. He could feel there was something there, hard against the ballcock. He twisted the stick, jiggered it from side to side, but still couldn't shift the obstruction, so he rolled up his right sleeve and shoved his hand into the cistern. He felt something soft, a kind of heavy fabric, rolled into a ball. He worked it free and carefully took it out.

Raoul stepped down from the seat, shook the excess water from his hand and wiped it on his trousers, then looked at the wad of dark green waterproof material. As he started to unwrap the package, something slipped out. His hand darted out, just catching it before it hit the uneven lino floor.

It was a small pale glass bottle, heavy and opaque, the hemispherical body patterned with a beautiful blue-green iridescence on one side, like the eye of a peacock's tail. On the other, a pattern in the glass that looked like leaves. It had a long thin neck with a small hole in the top, as if it had been worn on a chain or a thread, and a stopper of grey wool.

An unexpected explosion of knocking on the apartment door made him jump. He felt his heart lurch as he heard the rattling of keys in the lock.

'Monsieur,' came the shrill voice of the concierge, 'it's been more than ten minutes.'

'J'arrive,' he called out. *'Merci.'*

Raoul looked down at the exquisite tiny object in the palm of his hand, then, without thinking about it, quickly wrapped the bottle in his handkerchief and slipped it into his pocket. He put the damp cloth back in the cistern and was standing in the tiny lobby as the concierge pushed open the door.

'I lost track of time,' he said, dropping his last two coins into her open palm as he passed her. 'You know how it is.'

Aware of her suspicious eyes on his back as he ran down the stairs, he hoped she wasn't the type to call the police.

The sun was at its zenith. Keeping to the shadows, Raoul walked back towards the centre of town. He crossed the tram line and went down the boulevard Omer Sarraut past the Jardin des Plantes.

Outside the Café Terminus, a waiter was writing in chalk on a blackboard, advertising they had beer. Raoul stopped. The prices were exorbitant, but he was hot, thirsty and, for once, lucky to be in the right place at the right time. The thought of a cold beer – real beer – was too much to pass up.

He checked in his pockets. He'd given all his loose change to the concierge, but he had a note he'd been saving to buy food. Raoul looked at it and decided that beer beat the foul black bread they were selling hands down. He ordered at the bar, then took his drink outside to a table in the shade.

For a moment he just enjoyed the cold, sour taste on his tongue, on the back of his throat. Then, as usual, his thoughts started crowding in. Would the demonstration tomorrow change anything? He took another mouthful of beer, his mind turning, as it always did, on memories of war and revolution, resistance, like a permanent newsreel playing in his head.

From that, of course, to his brother. When Raoul had first arrived back in Carcassonne, he'd seen Bruno everywhere. Standing at the counter in the Café des Halles, or coming round the corner of the Quai Riquet, raising his hand to wave. So many men looked like him, reminded Raoul of his loss. As the days turned to weeks, to months, he'd seen Bruno less often. It made him miss him all the more.

Raoul raised his arm to attract the waiter's attention.

'*S'il vous plaît*,' he said, ordering a second glass.

The shadows moved round. Now, as the beer took hold, weak as it was, Raoul found his thoughts moving from grief to something different, something sweeter. To the girl at the river. The way her eyes fluttered open, just for an instant, and her wild black hair, all out of place. Her strong, determined features.

Chapter 17

'I know she's here, officer. Please check your records again.'

Sandrine looked down the corridor and saw Marianne standing at the desk in a blue dress, blue hat, matching gloves and bag. Immaculately turned out, as always.

'Marianne!' she cried, running to meet her.

Her sister immediately put her hand up to the cut on the side of Sandrine's head, staining the fingertips of her glove.

'Whatever happened? Are you all right?'

Sandrine winced. 'It's not too bad. How did you know I was here?'

'Lucie came to the Croix-Rouge to let me know what had happened. She told me she and Max had taken you home, but although your bike was there, Marieta said she hadn't seen you. I put two and two together ...'

'But how did you know I'd be at the police station?'

'Lucie said she'd persuaded you not to come,' Marianne said drily. 'Obviously, she didn't succeed.' She turned to the officer. 'Is my sister free to go?'

He nodded. 'Of course.'

Neither of the girls was aware of him watching them leave. Or that, as soon as they'd gone, Ramond tore up his notes and put the pieces into the rubbish bin.

Sandrine could tell Marianne was cross, although she wasn't quite sure why. She kept glancing at her, kept waiting for her to say something, but she walked fast and in silence. It wasn't until they had passed Artozouls, with its display of fishing nets, lines, rods and hunting equipment, and were standing outside the boulangerie next to the église des Carmes that Marianne spoke.

'Wait here,' she said, producing a coupon from her handbag and vanishing inside.

Sandrine was aware of the sharp eyes of an old woman in a first-floor apartment in the building on the opposite side of the street. She smiled, but *la vieille* stepped back behind her lace curtain.

Marianne reappeared holding a brown paper bag. 'It's still warm.'

Sandrine bit into the bun, which wasn't too bad at all. Solid, but thick with dried fruit so it tasted sweet despite the lack of sugar.

'You'd think they'd have a queue around the block if people knew she had these available so late in the day.'

'They don't,' said Marianne.

Sandrine frowned. 'Then how . . .?'

'It doesn't matter,' she said sharply.

'Why are you so cross?'

Marianne ignored the question. 'You'd better tell me what happened.'

'Didn't Lucie tell you?'

'No, all she said was that you'd had an accident down at the river, that she and Max had found you and taken you home.'

'She did try to talk me out of going to the police station,' Sandrine said, 'but I thought I should report it. Now I wish I'd listened to her.'

'Why?' Marianne said quickly. 'What happened? What did they do?'

'Do?' said Sandrine in surprise. 'They *did* nothing, that's the point. Nobody took me seriously.'

Marianne's shoulders relaxed a little.

Sandrine continued. 'In the end an officer took a few

notes, and that was that.' She pulled a face. 'I was an idiot, you don't have to rub it in. I know.'

To her astonishment, Marianne grabbed her arm. 'Do you, Sandrine? Really, I don't think you have any idea. That you would simply waltz into a police station – a police station, of all places – and make a scene. Didn't you even think about Max?'

'I didn't mention him,' she said, stung by how harsh Marianne sounded. 'I gave Lucie my word I wouldn't, though I don't understand why she made such a fuss.'

'Max is Jewish, Sandrine. Don't be so naïve.'

'Yes, but he's French. He's got all the right papers, hasn't he? He'll be all right.'

'No one is "all right", as you put it,' Marianne said. 'If he'd stayed in Paris, he'd have been arrested by now.'

'But Maréchal Pétain is protecting Jews in the *zone libre*, that's what it said in the paper.'

Marianne gave a sharp laugh. 'Every week the situation gets worse, can't you see? And because Lucie goes about with him, she has to be careful too. She gets spat at in the street; someone painted foul comments on her front door.'

'Oh,' said Sandrine, the fight going out of her. 'I didn't know.' She paused. 'Is that why she's worried about her father coming back?'

'Lucie said that?'

'Not in so many words.'

'Monsieur Ménard is a brute, an unpleasant man at the best of times,' said Marianne. 'Unkind to his wife. To Lucie, too. Belonged to a right-wing veterans' organisation for years, long before the war. In the LVF now.' She stopped. 'I'm just saying we have to be careful. You have to be careful. You put people at risk otherwise, even if you don't mean to.'

Sandrine felt a shiver go down her spine. On the surface,

Carcassonne and its people looked the same, but her perception was shifting, changing, slipping. Suddenly, it was no longer quite the town she loved.

'I thought I was doing the right thing,' she said, now thoroughly miserable.

'I know, darling,' sighed Marianne, the heat going out of her voice. 'But you don't see what's under your nose half the time.'

'How can I?' she protested. 'You never tell me anything. Besides, you're hardly ever home these days.'

'That's not fair, I …'

Sandrine stared at her, but whatever her sister might have been about to say, she'd thought better of it.

'What?'

Marianne shook her head. 'Nothing.'

They walked a little further in silence for a moment, then Sandrine pushed her hand into her pocket and pulled out the notes she'd written in the police station.

'Here,' she said.

'What's this?' Marianne asked.

'It's what happened,' she said. 'I was intending to give it to the police, but … well, I didn't get the chance. Anyway, you might as well read it.'

The sisters sat down on a bench beneath the plane trees lining the boulevard Maréchal Pétain. Sandrine watched as her sister turned the pages, but the expression on her face gave nothing away. When she had finished, Marianne leant back against the metal struts of the bench.

'At least do you see why I thought I should report what happened?' Sandrine said.

'To tell you the truth, darling, I don't know what to think.' Marianne tapped the papers in her lap. 'How much of this did you tell the policeman you talked to?'

'Not much. I simply said I'd pulled a man out of the river and that I thought someone had hit me. When I came to, there was no one there, so I made my way to the police station.'

'Did he believe you?'

Sandrine frowned. 'I don't know.'

Marianne paused. 'You didn't say anything about the … nature of the man's injuries?'

She shook her head. 'The thought of nobody knowing what had happened to him, after what he'd suffered, it didn't seem right,' she said quietly. 'I wasn't trying to cause trouble.'

At last, Marianne reached out and took her hand. 'No. It must have been dreadful. Horrible for you.'

Sandrine was furious to feel tears pricking in her eyes. 'You do believe me then,' she said. 'You don't think I'm making it up.'

Marianne shook her head. 'Even if you did bang your head, I can't see how you could invent all that.'

'What do you think happened?'

Her sister thought for a moment. 'Probably that the man, whoever he was, was being held nearby. Somehow he got away and made it down to the river. Perhaps he was trying to swim across. They came after him, saw you pull him out, were forced to put you out of action for long enough to retrieve the body.'

As much as anything, Sandrine was astonished by the matter-of-fact way her sister seemed to accept that such a thing could have happened in Carcassonne.

'As for the rest,' Marianne continued, 'honestly I don't know. It's hard to square the business of a second man pulling you out of the water. You're quite sure it wasn't the same person who hit you?'

'Quite sure.'

'How can you be certain? Did you see his face?'

'Why would he attack me first, then help me afterwards? It doesn't make sense.'

'True.' Marianne thought for a moment more. 'Would you recognise him if you saw him again?'

'Maybe. His voice, certainly.'

'What about the man who hit you?'

Sandrine shook her head. 'He came up behind me. I didn't see him at all.'

The girls sat in silence for a while longer. On the steps of the Palais de Justice opposite, a group of lawyers, like a murder of black crows, came flocking suddenly out of the court and down the steps to the cars waiting for them.

'What do you think has happened to the man I rescued from the river?' said Sandrine in a quiet voice.

'Try not to think about it.'

'I am, but it's hard. I've never seen anything so . . .'

Marianne folded the papers and gave them back to Sandrine.

'Put these away somewhere, somewhere safe. Better still, burn them.'

'But what do you think we should do?'

'Do? We should do nothing, nothing at all. Keep it to ourselves for now and hope nothing more comes of it.'

Chapter 18

The Haute Vallée

The doctor did not arrive at the Café des Halles until late in the afternoon, so it wasn't until after five that Baillard started the next stage of his journey.

He was heading for Rennes-les-Bains, a small town not far from Couiza and Coustaussa in the Salz valley. Baillard had lived there for some years in the 1890s, and continued to use it as his poste restante. He had been working on a book on the folklore and mythology of the valley. Gathering together antique stories of demons and ghosts and prehistoric creatures said to have stalked the mountains and hills before the Celts, before the Volcae, before the Romans. Before Christianity came and appropriated the old ways, the old shrines, for its own.

There wasn't a breath of wind as they drove north and the sun was still fierce, so they kept the windows wide open. The journey passed pleasantly enough. The doctor was good company and an engaging conversationalist, his interests ranging from midwifery in the mountain villages to the promise of a good harvest this year. He was careful to express no opinions about either Pétain or de Gaulle, and Baillard did not prompt him.

They drove into the town as the shadows were lengthening. The single bell of the church of Saint-Celse et Saint-Nazaire was ringing for vespers. The doctor set him down in the Place du Pérou. It had a new name now, but Baillard still thought of it in the old way. In those days, Abbé Boudet had preached from the tiny pulpit of the church of faith and ghosts and superstition, of trapped spirits and souls that could not rest. It was in this square that the old families of the village had waved their men to war in 1914, to Belgium and the Western Front, to their deaths – Jules Bousquet, Jean Bruet, Pierre and René Flamand, Joseph Saint-Loup. Baillard too, watching those he loved walk away – Louis-Anatole, who had survived the slaughter to start a new life in the Americas, and Marieta's beloved husband Pascal, who had not. *A Ses Glorieux Morts* read the inscription on the plaque in the church porch. Baillard knew, as did they all, that there was no glory in death.

For a moment he was tempted to climb up through the woods to see the old house that lived so vividly in his imagination, but the thought of gazing upon the burnt shell of the Domaine de la Cade saddened him. Nearly fifty years ago, but the memories were still sharp as glass. Too many people had died. Too many stories had changed their course. Here, more than anywhere else, Baillard felt the horror of that night in the landscape, the memory of ghosts and the earth torn open.

His thoughts returned again to the Codex. To the promise of those words, as well as the intimations of terror contained within them. Of what might be unleashed.

'*Las fantomas . . .*'

Baillard walked more quickly through the familiar streets to the bureau de poste, where he hoped the package from Antoine Déjean would be waiting for him. The office was closed, but he tapped on the window. Seconds later, a young woman came to the door and looked out. He saw her take in his pale suit, his panama hat and the yellow handkerchief he wore in his breast pocket.

'Monsieur Baillard?' she said.

He nodded. 'It's Geneviève, isn't it?'

'Yes, monsieur.'

'I knew your grandparents,' he said. 'Your parents, too.'

'Yes, my mother said so.'

'Please pass on my respects to Madame Saint-Loup when next you see her.' He dropped his voice. 'Now, I am hoping you have something for me?'

The girl's pretty face grew serious. 'I'm afraid that nothing has come, Monsieur Baillard. I've been here all weekend and today, but nothing has arrived for you.'

Baillard felt the air go out of his lungs. Only now did he realise how very much he had depended on the package being there.

'A message, perhaps?'

'I'm afraid not, monsieur.'

'No message,' he said softly. 'A pity, *damatge*.' He thought for a moment. 'Will you be here again tomorrow, Geneviève?'

'Every day except for Fridays, monsieur. My sister Eloise stands in for me then.'

Baillard nodded. 'I will be gone for a few days, but shall return at the beginning of next week. If anything comes for me, please keep it. Tell no one.'

'Yes, monsieur.'

He looked at her, seeing the steadfast expression behind her calm exterior. The Saint-Loup girls were all the same, took after their mother. As alike as grapes on the vine.

'Thank you, Geneviève.'

'I've done nothing, monsieur.'

'Ah, but you have, *filha*. You are here. That, in and of itself, is courageous.' He smiled. 'And for that, you have my thanks.'

'Any of us would do the same, Monsieur Baillard.'

With the sound of Geneviève bolting the door behind

him, Baillard walked back into the main street. He passed the Hôtel de la Reine, now down on its luck, so much less assured than it had been in the heyday of the spa town in the 1890s, when visitors from Paris, from Toulouse, from Carcassonne and Perpignan came to take the waters.

On the outskirts of the town, a farmer in a truck picked him up. Baillard was grateful for the lift. He was capable of walking great distances, even at his advanced age, but he felt burdened, particularly tired.

They left the village, following the cut of the river Salz. On the hills, jutting outcrops of rock kept watch over the valley. The glint of sunlight on water, the soft silver underside of leaves lifted by the breeze, yellow and blue and pink flowers clustering at the foot of fir trees and pines, juniper bushes and willow.

Unlike the doctor, his latest companion was a silent man, content to smoke and occasionally share a swig of red wine from the flask balanced on the dashboard in front of him, leaving Baillard at liberty to think. As the truck chugged its way through wooded valleys towards the tiny village of Los Seres, he wondered again what had gone wrong. He hoped that Antoine Déjean had only been delayed. That there was no cause for alarm.

As they drove higher into the mountains, Baillard thought about the Codex. A single sheet of papyrus between leather covers, according to contemporary records. Seven short verses, no more. Was it possible that so fragile a thing could have survived for so long? Fragments spoken, written down, words Antoine had seen? Enough for Baillard to hope they came from the Codex, but until the package arrived, he could not be sure.

Fanciful as it was, it seemed to him as though the story did not want to be told. A whispering, a trick of the light, hints and rumours, but the truth remaining stubbornly out of reach. He felt he was standing alone on a bare stage, with the characters waiting, invisible, in the wings.

Chapter 19

CARCASSONNE

'At least let me carry the plates to the sink,' Sandrine said again, after their evening meal was finished.

'I can manage,' Marieta said firmly, shooing her away. 'You should be resting.'

Sandrine's hand automatically went to the large sticking plaster on her head, the smell of iodine and antiseptic catching in her throat.

'I'm fine,' she said.

Marieta huffed. 'Well, I don't want you under my feet in the kitchen.'

Sandrine went to find Marianne in the salon at the front of the house. The largest room on the ground floor, before the war it had been used for special occasions only. After their father's death and the bitter winter of 1940 that followed, the girls had shut up the other rooms and set up camp here. Easier to heat just one room. By the time spring came, the habit was established. The dining room and their father's study remained closed, and the salon was a working room, magazines and books everywhere, a pleasant muddle.

In those days, acquaintances of Marianne had often stayed for a day or two, though Sandrine had rarely seen them. In the morning she went to college, and by the time she got home, they'd gone. Now, the stream of visitors had dried up. They mostly had the house to themselves.

Two tall windows gave on to the rue du Palais, with long yellow curtains skimming the wooden floorboards.

A fin-de-siècle fireplace of ornate marble, a little too large for the space, and a wrought-iron fire basket. Two oil paintings, one of their mother and one of their father, hung above the sideboard that smelt of beeswax and honey. Some time back, the plate and silver had been moved to the cellar for safe keeping, then left there even after the threat of bombing was over. In their place was a ceramic bowl with dried rose petals from the garden.

Marianne was reading on the sofa, with her legs curled up under her.

'I offered to wash up,' said Sandrine, throwing herself into the armchair, 'but Marieta sent me away.'

'Did you expect anything else?'

Sandrine shook her head. 'No, but she seems so tired.'

'She's not going to change her ways now.'

'I suppose not.'

Sandrine sat cross-legged in the chair and rested her head back. 'Are you going out?'

Marianne met her gaze. 'Not tonight,' she said, then went back to her book.

Sandrine couldn't settle. She swung her legs backwards and forwards, shifted position, picked up her book, put it down again.

'Do you mind if I put on the wireless?' she said in the end.

'Anything to stop you fidgeting. It's on the blink, though. Reception comes and goes.'

Sandrine went over to the highly polished wooden set and began to fiddle with the Bakelite dials, turning each in turn, but with no luck. The rattle of the airwaves cracked and pulsed. The hiss and spit of distant voices, echoing through the mesh of the speaker. Then there was a knock on the front door.

Marianne was immediately alert. 'Are you expecting a visitor?'

'No. Are you?'

Marianne shook her head. The girls listened as Marieta's wooden clogs clacked along the tiled corridor. Then the chain being taken off the door and the snick of the deadlock, followed by muffled conversation in the hall.

'Madomaisèla Lucie,' announced Marieta.

Lucie was wearing a smart red dress with wide sleeves, high heels and a matching bag. Her corn-coloured hair was perfectly waved and set and her lips were a flash of red in her pale face.

Marianne sighed with relief.

'Hope you don't mind me calling so late?'

'Not at all,' Marianne said. 'You look nice. Have you been out somewhere?'

'Sure thing.' Lucie pushed off her shoes and began to massage her toes. 'As a surprise, Max had bought tickets to a concert – our first-year anniversary, you see – and it was wonderful. No problems at all, it was a marvellous evening.' She turned to Sandrine. 'Max is a terrific amateur pianist, you know, good enough to be professional really, though he's so modest.'

'I didn't think classical music was quite your thing,' Marianne said.

'Oh well ...' Lucie waved her hand airily.

Marianne smiled. 'He's not with you?'

'No, he's gone home. He doesn't like leaving Liesl alone at night for long; there've been one or two ... problems. Well, you know.' Her look deepened. 'So, seeing as how I was at a loose end, I thought I'd come and see how the patient here was bearing up after this morning. Check she was all right.'

'I'm fine, thanks,' Sandrine said. 'And you were right about the police. No one wanted to listen to me. Kept me waiting for hours. One officer was nice, but that was it.'

‘You went to the police station?’ Lucie said quickly. ‘But you said you wouldn’t, you promised.’

‘There’s no harm done,’ Marianne said. ‘Sandrine didn’t say anything about you or Max. Really, there’s nothing to worry about.’

‘What kind of problems has Liesl had?’ Sandrine asked.

‘Boys throwing stones, shouting names,’ Marianne said.

‘Max says it isn’t serious,’ Lucie said, ‘but I think it’s awful. He’s reported it to the police, but of course they do nothing. It makes me furious.’

She leant back against the arm of the sofa, suddenly looking tired.

‘Thank you for bringing me home earlier,’ Sandrine said, feeling guilty now.

‘It’s all right, kid. You’re fine, that’s the main thing.’

‘Apart from the fact I can’t get the wireless to work.’

Lucie rubbed her eyes. ‘Want me to take a look?’

‘Can you fix it?’

‘I can try.’

She took off her gloves and went over to the cabinet. She crouched down and put her ear to the mesh, then started to adjust the settings.

‘Is it broken?’ asked Sandrine.

‘No, it’s just hard to pick up a signal. Well, that’s to say, it’s easy enough to get Radio Paris, but not other frequencies.’

Sandrine sat on the arm of the sofa, watching Lucie work. Voices in French, in German, echoing, then clear, then gone again. A burst of accordion music. Then four notes on a drum. Sharp, staccato, hollow.

‘Sounds like Beethoven’s Fifth,’ Sandrine joked.

Marianne stiffened. ‘God, you’re right!’

A high-pitched whistling filled the room, like an orchestra tuning up.

‘Perhaps it’s your concert, Lucie—’

'Shut up,' her sister said sharply. 'Listen!'

'Marianne!'

'Sorry,' she said quickly. 'It's just that at nine o'clock every night there's a broadcast from London. It's how de Gaulle and his supporters communicate with the Resistance. And how they pass on messages to one another in the *zone occupée*. Lucie's found it.'

Sandrine's heart skipped a beat. 'How do you know that?'

Marianne didn't answer, just sat forward to hear better. Lucie flapped her hand for silence as she tried to tune in. Then, through the hiss and crack of the radio waves, at last a clear voice.

'Ici Londres. Les Français Parlent aux Français.'

'Got it,' said Lucie.

'Demain, à Carcassonne … Tomorrow, in Carcassonne, in the *zone non-occupée* …'

Sandrine felt she was hardly breathing as she listened to a message she only half understood. She glanced at her sister, at Lucie, and saw expectation, nerves, concentration on their faces. Then, as quickly as it had begun, it was over. The English national anthem was played, and another burst of music, then the echo of space and a hissing. London fell silent.

Lucie leant forward and turned off the wireless.

'It is true then,' Marianne said under her breath. 'A demonstration tomorrow for Bastille Day.'

'Did you know about it?' Lucie asked.

Marianne flushed. 'Rumours, nothing definite,' she said. 'It's extraordinary you found the transmission.'

'So that's what he meant,' said Sandrine slowly.

'What who meant?' said Marianne sharply.

'The policeman, the one who listened to me – I think his name was Ramond. He said there was due to be a demonstration in support of de Gaulle.'

'He told you that?'

Sandrine nodded.

'And he was the officer you talked to about what happened to you?'

'Yes.'

'That's good, at least,' Marianne said, though she didn't explain.

'Max will want to go,' Lucie was saying, 'even though it's a risk.'

Marianne's expression softened. 'You'd think less of him if he didn't.'

Lucie laughed. 'I know that, I know.'

Sandrine felt a flutter of excitement in the pit of her stomach. 'I want to go too.'

Marianne's reaction was immediate, unequivocal. 'Absolutely not.'

'I want to show my support.'

'You're too young.'

'I'm eighteen!'

'Too young,' Marianne repeated firmly. 'I don't want you getting caught up in anything.'

Sandrine flushed. 'You were the one telling me I don't see what's going on under my nose. Well, this is my chance.' She turned to Lucie. 'May I come with you and Max?'

'No,' Marianne repeated.

'Look, I know I was an idiot today, but you can't wrap me up in cotton wool.'

'I am happy for Sandrine to come with us,' Lucie said carefully, looking at Marianne. 'Max won't let anything happen to her.'

Sandrine turned back to her sister. 'You see?'

Marianne didn't speak. The clock on the sideboard marked the seconds. Finally, she answered.

'All right, but you are to stay with me and do exactly – exactly – what I tell you. Do you hear?'

'You're going too?'

'Of course. Though quite what Marieta will have to say about it, I can't imagine.'

Sandrine grinned. 'Maybe she'll want to come. Wave a placard.'

There was a moment of silence as they each pictured the scene. Then all three girls burst out laughing.

Chapter 20

Los Seres

'This is as far as I go, monsieur. You'll be all right from here?'

Audric Baillard nodded. 'I will, *amic*,' he said, climbing out of the cab. 'My thanks for your kindness.'

Baillard watched the muffled tail lights of the lorry growing more and more faint, two pinpricks of weak light in the dark countryside. Then he turned away from the road and began to walk into the hills.

The world seemed to age with each step he took, following the old shepherds' tracks as he had done many times before. As so often, the familiar and ancient path brought back memories. At first they were memories of those against whom he had battled during his long life. But as he walked higher into the Sabarthès mountains, at his side were the ghosts of his allies, friends, the women and men of courage who, through the ages, had stood firm against tyranny. If the Codex yet survived to be found, then might he see them again in the even darker hours he knew lay ahead?

At last Baillard caught the first glimpse of the handful of buildings that made up Los Seres, silhouetted in the dark. His own small stone house was at the heart of the village. As he approached, he could see that no one had been there. No sign that Antoine had sought him here instead. He removed the wooden bar at the front door, propped it against the outer wall, then went inside.

Stale air rushed to greet him. He took off his hat and

his jacket, then lit the oil lamp. The match hissed, sparked, then a flame flared bright and set a pool of yellow light dancing across the polished wooden surface of the table. He went to the cupboard, took out a glass and an old-fashioned bottle with a rubber stopper, and poured himself a measure of Guignolet. The red liquid glinted and danced in the lamplight, sending a rainbow flickering across the bare walls of the house. He frowned, feeling something was not right, then realised it was the sound of the ticking of the clock that was missing. It had run down while he had been gone. He wound it up, let the music of the turning hands fill the silent space, then sat down at the table.

'And there shall come forth . . .'

The few words that had come down through the ages. One phrase in particular, recorded by a contemporary witness to the conflagration of texts destroyed by the early Christian Church in Gaul.

Was it a call to arms? An incantation? For all his scholarship and knowledge, Baillard was not certain. He feared the power contained within the words, of what might be set loose. France needed some intervention to help her cause, that was certain. But would the cost be too high?

'Come forth the spirits of the air.'

As he spoke the words again, Baillard had the sensation of something shifting. Imagination, hope, or something more tangible, he wasn't yet certain. The boundaries between the known and the unknown world beginning to crack, like ice in a melting river. He had an awareness of movement beyond the black of the mountains and the rock, beyond the fields and the plains.

Even now, in the caves of the Pic de Soularac, a shifting of bone and spirit. A girl and her lover, her husband, beginning to stir after eight hundred years of sleep.

'A ghost army . . .' he muttered. '*L'armada de fantomas.*'

Was it true? Could such things be true?

Baillard covered his eyes, in the hope that he might see more clearly. That he might hear better the voices trying to speak to him through the depths of recorded time. He almost felt he could hear the stirrings of the dead awakening, the remembrance of blood and sinew and muscle as the land came back to life.

But after a brief moment of promise, now only silence echoed. The graveyards, once more, were quiet. The time had not yet come. Might, he knew, never come.

Baillard took his hands from his face and placed them upon the table. Skin as thin as tissue, brown liver spots and ridged with blue veins. He was astonished to find his pulse was racing.

'Vertat . . .'

He couldn't allow himself to hope, because if he did and he was mistaken, the despair would weaken him. As rumours of what was happening in the East reached him – a genocide, a rewriting of what it meant to be human – Baillard feared he would not be able to find within himself the strength to fight such evil.

Outside, the moon continued to rise in a darkening sky above the Pic de Saint-Barthélémy, flooding the mountains with a silver light.

Chapter 21

CARCASSONNE

The windows and shutters of the bedroom were open. The black night sky was lit by ribbons of light from the glow of the full moon. Sandrine lay in her bed beneath the window, listening to the noises in the street and too stirred up to sleep. Comings and goings, men's voices, the sound of cars and feet on the pavements, the shriek of the last train leaving the station. Sounds of the Bastide, echoing off the stone walls of the old city, the cathedrals and alleyways, the lakes and trees in Square Gambetta.

Sandrine hated the blackout. No street lamps, no headlights. All official buildings had been issued with swathes of fabric to cover their long, high expanses of opaque glass. Two years after France's defeat, the blackout wasn't observed so rigorously in the *zone nono* now there was no longer the constant threat of German or Italian planes in the skies above Carcassonne. Even so, occasionally a zealous patrolman would knock on their door and tell them a sliver of light was showing through the gap in the shutters.

In some respects, life wasn't as bad as it had been during the war itself. There was no curfew in the South. There was rationing, of course, and endless queues, restrictions on travel and identity papers. But provided one didn't want to go over the demarcation line, it was possible to forget, if only for a moment, that France had been defeated. That, and the hollow absence in the heart of the house where her father had been.

But now Sandrine felt full of a wild, restless energy. She felt she had been lied to. That, beneath the surface of everyday life, everything was utterly changed. A dreary resignation etched on people's faces, the accretion of hundreds of tiny indignities. And what she had seen today at the river, at the police station too, signs of a harsher reality. She kicked off the sheet, stretching her long legs and arms to the furthest boundary of the bed, then she heard footsteps on the landing.

'I'm not asleep,' she called out.

The handle turned, and Marianne put her head round the door.

'Has Lucie gone?' asked Sandrine.

'About half an hour ago.'

'You've been ages. What were you talking about?'

Marianne sat down on the chair at the foot of the bed. 'Max. He's all Lucie talks about, really. About his life before the war, his experiences on the front line, their future plans.' She paused. 'She was down tonight, though, not like her usual self.'

'Max seems very nice.'

'Oh, he is. He's very good for her.'

'Where was he based during the war?'

'Metz, attached to the 42e Corps d'Armée.'

'Is that where Papa was?'

'No, Papa was much further north. Of course, Lucie didn't know Max then – they only met when he arrived in Carcassonne eighteen months ago. His father, Ralph Blum – you might have heard of him – was a well-known journalist. Anti-fascist, a vocal opponent of Hitler. He sent his family south when Paris fell.'

'Where's he now, still in Paris?'

'They don't know. He was arrested last August and sent to the camp at Beaune-la-Rolande. They've heard nothing since.' Marianne sighed. 'Lucie was talking about how much she wants to get married, but of course Max refuses. He says it will put her at risk.'

'Is he right?'

'Yes, even if they could find someone prepared to marry them in the first place. However, Lucie can't think about anything else. I'm terribly fond of her, but she seems to believe that rules don't apply to her.'

Sandrine thought for a moment. 'Lucie told me she'd introduced you and Thierry.'

'That's true, she did.'

'It made me realise you hardly ever mention him.'

Marianne went quiet for a moment. 'What's there to say? Lots of women in the same boat as me. No sense complaining.'

Sandrine sat up in bed and put her arms around her knees. 'Well, are you going to get married as soon as he comes back? Do you love him?'

Marianne hesitated. 'We're comfortable around each other.'

'Not love at first sight?'

Marianne laughed. 'I'm not sure that sort of thing exists outside of Hollywood or tatty *romans-feuilletons*!'

'How did it start? I don't think you ever told me.'

'Start? He was in our crowd. He's a cousin of my friend Suzanne. You remember Suzanne? Tall, cropped hair?'

'Yes, I like her.'

Marianne smiled. 'Well, Lucie was going dancing and Thierry was there, asked if I'd like to go with him. I did. It was pleasant. We went out again, and I suppose it went from that. You wouldn't guess to look at him, but he's very light on his feet. When he was called up, he wanted to make it official. As you know, he proposed. Rather caught me by surprise. He was so keen, I heard myself agreeing.' She shook her head. 'But as I said, it's not on the cards now.'

'It doesn't sound awfully romantic when you put it like that.'

'Why all these questions?' Marianne said suspiciously. 'Is there someone you like?'

'No,' Sandrine said quickly. 'No, just curious.'

The bells of Saint-Michel struck three. The air was cooler now and the rue du Palais was quiet at last, though there were still distant noises of men at work elsewhere in the town. The sound of a nightjar singing, the rasp of crickets in the cracks in the garden wall.

Marianne stood up. 'I'm all in.'

'You didn't answer my question,' Sandrine said. 'About getting married.'

'When Thierry comes home – if he comes home – we'll see.' She leant over and kissed Sandrine on the forehead. 'I promise you one thing, darling. War or no war, when you fall in love, you'll know.'

After the door had shut, Sandrine lay back on her pillows. What did she want? A steady and workaday arrangement, like Marianne seemed content with? Or the absolute and single-minded devotion Lucie had for Max? Or the loyalty her father had felt for their mother, spending his life mourning a wife who had died eighteen years before?

Sandrine felt a shimmering anticipation under the surface of her skin. It was absurd. Minutes, less than minutes, moments. She hadn't even seen his face. She knew nothing about him. In her half-waking state, her thoughts tumbled one over the other, racing, falling, soaring as she tried to recreate him. The sound of his voice, the sweet smell of sandalwood on his skin, the touch of his lips on her mouth.

Breathing life back into her.

‡

Codex IV

‡

GAUL
CARCASO
JULY AD 342

Arinius climbed the ladder to the top of the wall between the towers. Over the past days, the *limitanei* on the first watch of the day had become used to the company of this silent young monk. They nodded a greeting and continued their patrol.

He looked north, over the plain, to the river Atax, shimmering silver in the first light. Then he turned to the south. On clear mornings, before the burning heat of the sun fell over the town in a white haze, the peaks of the distant mountains were visible. Somewhere, someone was singing. A woman's voice, an old song about exile, about the endless sands of the deserts. About being far from home.

Arinius had become used to the different languages, the various smells of food and wine, the mixture of peoples who made their homes in Carcaso. He no longer heard the murmurings of the Liturgy of the Hours in his mind, but rather the whispering of the wind across the plains, the call of linnets and sparrows. The baleful howl of wolves in the hills at night.

From time to time, he unswaddled his precious cargo and stared at the beauty of the Coptic letters on the papyrus. He read Latin, but none of the other ancient languages. He wished he knew what the words meant, why they were considered so dangerous. But the letters, the pattern of them, the shape, imprinted themselves on his eyes and, through his eyes, on his soul. He feared them and revered them in equal measure.

Arinius felt God spoke to him through every line. His growing grief that Christianity had turned on itself had faded. His sorrow that, after the years of persecution by Rome, the new Church should have adopted the same weapons of oppression and judgement and martyrdom, this too had faded.

Here, in the frontier settlement of Carcaso, he felt at peace, even though the streets were not always tranquil. Arguments flared up easily out of nowhere, weapons drawn, then just as quickly sheathed. It felt like home and it saddened him that he had to leave. Even though his health had improved, the racking cough that tore through his thin frame and made his ribs ache was a constant reminder of how the illness still crouched within him. He did not believe he would live to make old bones.

Arinius was not afraid to die, though he feared the journey itself might kill him. All he could hope was God might grant him the time to ensure that the Codex was safe. In the future, in better times, he prayed, the holy words would be found and read, honoured and understood. Spoken as he had heard them spoken in the stone silence of the community in Lugdunum.

Arinius stood for a while longer, looking south towards the mountains, wondering what lay ahead.

Chapter 22

CARCASSONNE
JULY 1942

The man known as Leo Coursan knelt at the screen in the confessional in the cathédrale Saint-Michel, aware of the presence of the priest behind the grille.

'O God,' he continued, 'I am sorry for having offended you and I detest all my sins, because I dread the loss of heaven and the pains of hell. But most of all because I have offended you, my God, who are all good and deserving of all my love. I firmly resolve with the help of your grace, to confess my sins, to do penance and to amend my life. Amen.'

His hand went to the silver crucifix pinned to his left lapel. He had been obliged not to wear so visible a sign of his faith over the past few months and had felt naked without it. He had been forced to take on another name, another man's characteristics, and he had played his part well. Finally, this morning, he could return to himself once again.

The cathedral was deserted at this time of day. The only sounds were the song of the birds in the lime trees lining the boulevard Barbès. The plaster figures of St Bernard and St Benoît listened to him in contemplative silence.

'I have dissembled and lied for the purpose of bringing the enemies of the Church into plain view. I have consorted with those who deny God. I have neglected my spiritual salvation.' He paused. 'I am sorry for these and all the sins of my past life.'

His confession seemed to hang like mist in the air. The silence from behind the screen was deafening, so palpable that he almost felt he could reach out and touch it. Then, an intake of breath and the priest began to speak. A low, steady collection of vowels and syllables, intoned so very many times before, though he could hear the fear in the man's voice.

The words of absolution and forgiveness washed over him as white sound. He felt a lightness in his limbs, coursing through his veins, a sense of grace and of peace and the deep and certain knowledge that today he was doing God's work.

'Give thanks to the Lord for He is good.'

He could hear the relief in the priest's voice as he came to the end of the ritual.

'For His mercy endures for ever,' Coursan gave the response.

He made the sign of the cross, then stood up. He ran his hand over his newly cut hair, straightened his jacket and his trousers, then leant forward and whispered through the grille.

'Remain where you are for five minutes. Then leave and lock the cathedral behind you. Allow no one access today.'

'I cannot possibly—'

He smacked the wire mesh with his hand. The sound was loud, discordant, violent in the confined confessional. He felt the priest flinch behind the wire.

'Do it,' he said in a cold, level voice. 'You will thank me for this, Father. I give you my word.'

He pulled back the curtain, feeling the dust and imprint of ages in the thick material. Left, right, left, the heels of his shoes clipping loudly on the stone floor. He stopped, turned back to the altar, towards the rising sun, and made the sign of the cross with the holy water from the *bénitier*.

Then he pulled open the heavy wooden door and rejoined the world.

For an instant, he paused and looked out over the Garden of Remembrance. To the stone plaques of the war memorial commemorating the men of Carcassonne who'd given their lives in the Grande Guerre. He regretted the damage that would be done in this honoured place, but it was unavoidable.

He put his hands to his face, relishing the feel of smooth, clean skin after the weeks of not shaving properly. It was Leo Coursan, partisan, Occitan freedom fighter, who had entered the cathedral. A borrowed identity, stolen from a murdered man. It was Leo Authié, member of the Deuxième Bureau and servant of God, who left it and walked out into the early-morning sun.

Chapter 23

Raoul woke with a jolt. He had slept badly, his dreams haunted by Antoine and the girl, the sense of being too late. Always too late, failing to prevent some catastrophe or another. Arriving to find her dead in the water. His brother's tortured face shifting into Antoine's features. Antoine's silver chain in the girl's fingers. Coursan and César sitting at separate tables in a bar.

His hand shot out to his bedside table, checking the antique glass bottle was still there, lying wrapped in the handkerchief, then he slumped back against the headboard. He could see there was something inside the bottle, but had resisted the temptation last night to try to get it out. It was so fragile, he didn't want to damage whatever Antoine had hidden inside. He'd see what César thought.

Raoul lit his last cigarette, smoking it to the very end, then got up, washed and went into the kitchen. His mother was already there, standing at the window. Her blank eyes looked blindly out over the narrow street to the canal. Her thin arms were wrapped tight around her waist, as if she feared that if she let go she would shatter into pieces. In the sink, the tap was running into a china bowl filled with turnips.

For a moment, Raoul thought he saw her lips begin to form a smile or try to shape a greeting or acknowledge his presence, but she didn't. He kissed her on the cheek, then leant over and turned the tap off.

'I have to go out,' he said. 'Will you be all right?'

'Is he here yet?'

'No, there's no one, Maman.'

'Not Bruno?'

Raoul felt his heart contract, though he'd not expected anything else. It was the same every day. His once vivacious and kind mother had vanished when he'd told her Bruno had been killed. At first she hadn't believed it. Then, slowly and remorselessly, her world had begun to unravel, a little more every day, every week, every month.

Four years ago.

'No,' he said quietly. 'Only us.'

Now she rarely spoke, never seemed to notice anything. A neighbour came in each day to keep an eye and to do a little shopping, but Raoul didn't know if she even noticed. If she even knew a war had been fought and lost.

'Don't stay indoors all day,' he said. 'Go out, get some air.'

Raoul left the apartment and ran down the stairs, two at a time. On the Quai Riquet, he exhaled deeply, breathing out the sadness that choked his lungs, and let the sun and the soft morning air bring life back into his cheeks.

By seven thirty, he was sitting in the Café Saillan. The oldest café in Carcassonne, it was opposite Les Halles and only a few minutes' walk from boulevard Barbès, where the demonstrators were to gather. The air was thick with tobacco smoke and the grey faces of men come off the night shift. Hard-boiled eggs sat in a glass jar on the bar, as they always had, though these days they were china, not real.

Raoul found a table facing the door and ordered a *panaché*, not able to stomach the ersatz coffee on offer. He was queasy with nerves as it was. He scanned the room, wondering how many of the men in here were going to the demonstration. How many of them even knew what was about to happen. It was extraordinary how a day of such significance could look the same as any other, smell the same. Men in the tabac, women already queuing outside the boulangerie, the épicerie, a few standing in line outside the closed door of the haberdasher.

He raised his hand as he saw César appear in the doorway carrying a holdall. He looked drawn and there were bags under his eyes.

'No Gaston or Robert?' César asked, sitting down.

Raoul shook his head. 'Not yet. I waited for you at the Terminus last night, and later at the Continental, in case you went back to the print shop. I didn't see you.'

César's eyes sparked. 'Did you find Antoine then?'

Raoul shook his head. 'No. I went to the apartment straight after I left you. The concierge said she heard someone early yesterday morning, but didn't actually see him. What about you?'

César sighed. 'No luck either. Antoine didn't turn up at work yesterday. I tried his usual bars, but no one admitted to seeing him since last Friday.'

Raoul paused, then produced the white cotton handkerchief from his pocket with the bottle wrapped inside.

'I don't know if it's important, but I found this in Antoine's flat. It was hidden in the cistern.'

César frowned. 'In the cistern?'

Raoul nodded. 'That's why I took it. Antoine had gone to a lot of trouble to conceal it. I thought it might be important.' He looked across the table at César. 'It doesn't mean anything to you? He never mentioned he was looking after something for someone?'

César shook his head.

'There's something inside, a piece of paper maybe. I've been thinking we should try to get it out.'

'The bottle looks valuable,' César said doubtfully. 'It might break.'

'That's what worries me. On the other hand, if what's inside might—'

He broke off. César's eyes had sharpened, his face

settling into a scowl. Raoul turned round to see Sylvère Laval walking towards them, followed by the Bonnets. Quickly, he slipped the handkerchief and the bottle off the table and back into his pocket.

'Got the leaflets?' Gaston said when they drew level.

'For Christ's sake, Bonnet,' snapped César, 'don't broadcast it.'

'It's been all over the radio as it is,' Gaston said, but he lit a cigarette and shut up.

The group sat in silence. Laval watched the street. Gaston twisted a spent match round and round between his finger and thumb. Robert was tearing tiny shreds of paper from the corner of a copy of *L'Éclair*, another Vichyist newspaper.

Anticipation crawled over Raoul's skin like pins and needles. He wanted to get on with it. Seven forty-five, seven fifty-five. The hands of the clock above the counter ground slowly on, counting down the minutes to eight o'clock.

Finally Laval stood up. 'Time to go.'

Chapter 24

Sandrine looked at the drift of clothes heaped along the back of the Chinese silk settee, the discarded shoes on the floor by the bamboo plant stand. She had slept well for once – no nightmares – and she was full of anticipation.

'Darling, are you ready?' Marianne called up the stairs.

'Almost . . .'

She settled on a green dress with a white belt and buttons, which she thought made her look older. She paused for a moment to look at her reflection. The bruise on the side of her head was the colour of the sea at Narbonne in July, blue and green and purple, but the cut barely showed. She applied a little face powder, ran a comb through her hair, then began to search for a suitable pair of shoes.

'Sandrine!'

'*J'arrive*,' she shouted back. 'I'm coming . . .'

She buckled her shoes, then threw open the door and charged out on to the landing. The catch bounced in the latch and a funnel of warm air rushed into the room. It lifted the papers, her notes written in the police station and left abandoned on the tallboy, and sent them fluttering like a drift of autumn leaves. Sandrine picked them up and dropped them on the bed, then rushed back out.

The front door was open and Marianne was already waiting in the street. Marieta was hovering at the foot of the stairs.

'You stay with your sister,' she said. 'Don't do anything silly.'

'I won't, I won't,' Sandrine said, trying to get past her.

'And don't go getting yourself arrested again.'

Sandrine pulled a face. 'I wasn't arrested yesterday.'

'The first sign of trouble, you come home. Do you hear me?'

Sandrine grinned. 'And you put your feet up, do you hear me? You look all in.'

Then before Marieta could make any more fuss, Sandrine slipped past her and down the steps to the pavement.

'I'm sorry. Marieta was fussing, though I think she's proud of us actually.' She jerked her head. 'Which is more than can be said for that old witch next door.'

Marianne followed Sandrine's gaze to see their next-door neighbour, Madame Fournier, peering out from behind a voile curtain.

'She's an awful woman,' she said. 'Take no notice.'

The rue du Palais was quiet. But as soon as the girls reached the boulevard Maréchal Pétain, it was clear many Carcassonnais had heard the illicit broadcast or been told of it. Everywhere, people.

'Where are we meeting Lucie?' Sandrine said, raising her voice to make herself heard over the noise of the crowd.

'At the junction with rue Voltaire.'

Despite the serious purpose of the rally, there was something of a carnival atmosphere. Women in summer dresses, bare arms and flowered skirts, the clip of heels on the pavements. Men in their Sunday best, hats perched on the back of their heads, children carried on shoulders. As well as placards, there were flags – the red, white and blue of the murdered Republic, but also the scarlet and gold of the Languedoc. The colours of Viscount Trencavel. Some men had bottles of beer, women carried trays of cake or bread, biscuits, bonbons, each willing to share their meagre rations with those around them. For today, at least.

Sandrine felt a tap on the arm. She turned to see one of the teachers from the Lycée, a quiet and rather serious woman who taught the *première*. She had an idea she was married to a doctor.

'Madame Giraud, I'm sorry, I didn't see you.'

The woman held up her hand. *'Aujourd'hui, appelez-moi Jeanne,'* she replied.

Seeing her out of school, Sandrine realised Madame Giraud wasn't actually much older than Marianne.

'All right,' she smiled. 'Jeanne.'

'It's good to see you here, Sandrine.'

The crowd was continuing to build. Many people carried banners, words printed in block letters: *Ici France*, *Ici Londres*, *Vive la Résistance*, *Vivre Libre ou Mourir*.

'Live free or die,' Sandrine said, reading a placard carried by a veteran. She smiled at him. The medals pinned to his black jacket rattled as he leant forward and clasped her arm.

'I fought at Verdun, mademoiselle,' he said. 'But not for Vichy. Not for Berlin.' He waved at the people all round him. 'Today at least, today Carcassonne shows her true face.' He put his hand up and touched her cheek. 'It is up to you now. Old men should be put out to grass. Leave it to the young.'

'We'll do our best,' she said, oddly moved by the exchange.

At that moment, the marchers began to move off. The old man nodded to her, then raised his placard and, with his eyes fixed straight ahead, walked on.

Sandrine and Marianne turned the corner into boulevard Barbès, where the crowds were even denser, more tightly packed. Chalk marks had been drawn on the road. Slogans and symbols, the Cross of Lorraine and the Occitan cross, the letters FFL – for *les Forces Françaises Libres* – and the letter H for *Honneur*. White marks of defiance on the grey tarmac. Men outnumbered the women here, men with dark jumping eyes and thin shoulders, scanning the crowd. And lining the route along the pavements Sandrine saw a line of police, guns cradled in their arms. Watching, all the time watching. She stole a glance at her sister and saw Marianne had noticed too.

Swarms of children were running up and down the paths below the old city walls of the Bastide. Two little girls of seven or eight were playing *cache-cache*, until the mother of one of them appeared, smacked the child on the back of her legs and dragged her away. The march shuffled past the Jardin des Tilleuls, where the Foire aux Vins was held each November. On a normal day, she thought, the old veteran might be sitting with his comrades beneath the trees in his dark suit and beret. Today the benches were empty.

On the far side of the road, Sandrine caught sight of Max and Lucie, standing with Max's sister, Liesl. She had pale skin and wide brown eyes and wore her black hair long to the shoulder, not waved or pinned up.

'Liesl's rather beautiful, isn't she?' Sandrine said to Marianne.

'Very.'

Lucie was wearing the same dress she'd had on at the river. She looked bright and eye-catching, as if she was going to a fair. She waved and they pushed through the sea of people to join them. Lucie kissed them both. Max, formal as always in a sombre black suit, lifted his hat. Liesl gave a quick smile but said nothing.

Then Sandrine noticed Marianne's friend, Suzanne Peyre, Thierry's cousin. At nearly six foot tall and with cropped hair, she was very distinctive, towering head and shoulders above everyone else.

'There's Suzanne over there,' she said.

Sandrine tried to move forward, but she found her way blocked by Monsieur Fournier, their unpleasant next-door neighbour's equally unpleasant brother. Sandrine disliked him, not least because he always stood too close. She wondered why he'd come. He made no secret of his support for Pétain, and his outspoken opinions about 'the Jew conspiracy', as he called it, were well known.

'Mademoiselle Vidal,' he said.

'Monsieur Fournier.'

'I'm surprised your sister allowed you to come.'

Sandrine forced herself to smile. 'You're here, Monsieur Fournier.'

'What would your father have said?' he said, taking a step closer. Sandrine tried to move back, but the crowds were too dense and they were being pressed together in the crush. She could feel his sour breath, ripe with tobacco, on her cheek. 'Then again, he was another Jew lover, wasn't he?' he said. 'Like Ménard's girl over there.'

Sandrine was shocked by the blatancy of it all. Her mind went blank. She couldn't think of a single thing to say to defend either her father or Lucie.

'Problem?'

Somehow Suzanne had picked her way through the crowd and was now standing between her and Fournier.

'Not really,' Sandrine said.

'My friend doesn't want to talk to you,' Suzanne said, turning to him, 'so if you don't mind?'

'I'll talk to whoever I like, *éspèce de gouine*.'

Fournier's hand flashed out to grab Suzanne's elbow, but she batted it away and put her own hand up to warn him not to touch her again.

'Let's go,' she said, taking Sandrine's arm. 'Bad smell around here.'

'*Sale pute*,' Fournier hissed.

As Suzanne steered her back through the crowd, Sandrine couldn't help herself turning round. Fournier was still looking after them with hate-filled eyes.

'Don't let him get to you,' Suzanne said. 'Not worth it.'

'No. No, I won't,' she said, but she felt shaken all the same.

Some cafés were closed, but most on this section of boulevard Barbès had put out flags and bunting and banners. The Café du Nord was packed, people spilling out from the pavements into the road. The reason soon became clear. A display board was offering, at the price of only one franc, a special cocktail, '*la blanquette des Forces Françaises Libres*'. There were huddles of men standing around high bar tables set out on the street. Even though it was only just after eight o'clock in the morning, demand was already outstripping supply.

The house band from the Hôtel Terminus had set up on the terrace. The sheets of music, held in place by wooden pegs on the music stands, fluttered in the Tramontana breeze. Trumpet, horn, euphonium, brass glinting in the early sunshine, banjo, clarinet and drum, the accordionists apart from the others. The men wore black button-up uniforms and *képi* caps with their insignia on the brow.

Sandrine noticed an army of journalists and newspapermen camped on the opposite side of the street. Photographers with cameras and tripods jostled one another to get the best spot – first-floor balconies, the narrow perch of a wall. A reporter from *La Dépêche* was stopping people, asking why they had come, while a colleague snapped away.

'Hey, girl with the white belt. Over here!'

Sandrine turned round, in time to be caught as the flash went off. Quickly she dropped her head and hurried to catch up with Suzanne.

'Be in tomorrow's paper,' the journalist called after her.

'We wondered where you had got to,' said Marianne.

'A photographer just took my picture.'

'Sandrine!'

'It's all right, he didn't get a proper shot. Although what's the point in coming if we're not prepared to be seen?' She looked around. 'They can hardly arrest all of us, there must be three thousand people here.' She took a deep breath. 'In fact, I've a good mind to go back and give him my name.'

'Absolutely not,' Marianne said. 'No.'

Then someone started to shout. They all looked up. Sandrine felt nerves fluttering in the pit of her stomach and she reached for Marianne's hand. For a moment there was no response, then a quick squeeze and their fingers intertwined.

'They're here,' Marianne said. 'Someone's about to speak.'

Chapter 25

Raoul moved through the crowd, aware of César to his right and Gaston Bonnet somewhere up ahead. In the crush, he'd lost track of Laval and Robert Bonnet, and there was no sign of Coursan at all. He pressed leaflets into people's hands and shopping baskets. So far, it had gone well. People were reading them, looking at the photographs. Raoul slid one under a door, another beneath the windscreen wiper of a delivery truck parked at the bottom of boulevard Barbès. People would see the leaflet and start to understand what was really going on. Understand that the newspapers were all propaganda and lies.

His eyes darted from side to side to side, occasionally recognising a comrade, greeting one another by a glance or a slight nod of the head. There was a strong visible police presence, though they were clearly under instruction not to intervene or prevent the demonstration from marching. The plain-clothes men were harder to spot, though he did recognise Fournier, a well-known local *collabo*. Despite the carnival atmosphere, Raoul knew the crowd was thick with collaborators, police informers, with Deuxième Bureau.

Close to the Place des Armes, there were a couple of newspapermen with cameras. Raoul turned his face away and crossed to the opposite side of the street. Then there was an outbreak of applause up ahead and he stopped and looked towards the monument, like everyone else.

The crowd surged forward, then again. Through the forest of arms and shoulders and backs, Sandrine could just make out the clutch of men standing in front of the empty plinth.

She recognised Henri Gout, the former socialist deputy of the Aude. Each carried a green wreath. *Bons homes*, that was what Marieta had called them. Good men.

'Who's that with Docteur Gout?' she asked.

'Senator Bruguier,' replied Suzanne. 'A member of the Socialist Party before the war. He refused to support Pétain's dissolution of the constitution. Voted against the proposals. Like Docteur Gout, he's been relieved of his duties.'

Through a crackling loudhailer, Sandrine could hear Gout's voice, then another man, then another. She couldn't make out what any of them were saying, but the sentiment was clear. An outburst of applause, then another man, shouting and fierce, stirring up the crowd.

'Quite something,' said Suzanne.

'Wonderful.'

Suzanne looked at her. 'That clown earlier didn't upset you too much?'

She shook her head. 'It's why we're here, isn't it? People like him.'

'What happened earlier?' Marianne said, raising her voice to be heard over the noise.

'Fournier.'

Sandrine saw a flash of disgust in Marianne's eyes. Then up ahead there was a crescendo of applause and they all turned to look.

'*France libre*,' someone shouted. '*France libre. Vive la France.*'

Another outbreak of clapping, hand against hand against hand, growing louder. Cheering and yelling, the sound reverberating off the high stone walls of the old Bastion du Calvaire, the cathédrale Saint-Michel, the façade of the Caserne Laperrine on the far side of the Place des Armes.

'De Gaulle, de Gaulle, de Gaulle.'

The chanting grew stronger, braver.

'France libre, France libre.'

Sandrine's heart was pounding. All around her she felt the spirit of those courageous men and women who, in the past, had stood as she did now in the streets of Carcassonne, and who would do so again in the future. Voices raised in protest.

Then, above the noise, a woman began to sing.

'Allons, enfants de la Patrie, le jour de gloire est arrivé . . .'

Her voice floated above the crowd, a simple soprano line, as the words of 'La Marseillaise' filled the air. One by one, people joined in. Tainted by its adoption by Vichy, on this forbidden Bastille Day the anthem was being reclaimed by the daughters and sons of the Midi. Holding her sister's hand on one side and Suzanne's on the other, Sandrine joined in the final words of the song.

'Marchons, marchons, qu'un sang impur abreuve nos sillons!'

Applause, again. Another song began, the notes rippling like a wave through the crowd.

This time, the words caught in her throat. Sandrine was suddenly overwhelmed by affection for this band of women – Marianne and Suzanne, Lucie and Liesl, other friends and neighbours elsewhere in the crowd. And she knew that, whatever happened in the future, she would always remember this day. Standing together beneath the endless blue of the Midi singing for peace. For freedom.

'*Vive la France*,' she cried, punching the air with her fist. '*Vive Carcassonne!*'

Raoul had not intended to be drawn in, but the simple innocence of the crowd, the shouting and the singing, car horns beeping, touched him. He realised he was smiling. Bruno would have loved it. Been proud to be a part of it. The true Midi standing up for what they believed in. The pavements were five, six people deep, so Raoul climbed on to the base of a street lamp to get a better look. Now he could make out the distinctive features of Henri Gout. Could hear his rallying cry. His call for the crowd to fight for France, to resist the occupation of the North, to disregard Vichy. Raoul stuffed the remaining leaflets he was holding into his jacket pocket, moved by the emotion of it all. He pushed on to where the crowds were densest and climbed up on to a low wall.

'*Vive le Midi!*' The shout went up for the last time.

The band on the terrace of the Café du Nord struck up again, playing louder, faster, wilder, like a tarantella, notes spiralling, twisting in the air, as when dancers lose their footing at the Fête de l'Âne. Hats were being thrown in the air. Bellowing, shouting, berets and workers' caps and bonnets of straw and felt. Carcassonne in glorious colours. Around Raoul, the crowd on the boulevard Barbès, the Places des Armes, in the tiny side streets. Matrons and maîtres, men and women of all classes, all ages, united in the moment. Flags and placards, banners.

A woman's straw hat suddenly flew in front of his eyes, nearly hitting him in the face. Raoul instinctively flung out his hand to catch it.

Then all sound fell away, and all he could hear was the beating of the blood in his veins. He took in the elegant woman in a navy-blue dress, her very tall friend with cropped hair and the bottle blonde, all standing beside a girl in a green dress with a white belt. Wild black curls.

That girl.

Now she was turning around, reaching up to take the hat from his hand. A crack of light entered Raoul's numb heart.

Her eyes widened, as if she was trying to remember how or why she knew him.

'*Merci infiniment*,' she said politely.

He climbed down and handed her the hat. She took it, held his gaze a moment longer. Then turned away. Raoul saw her whisper something to the woman in blue, who then turned round to look at him too. Sisters? She was older, pale, with soft brown hair, but they had similar features.

Raoul didn't dare speak, for fear his voice would betray him. He had found her. Or, rather, Carcassonne had given her up.

The girl turned round again and now was staring directly at him, cautious but curious too.

Raoul was about to smile, about to try to speak, when out of the corner of his eye he saw a group of four thugs step forward and grab a man whose arm was raised in the communist salute. He was pushed to the ground. Someone screamed.

The mood of the day immediately changed, tightened, sharpened. A second man started to run, going against the tide of people. One of the officers hit him across the throat, and he fell. A woman shouted. Panic started to spread through the crowd. Then, the sound of glass breaking and tables being kicked over, chairs.

'I'm glad you're all right,' he said, allowing himself to touch her briefly on the arm. 'Very glad.'

'It's you,' Sandrine said.

But Raoul had already turned on his heel and charged towards the café.

Chapter 26

Sandrine felt a swooping sensation, as if she was up high and looking down on herself from a great height.

'Max has already gone ahead with Lucie and Liesl,' Marianne was saying. 'I think we should follow them.'

She stood stock-still, watching him go.

'Sandrine, come on,' said Marianne impatiently.

She didn't move. 'It was him,' she said, in a dazed voice.

'What, who?'

'The boy who gave me my hat back. It was him. From the river.'

Marianne stared at her. 'But you said you didn't see his face properly.'

'I didn't, not really.'

'Well, how do you know it was him? Did he say?'

Sandrine shook her head. 'He just said he was glad I was all right. But when I heard his voice, I was certain. It was him.'

There was another shout, then the shriek of a police siren. Marianne and Sandrine found themselves being pushed forward in the surge of the crowd.

Marianne grabbed her hand. 'We must get away from here, come on.'

Raoul ran to join César, who was standing outside the Café du Nord. All around on the terrace, tables and chairs were scattered, lying on their sides.

'What happened?' Raoul demanded, trying to concentrate on César, not think about the girl.

'As soon as Gout and the others had gone, the *flics*

moved in. Arrested someone. They'd obviously been watching him.'

'One of ours?'

'Ex-International Brigade, working with the Narbonne Resistance now.'

Raoul looked around. 'Where are the others?'

'Gaston and Robert were by the Place de l'Armistice earlier.'

'And Laval?'

'Saw him up by the Bastion du Calvaire about half an hour ago.'

'With Coursan?'

'Haven't seen him at all. You?'

Raoul shook his head. 'Keep looking. Make sure no one else is taken.'

'Fine,' said César.

Raoul continued up the boulevard Barbès. Most ordinary people, rattled by the altercation, were heading back into the safety of the maze of streets behind the Place des Armes. He caught another glimpse of Fournier, this time with a couple of men he recognised as members of the Fascist LVF.

He stepped back into the shadow of the building.

Then he saw Sylvère Laval was with them. At first, Raoul thought he'd been arrested, but as he watched, Laval pointed to a man in the crowd and spoke.

'That one, him.'

Immediately, the police reacted.

'*Attention, arrêtez*,' one of the officers yelled.

The target began to run, darting sideways, trying to find a path through the frightened men and women in his way, attempting to escape.

'*Arrêtez!*' the officer repeated. 'Stop!'

The partisan desperately pushed forward, launching himself into the sea of arms and legs. Someone fired into the air. A moment of silence, then people began to flee. Some dived for cover, others started running. Their quarry stopped. Slowly, he turned and put his hands above his head. Raoul saluted his bravery. There were women and children, old men who might get shot if he didn't give himself up.

The police were on him in a second, throwing him to the ground and cuffing his hands behind his back. Then hauling him to his feet and marching him towards a dark prison van parked beside the trees below the walls of the Bastion du Calvaire. As he was marched past the group, the partisan spat in Fournier's face.

Raoul leant against the wall for a second, his mind racing. Laval and Fournier. Undercover, working with the police, a trap. His thoughts tumbling one over the other in his mind.

He doubled back to where he'd last seen César. No sign of him. He skirted round the periphery of the dwindling crowd, watching all the time. He couldn't see any of the others. Then he caught sight of Laval again, now standing in front of the Garden of Remembrance by the cathédrale Saint-Michel. He was holding something in his hand.

Raoul watched as Laval bent down, then immediately stepped back into the sheltered west door of the cathedral. As if taking cover.

In an instant, he saw the whole plan laid out from the first act to the last. The full scale of it. This wasn't just about Laval infiltrating their group; it was part of a coordinated attempt to use the demonstration to turn the people of Carcassonne against the partisans. To paint the *résistants* as dangerous, careless of the lives of ordinary citizens. To portray them as the enemies of peace.

'Get down,' Raoul shouted at the top of his voice. 'Everyone, get down!'

His words were lost in the explosion.

For a second after the blast, nothing seemed to happen. Time stood still. Fistfuls of masonry, of stone and ballast seemed to hang suspended in the air for a moment, under the malevolent watch of the gargoyles, before suddenly crashing back to earth. And all around, copies of the leaflets Raoul was holding were fluttering like leaves blown by the wind. It seemed Laval had packed their tracts round the bomb to implicate them further.

Then, screaming and people shouting for help.

Raoul ran towards an old man lying dazed on the ground, still holding the placard he'd been carrying. A trickle of blood ran down his temple, but he was shocked rather than seriously hurt.

'*Vivre libre ou mourir*,' Raoul read, prising the veteran's thin fingers from the wooden handle. 'Are you all right, monsieur?'

'Never better, son,' he said. 'Shows we've got 'em on the run, *è*?'

A woman came to help, so Raoul moved on to the next. A teenage boy was propped against the wall, clutching his arm. He looked very grey, very pale. Raoul took off his jacket and swung it over the boy's shoulders. As he did, the few remaining tracts fell out of the pocket.

'Look!' a woman with a child was shouting. 'That's him. That's one of them, look!'

It was a split second before Raoul realised she was pointing at him, at the leaflets lying on the steps beside him. The same black and white images as were drifting all over the garden.

He heard sirens, distant but coming closer.

'No,' he began to say. Out of the corner of his eye, he saw Laval step out of the doorway and slip away into the crowd. He pointed. 'No, the man you want is—'

'He did it,' the woman shrieked. 'There!'

Now police were converging on the patch of garden from all angles and the woman was still shouting.

Raoul didn't like the pallor of the boy, but he knew there was nothing he could do.

'I'll try to get someone to help you,' he promised, then he ran into the cover of the streets beyond the square.

Chapter 27

'What was that?' said Sandrine, turning back in the direction of the noise. 'Firecrackers?'

A woman's scream drifted across the rooftops. Everyone around them paused, then carried on with what they were doing. Sandrine saw the owner of the Pharmacie Sarcos hesitate, before reaching up with his long wooden pole and hook to pull down the yellow and white awning as if he'd heard nothing. The mechanism squeaked as it unfurled.

'Why's no one taking any notice?'

Suzanne tapped the side of her head. 'See nothing, do nothing, that's how it is.'

'We should go back,' Sandrine said.

Another shout from the direction of the boulevard Barbès.

'We've got to help,' she said.

Before Marianne could stop her, Sandrine had started running. She raced back along the rue du Chartran, going against the tide. Marianne and Suzanne were now following behind.

The crowd was streaming away from the boulevard Barbès and into the safety of the Bastide. Men walking fast, women clutching the hands of frightened, crying children. In the distance, the wail of an ambulance.

Sandrine shot out her hand. 'What's going on? We heard an explosion and—'

'A bomb,' the man said. 'Might be another, no one knows.'

'Is anyone hurt?'

'Didn't stick around to find out,' he said, pulling his arm free and running on.

Sandrine's heart was thudding in her chest and her muscles were taut, but she kept going. Across rue Voltaire, then straight ahead she saw the devastation. The Garden of Remembrance looked like a quarry. Masonry, bricks. The rose trees lining the paths were snapped and twisted, there was rubble everywhere. The west door of the cathedral was obscured by a cloud of dust. The façade was still intact, but the semicircular stone surround and the pillars on one side were broken, torn apart by the impact of the blast.

Sandrine, Marianne and Suzanne looked in disbelief at one another, then went into action. Everywhere, injured people, dazed people, sitting on the ground. Some lying. Sandrine crouched down beside a teenage boy, who was nursing a wounded arm. His face was white with pain.

'Help's on its way,' she said.

The boy opened his eyes. 'My father will kill me. He didn't want me to come.'

'My sister didn't much want me to come either.'

'Then we're both for it.' He tried to grin, then closed his eyes. 'I'm cold,' he whispered.

As Sandrine adjusted the jacket on his shoulders, over his broken arm, she noticed his shirt was drenched. She lifted the jacket and saw, to her horror, a jagged piece of metal lodged in his side. Blood was pooling on the pavement beneath him.

'Am I going to be all right?' he said. 'I'm so cold.'

Sandrine tried to keep her voice steady. 'The ambulance is on its way,' she said. 'Try to keep still.'

She waited with him, watching him grow paler, more transparent, until at last the medics arrived. From the expression on their faces, she knew they didn't rate his chances either.

Shocked by what she was witnessing, Sandrine moved

on to the next person, then the next, doing what little she could. Smears of blood on the ground, turning brown in the heat of the sun, a child's shoe.

Suddenly all sound seemed to slip away from her. All heat, all colour, everything fading to grey, to white. And then, the same whispering she'd heard at the river.

'*Coratge*,' a girl's voice.

Sandrine spun round, then around again. There was no one there. No one anywhere near her. Yet the same sensation of cold air brushing her skin.

'*Coratge, sòrre*.' Courage, sister.

'Sandrine?'

A hand on her arm made her jump. She blinked and saw Jeanne Giraud looking at her.

'Are you all right? You're as white as a sheet.'

'I thought I heard someone calling me, but …' She stopped, seeing the look of concern on Jeanne's face. 'Yes, I'm fine.'

'I'm looking for my father-in-law, I don't suppose you've seen him? We got separated on the boulevard Barbès. Someone said they saw him here, by the cathedral, just before the explosion.'

'I don't know, I'm afraid.'

'He forgets he's not young any more,' she said, then moved off to continue looking.

Sandrine stood still. She saw the last of the wounded being helped into an ambulance. The door was slammed shut, then the siren rang and the ambulance pulled away. She noticed now there was a line of police cars in front of the Bastion du Calvaire. She turned to her right and saw the same at the top of the boulevard.

'Does anyone know what happened?' she asked, when Marianne and Suzanne joined her.

'No, reports are muddled,' Marianne replied, wiping her hands on her scarf.

'Some are blaming the partisans,' Suzanne said.

'You did well, darling,' Marianne said, giving her a brief smile. 'You kept your head.'

Sandrine looked at her big sister. Seeing the pride in Marianne's face, despite the tiredness, she felt something had changed between them. She smiled back, trying not to think about the boy and the blood on the ground. Another police car went past at top speed, its siren blaring, then a second.

'Where's everybody being taken?' she asked.

'Most have gone to the hospital,' Suzanne said, 'and those who can't risk it, in there.' She nodded in the direction of the Clinique du Bastion. 'Delteil or Giraud will patch them up, no questions asked.'

Chapter 28

César wasn't at the print shop. Raoul hesitated, then headed for his house. He was too late.

'Damn,' he said, throwing himself back into an open doorway opposite.

He watched as two policemen kicked their heavy boots against César's front door. The wood splintered and the lock gave. The door was flung back against the wall, the glass shattering over the hall tiles as the officers rushed in. Barely a minute or two later, they were back out in the blinding sun. César's hands were cuffed behind his back and blood was pouring from his nose. He was forced into the *panier à salade* and driven away.

Raoul waited until the road was clear, then quickly crossed the boulevard Marcou and over into rue Voltaire, not sure where to go next. He didn't know where Gaston and Robert Bonnet lived, so there was no way of warning them. No way of knowing if they'd already been arrested. He weighed up his options in the light of what he now knew, quickly realising the only sensible course of action was to get out of Carcassonne and try to make contact with other partisans in the region. He couldn't do anything to help César, but he could at least warn others about Laval and make sure they got the message that the bomb had not been detonated by *résistants*.

Raoul ran along the rue du Port towards the cathédrale Saint-Vincent, then right into the boulevard Omer Sarraut.

In the quartier de la Gare, the clean-up operation was already underway. Newspapers trampled underfoot, flags, greased-paper food wrappings and discarded caps from bottles of beer littered the ground, the squalid aftermath of the crowds. Bonfires lit in the SNCF sidings to dispose of the litter trapped by the wire railings belched grey smoke into the blue air.

The tram was loaded full of village husbands and their wives. The whistle shrieked, shrill and insistent, as the lines began to hum. But a procession of police cars was blocking the Pont Marengo and there were officers everywhere. A horde of people was standing outside the doors to the mainline station, everyone showing their papers. Lowered eyes, a flicker of fear, their moment of bravery was over.

There was no chance of Raoul getting on to a train, so he kept walking, heading for the apartment on the Quai Riquet and praying the police weren't already there. Muscle, skin, adrenalin, blood and bone, he took the stairs two at a time.

His mother was still standing at the kitchen sink. He rushed over and put his hands on her shoulders.

'Maman, listen to me. Maman? This is important.'

For a moment, he thought he saw a flicker of the woman she had been in her dead eyes.

'Bruno?' she whispered.

Raoul had to stop himself from shaking her. 'Bruno's gone,' he said in a level voice. 'He was killed, you know he was. Four years ago.'

Confusion flickered in her eyes, a spark of anger, grief, as if she was waking up. Then hope faded and her eyes clouded over again.

'Raoul,' she said.

He sighed. 'You have to listen. Soon, men will come here looking for me. Asking if you've seen me. If they do, tell them you don't know where I am. They won't hurt you. Tell them you haven't seen me for weeks, can you do that?' He tightened his grip on her shoulders. 'Do you understand?

If the police come, you tell them you don't know where I am. Yes?'

For an instant, she didn't react. Then, she nodded.

'Got to keep my boys safe,' she said softly. 'Keep Bruno safe.'

A wave of pity swept through Raoul, anger too. He put his arms around her, horrified by how thin she was, how fragile. He could feel every rib through the cotton dress. She did not hug him in return, but stood rigid, unyielding.

'That's right,' he said quietly. 'Keep your boys safe.'

Raoul ran into his bedroom. He got his papers and money from beneath the mattress, grabbed Bruno's rucksack from the back of the door and an old work jacket from the wardrobe. He pulled open the drawer in his bedside table and, from beneath a pile of laundered handkerchiefs, took out his service revolver and a box of ammunition. He put them in the rucksack too, then rushed back into the kitchen. His mother had returned to her vigil at the window, looking out for a son who would never return.

'They're coming,' she murmured.

Raoul rushed to look out, but the street was empty.

'Tell them you haven't seen me,' he repeated.

'They're coming,' she said again, crossing herself. 'The ghosts. I hear them. Waking, beginning to walk. They're coming.'

Raoul couldn't think of anything to say. His misgivings about leaving her were even stronger, but she'd be safer without him. At least he hoped he was right.

'You haven't seen me,' he said again.

He found an unopened bottle of red wine and hesitated over a loaf of dark bread. He left the bread.

'I'll be back, Maman,' he said gently. 'As soon as I can, I'll come back.'

*

Raoul headed down the rue des Études. He had a friend nearby he hoped might let him stay for a few hours, until it was dark at least. A third police car went past, its siren shrieking, this time heading towards the Caserne d'Iéna. The town was alive with police. As he crossed the street, he saw a *panier à salade* at the top of rue Voltaire. He glanced behind him, seeing there was another at the bottom of the street too.

He needed to get off the street before they saw him. Quickly, he slipped through the wrought-iron gates of the Jardin du Calvaire and pulled them shut behind him, hoping the deep green shadows of the garden would give him sanctuary.

Chapter 29

It took the girls less than ten minutes to get back to the rue du Palais. Marianne still looked passably respectable, but the knees of Suzanne's slacks were black from where she'd knelt on the ground. Her short hair was standing up in tufts where she'd run her fingers through it to shake out the dust.

Marieta shrieked when she saw them.

'We're all right,' Sandrine said quickly, seeing how weary Marianne looked. 'None of us is hurt.'

'You're covered in blood! Look at you!'

Sandrine caught sight of herself in the mirror of the hallstand and saw a wide smear, like a piece of ribbon, across her face.

'There was an explosion outside Saint-Michel,' she said. 'We went to help. We're fine.'

'Do you think you could make us some tea, Marieta?' Marianne said quietly. 'We could all do with something.' She put her hand on Suzanne's arm. 'You'll stay?'

'If there's enough to go round.'

Marianne smiled briefly. 'Is that all right, Marieta? A little bread and some ham, perhaps?'

Marieta stared for a moment longer, then nodded and tramped back down the corridor to the kitchen.

Marianne and Suzanne went into the salon. Marianne slipped off her shoes and sat on the sofa. Suzanne dropped down into the armchair and began to unlace her heavy boots. She pushed them off, revealing a hole in the heel of her left sock.

'Do either of you know what happened to Lucie?' Sandrine asked from the doorway.

Marianne shook her head. 'I lost track of her. I could telephone.'

Suzanne shook her head. 'I'll go round and check later.'

Sandrine watched them for a moment, then turned and went back into the hall. After all the noise and chaos and confusion, she wanted to be on her own. She took off her outdoor shoes, found a pair of espadrille sandals beneath the hallstand, then went upstairs to the bathroom to wash her face.

She heard Marieta carrying a tray of tea to the salon and the murmur of thanks and explanations, and took the chance to slip out through the kitchen and into the small courtyard garden. Her bicycle was still leaning against the fence where Max had left it yesterday morning.

Sandrine settled herself on one of the white wrought-iron chairs set at the table in partial shade beneath the fig tree and let the tranquillity of the garden wash over her. A hen blackbird was singing and there was a steady murmuring of cicadas, wasps buzzing around the ripe fruit. From time to time a lizard, quicksilver green, shot up the back wall of the house and disappeared into the cracks below the guttering.

She heard the rattle of the screen door. She looked up to see Marieta at the top of the steps, a glass in her hand. Holding tight to the railings, she made her way slowly down and placed the tumbler of lemonade in front of Sandrine.

'There,' she said.

Then, to Sandrine's astonishment, Marieta pulled out one of the heavy white chairs and sat down. Her expression was so solemn and so anxious that, despite her exhaustion, Sandrine sat up.

'What is it?' she said quickly.

'Madomaisèla, there's something I need to ask you.'

Unaccountably, Sandrine felt her heart skip a beat. 'Is something wrong?'

The old woman frowned. 'After you left this morning, I heard the shutters banging in your bedroom. I went upstairs. I couldn't help reading what you had written. I'm sorry.'

'Written?'

'The papers.'

At first, Sandrine had no idea what Marieta was talking about. Then she realised she was referring to the notes written in the police station.

'I'm sorry, I thought I'd picked them up. I'll clear them away later.'

'It's not that ...' Marieta paused again, clearly trying to find the right words. 'Some of the things you wrote – "a sea of glass" and "the spirits of the air" – those are the words he said?'

Despite the warmth of the day, a shiver went down Sandrine's spine, as the image of the man's face rushed back into her mind.

'Yes,' she said quietly. 'Kept saying the same things, over and over.'

'And he said Dame Carcas, you are sure?'

Sandrine frowned. 'Pretty sure. Why?'

'Also, to tell "the old man" it was all true?'

'Yes.' Sandrine kept her eyes fixed on Marieta's troubled face, trying to work out what she was really thinking. 'He said a name, but I can't remember it, so couldn't put it down.'

'Try, madomaisèla,' she said urgently.

Sandrine had never seen Marieta so jittery before. Even when the news came about her father, the older woman had kept her own emotions hidden. So having tried to forget, Sandrine forced herself instead to relive the moment.

She shut her eyes. 'It was an old-fashioned name. Bailleroux or Braillard, something like that.'

'Baillard?' Marieta said quickly. 'Was it Baillard, madomaisèla?'

Sandrine's eyes snapped open. 'Actually, it was. How on earth did you know?'

The housekeeper didn't answer. 'You did not tell the police? You did not give them Monsieur Baillard's name?'

'How could I? I've only just remembered it myself.'

The old woman sighed and sat back in her chair.

'What's this about, Marieta? You're making me nervous with your fierce looks.'

A breeze slipped through the garden, lifting the leaves on the fig tree and setting slats of golden sunlight down on to the table. Sandrine looked at Marieta, forced the housekeeper to meet her eye.

'Marieta?'

'It's so long ago,' she said, twisting the black material of her skirt between her fingers. 'My memory could be at fault. But the ghosts, Monsieur Baillard said he could hear … and those words, I'm sure …'

'You've heard them before?' Sandrine asked. 'Or read them? You know where they come from?'

But Marieta was locked in her own thoughts and wasn't listening. 'I shall write to him,' she muttered to herself. 'Those words. Ask him what to do.'

Sandrine touched her on the arm, making her jump.

'Who is Monsieur Baillard?' she said quietly.

The old woman's expression lightened for a moment. 'A good man, a good man and a true friend. He knew your father. It was Monsieur Baillard who recommended me for the position here. I came to know him in Rennes-les-Bains, many years ago. He was a regular visitor to the Domaine de la Cade.'

Sandrine's curiosity deepened. It was odd Marieta

hadn't mentioned Monsieur Baillard before, though she wasn't one to talk about herself. Sandrine did know plenty of stories about the Domaine de la Cade, stories picked up over many long summers in Coustaussa. How the house had burnt down in mysterious circumstances on 31 October 1897. How the entire estate, abandoned now, was said to be haunted. How the village children wouldn't go near it, especially at Hallowe'en.

She did the arithmetic in her head. 'If you knew Monsieur Baillard then,' she said, 'he must be incredibly old now.'

Marieta gave a brief smile. 'No one knows how old he is.'

But before Sandrine could ask anything else, Marieta was getting to her feet. She tucked the chair under the table and headed back towards the house.

'Marieta?' Sandrine called after her. 'Where does he live, this Monsieur Baillard? In Rennes-les-Bains?'

The old woman didn't turn round, but continued up the steps, pulling herself along the railings.

'Marieta! What are you going to ask him?'

The only answer was the rattle of the screen and the snick of the catch as the door closed, leaving Sandrine alone in the garden once more.

She sat back in her chair, hardly knowing what to think. All around her, secrets seemed to swoop and dive like fireflies, bright and dazzling. Unseen, but making their presence felt all the same.

Chapter 30

Leo Authié's office overlooked the Palais de Justice. It was the control centre from which he had run today's operation and an indication of the power he now held within the Deuxième Bureau.

A large mahogany desk and chair, wooden filing cabinets rather than functional regulation bullet-grey metal. The antique maps on the wall were originals, not reproductions. One showed the boundaries of Gaul in the fourth century, the point at which France became a Christian country. The second, the shifting boundaries of the Languedoc, from the historical territories of Septimania to the present day. The third illustrated the course of the medieval crusades in the Midi against the Cathar heretics.

Authié was not alone in believing that France's defeat in June 1940 was a direct consequence of successive administrations turning their backs on traditional Christian values. Too many immigrants, a lack of leadership, a corrosive dilution of what it meant to be French. However, after the shock of the quick and humiliating surrender had passed, Authié realised that in fact the occupation of the north and the collaboration between Vichy and Hitler would suit his purposes.

His hand went to the silver cross on his lapel. God had been with him today, as he had known He would. And it was with the Church that Authié's loyalties lay, not with the liberals and the socialists whose catastrophic godless government had led France to defeat.

Another prison van drew up at the door of the courthouse opposite. Everything had gone like clockwork.

The operation had been a triumph. The threat to Vichy's authority in Carcassonne had been contained, neutralised, undermined. Already there were fifty *résistants* in custody. By the end of the day, they'd have the rest of them. And although he knew some networks would regroup and new units would be formed, Authié believed he'd dealt the insurgents a blow from which they would not fully recover. The bomb had been effective. The wireless and newspapers were blaming the chaos on the partisans. Most local people would be less inclined to shield or support them now. He drew a deep breath. More important, the successful completion of today's strike against the terrorists meant he was at last free to return his attention to his pursuit of the Codex.

Authié went through the papers on his desk – letters, telegrams, official notifications, congratulations from his divisional commander, all of which he put to one side – until he found the envelope he was looking for. A long, thick fold of high-quality paper embossed with the name of a stationer in Chartres. No censor's stamp. It was from the head of one of the oldest and most influential Catholic families in France. François Cecil-Baptiste de l'Oradore was an immensely wealthy and knowledgeable investor. A collector of antiques and religious artefacts, he was prepared to pay a great deal for rare objects he wished to acquire. Certainly, he had invested hundreds of thousands of francs excavating in the mountains of the Ariège and the Aude.

When he had been approached to ask if he might be prepared to provide information, Authié had been both flattered and pleased. It was during the course of his work for de l'Oradore that he first heard rumours about a Codex, a text condemned as heretical in the fourth century that appeared to have escaped being destroyed with other non-orthodox writings. De l'Oradore himself had more pressing interests – key among them his obsession with the lost Grail books of the Cathars – but Authié had become preoccupied with the Codex. Its continued existence – if the rumours were true – was an affront to God. An evil.

Excavations had been suspended during the war, but as soon as the terms of the Armistice had been agreed and signed, de l'Oradore had reactivated the arrangement. Since then, Authié had provided him with various particular archaeological items, information too, and he had no doubt that his rapid rise through the Deuxième Bureau was due to de l'Oradore's patronage. He glanced again at the maps on his wall, each a gift for particular services rendered.

Authié hesitated for a moment, then broke the seal on the envelope. The header listed in striking Gothic type all the Catholic charities of which de l'Oradore was patron. The letter was, as he had been expecting, a request for a report into progress in the Ariège. Despite the difficult conditions in the Midi, de l'Oradore expected results – a return on his investment – and although the language was beautiful, the letter was an ultimatum.

Authié wondered how long he could delay before replying. Because he hadn't been able to give the matter his full attention in recent weeks, there was nothing new to report. His German partners had failed. And although he knew Antoine Déjean was involved, he had failed to find out how exactly. In the end, he'd had no choice but to give permission for him to be interrogated. Not only had Laval not learnt anything, but he'd made a mess of the business and allowed Déjean to escape.

'*Il a tout foiré*,' he swore under his breath.

More aggravating still was that the escape had only come to light because of Raoul Pelletier's presence at the river. And if Pelletier hadn't been there at the critical time,

Sylvère Laval could have dealt with the girl. That, at least, would have been one less loose end. It was a mess, all of it.

A knock at the door interrupted his reflections.

'Come.'

A young gendarme appeared, his skin raw from shaving. His heels clicked on the parquet floor as he crossed the office.

'Un télégramme.'

Authié put the letter down and held out his hand. His eyes scanned the information. His jaw tightened.

'When did this come in?'

'I brought it immediately, *mon capitaine*.'

Authié stood up, sending his chair flying. The gendarme rushed to right it, trying not to watch as Authié screwed up the telegram, put it in the ashtray on the desk and set a match to it.

'Is Laval on the premises?'

'I don't know, sir.'

'Well find out,' he shouted. 'Tell him to meet me downstairs. Immediately. And organise a driver and car. Now!'

The boy saluted, skidding on the parquet floor in his rush to be out of the room. Authié picked up the telephone, barked a number at the operator and waited for her to connect him. He listened to the voice at the end of the line for a moment, his face growing darker by the second.

'We need to meet.'

He held the receiver away from his ear. 'No, that's not acceptable. One hour. Usual place.'

Authié banged the receiver back in the cradle. He thought for a moment, then put de l'Oradore's letter back in the envelope and concealed it in the drawer of his desk, taking out his revolver at the same time. He slipped it into the pocket of his jacket, then strode out of the room and down the stairs to the main hall.

Everywhere the sound of muffled voices behind doors, the regular tap, tapping of the stenographers and the heels of women's shoes on the black and white tiles as they delivered messages from one office to another.

Sylvère Laval was waiting for him by the main entrance. He was back in uniform and his black hair had been cropped, revealing white skin round the rim of his cap.

'Why the hell did you hand Déjean over to Bauer?'

Laval looked confused. 'They were your orders.'

'I told you to keep him under guard until I could interrogate him.'

'I must have misunderstood.' Laval met his gaze. 'I was under the impression that because of the demonst—'

Authié raised his hand. 'I don't want to hear excuses, Laval. It's your second failure. I'm meeting Bauer now.'

'In Carcassonne?' Laval said quickly.

'Where else?'

Authié stared at his deputy for a moment, unable to interpret the expression on Laval's face, then walked towards the glass doors. The heat hit them the moment they were out on the street.

'What about Pelletier, have you found him?'

'Not yet, sir. We went to his apartment on the Quai Riquet. He lives with his mother.' Laval did a winding motion with his hand. 'Not all there. Kept asking if I'd seen Bruno and—'

'Where else?' Authié interrupted.

Laval's expression hardened. 'I tried the hospital, the usual cafés in town. No one remembers seeing him at the mainline station, or the tramway or the bus station.'

'I want him brought in tonight.'

'Posters with his photograph are being printed now, so—'

'Tonight, Laval. What about Sanchez?'

'He was arrested this afternoon,' he said in a tight voice.

'Good.' Then he paused. 'On second thoughts, has he been charged yet?'

'Not to my knowledge, sir.'

Authié thought for a moment longer. 'In which case, have him released.'

Laval's eyes widened. 'Sir?'

'Sanchez is more likely than anyone to know where Pelletier's gone to ground,' he said impatiently. 'They might have arranged to meet. Follow him.'

'But if we let him go—'

'Do as you're told, Laval,' Authié snapped. 'If, after twelve hours, he hasn't led us to Pelletier, he's not going to. Then you can talk to him. Find out what he knows. But I don't want him anywhere near the courthouse or the gaol. I don't want an official record of the interrogation.' He pointed at Laval. 'Don't make a mess of this too.'

Laval's face remained impassive. 'No, sir.'

'Anything else?'

'I've traced the car I saw at the river yesterday, sir. The vehicle is registered to a Monsieur Ménard, the garage man on boulevard Omer Sarraut. Ménard belongs to the LVF. He's currently in a POW camp in Germany, but there's a daughter with Gaullist sympathies. Goes about with a Jew by the name of Max Blum.'

The driver opened his door. Authié stood with his hand on the roof of the car.

'Was the Ménard woman driving the vehicle?'

'I was too far away to see.'

'She might know who the girl is.'

'Do you want me to speak to Mademoiselle Ménard, sir?'

'No, leave her to me. But talk to Blum. It's possible he saw Pelletier or knows him. Bring him in.'

'On what grounds, sir?'

Authié raised his eyebrows. 'He's a Jew, Laval. I'm sure you can find some reason.'

He got into the car and tapped the driver on the shoulder. 'Rue du cimetière Saint-Michel,' he ordered.

Chapter 31

'Let me do it,' Sandrine repeated, taking the envelope from Marieta's hands.

The housekeeper was standing in the open door wearing her hat and outdoor shoes. Her housecoat was hanging on the back of the kitchen door.

'I'll not have you running errands for me.'

Sandrine pushed the letter into her pocket and was out of the door before Marieta could raise any more objections.

'Won't be long,' she called.

The air seemed to crackle with anticipation, as if the streets were waiting for darkness to fall. A strange, expectant atmosphere. The boulevard Maréchal Pétain was deserted and all the small side streets in the Bastide were empty too. As if everyone had been warned to stay inside.

Sandrine propped her bicycle against the wall and got inside with minutes to spare before the post office shut. Only one counter was open.

'I'd like this to go tonight,' she said. 'It's urgent.'

The clerk, a middle-aged man with a pinched face, looked up at her over the top of his spectacles.

'Interzone?'

'No, Aude.'

He glanced at the address, then held out his hand. '*Carte d'identité*.'

'Why do you need to see that?'

He shrugged. 'I don't make the rules.'

Sandrine took her identity card from her pocket and pushed it under the glass. He peered at her personal details, looked up at her, then slid the card back.

'Not a very good likeness,' he said.

'How much will it be?'

'Fifty centimes.'

Sandrine pushed the money under the glass and was given a red stamp in return, which she licked and pressed to the envelope.

'The box is outside.'

'It will go tonight?'

'No reason not to,' the clerk replied. Then he pulled down his blind, leaving Sandrine staring at the blank glass.

She came out into the rue de la Préfecture, irritated by the peremptory manner of the clerk and by the fact that she'd had to show her *carte d'identité*. She dropped the letter into the box, then got on her bike.

The street was still empty, but the sense of watchfulness had intensified. As if there were eyes hidden behind every shutter, every door, waiting for what would happen when night came. Sandrine pushed off from the pavement. Then, without warning, a man rushed out from a tiny *ruelle*, right in front of her.

'Hey, watch what you're doing!' she shouted.

She swerved, jerking the handlebars to the left to avoid him. Her front wheel hit the kerb and she half toppled towards the pavement, grazing her knuckles. Furious, she looked up.

'You idiot . . .'

Then she stopped. Straightened up.

'You,' she said.

He was standing very still, his right hand holding the strap of his rucksack, his left clenched by his side. The same dark hair pushed back off his forehead. The same fierce, restless eyes. Tense, as if he might bolt at any moment.

'It is you, isn't it?' she said.

He looked dazed, but this time he answered.

'Yes.'

'At the demonstration.'

Now a hint of a smile on his lips. 'Yes.'

'And yesterday. At Païchérou.'

'Also me, yes.'

His voice was exactly as she remembered, and the presence of him, the memory of sandalwood and heat.

He looked down at her bike, then her scraped fingers. 'I should have been watching where I was going.'

'It doesn't matter.'

Sandrine felt his eyes travel her face, as if trying to commit every feature to memory. Then, as though it was all happening to somebody else, she watched him raise his hand and gently touch the bruise on the side of her head. The street, the day, real life, all of it slipped away.

'It's not so bad,' she said, aware her voice sounded high, odd even to her own ears. 'It doesn't hurt.'

He stepped back, let his hand fall to his side. She remembered to breathe.

'I'm Sandrine, by the way,' she managed to say. 'Sandrine Vidal.'

He was looking at her, staring as if she was speaking a foreign language, then he laughed.

'Raoul Pelletier,' he said. 'By the way.'

'Third time lucky.'

'Yes.'

He laughed again and ran his fingers over his hair. Sandrine realised, with a jolt, that the gesture was already familiar.

'I didn't think you'd recognised me earlier, in the boulevard Barbès.'

'I didn't at first,' she admitted. 'At least, I thought I knew you from somewhere, but … I wasn't sure.'

'No.' He paused. 'You were holding something. A necklace, chain. It belongs to a friend of mine.'

Sandrine's eyes widened. 'A friend? I …'

From further along the street there was the sound of footsteps, shouting. Then, a siren. Raoul's expression changed, sharpened. The wariness came back into his eyes.

'I'm sorry, I can't—'

'Why did you leave?' she said quickly, not wanting to lose him again. 'At the river?'

He caught his breath. 'I didn't want to.'

'Then why?'

He glanced down the street, then back to her. 'I heard the car, couldn't risk it … Could have been anyone. You were there today, you saw what was happening, how things are.'

Another siren. This time, they both reacted. Sandrine looked back at him.

'Where are you going?'

He shrugged. 'I can't stay in Carcassonne.'

'Why not?'

He dropped his voice. 'Most of my comrades have been arrested, others are missing. There's a warrant out for me. They'll be watching my flat, watching the homes of anyone, everyone I know. If I try to rent a room for the night, the moment I present my papers, they'll find me. I have to leave.'

Sandrine didn't realise what she was going to say until the words were out of her mouth.

'You could stay with us.'

Surprise flashed across his face. 'What? No, of course I can't.'

'We have plenty of room.'

'That's not the point,' he said.

Sandrine raised her chin. 'I won't turn you in, if that's what you're thinking.'

She saw a flash of anger in his eyes.

'That's not what I meant at all!'

'Then what?'

He stepped back from her. 'I'm not putting you – your family – at risk.'

'How would we be at risk? No one would suspect, why would they? We're not friends. There's no connection between us. No one would come looking for you at our house.'

'You don't know anything about me.'

Sandrine smiled. 'You saved my life.'

'Hardly.'

'I think you did,' she said simply.

Raoul was shaking his head. 'Look, I appreciate the offer, I do. But I can't let you get involved. You don't even know what I'm accused of doing.'

'Are you guilty?'

'No, but …'

'Well then.'

In an adjacent street, a car backfired. Sandrine jumped, looking towards the noise, then back to Raoul.

'The longer we stand here, the more likely it is you'll be caught. There are police everywhere, patrols watching all the main routes out of town and the station.' She held his gaze. 'Well? What do you say?'

Raoul was staring at her.

'What?'

The slightest smile crossed his lips. 'I don't think I've ever met a girl like you,' he said.

Sandrine flushed, but didn't waver. 'So you'll come?'

'You're either very brave or very stupid.'

Now a flicker of a smile on her face too. 'Stubborn, my sister would say. Not one to take no for an answer.'

In his eyes, she saw the battle he was waging with himself. A mixture of hope and temptation – and, she thought, something else she couldn't quite identify.

'What about your family?' Raoul said.

'It's only me, my sister and our housekeeper. They'll be pleased to help. My sister's friends sometimes stay.'

For another endless moment, the invitation hung between them. Sandrine looked at his expression and saw his resistance was weakening.

'Raoul,' she said softly. 'Please. Come.'

Finally, his resolve cracked. He dropped his shoulders. 'For one night only.'

'You can stay as long as you need,' she said, trying not to smile too broadly.

'Just tonight,' he said.

But he was smiling too.

Chapter 32

Leo Authié and Erik Bauer stood beneath the cypress trees in the centre of the cimetière Saint-Michel. The last of the sun struck the rows of white crosses and stone crescents in the military section of the graveyard, sending long, elongated shadows across the ground. Authié looked comfortable in the late-afternoon heat, his white shirt crisp and laundered. Bauer kept dabbing at his neck with a handkerchief, his pale skin flushed beneath the brim of his hat. Southern blood versus northern, old enemies. For now, finding themselves allies.

'He was weak.'

'Weak!' Authié said. 'You killed him and learnt nothing.'

'May I remind you, Herr Authié, that you handed Déjean to me when your attempts to extract information failed. If your men had done their job properly in the first instance, we would not be having this discussion. You are not in a position to criticise.'

Since Authié didn't want to acknowledge the original mistake had been Laval's, he didn't argue.

'What have you done with the body?'

'I shall deal with it.'

Authié's eyes narrowed. 'He can't be found in Carcassonne.'

'I shall deal with it,' Bauer repeated.

Authié pulled his cigarettes from his pocket, buying time while he thought about his next step. He offered the packet to Bauer.

'I do not smoke.'

'No, I don't suppose you do,' Authié said dismissively.

He lit up and watched the smoke circle upwards, light, into the sky. Bauer flapped it away with his hand, the heavy metal of his ring catching the light. Authié recognised the distinctive Totenkopfring worn by the SS elite, but was surprised at Bauer's indiscretion. It was common knowledge that there were thousands of Nazis operating south of the line, but they didn't usually broadcast their presence.

'Did Déjean mention the key?' Authié asked.

'He admitted knowing of it,' Bauer replied in the same tight, clipped voice, 'but no more. If Rahn did leave the key with him, Déjean did not confirm it.' He paused. 'You are satisfied your men searched Déjean's apartment properly?'

Authié met his gaze. 'Yes.'

'Today?'

He raised his eyebrows. 'We have been rather busy today, Bauer, doing your dirty work for you.'

Bauer's spongy skin flared red once more. 'We have no jurisdiction in the South, as you very well know, Herr Authié.'

'No official authority, but you have influence.'

Bauer stared at him a moment longer. 'I understand Déjean was seen at the river.'

It took every scrap of self-control Authié possessed to keep his voice neutral. 'Déjean tell you that?'

Bauer ignored the question. 'And there was a girl there also. They made contact, yes?'

Authié turned cold, wondering how much Bauer knew. How he knew anything at all.

'So Déjean did talk?' he said, still fishing for an answer.

'Who is she, Herr Authié? A courier?'

'I'm inclined to think not, but we are investigating. She's not a problem.'

'She is dead?'

'Don't be ridiculous, Bauer.'

'You left a witness to this matter? That was unwise.'

'A judgement call.'

'A poor one.'

Since he agreed, Authié didn't respond. 'She's just a girl who happened to be in the wrong place, at the wrong time. This is not Berlin.'

The Nazi took a step forward. This close up, Authié could see flecks of spittle in the corners of his mouth.

'This has been amateur. You have left too many loose ends.'

Authié met his gaze. 'The problem, as I see it, is that you have failed to find out anything. We needed to know who Déjean was working for and what, if anything, he knew, before the trail went cold.' He drew breath. 'You – we – have both failed. You assured me you were making good progress in the Ariège.'

Bauer frowned. 'When there is information to share, Herr Authié, I shall do so.'

'You are asking me to accept your assurances on that point?'

'It is difficult to proceed at the present time,' said Bauer. 'Do not pretend you don't understand.'

For a moment, the two adversaries faced each other down, neither man attempting to mask their mistrust or their dislike.

'Did Déjean say anything more about Otto Rahn?'

'Rahn was a fool,' Bauer said.

Authié smiled at having got a rise out of him. 'But one of yours, wasn't he? Same rank as you, Bauer, if I'm not mistaken.'

Bauer flushed. 'Rahn was a degenerate.'

'An Obersturmführer-SS all the same.'

Without warning, Bauer turned on his heel and strode back towards the entrance. His sudden departure took Authié by surprise, but it gave him a moment to gather his thoughts. The conversation had not gone as he had hoped. In truth, he was now more rather than less uneasy.

After a couple of moments more, he followed Bauer along the gravel path through the graves towards the rue du 24 Février. An unmarked car was waiting in the street.

'Are you going back to Tarascon tonight?' Authié said.

Bauer hesitated. 'Not directly. I am obliged to go north for a matter of days. After that I shall return to the Ariège, yes.'

'I expect to be kept informed of progress in the excavation.'

'If and when there is something to report, you will be told.'

'In person,' Authié said.

Bauer flushed. 'You are not in a position to dictate terms, Herr Authié. You seem to forget we are paying you. You work for us. My superiors expect a return on our investment. So far, your contribution has been disappointing.'

Authié held his gaze. 'I could say the same about your contribution, Bauer.' He gave a half-smile. 'There has been no difficulty with the local police?'

Bauer became still. Authié continued to stare at him.

'And no awkward questions about your presence in the area, I trust?'

'No,' the Nazi replied eventually, though the admission seemed to cost him a great deal. 'I am obliged to you for your assistance in this.'

'My pleasure,' Authié said sarcastically. 'So, as I was saying, you will keep me personally informed of any progress?'

For a moment, he thought Bauer would refuse to answer, but in the end he gave a tight nod, then got into the car and slammed the door.

Authié watched until the vehicle was out of sight, then, slowly, let his breath out. His pleasure at having won the final exchange of words was short-lived. Much of what

Bauer had said had hit home. The Resistance was increasingly using girls to carry messages, packages. He had assumed her presence was an unfortunate coincidence, but he was starting to reconsider. Could the girl and Déjean have arranged to meet?

Authié started to walk back towards the Bastide. Although the tip about Déjean's involvement with the Codex had, admittedly, come from Bauer in the first instance, he was starting to ask himself whether the collaboration was more trouble than it was worth. He paused outside the house where Déjean had been held, an unofficial prison that had come in useful on several occasions, then continued on. No one could possibly have known Déjean would be at the river at that point on Monday morning.

And what about Pelletier? Yesterday, at the meeting, he would hardly have shown everyone the necklace if there had been anything sinister about it. But had Authié underestimated him too? Perhaps it was a deliberate ploy to provoke a reaction? César had been more than usually belligerent at the meeting, and he and Pelletier were friends.

He looked across the Place des Armes towards the cathédrale Saint-Michel, golden in the light of the setting sun. Official tape had been stretched across the entrance to the Garden of Remembrance and two armed officers were keeping guard.

Authié turned right, following the road along the back of the Caserne Laperrine, mulling everything over in his mind. Pelletier and the girl and Déjean. What was the link between them? Was there any link at all?

Chapter 33

'Come on,' whispered Sandrine.

Raoul's edginess was contagious. Every sound, however innocent, was laden with threat, with danger. The empty streets she knew so well no longer felt safe.

'Where are we going?' he asked.

'Rue du Palais, it's not far.'

Raoul stopped. 'Not this way.'

'But it's quickest.'

'We can't go past the Palais de Justice,' he said. 'And that building opposite' – he pointed to an elegant white building past which Sandrine had walked a thousand times – 'that's the local headquarters of the Deuxième Bureau and where the Kundt Commission sets up shop when they're in Carcassonne.'

'What's the Kundt Commission?'

'Gestapo,' he said.

She hesitated, then nodded. 'We'll go via the rue de Lorraine then. Avoid the area altogether.'

Sandrine led him through the narrowest alleyways and short cuts, Raoul half carrying, half wheeling the damaged bike. They emerged opposite Square Gambetta. Between the fountains and lakes and stone balustrades and trees, the white marble statue of a warrior angel shone gauzy in the haze of the setting sun.

'After my father died, I got into the habit of sitting here and looking at her,' she said quietly. 'She's called *Y Penser Toujours* – Never Forget.'

'I didn't know she had a name,' he said.

They continued in silence through the square and into

the rue de Lorraine. Raoul suddenly stopped, rummaged in the front pocket of his rucksack and produced a rather twisted and bent home-made cigarette with tobacco spilling out of both ends.

'I forgot I had it,' he said, striking a match.

Sandrine watched as he pulled hard once or twice, until the paper sparked and started to burn. He exhaled a long white cloud of smoke, then offered the cigarette to her. She hesitated, then accepted.

She put it between her lips, aware of the taste of him on the paper, and took a puff. Heat hit the back of her throat as she inhaled, then immediately doubled over. Choking, as the smoke went down the wrong way. He thumped her on the back, until she stopped coughing. When she looked up at him, through streaming eyes, she saw he was trying not to laugh.

'First time?'

Sandrine nodded, unable to speak. She handed the cigarette back.

'Filthy habit anyway,' he said, though he was smiling. Then his expression grew thoughtful again. 'Before, you asked me why I didn't stay yesterday.'

'It's all right, you don't owe me an explanation.'

She wanted to ask him if he'd taken the chain, but she didn't know how to bring it up in case the man she'd tried to save was his friend.

'The thing is . . .' she began, but Raoul carried on.

'No, I want to explain.' He paused. 'You must have thought badly of me.'

Sandrine tilted her head to one side. 'And that bothered you?'

'I suppose it did.' He shrugged. 'I kept wondering if you were all right. You were on my mind – my conscience – all day.'

Sandrine glanced at him, then away again.

'You kissed me,' she said.

'I'm sorry,' he said, then added: 'Did you mind?'

'No,' she said quietly.

She heard him sigh. 'Well … good.'

They walked a little further, until they came to the corner of the rue Mazagran, where he stopped. Sandrine stopped too. Feeling as if she was watching the scene from the outside, she felt his hand on the back of her neck. Then he was drawing her gently towards him. She was aware of the steady pace of her breathing, in and out, in and out. The texture of his skin against hers, then the imprint of his lips on her forehead. Sandalwood, the memory of heat on his skin, tobacco.

'Since you didn't mind,' he said, when he released her.

They kissed again, then stood still for a while longer, bound together by stillness, by the calm of the moment. Raoul traced the line of her neck, over her shoulder, running his fingers down the length of her bare arm, over her elbow and wrist and hand, to empty air.

'We should keep going,' he said.

Time accelerated, catching up, returning Sandrine to the Bastide. She nodded, not trusting herself to speak.

They walked on through the square until they reached the crossroads.

'We can go in through the back,' she said, pointing at the side gate.

Her voice sounded thin, high, even to her own ears, but Raoul didn't seem to notice. He followed her into the garden, then propped the bike against the wall. For a moment, she couldn't see him.

'Raoul?' she whispered, terrified suddenly that he'd changed his mind.

He was standing beside the fig tree, half silhouetted in the fading light.

'I'm here,' he said.

Chapter 34

Raoul followed Sandrine into the house. Through a mesh screen door, the hiss of steam and pans clattering, a wooden spoon being banged against the side of a mixing bowl.

As they walked in, a medley of smells hit his senses – wild thyme and tarragon, sweet mashed turnip, even sausages. His heart tightened a notch. It reminded him of his mother's kitchen in the old days. An elderly woman, dressed in old-fashioned sabots and a long black dress beneath a patterned housecoat, looked up.

'Marieta, this is Raoul,' Sandrine said, her voice falsely bright. 'He's the one who helped after my … accident at the river.'

The housekeeper's expression didn't change. 'How does he come to be here now?'

Raoul was not surprised by the old woman's hostility, but he could see Sandrine was taken aback at her abrupt tone.

'We ran into each other in town, outside the post office,' Sandrine replied defensively. 'Can supper stretch to one more?'

'Madomaisèla Suzanne is still here. Madomaisèla Lucie too.'

'I'd like him to stay,' she said.

'I don't want to put anybody out …' he began.

'I invited you,' Sandrine said quickly, now evidently embarrassed.

Marieta continued to stare, but then turned and walked towards the table.

'In which case, I will lay an extra place.'

'I don't think she likes me,' Raoul said under his breath.

'Marieta's like that with everybody at first,' she whispered. 'Don't take it to heart. She's a lamb really.'

'She's looking out for you,' he said, touched Sandrine was trying to make him feel better. 'I don't blame her for that.'

They were standing close together now, close enough for him to smell the scent of her skin. His heart tightened another degree. There was a clatter of plates, then Marieta emerged from the larder carrying a wooden board with a large cut of ham in one hand, and the remains of a white loaf in the other.

Raoul stepped forward. 'Can I give you a hand?' he asked.

'I can manage.'

He swung the rucksack off his shoulder. 'I have some wine. It's not much, but I'd like you to have it.'

He took out the bottle and put it on the table. For the first time, Marieta looked directly at him. Then, finally, she nodded. Sandrine smiled with relief and Raoul stopped caring about anything else.

'Come on,' she said. 'I'll introduce you to everyone.'

'Is there anywhere I could clean up?' he said.

Marieta stood back from the sink. Raoul quickly put his hands under the tap and splashed water on his face, the worst of the grass stains and dust of the day. When he was ready, he followed Sandrine down a long dark corridor towards the front of the house.

The last of the day's light filtered through a large patterned glass window on the half-landing, illuminating three small black and white framed photographs. Raoul stopped and looked up. All were views of the countryside: the first, a village set high on a hill; the second, two or three odd flint huts, like tiny stone igloos. The third was a shot of a ruined castle.

'Where were they taken?'

Sandrine smiled. 'Coustaussa. We have a summer house there.'

'What are those strange buildings?'

'Our *capitelles* – *castillous*, the locals call them. They're actually quite famous. Visitors come from all over the place to photograph them.' She paused. 'Well, they did before the war.'

'What are they used for?'

'My father said they were a form of very old shepherds' shelter, for those taking their flocks south over the mountains in autumn and back again in the spring after the snows had melted. Truthfully, nobody even knows how old they are. When my sister and I were little, we used to play hide and seek in them, though we weren't allowed.'

In the darkness of the corridor, their fingers found one another. Just for a moment. Sandrine squeezed tight, then let go of his hand. Briefly, he caught sight of his reflection in the mirror. His face was gaunt, but for the first time in a very long time, he looked happy. Then he remembered the events of the day, remembered César and Antoine, and his eyes clouded over once more.

Behind a closed door to the left, he heard women's voices and the sound of a wireless in the background.

'Come on,' Sandrine said. 'Let's get it over with.'

Chapter 35

'*Arrêtez!*' Laval shouted. A single bulb illuminated the long, dark corridor that led to the holding cells in the gaol in Carcassonne. 'You, stop.'

This time, the guard turned round. Sylvère saw him take in his uniform, his rank. Confusion, then belligerence clouded his obdurate features.

'Are you talking to me?'

Laval's eyes slipped to the prisoner. The man's hands were cuffed behind his back, his knuckles were purple, swollen, and the thumb of his right hand was bleeding.

'Is this Max Blum?'

The prisoner raised his head and stared at Laval.

'What if it is?' demanded the guard.

'I need to question him.'

'You have no jurisdiction here.'

Laval strode along the corridor. The guard's hand slipped to his revolver, a spurt of defiance on his bovine face.

'I've no orders to release him into your custody.'

Laval stared at him. 'And somewhere private to have our conversation.'

'Unless you have written orders,' the guard spat the words out, 'I'm taking the prisoner to the cells, with all the others.'

Laval held his gaze for a moment longer, then, without warning, drove his fist into the guard's soft stomach. The man grunted and doubled over, but went for his gun. Sylvère grabbed his wrist and slammed it against the wall, once then again. He yelled and dropped his pistol, which skidded along the concrete floor. Before he had time to recover, Laval circled his arm around the man's fleshy neck and jerked his head back, then again. His cap fell to the ground. The guard's eyes bulged and the gasping sound grew fainter.

'Will this do in lieu of written orders?' said Laval, jerking his victim's neck back again. 'Yes?'

'Yes,' he choked.

Laval pushed the guard away from him, then crossed the corridor, picked up the weapon. He cocked it open, removed the bullets from the drum, clicked it shut again and threw it at the guard's feet.

'And somewhere to have the conversation,' he repeated.

Rubbing his throat, the guard put his cap back on his head. Without meeting Laval's eye, he walked a couple of steps back down the corridor, took a bunch of keys from his pocket and opened a door. Laval grabbed Blum by the arm and pushed him into the room.

'Wait outside,' he ordered the guard, taking the keys from the man's hands and shutting the door.

'Sit.'

Blum didn't move. 'Who are you?'

It was the first time he'd spoken. He was tall, but slight, so Laval was surprised at how deep his voice was.

'Sit down,' he said again, forcing the prisoner down into one of the chairs set either side of a plain wooden desk.

Laval sat on the corner, then leant forward and removed the glasses from Blum's face. This time, he saw clear protest in the prisoner's eyes, though still he didn't complain.

'Why have I been arrested? My papers are in order.'

'Are you long-sighted or short-sighted?'

'What?'

'Answer the question, Blum.'

'Short.'

'Your sister, Liesl, where's she tonight?'

Laval saw a flicker of alarm in Blum's eyes, though he hid it well. 'I don't know.'

'Well, now I know you're lying, Blum. Because it says here ...' he made a show of pulling some papers from his pocket and looking at them, 'that you keep a close eye on her. So, I have to ask, why you were out? Leaving her on her own.'

'There's no curfew,' he said shortly.

'Not for us, Blum, but for you?'

He saw the man struggle not to react to the provocation. He dropped his eyes to the papers again.

'We've had five or six complaints from your address. Even so, you left your sister alone?'

'The last time,' Blum said, 'those thugs were outside for three hours. Throwing stones at the window, shouting abuse.'

'High spirits.'

'Criminals.'

'The police aren't there to protect your kind, Blum.'

'French police are supposed to protect French citizens. All French citizens.'

Laval leant forward again. 'Tell me about Raoul Pelletier.'

'Who?' Blum said immediately. He sounded genuinely surprised.

'You heard me. Raoul Pelletier.'

'I don't know anybody of that name.'

From the look on Blum's face, Laval was certain he was telling the truth, but he needed to be sure. He drew back his arm and hit the other man on the side of his head with his open hand, taking him by surprise. Blum's head snapped back and his legs shot out in an attempt to stop the chair from toppling over.

'Raoul Pelletier,' repeated Laval. 'Who is he?'

'I've never heard of him.'

Laval laughed. 'Pelletier's name has been all over the wireless. There can't be a man, woman or child in Carcassonne who's not heard of him.'

'If you recall, we are no longer permitted to own a wireless,' said Blum, struggling to catch his breath.

Laval picked up Blum's glasses and twisted them between his thumb and forefinger.

'This morning, you attended the demonstration with your sister and your, what shall we call her, *salope*.'

Finally, a spark of anger. 'Don't talk about her like that.'

Laval hit him again, harder this time, splitting the skin beneath his eye. Blum swallowed a gasp, but said nothing as the blood trickled down his cheek.

'An illegal demonstration,' Laval continued. 'Pelletier was there.'

'I told you, I don't know anyone called Pelletier.'

Laval saw Blum brace himself for the blow, which didn't come.

'Where's Pelletier now?'

'I don't know anyone called Pelletier.'

'Who was the girl at the river?'

Laval saw the confusion at the abrupt change of subject and then, for the first time, the flicker of evasion.

'I don't know what you're talking about.'

'Yes you do, Blum. Think. We know you were there – we traced the number plate – you and your tart. Did you give the girl a lift somewhere?'

'I don't know what you're talking about.'

'How does she know Pelletier?'

Laval could see Blum was struggling, trying to put the different questions together. Trying not to get caught out.

'I don't know Pelletier,' he repeated for the third time.

This time, Laval went for his stomach, landing the punch just beneath the diaphragm. Blum grunted, but still managed to raise his head and stare at him.

'You're lying, Blum. Why was Pelletier at the river yesterday?'

The reaction was so quick, Laval almost missed it, but it was there. Confirmation that he genuinely didn't know Pelletier. Or at least, he didn't know that he had been at the river. He moved on with another question before Blum had time to think.

'This girl, is she a friend of "Mademoiselle" Ménard?'

'I don't know what you're talking about,' Max said, strain cracking his voice.

'Do you want me to ask Mademoiselle Ménard myself, Blum?'

'Leave her alone,' he said. 'She doesn't know anything. There's nothing to know!'

Blum flinched, clearly bracing himself for another blow, and relaxed a little when it didn't come. Laval stared at him – he was stronger than he'd expected – then leant forward and put the warped glasses back on his bruised face.

'She's got to know more than you, Blum. Maybe she'll be able to tell us the girl's name. Or that little sister of yours. Pretty girl, for a Jewess.'

Blum sprang out of the chair, even though his hands were still cuffed behind his back.

'Don't you go near her, either of them,' he warned. 'Or else I swear I'll . . .'

'You'll do what?' Laval laughed. 'You're here, Blum, she's out there. You can't protect her. Your sister, your whore, you're no use to either of them.'

Finally he saw fear in the other man's eyes. 'You can't hold me,' Blum said. 'I've done nothing wrong.'

'You're a Jew, Blum,' Laval said.

'I'm French.'

'Not in my eyes.'

'A Parisian.'

'Yet here in Carcassonne. Attending an illegal demonstration.'

'There were thousands there. You can't arrest everybody.'

Laval stood up and threw open the door. The guard, who had clearly been trying to listen in, sprang back.

'Process him. Put him on the deportation list with the others.'

'You can't do this,' Blum shouted. 'You've got no right!'

Laval walked out into the corridor. 'I can do anything I like, Blum. Send you anywhere I like. No one even knows you're here.'

He turned. 'And you,' he hissed to the guard, 'if you breathe a word of this to anyone, you'll be on that train tomorrow too.'

Chapter 36

'Marianne,' Sandrine said, leading Raoul into the salon. 'There's someone I want you to meet.'

An attractive woman sitting on a sofa looked up, a book in her lap. Raoul recognised her from boulevard Barbès. In an armchair to her left, a tall woman with cropped hair and slacks. A pretty bottle blonde was adjusting the dials on the wireless. All three immediately stopped what they were doing and looked at him with a mixture of suspicion and interest.

'Mesdames,' he said, wishing his throat wasn't so dry.

'Marianne,' Sandrine said, her voice too sharp, too fast, too high. 'This is Raoul. He's stuck, needs somewhere to stay. I said you wouldn't mind.'

'Darling, I'm not sure that's a . . .'

Sandrine carried on talking over her. 'It was Raoul who fished me out of the river yesterday,' she said. 'Without him, who knows how long I might have been lying there.' She put her hand on his arm and he felt how nervous she was. 'Raoul, my sister Marianne and our friends Lucie Ménard and Suzanne Peyre. Everyone, Raoul Pelletier.'

After a moment's hesitation, Suzanne stood up and offered her hand. 'How do you do.'

'Did you say Pelletier?' said Lucie.

Sandrine nodded. 'Yes, why?'

Lucie leant forward and turned up the volume on the wireless. The crackling voice of the presenter grew louder.

'Police in Carcassonne therefore request anyone who has any information pertaining to the whereabouts of the suspected bomber to contact them immediately. Following the discovery of a number of items in the apartment where the suspect resided …'

Raoul felt a trickle of dread. He knew they'd be after him, but to be set up for the whole thing? He couldn't work it out.

'… and the police advise that Pelletier may be dangerous. He should not be approached. The telephone number will be repeated at the end of this bulletin. We repeat, he may be dangerous and should not be approached. In other local news, the celebrations for the Fête de Saint-Nazaire will still go ahead in Carcassonne, despite the damage caused by this afternoon's outrage in the Bastide. Organisers say …'

Lucie flicked the dial off. 'They've been running bulletins every half-hour,' she said.

'You can't believe anything the wireless puts out,' Sandrine said, squeezing his arm. 'You're always saying as much, Marianne.'

His situation was even worse than he'd imagined but, despite that, despite everything, Raoul's spirits lifted a little at how Sandrine sprang unconditionally to his defence. Something inside him shifted.

He looked around the room, trying to work out what to say. How even to begin. He felt Marianne's eyes on him.

'Monsieur Pelletier?'

Raoul met her gaze. 'I wasn't responsible for the bomb.'

'Were you there?'

'Yes, and …' He hesitated. 'And I know who set it off, I saw him, though there's nothing I can do about it. No one will believe me.'

'Someone died,' Marianne said.

'A boy?' Raoul said, remembering the child's white face.

'Yes.'

'Marianne,' Sandrine said, sounding upset as well as

embarrassed. 'Raoul told me he was in trouble. I invited him. He doesn't have to answer to us.'

'Your sister has a right to know what happened,' he said. 'I'd expect the same in her position.'

'No,' Sandrine said firmly, 'she doesn't. You told me you didn't do anything and—'

'Darling, let him speak for himself.'

Sandrine threw her hands in the air. 'How can he possibly do that when you're sitting in judgement?'

Marianne patted the sofa cushion. 'Come and sit by me.'

Sandrine hesitated, then went to the sofa and sat down. Suzanne plonked herself back in the armchair. Lucie perched on the arm, swinging a shapely leg to and fro.

Raoul looked at Sandrine – her fierce eyes, the two spots of colour on her cheeks, her black curls framing her face – and the sight of her gave him courage. He knew without a shadow of a doubt that if there was ever to be something between them, he had to break the habit of deception he'd been forced to adopt and tell the truth. Trust Sandrine and her sister, their friends. Tell them what had happened, leave nothing out.

'May I sit down?' he asked.

'Of course,' Marianne replied.

Raoul pulled a wooden chair from next to the sideboard and put it in the middle of the room.

'The man who detonated the bomb is called Sylvère Laval,' he said. 'I know because he was a member of a group I was also in. I realised today – too late to do anything about it – he'd been working undercover with the police.'

'What kind of group?'

He was aware of Sandrine's dark eyes on him, but he continued to focus his attention on Marianne. He took a deep breath.

'A Resistance group.'

'And you, Monsieur Pelletier?'

He held her gaze. 'You're asking if I am a partisan?'

'I am.'

Raoul hesitated, then gave a sharp nod. 'Yes.' He almost expected an alarm to go off at the admission, or for the police to storm the house. 'I am a partisan. Of course.'

Marianne glanced at Suzanne. Raoul felt he could almost see the questions, the calculations flying unspoken through the air. He felt the force of Sandrine's steady gaze on him. Quickly he turned his head and risked a smile, was rewarded by the encouragement in her eyes.

'But the situation's complicated,' he said.

'Go on,' said Marianne.

'The march itself was genuine enough, but it seems many of the Resistance groups in the Aude had been infiltrated by Vichyists, by Deuxième Bureau, or . . .' He paused again. 'Or, like mine, set up by collaborators in the first place.'

'To trap *résistantes*,' Suzanne said, then quickly corrected herself. '*Résistants*.'

'Let Monsieur Pelletier continue,' Marianne jumped in. 'Who was in this group?'

Giving names went against everything he'd been taught. But again, Raoul knew he had no choice if he wanted to persuade her – them – to trust him.

'Two brothers, Gaston and Robert Bonnet; Antoine Déjean; and a former comrade of my brother from the International Brigade, César Sanchez.'

Raoul saw a glance pass between Suzanne and Marianne.

'What about your brother?'

'Bruno was murdered by the Nationalists in Spain in December 1938.'

Marianne paused. 'I'm sorry.'

'Thank you. The other members were Laval and the leader of the group, a man called Leo Coursan.'

Marianne looked at Suzanne again. 'Coursan, I know that name.'

Raoul glanced at each of the women in turn. Sandrine looked simply interested, curious. The blonde too. But Marianne and her friend? He was increasingly certain they knew precisely what he was talking about.

'I was aware there were tensions, but since I didn't know anyone except for César, and people are often on edge before something big like that, I didn't take it to mean anything. Unfortunately, I failed to listen to my own instincts.'

'Did you talk about your suspicions with anyone else?'

'I tried to talk to César. He clearly had something on his mind, but stupidly I didn't press him, so—'

'Where's César now?' Suzanne interrupted.

'He was arrested this afternoon. At his apartment.'

This time Marianne and Suzanne made no attempt to hide the glance that passed between them.

'Do you know him?' he asked.

Neither woman answered.

'Go on, Monsieur Pelletier,' said Marianne.

'I was outside Saint-Michel when the bomb went off. I shouted a warning to get people out of the way, but I was too late. Laval left a pile of the tracts we'd been distributing at the site, or packed them into the bomb, I'm not sure which. I had a few with me. I was trying to help the boy who was injured, they fell out of my pocket and a woman saw. Started screaming.'

'You have any proof of this?'

'Marianne!' Sandrine protested.

'No. But it's the truth.'

'A *bouc émissaire*, a scapegoat,' Suzanne said.

Marianne took no notice of the interruption. 'Is that all you were doing, handing out tracts? No – no other action?'

Raoul again held her gaze. 'Just handing out leaflets.'

'What was in them?'

'Photographs of the conditions in the camps at Argelès, Rivesaltes.'

'I saw them,' Sandrine said.

'So did I,' said Lucie. 'Awful.'

Marianne was silent for a moment. Raoul waited, feeling that the tide was turning in his favour, but not wanting to jeopardise anything.

'Do you think Coursan and Laval were working together?'

Raoul shook his head. 'I've been trying to work it out. I didn't see Coursan today and I don't know what's happened to him, but he and Laval are close . . .' He shrugged. 'It's hard to be sure.'

He paused, trying to decide whether to go on or not.

'Is there something else, Monsieur Pelletier?'

'I can see it was easy for Laval to frame me. I was right there at the critical moment. On the other hand, it's possible I'd been singled out anyway.'

'Why?' Marianne said quickly.

'Because of what happened yesterday at the river.'

Now Lucie started to pay more attention.

'Antoine Déjean is missing. Has been for several days.' Raoul risked a quick glance at Sandrine, who was sitting very still on the sofa with her arms wrapped around herself. 'You were holding his chain when I found you,' he said softly.

'It was in the pocket of a jacket abandoned down by the water,' Sandrine said, 'though that had gone when I came round.' She looked at Lucie. 'Do you remember, I asked you and Max to look for it?'

'I'm sorry we didn't believe you,' Lucie said. 'It just sounded so unlikely, all of it.'

Marianne leant towards Raoul. 'The man Sandrine helped at the river, do you think it was your friend?'

'I can't be sure. But he's still not turned up, and from Sandrine's description, it sounded like Antoine.'

'I didn't want to say anything in case I was wrong,' Sandrine said quietly. 'I'm sorry.'

Marianne thought for a moment. 'Are you saying you think Coursan attacked Déjean?'

Raoul shook his head. 'The timings don't work. He can't have been hauling Antoine up the bank, finding somewhere to hold him, then back at the rue de l'Aigle d'Or in time for the meeting. He was there before me.'

'What about Laval?' said Marianne.

'That's more likely. He arrived late, very late. Coursan was angry about it, though he didn't say anything until the rest of us had gone.'

Raoul stopped talking, suddenly weary of it all. The guessing games, how much to reveal, how much to conceal. He had done what he could to persuade them he could be trusted. He'd given them names. If Marianne still didn't believe him, he didn't see what more he could say.

'Mademoiselle Vidal, I accept you've only my word for any of this. And after everything, I can see how Sandrine turning up with me now, out of the blue, seems suspicious. I don't blame you. I'd be the same.' He glanced at Sandrine, then at Lucie and Suzanne, before letting his gaze come to rest on Marianne once more. 'But I've told you the truth.'

'I believe you,' Sandrine said firmly.

Raoul looked at her, fighting his corner so fiercely, so doggedly, and felt the knot of anxiety in his stomach loosen a little more.

'Darling,' Marianne said gently, 'you don't know him.'

Sandrine got up and came to stand beside him. 'I know enough,' she said. 'Raoul saved my life.'

Marianne placed her hands in her lap. 'You've only got his word for that. He was there at the river yesterday when you were attacked – you say by someone else, but there's no evidence it wasn't him.' She held up her hand to stop Sandrine interrupting. 'Again, he turns up today precisely where you happen to be, first at the demonstration, then in the rue de la Préfecture.'

'Are you suggesting he's been following me?' Sandrine said, her voice rising in disbelief. 'That's ridiculous. Why would anyone follow me?'

It was a simple question. That Sandrine asked it was, to Raoul, proof positive that she had no idea of what was going on. The blonde wasn't in the picture either. But the fact Marianne had raised such a suspicion in the first place – and the look on Suzanne's face – confirmed to Raoul once and for all that they were as involved as much as he was. He looked Marianne in the eye.

'I understand why you might think that, but I give you my word, I didn't know.'

'Know what?' Sandrine asked. She looked at her sister, then at Raoul, then back to her sister again. 'Know what, Marianne?'

All the theories and counter-theories, words and speculations and justifications, seemed to hang in the air.

'Marianne?' she repeated, sounding less certain.

Raoul ran his hands over his hair, feeling the strain of the day and the hours spent in the Jardin du Calvaire in the ache of his shoulders. He stood up.

'Look, I don't want to cause any trouble. I don't want to draw attention to the house. I should go.'

'You can't go now,' Sandrine said. 'If Raoul goes, I'm going with him.' She linked her arm through his. 'I mean it.'

Raoul felt the full force of Marianne's eyes on him, summing him up. Everyone else was looking at her, waiting to see what she would decide. The carriage clock on the mantelpiece was deafening, suddenly, in the expectant quiet.

Finally Marianne sighed. 'All right, he can sleep in Papa's room. Only for tonight.'

Sandrine immediately rushed to her sister and threw her arms around her.

'Thank you, I knew you'd come round.'

Raoul let out a long deep sigh. 'Thank you, Mademoiselle Vidal.'

Marianne was still staring at him. 'But you need to be gone first thing in the morning, Monsieur Pelletier.'

Chapter 37

Reluctantly, Sandrine followed Marianne upstairs. She stood on the threshold of their father's room, while Marianne fetched clean linen from the airing cupboard. Even though there had been plenty of occupants in the past couple of years, the room still smelt of him. A mixture of hair oil and old books and his favourite cologne. She sighed.

'Come on,' said Marianne.

'I don't see why I've got to help,' she said. 'Marieta was happy to make up the bed.'

'She's seeing to supper,' Marianne said calmly. 'Put the slip on the pillow first, then the pillowcase.'

Sandrine pulled off the heavy white cotton pillowcase, tossed it on the bed and started again.

'It's rude leaving Raoul alone downstairs,' she said.

'He's not on his own. Lucie and Suzanne are with him.'

'It's our house. He's our guest,' Sandrine said irritably. 'One of us should be looking after him.'

Marianne handed Sandrine the corners of the sheet and they shook it out, letting the air hold it before it floated down to the mattress.

'No one's stayed in here for a while,' Sandrine said.

'No.'

'Why is that?' she asked. 'We used to have all sorts dropping by, but not so much now.'

Marianne didn't answer. Sandrine looked at her sister, doubled over the bed. She looked so tired and was actually being pretty decent about having a last-minute guest sprung upon her. Sandrine suddenly felt guilty she was behaving so badly.

'I'm sorry, I don't mean to be foul-tempered,' she said. 'It's just that I like him.'

Her sister straightened up, hand in the small of her back. 'I know.'

Sandrine stared at her. 'I mean, I really like him, Marianne.'

Finally, her sister's expression gave a little. 'Darling, that's obvious.'

'That's the reason I was upset at you firing all those questions at him. I know you're being careful, but I want him to like you too.'

'Raoul understands,' Marianne said quietly. 'He understands how things are.'

Sandrine finished putting the second pillow in its case and dropped it on the bed.

'What do you think, though? You do like him, don't you?'

Marianne sighed. 'I don't know him,' she replied, running her hand over the sheet to iron out any creases.

'Don't you believe what he said?' Sandrine said quickly. 'I thought you did.'

'That's not what I meant.'

'What then? I want to know what you think, Marianne.'

'Do you?'

'Yes.'

Marianne straightened up. 'All right,' she said. 'I'm not making a judgement on the rights and wrongs of the situation, so don't jump down my throat, but the fact of the matter is that whatever the reason, he did run off and leave you at the river.'

'But you can't—'

Marianne raised her hand. 'Let me finish. Raoul's explanation of why he did that makes complete sense, I'm not saying it doesn't, only you have to ask yourself, with a man like that, where do his loyalties lie? With the people he cares about, or with a cause?'

'I don't think—'

'I don't want you to get hurt, that's all,' Marianne continued. 'Love at first sight, it's not real life.'

Sandrine took a deep breath. 'I know you'll say I've only known him a few hours – and that's true, no time at all.' She paused. 'The thing is, it doesn't matter what his motives are, I don't care. It doesn't seem relevant.' She hesitated, willing her sister to understand. 'Do you see?'

For a moment, Marianne didn't answer. 'There's no future in it,' she said in the end. 'Raoul can't stay in Carcassonne, he'll have to disappear. There's no chance of you being together.'

'I'll wait.'

'It's not a matter of waiting, Sandrine,' she said wearily. 'He's got a murder charge hanging over him. He's not going to be able to come back.'

'He'll clear his name.'

Marianne stared at her for a moment longer, then she sighed. 'Just promise me you'll be careful.'

Sandrine nodded. 'I promise,' she said. She straightened the pillows. 'There, finished. Is there anything else to do up here?'

'No,' said Marianne, sounding even more tired.

'Can I go?'

'Of course. I'll be down in a minute.'

Sandrine raced round the bed and hugged her. 'Thank you for letting him stay,' she said. Then she bounded out of the room and back down the stairs, to where Raoul was waiting for her in the salon.

‡

Codex V

‡

Gaul
Plains of Carsac
July AD 342

Arinius went to take his leave of the two soldiers on the night watch. A father and son, they had become friends during his time in Carcaso. They told him of their wandering lives, spent in fortified towns and garrisons. Marching from one side of the crumbling empire to another. He told them of his God, shared stories of mercy and grace and transformation. As they clasped hands one last time, the father gave him a pair of leather sandals for the journey south and warned him to be careful.

Arinius returned to his lodgings. He did not wish to leave, but he felt the broad hand of time at his back. He wrapped his arms around his thin frame, feeling the familiar crackle of the Codex against his skin, then settled his debt with the innkeeper and left.

The long journey from Lugdunum to the furthest reaches of Gaul had aged him. Every stone, every twist of the path, had left its mark on his bones, on the surface of his skin. But his time in the fortified town had restored his health. The blisters on his feet had healed and the cough that had plagued him since the salt lakes of the flat lands of Narbonensis, if no better, was at least no worse. More often than not, he slept through the night, no longer woken by fever or the sweating that left his bed drenched.

'*Pater noster, qui es in caelis*,' Arinius said, murmuring the comforting words of the Lord's Prayer as he waited for the gates to be opened. 'Hallowèd be Thy name.'

His fingers wrapped around his mother's brooch. She was the wisest, kindest person he had ever known. Arinius knew she would have understood his mission, would have been proud of his fortitude. He felt her beside him, encouraging him on.

'*Et dimitte nobis debita nostra*,' he recited. 'Forgive us our trespasses, as we forgive those who trespass against us.'

Arinius pulled his cloak around him and walked reluctantly through the streets that he had come to call home. He knew it was unlikely he would ever pass this way again. In the silence of the morning, for an instant he heard the voice of God speaking to him. A whispering, a sibilance on the wind. It was, he felt, a moment of grace. A sign.

'Amen,' he whispered. 'So be it.'

He joined the crowds at the main gates. The sound of the wooden bars being removed, the creak of the metal hinges as the night watch pulled open the heavy gates and opened the castellum to the world once more. The movement and surge of men's feet shuffling forward.

Ahead on the plains of Carsac, the Atax glinted brightly in the early-morning sunlight. Arinius prayed that God would give him strength, would guide him safely to the mountains that divided Gaul from Hispania.

Step by step towards the mountains of Pyrène.

Chapter 38

CARCASSONNE
JULY 1942

The sun was rising over the fortified city of Carcassonne. Filigree rays pierced the clouds and dappled the stone face of the Narbonnaise towers, catching the shards of red tile in the Roman section of the walls and painting the Cité amber and bronze in the shimmering light of dawn.

The river was still in the hazy morning air. On the far side of the Aude, the shops and offices of the Bastide were beginning to stir. The house in rue du Palais was still sleeping. Marianne and Marieta were in their own beds, Lucie was curled up under the pink day blanket on the settee and Suzanne was asleep in the armchair, her arms crossed and her head resting on her chest. Wine and the adrenalin of the previous day – and the sense that it would be better not to be out on the streets – had kept the women there together.

Sandrine and Raoul were sitting on the terrace at the rear of the house, where they had been all night. Close together, her cardigan and his jacket serving as bedclothes, his head upon her shoulder. They had dozed a little, resting arm to arm. Mostly, they had talked. Shared fragments of autobiography, their stories. Occasionally touching each other's hands, arms, the lightest of movements before a shy retreat, a dance every bit as complex as the skimming of the swifts over the surface of the river and up, higher and higher, into the sky.

Sandrine glanced at Raoul's sleeping head, then back

out over the garden once more. It was the same sun that had greeted her on Monday and on Tuesday, but it rose now on a different world. Everything had changed, for both the better and the worse, revealing a world at once more perfect and more treacherous. The blue of midday, the white heat haze of the early afternoon, the shifting of light and the purple dusk, setting the shadows to flight. Sandrine felt she had lived lifetimes in the space of the past two days.

Raoul stirred and sat up, stretched.

'Good morning.' She smiled at him.

He rubbed his eyes, turned and looked straight at her. 'Sandrine.'

'I wish I had coffee to offer you, but …'

'I know.'

'We have tea?'

'Thank you.'

Sandrine got up and ran into the house, resenting the time it took the kettle to reach the boil on the stove. She returned a few minutes later with a tray, a metal teapot and two cups. 'I found some biscuits. They don't look too bad.'

'What time is it?'

'Early still.'

He took a mouthful of tea. 'This is the time of day I always like best,' he said. 'After I was demobbed, I lived down on the coast near Perpignan. We helped refugees, escapees, over the mountains up to the border. We left at three or four o'clock in the morning, when it was still dark, and used to get back to Banyuls-sur-Mer just as the sun was rising. The relief at not being caught, every time …'

'I like this time of day too,' she said. 'No one about.'

Raoul put his cup down between his feet and took one of the cigarettes Suzanne had given him from his pocket. 'It was generous of her to give me these,' he said, inhaling deeply. 'How come she has tobacco?'

'She claims her father's ration, I think. He doesn't smoke.'

Sandrine took another mouthful of her tea. Thick with sugar, hot, after their long night of talking it tasted wonderful.

'Why did you go to Banyuls in 1940, rather than coming back to Carcassonne?'

'Bruno.'

Sandrine frowned. 'But by then, wasn't he …'

Raoul nodded. 'Yes, he was killed two years before that. I'd been in Banyuls before, before the war broke out. I used to get these letters from Bruno, telling me what was going on. He was fighting for what he believed in, putting his life on the line. I wanted to be like him. Do you see?'

'Yes.' Sandrine nodded, knowing that if she'd been asked the same question a few days ago, she might have given a different answer.

'So I threw in my studies and went to join him, December 1938. I knew there was a crossing point south of Banyuls-sur-Mer, on the coast, so I headed there. I went straight to a down-at-heel bar on the waterfront, where I'd been told a guide would meet me and take me over the Pyrenees. I had fifty francs to pay for my passage, all the money I had in the world.' He flicked the end of the cigarette down on to the paving stones. 'I waited and waited, but the guide never came. Not that day, nor the day after. I heard nothing, got no explanation other than these things happened.' He stopped, his eyes fixed on a distant point in the garden. 'A week later, I heard that a unit of French and British Republican sympathisers had been ambushed, their route betrayed by their own side. Bruno was one of them. Their bodies were doused in petrol and set alight.'

Sandrine took his hand.

'Photographs of the massacre were circulated as a warning and the names published,' he said quietly. 'I was in shock. I was eighteen, on my own, a long way from home. I drank all night and all the following day and into the next night, stumbling from bar to bar, until the money I'd got together to pay the *passeur* was spent. Christmas found me on the jetty at Banyuls contemplating the black winter sea.' He gave a deep sigh. 'I stood there for hours. The cold penetrated right down to my bones, but I barely noticed. Trying to be brave enough.'

Sandrine squeezed his fingers, encouraging him to keep going.

'I wish I could say it was the thought of my mother, God even, anything. But, truthfully, I lacked the courage to jump.'

'Perhaps it takes more courage not to,' Sandrine said, pushing away the image of a world in which they had never met. 'Harder to keep going.'

'Perhaps.' He gave a fleeting smile. 'In the end, I think it was the idea that someone should pay for what had happened to Bruno. Revenge, I suppose. So I walked back to the bar and the proprietor's wife took pity on me. Gave me coffee and rolls and a few francs to tide me over until I got back to Carcassonne. I didn't want to come back, but I knew my mother would take Bruno's death badly – he was always her favourite – and I thought I owed it to her to tell her myself, face to face.'

'Did you mind that? It didn't make you jealous of him?'

Raoul put his head on one side. 'Not at all. I looked up to him too. Our father died when I was three – I have no memories of him at all. Bruno was the man of the house, he looked after us both. We relied on him.' He sighed. 'He was always so certain, so clear about right and wrong, whereas things never seemed so black and white to me. Not then, at any rate.'

Sandrine smiled, but didn't say anything. She didn't want him to stop talking.

'I always intended to go back to Banyuls,' he continued. 'Stupid, but I felt close to Bruno there.' He shook his head. 'Then of course war broke out and I was called up. Caserne d'Iéna.' He sighed. 'Sunday the third of September. It was so hot that day.'

Sandrine nodded. 'Yes. Marianne and I went to see Papa off. We stood out on the parade ground for hours with the sun beating down on the back of our necks. Then, after all the buses had gone, we went to Place Carnot to listen to the news from *L'Indépendant* being broadcast over the loudspeakers. About how the Maginot Line would keep France safe. I believed it. It didn't occur to me that Papa would ...'

She broke off.

'You miss him a great deal,' he said softly, turning her hand over in his and kissing her palm.

She sighed. 'Not all the time, but then something will happen and I'll think to myself that I must tell him, then I remember.'

They sat in silence for a moment, until Sandrine released her hand and took another sip of her tea. 'What happened to you then?'

'We sat in barracks for what seemed like months. What I remember most about the *drôle de guerre* is the boredom. Being confined to quarters, the daily drill and pointless kit and weapon inspections. We spent most of our time playing football and cards. The farmers in my unit were more worried about the harvest and their crops than German bullets.'

'It was the topic of conversation here too. That autumn, everyone joined in with the *vendanges*. Even the Spanish refugees from the camps at Couiza and Bram were allowed out to help.'

'When finally we were sent north, we found ourselves in this strange deserted land. Walking through the villages, all evacuated, desolate, abandoned to the animals. Cows and pigs and goats wandering through deserted streets. Everyone had gone, been sent away. The only sound was the distant wail of sirens, the sound of the Stukas in the sky.'

They both fell silent, the ghosts of their past close to them in the early-morning light. There was so much more Sandrine wanted to hear and to tell him, but she could feel the intimacy of the dawn was already melting away. The sky was turning from white to the glorious blue of summer. The outlines of the trees and rooftops beyond the garden were stronger, clearer.

The easy atmosphere between them changed. There was no more time for reminiscence and stories.

Beyond the walls of the garden, the bells of Saint-Michel began to ring for six o'clock.

Raoul sighed. 'I have to go.'

'I know.'

He didn't move.

'Wait a minute,' she said, jumping up. 'There's something I want you to have.'

She vanished into the house, reappearing a few minutes later with a brown trilby and a light summer jacket.

'Your father's?'

She nodded. 'He wouldn't mind,' she said, helping him into the jacket. 'There. It's a good fit.'

He touched her cheek with his hand. 'If you're sure.' He sighed again. 'This is it, then.'

'Yes.'

'Say goodbye to Lucie and Suzanne. And thank your sister for me.' Raoul grinned. 'Does it often end up like that here? Everybody getting tight then sleeping it off in the salon?'

Sandrine smiled back. 'No. Last night was unusual. Lucie only stayed because Max was spending the evening with his sister, so she was at a loose end. As for Suzanne, she's a law unto herself.'

'I like her. Straightforward. You could rely on her.'

'Yes,' she agreed, remembering how Suzanne had come to her rescue with Monsieur Fournier. 'Lucie's fun, though.'

'Yes, she seems nice.' His face clouded over, as if he was struggling to find the right words.

'What is it?' she said quickly.

'It's . . .' Raoul paused. 'Get Marianne to talk to you.'

Sandrine laughed. 'We're always talking, what do you mean? We never stop.' Then she looked at his expression and saw he was serious. The smile slipped from her face. 'Talk to me about what?'

Raoul took her hand. 'Just talk to her.'

Behind them, a rattle of pans in the kitchen.

'Someone's already up,' he said. 'I must go.'

'It's only Marieta.'

'Even so.'

Sandrine stood on tiptoe to straighten his collar, then stepped back again.

'Where will you go?' she said quietly. 'Back to Banyuls?'

'Maybe. Anywhere, as far away from Carcassonne and Laval as I can manage.'

'Until it's blown over.'

Raoul sighed. 'It's not going to blow over,' he said. 'There's a murder charge against me. That won't go away.'

Sandrine didn't know for sure what she was going to say until she'd said it, and the moment the words were out of her mouth she knew Marianne would be furious. But she didn't care.

'If you're stuck or need somewhere to stay in an emergency, you could go to our house in Coustaussa.'

'No,' he objected immediately, as she'd known he would.

'No question of it. You've done more than enough already. I've put you at risk simply by being here. I'm not going to do it again.'

Sandrine continued as if he'd not spoken. 'The house is standing empty. It's out of the way. People mind their own business in the valley.'

'No,' he said forcefully.

'Once you're in Coustaussa, coming from Couiza, head through the village towards the back road towards Cassaignes. It's a stone house, three steps up to the front door, yellow paintwork. Everyone knows it. Wooden sign outside – CITADELLE – though it came down in the storms a couple of years ago and I'm not sure it was ever put back up. There's a key under the geranium pot on the terrace at the back.'

'Sandrine, enough,' he said, putting his hands on her shoulders.

'Just consider it.'

He placed a kiss on her forehead, then drew her close against him. Sandrine threw her arms around his waist, holding on tight as if her life depended on it.

'You're shivering,' he said.

'I'm cold, don't know why,' she whispered.

They stood there for a short while, greedy for even a few seconds more. Bound together, not speaking, just feeling the beat of one another's heart through the thin cotton of their clothes.

Then he took her chin in his hand and tilted her face to his and slowly, sweetly, began to kiss her. She felt heat rushing through her, desire lightening every artery and vein and muscle, every tiny nerve ending.

Then, the unremitting and unwelcome sound of Saint-Michel striking the quarter. Raoul stepped back.

'I don't want you to go,' she said.

'I don't want to go,' he said, though he was trying to

smile. 'Whatever happens in the days, weeks ahead, the time I've spent with—'

Sandrine couldn't bear it. 'Don't,' she said quickly, with a catch in her voice. 'Please, don't say anything more. Don't.'

He nodded, understanding. The stolen seconds stretched into minutes. Finally, Sandrine dropped his hand.

'Go,' she said, amazed her voice sounded so steady, so determined, when she felt she was breaking into a thousand pieces.

'You'll be all right?' he asked.

Sandrine nodded, not trusting herself to speak. She watched as he swung his rucksack on to his shoulder, adjusted the straps over the borrowed jacket, straightened the hat.

'This is it, then.'

'Remember,' she said, 'through the village. The last house.'

She painted a smile on her face and Raoul did the same, though she could see he was struggling too.

Then he was walking away. Down the steps and across the garden and out through the gate, away from her and into the Bastide.

For a moment, Sandrine stood motionless, still feeling the echo of his hands on her skin. Then, dizzy with desire and lack of sleep, she sat back on the bench, put her head in her hands and wept.

Chapter 39

'Sanchez.'

César spun round at the sound of his name to see Sylvère Laval stepping out from beside the loading sheds in the station sidings. Like César, he was in the same clothes as yesterday, though he had a beret pulled low on his head.

'Christ, Laval,' Sanchez hissed, 'what the hell do you think you're playing at, sneaking up like that?'

Laval shrugged an apology.

'What're you doing here anyway?'

'Same as you, I imagine. Waiting for the first train out. Safer up here than down in the station, less chance of being seen. The town's crawling with *flics*.'

'There are roadblocks everywhere. Checking papers.'

'Not so bad this morning, though.'

'Let's at least wait inside,' César said, still irritable Laval had made him jump.

Laval pulled open the large sliding doors a fraction, just enough for them both to slip through. César found a couple of packing crates and they both sat down.

'There's a train due at seven thirty,' he said.

'So I heard.' Laval got out his cigarettes. 'Smoke?'

César noticed the packet was full, even though he'd had no cigarettes yesterday morning, and wondered where Laval had got new supplies. He accepted anyway. Black market or not, they'd taste the same. He cupped his hand round the match, drew hard on the cigarette, then sat back and waited for the nicotine to hit the back of his throat.

'They didn't get you either?'

'I was lucky,' Laval said. 'You too, by the look of it.'

César shook his head. 'I was arrested, but they let me go.'

Laval narrowed his eyes. 'Why?'

'I don't honestly know,' he said. Truthfully, it had been preying on his mind all night. One minute he was in the holding cells with the other prisoners, the next he was being frogmarched out of the station and thrown out on to the street. The officer who'd released him didn't look like he'd known what was going on either. It didn't make sense, though César wasn't about to complain.

'Couldn't make anything stick, I suppose. There was no evidence I'd done anything other than attend the demonstration.'

'You and a couple of thousand others.'

César nodded. Maybe that was all there was to it. 'They got the Bonnets, though. They both had a stack of the tracts left. Last I saw, they were being put in a prison van.'

'Is that so?'

There was something about Laval's tone that snagged César's attention. He stared at the other man, trying – failing – to decipher the look on his face. He didn't think it was fear or concern for his own skin. If anything, Laval seemed less on edge than usual.

'What about Coursan?' César asked. 'Any news of him?'

Laval shook his head. 'No, but they've been putting bulletins out for Pelletier all night. They think he set the bomb off.' He paused. 'What do you think, Sanchez? Do you reckon he's capable of doing such a thing? A kid died ...'

César looked at him. 'Not a chance. The town was crowded, civilians everywhere. Raoul wouldn't put innocent people at risk.'

'Not even to make a point ...?'

'No.'

'He was in the International Brigade,' Laval said. 'Ends justify the means and all that.'

'His brother was. Not Raoul.'

'You were too,' Laval said mildly. 'Do you know where Pelletier is?'

César's head snapped up. 'No, why would I?'

Laval shrugged. 'You're friends. Natural he'd turn to you if he needed somewhere to stay.'

'He's not stupid,' César said. 'He'll be long gone.'

The noise of a car straining up the hill towards the cimetière Saint-Vincent caught their attention. Both men immediately stopped talking, even though there was no way anyone would hear them.

'You did a good job with the leaflets,' Laval said, when the sound of the engine had faded away. 'Must have been difficult finding somewhere to print them.'

'Not really,' César replied. 'Owner's never there.'

'I heard Robert Bonnet's been helping you,' said Laval. 'That right?'

'No,' César said abruptly. 'Don't know where you heard that. All my own work.' He was unnerved by Laval's unswerving gaze. Like a snake about to strike. 'All my own work,' he repeated.

He felt a prickling on his skin, realised his heart was racing. He glanced at the sliding doors, only now noticing Laval had pulled them shut after them.

'It's stupid us being together,' he said, standing up. 'I'm going to head down to the station. Take my chances.'

Laval also stood up. César tensed, he couldn't help himself.

'Where did you spend last night, Sanchez?'

'Here,' he said. He glanced again to the door, judging the distance.

'Not in Déjean's apartment?'

César turned cold. How could Laval possibly know he'd been there? He couldn't, surely, not unless he'd followed him. But that would have meant following him from the police station, and how would he know he'd been released?

The truth hit him like a fist, taking the wind from him.

'You're working for them,' he said slowly. 'I suspected Coursan, but—'

Laval moved so quickly round behind him, César didn't realise what was happening until the knife was at his throat, the blade tilted sharp against his windpipe.

'Why did you go back there?' Laval whispered in his ear. 'Tell me.'

'You know why,' César said desperately.

He tried to struggle free, but Laval increased the pressure on the knife and Sanchez felt his skin split. A trickle of blood ran down his neck.

'And Pelletier? He was there for ages, according to the concierge. What was he looking for, Sanchez?'

'Nothing. The same. We were both looking for Antoine.'

Laval increased the pressure on the blade. Another bead of blood bubbled on César's skin. A pop of air, catching in his throat.

'Don't play games, Sanchez. You were looking for the key.'

'Key? I don't know what you're talking about.'

'We can do this quickly,' Laval said in a cold voice, 'or very slowly indeed, it's up to you. So, I'm going to ask you again. Did Pelletier find the key? Did you?'

César felt like he was drowning, a swimmer gasping for air. He couldn't breathe properly. His eyes started to flicker shut. He remembered being in the Café Saillan. Raoul had shown him something, but it wasn't a key.

'No,' he gasped.

Laval put the tip of the knife into the gash and pressed until it hit jawbone. This time, César couldn't stop himself screaming.

'Did he find the key?'

César didn't understand anything other than he mustn't

reveal what Raoul had shown him. Was that yesterday? The day before? He'd been an idiot. He should have confided in Raoul, but he'd held back. Kept his suspicions about Coursan to himself and not paid enough attention to Laval.

'Where's Antoine?' he managed to say.

'You'll see him soon enough,' Laval said. 'Last chance, Sanchez. Tell me what he found.'

César felt his eyes closing. 'Nothing. I swear.'

For a moment Laval released the pressure. César swayed forward, his legs too weak to hold him. The whistle of a train penetrated the gloom of the shed. He tried to raise his head.

At first he thought Laval had winded him. Then he felt a violent, snaking pain in his back as the knife was withdrawn, leaving a vacuum. After that, a ferocious aching. He was losing consciousness, but he couldn't help himself. As he slumped to his knees, he felt Laval's hands searching his pockets, an act both gruesome and intimate. Then the sensation of being dragged backwards, the rough scratch of grit and dust on his heels, to the furthest grey corner of the loading shed. Laval let him drop. César felt his head hit the ground with a thud, then the sound of the doors sliding open and shut once more.

Then, silence.

He tried to move. He rolled over on to his side, then hauled himself up on all fours and tried to crawl towards the door. But colours were dancing in front of his eyes, red and green and stripes. He had no strength in his arms or his legs.

He heard the shriek of the train whistle and the belch of steam as another locomotive pulled out of the station. He slumped beside a stack of dirty crates and boxes. The fingers of his right hand were twitching as he clutched at the musty air.

He was finding it hard to breathe. Now all he could think about was how thirsty he was, a glass of beer or wine, anything would do. His eyes fluttered shut, then open. Shut. He imagined himself swimming at Saissac, could almost feel the ice-cold mountain water on his arms and back, running over his lips, his face.

His legs began to shake, jerk, no longer his to control. Not swimming, choking. The skin of his bare feet patterning the dust, recording his final moments. As his eyes closed for the last time, César thought how he should have trusted his instincts.

Chapter 40

Marieta looked out of the kitchen window. Sandrine was still out there on the bench, wrapped in the blanket. She was glad the boy had kept his word and gone, but the sight pulled at her heart.

The sound of Sandrine rattling through the wardrobe in Monsieur Vidal's room had woken Marieta at six. From the house, she had watched Raoul leave, then gone into the garden in her nightclothes to try and coax Sandrine inside. She wouldn't come, but she had accepted the blanket and a cup of lime-flower tea laced with brandy.

Marieta felt a sudden stab of pain in her chest, taking her breath away. She clutched at the sink, the cold porcelain comforting beneath her fingers. Her heart felt as if it was struggling to keep its regular beat. She pressed the heel of her hand against her ribs, waiting for the spasm to pass. It always did. A few seconds more, and the ache faded to nothing.

Marieta lowered herself heavily down on a kitchen chair, sipping at a tisane of lime tea and saccharine. The letter should arrive in Rennes-les-Bains in a day or two. Monsieur Baillard collected all his letters from the *poste restante* there, as he had always done – there had never been a postal service to the remote village of Los Seres, even before the war – but even if it did arrive quickly, there was no telling when he might pick the letter up. It could be days, weeks even. She felt her anxious heart stumble and trip once more.

She wasn't sure why she was so fearful. Because of what Monsieur Baillard had told her long ago about the legend of Dame Carcas? Or because the matter brought back the memories of that dreadful Hallowe'en at La Domaine de la Cade when her beloved mistress Léonie had died? Of the screaming heard all through the valley and the little boy crying and holding tight to her skirts? Of all those who had died that night? Or because of how worried she was now about what would happen to the girls when she was gone? About Sandrine and the risks Marianne took?

'All these things . . .' she muttered.

Marieta took another sip of her tisane and felt the pressure in her chest ease a little. Monsieur Baillard would find a way to be in touch with her if he thought what she had to say was important. Her expression softened. Whatever the circumstances, the thought of seeing him again lifted her spirits. Like her, his roots were in the ancient stories and landscape of the Languedoc, not these headlong, modern times.

She had first met Audric Baillard in the 1890s, when he had been a regular visitor to the Domaine de la Cade, the old estate outside Rennes-les-Bains where she'd been in service. In those days, Marieta had been a curious girl, unwilling to let things lie. She had asked her friends about him, most of whom were, like her, servants at the good houses. Agnès, parlour maid for old Abbé Boudet, one of Monsieur Baillard's constant friends, said her master was too discreet to let anything slip. A cousin of Marieta's was friends with the girls who did for the *ritou*, the priest, of neighbouring Rennes-le-Château. But even she couldn't find anything out about Monsieur Baillard.

Marieta's late husband Pascal was of the opinion he had been a soldier, even though Monsieur Baillard never talked about his time in the army or where he had served. He was a famous scholar, a respected author, a gentleman. As well as Occitan and French, he spoke Hebrew, Arabic, Spanish,

Greek. He could read Latin and decipher hieroglyphs, Aramaic and Coptic texts.

Marieta took off her hairnet, twisting her long grey hair into a bun at the nape of her neck. Then, taking grips from her dressing-gown pocket, she pinned it in its usual style. She knew she should go upstairs to dress, before anyone came down and found her sitting in the kitchen in her nightclothes, but her legs were tired and she was so short of breath.

'Today is Wednesday,' she muttered. The post was unreliable now. The earliest he might receive the letter would be Friday. Probably it would take longer, if it arrived at all.

Marieta's thoughts again drifted to the past. After the fire in 1897 that had seen the Domaine de la Cade razed to the ground, she and Pascal had gone to work for Monsieur Baillard in Los Seres. She learnt then for certain that he had never married or had children of his own, though he had stood as guardian on more than one occasion. The letters he received from abroad were testament to that.

Marieta knew there had been someone he'd loved many years ago. It had come to nothing – she fancied the girl might have been married to somebody else – but even now, it pained her to remember how often Monsieur Baillard sat looking out over the Pyrenees, as night turned to day, as if he was still waiting for her to come back to him.

The old housekeeper settled her shoulders, trying to shake herself free of the ache in her neck and arm. To get rid of the knot of worry in the pit of her stomach.

'Perhaps Friday,' she muttered again. '*Benlèu divendres.*'

Chapter 41

In the small rented apartment in the rue Georges Clemenceau, Liesl Blum glanced at the clock for the third time. She didn't understand why Max hadn't come home last night when they had arranged to have supper together. Nor this morning either. This was how it had started in Paris. Men disappearing in the night or being arrested at dawn. Her father, their friends and neighbours. But not in Carcassonne.

Liesl had fallen asleep on the settee waiting, but when she'd woken and checked Max's room, his bed hadn't been slept in. She was trying to carry on as usual, though the dread was hard in her chest. She drank a glass of water and ate some bread, though she had no appetite, returning every few minutes to look out of the window. Willing herself to see her brother's long, lean figure striding along the pavement.

Still Max did not come.

Liesl made herself sit down at the table in the living room, which was already covered with paste and scissors and paper. Her camera too, though it was hard to have film developed now. There was no ink, no good-quality photographic paper.

Since they had arrived in Carcassonne, Liesl had kept a scrapbook, everything that had happened since she and Max had left Paris two years ago when the Nazis marched in. It was foolish, in a way, but their father had always impressed upon them the importance of recording everything, writing things down. That whatever new laws were brought in, each new iniquity, they should continue to behave as they saw fit in the privacy of their own home. Liesl tried to live by his example. This scrapbook was her own small act of defiance.

She turned the pages, looking at the black and white photographs. Her eyes stopped on a portrait of her parents, her father's arm proprietorial around her mother's waist. Both elegant, both serious, staring straight into the camera. They had heard nothing from him – about him – for over a year. Liesl had been a little scared of him. Neither of their parents had paid much attention to her or to Max, farming them out to the care of neighbours while they campaigned and electioneered and organised rallies.

But Liesl felt she was carrying on her father's tradition. He used words, she used images. He had been a prominent anti-Nazi campaigner, working tirelessly to expose what was happening to Jews in the countries annexed by Germany. Individual arrests at first, then the *rafles*, everybody rounded up at the same time and confined in ghettos. Now the same was happening in France. Little by little by little, the poison was spreading.

She turned the page, running her hand over the rough blotting paper, this section a record of the mass arrests of Jewish families, of the thousands of Jewish men sent to camps. She stuck another cutting in, this one taken from *La Dépêche*. An old but poignant image. Students in Paris had taken to wearing 'butterflies', anti-German stickers, and carrying their books against their chests, obscuring the yellow stars that Jews in the *zone occupée* were forced to wear.

Liesl glanced at the clock again, the trepidation building in her chest with every minute that passed without Max.

'Jew!'

She jumped in alarm as a stone hit the wall next to the sitting-room window with a loud thud.

'*Putain*, we know you're in there.'

Liesl turned. The boys hadn't come last night – perhaps because there'd been too many police on the streets – but she hadn't expected them this morning.

'We know you're in there, *juive*.'

Ugly voices shouting up at the window from the street. Another stone ricocheted off the woodwork. Liesl tried not to take any notice. They might be out there for up to half an hour, depending on who came along the street and was brave enough to make them stop.

'Let us in, Jew. You know you want to.'

Raucous laughter. Liesl tried to stop her ears, tried to concentrate on what she was doing. They'd get bored. They usually did. What had changed? It was a normal day, why was nobody doing anything to stop them? Then another stone and the sound of the window shattering. Liesl leapt up as a shard of glass struck her on the cheek. Felt the trickle of first blood.

She ran to the door to the apartment to check it was locked and bolted. As she did so, she heard the street door downstairs bang back against the wall, and a cheer. For a moment she froze. How had they got in? Had someone let them in?

The sound of boots on the stairs propelled her into action. Liesl rushed to the table, her terrified hands trying to clear away her precious scrapbook. The smash of a fist on the inner door to the apartment made her jump, the papers slipping through her fingers. She realised she was holding her breath, as if that would keep her presence a secret.

'We know you're in there, *garce*.' The same vile voice, now just the other side of the front door.

Another thud, a fist against wood. Then a boot. The entire door shook, the reverberations skimming along the wall.

Liesl swallowed a cry. She couldn't believe they would break in, attack her in broad daylight. She didn't see how such a thing could be happening. Then, the crack of wood as one of the panels in the door split. A roar of triumph went up from the boys outside. How many were there? Three? Four? More? Hateful voices getting louder, more frenzied.

'We're going to teach you a lesson, Jew girl.'

The boots harder against the door, the lock wouldn't hold. They were almost inside.

Un, deux, trois, loup, the words of the children's playground rhyme went round and round in Liesl's head. 'Coming to get you, ready or not.'

The sound of the front door splintering, the sound of blind hands reaching into the apartment, turning the lock. The rasp of the bolt, then a cheer as the door was flung open and the mob of boys stormed into the flat.

Chapter 42

'Wake up, darling.'

Sandrine heard Marianne's voice, then felt the weight of her sister's hand on her shoulder, shaking her awake.

'What time is it?' she said, sitting up. Her neck was stiff and the bruise from Monday was throbbing where she'd leant against it.

'Half past ten.'

For a moment, Sandrine felt all right. Normal. Then she remembered, and misery pressed down on her shoulders.

'He's gone,' she said.

'I know, Marieta told me.'

'I didn't want him to go.'

Marianne nodded. 'I know, but it's for the best. Come inside, have something to eat.'

'I'm not hungry.'

'There's a little bread left, and some butter.'

'I'm not hungry,' she repeated.

Marianne held out her hand to pull her up. 'Don't be silly.'

Sandrine followed her back into the kitchen. She felt cold and woolly from lack of sleep. She sat down heavily on a chair, watching as her sister poured them both a cup of ersatz coffee from the pot Marieta had left on the stove, then got out a plate and knife.

Marianne sat down on the opposite side of the table. Sandrine sipped at the coffee and started to wake up. She took a piece of bread, dipping it in her cup to soften the crust, surprised to find that she had an appetite after all.

'Have Lucie and Suzanne gone?' she asked.

'Suzanne, yes, about half an hour ago. Lucie felt rather unwell, so I've put her in Papa's room to sleep it off.' She paused. 'Since the bed hadn't been slept in ...'

Sandrine flushed. 'We stayed up talking all night. In the garden. That's all.'

Marianne stared at her. 'Glad to hear it.'

'I gave him one of Papa's jackets and a hat. I hope that was all right.'

'Of course. No sense wasting things.'

Sandrine ate a little more. 'Just as he was going, Raoul told me I should talk to you.' She watched Marianne's reaction. 'I said we were always talking, but I think he meant something in particular.'

On the other side of the table, her sister became very still.

'What else did he say?' Marianne asked. Her voice was measured, but the atmosphere was suddenly taut.

'Just that.'

Marianne still didn't move.

'What did he mean?' Sandrine asked.

Marianne hesitated a moment more, then got to her feet, went to the door and closed it. She turned round with her arms crossed. Sandrine's heart started to hammer against her ribs. Her sister looked so determined, so resolute. And the door between the kitchen and the hall was never shut.

'What?' she said quickly, nervous now.

'Listen carefully. Don't interrupt. You have to promise that you will never breathe a word of what I'm about to tell you to anyone. No one, not a soul.'

Sandrine felt her stomach lurch. 'I promise.'

Marianne sat down again and placed both hands flat on the table, as if trying to anchor herself.

'Raoul guessed. Almost straight away, I could see he knew.'

'Knew what ...?' Sandrine began to say, then she stopped. She felt a strange calm come over her. She knew what Marianne was going to say. All those nights her sister was late back from work and with mud on her shoes, disappearing for an hour here or there without explanation. The 'friends' who arrived after dark and went before it was light.

'You've been helping them too,' she said.

Marianne's eyes flicked up. 'You knew? But you never said anything.'

Sandrine shook her head. 'No, not until now.' She paused. 'Just you?'

'Suzanne too.'

'Not Lucie?'

A smile flickered across Marianne's lips. 'She only cares about Max, nothing else matters. She hopes if she closes her eyes to what's happening, it will go away.'

'Max doesn't know?'

'Nobody else knows,' Marianne replied.

'Not even Marieta?'

Marianne hesitated. 'I'm sure she does, but she acts as if she doesn't. She clears things away, things that get forgotten.'

'I found a man's razor in the bathroom once. It wasn't Papa's.'

Marianne smiled. 'Marieta carries on in her usual way. Posts letters for me, drops things off if I ask her. I try not to call upon her too much.' She shrugged. 'And I go along with her pretending she doesn't know. It's safer that way.'

Sandrine's head was spinning as she tried to take everything in. A snapshot of so many tiny incidents, none of them big enough to have drawn her attention at the time, but now combining to make a clearer picture.

'Why didn't you tell me?' she asked quietly. 'Didn't you trust me?'

Marianne sighed. 'I wanted to, but I didn't want to put you at risk, and besides …'

'… you were worried I'd let something out.' Sandrine finished the sentence for her.

Marianne nodded. 'Yes,' she said, holding her gaze. 'I'm sorry. Can you understand?'

Strangely, Sandrine realised she did. A few days ago, she would have lost her temper or sulked or argued. Not now. After a night of talking with Raoul, listening to what he had done, how he had been forced to live, she thought she did understand.

'I feel such an idiot. Not noticing.'

'I did my best to make sure you didn't notice anything. That you could carry on as usual.'

Sandrine thought for a moment. 'Why are you telling me now?' she asked. 'Simply because of Raoul?'

Marianne shook her head. 'I'd decided to tell you anyway,' she said. 'I was just waiting for the right moment. The way you marched into the police station – although I was cross with you about that too – the way you coped with what happened at the river. Then at the cathedral yesterday …' She shrugged. 'You held your nerve, you didn't make a fuss. You were a help and it made me realise that …'

'… I'd grown up.'

Marianne smiled. 'I wouldn't have put it quite like that, but I suppose so, yes.'

Despite her exhaustion and all the complicated emotions battling inside her head, Sandrine felt a shot of pride.

'Thank you,' she said quietly.

She sat in silence for a moment, letting her sister's words take root in her mind. Looking back on everything that had happened, trying to make it fit. Finally putting two and two together.

'The people you work with,' she said after a while, 'do you know who they are?'

'No, we never meet. No one knows anyone except their immediate contact. It's safest. That way, if we were caught, we couldn't give much away.'

Sandrine felt sick as the reality of the risks Marianne and Suzanne had been taking started to sink in.

'That's what made Raoul suspicious,' her sister continued. 'He mentioned César Sanchez and Suzanne reacted. He noticed. Sanchez is a good friend of hers too – that's where she's gone now, to see if she can find out what's happened to him.'

Sandrine thought for a moment. 'How long have you been … helping?'

'I can't even remember quite how it started. Right at the beginning, the autumn of 1939 and the following spring, there were lots of German émigrés and Jewish dissidents, a few members of the Dutch Resistance, all trying to get out of France this way. We had plenty of space here.' She shrugged. 'Suzanne asked me if I could help from time to time, and it seemed such a small thing to do, to give someone a bed for the night. After we surrendered and the North was occupied, things changed. I volunteered for the Croix-Rouge, helped in that way instead.' She paused. 'But things have been getting worse. In January this year, the last few of my Jewish pupils simply disappeared from class. One day they were there, the next they'd gone and no one could – would – tell me what had happened to them. I was appalled and said as much to Suzanne, who admitted she was running a few errands for the Resistance – that's how they put it – so I decided to do the same.'

'When you say errands, what do you mean?'

'Delivering papers, mostly. False documents, *sauf-conduits*, identity cards, ration books, coupons. Dropping off leaflets to collection points – *boîtes aux lettres* – for someone else to pick up and distribute, all sorts.'

'In Carcassonne?'

Marianne smiled. 'Yes, darling. There are several places in the Bastide, in the Cité too.'

'Why don't people stay here any more?'

'As I said, fewer people come through Carcassonne. But mostly since Madame Fournier moved in next door to keep house for her brother. She's always snooping, reports everything to him.'

'He's a vile man,' Sandrine said, remembering how he had spoken to her and Suzanne.

'Worse, he's dangerous. He's an informer.'

'Oh.'

Marianne let her shoulders drop, clearly relieved that the secret was out in the open. Sandrine had a hundred questions racing around her head, but her sister had stood up.

'You have to forget I ever told you any of this. I mean it. Say nothing, don't think about it. Don't bring it up, even with Suzanne.'

'I won't.'

Marianne opened the door to the corridor. 'I'm going to check on Lucie, she was awfully sick in the night. Then I am due to go to the station. To meet other Red Cross volunteers.' She paused. 'You can come with me if you want.'

Sandrine looked up. 'You mean it?'

'If you do precisely what I tell you, then yes. Why not? But we have to go in ten minutes. I won't wait if you're not ready.'

'Marianne …'

Her sister turned again. 'What is it?'

'I just want to say … I'm proud of you,' she said in a rush, feeling ridiculous to be saying such things to her older sister. 'Proud of you for being so brave, for standing up for—'

Marianne shook her head. 'No,' she said quietly. 'I'm not brave. I hate it, I hate it all. But there's no choice.'

Chapter 43

'Where the hell have you been?' demanded Authié.

Laval stood with his hands in front of him. 'Interviewing Blum.'

'All night?'

'And then Sanchez, sir, as per your orders.'

Authié raised his head, noting Laval was back in civilian clothes. He waved his hand impatiently for him to continue.

'Well, does Blum know where Pelletier is?'

'I believe not, sir.'

Authié drummed his fingers on the desk. 'Did he admit he was at the river?'

'Eventually, yes, he did. He says he doesn't know the girl's name, though he admits he saw her. That could be true, but I think we'll learn more from the Ménard girl in any case. Blum was more concerned about protecting her than anything else.'

'What have you done with him?'

'On the list to be deported today.'

'Le Vernet?'

'In the first instance, yes.'

Authié nodded again. 'What else?'

'After the wireless bulletins, the switchboard took a dozen calls from people claiming to have seen Pelletier – in Narbonne, in Toulouse, in Perpignan – but nothing credible. We had a permanent watch at the station and patrols checking bars, restaurants, churches and the cinema, anywhere he might have been hiding. There was a lot of trouble last night – looting, broken windows – so there were plenty of police on the streets, but no one matching

Pelletier's description. However, now the posters are ready to be put up, it will be harder for him to evade notice.'

'If he's still in Carcassonne,' Authié interrupted, 'which I doubt. What about Sanchez?'

Laval flushed at Authié's peremptory tone, but he kept his irritation hidden.

'Sanchez was released at midnight. He went to Pelletier's apartment on the Quai Riquet, was there for no more than a couple of minutes, then went to Déjean's apartment, where he spent the night. At approximately five o'clock this morning, he made his way to the sidings on the far side of the railway station. I approached him. He said he didn't know where Pelletier was and claimed to know nothing about what – if anything – he might have found at Déjean's apartment.'

'Nothing about the key?'

'No, sir.'

'So that's it, Laval? In twelve hours you've learnt precisely nothing.'

Laval didn't answer. Authié pulled out a cigarette and tapped it on the packet, then lit it. 'Where's Sanchez now?'

'No loose ends, you said.'

Authié stared at him. 'What are you saying, Laval? Are you telling me he's dead?'

'Yes, sir.'

He dropped the matches back on the desk. 'You killed him?'

'To prevent him talking.'

'Why the hell didn't you say so sooner?'

'I was answering your questions. You asked me about Blum.'

'Sanchez's death can't be traced back here?'

'It will be written up as a knife fight, communists brawling among themselves. There're a lot of Spanish workers in the quartier de la Gare.'

Authié smoked half the cigarette in silence, then flicked the remainder out of the window. He watched it drop to the pavement below, then turned back to face the room.

'For your sake, Laval, you'd better be right.'

Authié went back to his desk and opened the top drawer.

'Is my transport into the *zone occupée* arranged?'

'The car will be here at midday, sir.'

'Good.'

'How long will you be gone?'

Authié shot him a sharp look. 'What business is it of yours, Laval?'

'I only wanted to be sure of my orders in your absence.'

'You know what I want you to do. I want to know what Pelletier found in Déjean's apartment.'

For an instant Authié saw the dislike in Laval's eyes, but then the shutters came down again.

'Yes, sir,' he said in a dead voice. 'Do you want me to keep a watch on Bauer and operations in Tarascon as well?'

Authié hesitated. He did want to know what Bauer was doing, but over the past few days Laval had made mistakes. This situation required subtlety.

'No,' he said. 'Concentrate on finding Pelletier.'

Chapter 44

Roullens

Once the patrol had passed, Raoul climbed out of the deep ditch where he'd concealed himself. Every siren, every green flash of a *panier à salade*, set his pulse racing. By this time, he had no doubt, posters with his face slapped on them would be plastered all over Carcassonne, denouncing him as a murderer, a fugitive. His situation was desperate. If the police caught him, he knew they'd shoot on sight. He glanced along the route de Limoux in both directions. Only when he was sure the road was empty, did he emerge and carry on walking. The hope he'd felt when he was with Sandrine had gone. Now, he felt hunted.

Raoul had taken an indirect route west out of Carcassonne, doubling back on himself so if anyone did report seeing him, it would be hard for Laval to pinpoint precisely where he was heading. His destination was the village of Roullens, some seven kilometres to the south-west of the town. One of Bruno's former comrades in the International Brigade, Ramón, had family there and Raoul was hoping they'd let him stay for a night or two. He was gambling that Laval – and Coursan – would expect him to try to get as far as possible, as quickly as possible. By staying closer to Carcassonne, Raoul hoped to buy himself a little time while he worked out what the hell he was going to do in the long run. He had no idea if the plan would work, but he couldn't think of a better one.

The pretty country road to Roullens was deserted, but birdsong filled the air and the sun was warm on his face.

Raoul passed the beautiful and imposing Château de Baudrigues, its tranquil green parkland and elegant white façade glimpsed through the trees a welcome sight after the tense grey streets of Carcassonne. For a moment, he was tempted to go into the domaine. Sleep for an hour or two in the deep shade of the woods. But he had a memory Baudrigues had been requisitioned at the beginning of the war, and he didn't know if it was still in use or had been handed back to the owners. There was no sense taking the risk.

Raoul kept walking. He wondered if Sandrine was thinking of him as he was thinking of her. He remembered her tumbling black hair, the feel of it between his fingers, and her bright, sharp eyes. He wondered if she had spoken to her sister, and if she had, what had been said. He hated that every step was taking him one step further away from the rue du Palais. Most of all, he hated the fact that with a murder charge hanging over him, he would never be able to go back.

Behind him on the road, he heard an engine. His thoughts scattered and he immediately stepped out of sight, watching as the vehicle came into view. When it was closer, he could see it was a blue Simca truck. Local, not military, he thought. A safe bet. Hoping he was right, Raoul stepped back out on to the road and raised his arm.

Chapter 45

Carcassonne

Leo Authié faced the west door of the cathédrale Saint-Michel and ran his hand over the battered stonework. He was pleased to see the damage wasn't too extensive. At least Laval had carried out those orders effectively.

He went inside. Although there was evidence of the explosion, in the layer of white dust that covered the hymnals and votive candles for sale on the table, the calm and tranquillity of the cathedral was unaffected.

Authié dipped his finger into the *bénitier* of holy water and made the sign of the cross on his forehead. For a moment, he allowed the burden of his responsibilities to lift. Here, he felt certain of his mission. Here, everything was unequivocal. Absolute.

'The cathedral's closed.'

Authié looked in the direction of the voice and saw a charwoman mopping the flagstone tiles. He ignored her and walked up the nave, pausing only to make obeisance, then strode to the confessional.

'Hey, didn't you hear what I said?' she called after him.

Authié walked round to the far side, pulled back the curtain and peered inside. It was empty.

'Where's the priest?' he said, his voice echoing in the cavernous stone spaces.

'I told you, the cathedral's closed. Come back on Sunday.'

Authié walked back towards her, sharp heels, sharp eyes. She held her ground.

'Get out,' he said.

The woman's eyes narrowed. 'Who are you to talk to me like that?' she said. 'See the mess they've made? I've got to get things straight.'

Authié put his hand to his breast pocket and produced his identification.

'Do as you're told.'

The char peered at the card, and Authié saw her knuckles tighten on the handle of the mop. Without another word she picked up her pail and walked back towards the small room behind the choir.

Authié stepped into the pew third from the front on the left-hand side. As he waited, he let his gaze move over each of the high side chapels in turn. He looked at the soaring stained-glass windows dedicated to St Bernard and St Benedict and at the unlit thick tallow candles on the high altar. All of it spoke of the magnificence of grace, the power of God.

The bells in the tower struck the half-hour. He glanced behind him, but the west door remained firmly closed. The car to take him north was ordered for midday.

His thoughts returned to Erik Bauer. Authié knew Bauer had no interest in the Codex other than to placate his masters in Berlin. The ambitions of the Reich were writ large in its headlong acquisition of everything and anything.

Authié considered the Nazi attempts to extirpate God from civil life both childish and pointless. He believed in a theocracy. His mission was to re-establish God at the heart of daily life. The absolute rule of religious law and obedience to the Church. His God was the God of the Old Testament, a God of judgement and wrath and punishment for those who transgressed the laws. Not a God of light or tolerance or one who postulated the equality of all men.

He believed the time was at hand for Europe to return to Christian rule. A new crusade against the Jews and the Moslems, any who refused to accept the one true faith. Those who had turned their faces away, as well as those who supported them. Authié had ensured that clerics of his rigorous persuasion were appointed to the key positions in the diocese, although he'd not yet been able to get rid of Abbé Gau. He'd made it impossible for Jewish businesses to continue to thrive, made sure that the schools of Moslem learning were shut down. He had done everything he could to turn the local population against anyone not prepared to return to the waiting arms of the Church.

To start with, his strategy had worked. The majority of Carcassonnais were inclined to put their trust in Pétain. They disliked Hitler and his Nazi party, but they wanted their sons, their husbands, their brothers returned from German POW camps and so were prepared to see Vichy work with Berlin to achieve that.

But signs were that ordinary citizens were becoming impatient. As the stringencies of rationing had begun to bite and fewer POWs than promised had been repatriated to France, views were changing. The endless queues and checkpoints, the lack of freedom to travel over the line or communicate with relatives in the north: citizens were starting to criticise and question whether the '*voie de collaboration*' was working to their advantage. The churches were still empty and time was running out. Authié knew the status quo would not hold for very much longer.

He needed to find the Codex. It was a heresy, a proscribed text. If the authority ascribed to those verses was to be believed, the man who possessed it could be a modern-day Joshua, before the walls of Jericho, powerful and invincible. But Authié would not make use of it. His faith was strong enough to resist such temptation.

He would, of course, destroy it, in accordance with the church's wishes.

At last, Authié heard the creak of the door and the scrape of the wood on the stone steps. He did not turn and he did not react, but waited and listened as the footsteps came closer, closer until they stopped. The man stepped into the far end of the pew and knelt down.

'I came as soon as I got your message,' he said.

Authié pushed the hymn book along the wooden rail. The sepia border of a hundred-franc note just visible between the pages.

'Fournier, I have a job for you.'

Chapter 46

Sandrine walked across the Pont Marengo towards the mainline station. The streets were oddly quiet for a weekday morning, as if Carcassonne itself was waiting to see what the day might hold. She was pleased Marianne had let her come, but her past ignorance of the true state of affairs had made her confident and bold. Now, she was scared. She expected at every moment to be stopped and challenged.

'Where do we go?' she asked.

'Just do what I do,' Marianne replied.

There were hardly any passengers, but there were scores of police checking the papers of anybody trying to go in or come out of the railway station. Sandrine hoped Raoul was already many kilometres clear of Carcassonne.

The officers checked their *cartes d'identité* in silence, then waved them through to Marianne's Croix-Rouge colleagues who were already on the platform. As well as food and drink, they had blankets, various bits and pieces of clothing, a few pairs of men's shoes and, oddly, a pile of spectacles.

'This is my sister, Sandrine,' Marianne said.

Everyone was friendly, though quiet. Sandrine said her hellos. A woman in a broad-brimmed straw hat smiled back, another nodded and handed Sandrine a pail of water and three tin cups. Marianne picked up a *panier* that contained medical supplies: bandages and iodine swabs and sticking plasters.

'How many are we expecting?' Marianne asked.

'Originally we were told twenty prisoners would be deported to camps in the Ariège today,' said a tall, dignified woman in uniform. 'But after yesterday's arrests, I'm expecting more.'

On the way from the rue du Palais, Marianne had explained that the Red Cross was allowed to see the prisoners on humanitarian grounds only. They were not allowed to intervene or talk to them about the charges against them, discuss politics or anything else, otherwise they would be forbidden access in the future. All they could do was to try to make the men's journey less uncomfortable. Still surprised that Marianne had let her come in the first place, Sandrine hadn't wanted to admit she was nervous about what she might see.

'How long before the prisoners get here?' she asked.

Marianne shrugged. 'It could be soon, might not be until the end of the afternoon. They always get us here much earlier than necessary.'

'What's the point in that?'

Marianne gave a tired smile. 'To make it as difficult as possible. The authorities have to allow the Croix-Rouge to monitor the situation, but they'd prefer it if we didn't. Keeping us waiting for hours, it's just one way to put people off. Lots of the women have children, can't get away for so long.'

Sandrine noticed how deep the worry lines around her sister's eyes were and again felt stupid at how she'd managed to miss the signs of the burden Marianne had been under. Not only the work itself, but also the strain of keeping up appearances. Ensuring that life seemed to be carrying on as usual. Sandrine wondered if she'd have the courage to do the same. To risk her life for the sake of people she didn't even know.

'Where are they being sent?' she said, talking to keep her nerves under control.

'To internment camps in Ariège and Roussillon,' Marianne replied.

'And then? Do they stay there?'

'It depends on the charges against them,' she said. 'Those classified as undesirables or enemy aliens will be sent over the line to camps in the north.' She hesitated. 'Perhaps even into Germany, I'm not sure. There are lots of stories we've not been able to verify yet.'

The sound of the guard shouting disrupted their conversation. The sisters looked round to see the train driver leaning out of the cab of the engine.

'Looks like they're coming,' Marianne said. 'They walk the prisoners from the gaol on the route de Narbonne.' She lowered her voice. 'Some of them will try to give you letters, trinkets to pass on. We're not supposed to take them, but if the guards don't see, it's all right. It's a great comfort to them, but we only get a few minutes to hand over clothes or shoes to those who need them and to check they are fit to travel before they're put on the train, so don't get caught up with one person for too long.'

'And if someone's not fit to travel?' Sandrine asked. 'What do we do then?'

Marianne didn't answer.

There was a belch of smoke. A heavy hiss and a grinding of brakes and iron on the tracks, as more third-class carriages were shunted towards the engine. The guard jumped down, then began to lift the heavy chains to connect the new rolling stock to the rest of the train. All the windows in the third-class carriages had been painted over, making it impossible to see in.

Then, at the outer edges of the station compound, above the Quai Riquet, Sandrine heard shouting and the sound of feet. Moments later a unit of armed *gardes mobiles* came into view, herding a line of prisoners through a side gate and across the rails towards the transit carriages at the back of the train.

The guards were shouting, even though there was no

trouble, pushing the prisoners with their sticks, the butts of their machine guns. Sandrine felt her fingers clench around the thin handle of the bucket. Some of the other ladies walked to the far end of the station to help those at the back. Sandrine and Marianne moved to the head of the line.

'Remember,' Marianne said, 'our job is to be kind. To patch them up. Do the best we can, as quickly as we can, then move on.'

'But there are so many of them,' Sandrine said, looking up and down the long platform, aghast at the sight.

'Just do what you can.'

As they came closer, Sandrine saw the men were handcuffed, though not chained together. They looked disreputable, dirty, in filthy clothes, their faces grey. Marianne had warned her that they were held in unhygienic and unsanitary conditions, but Sandrine was shocked to acknowledge her first reaction was disgust rather than pity.

Then she recognised the older brother of one of the boys in her class at school. A quiet, gentle boy, not one to cause trouble. Straight away the mass of prisoners became individuals and she rushed to help. He had a cut on his head, the blood brown on his temple, and his knuckles were bruised and swollen.

'My God, Xavier,' she said. 'What happened?'

He tried to smile, revealing a couple of broken teeth.

'They came for a friend of mine. Said his papers weren't in order. The police didn't take kindly to me trying to intervene.'

'That was brave,' she said, dipping a metal cup in the pail and giving him a sip of water. She waved to attract her sister's attention. 'What happened to your friend? Where's he now?'

Xavier shrugged, then winced. 'I haven't seen him since we were arrested. Could you try to find out?'

'What's his name?'

'Marc Filaquier.'

'I'll try,' she promised, then waved again. 'Marianne, over here.'

Marianne quickly appeared, took a look at Xavier's injuries and started to patch him up.

'Go,' she said to Sandrine. 'There are plenty of others who need help.'

Sandrine threw herself into the thick of things. Rushing up and down the line, giving everybody water, handing out dry biscuits, calling for medical assistance, accepting letters and rings when the guards weren't looking.

'I was going to propose,' one boy was saying. 'But we quarrelled, and now . . .' Tears began to run down his dirty cheeks. 'Never got the chance to make it up.'

'Write a note and I'll take it to her,' she said. She pulled a piece of paper and a pencil from her pocket, then noticed he was cradling his right hand in his left. She licked the end of the pencil. 'On second thoughts, tell me what to say.'

He tried to smile. 'She's called Maude Lagarde, rue Courtejaire. Red door, just past Artozouls.'

'All right.'

'Tell her I love her – I'm Pierre-Jacques – and I'll write. They allow letters, don't they?' he said, his voice rising. 'They do allow letters.'

A police officer appeared, poked him in the ribs with his stick.

'Enough. Get on the train.'

Sandrine couldn't stop herself. 'He needs medical attention.'

'Are you trying to tell me what to do?'

'No, of course not,' Sandrine said quickly, stepping back. 'But his wrist is broken. He should be in hospital.'

The guard moved closer. 'Unless you want to find

yourself going with him, mademoiselle, I suggest you get out of the way and let me do my job.'

Sandrine could do nothing but step back as Pierre-Jacques was forced on to the train with the others. She tried to catch the boy's eye, but his head was bowed and he didn't look back.

'You said they had to be fit to travel,' Sandrine said, when she found Marianne, 'but there's someone with a broken wrist. He should have been taken to hospital, but the guard just didn't care.'

She felt her sister's arm go around her waist. 'Come on,' Marianne said quietly. 'There's nothing more we can do.'

Sandrine turned away. The remaining prisoners were being loaded into the last carriage at the far end of the train. The woman with the broad-brimmed hat stepped forward and put a blanket around the shoulders of a tall, stooped man at the end of the line. He had his back to her, but Sandrine briefly glimpsed his aquiline features and black hair. She frowned. Was there something familiar about his profile? Then the woman moved and blocked her view.

Sandrine quickly started to walk down the long platform towards the group, trying to look past the Red Cross ladies standing between her and the man. Although he was covered by the blanket now, she could make out his cuffed hands were held out in front of him. Sandrine saw him slip. The woman tried to help. The warder pushed her roughly away.

Sandrine started to run, suddenly desperate to get to them before the doors were shut, but Marianne put out her hand and stopped her. She watched in despair as the warder raised his baton and struck the man across his shoulders, then shoved him on to the train.

'No!' she shouted, but the guard took no notice.

The woman raised her hand to warn Sandrine not to say anything more.

'That's the lot,' the warder said, slamming the door and walking back up the platform towards the front of the train.

The driver nodded and sat back in his cab. The guard banged the side of the engine, then blew his whistle and waved his flag. Slowly, the wheels began to move, metal grinding on metal, steam belching out into the clear blue sky.

The women were left standing on the platform, watching as the train disappeared around the bend in the track.

'Is it always like this?' Sandrine said to Marianne.

'It was particularly awful today. There were many more prisoners than we'd been told to expect and they were in a worse condition than usual.' She paused. 'Do you wish you hadn't come?'

Sandrine looked along the empty platform, then up towards the white stone crosses and tombs in the cimetière Saint-Vincent on the hill above the station. She thought of the risks Marianne and Suzanne took every day, of how Raoul kept fighting against the injustice they saw all around them. Then she thought of Xavier and Pierre-Jacques. She'd hardly done much, but it was better than doing nothing.

'No,' she said. 'Quite the opposite.'

Chapter 47

Sandrine and Marianne walked over the boulevard Omer Sarraut. Ahead of them, to their right, was the Café Continental, traditionally a leftist meeting place. On the opposite side of the road, the Café Edouard where the LVF and the Jeunes Doriotistes met. Sandrine realised she was already starting to divide the Bastide into them and us.

'What is it?' Marianne asked.

'Nothing,' she said quickly. 'I'm fine.'

Sandrine looked down at the sad collection of objects, letters, notes in her hand.

'I promised I'd deliver these,' she said.

'That was nice of you.'

'You said it was all right,' she said quickly, 'if the guards didn't see.'

Marianne put her hand on Sandrine's arm. 'I mean it, it was a good thing to do. It makes all the difference to the prisoners.'

'Good,' she said. 'I'll meet you at home later.'

'It's all right, I'll walk with you,' Marianne said. 'Before we left, I promised Lucie I'd drop a note from her to Max, but there wasn't time. She promised to have supper with him, but she is still feeling awful.'

They walked down into rue Georges Clemenceau, towards the building where Max and Liesl were living. When they were level with Artozouls, Sandrine stopped.

'I've got something to drop off here. Won't be a moment.'

'All right?' asked Marianne, when she got back.

'No one was there,' she said. 'I pushed the note under the door. I hope she gets it all right.'

As they carried on, Sandrine realised she was looking into everyone's faces – wondering what they were thinking, what sort of person they might be. There were plenty of people about in the heart of the Bastide, though she thought everyone looked nervous, scuttling to and fro, heads down, trying not to attract attention.

They arrived at Max and Liesl's building to find the door on to the street was standing open.

'That's peculiar,' Marianne said. 'They've had a bit of trouble recently, so Lucie said they kept it locked.'

'Even during the day?'

'I thought that's what she told me, but I might be wrong.'

Sandrine went inside first, stepping into the dark hall. She had a bad feeling, the sense that something wasn't right. And there was a peculiar smell, like blocked drains. She took the stairs two by two, dread building in her chest, until she reached Max and Liesl's apartment.

'Marianne,' she called, 'quickly.'

The front door was kicked in, hanging off at the hinges, and bore the imprint of boots. There were splinters of wood everywhere and splashes of blood on the jamb.

Sandrine rushed into the living room, then stopped dead. She put her hand over her nose and mouth. The walls were covered with graffiti – the words JUIVE, JUDEN, JUIF daubed in black paint, crude swastikas and Nazi slogans, crossed-out Stars of David. Worse, the stench of excrement and the ammoniac smell of urine.

In the centre of the room was a heap of clothes mixed with smashed glass from the windows, the stuffing from the cushions on the sofa, which had been ripped open. On the floor, a black and white photograph of Max's father and mother with a swastika scrawled across it. Sandrine bent down and picked it up, then turned round as Marianne came into the room behind her.

'Oh God,' she said.

Suddenly they heard a noise. Sandrine froze, threw a glance at Marianne, who pointed to the rear of the apartment. Sandrine nodded, then slowly went towards the sound.

She looked into the first bedroom. The window was open and the room had been turned over, but it was empty.

'There's no one here,' she said.

She heard the same sound, a shuffling and the creaking of a floorboard.

'It's coming from here,' she said, going quickly into a smaller second room.

'It doesn't look as if they came in here at all,' said Marianne.

'Listen,' said Sandrine. 'Over there. Behind the bedside table.'

The sisters pulled the piece of furniture forward, surprised as it rolled away from the wall.

'There's some kind of storage cupboard or something,' Sandrine said, crouching down.

'Is there a handle?'

'Can't see one,' said Sandrine, rapping her knuckles on the white and pink paper, 'but it sounds hollow.'

Then, more clearly this time, the same shuffling, and the sound of a bolt being shot open. Slowly the hatch door opened and Liesl crawled out.

'Oh my God,' Marianne said, immediately putting her arms around the girl. 'What happened?'

Liesl emerged, blinking, into the light, then slowly stood up. Her pale face was white, strained, and her eyes were blank. She was clutching a photograph album.

'Liesl,' Marianne said, 'look at me. What happened to you?'

For a moment, it seemed the girl hadn't heard. Then, slowly, she raised her head.

'I hid,' she said in a stunned voice. 'Max told me if anyone came I should hide. So I hid.'

'Who came?' Sandrine said. 'Who did this?'

Liesl carried on as if she hadn't heard. 'There's a compartment, you see. It was part of a corridor, but when the house was divided up, there was an awkward space left between the two apartments. Max built it. Said to hide if the police came. I bolted the door from the inside like he told me.' She looked at Sandrine, as if noticing her for the first time. 'Where's Max? Why wasn't he here? Where is he?'

Sandrine looked down at the photograph she was still holding, then turned cold. Now she realised with a sinking feeling why the man on the station platform had been familiar. The same aquiline profile, the same dark hair as his father. She had only met Max twice before and without his heavy spectacles obscuring his face, she hadn't properly recognised him.

'He was one of the prisoners,' she whispered to Marianne, so that Liesl couldn't hear. 'I couldn't work out if I knew him or not.'

'What, are you certain?' Marianne said quickly.

'Not at the time. He was at the far end of the platform, half covered by a blanket, and there was someone in the way.' She looked at the black and white image. 'But, now I'm sure. Look.' She frowned. 'I should have said something. Told him I'd get a message to Liesl and Lucie, at the very least.'

'Don't blame yourself,' Marianne whispered. 'It might not even have been him anyway. For now, let's get Liesl out of here.' She put her arm around the girl's shoulders and raised her voice. 'We'll try to find out what's happened to Max. But for now we're going to take you home with us. You can't stay here.'

Liesl stared blankly at her for a moment, but she

allowed Marianne to steer her out of the bedroom and into the living room. She stopped for a moment, staring at the defaced walls and the devastation, then carried on to the hall without saying a word.

Sandrine crouched down and picked up one of Liesl's cardigans, then hung it on the back of a chair. 'I'll stay here and clean up.'

'All right,' Marianne said, dropping her voice again. 'But be quick. It's possible they'll come back.'

Chapter 48

TARASCON

The elderly couple stood in front of a table at the Café Bernadac in the Place de la Samaritaine in Tarascon.

'Please, Achille,' Pierre Déjean said again.

Achille Pujol looked at his beer, cloudy yellow, rough, popular in the Vicdessos valley, then put the glass down on the table. Beads of sweat gathered on his upper lip, caught in the grey hairs of his moustache. He looked every inch the retired police inspector he was. Solid, strong, steadfast and, at this precise moment, immensely worried.

'I don't do that sort of thing any more,' he said.

'Just listen to us,' Madame Déjean said quickly, 'that's all we're asking. If you still don't think you can help, then say no.'

Pujol looked into the defeated face of his friend, then drained his glass and stood up. 'We can't talk here.'

Between semi-retiring from the police force and the outbreak of war, Pujol had spent a few fruitless years as a private detective. There hadn't been much call for his services in Tarascon. Disputes tended to be sorted in the old ways and his only proper client had been the Péchiney-Sabart aluminium factory in the mouth of the valley a few miles away, keen to stop pilfering. After that, the director of the largest of the region's plaster producers had hired him to investigate losses from his Arignac factory. He'd also had a case of shoplifting from the épicerie Rousse here in the town. The work hadn't satisfied him and he'd resigned after five years to devote himself to his garden and his hunting.

The Déjeans followed him across the square and into a three-storey house at the end of the row. Pujol pushed open the front door and led the sombre party along a corridor, chill despite the heat of the afternoon. He let himself into a small, dark room on the ground floor with a latch key.

'I've been using this as an office,' he said, by way of apology. 'Take a seat.'

Pierre and Célestine Déjean perched themselves on the edges of their chairs, Célestine clutching her felt hat tight in her lap.

'We want you to look into it,' Pierre said, placing his broad pink hands on his knees. 'Investigate Antoine's disappearance.'

Pujol shook his head. 'You're saying he's disappeared, but you don't know that for certain. All you do know is Antoine didn't arrive when he said he would.'

'He never lets us down, not if he says he's coming.'

'Things are different now, Célestine,' Pujol said quietly. 'You know that.'

'He would have sent a message,' she said stubbornly.

Her husband cleared his throat and spat a thread of tobacco to the floor. Then he fixed Pujol with a look that carried the long story of their friendship – in the army at Verdun as young men, as neighbours in Tarascon in times of peace, their lives lived side by side in the valleys of the Ariège.

Pujol pulled his notepad towards him. 'When were you expecting him?'

'This weekend just gone. He works in Carcassonne. He's doing well.'

Pujol made a note. 'What's Antoine do for a living? Didn't he want to train as a teacher? History, was it?'

'Latin and Greek,' Célestine said, unable to keep the

pride from her voice, 'but of course there's no call for it these days.'

'It's a good job,' Pierre said firmly. 'He's a representative for Artozouls, fishing tackle, hunting equipment, that kind of thing.'

Pujol nodded. 'I've heard of it.'

'He told us he'd be coming this way for work, so he'd pay a visit. It was Célestine's birthday last Sunday.'

'He's a good boy,' she murmured. 'If he said he'd be here, he'd be here.'

Inwardly Pujol marvelled at her naïvety. Even with all the correct papers, travelling took time these days. The buses that ran on the foul-smelling gasoline often broke down, the railway timetable was unreliable. Then again, who was to say? There might be more to it.

'How long was Antoine intending to stay?' he asked.

'A few days,' Pierre replied. 'At least, he asked me to look out his old hiking equipment. You know, boots, ropes. I assumed he was hoping to get out into the mountains. Not a proper expedition, but you know how keen he is on climbing.'

'I do,' Pujol said darkly.

He remembered the numerous occasions in the past when he'd had to warn Antoine and his friends off trespassing in the caves of Lombrives and Ussat. Treasure-hunting. That German boy, Otto Rahn, with his peculiar ideas. Took over the inn for a while, Pujol seemed to remember. Good friends, they were, the German boy and Antoine.

'I know what you're thinking, Achille,' Pierre said, 'but that was years ago. He did well in the war. Done well for himself since.'

'I know,' said Pujol.

'We didn't worry when he failed to arrive,' Célestine said quietly. 'Not at first. I know you think we don't understand how things are, Achille, but we know well enough. But it's been three days and still no message.' Her hands were clawing the material of her skirt. 'If he couldn't come, he'd find a way to let us know.'

Pujol sighed. 'What exactly do you want me to do?'

'Speak to your contacts in the police,' Pierre said. 'In case there's been an accident. Any reports of . . . anything.'

Achille met his old friend's eye and realised there was something Déjean wanted to say about his son, but couldn't with his wife listening.

'Célestine,' he said lightly, 'there's a bottle of wine in the kitchen. Would you mind fetching it? I think we could all do with something.'

She was reluctant to leave, but she did what he asked. Pujol waited until she had gone out of the room before continuing.

'What's going on, Pierre?'

Monsieur Déjean glanced at the door, then dropped his voice.

'I know he was involved in something, Achille. I don't know what. Better not to ask questions. The thing is, a week ago, a man came looking for Antoine. Foreign. Célestine doesn't know.'

Pujol's attention sharpened. 'Go on.'

'German, though his French was excellent. Said he was a friend.'

'He didn't leave a name?'

'No.'

'Or say what he wanted?'

Déjean shook his head.

'What did he look like?'

'Northern skin, medium height, formal. And a ring, showy.'

Pujol's eyes narrowed. 'SS?'

'I don't know. Could be.' Pierre shrugged. 'A neighbour

was going to Carcassonne to visit her daughter, so I asked her to warn Antoine that someone had been sniffing around.'

'Did she manage to see him?'

Pierre nodded. 'And this is what is odd. When she told him a man had been looking for him, Antoine asked if it was an old man. If he was wearing a pale suit.'

Pujol's hand froze in mid-sentence. 'Why did he ask that?'

'She didn't say, only that when she said he wasn't, Antoine lost interest.'

'Was he worried?'

'Thoughtful more like, that's the word she used.'

'You'd told her to say the visitor was German?'

'Yes.'

Pujol scribbled a few more words on his pad. 'Anything else?'

'No.'

Now that Célestine wasn't in the room, Pierre made no attempt to hide his fear. In five minutes, he seemed to have aged fifty years. Pujol's heart went out to him.

'I'm worried, Achille,' he said, his voice suddenly cracking.

'Antoine's a good lad.'

'But always one to take risks. Act first, think later.'

'It's seen him through so far, Pierre,' Pujol said gently, wanting to give what crumbs of comfort he could.

The truth was, Pujol didn't like the sound of it. Antoine was the sort of young man who would be involved with the Resistance. Rightly, in Pujol's opinion. He was brave and moral, but the type to think he was invulnerable.

'I'll ask around,' he said quietly. 'Of course I can.'

Pierre's shoulders sagged with relief. 'I hope it's nothing,' he said. 'That we're making a fuss about nothing, but . . .'

'I'm not promising anything,' Achille said. 'But I'll do my best.'

The door swung open and Célestine came in carrying the wine and glasses. Pujol wondered how long she'd been listening outside.

'Have you finished talking behind my back?' she said, though there was no complaint in her voice.

'Celsie,' murmured her husband.

'Are you going to help us?' she said, looking Pujol in the eye.

'I'll do what I can, Célestine,' he said.

She held his gaze a moment longer, then nodded. 'We'll drink to that, then.'

After the Déjeans had left, Pujol emptied the remainder of the bottle into his glass, sat back in his chair and looked over the notes he'd written. He drew a ring around a couple of the words in the middle of the page, then ringed them again.

'I wonder ...'

He couldn't be certain, especially at three steps removed, but he'd bet his last *sou* that when Antoine mentioned an old man in a pale suit, he'd been referring to Audric Baillard. He thought for a moment, then ripped a clean sheet of paper from his notepad and began to write a letter.

Chapter 49

CARCASSONNE

Sandrine cleared up all she could, then packed a case for Liesl and left. She walked through the Bastide, delivering the remaining prisoners' letters on her way back to the rue du Palais.

She put her head round the door of the salon to tell Marianne she was home, then went upstairs to the bathroom to wash and change her clothes.

'I never thought I'd get rid of the smell,' she said when she came back down. 'Not that cold water and what passes for soap help much.'

She sat down in the armchair and crossed her legs. 'I couldn't do anything about the graffiti on the walls – it will need painting over – but I salvaged most of the clothes and photographs.'

Marianne nodded. 'Well done.'

'Where is Liesl?'

'Resting.' Marianne sighed. 'Lucie's still here, too. Marieta said she's been asleep most of the day. It must have been something she ate, she didn't drink much wine last night.'

'How is she? Liesl, I mean.'

'Not so bad, given the circumstances. She's tougher than she looks.' Marianne sighed. 'Of course, she's been through a lot already.'

'Did you tell her I thought I saw Max?'

'No, I thought we should wait until we were sure. I telephoned Suzanne, though, and asked her to go to the police station.' She sighed again. 'She's already been there once today, trying to find out what's happened to César Sanchez.'

'Any luck?'

Marianne shook her head. 'No, which could be good news or not. Impossible to say.'

Sandrine thought for a moment. 'Will they tell Suzanne about Max, given she's not a relative?'

'Whenever a train leaves Carcassonne,' Marianne said, 'the police are supposed to post a list of names of prisoners being deported and where they're being sent.'

'Do they?'

'Sometimes.'

'Did you tell Suzanne what happened to Liesl?'

'Yes.'

'What about Lucie?'

'She was asleep,' said Marianne, 'which I admit was a relief. The news – if it's true – will hit her hard.'

She stood up. 'Do you want something to drink? You look all in.'

Sandrine smiled. 'Please. Whatever there is.'

She shut her eyes and leant back against the chair, as exhausted as she'd ever felt in her life.

'Here you go,' said Marianne, handing her a glass of red wine. 'I think you've earned it, don't you?'

'Thank you.'

Sandrine took a sip of wine, then another, feeling the immediate effects of the alcohol warming her blood. Despite the temperature, she was cold. Tiredness, she supposed.

Marianne returned to her usual spot on the sofa. 'I've just had a rather peculiar exchange with Marieta, who asked, apropos of nothing, if we might be going to Coustaussa this summer. Extraordinary! As if we can suddenly up sticks and go like we used to.' She shook her head. 'I can't imagine what's brought that on.'

'I can,' Sandrine said. 'I meant to tell you about a conversation we had yesterday, but then I saw Raoul and it put everything else out of my mind.'

'Yes,' Marianne said wryly.

Sandrine smiled, then explained what had happened in the garden. 'The thing is, I'd never seen Marieta so rattled before. Having slept on it, I'm sure she's now decided she wants to see Monsieur Baillard in person rather than rely on the post.'

'How odd,' Marianne said. 'And you're sure "Baillard" was the name Déjean said?'

'Pretty sure. Have you ever heard of him?'

'I think Papa might have mentioned him once or twice.'

For a while the girls sat in silence. Sandrine sipped her wine and allowed herself, for almost the first time in the headlong day, to think about Raoul.

She felt a wave of exhilaration, followed fast on its heels by a suffocating thought that she might not see him again for weeks, months.

'Do you think he'll be all right?' she said quietly.

'Raoul?'

Sandrine nodded.

Marianne paused. 'Honestly, darling, I don't know. You saw what it was like today, what happened to Liesl. Things are getting worse.'

The sound of a door opening upstairs brought the conversation to a halt. Marianne got up and went into the hall.

'It's Liesl,' she said, then raised her voice and called up the stairs. 'We're in here. Come down when you're ready.'

A few moments later, the girl appeared. She was pale, and there were dark circles under her eyes, but she seemed calm.

'How are you feeling?' Marianne asked, patting the sofa beside her.

'A little better,' she said in her quiet voice. She sat down.

'Would you like something to drink? Are you hungry?'

'Nothing, thank you.'

'Do you want to tell us what happened?' Sandrine said. 'Or would you rather not?'

'No, I don't mind.'

Liesl took a deep breath, then began to talk in a steady, clear voice. With no self-pity at all. The more she heard, the more angry Sandrine became.

'We should report them,' she said fiercely, when Liesl had finished.

'Max has tried to report them, many times,' Liesl said. 'The police always say there's nothing they can do.'

'But this isn't just name-calling, throwing stones – though that's bad enough. This is criminal.'

'I could hear them breaking things, smashing the windows, ruining everything,' Liesl said quietly, 'but I didn't see them. I couldn't identify them.'

'It's beyond belief that this could happen in the middle of the day,' said Sandrine. 'What about the neighbours? Didn't they notice?'

From the look on Liesl's face, it was clear the neighbours had heard, but had decided not to intervene all the same.

'I cleared up as much as I could,' Sandrine said, now disillusioned as well as angry. 'It was pretty foul, but apart from the graffiti, it wasn't as bad as it looked at first glance. I brought what I could back with me.'

'My camera?' Liesl said quickly. 'Max bought it for me. It's a Furet.'

'Yes, I got that. The thugs had turned the table over and the camera was underneath, so they missed it,' Sandrine said. 'I'll fetch it.'

She went out into the hall. Someone was moving around on the first floor. She heard the chain flushing in the bathroom, then footsteps on the landing. Sandrine caught her breath. Even after two years, she half expected to see her father standing at the top of the stairs. His glasses in one hand and his newspaper in the other. She smiled. He'd never gone anywhere without his newspaper.

She stared into the empty space for a moment, the light fading from her face. She sighed, then picked up the case with Liesl's things and went back into the salon.

'Lucie's up,' she said to Marianne.

'Lucie's here? She'll know where Max is,' Liesl said with a spark of hope. 'Have you asked her?'

'Asked me what?'

Lucie looked dreadful. Pale, her lips cracked and tiny blue veins on her eyelids. She hadn't even brushed her hair, let alone waved it, and her dress was crumpled.

'Lucie!' Sandrine blurted, before she could check herself.

She pulled a face. 'I know, I look awful.'

'I'll get Marieta to bring some tea,' Marianne said.

Lucie gave a wan smile, then noticed Liesl and her suitcase and became very still.

'What's going on? Why's Liesl here? Where's Max?'

'Don't you know where he is?' Liesl said. 'I thought – hoped – he was with you.'

'What do you mean? He went straight home after the demonstration to have supper with you.' Lucie turned to Marianne. 'And why are you all sitting here like this? What's going on?'

'Let's wait and see what Suzanne has to say,' Marianne said. 'No sense jumping to conclusions.'

'What's Suzanne got to do with it?'

'We don't know where Max is,' Liesl said in a small voice.

'Are you saying he didn't come home?' Lucie's voice was rising. 'Max is missing, is that what you're saying? Max is missing?'

'Come and sit down,' Marianne said. 'It won't do any good to get worked up.'

'I don't want to sit down,' Lucie threw back. 'I want to know where Max is.'

'We all do,' Sandrine said, less sympathetically than Marianne. She put her hand on Lucie's shoulder, who shrugged it off. 'If you sit down, we'll tell you what we do know. It's impossible with you like this.'

For a moment, she thought she'd been too unkind. Lucie looked as if she was about to burst into tears. But then the hysteria seemed to go out of her and she crumpled into the armchair.

'I'm sorry, I don't know what's got into me.'

'It's all right,' Sandrine said more gently, sitting down beside her and taking her hand.

'But will someone please tell me what's going on?'

Still holding her hand, Sandrine told Lucie about what had happened at the apartment.

'Oh my God,' Lucie said. 'It must have been awful.'

Liesl nodded.

'So that's partly why Suzanne's gone to the police station,' Marianne said when she'd finished.

'But Max must have had an accident,' Lucie said, starting to stand up. 'He was going straight home. We must ring the hospital. Not the police station.' Then, seeing the expression on Sandrine and Marianne's faces, her face froze. 'What, you think he's been arrested, is that it?' she said slowly. 'But why, why would he be arrested? Max is careful. He's always so careful, isn't he, Liesl? He'd never go out without his papers.'

'Never.'

'There's no reason for him to be arrested,' Lucie said

again, but the panic in her voice revealed how scared she was.

Sandrine caught Marianne's eye and could see she was thinking the same thing. Given that Lucie was in such a state already, there was no point in continuing to keep their suspicions to themselves.

'The thing is,' Sandrine said carefully, 'I think I might have seen him at the railway station earlier. He was a long way off and there was a woman in my way, blocking my view, but—'

'The railway station?' Lucie jumped in. 'Why were you there?'

'A group of prisoners were deported this morning,' Marianne answered. 'Sandrine thinks Max might have been one of them.'

The tiniest of cries escaped from Liesl's mouth. The last vestiges of colour drained from Lucie's cheeks.

'He was a long way off,' Sandrine said, feeling awful. 'I didn't want to say anything until I was sure it was him.'

'It can't have been Max . . .' whispered Lucie.

'Suzanne will be back any moment now,' Marianne said. 'Let's wait until we know for certain. In the meantime, Liesl can't go back to the flat, that much is obvious. The windows are broken and the door needs securing.'

In the hall, the telephone began to ring. Sandrine looked at Marianne, who got up and went to answer. In the salon, no one spoke.

Marianne came back into the room.

'Was that Suzanne?' Sandrine asked, feeling her heart speed up.

Her sister nodded.

'Well?' said Lucie, unable to keep the hope from her voice. 'What did she say? His name wasn't on the list, was it? It can't have been on the list.'

'I'm sorry,' Marianne said quietly.

'No . . .' Lucie whispered.

Liesl caught her breath. 'Where's he been taken?' she managed to ask.

'They hadn't a record of it,' Marianne said in a steady voice. 'Suzanne said they wouldn't tell her.'

'Wouldn't or couldn't?' said Sandrine.

'We don't know where he's been taken?' Liesl said, her self-possession finally cracking.

'What are we going to do?' Lucie wailed. 'If we don't know where . . .'

Marianne put her arms around Liesl's shoulders and finally the girl allowed herself to cry. Liesl's distress seemed to prompt Lucie to try to pull herself together. She reached out and took her hand.

'Hey, kid. It'll be all right.'

Sandrine looked desperately at Marianne, who gestured for her to follow her out into the hall and leave Lucie and Liesl together for a moment. Marianne gently shut the door.

'What are we going to do?' Sandrine whispered.

'The whole situation is peculiar,' Marianne said in a low voice. 'Suzanne said Max was the only person without a destination recorded on the list.'

'Why would they keep it secret?'

'I'm not sure. Suzanne got the impression that the police didn't actually know where Max was being sent.' She looked at the closed door. 'We have to think seriously about what to do with Liesl. She can stay here for now, but she can't go back to the flat. Possibly not at all, not until we know why Max was arrested.'

'But she's only sixteen. Her papers are in order.'

Marianne shrugged. 'So were Max's papers. Honestly, I can't begin to work out what's going on. This could be to do with their father, or something else entirely.'

Sandrine thought for a moment, then an idea started to take shape in her mind.

'What about Coustaussa?' she said slowly. 'Marieta's desperate to go and see her Monsieur Baillard. Liesl could go with her. At least until we find out where Max has been taken and why. She'll be safer away from Carcassonne, especially with Madame Fournier next door.'

Marianne shook her head. 'It would be so complicated to arrange,' she said. 'Changing the ration books, coupons, travel documents, too much to organise. I'm worried enough about Marieta as it is. I can't ask her to take all that on.'

Sandrine felt a spark of possibility. She'd told Raoul he could go to Coustaussa if he was stuck. Of course, there was no reason for him to take her up on the offer. He'd head for Banyuls or any of the other places where he had friends who could help. But what if he couldn't get that far south? What if he had nowhere else to go?

'Well, how about if I went with them?' Sandrine said in a level voice, though her heart was racing. 'I could sort things out with the Mairie in Couiza, so the responsibility wouldn't fall on Marieta's shoulders.' She paused. 'As for Liesl, you or Suzanne could get her some alternative papers, couldn't you?'

Marianne stared. 'Well, yes. It would take a few days, but yes, we could manage that.'

'Well then. As soon as that's done, the three of us could go. I'll get them settled in, then come back. Simple. The country air would do Marieta good in any case.'

Her sister was still frowning, though Sandrine could see she was considering the idea.

'Would you mind?' Marianne said eventually. 'It will be a lot of work for you.'

Sandrine smiled. 'I wouldn't mind at all.'

*

By ten o'clock, the girls had worn themselves out with talking and planning and discussing. Marianne had convinced Liesl she couldn't stay in Carcassonne, Sandrine had persuaded Lucie to stay another night with them and leave it to Suzanne to find out where Max had been sent. The plan was straightforward – Marieta, Liesl and Sandrine would leave for Coustaussa at the beginning of August, just as the family had done in the old days, while Lucie, Marianne and Suzanne would stay put in Carcassonne.

It was well past eleven when Sandrine and Marianne turned in. Her sister looked so tired, Sandrine offered to lock up. As she checked the shutters in the salon, she thought about how, in a matter of three days, her entire life had been turned on its head. And as she double-bolted the back and front doors and checked the blackout was in place, she realised it felt as if a layer of skin had been stripped from her bones.

She walked slowly upstairs. She hesitated a moment outside her father's room, hearing the sound of Lucie crying behind the closed door. She was on the point of going in, then stopped herself. Grief was a private business. She suspected Lucie would rather be left alone. There was no noise coming from the box room where Liesl was sleeping.

Sandrine looked out through the landing window to where the stars shone bright in the clear July night sky. The full moon sent diamonds of coloured light dancing across the wall. For a moment she felt something shift inside her. Hearing an echo of other hearts and spirits as they fluttered and sighed and breathed. A consciousness of other lives once lived in the narrow streets of the medieval Cité or in the Bastide Saint-Louis.

'*Coratge*,' she murmured. 'Courage.'

The moment passed. Everything returned to normal. Sandrine sighed, then went into her bedroom and closed the door. The house fell silent.

Chapter 50

THE HAUTE VALLÉE

As soon as the broadcast had finished, Audric Baillard began to dismantle the wireless transmitter. Standing the small brown cardboard outer case of the receiver on the table, he wrapped the antenna in a lightweight jacket and pushed the headphones into the toe of a large woollen sock. He did not think the police would venture this high up into the mountains, but who was to say?

In between the usual code words and messages from the Free French to their colleagues in occupied France, Baillard had picked up news of yesterday's Bastille Day demonstration in Carcassonne. The Midi was showing her true colours. He smiled for a moment, then went back to work.

He wrapped the four wire segments between the folds of an old copy of *La Dépêche* and put them at the bottom of a suitcase lying open on the chair beside him, then packed clothes on top of them. The smile slipped from his lips. If the news from Carcassonne was encouraging, the news from the North was the opposite. In the past months, whole families had been coming from Paris and Chartres to Ax-les-Thermes, in the hope of escaping over the mountains to Spain. From Spain to Portugal, then to England or America, even though America had closed her borders some time ago. Now, according to the wireless, there had been another mass round-up in Paris, this time involving thousands of police. Tens of thousands of Jewish men, women and children were incarcerated in the Vélodrome d'Hiver on the outskirts of the city. He hoped the rumours were exaggerated, though he feared they were not.

Baillard clipped shut the catch on his suitcase and put the case on the floor. He poured himself a glass of Guignolet and took it outside to watch the silver moon on the peaks of the Sabarthès mountains, as he had done so very many times before. Sometimes in the company of those he had loved and who had loved him. More often, alone.

He had intended to rest in Los Seres for a few days and gather his strength, ready to guide the next group of refugees to safety over the Pyrenees. But Antoine Déjean was much on his mind and the news on the wireless had caused him to change his plans. Baillard hoped that the demonstration was the reason Antoine had been unable to deliver the package as promised. He would return to Rennes-les-Bains. If there was still no letter, once he had taken the next group of refugees over the mountains to Spain, as he had promised, then he would go to Carcassonne and search for Déjean there.

Baillard had to act. He could not leave things to chance. Despite the propaganda printed by the collaborationist newspapers, Nazi victory was by no means assured. But if their enemies gained possession of the Codex, there would be nothing anyone could do to stem the tide of evil.

All of Europe would fall. And beyond.

Baillard stood a while longer, letting the alcohol warm his bones and the sight of the mountains calm his spirits. At midnight, he went back inside. He washed his lone glass and set it to drain beside the sink, then fastened all the shutters and locked and bolted the front door. Finally, with the weight of the heavy suitcase in his hand, he began the long, dark walk back down to the valley below.

Pas a pas … Step by step.

PART II

Shadows in the Mountains
August 1942

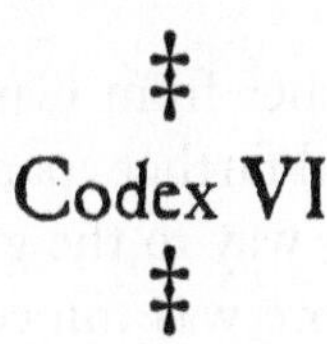

Codex VI

GAUL
COUZANIUM
AUGUST AD 342

Arinius waited until he could no longer hear the hooves of the horses before emerging from his hiding place. He stepped out into the silence. The air that moments earlier seemed to bristle with threat, settled gently back around him.

Caution had become habitual. It was not that he believed the Abbot would send soldiers after him to retrieve what was rightfully his. He had been gone too long, more than four months. But Arinius had been warned that *bagaudes*, bandits, roamed the countryside in the foothills of the mountains. Mostly gangs of soldiers deserting their commissions. He could not jeopardise the safety of the Codex, so he was careful, took no risks.

The young monk knelt down beside the river, feeling the dry corners of the papyrus poking into his ribs, and splashed water on his face. He cupped his hands and drank, the cold water soothing his raw throat. His cough was worse again, he didn't know why. Although it was cooler by the water, the midges and mosquitoes and flies had bitten and sucked and irritated him all night long.

Another dawn, the sky clear and white, promising another day of fierce heat. This morning he was tired, but he picked up the pace once more, following the path along the tributary of the river, then climbing up out of the valley to the high land. Another of Caesar's marching routes, the road ran due south and was lined on either side by trees.

As he travelled further from Carcaso, the settlements had become smaller and farther apart. The green river valleys of the Atax giving way to the gullies of the Salz, the red earth where iron ore was mined, the forests of trees with black bark, older than time itself. The forgotten communities of the rocks and the peaks, tribes who had survived each occupation of Celt or Roman, holding fast to their mountain traditions, their mountain ways.

Now here, in the high valleys, were tiny villages untouched by civilisation. Here older religions still reigned, mythologies, stories of Hercules and his lover Pyrène, Abellio and the spirits of the air, tales never written down but handed from father to daughter, mother to son. Here they spoke no Latin, not even Iberian, but rather a strange dialect of the Volcae as grating to Arinius' ears as the jackdaw chattering of the sailors at the port in Massilia.

He heard wheels behind him. He glanced round, to see only a cart driven by an old man with skin the colour of leather.

He raised his hand. '*Salve, mercator.*'

The man pulled up. 'I only trade for money,' he said immediately.

Arinius smiled. He had little to trade in any case. He reached into his bag and pulled out a denarius. The merchant jumped down and took it, bit it, then threw back the blanket covering his wares to reveal a selection of glass bottles and earthenware jars.

'For that, I can do you a draught of *posca*. Or *cervesa*. You'd get more for your money.'

Arinius had been brought up to think *cervesa* vulgar, a drink fit only for the barbarian countryside. Nobody in Lugdunum would drink it. But during his travels he had grown to like the gritty, malt taste of the beer. If anything now he preferred it to *posca,* the watered-down wine-and-vinegar concoction so popular in Carcaso.

'I don't suppose you have true wine?' he asked, holding out another coin.

'Won't get much for that.'

'I don't need much,' he replied.

He had not been lonely in Carcaso, but after two weeks of travelling alone on the open road, he had started to miss the community of his brother monks. The taste of wine on his tongue, he thought, would remind him of companionship.

The merchant rummaged through the dazzling and precarious pile of bottles and jars and mirrors, and extracted a small bottle. Fashioned from pale green glass, the hemispherical body was patterned with a beautiful blue-green iridescence on one side, like the eye of a peacock's tail. It had a long thin neck and a stopper of soft wood, and a leather thong threaded through the top so it could be carried or worn around the neck.

'It's beautiful,' said Arinius, smiling at the trader.

The merchant shrugged. 'Do you want it or not?'

Arinius handed over his money.

'Thanking you, *frater.* Anything else for you?'

Arinius looked at the empty land all around. 'If you could point me in the direction of the nearest settlement? Is there anything hereabouts?'

'Couzanium's not far,' he replied. 'About half a day's walk.'

'A town?'

The man shook his head. 'No, just a few houses. But there's a larger settlement to the east of Couzanium, Aquis Calidis. Some two hours' walk, perhaps three. Hot and cold water springs, salt water and fresh, a proper bathhouse there. It used to be popular with soldiers from the garrisons past the Sinus Gallicus. Not much visited now.'

‘I might try it.’

The merchant threw the covering back over his wares, climbed up and tapped his animal on the haunches. The cart moved forward in a rattle of clinker and glass.

Arinius took the stopper from the neck of the bottle and drank, letting the heat of the rough wine soothe his throat. He wiped his mouth with the back of his hand, replaced the wooden bung, then put the thin strip of leather around his neck and shoulder, already thinking of how welcome it would be to let the hot waters relieve his tired bones.

He hesitated for a moment, then, with the glass bottle tapping against his hip, Arinius continued on the Roman road towards the green valleys of Couzanium.

Chapter 51

CARCASSONNE
AUGUST 1942

Sandrine stood with her arms resting on the open window of the second-class carriage. She was wearing one of Marianne's travelling outfits, a green jacket and pleated skirt. With her black curly hair pinned and set back off her face, she looked older. She felt older.

'Won't be long now,' Marianne said.

Sandrine patted her pocket, checking again that she had all the tickets and papers, then looked back to the knot of women standing on the platform waiting to see them off. Try as she might, she couldn't stop her gaze returning to the far end of the platform, where three weeks ago she had witnessed the police herding prisoners like animals on to the train. Max among them, though she'd not realised in time to be able to do anything to help him. Suzanne had been unable to find out where he had been sent or why he had been arrested. César Sanchez and Antoine Déjean were also both still missing. No one had heard anything, no gossip, no rumours. And because they didn't know why Max had been arrested, they had kept Liesl out of sight, in case the police came for her too.

Every knock at the door had put Sandrine's nerves on edge. And every morning since Raoul had left, she checked the mat the instant she heard the sharp metal click of the letter box. For a letter, a postcard, anything. She knew he wouldn't write, he couldn't risk writing, but hope was stronger than common sense. She had kept busy.

At first she tried to identify the words she'd heard at the river, the words that had so frightened Marieta, but that had led nowhere. The municipal library was shut for the summer – in any case, many books that could have been useful had disappeared from the shelves – and Marieta refused to discuss it. The only indication the conversation had ever happened was the fact that Marieta, too, checked for a letter every morning. Sandrine had even visited the cathedral in the hope of speaking to Abbé Gau, but he was nowhere to be found. As July had tipped into August, the days seemed to drag. It had been an uneasy, unnerving few weeks, and Sandrine longed to be gone from Carcassonne.

Even though it was late morning, the station was as quiet as a Sunday night. The lingering consequences of the Bastille Day demonstration and the fierce August heat kept everyone indoors. There were still large numbers of *police d'occasion* on the streets, and regular checks and road-blocks. And although the broadcasts from London gave news of Nazi setbacks, there had been a flurry of rumours that Hitler was preparing a new offensive. Against whom, no one was certain, but the *bobards* were widespread and the atmosphere in Carcassonne brittle.

'I wish you were coming with us,' Sandrine said, suddenly reluctant to leave now the moment had come.

Marianne smiled. 'You'll be fine. Telephone from Couiza to let me know you've arrived safely.'

'I will,' she said.

The guard's whistle shrilled. Sandrine blew her sister a kiss, waved to Suzanne and Lucie, then ducked back inside the carriage as the train began to move off.

'That's that, then,' she said.

Liesl sat reading and cradling her precious camera on her lap. Marieta claimed the opposite seat, looking rather grey and breathless. Her hair was neat beneath a black felt hat. She had dressed her light grey summer coat with a spray of red glass beads at the lapel. Her sturdy feet were planted firmly on the floor, outdoor shoes rather than her customary wooden clogs, and she was darning a pair of socks that would not be needed until winter. The strand of grey wool swished and flicked like a kitten's tail as the thick needle went in and out of the heel.

Sandrine set her eyes on the landscape outside the window, yellow and brown and green, and tried to ignore the fluttering of expectation in the pit of her stomach. She leant her head against the glass. The train rattled its lulling song along the metal tracks, at first running parallel to the river. Beyond the smeared carriage window she caught glimpses of Maquens, Leuc, Verzeille, Roullens. Familiar names, but places she had never visited.

In September, the fields would be alive with farm workers and labourers, children as young as eight or nine helping their parents to bring in the harvest. Wheat and barley in the plains, vines for as far as the eye could see. The air would bristle with tension and expectation as the *vendanges* tiptoed closer, closer, everyone waiting for the moment when the wine harvest began. Now, the fields were mostly deserted. From time to time, a man in corduroy trousers and checked shirt pushing a bike along a straight, featureless country road. Pairs of women in wide-brimmed straw hats with baskets, making the long walk from the omnibus to farms in the folds of the countryside. In small market gardens beside the line, goats and chickens grazing, scratching. Fields of yellow sunflowers, their faces tilted to the sun. A wooden cart and a white delivery truck, the unchanging pace of the countryside, war or no war.

In the *zone occupée*, Sandrine knew, soldiers patrolled the trains, particularly those passing close to the demarcation line. At least things here were not that bad.

Not yet. Not quite.

*

The train stuttered to a halt.

'Limoux. Limoux. Cinq minutes d'arrêt.'

Marieta's eyes fluttered half open, woken by the station master's announcement, then shut again.

'Do you want to get out and stretch your legs, Liesl?' Sandrine asked.

The girl shook her head. She seemed composed and her features were calm, but Sandrine knew better. She tried not to pry.

Sandrine stepped down to the platform, looking at the colourful summer dresses and two-pieces, the headscarves and shallow-brimmed straw hats with bright ribbons. All along the platform doors opened, were propped back, then slammed shut. Leave-takings and greetings, the songs of summer.

The guard blew the whistle, Sandrine climbed back in and they were off once more, the train climbing higher, slower, into the hills, the first view of the mountains. The air changed. Even Liesl stopped reading and was looking out of the window.

'It's so beautiful,' she said. 'I didn't realise.'

As the train pulled out of Alet-les-Bains, Sandrine felt the familiar tug at her heart. They left behind the sunflowers and began the steady climb into the Haute Vallée. The solid grey stone of the railway bridges over which the train jerked, hauled, heaved its carriages. The countryside became steeper, less forgiving. Birch trees and beech, holm oak and hazel. Through the open window slipped the remembered scent of cedar and laurel, the damp air of the deep woods.

The train emerged from the green shadow of the wooded banks of the crystal river, blinking into the light. Sandrine caught her first glimpse of the limestone hills and jagged crests, rock and fir trees on the plateau of the Salz, and the sharp ridges of the foothills of the Pyrenees beyond.

She thought of the times in the past when she had done this same journey to and from Carcassonne, looking out over these fields and skies and rivers, almost sensing the ghosts of fellow travellers heading south into the Corbières. The bustle of the railways, the antique hiss of engine and whistle.

The whispering of generations past.

Chapter 52

TARASCON

Audric Baillard entered Tarascon by way of the Avenue de Foix. Ahead of him, the Tour du Castella sat perched high on its hill, calling the weary traveller home as it had for more than a century and a half.

In the distance, beyond the town, the Pic de Vicdessos. It dominated the valley, the town, the rivers and the woods, a reminder that this was an ancient landscape that had survived without mankind for many hundreds of thousands of years. Timeless, impervious to the follies of men.

Baillard was heading for the Grand Café Oliverot, opposite the bureau de poste, which had occupied the same site on the right bank of the river Ariège since the turn of the century. Indeed, he had been one of its first customers. It was a favourite haunt of Achille Pujol's in the old days.

Audric was fond of Tarascon, with its cobbled streets and quiet acceptance of its place in the world. There was a suggestion of old values and time unchanging for generations, which chimed harmoniously with Baillard's view of the world. If anything, the little mountain town seemed more prosperous, more confident than last time he had visited. The Grand Hôtel de la Poste looked freshly painted. Some, at least, of its rooms might be occupied. He frowned, wondering what that signified. German visitors? Guests of Vichy? He hoped not.

Baillard turned the corner and straight away saw his old friend sitting at his usual spot at the end of the terrace, overlooking the river Ariège and the Pont Vieux. He looked a little heavier and was grey now, but it was the same grizzled profile, the high forehead and tufts of hair that wouldn't lie flat.

He walked over to the table. '*Bonjorn*, Achille,' he said.

Pujol frowned at the interruption, then broke into a wide smile. 'Audric Baillard, I'll be damned. You got my letter, then?'

Audric nodded. 'How go things with you, *amic*?'

'Could be worse,' Pujol said, gesturing with his hand. 'Then again, could be better.' He reached over and dragged a chair across from the adjacent table. 'I'm glad you came.'

'Your letter said it was urgent,' said Baillard, sitting down. He put his hat on the table. '*Qu'es aquò?*' What is it?

'Antoine Déjean,' Pujol said. 'Do you know him?'

Baillard became still. 'What have you heard?'

He listened without interrupting as Pujol gave a clear and concise précis of his conversation with Pierre and Célestine.

'But in over three weeks, nothing,' Pujol finished. 'Boy seems to have vanished off the face of the earth. No one knows anything.'

Baillard frowned. 'And Sénher Déjean said the man looking for Antoine was German?'

Pujol nodded. 'Time was, Audric, do you remember, when we couldn't move for Germans down this way. All those expeditions grubbing about, the spring and early summer of 1939.'

'I do.'

'There was also that odd lot – the Polaires, they called themselves – claiming to be after evidence of some kind of ancient super race or something. And that French expedition from Chartres, funded by . . .' He clicked his fingers. 'What was the man's name?'

'François Cecil-Baptiste de l'Oradore.'

'That's it. Quite a memory you've got.'

Baillard's eyes darkened. 'I had some association with the family in the past,' he said. 'Though they went by a different name in those days.'

'De l'Oradore lodged a complaint about the Germans, must have been July 1939, maybe August. Ironic that, now, when you come to think about it. Claimed they were after the Cathar treasure, would you believe it?'

Baillard looked at him, but said nothing.

'The point is, when Pierre's neighbour saw Antoine in Carcassonne, she reported the first thing he said, when he heard there had been someone asking after him, was – and I'm quoting here – was he "an old man in a pale suit"?' He paused. 'I assumed he was referring to you, Audric. I hoped you might know something.'

Baillard nodded. 'Antoine was working for me, Achille. He was supposed to leave a package for me in Rennes-les-Bains, but it didn't arrive. He didn't arrive.'

'Oh.'

'And no word.'

'What was in this package?'

'A map.'

'Of what?'

'The hiding place of something of enormous importance,' he replied. 'Something that might – could – change the course of the war.'

Pujol's eyebrows shot up, but something in the tenor of Baillard's voice dissuaded him from asking anything else. He took another mouthful of beer.

'Do you remember Otto Rahn, Achille?' Baillard said quietly.

'I heard he did for himself. Sleeping pills, wasn't it?'

'Possibly.'

Pujol's gaze sharpened. 'It's like that, is it?'

'Benlèu,' Baillard said. Perhaps.

Pujol took another gulp of beer. 'Can't say I'm surprised,

a very nervy chap. They were always hanging about together, Rahn and Déjean, thick as thieves the pair of them. Poking about in the caves without any kind of permission, looking for God knows what. Lombrives, Niaux, further over to Lavelanet and Montférrier, all the way up to Montségur. Spouting all sorts of nonsense, calling each other by odd names.'

'*Gottesfreunde*,' said Baillard. 'The German equivalent of *bons homes*. What people are now inclined to call Cathars. Rahn put his thoughts down in two rather peculiar books, *The Crusade Against the Grail* being one. Later, he wrote about the time he spent in Montségur, though he doesn't mention Antoine by name. It was published in 1936, the same year Rahn was accepted into the SS.'

'Yes, I heard they got their hooks into him.'

'Rahn was a naïve young man, easily influenced. He was flattered to be taken seriously. He did not realise what they wanted from him.'

'Are you telling me all that back then is tied up with Antoine's disappearance now?'

'Yes.'

Pujol looked hard at him, his eyes sharp. For a moment, Baillard got a glimpse of the high-ranking police detective he once had been. Astute, principled and determined.

Pujol stood up and threw a note down on the table. 'I have a bottle of wine at home. We can continue our conversation there. What do you say?' He looked up at the sky. 'Get back before the storm hits.'

'I think it is still some way off,' Baillard said, 'but yes. This is a conversation we should have in private.'

Chapter 53

COUIZA

With mixed feelings, Sandrine opened the carriage door and stepped down on to the platform. She felt as if she might see her old self, the girl she had been three summers before, waiting to meet her. Long socks, her hair in plaits still. Her father in his light summer suit and Marianne, fresh from her first term of teaching, their cases piled high for a month of swimming and playing cards and lazy, long summer days and nights.

'Can you help me with the bags, Liesl?'

Marieta was gathering her things. Sandrine smiled. She, at least, never changed. Then Sandrine saw another familiar face. Ernest, the station master, waving and pushing a rattling luggage trolley fast along the empty platform to greet them. His uniform strained across his broad chest. His black handlebar moustache seemed more impressive.

'Madomaisèla Sandrine, a pleasure to see you. We got your message saying you were on your way.' He stood back. 'And look at you! So tall.'

'Thank you.'

His face grew solemn. 'May I say, we were all very sad to hear of your father's death. He was a fine man.'

She accepted his condolences with a quiet smile. 'He was.'

'Will Madomaisèla Marianne be joining you?'

'Not for the time being.' Then, aware of a flutter of nerves in her stomach, she turned to Liesl. 'But this is a cousin of ours, from Paris. In case anyone asks.'

Ernest peered over the top of his spectacles. Sandrine hated lying to him, but over the past couple of weeks it had become clear how precarious Liesl's situation was. They still had no idea where Max had been taken, and rumours were circulating, terrible stories, unbelievable, that even children were now being arrested in Paris with their parents and sent to camps. Even with the oldest of friends, they could take no risk.

Ernest held her gaze for a long moment, then tipped his hat to Liesl.

'Nice to meet you, Mademoiselle Vidal.'

Sandrine gave a sigh of relief. It was the first hurdle. If he was prepared to collude with the pretence, then she hoped their neighbours would do the same.

Liesl smiled. 'Oh, it's not . . .' She turned pale, stopped, remembered what she was supposed to say. 'It's a pleasure to be here, monsieur. And please, call me Liesl.'

Marieta finally descended from the carriage.

'*Bonjorn!*' Ernest cried, lapsing immediately into Occitan. '*Benvenguda.*' He held out his hand to help her down the steps.

'*Bonjorn*,' she replied, then prodded his corpulent stomach with her finger. 'I see rationing agrees with you.'

Ernest roared with laughter, and even Liesl smiled. Sandrine felt the knot of tension below her ribs loosen a little more as she listened to the two old friends exchanging news.

'Will you be staying long, Madomaisèla Sandrine?' Ernest asked, piling the cases on to the trolley.

'A week or so at least. Marieta and Liesl will be here for longer.'

'If you need any help, the new mayor here is not so bad. He can be trusted.'

'I need to sort out our papers and rations,' she sighed. 'I suppose I'd better come back to the Mairie later, once I've seen Liesl and Marieta settled in the house.'

'My brother assists at the town hall,' Ernest said in a low voice. 'How about I tell him you will be in to see him later in the week, with your *cartes d'identités* and your ration books?'

'Could you arrange that?' she said hopefully. 'I'd be so grateful.' Going all the way up the hill, then coming all the way back to stand in another queue was the last thing she felt like.

'A few days here or there, I can't see that will be a problem. And if there's anything extra you need,' he said, dropping his voice even lower, 'you just let me know.'

'I will,' she said with a broad smile. 'If we're stuck, we'll come to you. Thank you.' Sandrine looked out to the concourse. 'Is there likely to be a bus this afternoon?'

Before the war, there had been two buses a day that ran along the valley of the Salz, one from Couiza to Arques, the other from Couiza to Rennes-les-Bains. Since Coustaussa was early on the route, they could catch either one.

'Not every day, but you're in luck. And Madame Rousset has arranged for Yves to meet you at the stop below Coustaussa and take you up to the village.'

Sandrine glanced at Marieta, enormously relieved to hear that they weren't going to have to walk up the steep hill with their luggage.

'That was thoughtful, thank you.'

Sandrine went to pick up her case, but Ernest got there first.

'We still have standards, mademoiselle. We're not going to let those criminals in Vichy change everything, *è*.'

He accompanied them down the platform and through the ticket hall, then loaded the bags on to a bus waiting at the front of the station.

'The driver should be here any minute,' he said, tipping his hat. 'Let me know if there's anything you need, I'm sure we will be able to come to some arrangement.'

'I will, of course,' she said, biting her lip to stop herself smiling at the idea of sweet, honest Ernest being part of the *marché noir*.

The fierce Midi sun hit Sandrine the moment she stepped out of the shade of the station building. The Tramontana was whipping up the dust, brown clouds of grit and clogged air, scraps of paper and a few dry leaves spiralling in the wind in circles.

'It's so humid,' Liesl said. 'Will there be a storm?'

Marieta shook her head. 'Tomorrow, maybe.'

Sandrine could see that Liesl felt terribly out of place. Here, more than in Carcassonne, she looked like a Parisian. A girl who belonged in a white dress and hat strolling along Haussmann's elegant boulevards. Not in the dusty garrigue of summer in the Languedoc.

'Are you all right?' she asked quietly.

Liesl nodded.

Sandrine looked at the other people milling around the square. Women in flowered dresses and children sucking iced lollies, a few old men. A young priest stood a little apart from the others, his complexion like wax, in a black soutane, his nose stuck in a book. At first glance things seemed much the same, but the atmosphere was different. Before the war there were always plenty of summer tourists. Now it was a local crowd. But there was also a kind of watchfulness. As if no one quite trusted anyone any more.

The driver emerged from the café and shambled towards his bus, cigarette stuck to his bottom lip, a newspaper under his arm and his napkin still tucked into his collar. Within minutes, all the fares had been paid and everyone was seated in a muddle of packages and parcels, dogs on laps, children standing between their mothers' legs, cycles fixed on the rack at the back. The tiny glass windows were tilted open as far as they would go, but it was still stiflingly hot. Two elderly women in hairnets and heavy seersucker dresses wafted paper fans backwards and forwards, sending a welcome draught Sandrine's way.

The bus wheezed and belched its way out of the station and soon they were on the route de Coustaussa, heading east. Napoleon's marching trees gave welcome shade from the hot August sun. Neighbour began to chat to neighbour, a whining child was slapped and started to grizzle, an old man carrying a can of cooking oil like a baby in his arms began, softly, to snore.

Sandrine smiled, despite everything. It was hard to believe that anything could ever affect the quiet and tranquillity of this ancient place.

‡

Codex VII

‡

GAUL
COUZANIUM
AUGUST AD 342

Arinius reached the small settlement of Couzanium in the middle of the afternoon. He set up a makeshift camp by the river Atax, the same river that flowed through the Carsac plains. Removing his sandals, he dipped his tired feet in the water, letting the current cool his blistered skin. Then he rinsed his handkerchief, thick with dust from the journey. He couldn't shift the spots of blood. They were faint, barely visible, but still there all the same.

The hour and time of his passing was in God's hands. Arinius did not know how much time might be given to him. He had seen men die quickly of the illness he carried within him, or survive for some time, in a few cases, for years. He did not know how long the precious text would need to remain hidden. For one lifetime, or a thousand? The simple truth was that if he did not ensure the Codex could be found again when the time was right, then it might as well have been consigned to the fires in the community at Lugdunum. He had to survive long enough to achieve these things.

He spread the handkerchief out on a rock to dry in the sun, weighted to stop it blowing away, then sat back to eat. The wine was almost gone, but he ate the last of his cured ham and almonds, then set out to explore the modest collection of dwellings.

In these furthest reaches of the Empire, principles of

trade and commerce still held strong. Drawn by the noise, Arinius walked towards the heart of the settlement, where itinerant merchants had set up an informal market in the shadow of the bridge. He perused the stalls – furs and cloth, rabbits for the pot, herbs and strings of red beads.

He knew what he was looking for. First, a small cedarwood box. He would need to wrap it in furs or cloth before he buried it in a dry place, away from the air and the damp. He hoped it would be sufficient. He knew how to mix ink and how to style a quill from a hollow bird's feather. He was pleasantly surprised to be able to buy what he needed. He couldn't afford papyrus or a scroll, but he bought a square of spun wool, the length of his arm and the colour of goat's milk, in a fine weave. Wool would hold an image better and was easier to preserve intact than a wax tablet or wooden board that might crack or warp or burn.

The hours he spent at the market were pleasant, reminding him of the boy he had been. Often he had been called upon to accompany older monks to the forum in Lugdunum, a pair of willing arms and strong legs. Having purchased what he needed, Arinius returned to the river, gathered everything together and walked back to the crossroads.

He was in two minds where to go next. Ahead of him, the mountains. Behind him, Carcaso. To either side, green hills and empty space. But the merchant's comment that there were baths at Aquis Calidis had lodged in his mind. How much good the waters would do his aching bones. Perhaps the healing hot springs would improve his lungs. He would never be cured, he accepted that, but the waters might slow the pace of his illness.

Arinius turned to the east. The road followed the river valley between high hills. Lush pastures, thick wooded forests of beech, holm oak, hazel and chestnut that came right down to the road. High on a hill to his right, on a stark and rocky outcrop, he spied a small hilltop oppidum. Grey stone against the blue of the sky and a landscape scarred through with red iron ore, limestone fissures.

'A place of beauty,' he said, feeling his spirits lift. 'And, God willing, a place of safety.'

Chapter 54

Coustaussa
August 1942

'There it is,' Sandrine said, as the bus shuddered to a halt.

Coustaussa was a pretty hamlet, perched on a ledge in the hillside overlooking the river Salz. There was a small mairie and a war memorial, as well as the ruins of a twelfth-century château-fort that once had kept watch over the valley, built on older Roman remains. The view across the valley was to Rhedae, Rennes-le-Château as it was now known.

Coming up from the main road, it was the ruins of the castle a visitor glimpsed first. Only as one drew closer did the houses and the small seventeenth-century church reveal themselves. There was no café, no boulangerie. The town crier still announced the arrival of the cobbler or the knife-grinder or the baker's van doing its rounds.

The village's only notoriety was the violent killing of the village priest, Antoine Gélis, murdered in his presbytery on Hallowe'en 1897. Marieta remembered him from when she was in service in neighbouring Rennes-les-Bains, and one or two of the oldest residents of the village talked of him as a solitary, reclusive man who played little part in the life of the village. Frightened of his own shadow, hiding from ghosts.

The driver opened the concertina doors. Sandrine jumped down, Liesl handed down the bags, then held out her hand to Marieta to help her on the steep metal steps.

Yves Rousset was waiting with his grandmother's donkey and trap. Sandrine raised her hand in greeting, hoping it wasn't going to be awkward. She hadn't seen him since an uncomfortable kiss in the fields three summers ago.

'Hello,' she said in a bright voice. 'How are you?'

Yves didn't meet her eye. 'Nothing to complain about.'

'This is one of my cousins, Liesl. From Paris.'

He looked at Liesl, clearly seeing no family resemblance, but made no comment.

'How is Madame Rousset?' Sandrine said quickly.

'So-so,' he said, putting the first of the cases into the trap.

Slowly, the donkey pulled its load up the earth track, Yves holding the reins, Marieta riding in the trap and Sandrine and Liesl walking alongside. Despite the heady green of the valley down by the river, the grass here was brown, dry from lack of rain, and the heavy wheels threw up tiny stones, fragments of twigs and leaves between its spokes.

Their house sat on its own patch of land, slightly below the village and to the south-east. It was one of the larger houses, built from stone and quarry pillaged from the ruins of the castle some eighty years ago. Three narrow, high stone steps led to a tall double front door painted yellow, with the grimacing metal gargoyle she had hated as a child. Yellow-painted window frames either side of the door and planters of geraniums on the sills, with their heads snapped and hanging down. The sign was still broken, the pieces dividing the single word – CITADELLE – in two. Picking them up, Sandrine made a mental note to ask Yves to mend it.

'So, here we are,' she said.

While Liesl and Yves unloaded the baggage, Sandrine hesitated, memories of summers past at her heels. Then she climbed the steps, unlocked the door and went inside. Straight away, the familiar smell of beeswax and polish, the mustiness that permeated the hall from the cellar and kitchen, assaulted her and made her heart strings crack. Remembering her father, polishing his glasses and smiling as Marieta bustled, fussed, complained about the plumbing or the stove smoking or the quality of the bread from the Spanish baker.

Yves brought the bags into the hall.

'Thank you,' Sandrine said, still a little uncomfortable.

He met her eye for a moment, then turned to Marieta. 'My mother invites you to call, once you are settled in.'

'Tell Madame Rousset I shall be delighted,' Marieta replied formally.

Leaving Liesl and Marieta for a moment, Sandrine went further into the house. She wanted to reacquaint herself with the feel of it, the smell of it, without anyone looking on.

A narrow central staircase led upstairs to three small bedrooms and an even smaller bathroom, a recent addition. When her grandfather had bought the house, there had been no running water and no electricity. Now they had both, even though the generator often broke down, so they mostly relied on the lamps and still heated the water with an old wood stove fuelled by vine roots and hawthorn prunings. Left alone, the fire went out. Marianne and Marieta grumbled about the inconvenience, but for Sandrine it was all part of the romance of the summer. She wouldn't change a thing.

The dining room and kitchen were either side of the hall at the front. Quickly, to get it over with, Sandrine opened both doors and looked inside, half expecting to see her father sitting in his usual chair.

It was empty, of course.

She took a deep breath, felt the familiar clutch of her

heart. At the same time she realised with relief that she was glad to be here again. She took off her coat and her hat, shaking out her hair, then walked down the corridor. Conscious of the echo of her father in the empty spaces, but not distressed by it.

The sitting room filled the whole of the back of the house, facing north towards the Camp Grand and the stone shepherds' huts. They'd fallen into disrepair, but she and Marianne had loved playing in the ruins when they were children. For a moment, a snapshot of her and Raoul standing in the twilight in the rue du Palais and looking up at the black and white photographs. Was it ridiculous to hope he would ever come to Coustaussa and see the *capitelles* for himself?

Absurd to even think of it ...

This room, too, smelt of her father. His cologne, the mixture of his tobacco and hair oil. Sandrine closed her eyes for a moment, summoning his face to her mind, remembering his smile and his laugh and the way he frowned when he was reading. Then, purposefully, she walked over to the windows and threw them wide, letting the light in.

In the distance, thunder rumbled in the hills.

‡ Codex VIII ‡

Gaul
Couzanium
August AD 342

Arinius rubbed his temples, trying to soothe away the headache pricking behind his eyes. He felt the storm getting closer all the time, like a living, breathing thing at his heels. The clouds were marching fast across an increasingly angry sky.

Another rumble of thunder, a growling in the hills, like an animal waking from its winter hibernation.

The road ran on out of sight. If the merchant had been right about the distance between Couzanium and Aquis Calidis, Arinius realised he was at risk of being caught out in the open when the storm hit. His earlier sense of contentment and calm had gone, chased away by the threatening voice of the thunder. There was nothing to fear from the storm, or so he told himself. Even so, he picked up his pace, all the time looking around for a suitable place to take shelter.

'Our Father,' the words keeping pace with the accelerated beating of his heart, 'who art in Heaven …'

On his left, set above a low ridge of hills, Arinius noticed a number of small, plain dwellings. Roofs of thatch and branch, low stone buildings. It was impossible to tell from down below whether it was a village, another watch point to guard the road, or a temple. Here, in the green folds of this ancient river valley, his Christian faith had no hold. The old gods of the Romans and the Volcae before them still held sway. Temples and shrines to Minerva and Pyrène, to Jupiter and Abellios.

Arinius lifted his face to the sky. The day darkened from white to purple, purple to black. Another crack of thunder, then a golden fork of lightning split the black sky. Seconds later, the first drop of water fell, then another and another, patterning the cobbled surface of the road. He pulled his hood up over his head as the rain grew harder, more insistent.

He had to find shelter. Arinius stepped off the road and began to climb, as fast as he could, up towards the woods and the tiny collection of flint shepherds' huts and *villae* half hidden in the trees beyond.

Chapter 55

Coustaussa
August 1942

Sandrine and Liesl helped Marieta clear the supper plates, a scratch meal of fresh vegetables and rice that Madame Rousset had brought for them, then retired to the salon. Low growls of thunder rumbled in the hills and the air had grown cooler.

'Are you sure there won't be a storm?' Liesl said anxiously. 'It sounds so close.'

'This house has withstood Midi storms for a hundred years and will cope with a good few more. Try not to worry,' Sandrine replied.

The evening passed quietly and at nine o'clock they turned in. Marieta was clearly exhausted, Liesl kept yawning and Sandrine herself was struggling to stay awake.

'I can lock up, Marieta,' she said. 'You go to bed.'

'I'm not having you running around after me, so there's no cause to go asking.'

'There's nothing that won't wait until the morning,' Sandrine said firmly. 'It's been a long day. I don't want you up all hours, banging about down here.'

'I'll be up in a moment, madomaisèla.'

She put her hand on the old woman's shoulder. 'All right. But don't be too long,' she said softly. 'Come on, Liesl, I'll show you to your room.'

She left Liesl unpacking her clothes and walked to her father's room. After a deal of soul-searching, Sandrine had decided she would sleep in here. It could not be a shrine. She'd understood the moment she arrived that, if her memories of so many wonderful summers in Coustaussa were not to be permanently overlaid with sadness, no corner of the house could be out of bounds.

She took a deep breath, then pushed open the door and walked in. His summer jacket was hanging on a hook. She ran her hands over the chest of drawers, the counterpane on the bed, the collection of curios and ornaments gathered from his travels. A wooden walking stick propped in the corner, an old brooch found in the rubble of the castle ruins, a statue of Joan of Arc in papier-mâché she'd made at school ...

She undressed and got into the unfamiliar bed. For while she lay there with her eyes open, looking at the ceiling and listening to the silence. She missed the noises of the city, the rattle of trains and delivery carts, the early-morning sounds of the *péniches* on the Canal du Midi.

The air cooled a little, the wind dropped and Sandrine slept. Tonight, the nightmares didn't come. Instead her dreams were possessed by armies and war, women and men from antiquity, long hair streaming, swords and insignia gleaming, in a bright landscape that was neither familiar nor yet entirely unknown. Vivid shimmering faces of people she did not know: a woman in a green dress with a red cloak, a monk with a grey woollen cloak around his thin shoulders holding an ancient script in his hands, words like black birds, and a girl with copper curls tumbling down her back. Shadows, shades of people known and yet not known. The rattling of bones in the earth, the shift and movement of the dead awakening.

As the rumbling wind passed over and brought a smattering of light rain, Sandrine half woke and thought of Raoul. The same questions, always the same. Wondering where he was, if he thought of her as she remembered him. Hoping he was safe.

As the hours of night passed, finally the lullaby of the rain sent her into a deep and restful sleep.

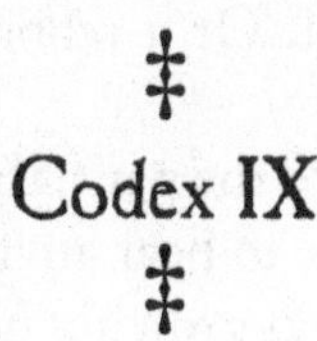

Codex IX

GAUL
COUZANIUM
AUGUST AD 342

Arinius had never heard such noise, such anger in the skies. A crack of lightning, then the thunder growling at his back like a wild animal. Another jag of lightning. The storm was coming at him from every angle, the rain beating down on the back of his neck. He pulled his hood over his head, but the force of the wind kept ripping it back. He tried to walk faster, but his legs were unwilling and several times he slipped.

The words of the Revelation of St John the Divine came into his mind. With such a storm, who could doubt the old battle between dark and light? Seven seals broken bringing war and famine and death and victory. Four horsemen, the blast of seven trumpets and seven bowls emptied upon the earth. The seas turned to blood, fish suffocating upon the shore. The white bones of men on the battlefield. Blackened skies and the green world turned to dust. Mountains as they collapsed into the dead oceans.

In fear, Arinius began to pray. Struggling to be heard above the noise of the tempest and the crack of the wind, above the beating of his heart. Already, rivulets of water were running down the hillside, opals of rain battering down on him, and always, the thunder snarling in the hills.

Then, over the cacophony of the storm, the crack of a branch underfoot, a rustle in the undergrowth. Another breaking of a twig, close by. He caught his breath, seized by a new dread. A wild boar? These woods were rich for hunting, he'd no doubt. Or a rabbit, a snake? Pray God not a wolf.

He froze, listening for the pant, the gasp of a beast waiting to attack, but unable to hear anything over the noise of the tempest. The rain was growing heavier, harder, pounding down and sending clods of mud and wet leaves and branches skidding down the hillside, but Arinius continued on, murmuring the Lord's words, mixed now with memories of stories, of older tales, like a spell to guard against any ungodly inhabitant of the woods.

He slipped, then slipped again, sliding back down the slope in a roll of wet wool and leather. He struggled to find purchase and get back on his feet. The Codex was safe beneath his tunic and the bottle was still on its leather tie around his shoulder, but he realised he was in danger of doing himself serious injury if he carried on. He had to find shelter and see the storm out.

Head down against the wind and the rain, Arinius wrapped his arms round an oak tree. He lost track of time, clinging to the trunk as a sailor to a mast in a storm-tossed sea. The edges between the darkness of the day and the blackness of night blurred.

Gradually, the thunder quietened, then stopped altogether. Over the noise of the rain and the wind, he could hear the howls of wolves in the distant hills. A screech owl returning from the hunt and the sounds of night jays.

Finally, the rain also began to ease and Arinius sank to the ground in precarious sleep. He dreamt of deliverance and heaven, imaginings of white figures standing before triumphant gates with sword or scroll in their hands. And in the centre, a single figure, lit by the sun and by the moon.

Silver and gold.

‡

Chapter 56

Tarascon
August 1942

'Monsieur? Monsieur Audric, wake up.'

Baillard heard the child and his heart leapt. For a moment, forgetting where he was, who he was. He was back in the distant past, hearing another child's voice calling to him.

'Bertrande?' he said, a lift in his voice.

'No, it's Aurélie, monsieur.'

Baillard opened his eyes to see the youngest of the Saint-Loup girls standing at the bottom of the bed with a candle in her hand. Disappointment rushed through his old bones. Of course it wasn't Bertrande, how could it be? She had died many years ago. So very, very many years ago.

'What time is it, *filha*?' he said softly. 'It's dark still.'

'Some time after four, monsieur. My sister Eloise sent me to fetch you. She says you should come.'

Immediately, Baillard sat up. 'What's happened?'

'They've found something,' she said.

'Something or someone?' he asked quickly.

'I don't know, only Eloise said you should come straight away. There's a *charreton* waiting.'

Quickly, Baillard straightened his clothes, pushed his feet into his shoes and took up his hat and coat.

'Have you told Inspector Pujol?' he asked, following Aurélie through the sleeping house.

'I couldn't wake him, monsieur.'

Baillard stopped, listening to the stertorous snoring

coming from behind the closed door of Pujol's bedroom.

'No, I dare say you couldn't.'

Five minutes later, Pujol was lumbering down the corridor with Baillard and Aurélie, nursing a hangover. A sour smell of sweat and red wine seeped through his pores, and his general lack of fitness and lungs full of tobacco meant he moved heavily. Baillard knew he would wake up as soon as the morning air hit his face.

'How did she get in?' he growled, rubbing his eyes.

'You left a window open at the back, Monsieur l'Inspecteur,' Aurélie said, then added: 'You should be more careful.'

Baillard laughed.

Pujol unbolted the front door and they stepped outside into the street. Straight away Baillard heard the sound of dogs howling in the hills to the south of the town. Pujol glanced at him, and they both started to walk a little faster.

'Did you say someone was waiting for us, Aurélie?'

'By the bridge,' she said. 'My uncle.'

It was as dark as pitch. The blackout was not rigorously enforced in the countryside, but it was late and few people were awake. Baillard's heart was thudding as they made their way through the sleeping streets. Ahead, in the distance, he saw the outline of a donkey and cart.

Although many of the vehicles requisitioned by the army in 1939 had been returned, there was little fuel, and in the Haute Vallée people relied on the old ways of getting from village to village. Ox and cart, pony and trap. As they drew closer, Baillard saw their driver was a young man, broad and tall, his face weathered by the wind and the sun. The two Ariégeois greeted one another, then Pujol made the introductions.

'Audric, this is Guillaume Breillac. He's married to Eloise Saint-Loup.'

'I have heard of you, Sénher Baillard,' Guillaume said, tipping his hat.

'His father and I served together in the last war,' Pujol said. 'Me, him and Déjean. Signed up together, September 1914.' He turned back to Breillac. 'How is the old rogue, still going strong?'

'The same as ever, Monsieur l'Inspecteur. He and my brother are waiting for you above the Larnat road.'

'What's Pierre doing up there at this time of night,' he said, raising his eyebrows. 'Hunting, no doubt?'

Guillaume shrugged. 'It's hard for him.'

Pujol turned to Baillard. 'Took a hit from a shell, May 1940. Came out of it all right, but doesn't like to be around people much any more.'

'I am sorry to hear it.'

'Whereas Guillaume's something of a local hero,' Pujol continued. 'He was involved in the discovery, what, ten years ago now, of a mass grave in the caves not far from here. You must have heard about it. Hundreds of bodies, been there seven hundred years or so. A bad business.' Pujol shook his head. 'But no more ghosts in the hills now, *è*, Guillaume? Old Breillac's a great one for holding that the mountains are haunted.'

Pujol slapped Guillaume on the shoulder once more, before walking round to the back of the cart. Throughout the exchange Baillard had watched Guillaume's honest, intelligent face closely, and saw a different emotion mirrored there. Tolerance for Pujol's teasing, but no modern disdain for old wives' tales. Something sharper.

'I heard something of it,' he said, looking at Guillaume.

For a moment Guillaume did not react. Then he nodded, the briefest acknowledgement of a shared knowledge. Baillard smiled. They understood one another.

Pujol made heavy weather of clambering up the single frame step, causing the cart to tilt perilously to one side.

The shovels and digging equipment slid across the floor of the trap. He lowered his hefty frame down on the narrow wooden cross bench, then shuffled along to make room, breathing heavily. Baillard climbed easily into the cart and sat down next to him, a slight, neat figure, his pale suit with a yellow handkerchief in the breast pocket just visible beneath his trench coat. Guillaume tapped the donkey's flank with his stick, clicked, and gave a tug on the reins. The animal dropped its head, lifted its foot and began to pull. The harness strained, leather and bridle clinking against the wood.

In the distance, the first vestiges of light appeared in the sky, flecks of white, silver, the air fragrant with the scents of pine and oak. It was a timeless scene, the spark of the animal's hooves on the path, puffs of breath, the early song of birds in the forest around them.

Guillaume came to a halt. Baillard looked up at the path, memories of other such journeys vivid in his mind. To the peak of Montségur, to the Mont d'Alaric above the plains east of Carcassonne, to the highest reach of the Pic de Saint-Barthélémy.

'We have to walk from here.'

'How far is it?' said Pujol.

'About ten minutes to the plateau. My father and brother are waiting there.'

Guillaume tied the donkey to a tree. Baillard looked at Pujol's face, moist around the temples, and smiled sympathetically.

Pujol grunted. 'I can't imagine why I let you talk me into this, Audric,' he grunted. 'Two old men clambering about the rocks like a pair of schoolboys.'

'Courage, my friend,' Baillard said. '*Coratge.*'

Pujol was panting heavily by the time they reached the ridge. Baillard saw the pinpricks of light from the hunting lamps, pale against the dawn sky, and three men standing looking down into the gully below.

'Breillac,' said Pujol, offering his hand.

The old man turned round. His face was riven with white crease lines in his brown skin, but his eyes were clear, sharp. A cigarette was wedged into the corner of his mouth. He nodded, then turned to Baillard.

'*Peyre*, this is Monsieur Baillard,' Guillaume said, in the dialect of the mountains. 'And my brother, Pierre.'

Baillard nodded a greeting. '*Bonjorn.*'

The old man's eyes fixed on Baillard, as if he knew of his reputation, but he said nothing. The young man nodded.

'What's happened, Breillac?' asked Pujol.

'About an hour ago, Pierre heard a noise.'

'What was he doing up here?' Pujol demanded.

Since two rabbits hung from his belt and the blade of his knife glistened in the early-morning light, the question was unnecessary.

Baillard put his hand on his friend's arm. 'You are retired now, *amic.*'

'We don't want any trouble,' Breillac said, his voice thick with red wine and tobacco.

Baillard nodded. 'We understand.'

'Pierre was setting traps. Might have used something to flush the rabbits out.'

'Something?' Pujol demanded.

'To help things on their way.'

Pujol was about to turn on Pierre, but one look at Baillard's expression warned him not to.

'So Pierre didn't notice anything different at first,' Breillac continued in his steady way. 'Then he saw something.' He pointed down into the gully. 'Down there. Looks like a body. Pierre fetched me, I sent Guillaume to find you.'

'You did the right thing, Sénher Breillac,' said Baillard quickly.

Pujol nodded. 'Shall we see?'

Breillac gestured to his sons. Pierre had a coil of rope hooked over his shoulder and Guillaume produced a leashed axe from a hessian sack on his back. Without a word, they went to the edge of the gully.

The three old men watched in silence as the boys climbed down, Breillac sucking on the end of a thin rolled cigarette.

'*Aquí*,' Guillaume called out from below.

'What is it?' Pujol called.

'A man.'

'Alive?' Baillard said quickly.

'No, sénher.'

Moments later Guillaume appeared back at the top of the ridge. Wrapping the end of the rope around his waist, he steadied himself against the side of a rock and, with the help of his father and Pujol, slowly began to haul the body up the side of the cliff. Baillard watched, feeling as if a fist was tightening around his throat.

'God save us . . .' Pujol said, crossing himself.

Baillard stared in pity at the battered body. He helped lower it from Guillaume's shoulders and lay it on the ground. Struggling to keep his anger in check, he put his hand on Antoine Déjean's forehead.

'Look, Audric,' Pujol muttered, pointing at the rope burns on Antoine's wrists, then the bruises on his stomach and face. 'These aren't the result of a fall.'

'No.'

Baillard began to speak, an old mountain prayer for the passing of a soul.

'*Peyre Sant, Dieu . . .*'

Old Breillac bowed his head. His sons stood beside him, looking down at the broken body of the young man.

'Amen.'

Baillard leant forward and laid his yellow handkerchief over Antoine's face, then turned to Pujol.

'Why here, Achille?'

'It's obvious when Pierre set a charge in one of the burrows, he misjudged it.' He pointed to a crumbled section of path further along. 'Caused a landslide, look. The trees have come down.'

'No, not why did it happen. I mean why bury the body this far up in the hills in the first instance. There are plenty of other places that would have served as well. Antoine might not have been found for months.'

'It's very remote,' Pujol suggested.

Baillard was frowning. 'Is there anything special about this place, Achille? Something significant?'

Pujol started to shake his head, then stopped. 'It's not that far from where de l'Oradore set up camp. Could that be relevant?'

'It could be ...' Baillard murmured.

'What will I tell Célestine and Pierre?' Pujol said quietly.

'The truth, *amic*, which is that their son is dead and we do not know why.' He sighed. 'But it might be as well to put it about that it was a climbing accident. If his killers believe the matter closed, it will be easier for us.'

'Easier for us to do what?'

'To find out what happened without interference.'

The Breillacs were talking quietly to one another. Their storm lamps, the light extinguished now the day had started, were on the ground beside the rope.

'They'll hold their tongues.'

Baillard nodded. 'Breillac strikes me as a man who keeps his own counsel. Pierre too. And Guillaume, he understands more than most, I would say.'

Pujol looked at him for a moment. 'Never have half an idea what you're talking about, but I suppose you know what you mean.' He waved at Breillac. 'We're going to take him down.'

Guillaume and Pierre carried Antoine down the path to where the donkey and trap were still standing. Baillard took off his coat and laid it across the body. Then they walked slowly behind the *charreton* into Tarascon in the pale light of early morning.

Codex X

Gaul
Couzanium
August AD 342

Arinius woke, stiff and cold, at first light. Dawn was just starting to give shape back to the land. The black outline of trees on the horizon, the purple silhouette of the hills, the pinpricks of colour of wild flowers in the garrigue, a world made clean and beautiful and bright. He had climbed further than he'd realised and was in fact much closer to the top of the hill than the valley below. The overwhelming force of the storm and the rain had refashioned the landscape, the torrent carving channels in the hillside, exposing mud and the shallow roots of trees. Drifts of sodden leaves and detritus covered the ground, and the undergrowth was sodden and tangled, twisted into strange shapes by the wind.

Arinius started to climb up towards the settlement. When he cleared the brow of the hill, he saw straight away that the curved buildings he'd glimpsed from the road were not houses at all, but rather a strange collection of stone huts. Each had a domed roof and a low opening, though no windows.

He ducked his head and went inside the first of them. The roof had collapsed. He tried the second, which was flooded. But the third was spacious and dry, with plenty of room. He removed his belongings from his bag – the cedarwood box and the writing materials – and laid everything out on the ground. Nothing was spoiled but he didn't wish to run the risk of rot. He draped his cloak and his tunic over the dome of the hut. The air was cool, but it was dry and it would be hot again later.

Then Arinius sat down and looked out across the blue and green valley and waited for the sun to rise.

‡

Chapter 57

Tarascon
August 1942

Audric Baillard and Achille Pujol walked across the Place de la Daurade and stopped in front of the small terraced house where the Déjeans lived. Pujol lifted his hand and knocked.

'Célestine,' he said, removing his hat. 'May we come in?'

'You have news?' she said quickly.

'If we could come in,' Pujol said.

The light faded from Célestine's face. She nodded, and stood back to let them enter.

'This is an old friend,' he said, 'Audric Baillard.'

Baillard saw Célestine take in his pale suit, the yellow handkerchief he wore always in his left breast pocket. With a jolt, he realised she had been expecting him.

'Monsieur Baillard,' she said.

Baillard took off his hat. 'Madame Déjean.'

'Is Pierre here?' Pujol continued.

Célestine tore her gaze away from Baillard. 'You have news,' she said, more a statement than a question.

'Célestine, please. If you could fetch Pierre,' Pujol said.

Célestine led them down the narrow corridor. She gestured for them to enter the parlour, then went in search of her husband.

Baillard looked around the small room. Every surface was covered in framed photographs: a chubby boy in short trousers, holding two metal soldiers out towards the camera; Antoine in his Sunday best with his parents on

La Fête-Dieu, the most important saint's day celebrated in Tarascon; Antoine posing with a rope slung over one shoulder and climbing boots, making a thumbs-up sign; smiling and waving his *fascicule de mobilisation* papers in 1939. Baillard glanced at Pujol and saw that he was thinking the same thing. The room felt like a shrine already.

'Look at this one, Audric,' Pujol said, passing him a photograph in a black ash frame. He pointed to a soldier in uniform standing at the back of a group of eight young men. 'That's me.' He was twenty-eight years younger, slimmer, with thick brown hair just visible beneath the rim of his regulation cap, but it was unmistakably Pujol. 'And that's Pierre Déjean at the front. A photographer went round all the villages that day.'

'I remember it.'

'We were so young,' Pujol said, continuing to stare at the black and white image. 'Went off so pleased with ourselves, cocks of the walk. Women throwing flowers, cheering us like we were heroes. Heads stuffed full of patriotic nonsense. So much mud. And the woods, trees all shot to pieces, bark, trunks shattered. Never saw anything like it.'

'No,' Baillard said quietly.

His friend sighed, then gently put the frame back in its place. 'Me and Pierre Déjean, we were the only two who made it back. Thought we'd be home in time for Christmas. Remember?'

'I do.'

'Different this time.'

'Yes.'

Pierre burst into the room. 'You have news about Antoine?'

Baillard watched Pujol revert to his former role. Gone was the nostalgia of seconds before and in its place, a steady and reassuring authority.

'You've found him,' Célestine said in a dull voice.

Pujol nodded. 'I'm sorry.'

Pierre slumped in a chair, his hands hanging between his knees. 'Where?'

'In the mountains. Not far from Larnat.'

'He fell?'

'It's too soon to say,' Pujol said.

Baillard drew his breath. 'You have my condolences, Sénher Déjean, Na Déjean. I knew your son. He was a courageous man.'

'Where is he?'

'Guillaume Breillac has taken his body to the church.'

Pierre nodded, but without looking up. Célestine, despite her grief, raised her eyes to Baillard's and looked at him. Baillard was certain she had something she wished to say. Equally sure that she would not speak in front of her husband or Pujol.

Baillard stood up and gave a small bow. 'We will intrude on your grief no longer.'

Pujol glanced at him in surprise, but also got up. As the quartet moved towards the door, he managed to draw Pujol aside.

'I need to talk to Célestine alone.'

Pujol gave him an inquisitive look, but nodded and immediately strode forward and put his arm around Pierre's shoulder.

'I was looking at the photograph of us all,' he said, somehow turning Déjean around and keeping him in the room. Baillard could see Pierre was reluctant to be taken aside, but his natural courtesy kept him there, long enough for Baillard to leave the room with Célestine.

Sure enough, rather than turning left towards the front door, she turned right and beckoned him to follow. She led him to the kitchen, then closed the door behind them.

Baillard felt the short hairs on the back of his neck stand on end. 'Do you have something for me?'

Célestine nodded. 'He told me you might come. A man in a pale suit, yellow handkerchief. That I wasn't to give it to anyone else, tell no one else. Not even his father.'

'Go on.'

'Pierre is a good man,' she said, 'but he doesn't see what's under his nose. He doesn't think I know what Antoine was doing.'

She gave a broken smile. Baillard's heart went out to her, understanding that she had already accepted the worst, since the day her son failed to arrive for her birthday three weeks ago.

'As if I wouldn't be proud of him.'

'He had a great sense of honour,' Baillard said simply.

'He told me he was working for you, Monsieur Baillard. Oh, not your name of course, but how to recognise you. And that if anything happened to him ...' She stopped, a catch in her voice, then steadied herself. 'That if anything happened to him, I should give you this.'

Célestine went to the sink, drew back the green and white piece of fabric that concealed the shelf beneath and pulled out an open wooden box filled with cleaning materials. Brushes, a tin of polish, a bottle of vinegar and another containing liquid ammonia.

'Pierre would never think to look here,' she said. 'It seemed the safest place.'

She put her hand into the box and lifted out a white envelope. She handed it to Baillard, then returned the cleaning box to its home under the sink.

Baillard carefully opened the envelope, hardly daring to hope it could be the map itself. Straight away, disappointment rushed through him. It was simply a brief scribbled note, clearly written in a hurry.

'When did Antoine give this to you?'

'A month ago.' She dropped her head. 'He said he now knew where to look.'

'Did he say why he didn't come to me in person?'

'He thought he was being watched. He didn't want to lead them to you.'

Guilt pinched at Baillard's heart. 'Thank you, Célestine,' he said.

She hesitated. 'Antoine was killed, wasn't he? Not a climbing accident.'

Baillard looked at her proud face. Her expression unwavering, already resigned to loss, but with an infinitesimal flickering of steel in her eyes.

'Monsieur Baillard,' she said, reproach in her voice.

'Yes.'

She put her hand to her heart, struggling, he could see, to contain her grief.

'Did he suffer?' she asked, needing to know. Not wanting to know.

More than anything, Baillard wanted to spare her the dreadful knowledge of her son's final moments. But he understood, more than most, that it was better to know the truth, however painful or hard, than to live with uncertainty. Always wondering what might or might not have happened. Doubt ate away at the soul, left holes in the heart.

'Your son was a man of courage,' he said again. 'He did not betray his friends.'

Célestine met his steady gaze. 'Thank you.'

Overwhelmed with pity, Baillard put his hand on her shoulder.

'*Desconsolat*,' he said. 'I am so very sorry.'

Célestine nodded, then stepped away and raised her chin. 'Don't let it be that he died for nothing, Monsieur Baillard. Do you hear? Make his death count. It is the only way to bear the loss.'

Chapter 58

'What did Célestine want?'

The sky was black and they hurried across the square, collars up against the wind. Baillard looked up at the glowering clouds skimming the mountains opposite.

'Antoine left a note for me in her safe keeping.'

'Why the hell didn't she tell me that two weeks ago?' Pujol said.

'She gave her word she would tell no one, not even her husband, unless something happened to him.'

'What's it say?'

'That he thought he was being followed.' He paused. 'Rahn's writings were often obscure, deliberately ambiguous, so when he wrote about a skeleton key, it was assumed it was symbolic, allegorical even. Déjean, it seems, gave out that it was real, to throw his enemies off the trail.'

Pujol's face darkened. 'Are you telling me he was murdered for something that doesn't even exist?'

For a moment, both men were silent. At their back, purple storm clouds moved fast across the blackening sky.

'You have had Antoine taken to which church?' Baillard said.

'La Daurade,' Pujol replied. 'Madame Saint-Loup will lay him out, make him … make it possible for Célestine and Pierre to see him.' He paused. 'And it will keep him away from the police station – it's hard to know who to trust, *è*?'

They walked a few steps further, then Pujol stopped again.

'What I don't understand is why Antoine approached you in the first place, Audric.'

'I approached him. There are events in the past – the far distant past – that mean I have for many years kept a close watch on these mountains. Lombrives, the Pic de Vicdessos, further west to Montségur and the Pic de Soularac. I observed what Rahn and Antoine were doing. When Rahn left, Déjean went to university, little happened. However, when he was demobbed, he made repeated trips to the mountains.'

'You think Rahn sent him something before he died?'

'Yes, or information that made Antoine reconsider something he had overlooked before,' Baillard answered. 'When I was sure of where Antoine's sympathies lay – given his friendship with Rahn, I had to be certain he had not been coaxed into the same attitude of mind – I approached him. Déjean was clever, he could read both Latin and Greek. He told me about the map and that he thought he knew where to find it.'

'But he didn't tell you where it was?'

Baillard smiled. 'He liked to keep his secrets close. I asked him several times, but he always said he would bring it to me as soon as he had it.' His face clouded over. 'I encouraged him, Achille, and I greatly regret it.'

'You can't blame yourself, Audric. He knew what he was letting himself in for.'

'I feel responsible.'

'The men who murdered him are responsible,' Pujol said firmly. 'Do you know who they are?'

'No,' said Baillard. 'But I will find out.'

They walked the last few metres to the house quickly and in silence. Pujol took his latch key from his pocket.

'Find out who killed him. I mean it, Baillard,' he said, his voice cracking with anger. 'Find out who did such things to him. He died badly.'

The wind had fallen, but now the sky began to growl and shudder. Warning shots of thunder, several minutes apart, ricocheted between the mountains and the hollows of the valleys. Baillard looked up at the Pic de Vicdessos, now shrouded in angry purple clouds.

'Not so hard to believe in Sénher Breillac's ghosts now,' he said quietly.

Chapter 59

Carcassonne

'Ghosts?'

Leo Authié tapped the razor on the side of the basin, then put it on the glass shelf. He patted his face with the towel, then ran his hand over his skin before pulling out the plug. He disliked interrogations, the stench of fear and stupidity. He felt filthy the moment he walked into the prison. The water drained, leaving a skim of grey foam and dark bristles around the rim of the porcelain.

'Yes, sir,' came Laval's voice from the other room.

Authié straightened his tie and collar, then walked out of the tiny closet into his office.

'You're saying operations have been suspended because of ghosts?'

'Yes, sir.'

Authié had only been back in Carcassonne for twenty-four hours but already the heat was getting to him. The temperature had been pleasant in Chartres, and the time he'd spent there, as the guest of François-Cecil de l'Oradore, had been both informative and productive. For those prepared to work within the new realities, daily life under occupation was comfortable. Between de l'Oradore and his German friends, there was a natural alliance. They were men of similar views and attitudes.

During the course of his sojourn in Chartres, Authié had learnt more about de l'Oradore's interest in the Languedoc. His focus – obsession – was a trilogy of medieval books said to have been smuggled from the citadel of

Montségur in the thirteenth century by the Cathars. De l'Oradore already possessed one of the books and was prepared to spend a great deal of money acquiring the others. His interest in anything else was secondary.

It had become clear that de l'Oradore's purpose in summoning Authié to Chartres was to consolidate his position within the emerging new structures of enforcing law and order. Having set up Authié as his eyes and ears in the Languedoc, he did not wish to lose him. At his instigation, Authié had travelled to the Préfecture de Police in Paris to meet members of the Brigades Spéciales who were involved in breaking Resistance networks and organisations, and had been given an insight into how the war against the terrorists – the partisans – was being conducted.

Authié's sense, in both Chartres and Paris, was of order restored. It was at first disquieting to see road signs in German and the swastika flying in place of the Tricolore above official buildings. To see the grey and green uniforms of the Gestapo and the Wehrmacht paraded so openly. But there was no doubt the *rafles* in July and the mass deportation of Jewish families had resulted in quiet, calm streets. Life felt disciplined, everything and everyone in their rightful place. Most important, the churches were full and the synagogues empty. Paris had adapted. Parisians had adapted. Not all, but many.

He had returned to Carcassonne with a sense of what the future might hold. Almost immediately, the bad news started. Although Fournier had done what Authié asked of him, a fire at the police depot had resulted in the wanted posters for Pelletier all being destroyed. They had now been reprinted and distributed, but three valuable weeks had been lost. The result was that there had been no reports of sightings of Pelletier since July.

Authié rolled down the sleeves of his shirt, noticing there was a speck of blood on his cuff.

'You're telling me Bauer has suspended the dig outside Tarascon because his men refuse to continue working?'

'Temporarily, yes, *mon capitaine*,' Laval said. 'They say the mountains are haunted. Bauer is waiting for new engineers to arrive from Munich.'

Authié took his jacket from the back of his chair and shrugged his arms into the sleeves.

'It's ridiculous.'

He glanced down at the report Fournier had given him once more, then put it in his pocket.

'I shall be an hour, no more,' he said.

'Do you want me to come with you, sir?'

'No,' he said, raising his eyebrows. 'A light touch is what's needed.'

Authié left the office and walked along the boulevard Maréchal Pétain. On the opposite corner, the Palais de Justice stood impassive and grand in the afternoon sun. Quiet today. He paused a moment, realising he was pleased to be back, then continued along the boulevard in the shade of the *platanes*, turned left on to the boulevard Omer Sarraut and carried on until he arrived at the Ménard garage.

A pair of legs were sticking out from beneath the chassis of a car up on bricks. Authié walked straight to the door leading to the domestic accommodation beyond the workshop and rapped on the glass.

Lucie heard the knock and hesitated before answering. She peered through the gap between the glass and the frame. A well-dressed man of average height, in an expensive grey suit and hat, well-cut clothes. She was sure she'd not met him before. She would have remembered.

'Mademoiselle Ménard?'

'Yes?'

'May I have a few minutes of your time?'

'Who are you?'

'Police,' he said.

A shiver went down her spine. 'I need to see some identification. You could be anyone,' she said.

He held his card up to the door, then withdrew it before Lucie could read it.

'If I might now come in, mademoiselle,' he said.

He did not raise his voice and his smile did not slip, but at the same time Lucie didn't feel able to refuse. She knew she looked dreadful. Her eyes were red and her hair was a mess. She had not bothered with powder or lipstick, and she was wearing an old red cardigan over the same summer dress she'd been wearing to see Sandrine, Liesl and Marieta off.

'I'm sorry,' she said, touching her hair. 'I wasn't expecting visitors.'

He took off his hat. 'Is there somewhere we can talk?'

Lucie glanced towards the kitchen, where her mother and a neighbour were discussing the release of their husbands from German POW camps. The train was due any day now. Whatever the man wanted, she didn't want her mother to know about it. She pulled the door to.

'We can talk in the workshop,' she said.

She led him through the house to the garage at the back, slid closed the heavy door separating the house from the *atelier*, then turned round, arms crossed, feeling as if she was holding herself together. Her heart was hammering and her throat was suddenly dry. Had he come to arrest her too? Surely not like this? Not just one man?

'Shall we sit down?' he said, gesturing to the long wooden bench that ran along one side of the garage wall.

'I'd rather stand, monsieur …'

'Authié,' he said. 'Captain Authié.'

'I'm sorry. Please make yourself at home.'

'Thank you.'

Lucie relaxed a little. If he had come to arrest her, he wouldn't be so polite, surely? He wouldn't have come alone?

'I have one or two questions I need to ask, if you don't mind.'

I do mind, Lucie wanted to scream, I mind very much. But she kept her expression neutral, her eyes blank.

'On Monday the thirteenth of July,' he began, 'you were driving past Païchérou at about ten o'clock in the morning. Is that correct?'

The words 'before Max ...' came into her mind, though she didn't speak. Everything, now, was divided into the time before Max had been arrested and the endless time since then.

'In a blue Peugeot 202,' he added, his eyes glancing to the far side of the workshop where the car was sitting in plain view.

'Yes,' she admitted.

'I'm not in the slightest bit interested in what you were doing, Mademoiselle Ménard, or who you were with. I merely want to know the name of the girl you picked up.'

'It was three weeks ago,' she said.

For a moment, Lucie saw a glint of irritation in his eyes, but he quickly smothered it and continued in the same pleasant tone. She dug in her pocket and pulled out a packet of cigarettes and a box of matches. She took out a cigarette and tried to open the matches, but her hands were shaking and they spilled all over the floor. She bent down, started to try to pick them up.

Authié stepped forward with a lighter. 'Here,' he said, then collected the scattered matches and put them on the workbench beside her.

Lucie tried to laugh. 'I'm sorry, I don't know what's got into me. I'm not sleeping very well, I ...' She drew on the cigarette.

'To be clear, you were driving past Païchérou on that Monday morning and you picked up a passenger, am I right?'

'I don't . . . I may have done.'

'Come now,' he said, sounding amused.

She wrapped her arms tightly around herself, feeling the ladder of her ribs beneath the thin cotton. 'Yes, all right, I did.'

'And what was her name?'

She tried to shrug. 'I didn't ask.'

Authié raised his eyebrows. 'You helped a girl, took her home, without ever asking her name?'

'It wasn't my business.'

'All right,' he said. 'Can you tell me where you took her, at least?'

'I . . . I can't rightly remember. As I say, it was more than a fortnight ago. Nearly three weeks.'

Lucie felt herself growing red under his scrutiny. She took another drag of the cigarette, but it didn't help. If anything, it was making her feel more sick. She hadn't eaten today. Had very little appetite at all these days. She stubbed the cigarette out on the edge of the bench, then put the stub in her pocket.

'You weren't alone that day, though, were you?' he said quietly.

Lucie felt the floor go out from under her. 'I – I can't remember, really I can't.'

'Wouldn't you like to know where he is, Mademoiselle Ménard?' he said softly. 'Your friend.'

Lucie stared at him. Could this man tell her what had happened to Max? Even Suzanne had failed to find out anything. This Authié might help her. She had no status, she wasn't a relative or his wife, they didn't have to tell her anything.

'Do you know where he is?' she said in a rush, all caution

forgotten. 'I'm going out of my mind with worry and no one will tell me anything.'

Authié stared at her, then carried on as if she hadn't spoken.

'We have reason to believe the young lady you helped was the victim of an assault. I understand your discretion, of course I do. I applaud it. But there have been one or two attacks on women recently. Unpleasant. If she saw something, it might help us catch this man.'

Lucie's hand stole to her stomach. What if she never found out where Max had been taken? Whether he was even still alive? In any case, what harm could it do to give him Sandrine's name? She'd gone to the police station herself. Lucie would only be passing on information they already had.

'She reported the attack to the police the day it happened,' she said. 'You must already have her details on file.'

For an instant, she thought she saw surprise flicker in the man's eyes, though it was masked immediately.

'It takes time for information to work its way through the system,' Authié said casually, 'as you can imagine. That's why I'm here now. To speed things along.'

'I see.'

'As regards Monsieur Blum,' Authié said, 'I can make no promises, but it's possible I could expedite matters.' He leant back against the wooden strut of the workbench. 'A name for a name, as it were. A fair exchange, wouldn't you say?'

'It's been nearly three weeks,' Lucie said, a catch in her voice. 'No one will tell me anything.'

Authié spread his hands wide. 'So, now. Are you sure you don't remember her name?'

Lucie's head told her not to say anything. Let Captain Authié find things out on his own. But her heart sang a different tune. Since the day of the demonstration, she'd barely slept. The instant her head touched the pillow at night, her mind was filled with images of Max handcuffed and beaten, imprisoned on a train, being sent she didn't know where.

The worst thing of all was that she felt guilty. Guilty that she had been with Marianne and Sandrine the evening he had been arrested, had drunk too much and fallen asleep on the sofa. If she had known what had happened earlier, perhaps she would have been able to do something. Get him released. Done something, anything.

'Mademoiselle Ménard?'

Captain Authié was offering her a chance to find out where Max had been taken. Then, at least, she could write to him. Start to try to get him home, sort out the misunderstanding.

'Her name's Vidal,' she said. 'Sandrine Vidal.'

Chapter 60

For a moment, the words seem to hang in the air between them.

'A name for a name, you said,' Lucie said desperately.

'I am a man of my word, Mademoiselle Ménard.'

Lucie flushed. 'Of course. I'm sorry, I didn't mean to suggest otherwise.' She faltered. 'Please.'

'Blum was in a consignment of prisoners sent to Le Vernet on the fifteenth of July.'

Lucie felt the air go out of her. She dropped her hand to the bench to steady herself. Of all the camps, she'd heard Le Vernet was the most notorious.

'His papers are in order,' she said in a hollow voice. 'Why was he arrested?'

'The details are not clear.'

'But what am I going to do?' she cried. 'Really, I can't bear it.'

Authié looked at her. 'If Monsieur Blum has done nothing and his papers are in order, then he has nothing to fear. You, Mademoiselle Ménard, have nothing to fear.'

'If that was true, I—'

'It's even possible I could arrange for you to see him.'

Colour flooded Lucie's pale face. 'Oh …'

'In return for a little help, Mademoiselle Ménard.'

'But I told you Sandrine's name.'

'I would like to speak to Mademoiselle Vidal,' he continued smoothly. 'We have her address on file, of course, as you said. But if you know it, that would be a great help. Speed everything up.'

'Rue du Palais,' she said. 'She lives with her sister

and housekeeper. The house with coloured tiles.'

Again the words – Judas words – seemed to hover in the air.

'You see?' he said pleasantly. 'That wasn't so hard, was it?'

'What about Max?' she said quickly. 'Can you arrange for me to see him?'

Authié put on his hat. 'I shall look into the situation. I'll be in touch if there is any news.'

'When will that be?' she said, desperate not to let him go until she had an answer.

He pulled open the sliding doors. 'Thank you for your help, mademoiselle. I'll see myself out.'

Lucie listened to his footsteps echoing down the corridor, then the sound of the front door opening and closing. She slumped down against the bench. She felt hollow and weak, but for the first time in three weeks, there was hope.

She took the stub of the cigarette from her pocket and managed to strike and hold the match. This time, it calmed her beating heart. She kept telling herself she'd done nothing wrong.

He had Sandrine's name already. He only had to check the files.

Lucie thought for a moment more, then went into the house to the telephone. She should at least tell Marianne what had happened. She'd not seen much of her or Suzanne since Sandrine left. She'd not visited the rue du Palais.

She dialled the number. The line was busy. Lucie shut her eyes and tried to picture Max's face. Captain Authié hadn't come flanked by officers or threatened her. And he could help Max. He had promised. Almost promised, at least.

'A name for a name,' she murmured, dialling again.

This time, the number rang, but nobody answered. If she couldn't get through, she'd have to go to the rue du

Palais in person. She didn't want to. Marianne would be impatient and high-minded. She always was. She wouldn't understand how finding Max had to take priority over everything else. And it was so hot and she felt so unwell.

Lucie's hand went to her stomach again. She had to think of the future.

Chapter 61

Authié went directly from the boulevard Omer Sarraut to the Commissariat to check the police files. There was nothing on Sandrine Vidal, but it appeared there was a substantial surveillance file on her sister, Marianne.

A teacher at the Lycée des Filles on Square Gambetta, her name was on a list of teachers who had refused to implement the new academic curriculum. She had continued to teach Jews alongside French students, declined to carry out monitoring. Undesirable authors such as Brecht, Zweig and Heine remained on the shelves in her classroom. The father and mother were both dead. The only other resident of the house was a housekeeper, who had been with the family for years.

Authié re-emerged into the sunlight and looked at his wristwatch. He had plenty of time before Bauer was due to call, enough time to visit the house himself. Five minutes later he was standing in the rue du Palais looking up at the impressive façade. Vidal had clearly left his daughters well provided for. Plenty of space, he thought. The sort of house that might well be used by partisans for any number of purposes.

Authié walked up the steps and knocked. He heard muffled voices, then footsteps. The door was opened by a tall woman with short cropped hair and slacks.

'Mademoiselle Vidal?'

The woman folded her arms. 'No.'

'Is Mademoiselle Vidal at home?'

'Who wants to know?'

Authié reached into his pocket and produced his identification. The woman read it, hesitated, then stood back to let him in.

'Who is it?' came a voice from inside.

'Police,' the tall woman said, closing the front door.

Authié walked into the salon before she could stop him. A slender, brown-haired woman sitting on a sofa beneath the window immediately got to her feet.

'Marianne Vidal?'

'Yes.'

'And your friend?'

'A guest,' she said. 'What can I do for you, monsieur?'

'Authié. Captain, in fact,' he said. 'And your guest's name?'

'Is this relevant, Captain Authié?'

Authié's interest quickened. Her expression was wary. Most ordinary citizens were nervous in the presence of the police, but there was a watchfulness in this woman's eyes that suggested something more guarded.

'Don't be obstructive, Mademoiselle Vidal.'

'I'm sorry, I didn't mean to give that impression.'

Authié turned to the other woman, who answered.

'Suzanne Peyre.'

'What can I do for you, Captain Authié?' asked Marianne.

'It's your sister, Sandrine, I want to talk to. Is she here?'

Again the same flash of alarm, though her voice gave no indication of it.

'I'm afraid not.'

'Do you have any idea how long she might be?'

'I'm sorry, no.' She smiled pleasantly.

Authié's gaze hardened. 'Where is she, Mademoiselle Vidal?'

Marianne kept her expression in place. 'I don't know,

I'm afraid. She went out first thing this morning. I didn't see her leave.'

'Perhaps your housekeeper might know,' he said. 'Fetch her, please.'

'I'll go,' said Suzanne, immediately leaving the room.

Marianne paused. 'May I ask why you want to talk to my sister?'

'I believe it was someone called Lucie Ménard and her friend – a Jew – who came to the help of your sister after her unfortunate accident.'

'I beg your pardon?'

'You were aware your sister was the victim of a crime committed three weeks ago. Monday the thirteenth of July?'

'Not a crime, Captain Authié,' she said calmly. 'She had an accident. Came off her bike, that's all.'

'Mademoiselle Ménard told me she was attacked.'

'Mademoiselle Ménard is mistaken.'

'The report at the police station says your sister claimed to have been attacked.'

The reaction was tiny, immediately masked, but it was there all the same.

'It's true my sister went to the Commissariat straight away, Captain Authié, but frankly I was cross with her for wasting police time. I believed – and still do – that her injury was the result of an accident.'

Despite himself, Authié was impressed with her self-control. 'You thought she was making it up?'

'I think she was muddled after the accident.'

'So you were not aware there have been several attacks on women in Carcassonne, Mademoiselle Vidal?'

Marianne held his gaze. 'I was also under the impression that since the victims have all been Jewish, the police were not taking the matter seriously.'

Authié raised his eyebrows. 'Are you criticising the police, mademoiselle?'

'An observation, Captain Authié.'

'You confuse Carcassonne with Paris, Mademoiselle Vidal.'

'I hope that's the case, Captain Authié.'

He paused. 'Your sister did not say anything about her assailant?'

'She said all sorts of things, which, as I mentioned, I'm afraid I didn't take seriously. I no longer recall the ins and outs of the conversation. It's nearly three weeks ago.'

'She did not mention the name Raoul Pelletier, for example?'

And there it was for the third time, Authié thought, a spark of knowledge.

'Marieta seems to have slipped out,' Suzanne Peyre said, appearing in the doorway.

Authié looked from one woman to the other. 'I appear to be out of luck,' he said wryly. 'I shall have to come back later and hope your sister will be back. Or perhaps return to speak to Mademoiselle Ménard. She was inclined to be helpful. She might remember something else.'

He lifted his hat, then strode back into the hallway and out of the house without giving them the chance to respond. Authié crossed the street and turned to look back at the building. Had the girl been sent away, perhaps? It seemed strange that both she and the housekeeper were not at home. He wondered what Suzanne Peyre had been doing to have been away from the room for so long. He was impatient to return to the office to see if there was a file on her too.

He felt a prickling on the back of his neck, certain he was being watched. In the house next door to the Vidals, a curtain dropped back into place, but it was long enough for him to recognise the woman inside. He knew one of his informers lived in the quartier du Palais, but hadn't realised it was this house. He walked up the steps.

'Madame Fournier, ' he said, when she answered the door. 'I wonder if I might prevail upon you?'

Chapter 62

TARASCON

Erik Bauer dabbed at his neck with his handkerchief, the flattening August sun too much for his northern blood. He took off his hat, fanned his face, shifting the still air, then put it back on his head.

Bauer was proud to be a member of the Ahnenerbe. As a boy, he had read Wolfram von Eschenbach's grail writings and the great Germanic legends, celebrated the music of the *Minnesänger*. Like the Führer himself, Bauer had stood before the Spear of Longinius in its glass case in the Hofburg Museum in Vienna. When the Habsburg Treasures were moved from Austria to Nuremberg after the Anschluss, Bauer had applied to the Ancestral Heritage Research and Teaching Society, under the leadership of Reichsführer Himmler, and finally been accepted. He was one of thousands of scientists and historians all over the world – Egypt, South America, France – seeking artefacts to prove the historic existence of a superior, an Aryan, race and to substantiate its claims. The grail books of the Cathars, the lost treasure taken from the Temple of Solomon after the Sack of Jerusalem, other objects of antiquity said to be hidden within the mountains of the Languedoc. He despised Rahn and had been one of those who'd denounced him for his degeneracy, but he had found the man's writings compelling all the same. Bauer hoped that if he could find the key, even the Codex itself, then he would come to the attention of those higher in the party.

He was convinced that this particular network of caves

between Niaux and Tarascon was not going to yield results. They had been thoroughly excavated before the war with no significant success. Even so, he wished to guard against anyone else getting in, in case he was mistaken. He knew the locals would swarm all over the site as soon as they had gone.

'Obersturmführer?'

The chief engineer, a stocky, bull-like man, was waiting for orders.

Bauer nodded. '*Beginnen Sie.*'

Bauer watched the foreman instruct his men to place the dynamite charges at equal intervals along the opening to the cave, a little distance from the ground. Once set, another man climbed above and placed three along the upper edge of the rock face. In natural rock falls and landslides, there was usually a section where the rock was thinner. Bauer wanted to make sure there were no weak places through which someone could gain access.

The foreman uncoiled the wires that led to the charge box, then carried the device as far away from the opening to the caves as he could.

'*Ist es bereit?*' Bauer asked. It's ready?

The foreman nodded. Bauer and the three other men took cover, then the foreman depressed the handle. The dynamite did its work. An immediate crump, then the force of the explosion snaking through the ground. A moment of suspended silence, then the rumble of rock as the cave entrance began to collapse in upon itself.

Only when the aftershock of white clouds of dust mushroomed up into the hot air did Bauer emerge from his hiding place.

He looked at the entrance, now entirely blocked, then nodded.

'*Gut gemacht.* You have done well,' he said. He dabbed

the back of his neck again with his damp handkerchief. 'Tell your men to pack up. Clear everything. We move north tonight.'

Chapter 63

CARCASSONNE

Marianne dropped the last of the false identity papers into the sink. She put a match to them, watched the flames flare and die, then turned on the tap. The kitchen was filled with the stink of damp ash.

'That's the lot,' she said. 'What a waste.'

Suzanne nodded. Her hands were stained black where she had carried each sodden, pulpy armful outside. There was a small patch of earth beneath the kitchen window where she'd buried the evidence, hidden from the Fournier house by the overhang of the balcony. She went back to the sink and washed her hands, scrubbing at them until the last of the ink and ash was gone.

'What are you going to do now?' she said, shaking them dry.

'Send a telegram to Sandrine to warn her about Authié.'

'What about Lucie?'

Marianne's face grew still. 'I can't believe she'd do such a thing.'

Suzanne put her hand on her friend's shoulder. 'Why don't I go and see what she's got to say? But I've got to find Robert Bonnet first and tell him we've had to get rid of this lot.'

Marianne sighed. 'After all your hard work.'

'Better safe than sorry.'

'I know. Even so.'

Suzanne leant forward, gave Marianne a peck on the cheek. 'Be back as soon as I can.'

Marianne bolted the door after she'd gone, then walked briskly through the house to collect her purse, hat and gloves. The silence seemed to echo around her. When the others first left for Coustaussa, frankly it had been a relief and she'd enjoyed the peace. Liesl was no trouble, but her unhappy presence cast a pall over the house. Sandrine had been the opposite, rushing around to check the post each morning, then going to the library and the cathedral, trying to do too many things at once. Marieta had been withdrawn and anxious. But now she hated the quiet. And every day, she felt more tired. Less able to cope. If it hadn't been for Suzanne, she would have gone out of her mind with the strain.

A knock on the front door made her jump. For a moment she was tempted to ignore it, then she heard Lucie's voice.

'I need to talk to you,' she said in a loud whisper.

'Talk? Don't you mean apologise?' muttered Marianne.

'Please.'

With a sigh, she opened the door and Lucie stepped inside. Marianne was shocked at her appearance. She looked wan and drawn, with dark roots showing through her corn-coloured hair.

'Your Captain Authié has just left.'

Lucie's eyes widened. 'He's been here already?'

'What do you expect?' she said sharply. 'You could have at least telephoned to warn us you'd blabbed to the police.'

Lucie flushed. 'I tried to, but the line was occupied.'

'You can't have tried awfully hard.'

Lucie lifted her chin. 'I'm here now, aren't I?'

Marianne's self-control snapped. 'Whatever were you thinking? Authié's with the police. Deuxième Bureau, more likely than not. How could you tell him anything?'

'You say that as if I'm supposed to know what it means,'

Lucie said, 'but I don't. I don't care about all that kind of thing. He was civil to me, that's all I know. He says he can help me find Max.'

'Help you?' Marianne said in disbelief. 'Don't be so naïve.'

'Don't grumble at me, I can't bear it,' Lucie said. 'It was Sandrine who went to the police in the first instance. *She* was the one who made a report, not me. I begged her not to. It's not my fault.'

Marianne took a deep breath. Tried to get her temper under control, knowing there was a grain of truth in what Lucie said. Knowing she was angry with herself, too. Because nearly three weeks had gone by, she'd allowed herself to think the danger had passed.

'All right,' she said, holding up her hands. 'All right, all right.'

'He knows where Max has been taken,' Lucie said, her voice threatening to break. 'I can't bear not knowing, Marianne. After all these weeks with no news. I couldn't bear it a moment longer.'

Marianne sighed, then chose her words with care. 'I understand you're desperate – and although Suzanne and I have done our best, it's true we've failed to find anything out – but even so, you know better than to tell the authorities anything. It's why you advised Sandrine against going to the police in the first place.'

'Well,' Lucie said, regaining a little of her spirit, 'Captain Authié said that what happened to Sandrine is connected to the other attacks on women. That's the only reason he wants to talk to her.'

'You don't believe that, surely?'

Lucie's chin shot up. 'Why not? He seemed decent enough. I don't see why you have to mistrust everyone.'

Marianne narrowed her eyes. 'What else did you tell him?'

'Nothing,' she said quickly. 'Only Sandrine's name. And address, but she'd already given that to the police anyway.'

'You didn't say she'd gone to Coustaussa?'

'As if.' Lucie's eyes flashed. 'Oh, I suppose you're not going to trust me or tell me anything?'

'Do you blame me? Obviously I don't trust you. Why would I? There, I've said it. Is that what you wanted to hear?'

'I came here to own up,' Lucie shouted. 'I've been worrying about it all day, even though it wasn't me that started it.' She paused. 'And I'll tell you this for nothing. If Sandrine had been arrested, taken somewhere and you didn't know where, you would do the same. You'd do anything to find her.'

Marianne dropped her shoulders. 'You see, that's it, Lucie,' she said quietly. 'I wouldn't. I wouldn't betray my friends.'

Lucie stared at her for an instant, then ran out of the house, slamming the door behind her. Marianne sank down on the seat of the hat stand and put her head in her hands. Lucie didn't think she'd done anything wrong. She hadn't told the police anything Sandrine hadn't told them herself, and there were some who weren't in Vichy's pocket. Gaullists not Pétainists. She had been harsh on her, she knew it. Lucie had never shown the slightest interest in anything around her: politics, the town council, laws and rules and regulations, all went over her head. She'd always been like that.

But for the first time, Marianne was genuinely frightened, cold down to her bones. Everything seemed to be spiralling out of control. The worst of it was, she didn't know what she could do to stop it. She wished she was in Coustaussa too. At least then she would know Sandrine was all right. There, she could forget real life and go back to how things used to be. Play a game of cards or listen to the wireless. Ordinary, humdrum things.

All she wanted was to feel safe again.

Chapter 64

COUSTAUSSA

Sandrine opened the shutters on another humid and overcast morning. Grey clouds scudding the hills, a sense of bristling threat carried on the breeze. Perhaps at last the weather would break. They needed a thunderstorm to clear the air.

It had been a busy three days, she'd hardly had a chance to miss Raoul or Marianne at all. She had visited each of their neighbours in turn, receiving condolences, accepting gifts of food, catching up on the life of Coustaussa since they had last been there. She had introduced Liesl to everyone and, although a few had raised their eyebrows at the arrival of a Parisian cousin, nobody said anything.

Between them she, Liesl and Marieta had got the house straight and stocked the larder as best they could, cleaned out the plumbing and chased spiders from the house. Sandrine had also rearranged the furniture in the salon, moving her father's favourite chair so that it wasn't the first thing she saw when she went into the room. The little house felt like home again.

It was Friday already and she couldn't put off going to Couiza any longer. Ernest had rung Marianne on the day of their arrival, just to let her know they'd arrived safely, and he had spoken to his brother in the town hall. But Sandrine had to go in and present their papers in person – they needed temporary ration books, there were all sorts of forms to be filled in, filed, ticked, stamped. Yellow, red, white, blue, all of life recorded and recorded again. She was dreading it, all the queuing and bad tempers in the heat. On top of everything else, Marieta seemed particularly tired this morning.

'I'm not sure we should leave you,' Sandrine said again. 'You look all in.'

Marieta clasped her hands in front of her. 'There's still plenty to be done and I don't want you under my feet, getting in the way,' she replied. 'In any case, the storm's coming.'

'Are you sure?' Liesl peered out at the hazy sky, white and flat and lowering. 'It's been like this ever since we got here.'

'Blowing up from the south,' Marieta said doggedly. 'Best to go now, madomaisèla.'

Sandrine sighed, knowing Marieta was always right about the weather. 'Well, all right. We'll be as quick as we can, but please, please promise me you won't overdo it. Marianne would never forgive me if she thought I was running you ragged.'

Marieta smiled. 'As if,' she said. 'Besides, how will she know, *è*?'

Sandrine smiled back, but she was on edge as she walked to the lean-to at the end of the garden and got out the bikes.

'Is Marieta all right?' Liesl said.

'She's tired, but she won't ease up.'

She noticed Liesl had the camera Max had given her in its case on a strap around her neck.

'Isn't that rather heavy? Are you sure you want to bring it?' she said.

'It reminds me of . . .' Liesl began, then stopped. 'I like to keep it with me,' in a quieter voice. 'In case there's something to photograph.'

'I'm going to call Marianne from Couiza,' Sandrine

said quickly. 'I'm sure there'll be news by now.'

Liesl said nothing.

It took fifteen minutes to get down to the town. It was very humid, oppressive air, so they were both out of breath by the time they arrived at the Mairie.

'You have your new papers, your *carte d'identité*?' Sandrine asked Liesl for the third time.

'Everything.'

They joined the long queue of people waiting to be seen, shuffling forward step by step. Suzanne had acquired false papers for Liesl, but this would be the first time they had tried to use them. What would happen if the official noticed something wrong and challenged them? Sandrine knew there was nothing she could do, she had simply to hold her nerve and hope Liesl did the same, but she kept checking and checking everything again.

'Good morning,' she said brightly, when they reached the head of the queue. She handed over all three sets of papers.

'There's only two of you,' the official said, peering at her over the top of his spectacles.

'Marieta Barthès remained in Coustaussa. Ernest said he—'

The man's face lightened. 'Ah, you're Mademoiselle Vidal.'

'That's right,' said Sandrine, the words coming out in a rush. 'Sandrine Vidal.'

'And this is,' he glanced at the photograph, then up at Liesl, 'the other Mademoiselle Vidal.'

He stamped the documents quickly, then handed the papers back. 'Third door on the left.'

Thanks to Ernest's brother, they found themselves moving swiftly through the system. Even so, it took a long time. They were sent from bureau to bureau, answering the same questions over and again. Presenting Marieta's papers, explaining she was too old to come in person. It got easier, but each time Sandrine's heart was in her mouth.

Finally, after three hours, they emerged with temporary ration books and *permis de séjour.*

'We did it,' Sandrine said, under her breath. She squeezed Liesl's hand. 'So what do you say to some lunch? I'm starving.'

Liesl smiled. 'I could manage something,' she admitted.

The Grand Café Guilhem on the bridge by the railway station was serving lunch – tomatoes, black bread, white goat's cheese and cured ham. Liesl left the ham, but was persuaded to order a cherry ice to follow. Sandrine tried a little, but it tasted of saccharine.

'I'm going to try to get through to Marianne. Find out how things are at home and let her know everything's gone all right at our end,' Sandrine said when they'd finished. 'It's bound to take a while. Will you be all right for an hour or so?'

Agreeing to meet outside the post office in an hour, the girls separated. Liesl went off in the direction of the river with her camera and Sandrine joined yet another queue. The Tramontana was still twisting up the dust and the thermometer was pushing ever higher.

It was a slow, hot business as the line moved slowly forward. The three customers ahead of Sandrine all wanted to place calls interzone and the operator was struggling to cope. Tempers were fraying. The closer people got to the front, the more anxious they became that whatever they wanted would sell out – stamps, envelopes – and there were a few near arguments, sharp elbows and *paniers*, each person determined to have her rights.

As Sandrine moved forward, one step at a time, she thought about how she could persuade Marieta not to work so hard all the time. She wondered where Raoul might be now. As the days passed with no word of him, the sharp pain of his absence had dulled into a regretful ache. She missed him, but she couldn't allow herself to pine. There was too much to do. Another shuffle forward. From time to time, fragments of conversations broke into her reflections.

'Nine thousand police and gendarmes, so I heard,' said a woman, joining her husband in the queue. 'Herded them all in some cycling stadium, north of Paris. It's been in all the papers.'

'Was it the Vélodrome d'Hiver?'

'I don't know.'

The man sighed, pushing his hat back on his head. 'Lovely racing track, that. Went there once. Saw Antonin Magne take his Grand Prix.'

'Twenty-five thousand of them, Jews, all packed in there.'

'That happened three weeks ago,' said a middle-aged woman in a garish housecoat. 'Day after Bastille Day, or that's what it said in the papers.'

'Foreigners, were they?'

'I suppose so,' the wife said. 'Wouldn't be French, would they? I mean to say.'

'If they're foreign,' said the man, 'then I'm for it. We should send them all home. It's always France that has to put up with the riff-raff, thieves the lot of them.'

Sandrine realised her nails were digging into her palms. She had become used to hearing such sentiments in Carcassonne, but she had expected – hoped – things would be different here.

The queue moved forward again. Then, without warning, she saw Raoul staring at her.

'Oh …'

Looking straight at her from the pillar, a black and white poster with his face on it. Above the photograph, a single word in capital letters: RÉCOMPENSE.

Sandrine had expected to see something like this in Carcassonne. Raoul had warned her she might. But even though she'd been on the lookout, she'd not seen a thing and, as the days passed and still his face was absent from the police posters papering the town, she hoped they'd given up trying to find him. RÉCOMPENSE. PELLETIER, RAOUL.

Her pulse started to race and she felt dizzy, blindsided by the sight of him.

'Mademoiselle?'

At first, Sandrine didn't hear. She wanted to reach out and touch the poster, but she dared not. Then she felt a finger poking into her back.

'It's your turn,' said the woman behind her in the queue.

'*Pardon*,' Sandrine said, tearing her eyes away. 'Sorry, I'm sorry.'

She stepped up to the window, feeling sick. If there was a poster in Couiza, all the way down here, then that was bound to mean there were posters everywhere. All the towns and villages. Raoul wouldn't stand a chance.

'How can I help, mademoiselle?'

All those pairs of eyes, somebody would see him and take the chance to claim the reward. It was so much money.

'Mademoiselle?' the operator said, more sharply.

Sandrine forced herself to concentrate. With a last glance back at Raoul's face, she put her purse on the counter and got out her papers once more.

'I need to place a call to Carcassonne.'

Chapter 65

Coustaussa

Marieta looked around. She had spent the morning cleaning, but there was still dust everywhere. The consequences of a house left unlived in for two years, as if it was getting its own back for being abandoned. She moved the empty vase on the hall table. She had done it earlier, but there was still a ring on the table. The banisters, too, could do with another layer of polish.

The thunder was closer. It wouldn't be long before the rain started. Marieta knew she should go and check that all the shutters were securely fastened, but she was so weary.

'*Apuèi*,' she murmured.

Why was there no word from Monsieur Baillard? No letter? It had been three weeks. And all of Sandrine's endless questions, always questions she couldn't answer. Marieta lowered herself down to the chair in the hall, hearing the wood creak and sigh. Maybe he had received the letter and was making his way to Coustaussa? The thought gave her some spark of comfort, even though there was no reason for him to know she was here.

It was so close, so humid, she could barely breathe. She felt the sheen of sweat on her brow. The rain would clear the air. The burden of her knowledge, scant as it was, was growing heavier. Not knowing whether he'd even received the letter. She couldn't wait a moment longer. There was no question of making the journey herself to Rennes-les-Bains. It was too far to walk on her tired legs. Perhaps Madame Rousset could ask Yves to take her in the trap?

She took her Bible from the pocket of her housecoat and placed it on the table, her work-worn hand resting on the black leather cover. Last night, as the Tramontana rattled between the hills, she had sat up in bed in her room under the eaves and, by candlelight, turned to the Book of the Revelation of St John the Divine, the last book of the New Testament. A text Marieta both loved and feared, the words had nonetheless brought her some measure of peace.

Her head jerked up as another warning gust sent something scuttling in the road outside. A flowerpot, perhaps? She hoped it wasn't a tile coming off the roof. Then she realised it was someone knocking on the door.

'Monsieur Baillard,' she said quickly, the wish father to the deed.

As she pulled herself to her feet, a jab of pain snaked down her left arm. Marieta ignored it as she hurried to the front door and pulled it open.

'*Perfin …*'

A wave of disappointment swept through her at the sight of Geneviève Saint-Loup standing on the step, smiling.

'*Bonjorn*, Marieta, I heard you were back in Coustaussa. Is Sandrine here?'

Marieta caught her breath. 'No, she and …' She broke off, not sure what she was allowed to say, not even to Sandrine's oldest friend. 'She's not here.'

Geneviève was frowning. 'Are you all right, Marieta? You look awfully pale.'

'Quite fine.' She made an effort to smile. 'Madomaisèla Sandrine has gone to Couiza to arrange our *permis de séjour*.'

'The new mayor is all right,' Geneviève said, still looking concerned.

'Good.'

'I have a telegram for Sandrine from Marianne. She wants her to telephone as soon as she can.'

'Is something wrong in Carca ...?' Marieta began to say, but another stab of pain stole her words from her. 'In Carcassonne?'

'Are you sure you're all right?' Geneviève said. 'Is there anything I can do?'

'It's the humidity, nothing more. I'll be fine as soon as the weather breaks, and it will.'

Geneviève didn't looked convinced. 'Well, will you tell Sandrine that Friday's my day off. The rest of the week she can find me in the post office in Rennes-les-Bains if she wants to come down.'

Marieta shot out her hand and grasped Geneviève's arm. 'The post office?'

Geneviève nodded. 'That's right, I've been working there for six months now.'

'I sent a letter from Carcassonne to the post office,' Marieta said urgently. 'For Monsieur Baillard. Has it arrived, can you recall? Three weeks past.'

'He had a letter from Tarascon round about that time, but nothing from Carcassonne. I'm sorry.'

'Are you sure?'

'Quite sure. I've been looking out especially for ... He came in person.'

'You've seen him?'

'Yes. It was around Bastille Day, then again a few days after that. He said he was going south, then on to Tarascon.'

A wave of relief rushed through Marieta's tired body. She gave a long sigh.

'Did he seem well to you?'

'Yes, he looked in good health, given his age ...' Geneviève tailed off. 'If I see him, do you want me to tell him you were asking after him?'

'Yes, yes. Tell him ...' She hesitated, not sure what to say. 'Tell him I must see him. That it is urgent. You won't forget?'

'No, of course not, but . . . Are you sure you are all right, Na Marieta? Can I get you a glass of water, perhaps?'

'Perhaps I will lie down,' she said, keen for the girl to go. 'You should get off before the storm, *è*. Thank you for coming.'

Marieta forced herself to stand on the front step and wave while Geneviève disappeared down the hill, then she went back inside. She was light-headed with the relief of knowing that Monsieur Baillard was all right. That he was close at hand. Only now did she realise how much she had been worrying that something had happened to him – injured during the war, or even captured, she didn't know what. But now, now she didn't have to worry any more. Geneviève would tell Monsieur Baillard she was here and he would come to Coustaussa.

'*A la perfin*,' she murmured. 'At last.'

Pressing the heel of her hand to her chest, Marieta lowered herself back on to the same tattered chair at the foot of the stairs. A gust of wind shrieked under the door. She hoped that if the storm reached as far north as Carcassonne, Marianne would close the windows in the kitchen. She remembered she still hadn't checked the shutters at the back of the house were secure, but she hadn't the strength to move. She picked up the Bible from the hall table and turned to read from the Book of Revelation.

'*Voici ce que dit celui qui a les sept esprits de Dieu et les sept étoiles: Je connais tes oeuvres. Je sais que tu passes pour être vivant, et tu es mort.*'

Some of the words Sandrine had written reminded her of these ancient verses. Marieta didn't understand how that could be, but had faith Monsieur Baillard would explain.

'These things say he who has the seven spirits of God and the seven stars: I have knowledge of your works, that you seem to be living but are dead.'

Another rumble of dry thunder. Marieta thought the

storm was still some way off, but hoped the girls wouldn't be caught out in the open. Her arm was aching so much, it hurt to hold the Bible steady in her hands.

'*Puis je vis le ciel ouvert*,' she recited. '*Le ciel ouvert* … Then I saw that heaven was open …'

Marieta felt a sudden sharp pain in her chest, clean and precise. She tried to focus on the spidery words written on the thin pages. The Bible fell from her lap to the ground. The tissue-thin pages of the Book of Revelation fluttered, stirred up by the wind, like the wings of a trapped moth battling against the glass to be free.

Chapter 66

Couiza

Liesl was waiting for Sandrine outside the post office when she came out.

'Did you get through?'

Sandrine didn't hear. She was still poleaxed by the sight of Raoul's face on the poster.

'Sandrine?'

'No, I'm sorry, I'm afraid not,' she said. 'No one answered.'

'So, no news,' Liesl said in a small voice.

'I'll try again tomorrow. I want to speak to Marianne anyway, I don't mind coming back.'

Liesl turned away, busying herself with the strap on her camera case. Sandrine's heart went out to the girl, realising how hard she was trying not to let her emotions show.

'What would you say to another ice?' Sandrine said. 'Give us an extra push before we head off back up the hill?'

'I'm not hungry.'

'No, but something to drink, at least. It's the wrong way around, I always think. Downhill when you're starting out, and uphill when it's time to go home.'

'Shouldn't we get back to Marieta?'

Sandrine glanced up at the glowering sky, then back to Liesl. 'I don't want to be caught out in the open,' she said. 'Might be better to wait it out here, then go home. Half an hour here or there won't make much difference.'

They got back to the Grand Café Guilhem, where they'd left their bikes, just as the heavens opened. They sheltered under the awning of the café, but the wind was coming from all angles and they were soaked all the same. Inside, the lights flickered with each tremble of thunder. Sandrine considered going in, but then she noticed two policemen standing at the zinc counter. Liesl was nervous enough as it was. It would be so easy to say the wrong thing or be rattled into letting her real name slip.

'Are you all right out here?' she said.

Liesl nodded, understanding, though her face was white.

'You didn't have any trouble while I was in the post office?' Sandrine said, realising she should have asked before.

'No one took any notice of me.'

Sandrine sighed. 'That's good. So, do you think you'll be happy enough here for the time being? You won't miss Carcassonne too much?'

'Until Max comes back, yes.'

A sudden clap of thunder overhead made Liesl jump.

'Our neighbours in Coustaussa are nice, most of them at least,' Sandrine hurried on, talking to keep the younger girl's mind off the impending storm. 'Monsieur Andrieu, who we met on Wednesday, he owns most of the fields to the north and the large white farm on the edge of the village. You wouldn't know it. Never throws his weight around. My father's closest friend was Monsieur Sauzède, one of those very proper, very old-fashioned men, but with a wonderful sense of humour.'

Liesl looked at her. 'You miss your father?'

'All the time,' she said. She took a deep breath, then carried on. 'Ernestine Cassou, she's a different matter. Lives in the end house in the rue de l'Empereur with her father. Never without a grievance, as Marieta would say.'

Liesl managed a smile. 'I admit, I didn't take to her.'

'My closest friend is Geneviève Saint-Loup. One of four sisters, she lives in Rennes-les-Bains. I hope you'll meet her at the weekend. When we were little we spent all of our time in Coustaussa, playing *cache-cache* in the ruins of the castle with the village boys.'

Liesl looked up briefly. 'Like the boy who met us off the bus?'

'Yves Rousset?' Sandrine said. 'Yes, him and his older brother, all of their friends. Pierre Rousset was killed at the beginning of the war.'

'Yves seems nice.'

'He is nice,' Sandrine replied, momentarily hearing something lighter in Liesl's voice. 'Quiet, but kind. Reliable.'

'Is he . . .?'

'The Roussets are decent types. The kind that help if asked, but otherwise mind their own business.'

A torrent was cascading down the street, a mass of swirling black water hurtling into the storm drains and towards the river. Another crack of thunder, followed, hard on its heels, by a white jag of lightning. Liesl's eyes flared wide with terror.

'When I was little,' Sandrine said quickly, 'Marieta used to tell me the thunder was God rearranging his furniture, dragging a chair across the sky. The lightning was angels turning the lights on and off.'

Liesl clutched her camera even tighter.

'It won't last much longer,' Sandrine said.

The storm was now directly overhead, swallowing Couiza up within the clouds. The driving rain pounded down on the road like sparks from an anvil. Liesl trembled at each new assault, peering out at the furious black sky.

'This is the worst of it, then it will move on.'

'To Carcassonne?'

'Maybe. Limoux, certainly.'

They stood in silence, Sandrine enjoying the relief of being cold and damp after the hot, humid days. The sight of Raoul's face had brought all those buried feelings back to the surface. The memory of the touch of his hand on her skin. Watching the sun rise over the Cité. She sighed. Where was he? Sitting out the storm like them, or miles away on the Vermilion Coast? In Banyuls or Perpignan?

At first, the shock of seeing the poster when she wasn't expecting it had driven any other thought from her mind. Now it had had time to sink in, she realised what puzzled her the most was that the reward was so large. It wasn't unusual these days to see WANTED notices stuck up all over the place – on lamp posts, walls, pinned on the noticeboard outside the Commissariat de Police – offering money for information. But five hundred francs?

So much. Too much.

Another collision of thunder in the sky directly above them, and Liesl grabbed at Sandrine's arm.

'I can't bear it,' she said in a whisper. 'It's so wild, so … so angry. I've never heard anything like it.'

Sandrine put her arms around Liesl and held her close.

Chapter 67

TARASCON

Aurélie Saint-Loup was sitting on the front doorstep, looking aggrieved.

'I've been waiting for ages,' she complained.

Baillard bent down to the child's level. 'What is it, *filha*?'

'My sister Geneviève telephoned from Rennes-les-Bains.'

'Has a package arrived for me?' he said quickly.

Even now he hoped Antoine might have managed to keep the package safe before he was captured.

'A package?' the little girl asked. 'I don't know about that. Geneviève wanted you to know Marieta Barthès is in Coustaussa and asking urgently after you. She sent me to find you.'

Baillard stood up and glanced at Pujol, who'd drawn level. He looked tired, the result of several days of asking questions and getting nowhere. Célestine was coping, but Pierre was not. Pujol felt he was letting his friend down.

'Marieta Barthès . . .' Baillard smiled at the thought of seeing her. 'And the family also?'

Aurélie shrugged. 'I don't know, only that it was important. She didn't think Madame Barthès looked very well.' The child frowned. 'Geneviève sounded a bit funny, actually.'

'Is it possible, Achille?' Baillard asked.

Pujol took a moment to realise, then his expression altered.

'You're not seriously suggesting we go to Coustaussa now, Audric? The storm's heading that way. The roads will be impassable, you know what those valleys are like.'

'Marieta is not the sort of woman to make a fuss. If she says it is urgent, then it will be.' He paused. 'And if she is ill . . .'

Pujol looked at him, then sighed with resignation. 'I'll go and see if I can find a car. And enough petrol to get us there and back.'

They'd been driving for an hour. Baillard had been thinking of a girl he'd loved when he was young. Loved still. Remembering the banners and colours and the towers of the Cité. He looked down at his hands and flexed his fingers. He could almost feel the warm metal of his sword in his hand.

The Midi had lost the battle then, but what of now?

'E ara?'

'What's that, Audric?' said Pujol, peering through the windscreen at the rain.

Baillard shook his head. 'Nothing, my friend. Talking to myself.'

'Don't wonder at it. Clambering all over the hills at four o'clock in the morning, yesterday, the day before, the day before that. We're too old for it, Audric. I keep telling you, but do you listen?'

Baillard peered out of the window. 'Where are we?'

'Just gone through Espéraza. The roads are worse than I was expecting.'

Evidence of the storm was everywhere. Broken branches, pools of standing water, mud the colour of gingerbread where rainwater had cascaded down the hillside. Baillard looked out of the window and saw the land as a living, sentient thing. A sleeping giant brought to life by the whisperings and stirrings of bones in the earth. In the graveyards of the Haute Vallée and the mountains where no tombstone marked the place where warriors had fallen.

'The glorious dead awakened,' he murmured.

Could it be true? Could such things yet be true? With every passing day, the evil from the north was coming closer and closer. Such evil.

'Malfança . . .'

They entered Couiza. A woman in black was sweeping the debris from her steps. She stopped and stared at the solitary car.

The road was carpeted with twigs and leaves. As Pujol negotiated the winding, slippery road up to Coustaussa, Baillard gripped the dashboard. He had faced many perilous situations in his long life, battles for faith and tolerance, survived siege and torture, but the fear in his stomach with the wheels of the car slippery under Pujol's clumsy touch was just as sharp.

'Go through the village,' he instructed, trying to keep his voice calm. 'Almost out to the other side. Last house.'

A small white dog barked at them, then shot away as they drew up outside the house. The geraniums in the window box looked battered from the storm, their heads bowed and red petals scattered on the sill.

'Funny-looking thing,' said Pujol, pointing at the brass door knocker.

'François Vidal told me it was modelled on one of the gargoyles above the north door of the cathédrale Saint-Michel in Carcassonne.'

'Would have thought it put callers off,' grunted Pujol. 'But then perhaps that's the idea.'

Baillard got out of the car and walked up the stone steps, lifted the brass knocker and rapped three times. He waited, his white panama hat in his hand, knowing Marieta would take her time, even if she was there. After a minute or so, he knocked again. Still nothing stirred in the little house. The dread that had been building in his chest all afternoon took on a life of its own.

He reached for the handle and turned.

Baillard saw Marieta straight away, sitting on the chair at the bottom of the stairs, her grey head bowed against the spindle and the Bible on the floor at her feet. A still figure in black.

'Pujol,' he shouted, 'in here!'

Baillard grabbed Marieta's wrist and felt a flutter of relief when he found her pulse. It was weak and erratic, but there still. He looked at the blue tinge around her lips, at the jagged rise and fall of her chest, and realised what had happened. He loosened her collar and tried to help her to sit up.

'Her heart,' he said, as Pujol appeared in the hall behind him.

'Is she . . .?'

'No, but she's very weak.'

Together they laid Marieta on the floor. Baillard put the heel of his hand on her chest, put his other hand on top and interlocked his fingers. Then, using the whole weight of his body, he began to press.

'One, two, three . . .'

After a while, he stopped. He laid his ear to Marieta's ribs, as he had seen his old friend Harif do, listening. Nothing. He paused, then put his mouth to hers and sent the breath from his lungs into hers. He watched, desperately looking for signs of change. None. He repositioned his hands, then continued to press down on her chest.

'What are you doing, Baillard?' Pujol said.

'It's something I was taught, many, many years ago. A technique used by the Egyptians, so I was told, lost to our modern times.' He glanced up at Pujol's doubtful face. 'But if you could fetch a doctor,' he said urgently. 'Madame Rousset, in the blue house on the corner of the rue de la Condamine. She will know.'

'Got it,' said Pujol, immediately leaving.

Baillard started again. One, two, three, counting each beat of her struggling heart. His arms grew tired, his shoulders ached, but he didn't stop. Still thinking of Harif, who, many years ago, had shown him how to save a life this way. Ten, eleven, twelve. He thought of his grandmother, Esclarmonde, who had taught him to dress a wound. Eighteen, nineteen, twenty. Of Alais, the greatest healer the Midi had ever known. Thirty-seven, thirty-eight, thirty-nine. Harif, Esclarmonde, Alais, he kept all three of them close at his side while his aching muscles worked and worked.

'One hundred and three, one hundred and four, one hundred and five . . .'

Finally, Baillard felt Marieta's breathing change. The rasping, tattered gasps yielded to a regular rhythm as her heart returned to normal.

'*Peyre* . . .' he muttered, sinking exhausted to the ground beside her. 'Welcome back, *amica*.'

For a few moments Baillard sat quietly in the company of his friend, an old woman now. He realised that the wind had dropped. That there was no longer the sound of rain on the glass.

Finally he got to his feet and walked into the salon to open the shutters and let the daylight in.

Chapter 68

Coustaussa

Sandrine and Liesl propped their bikes against the gate at the back of the house. It had taken them a long time to get back from Couiza in the wet. Even though the rain had stopped, the steep roads were slippery, covered with detritus and leaves and broken branches.

As they approached the house, Sandrine saw the shutters were unsecured at the back, banging open in the wind. She frowned.

'That's odd …'

She dropped her bike on the grass and ran up the path and into the house, Liesl following close on her heels.

'*Coucou?*' she called. 'Marieta?'

Liesl flicked the switch. 'The lights don't seem to be working.'

'The generator often packs up,' Sandrine said, struggling to keep her voice calm. 'It's easy to fix.'

She heard a noise in the hall. 'Marieta?' she called with relief. 'Marieta, is that you?'

Sandrine rushed into the corridor, then stopped dead. Marieta was lying on the floor in the hall, with a jowly, heavy-set man standing over her. Without thinking, she flew at the intruder.

'Get away from her,' she shouted, shoving him out of the way and crouching down beside the unconscious woman. 'What have you done to her?'

'Mademoiselle, *calmez-vous*,' the man was trying to say.

'Marieta, what happened?'

The old woman shifted. 'Léonie?'

'It's me, Sandrine.'

Marieta's eyes were milky, unfocused. 'Léonie?' she said again.

'Who's Léonie?' whispered Liesl, who'd come into the hall behind Sandrine.

'I don't know.'

'Is she all right?'

Only now did Sandrine notice that there was a pillow under Marieta's head and a blanket covering her. Then, a quiet and reassuring voice at her back.

'She will be, madomaisèla.'

Sandrine swung round to see a second man, in a pale linen suit, coming out of the doorway to the salon.

'Who are you?' she demanded.

'Monsieur Baillard,' Marieta was saying, trying to sit up. 'I apologise, I should have ... she doesn't ...'

'Baillard?'

Sandrine turned back to Marieta, furious, now she realised she was all right, rather than terrified. 'I told you,' she said. 'I told you not to do too much, and now look, look what's happened. You've worn yourself out.'

Marieta's face softened. 'So you are the one to scold me?'

'Madomaisèla,' the man in the pale suit said in a steady, calm voice. 'She's given us all a scare, but all will be well. She is strong. It is not yet her time.'

Sandrine glared at him, at Marieta, then burst into tears.

'She's stable,' said the doctor. 'Is there someone who can sit with her?'

Baillard nodded. 'We will all be here.'

'Good.' He began to pack up his bag. 'She was lucky you were here, Monsieur Baillard, and lucky Geneviève Saint-Loup was worried and telephoned. It might have been a very different story if she'd been here on her own for very much longer.'

'It was a heart attack?'

The doctor nodded. 'A mild one, more of a warning. I can't be sure without an X-ray examination, but I suspect Madame Barthès has been having symptoms for some time.'

'What is her long-term prognosis?'

The doctor shrugged. 'She'd be better in hospital, but no reason she shouldn't make a full recovery.'

'She has no time for hospitals,' Sandrine said. 'Nor doctors, come to that.'

'These village types never do,' he said drily. 'Nevertheless, I'll be in to check on her tomorrow. Do you have ration cards and so forth? Marieta certainly won't be fit to travel for some considerable time.'

Sandrine nodded. 'Our papers are in order.'

'That's one thing at least,' the doctor said.

Pujol nodded. 'I'll drive you back to Couiza, doctor,' he said.

Baillard watched the car pull away, then closed the door and came back inside.

'And now, madomaisèla, if you are not too tired – and Liesl might sit with Marieta for a while – perhaps you and I should talk.'

'She's been overdoing it,' Sandrine said, looking into the salon where Marieta was sleeping peacefully on the daybed. Her eyes were closed and her hands folded neatly above the sheet. 'We've all told her, but she won't listen.'

'No, she never did,' he said with a gentle smile.

Sandrine looked at him. 'You've known her a long time, Monsieur Baillard.'

'She told you so?'

'Yes, though not much.'

Baillard put his head on one side. 'Did Marieta tell you she sent for me?'

'I knew she'd written to you – I took the letter to the post office myself three weeks ago – but not what she said. And ever since we've been here, she's watched the letter box like a hawk.'

'The missive did not arrive.'

'No?'

Now Sandrine was looking at him properly, she realised Monsieur Baillard was even older than she'd originally thought from Marieta's description. A halo of white hair, his face deeply lined, his skin translucent almost, though his eyes were quick and intelligent and clear.

'No,' he said in his quiet voice, 'so it's time you found out why Marieta was so disturbed by what happened. Shall we move somewhere quieter, so we don't disturb her or your young friend?'

'My cousin …' she began automatically, then stopped. There seemed little point lying to Monsieur Baillard. She smiled. 'A friend. Would you like something to drink?'

'If you have wine?'

She led him to the kitchen. 'My father's cellar is still untouched,' she said.

Choosing a bottle of red Tarascon wine, Sandrine poured two glasses, then sat down in the chair opposite him.

'I am sorry to hear about your father's death. He was a good man.'

She smiled. 'I didn't know you knew him, Monsieur Baillard.'

'More by reputation than in person, I regret to say. We talked on one or two occasions. He had a profound love of architecture, buildings that tell the story of the past. A passion I also share.' Again he fixed his steady gaze on her. 'You miss him greatly.'

It was a statement rather than a question. Sandrine nodded.

'It's better, of course, less painful. But here, it's hard to believe I won't see him sitting in this chair, reading one of his local history pamphlets, a glass of whisky by his side.' She laughed. 'He developed a taste for it after he'd been to Scotland. Filthy stuff, Marieta called it.'

For a moment, they sat in silence. Sandrine wasn't sure what to say, how to begin. If she was supposed to begin. Time passed, marked by the ticking of the clock on the wooden shelf above the big open fireplace.

'So you don't know why Marieta wrote to you?' she said.

Instantly the atmosphere in the room seemed to change, shifting from the memories of old friends and family to something else.

Baillard placed his glass on the table beside him. 'I think, perhaps, it would be better if you told me what prompted the letter in the first instance.'

Sandrine was soothed by his old-fashioned way of talking, by his formal and precise language and calm, steady tone. She felt the knot in her chest begin to loosen.

'So much has happened since then.'

'Stories shift their shape, change character, madomaisèla. They acquire different complexions, different colours, depending on the storyteller.' He shrugged. 'Why not simply tell the story as it comes back to you.'

She took a mouthful of wine, then drew a deep breath. 'It was the day before the demonstration in Carcassonne. Monday the thirteenth of July . . .'

Chapter 69

In the world outside the window, as Sandrine talked, the sounds began to change. Cicadas, nightingales, scuttling hares, mice. In the fields beyond the village, mountain foxes. All around were the light scents of the countryside after a storm, the green perfume of wild rosemary, mint and thyme. The *martinets* were beginning their nightly courtship, feeding, swooping, spiralling and spinning like dancers in the air. On the outskirts of the village, the beech trees and laurel, wet in the fading day, threw long shadows.

When Sandrine had finished, she took another mouthful of wine and looked at Monsieur Baillard. He did not move and he did not speak.

'Everything's happened so fast, one thing after the other,' she said. 'Finding Antoine in the river, meeting Raoul, learning what Marianne and Suzanne were doing, trying to keep Liesl safe. So fast.'

Baillard nodded. 'I am afraid to tell you that Antoine Déjean has been found.'

'Alive?' she said, though she had no hope of it.

'No.'

'No.' She sighed. 'Where?'

'In the mountains not far from Tarascon.'

'It was dreadful,' she said quietly. 'The moment when he opened his eyes and stared at me, and I realised I could do nothing. I felt useless, quite useless.'

Baillard nodded. 'There is an intensity of connection between the living and the dying so powerful, that it makes all that has gone before insignificant. The ancients called this gnosis – knowledge – a single moment of enlightenment, dazzling. For an instant all things are clear, the perfect, ineffable pattern revealed in the time between the sighs of a beating heart. Truth and the spirit, the connection between this world and the next.'

'He'd been tortured.'

Baillard did not answer. Sandrine exhaled, aware of the heavy beat of her pulse, the thrumming of the blood in her ears.

'This young man, Raoul Pelletier,' Baillard said. 'He came to your rescue at the river and you gave him shelter. You helped him get away. Yet he stands accused?'

'He was set up.'

'Do you trust him?'

'I do. Marianne couldn't understand how I was so sure. It's true that I know little about him and I don't know where he is now. But, yes. I do trust him.'

'Completely?'

'Yes,' she said without hesitation. 'With my life.'

Baillard stared at her for a moment, pressing the tips of his fingers together as he thought.

'It is an old and distinguished name he carries. A very old name.'

Sandrine watched him, waiting for him to speak again. He sat so still, looking out over the dark garrigue beyond the window and the outskirts of the village, as if he'd forgotten she was there.

'Monsieur Baillard,' she whispered. 'Why was Marieta so scared? I tried to find out, but she wouldn't tell me.'

'No.'

She waited a few moments more. 'Why was Antoine murdered?'

He sighed. And it seemed to Sandrine that single sound contained all the knowledge of the world, of civilisations, of everything that had been and was yet to come.

'Antoine was killed in his attempt to find – and protect

– something of great power, of great antiquity,' he said. 'Something that is capable of changing the course of the war.'

'A weapon?'

Baillard shook his head. 'No. At least, not in the way you mean, *filha*.'

'Then what?'

'He had discovered a map that reveals the final resting place of an ancient religious text, a Codex. He was due to deliver the map to me in person some weeks ago, but he never arrived.'

'Where's the map now?'

Baillard raised his hands in a gesture of ignorance, then let them fall.

'Even if you find the map, are you sure the Codex itself actually survives?'

'Instinct says it does, but I have no proof.'

Sandrine frowned. 'In any case, how did Antoine know what was in the Codex if no one's even seen it?'

'Fragments are known. My belief is that some verses were—'

'Written on the map itself,' she jumped in, then turned red. 'Sorry, I didn't mean to interrupt.'

Baillard smiled. 'I came to that same conclusion myself,' he said with a momentary sparkle in his eye. 'Antoine could read Latin and Greek. I am certain he found the map – had sight of it at least. It is the only explanation that serves.'

'I tried to do some research,' Sandrine said, 'though it didn't get me very far. When I badgered her, Marieta finally admitted that the words reminded her of certain lines in the Book of Revelation, but she wouldn't say any more than that. I went to the municipal library in Carcassonne to see if I could find any mention of such a connection, but it was closed for the summer.' She paused.

'Marieta seemed terrified, Monsieur Baillard, even at the thought of it.'

'Yes.'

'Is she right to be?'

He did not answer the question. 'The Codex is a Gnostic text, condemned in the fourth century as heretical. The authorship is unknown although, as Marieta told you, the verses are believed to bear some similarity to the only Gnostic text included in the Bible, the Book of the Revelation of St John the Divine.'

'Are there other books that might have been included in the Bible but were left out?'

'The Bible is a collection of writings, not a single unified text.'

'But that's not right . . .'

Baillard allowed himself a smile. 'For the first few centuries of its mission, the Christian Church was under attack – not least from the continued Roman occupation of the Holy Land – so the need to strengthen and unite was paramount. It was important to establish an incontrovertible, agreed holy book. The matter of which texts should be viewed as legitimate, which not, was the subject of much heated debate. The texts chosen to form the Bible were standardised in Greek, then translated into other languages. In Egypt, for example, into the Coptic language of the early Egyptian Christians. As communities developed – monasteries, places of worship – other key texts were translated and disseminated. Often on papyrus, gathered into individual leather-bound books known as codices, to keep them safe.'

He took another sip of his drink. 'The orthodox lobby won. A certain interpretation of Christianity triumphed. Despite this, the doctrine of equality under faith never entirely went away, though it was driven underground.' He paused, a gentle smile lighting his face. 'In the past, I had many friends who were of the Albigensian faith – Cathars, as they are sometimes called now, although at the time they referred to themselves as *bons homes*, good men, good women. Some consider them Gnostics and argue that they are the natural descendants of those early Christians.'

While they had been talking, night had fallen over Coustaussa. Sandrine got up to close the shutters, then lit the old brass lamps as she'd seen Marieta do a thousand times. The hiss and spit of the oil, then haloes of yellow light flared and warmed the corners of the room. She glanced across at her guest, realising he had removed himself. Memories of the past, friends lost, in the presence of ghosts. Echoes in the landscape.

'Go on, Monsieur Baillard,' she said gently.

He looked up again and nodded. 'The battles between Gnostic and orthodox thinking lasted some two hundred years – a little more or less in different parts of the world – but the time that concerns us now is the fourth century, when many of the Gnostic texts were destroyed. We have no way of knowing how many priceless works were consigned to the fire, only that much knowledge was lost.'

'How do we know of their existence in the first place?'

'A good question. In AD 367, an edict went out from Athanasius – the powerful Bishop of Alexandria – that heretical texts were to be burnt. However, the threat preceded this by some years. Athanasius was a controversial figure – sometimes his views were in favour, sometimes not – but Christian leaders took matters into their own hands well before this edict and ravaged their own libraries.'

'So Gnostics were already taking steps to hide or protect texts they thought were at risk,' Sandrine said.

Baillard nodded. 'According to contemporary records, there was a mass burning of books in 342 in Lyon – Lugdunum as it then was – but some texts were successfully smuggled to safety. To Egypt, to Jordan, and hidden there.' Baillard paused. 'Only very recently has it come to light that the Codex considered by the Abbot to be the most dangerous of all the proscribed texts might never have left these shores.'

'And Antoine died because of this,' Sandrine said quietly. 'For a book.'

'Not even a book,' he said. 'A single sheet of papyrus, seven verses.'

Sandrine shook her head. 'Given our situation now, and with everything that is happening, it seems so ... not irrelevant exactly but ...'

Baillard stared. 'Pujol thinks the same. But the knowledge contained within those seven verses is said to be as powerful, as terrifying, as anything in the Old Testament or the prophecies of Revelation.'

Sandrine leant forward and met his gaze. 'What knowledge?' she asked, surprised to hear her voice so steady when her heart was beating so fast.

'Christians believe that, at the final reckoning, we shall all be reunited at one unique moment of apocalypse. Such belief is fundamental to many faiths, in fact. To our modern minds, this idea is strange. Dismissed as magic or superstition or fairy tale. But to those who have walked this earth before us, down the generations, such concourse between this world and the next was seen as natural, evident.'

'But what, precisely, does the Codex promise?' she said again.

'That, in times of great need, in times of great hardship, there is an army of spirits that can be called upon to intercede in the affairs of men.'

'Ghosts, do you mean? But that's impossible!'

'The dead are all around us, Sandrine,' Baillard said in his soft, measured voice. 'You know this. You feel your father close to you here, do you not?'

'Yes, but that's different ...'

'Is it?'

She stopped, not sure what she was trying to say. Was it different or the same? Her dreams were filled with ghosts, memories. She sometimes thought she saw her father on the turn of the stairs, the outline of him in his chair by the fireplace.

'Has this . . .' She hesitated, working out how to frame the question. 'Has this army ever been called upon before?'

'Once,' Baillard replied. 'Only once.'

'When?' she said quickly.

'In these lands,' he said. 'In Carcassonne.'

For an instant Sandrine thought she could hear the words beyond the words, feel the presence of an older system of belief that lay beneath the tangible world she saw around her.

'The spirits of the air . . .' she murmured. 'Dame Carcas?'

She spoke without thinking, and as she did so, Sandrine experienced a moment of sudden illumination. In that one instant, she thought she understood. Saw it all clearly, the ineffable pattern of things, the past and present woven together in many dimensions, in colour vivid and sure. But before she could catch hold of the memory, the moment had passed. She looked up and saw Baillard was staring at her.

'You do understand,' he said softly.

'I don't know, I thought I did . . .' She hesitated, not sure what she felt. 'But even if the Codex did survive and is here, somewhere, waiting to be found . . .' She stopped again. 'Our enemies are real, and this . . .'

Now it was Baillard's turn to hesitate. 'The war is far from over,' he said in a quiet voice. 'Here in France, in the world beyond our borders, I fear the worst is yet before us. Decisions are being made that are beyond human comprehension. But . . .' He paused. 'Evil has not yet won. We have not yet passed the point of no return. If we can find the Codex – and understand the words it contains, harness them to our needs – then there might still be a chance.'

Sandrine looked at him with despair. 'England fights on, I know, but we have lost, Monsieur Baillard. France is defeated. People – even in Carcassonne, in Coustaussa – seem to be prepared to accept that.'

Baillard looked suddenly older. The skin on his face seemed stretched tighter, pale and transparent, a record of all the things he had seen and done.

'They do not think they have a choice,' he said softly. 'But I do not believe Hitler and his collaborators will be satisfied with what they have, whatever compromises Pétain has offered. And that, *filha*, will be when the real battle will begin.'

'The Nazis will cross the line,' she said, a statement not a question. 'They will occupy the Midi.'

Baillard nodded. 'This status quo will not hold for much longer. And that is when possession of the Codex, for good or ill, could make – will make – the difference. Between certain failure and the slightest possibility of victory.'

'A ghost army,' Sandrine whispered.

Baillard nodded. 'One that has not walked for more than a thousand years.'

‡

Codex XI

‡

GAUL
COUZANIUM
AUGUST AD 342

Arinius emerged from his stone shelter to another perfect morning. A gentle wind whispered in the air and the dawn sky was an endless pale blue. All around him the colours of summer were now painted bright. Yellow *Ulex gallii*, its scent gentle in the dawn, the tiny pink heads of orchids blinking out from between the grasslands. Three days had passed since the storm, and, although he sensed a change in the air, a hint of more rain to come, there was not a cloud to be seen.

He turned to face the sun. Arinius no longer knelt to pray, but rather stood with his arms outstretched and his face lifted to heaven. He thought of his brother monks observing Lauds in the cool grey spaces of the community in Lugdunum and did not envy them their confinement.

'In the morning, Lord, I offer you my prayer.'

He no longer needed the tolling of the bell in the forum to remind him of his obligations. Now, after his months alone with God, Arinius spoke words of his own devising. He gave thanks for the new day, for his safe delivery through the storm, for the sanctuary of the gentle and hospitable land in which he found himself.

'Amen,' he said, making the sign of the cross with the fingers of his right hand. 'Amen.'

When his offices were over, Arinius went back inside to fetch his bag. He broke his fast with the victuals he had purchased in Couzanium: a portion of wheaten bread ground with millet, a handful of walnuts, washed down with the *posca* infused with the memory of the wine he had bought from the merchant. The iridescent glass glinted in the morning sunlight, reflecting blue and green and silver.

The young monk sat and looked out across the valley. At the earth slashed through with red iron ore on the hills on the far side of the river, the expanse of grassland and woods. The land was evidently rich with fruit and nuts and, last night's storm notwithstanding, it seemed to be a tranquil place to rest a while. To prepare for the final stage of his journey into the mountains.

As the sun rose higher in the sky, Arinius decided to prepare his writing materials. He did not want to carry his tools into the mountains, only those things he would need for the journey. He got out the square of spun wool he had purchased in the travelling market in Couzanium and spread the yellow-white yarn flat on the ground. Grasping the iron handle of his hunting knife, he began to cut the fabric into squares.

It was hard and repetitive work. He felt the sweat pooling in the hollow at the base of his throat and on the back of his neck. The muscles at the top of his arm and in his shoulders began to complain, to ache. From time to time he paused to add another cut section to the pile, before returning to the diminishing square of fabric.

Finally, he had finished. He stood up to stretch his legs, clenching and unclenching his fingers. He drank the last of the *posca*, ate another portion of bread, then gathered his basket to go out in search of the materials he required for the next stage of the operation. In the community in Lugdunum, Arinius had been taught to create a form of ink, a mixture of iron salt and nutgall, and a gum from pine resin. He hoped in this valley to be able to find everything he needed. The liquid looked blue-black when it was first used, but quickly faded to a pale brown. He also needed to find the right sort of feather to fashion a crude reed pen. In the past he had tried crow's feathers and those of geese, but through trial and error had discovered that blackbirds' feathers were the easiest to use.

With the Codex still carried beneath his tunic, and his leather bag over his shoulder once more, Arinius ventured out into the valley to find what he needed.

Chapter 70

COUSTAUSSA
AUGUST 1942

Sandrine took the shopping list Monsieur Baillard had written and cycled down to Couiza. The storm had cleared the air and the morning was fresh and pleasant. A few clouds, the trees green and glistening on the horizon, the sky an endless blue. The sort of day one remembers.

Marieta seemed none the worse for her ordeal, but Sandrine wanted to let Marianne know what had happened all the same. By ten o'clock she was again standing in a slow-moving queue in the post office. Although the phone rang in the rue du Palais, no one answered. It meant she would have to try again.

On her way out, she stopped in front of the poster. Raoul's face stared blindly at her. Stay away, she whispered under her breath, even though before she'd been desperate for him to come to Coustaussa.

'Villainous-looking creature,' a woman said.

'Do you think so?' replied Sandrine, keeping her voice steady.

She went to each of the shops in turn, then pushed her heavily laden bicycle home, past gardens filled with vegetables beneath wire cages guarded by old women. No one grew flowers any more, only food to eat. Past the electricity substation. The door was ajar, revealing the white porcelain shields protecting the connectors on the upper storey, like a row of upturned vases.

It was hotter now and there was little shade on the

steepest part of the hill. Sandrine turned over in her mind the many things Monsieur Baillard had told her. While he was talking, she had accepted everything he said without question. Now, in the bright light of a summer's morning, the whole conversation seemed like a dream.

A ghost army?

Of course she didn't believe it was real, couldn't believe it was real. But did he? Sandrine wasn't sure.

Even after a few hours' acquaintance, she understood how Monsieur Baillard gave the same weight to stories of antiquity as he did to those things that had happened yesterday or the day before that. But whatever he believed, the consequences of the hunt for the Codex, on both sides, were real enough.

She cleared the crest of the hill, then stopped and looked around, casting her eye to each of the four points of the compass. Rennes-les-Bains to the south-east, Couiza to the west, the turrets and towers of Carcassonne many kilometres to the north, out of sight. And ahead, Coustaussa. From this distance, everything looked as it always had. She'd been to Paris once, to Toulouse and to Narbonne, but no further than that. These were the foundations on which her life was built.

If Monsieur Baillard was right and the Nazis crossed the line, the tranquillity of the valley would be lost for ever. Of the Aude. She would not let that happen. She would fight to stop it happening.

'Live free or die,' she said, remembering the placard the old veteran had carried at the Bastille Day demonstration.

It seemed a lifetime ago. Sandrine understood what was at stake now. She understood what it meant to resist. Whether she was here in Coustaussa, or back in Carcassonne with Marianne and Suzanne. With Raoul.

Last night she had listened and listened to what Monsieur Baillard was telling her. Now her mind buzzed with questions, like flies in a jar, one question above all others. Monsieur Baillard had said the Codex had been called upon once before. More than a thousand years ago.

Was it true? And if it was, what had happened to the Codex over the intervening years? Lost again? Now to be found once more? Despite the heat of noon, Sandrine felt goosebumps prickling on her skin.

'Vivre libre ou mourir,' she repeated.

Chapter 71

LIMOUX

Raoul Pelletier ran his hands over his chin, uncomfortable in the heat. He'd not shaved since leaving Carcassonne because the beard and moustache disguised the shape of his face. It wasn't much, but it was the best he could do, especially since he'd seen a poster asking for information, with a huge reward being offered. He'd been expecting it for weeks, was surprised that it was the first he'd seen. Although he looked different after three weeks of living rough, if someone put their mind to it, he'd be recognised. So far as he knew, at least there hadn't been anything on the wireless since the end of July.

Raoul was sitting in the café by Les Halles in Limoux, with a clear view of the front door of the Hôtel Moderne et Pigeon. Local *résistants* used the hotel as a safe house and he had been told there was someone who might give him a ride south. The man he was looking out for was Spanish, a comrade of Ramón with whom he'd stayed in Roullens three weeks ago.

He had bought the morning edition of *La Dépêche*. It was a Pétainist publication, but it served his purpose. He flicked through the paper, glancing up at the door to the hotel, which remained stubbornly closed. As he looked back down, his attention was drawn by a STOP PRESS item on the inside back page.

TRAGIC CLIMBING ACCIDENT

It is with great regret that we report that the body of

a local man, identified as Monsieur Antoine Déjean – originally of Tarascon – has been found in a gully to the north of the village of Larnat, in Ariège.

Raoul turned cold. From the moment he'd found Sandrine clutching Antoine's necklace at the river, he had expected this. But the black and white reality of it still hit him.

Monsieur Déjean's body was discovered by a poacher, who alerted the appropriate authorities. Retired Inspecteur Pujol, formerly of the gendarmerie in Foix, hypothesised that the young man had lost his footing and fallen. The extent of his injuries were such that it appeared he had died instantly some weeks previously. When asked if Monsieur Déjean might have been investigating the caves for some illegal purpose, Inspecteur Pujol replied in the negative. 'Although it is the case that the Lombrives caves and other adjacent sites have become the unfortunate focus for unscrupulous treasure-hunters and cultists, there is no evidence to suggest that Monsieur Déjean was involved with any such group.'

Raoul glanced up again. No one was going in or out of the hotel. He continued reading.

Monsieur Déjean, who was unmarried, was a resident of Carcassonne and worked for Artozouls, the hunting and fishing suppliers. The funeral will be held at ten o'clock on Wednesday 19 August at the Église de la Daurade, Tarascon. No flowers by request.

In his pocket, Raoul's fingers tightened around the handkerchief containing the tiny bottle he'd retrieved from

Antoine's apartment. It had become an habitual action on his part, a talisman almost.

At last, he heard the door of the hotel open and a dark-haired man, matching the description of the man he was waiting for, came out. Raoul dropped the newspaper on the table, quickly crossed the street and fell into step beside him.

'Le temps est bouché à l'horizon.'

The slightest nod, to indicate that the password had been heard and accepted.

'Where do you need to go, *compañero*?' the Spaniard replied, without breaking his stride.

'Banyuls,' Raoul began to say, then he stopped. The newspaper article changed things. He was now convinced that Leo Coursan – with Laval's help – was responsible for Antoine's abduction and murder. If he was right, Sandrine was in danger. His intention had been to stay as far away from her as possible, not to drag her into his situation. But now he realised he couldn't leave.

'On second thoughts, Coustaussa,' he said.

'I can take you to Couiza. Two kilometres from there?'

'Sí gracias.'

The man nodded. 'Red van at end of alley. BONFILS on the side. We leave in fifteen minutes.'

Carcassonne

'Did you know about this, Laval?' said Authié, pushing the copy of *La Dépêche* towards him.

'I've seen it, sir.'

'What the hell's Bauer playing at? How could he be so incompetent as to dispose of the body where it would be found so soon?'

'There have been storms in the Haute Vallée, perhaps that caused a mud slide. Disturbed the grave.'

Authié realised it was close to where de l'Oradore's excavation had been three years previously. Was that deliberate or another unfortunate coincidence?

'What's Bauer got to say about it?' he demanded.

'I have not spoken to him,' Laval said in a level voice.

Authié stared at his deputy, hearing something in his tone, then dropped his eyes back to the newspaper.

'Who's this Inspector Pujol?'

'A retired local policeman.'

'One of ours?'

Laval shook his head. 'The opposite, sir. Sympathies are with the partisans.'

'Why was he called rather than a serving officer?'

'The locals trust him. They don't like the authorities. A place like Tarascon, people stick to their own kind.'

'Like the Middle Ages. It's ridiculous,' Authié snapped. He looked back at the article. 'According to this, the death's being treated as a climbing accident. Do people believe that?'

'From what little I've been able to gather. Do you want me to go back to Tarascon, sir?'

Authié considered. 'On balance, it's a good idea,' he said eventually. 'I'll put someone else on surveillance of the Vidal house for the time being. What's happening there?'

'It continues the same, sir. The tall woman, Suzanne Peyre, is often there. Mademoiselle Vidal spends most of her time at the Croix-Rouge in rue de Verdun, then returns home in the evenings. No sign of the younger girl or the housekeeper.'

'Lucie Ménard?'

'I haven't seen her at all.'

Authié glanced again at the paper. 'Go to Tarascon today, Laval. Report back as soon as you can. I intend to go myself on Wednesday, but I want information before that.'

'Wednesday?'

'The funeral,' he said impatiently. 'It will be a good opportunity to take the measure of things for myself.' He paused again, then raised his eyes and looked at Laval standing on the other side of the desk. 'As regards Bauer, I think the arrangement has run its course. Not until after Wednesday, but then I need you to act. You understand me?'

Laval met his gaze. 'Yes, sir.'

Couiza

The Tramontana was stirring up the dust outside the railway station when Raoul walked into Couiza. He couldn't see any police checking papers, but even so he didn't want to risk going into the station to ask for directions to Coustaussa. But road signs had been taken down in 1939, and he didn't want to waste his time striking out in the wrong direction. He noticed the door to the tabac on the far side of the square was open.

There was a man in front of him complaining about the length of the queues in the post office. He turned, half knocked into Raoul, then frowned. He exchanged a look with the tobacconist, looked hard at Raoul, then left quickly. Raoul told himself not to read anything into it, it was just one of those things. Small towns like this, all strangers were treated with suspicion.

'Do you have tobacco to buy?' he said. 'Cigarettes?'

'Rations only.'

'Not for cash?'

The tobacconist looked at him. 'I can't help.'

Raoul shrugged. 'A box of matches anyway,' he said, handing over a note. 'And if you could point me in the direction of Coustaussa.'

The tobacconist looked at him. 'New around here?'

'Passing through.'

He came out from behind his counter. 'Right out of the door. Long road with trees. You'll see Coustaussa on the hill, left-hand side.'

The tobacconist stood in the doorway, watching him go. Raoul felt his eyes on the back of his neck. He looked back in time to see the man turn the sign on the door to CLOSED, leave the tabac and cross the square in the opposite direction.

Already Raoul regretted mentioning Coustaussa, but he told himself he was making something out of nothing. He found an unmade path running parallel to the main road running east. Bicycle tracks suggested someone had taken the same route earlier, a single line snaking up towards the village. He hadn't seen a single patrol, but he'd be less visible away in this quiet neighbourhood. Small houses with neat back gardens, neither quite in the town nor properly in the countryside.

Raoul tried to bring Sandrine's face to mind. She'd been his constant companion over the past three weeks, snapshots of their brief time together carried in his head like treasured photographs in an album. But today, it didn't work. His memories were less strong than the twist of fear in his stomach. What if Coursan had already tracked Sandrine down in Carcassonne? His fault. What if she was in Coustaussa, but was horrified to see him? She'd had three weeks to regret the invitation, more than three weeks when anything might have happened.

In the distance, Raoul heard the thrum of an engine. His reactions sharpened. A car driving in the same direction he was walking. Thoughts about the future gave way to the needs of the present. He glanced around, but there was nowhere obvious to hide. Gardens, the open track, few trees for cover. Then he noticed, a little way ahead, a small, squat building, an electricity substation.

He sped up, covering the last few metres quickly, and

stepped into the shadow of the building, moments before a police car appeared on the track behind him. Sending gravel skidding, the tyres crunching on the rough surface, disappearing in a cloud of dust on the road leading up to Coustaussa. Raoul leant back against the whitewashed wall, his heart thudding in his chest, remembering the sharp eyes of the customer in the tabac and the glance he'd exchanged with the owner. He'd no way of knowing whether they'd recognised him or simply reported him because he was a stranger in a town that did not welcome outsiders. He looked down at his clothes, dirty from the road, remembered his unshaven, sun-worn face.

Should he go on? The police car was heading in the same direction. Was he a coward to contemplate turning back or simply being prudent?

He looked back at the houses on the outskirts of Couiza, trying to decide what to do. Then he turned and looked along the empty road. There was a slight trace of dust still hanging in the air, whipped up by the tyres. The memory of sitting side by side in the garden of the rue du Palais came back to him. How when he'd described standing on the jetty in Banyuls, being too much of a coward to jump, Sandrine had said she thought it took more courage to go on than to give up.

He carried on walking.

Chapter 72

COUSTAUSSA

'How do you feel now?' Sandrine said, joining Monsieur Baillard and Marieta on the terrace.

'I would feel better if everyone stopped fussing,' Marieta said, though she didn't look like she really minded.

'Doctor's orders,' Sandrine smiled. 'We're not going to let you lift a finger.'

'Doctors, what do they know?' she said gruffly. 'Now, did you speak to Madomaisèla Marianne?'

The smile slipped from Sandrine's face. 'No, as a matter of fact. No one there. I'll go back later. She doesn't even know what happened to you and . . .' She stopped. 'I'd like to be sure everything's all right.'

'And why wouldn't it be?' Marieta said sharply.

'No reason. It's just odd that there wasn't anyone there again, that's all.' She looked around. 'Where's Liesl?'

'She went to call on Madame Rousset,' Baillard replied. 'Her son – Yves, is it? – came for her.'

Sandrine grinned. 'Did he indeed?'

She put her *panier* down on the table. 'I got everything you asked for, Monsieur Baillard. And this package they had put by for you in the bookshop, as you'd asked.' She took a parcel wrapped in brown paper from the basket. 'There was more in the shops than I'd expected. It's not like that in Carcassonne.'

Baillard slit the string with a knife and opened the package, then nodded with satisfaction.

'Yes, this will do.'

'What is it?'

'It is a stock of paper they were keeping for me. Nowhere near old enough, of course but, with modification, I think it will pass.'

'The bookshop owner said she had been keeping it for you for some time, but how is that—'

'It was kind of her to remember,' Baillard said, forestalling Sandrine's question. He put his hand on Marieta's shoulder. 'Do you need anything, *amica*, otherwise, if you will beg our patience, Madomaisèla Sandrine and I have things to discuss.'

'Go, go,' she smiled, making a shooing motion with her hands. 'I will be quite all right.'

Sandrine picked up her basket and she and Baillard carried everything into the house and unpacked it. As well as provisions and several sheets of woven cream paper, there was a heavy bottle of *sirop*, a bottle of Indian ink and a horsehair brush.

'So do you know who murdered Antoine, Monsieur Baillard?'

'No, not for certain,' he said. 'Over the past twenty years or so there has been a great deal of activity in the area around the caves of Lombrives and the Pic de Vicdessos. All such licences were rescinded when war was declared but, once the Armistice was signed, several expeditions returned. A French team funded by the head of an old Chartres family – a man called de l'Oradore – among them. But Antoine's father said the man asking after his son was German, so . . .' He shrugged.

'Surely there can't be German teams allowed here now?'

'Not officially, of course, but unofficially, I think it's probable,' Baillard replied. 'The question is whether they are collaborating with one another or working independently.' He thought for a moment. 'It is common knowledge that the Ahnenerbe are in the region.'

'What's the Ahnenerbe?'

Baillard's face hardened. 'An organisation dedicated to finding evidence validating Nazi beliefs of an Aryan race. To that end they have archaeologists all over the world searching for artefacts, for religious texts.'

He broke off and Sandrine saw his amber eyes darken, as if some other, more powerful story had claimed his attention. Then he waved his hand, chasing away his memories.

'Antoine was friends with a young German, Otto Rahn, who lived at Montségur for some time. A young man in search of meaning. Rahn believed he had found it here, in the Pays d'Oc. Flattered into joining the SS, he was coerced into feeding information back to Berlin.' The thought lines furrowed deeper on his forehead. 'It is my intention to do the same, except of course the information we will provide will be false.'

Sandrine looked at the antique paper, then suddenly understood Baillard's odd shopping list.

'You're going to create a forgery,' she said.

He smiled, clearly pleased she had worked it out so quickly.

'And put out that it's been found in order to flush out Antoine's killers . . .' She paused. 'Or . . . to leave you free to search unhindered for the real Codex? Is that it?'

He nodded. 'Yes.'

'So you do believe it survived,' she murmured. 'I wasn't certain if you did.'

Sandrine looked down at the materials on the table. 'But can you really make something convincing enough to persuade an expert?'

'I think I can do well enough for our immediate purposes. Why Antoine's body has been found now, whether it was deliberate or unintended, I do not know. However, I think matters will accelerate because of it. I have a contact in Toulouse who will help, a leading French expert on ancient manuscripts and documents in the Languedoc. He will verify its authenticity.'

'But if you're right, and it's Nazi money behind this – or even a mixture of French and German – surely they'll send it to their own experts? However cleverly you produce the forgery, it's obviously not parchment or papyrus, or whatever the real Codex was made of.'

'Eventually they will send it to the Ahnenerbe, yes. But they will not wish to run the risk of drawing Reichsführer Himmler's attention to it until they are completely certain it is genuine.'

Sandrine thought for a moment, but since she realised she would go along with whatever plan Monsieur Baillard put in place anyway, she then sat down and folded her arms on the table.

'What do you need me to do?'

Baillard stared at her. 'This is not a game, madomaisèla,' he said sternly. 'You cannot be under any illusions. If you become involved with this deception, you put yourself in danger. You understand this?'

Sandrine thought of Antoine's desperate face, the weight of his body as she dragged him to the riverbank, the words he had fought so hard to say.

'I'm already involved, Monsieur Baillard,' she said quietly. 'So, tell me what I can do.'

She saw his eyes soften.

'What?' she said quickly. 'What is it?'

He smiled. 'Nothing, *filha*. It is merely that you remind me of someone.'

'Léonie, yes,' Sandrine said. 'Marieta mentioned her yesterday. She thought I was her, I think.'

Baillard shook his head. 'I wasn't thinking of Léonie.'

'Then who?'

For an instant, she thought he hadn't heard. He sat

so still, his hands resting flat on the table, not a muscle moving. Then he gave a long and weary sigh.

'Alaïs,' he said finally. 'Her name was Alaïs.'

Chapter 73

TARASCON

The two men stood beside Bauer's car outside the railway station in Tarascon. Laval's motorbike was parked in the shadow of the trees a little further away. There were freight deliveries coming in and the station was busier than usual. No one noticed them.

Laval handed over the file on Marianne Vidal – with additional information on Lucie Ménard and Sandrine Vidal – then reported what had taken place since Bauer and Authié's meeting at the cimetière Saint-Michel.

'Pelletier has the key?'

Laval shrugged. 'Sanchez had no idea.'

The German looked down at the file in his hand. 'Herr Authié told me he thought the girl was not involved. He was lying?'

'No, that was his opinion then. Subsequently he has reconsidered.'

'You are certain she cannot identify you.'

'Yes.'

Bauer stared at him. 'Do you think Déjean said anything to her?'

'I don't know.'

'You have spoken to this girl?'

'No. As soon as we'd identified her, the house in Carcassonne was put under surveillance. She isn't there, though her sister is. Authié's trying to find her.'

'And this Pelletier?'

'We're still looking for him.'

'What about the Jew and his girlfriend?'

'Blum is in Le Vernet. Lucie Ménard is in Carcassonne. She was the one who identified Sandrine Vidal for us.'

Bauer frowned. 'In my absence, two of my men were arrested and taken there also. Do you know anything about this incident?'

'I wasn't in Tarascon when it happened, Herr Bauer.'

Bauer waved his hand impatiently. 'You hear things, Laval.'

Laval shrugged. 'As I heard it, they were indiscreet. Got into a fight in a bar over a girl. The local police, unaware of their privileged status, arrested them.'

'I shall expect Authié to expedite their release.'

Laval nodded. 'I will make sure he is apprised of the situation.' He could see Bauer suspected some kind of sleight of hand, but was struggling to work out what it was.

'Herr Authié has returned to Carcassonne?'

'On Tuesday,' Laval replied. 'He's suspicious.'

'Of you?'

'Of *you*, Bauer. He thinks you intended Déjean's body to be found.'

'That's absurd.' Bauer's pupils dilated slightly. 'Has he any reason for thinking so?'

Laval held his gaze. 'Not from me. I can't answer for your men.'

'They know how to hold their tongues.'

'The guards in Le Vernet can be persuasive.'

'They will not talk.'

Laval paused, then said: 'Did you intend Déjean to be found?'

'Of course I did not,' Bauer snapped. He dabbed again at his neck, which was glistening with sweat. 'A poacher was using dynamite for setting traps. It caused the land to give way.'

'It was a coincidence that you buried the body where the French team was working.'

Bauer didn't answer.

'It's what Authié thinks.'

'It is none of your concern, Laval,' Bauer said, spittle forming in the corner of his mouth. 'You are in the business of buying and selling information. That is the limit of your interest.'

He put his hand into the inside breast pocket of his jacket and pulled out an envelope. 'It is as agreed.'

Laval slit open the package with his bone-handled clasp knife and counted the notes. He was not unhappy with the situation. It was easy to fan Bauer's suspicions about Authié's reliability. The less they trusted one another, the better for him in the long run. He put the knife back on his belt and looked up to see Bauer staring at him.

'I do not either like or trust Authié,' Bauer said, 'but I do understand him. You, Laval, your motivation is not clear to me.'

'Nothing to understand, Herr Bauer,' he said, rubbing his fingers together. 'You claim to act out of duty to your masters in Berlin, that you're following orders. Authié claims to act in the name of faith. You both make pretence of higher motives to justify what you are doing. You are both prepared to torture, to kill, to do anything to get what you want.' Laval put the envelope in his pocket. 'I, at least, am not a hypocrite.'

Chapter 74

COUSTAUSSA

Sandrine and Audric Baillard looked up at the sound of knocking at the door, both immediately alert. The evidence of their labours – paper, a dish filled with castor oil and hair dye, ink, old tallow wax candles and a box of matches – covered the table.

Sandrine didn't expect trouble in Coustaussa, but her stomach lurched all the same.

'Do you want me to go?' called Liesl from the terrace. She had come back from visiting the Roussets in a cheerful mood.

'Best if I do,' Sandrine answered, standing up.

Without appearing to hurry, Baillard gathered up the things and carried them across the room. Sandrine opened the sideboard, moved a couple of boxes to one side to make space, then helped him put everything away out of sight.

'I shall sit with Marieta,' he said.

'I'm sure it's only a neighbour,' said Sandrine, though she felt nervous as she walked along the corridor to the front door. In the old days, it always stood open. Now, they kept it closed.

Marieta's Bible was still lying on the hall table. Sandrine's hand hovered over it, suddenly tempted to look inside. She traced her fingers over the battered leather cover, rough beneath her skin, then jumped at three more heavy blows on the door.

'All right, all right,' she muttered under her breath.

Cross with herself for being so edgy, she covered the last

few steps quickly and pulled open the door more forcefully than she intended.

'Mademoiselle.'

Sandrine felt the air had been sucked from her lungs. For a split second she struggled to catch her breath, staring at the uniforms, the police car in the empty street behind. What did they want? Why were they here? She didn't recognise either of the officials, though she supposed they came from Couiza.

She forced herself to smile, not to shake. 'What can I do for you, officers?'

To her own ears her voice sounded unnaturally high, but they didn't seem to notice.

'We have reason to believe a fugitive is in the vicinity and heading for Coustaussa,' the younger man said. 'We're here to warn residents.'

'Have you seen any strangers in the village?' the older man demanded. 'It's your duty to report anything suspicious.'

Sandrine had to stop herself from laughing out loud. They hadn't come for Liesl or to question her about the false papers. Nothing to do with them.

'I'm sorry,' she said, shaking her head. 'I haven't seen anyone.'

'The man in question has dark hair and a beard, wearing a brown trilby hat.'

Sandrine gave a jolt as a thought scuttled across her mind, but it was gone before she could catch hold of it.

The older officer narrowed his eyes. 'Have you seen anyone fitting that description, mademoiselle?'

'No, I haven't,' Sandrine said. 'It's so hot, we've been inside all afternoon.'

'We?'

Sandrine quickly tried to decide what to say. Should she mention Monsieur Baillard? Liesl? Marianne had counselled her to stick as close to the truth as possible, while at the same time saying nothing more than was needed.

'Our housekeeper, Marieta, is here. She's in her sixties and had a heart scare a few days ago. She's under doctor's orders to stay as quiet as possible. One of Marieta's oldest friends is sitting with her, and my cousin, that's it.' She carried on talking before they could ask to speak to the others in person. 'It's kind of you to warn us, but I wonder how you know this man is heading for Coustaussa?'

'He asked for directions in the tabac in Couiza. The owner was suspicious and informed us.'

'I see,' said Sandrine, making a mental note to avoid the tabac in future. 'How fortunate the owner was on his guard.'

'Keep your doors locked, mademoiselle,' the younger man advised.

'And if you or anyone else in your household sees anything, contact us immediately. Do not approach him. Pelletier is dangerous.'

Sandrine felt the ground drop from under her. She swayed slightly on her feet, letting her shoulder lean against the solid door frame.

'Are you all right, mademoiselle?'

She fanned herself with her hand. 'Just the heat, it's so … And of course, it's frightening to think of someone so close by. We're quite isolated here.'

She forced herself to stand still as he nodded and they walked down the steps and got back into the car. Forced herself to listen as they fired the engine and pulled away, heading on towards Cassaignes. Everything in slow motion as she slowly and carefully stepped back inside and closed the door.

Only then did her shaking legs give way. She leant back against the wall, her heart galloping, her skin flushed cold and hot at the same time. It was the worst news. The police were hunting Raoul. Someone had informed on him. He was heading for Coustaussa. Then, she couldn't help it. She put her hand over her mouth. The worst of news, yes, but also the very best news. What she'd been desperate to know for the past three weeks. That Raoul was alive, that they hadn't caught him yet. She started to smile.

And that he was here. Heading for Coustaussa.

Raoul stopped. The heat hung heavy over the fields, the sun blazed down, brutal and remorseless. The wind shimmered through the fields of wheat at the top of the hill, making the dry stalks whisper. He pulled a bottle of water from his rucksack and drank enough to take the edge off his thirst, then splashed the rest of the water into his hands and on to his face and neck.

He cleared the brow of the hill and saw the stone shepherds' huts from the photographs on the stairs at the rue du Palais. He stopped. In the distance he could hear the engine of a car, somewhere across the valley. The police coming back? He stepped into the shade of one of the *capitelles*, listening and waiting until the sound died away, going in the opposite direction. He looked back the way he'd come, down to the main road. No one, nothing, for as far as the eye could see.

Raoul stepped back on to the road, then heard an older, more timeless sound. He held back until a young man leading a donkey and cart came into view at the brow of the hill. Dark-haired, with an open shirt and corduroy trousers and a red handkerchief tied at his neck, he didn't look the type to cause trouble. Not police.

Raoul hesitated, then decided to risk it. He'd attract more attention ambling around the village looking for the house. Better to take a chance.

He nodded a greeting. 'I'm looking for the Vidal house. Do you know it?'

'Who wants to know?'

'A friend,' Raoul said lightly. 'Can you tell me where it is?'

The young man continued to stare at him, sizing him up. Raoul waited, keeping his expression neutral, letting him come to his own decision in his own time.

'Carry on down into the village,' the young man said eventually, 'right into rue de la Condamine, then straight on. Set back on its own.'

'Thanks,' Raoul started to say, but he'd already walked on.

He found the house easily enough. The incongruous gargoyle door knocker, the yellow-painted woodwork. A riot of geraniums ran wild in the window boxes, red and white, their heads rather battered by the wind. Raoul tucked himself into the shadow of a barn across the road from the house and waited. He saw no signs of life, no indication that anyone was keeping watch, but he had to be sure.

He was also building up his courage. At this moment, there was still hope. Hope that Sandrine was here in Coustaussa, hope that she would be pleased to see him. As soon as he lifted his hand and knocked on the door, he'd know for certain one way or the other.

He took a deep breath. Then, keeping his head down, he walked quickly out of the cover of the barn and up the steps to Sandrine's house.

Sandrine, Liesl, Marieta and Baillard heard the knock from the back terrace.

'Is it them?' Liesl said with panic in her voice. 'Have they come back?'

'No,' Sandrine said quickly. 'Why would they be back

so soon? In any case, even if it is the police, there's nothing for you to worry about. They're not looking for you, Liesl, I promise.'

'I'm going upstairs,' said Liesl, slipping out of her chair and running into the house.

'Liesl, really, it's not necessary …' Sandrine began to say, but the girl had already gone.

'Let her go,' Monsieur Baillard said. 'There is nothing you will be able to say to reassure her. Better she should feel safe.'

'Yes. Of course,' Sandrine replied, trying not to let Liesl's fears get into her bones too.

For the second time in an hour, Sandrine walked back through the house, queasy with nerves, and opened the door.

She stopped. Her heart stopped. Everything stopped. Like the shutter on a camera imprinting one precise, unique, moment.

His skin was darker, a beard, and his hair was longer, but it was him.

'Raoul,' she said, her face breaking into a smile. 'Raoul.'

Nothing more needed to be said. Sandrine saw the anxiety vanish from his face, like the sun coming out from behind the clouds, and he smiled. The same crooked smile she'd carried as a keepsake next to her heart every day since he'd left.

'If I was stuck, you said to come.' He raised his arms, then let them fall back by his sides. 'So, here I am.'

Chapter 75

They stood in silence for a moment, each hardly able to trust the evidence of their eyes. Then Sandrine reached out and took his hand, felt the flesh-and-blood reality of his fingers in hers.

'Here you are,' she said, finally remembering how to talk. 'Yes.'

Raoul nodded. 'All the way, I kept telling myself there was no reason you would be here. Yet, somehow …'

Sandrine stared at him, seeing her delight mirrored back in his face. Smiling, reminding each other and themselves of how they looked and sounded, until Sandrine realised how stupid they were being.

Quickly she pulled him inside and closed the door. 'The police have been here. They're looking for you.'

'Why here? Why did they come here?'

'They were going to every house, not just us. Someone in Couiza saw you.'

'I heard the siren an hour back, but hoped …' Raoul put his hand to his face and rubbed his stubble. 'I hoped this would be enough.'

She smiled. 'I rather like it.' Still holding his hand, she took a step back. 'How did you know I was here? Did Marianne tell you?'

'No, I just thought I'd try my luck.'

'What would you have done if I hadn't been here?'

He shrugged. 'I don't know. Though I shouldn't have come—'

'Where have you been all this time?' she interrupted, the words coming out in a rush. 'What's been happening?'

‘In a moment,’ he said, pulling her to him.

Raoul put his hand around her waist, the other around her neck. She felt the touch of his lips on hers and the salt of his skin, and the memory of the time spent without him faded away into the haze of the day.

‘Come on,’ she said quietly, finally slipping out of his arms. ‘Let’s join the others.’

‘Others? Who else is here?’

‘Marieta, of course. Also Max’s sister Liesl, as well as an old friend of Marieta’s.’ She caught her breath. ‘Marieta’s not been at all well.’

Quickly she explained what had happened.

‘But she’s going to be all right?’ he said. ‘She’ll make a full recovery?’

She nodded. ‘The doctor says she’ll be fine, provided she rests and doesn’t overdo things.’

‘And how’s Liesl holding up?’

‘Given what’s she’s been through, well.’ Sandrine glanced up the stairs to the girl’s closed door, then back to Raoul. ‘I’ll go and bring her down in a moment. Suzanne tried to find out where Max has been taken, but hit a brick wall. There’s been no news about César Sanchez. He’s gone to ground somewhere too.’ She paused. ‘Unless you know where he is?’

Raoul frowned. ‘César was arrested after the demonstration.’

Sandrine shook her head. ‘When Suzanne went to the police, then the Palais de Justice, they denied all knowledge of him.’

‘But I saw them take him.’

‘I remember you saying that, but there’s no record of him being arrested.’ She paused, then carried on. ‘There is one thing. Antoine’s been found dead, outside Tarascon,’ she said, watching his face. ‘I’m sorry to be the one to tell you.’

Raoul nodded. 'It's all right,' he said. 'I already know.' He pulled the copy of *La Dépêche* out of his rucksack. 'It's what tipped the balance and made me decide to come to find you. I wanted to warn you.'

'Monsieur Baillard thinks it will set things moving too.'

'Monsieur Baillard?'

'He was with Inspector Pujol when Antoine's body was found. So far as I know, no one's been trying to find me, though.'

'Who's Monsieur Baillard?' he asked again.

Sandrine smiled. 'Come and meet him. He'll be able to explain better than I can.'

She pushed open the wire mesh screen and went out on to the terrace. Baillard was sitting in the shade, looking out over the garrigue.

'Monsieur Baillard,' Sandrine said, 'this is Raoul. He saw the report of Antoine's death in *La Dépêche*.'

Baillard stood up. 'Do you usually act on what you read in *La Dépêche*?'

'Not usually, sir.'

As the two men shook hands, Sandrine noticed how closely Monsieur Baillard was scrutinising Raoul's face. As if searching for something, some sense of recognition or familiarity. 'It is an honourable local name you have,' Baillard said.

Raoul nodded. 'The steward to Raymond-Roger Trencavel was called Bertrand Pelletier, I know. My brother used to tell me stories about him. Viscount Trencavel, Guilhem du Mas and Sajhë de Servian, others. The great heroes of the Midi, he called them.'

For a moment, something flickered in Baillard's amber eyes, a window to another story, an older story, but then it was gone.

'My father was always pointing out street signs to me when I was little,' Sandrine said. 'It was something of a crusade of his to have local men remembered in practical, visible ways. Not just Viscount Trencavel, but also Courtejaire, Cros-Mayreveille, Riquet, Jean-Jaurès. He thought it was the best way to keep the past alive in our memories.'

Raoul nodded. 'My brother thought the same, though it is confusing when streets are forever being renamed.'

'You won't say that when it's your name up on the wall for some heroic act of bravery,' Sandrine teased. 'You'll be all for it then.'

They both laughed. Baillard did not.

'Your father was right,' he said. 'We should remember the dead, those who gave their lives for others. These lands have suffered more than their fair share of occupation and violence. If we do not remember those who have gone before us, we are destined to repeat the same mistakes. We walk blind through time.'

His voice sobered them, brought a different atmosphere to their conversation. Sandrine frowned.

'Surely it's better to look forward?'

'Sometimes, *filha*, yes. But history is perspective. Those who come after us will – may – look back on these times we are living through now and see the situation clearly. It is possible to see the span and the duration of things – a war of two weeks, two months, two years, two hundred years even. It will seem obvious to them which of the decisions we are making today are right and which are not. In the heat of the battle, it can be difficult for good people to act for the best.'

'Only if you have no sense of right and wrong, she said.'

Baillard gave the slightest of smiles. 'Some are fortunate enough to see the world in black and white. Others might perceive the situation the same way, yet feel their actions must be guided by different considerations.' He glanced at Raoul. 'So some view the partisans as freedom fighters, for example. Brave and honourable men and women, refusing to collude with an occupying force. Others think it is the partisans who are the terrorists, preventing France from enjoying peace.'

'But that's ridiculous. Nobody could possibly believe that.'

'Ah, but you know there are some who do.'

Sandrine shook her head. 'I don't accept that there are always two sides to every story. I won't. What happened to Liesl, the way the prisoners were forced on to the train, that was wrong. What's happening in Paris – everywhere – it's wrong. You have to choose.'

Baillard tilted his head to one side. 'Do you think things are so simple, madomaisèla?'

Sandrine raised her chin. 'Yes.'

Baillard smiled, then turned to Raoul. 'And you, Sénher Pelletier?'

He hesitated. 'Most of the time, yes.'

Baillard's eyes rested on Raoul for a moment longer, then he nodded. 'Good. It is good to be steadfast. It is to be hoped your certainty will serve you – serve us all – well.'

Chapter 76

For a moment, Baillard's words hung in the air between them. Then he nodded and, when he spoke again, his voice was practical. The reverie of moments before had gone.

'Sénher Pelletier, I am glad to see you are safe. As, I am sure, is Madomaisèla Sandrine.'

She smiled. 'But where have you been?'

'When I left you, I decided that Coursan would assume I'd head immediately south. So I stayed close to Carcassonne instead. Roullens first, then Montclar, down to Cépie, then Limoux.'

'So close,' she sighed. 'I pictured you in the mountains, on the coast.'

He nodded. 'It was so hard not to turn round and come back,' he said quietly. 'Hardest thing of all.'

'Is there any reason to believe the police are aware of your connection with this house, Monsieur Pelletier?'

'Not from me, sir, no.' He paused, then said: 'Sandrine told me you were there when Antoine was found.'

Baillard nodded. 'He died bravely.'

Raoul briefly bowed his head, but said nothing.

'Did she also tell you that Antoine was working for me?'

'I haven't had a chance.' She turned to Raoul. 'He was supposed to be delivering something to Monsieur Baillard.' She saw his expression change. 'What?' she said quickly. 'Do you know what it was?'

Baillard also sat forward. 'Sénher Pelletier?'

'No, but I found this.'

Raoul opened his rucksack and pulled out the white

handkerchief, grey now from its long journey in the belly of the bag. Baillard's eyes glinted with unexpected hope. Raoul unwrapped the package and placed an iridescent glass bottle in the older man's palm.

'Is it what you were waiting for, Monsieur Baillard?' said Sandrine eagerly.

Baillard let out a long exhalation of breath. 'It might be.'

'Where did you find it?' Sandrine asked Raoul.

'In Antoine's apartment. When he didn't show up, I went to look for him. It was hidden in the cistern, so I figured it was important. It's beautiful, probably valuable, but I thought there had to be more than that. There's something inside.'

Baillard turned the object over in his hands. 'At first glance, this looks as if it could date back to the fourth century of the Christian era. A great deal of evidence of the Roman occupation of this region has come to light. When the land has been ploughed, or in fields where vines were planted and replanted.'

'I found an old brooch in the ruins of the château-fort,' Sandrine said, 'years and years ago. I gave it to my father as a present. He thought it was Roman.' She smiled. 'He said we had to give it to the museum. But later, I discovered he'd kept it, the paper wrapping and the ribbon as well.'

'Humankind has a habit of occupying and reoccupying the same territory over and again. Houses built where once there were temples, shrines to Christian saints on the sites dedicated to the old Roman gods along the routes most travelled.' Baillard lifted the bottle to the light. 'Imagine all the many men and women through whose hands this one small object has passed.'

'Or maybe not so many,' Sandrine said, 'if it has been hidden all this time.'

Baillard smiled. 'True.'

'Why is it so important?' Raoul asked.

'Not of itself, but rather because of what it contains, Sénher Pelletier.'

Sandrine stared at Raoul. 'Why didn't you try to get it out?' she said. 'I would have done.'

'I was tempted, but I was worried about damaging it. And I suppose I wanted to carry on thinking I'd be able to give it back to Antoine in person, so ...'

Baillard nodded. 'Madomaisèla, do you have a pair of tweezers?'

Sandrine charged inside, her footsteps clattering on the wooden steps, and was back in no time.

'Here you are.'

Baillard hooked the piece of grey fabric in the neck of the bottle with the metal points and slowly, carefully, eased it out.

'Wool,' he said. 'Wool was widely used, especially in the colder western territories of the Roman Empire. This is quite thick, so it probably comes from a cloak or an outer garment.'

'Wouldn't it have rotted?'

'That depends on where it has been all this time.'

Baillard sniffed the bottle, in case there was some perfume or liquid inside, then tipped it gently into the palm of his hand. Nothing came. He held it closer to the flame, trying to see inside the narrow neck.

Sandrine watched him pinch the points of the tweezers together and, with a steady hand, thread them into the neck. He released the pressure a little to try to grasp what was inside, then withdrew the tweezers again. Little by little he gained purchase, until finally he managed to draw the tweezers out of the neck of the bottle.

'*Aquí*,' he whispered. 'There.'

Baillard carefully put the bottle down, then, laying the yellow handkerchief from his breast pocket on the table, he even more delicately placed the piece of fabric on it.

'It will be very fragile in the air after so long confined,' he said. 'We must be so careful.'

'Is it the map?' she said.

Baillard didn't answer. 'This, also, is wool, but of a much lighter weave. Perhaps from an undergarment.'

Gently, corner by corner, he opened the square of fabric out with the tweezers. Sandrine leant forward to see better. It was a faded white, yellow in places and brown along the main creases, with simple images. Like a child's drawing.

'It is what you were waiting for, Monsieur Baillard?'

The old man sighed with relief. 'I think so,' he said softly. 'Look, the sun and her shadow to show direction, trees identified by delicate leaves sketched alongside – oak, ash, pine and beech.' He paused. 'And here, a double cross.'

'But even supposing it is genuine, the landscape will surely have changed beyond recognition after all this time. Will it be any use?'

'It is true, *filha*, that rock is quarried, that rivers change their course and that forests are cut down for timber, for houses.' He smiled. 'But the mountains, they change their shape less than anything else. The Pyrenees are much as they ever were.' He pointed with the end of the tweezers. 'So you see, I rather think that might be the Pic de Vicdessos, outside Tarascon. And can you see there, and there, that sequence of ridges. It is very distinctive, this combination of woodland, outcrop and the cave below.'

'I suppose so,' Sandrine said, still looking doubtful.

'Does anyone else know you have this, Sénher Pelletier?'

Raoul shook his head. 'No. At least, I showed César the bottle, though he wasn't very interested.'

'Would he have told anyone?'

'I don't think so.' He frowned, remembering that Sandrine had told him César was also missing. 'I hope not.'

Baillard studied the map for a while longer, then looked

up. 'I am greatly in your debt, Sénher Pelletier. We all are.'

'What are we going to do now?' asked Sandrine.

'Put our plan into action,' Baillard replied.

Sandrine frowned. 'But surely we should start looking for the Codex straight away?'

'*Pas a pas*,' he murmured. 'All in good time. There is everything to be gained by continuing along the path we have set ourselves. The difference is, now we have sight of the map, we can lay our trap in another part of the mountains altogether.' Baillard hesitated for a moment, then said: 'Do you know how to handle a gun, madomaisèla?'

Sandrine's eyebrows shot up. 'I beg your pardon?' She stared at Monsieur Baillard, then realised he was utterly serious. 'I suppose I do. I've fired a shotgun. And a pistol once. Why?'

'It is time you learnt properly.' Baillard turned to Raoul. 'Do you have your service revolver, Sénher Pelletier?'

'Yes.'

Sandrine looked at Raoul, then back to Monsieur Baillard. 'You're not suggesting …' she said, her voice rising. 'But that's madness. Someone's bound to hear us. What if the police are still around? It's too much of a risk.'

'You wish to help, do you not?'

'Yes, but …'

'In which case,' he said quietly, 'it is more of a risk if you cannot defend yourself, should the need arise.'

Sandrine turned cold. 'But if anyone hears us and sees Raoul, they might – will – turn him in.' She shook her head. 'I won't risk it.'

Raoul put his hand on her arm. 'Monsieur Baillard's right, you need to be able to use a gun. We'll be careful. It's a good time of day for it, most people are indoors, sheltering from the heat. And if anyone does hear us, they'll more likely than not think it's a farmer out shooting rabbits. There must be plenty of secluded places around here.'

Sandrine stared at him. 'Raoul, the police were here in Coustaussa. Today. It's not any ordinary day. It's too dangerous. We should wait.'

'We do not have time to wait,' Baillard said. 'There will be no other opportunity.'

'Why?' she said quickly. 'When do you intend to go?'

'Raoul, at first light,' he said. 'I shall follow later in the morning.'

Distress rushed through her. She knew Raoul couldn't stay, but at the same time she had hoped they would have more than a day together. She looked from one to the other, then gave a sharp nod of her head and stood up.

'All right, if you both think it's a risk worth taking. But on one condition.'

'What's that?' said Raoul.

Sandrine held out her hand. 'Come on,' she said. 'Marieta will help.'

Chapter 77

CARCASSONNE

'May I come in?'

Marianne stared at Lucie. Her blonde hair was immaculate and her red lipstick perfectly applied, but she was a shadow of the bright, vivacious girl she had been. She was also holding a suitcase.

'Oh Lucie,' she sighed wearily. 'I don't want to argue.'

'Please, Marianne, I've got nowhere else to go.'

Marianne could see Lucie had done her best to disguise the fact she'd been crying. But her eyes were red and swollen and the powder failed to disguise how pale she was. Marianne was still angry, but their years of friendship pulled at her heart strings. With a sigh, she leant forward and took the suitcase from Lucie's hand and drew her inside.

'What's happened now?' she said.

'My father's back.'

'Oh,' Marianne said. She put the suitcase down at the foot of the stairs, then linked her arm through Lucie's. 'Come into the kitchen,' she said. 'I've got apples stewing on the stove.'

'Wherever did you get apples?'

Marianne didn't reply. 'Sit down, I'll be done in a moment.'

Lucie took off her hat and gloves. 'They smell delicious.'

Marianne continued to stir, the wooden spoon banging against the metal side of the saucepan.

'I found a little cooking brandy Marieta had squirrelled

away at the back of the larder,' she said.

Lucie waited patiently while she took the pan off the heat, covered it with muslin cloth, then left it to stand on the dresser.

'So,' Marianne said. 'Your father.'

Lucie nodded. 'He and six other POWs arrived in Carcassonne yesterday. I'd forgotten what it was like. Tiptoeing around him, trying to second-guess his mood.'

'What happened?'

'At lunchtime he went to find some of his old LVF buddies at the Café Edouard. No doubt to boast about how tough he was, how he'd survived being in prison, how he ran rings around the guards.'

'I can imagine.'

'Well, of course everyone wanted to buy him a drink, and so ...' Lucie shrugged.

'Someone said something about Max?'

'Your neighbour,' Lucie said, jerking her head in the direction of the house next door. 'What's he called?'

'Fournier.'

'That's right. They got talking and Fournier said something about how ashamed my father must be ...' Lucie broke off. 'Well, you can imagine. The next thing, he was storming back into the house, shouting at my mother, demanding to know if it's true.'

'Lord,' Marianne said softly, taking her hand.

'My mother tried to calm him down, told him I was out, but he was in no mood to listen. She cut her head on the corner of the cupboard, but she stuck up for me.' She stopped. 'For once, Marianne, my mother stuck up for me. Told him it was gossip. That I'd hardly left the house for weeks.' She paused again. 'When he demanded to know where I was, she said I'd gone to the market.'

'Did he believe her?'

Lucie shrugged. 'I don't know. He was so drunk, he

could barely stand up. I could hear him banging into the furniture. I stayed in the bathroom, praying he wouldn't be able to get up the stairs. I knew he'd pass out eventually. Once I heard him snoring, I crept out and my mother told me to go before he woke up.' She looked at Marianne, tears brimming in her eyes. 'I packed and came here. I'm sorry.'

'Are you saying that she's turned you out for good?'

'It's him or me,' Lucie said. 'It's always been that way. What's she to do?'

'Oh, Lucie.'

'I know you don't want me here, I know you hate me at the moment. But I didn't know where else to go.'

'I don't hate you, you little fool,' Marianne said, 'I just . . .'

She stopped. There was no point going over it all again.

'I did try to telephone to warn you about Captain Authié. I was telling the truth. And I swear I didn't tell him anything else. He's going to help me, I know he'll keep his word.'

Marianne swallowed a sigh, realising Lucie was determined to hold on to the only chance she thought she had. She got up, went to the larder and poured two small glasses of red wine.

'Still no news about Max then?' she said.

Lucie shook her head. 'I have no rights, I'm not his wife or a relation. No one will tell me anything.' She glanced at Marianne, then let her gaze slide back to her lap. 'Captain Authié is the only person, the only one who's offered to help at all. And I have to know how Max is, I have to. That everything's going to be all right.'

'It will be,' Marianne said mechanically, knowing the odds were against it. Every day the news was worse. 'It might take a little time, but we will find out what's happening.'

'That's the thing,' Lucie said desperately. 'I don't have time.'

'Of course you do. We'll find out why Max has been arrested, and then you can at least write to him. I know it's dreadful waiting, but a few days here or there won't make any difference.'

Lucie shook her head. 'You don't understand.'

'Understand what?'

Lucie drew in her breath. 'I'm pregnant,' she said.

'Oh.' Marianne sat back in her chair. 'I see.'

'We were careful. I don't understand how it happened.'

'Oh,' she said again, then, 'Does Max know?'

She shook her head. 'I wanted him to be the first to know.' She looked up. 'We wanted to get married, you know we did, but … he didn't want to put me at risk. He was thinking of me.'

'Do you think your mother guessed?'

'I have been dreadfully sick.'

'Perhaps she was thinking of you after all.'

'Maybe.'

They heard the kitchen door open and Suzanne came in from the garden. She looked at Lucie with surprise, then put her hand on Marianne's shoulder.

'Everything all right?'

'Lucie's pregnant,' Marianne replied.

'What!' said Suzanne.

'Her father's back and Fournier told him she'd been seen out with Max. She came here to get away from him.'

'I've nowhere else to go,' Lucie said.

Suzanne folded her arms and leant back against the dresser. 'You can't stay here. Fournier's next door and his sister's always at the window, snooping and passing on information.'

Lucie rubbed her face with her handkerchief. 'But what am I going to do? No one can know.'

Marianne and Suzanne exchanged glances. Suzanne shrugged. 'It's up to you,' she said.

Marianne thought for a moment, then she sighed.

'Lucie, listen. I've heard nothing from Sandrine, and that's unlike her. And she needs to know that someone's looking for her. I sent a telegram, but we were thinking of going to see if things are all right.'

For a moment, hurt shone in Lucie's eyes. 'You were going to go without telling me?'

'Do you blame us?' Suzanne said sharply.

'But I . . .' she began, then shook her head. 'No, I suppose I don't.' She paused. 'When were you going to go?'

'As soon as we can,' Marianne replied. 'You'd better come with us. You'll be safer there with Liesl and Marieta until . . .'

For a moment Lucie looked relieved, then her expression changed. 'But if I leave Carcassonne,' she said, anxiety mounting in her voice, 'how will Captain Authié contact me when he gets permission for me to visit Max? I can't leave.'

'Lucie, stop,' Marianne said sharply. 'You've got to get it into your head that you can't trust Authié. He only made the promise to get you to talk about Sandrine. He's not on your side. Certainly not on Max's side.'

'But I'm not interested in politics,' Lucie protested. 'I'm not trying to cause trouble. I just want to get on with my life with Max, that's all.'

'Those days are gone. The occupation affects everything we do, whether you choose to accept it or not.'

Finally, tears began to roll down Lucie's cheeks. 'There must be something.'

'You need to think of yourself now,' Marianne said firmly. 'Of the baby. That's what Max would want you to do.'

'How far gone are you?' said Suzanne in her abrupt way.

'Three months.'

She did the arithmetic. 'Due in January.'

'I suppose so.'

'Haven't you seen a doctor?'

'How can I?' she wailed. 'I'm not married. They'd want to know who the father is. I can't.'

'You don't show,' Suzanne said.

'I haven't been able to keep anything down for weeks.'

'All the more reason to get you to the country,' Marianne said. 'A few weeks of Marieta's cooking and you'll be your old self. We'll carry on trying to find out what's happened to Max, without Authié's help. You mustn't worry any more.'

Lucie was picking at a thread of cotton on her sleeve, thinking about what to do. Marianne smiled. Lucie had always been the same. Holding any set of views passionately, but just as likely to turn round and do the precise opposite.

'What do you say?' she asked.

When Lucie raised her head, Marianne saw her eyes were now dry.

'Would it help if I could get hold of a car?' she asked.

Marianne looked at her, then at Suzanne, then burst out laughing.

Chapter 78

COUSTAUSSA

Sandrine and Raoul were in the woods beyond the Andrieu farm, with six empty glass jars, Raoul's service revolver and some ammunition. Sandrine had tied her hair back off her face and was wearing an old shirt and a pair of slacks of her father's, held up with a leather belt. Raoul's hair was short – cut by Sandrine in the bathroom – and he'd shaved off his beard. He looked more like his old self, the face on the poster, but nothing like the man the Couiza police were looking for.

'Bend your knees and set your feet further apart,' he said. 'No wider than your shoulders. The first rule of marksmanship is that the position and hold must be firm enough to support the weapon.' He paused. 'So, are you comfortable?'

'I suppose so.'

'Raise your right arm, straight in front of you,' he said. 'The gun's got to point naturally at the target. Otherwise the recoil will knock you off balance.'

'It feels all right.'

'Good. Now, close your left eye, focus with your right. Look down the barrel, through the sight. Make yourself breathe, slowly, in and out, get used to the position.'

'Can I shoot?'

'Be patient!' he laughed. 'This isn't about firing a shotgun at a rabbit, whatever lessons those country boys might have taught you. It's about precision, putting the bullet where you want it to go. About being patient.'

'I am being patient,' Sandrine protested.

He laughed again. 'Now slowly, very slowly, squeeze your finger towards you; you're gently pulling the trigger, not jerking at it. Squeeze it. Keep your eye all the time on the target, don't look at anything else, just keep the target in your sight. Then, and only then, when you're ready, shoot.'

Sandrine felt a strange calm go through her. The steady beating of her blood in her ears, an awareness of each of the muscles in her neck, her arm, connected all the way down to the tip of her right index finger on the metal trigger. She ceased to be aware of Raoul or that he was watching her. She exhaled, then, slowly, squeezed. At the last moment, the barrel jumped and the bullet went high.

Frustrated, she let her arm drop. 'What happened?' she said, cross with herself.

'It's what always happens to start with.'

'It didn't used to happen.'

'A shotgun's a very different weapon.'

'I meant Yves' father's revolver, a souvenir of the war.' She paused. 'The last war, I mean.'

'Who's Yves?'

'Just a boy from the village,' she said quickly. 'It was a long time ago.'

'I see.' Raoul looked at her. 'The shot must be released and followed through without any change to your firing position. You anticipated the shot, so at the very last second you lost your aim.'

'I didn't.'

'It's a common mistake. You blink, your arm moves, the bullet misses its target.'

Raoul came round and stood close behind her, touching her shoulder, her elbow, moving her arm a little higher. Sandrine could feel his breath on her cheek, the sweet smell of soap and tobacco. She felt herself blush.

'Now,' Raoul said, once he was satisfied with her position. 'Try again.'

Sandrine took aim. Determined to do it right, she counted down in her head, like swimming in the deeper part of the river at Rennes-les-Bains, slow and steady, breathing in, breathing out. This time, she squeezed the trigger and imagined the bullet shooting down the barrel and out. This time, the glass shattered.

'There!' she said with triumph, turning round to face him.

'Not bad,' he said. 'We'll make a marksman of you yet.'

'Haven't we practised enough?' she said. 'It makes me nervous being out here.'

He smiled. 'There's no one about.'

Raoul leant forward, aligning his arm with the length of hers. Now he was folding his hand over hers, helping her to raise the gun, her exact shadow. Heat flooded through her, making her aware of every inch of her skin, of his skin, of his breath on the back of her neck.

'Now,' he whispered in her ear. 'Try again.'

When the shadows were beginning to lengthen, Raoul and Sandrine returned to the house.

She put her head around the door into the salon. Liesl and Marieta were playing 'vingt-et-un'. Marieta had more colour in her cheeks. Liesl seemed to have recovered from her attack of nerves. Sandrine went back into the hall.

'I can't find Monsieur Baillard,' Raoul said, appearing at the end of the corridor. 'I wanted to tell him about my star pupil.' He took her hand and held it tight.

'What is it?' she said, feeling the urgency in his grasp.

'I was going out of my mind at the thought of not seeing you again.'

Sandrine raised her hand to his cheek, and all the words, spoken and unspoken, shimmered in the air between them. Then, sharp, a glimpse of how life might have been. In different times, not these times, the vision of years of marriage and love and company. The smile slipped from her lips.

'If something happened to you, I don't think I could bear it,' she said.

'Nothing's going to happen to me,' he said.

'You can't say that.'

'I can look after myself.'

Sandrine sat down at the bottom of the stairs. 'When you were taking refugees across the border, when you were risking your life for people you didn't even know, probably wouldn't see again, what were you thinking?'

He sat down beside her. 'Mostly you're not thinking at all, only about where to sleep, where the next meal's coming from, if there are police or patrols about.'

'Were you scared?'

He laughed. 'All the time. It's how you survive. Fear keeps you on your guard, keeps you safe.' He threaded her fingers through his. 'You think about one day at a time. Today's the only day that matters.'

'And if things never change?'

'They will,' he said quickly. 'They have to. We'll keep fighting, more people will come over to our way of seeing things, we won't …' He stopped. 'Things will get better, you'll see.'

Sandrine looked at his serious, proud face, his restless eyes bright in his tanned face, then put her arm around his waist. Sensing a change in her, perhaps, Raoul felt suddenly awkward.

'What?' he said, nervous now.

Sandrine stood up and took a couple of steps up the stairs. 'Today is what matters, that's what you said.'

'Yes …'

'And you can't say you'll be all right, because you don't

know. We don't know what will happen when the sun rises tomorrow.'

She kicked off her shoes, which fell clattering back down to the floor, then turned and walked up the narrow stairs, feeling his eyes on her. She didn't know what she intended, not really. Only a voice in her head telling her how little time they might have.

Sandrine stopped, turned then. Looked back at him. Watched as Raoul ran his fingers over his hair, glanced at the shoes lying like an invitation on the floor, not sure what he was supposed to do.

She smiled. In slow motion, it seemed to her, he started to walk up the stairs, then faster, taking them two at a time, until he was standing in front of her.

'Today is what matters,' she said again.

Chapter 79

The sun was sinking down to earth, covering the garrigue in a golden light. Everything was sharp, outlined against the whitening sky.

Audric Baillard stood beside the largest of the *capitelles*, his hand resting on the stone, still warm from the heat of the day. He looked down the low wall that ran alongside the track back towards Coustaussa. Past the old holm oak, past the white walls of the outbuildings of the Andrieu farm, to the cemetery.

To the west, the ruins of the old château-fort. To the east, Arques and Rennes-les-Bains hidden in the green folds of the woods. Ahead, on the far side of the valley, the village of Rennes-le-Château, a semicircle of green houses and the flat red turrets and towers of the ancient Château des seigneurs de Hautpoul. The Visigoths had made the hilltop the capital of their spreading empire, building on older remains. The square towers and high arched windows of the more recent castle were reminiscent of the oldest sections of the walls of the medieval Cité of Carcassonne.

Baillard took the fragile scrap of woollen cloth from its linen shroud in his pocket and held it before him, still unable to believe the turn of fate that had brought it into his hands. Crude though the picture undoubtedly was, he was certain the tallest of the peaks shown was the Pic de Vicdessos. He followed the line to the hiding place at its centre with his eye. Hard to tell without an indication of scale, but he estimated it might be some three or four kilometres north of there. Even so, it was a large area, filled with caves and labyrinthine fissures in the rocks. Once, most of the lower slopes would have been forest. Today, open spaces punctuated the woods.

'*A la perfin*,' he murmured. At last.

Baillard took a deep breath, then began to read out loud the few Latin phrases written on the map. Repeating the words once, then again, hoping to hear the voices calling to him from deep within the earth. He closed his eyes.

'Come forth ...'

And this time, although the sound was still indistinct and blurred and distorted, Baillard perceived the shift of bones within the land. For an instant, a cooling of the air and the light metamorphosing from pink to silver to white. He caught his breath. The rattle of metal and leather, of swords and marching feet. Banners and battle colours, one row behind another behind another, shimmering like a reflection in a mirror. The heroines of antiquity, Pyrène and Bramimonde, the Queen of Saragossa, Esclarmonde de Servian and Esclarmonde de Lavaur. The song of the dead awakening.

'... the spirits of the air.'

Harif, Guilhem du Mas and Pascal Barthès, all those who dedicated their lives so that others might live. The Franks and the Saracens, the battles of Christianity against another new faith. Stories of treachery and betrayal in the eighth century as in the fourth, Septimania conquered and subjugated and occupied once more. The force of arms and the clash of belief.

'A sea of glass ...'

In his mind's eye, Baillard could see the walls of Carcassonne. Charlemagne's army camped on the green plain beside the river Atax. Looking out over the plains of Carsac, the widow of King Balaak, the sole survivor in the besieged Cité. Straw soldiers set along the ramparts to protect Carcas, the Saracen queen, from the power of the Holy Roman Emperor. No man left living to send out to parley. Burning what little remained for warmth.

'A sea of fire.'

Baillard closed his eyes as the legend took shape in his mind. Every schoolchild knew the story. How Dame Carcas fed the very last grains of food in the starving city to a pig, then tossed the animal over the wall. When its sides split open, and undigested food spilled out, the deception was sufficient to persuade Charlemagne that the Cité had food and water enough to withstand. He lifted the siege and struck camp, until the single note of an elephant-tusk horn called him back and the Tour Pinte bowed down in homage at Dame Carcas' behest.

Carcas sonne, so went the phrase. Carcas is calling.

A story to explain how Carcassonne got its name. A fairy tale about a brave woman and an army of straw men defeating the might of the army of the Holy Roman Emperor. A myth, no more.

And yet.

Baillard took a deep breath. However impossible the legend of Carcas might be, the Cité itself never did fall to Charlemagne. What had saved Carcassonne? Could it be that, behind this schoolboy legend, lay a deeper and different truth?

'And come forth the armies of the air.'

Now, in the smallest of spaces between one beat of the heart and the next, Baillard thought he could see the transparent imprint of those he had loved. Foot soldiers in the shimmering ranks of the ghost army as it began to breathe and take form. Viscount Trencavel and the *seigneurs* of the Midi. From Mirepoix and Fanjeaux, Saissac and Termenès, Albi and Mazamet. And further back in the serried ranks, the *cavaliers* alongside whom he had once fought.

He caught his breath. Could he see Léonie's copper hair, like a skein of burnished cloth? The *chanson de geste*, earlier than the Song of Roland, earlier even than *la canso* of Guilhèm de Tudèla, a poem that Baillard himself had completed. And her? Might he yet see her? The girl in a red cloak and a green dress, for whom he had waited for eight hundred years.

'Alaïs,' he murmured.

Baillard spoke the words once more, but the atmosphere was different. The boundaries of what was and what might be no longer merged one into the other. A diminuendo, the voices fainter now, the outlines faded to grey.

He opened his eyes. He was left with the promise of what might be, nothing more. He understood. The fragments he had spoken were not enough, not sufficient unto the task. He clenched his fist. These times had been foretold by Ezekiel and Enoch. By Revelation. Of the seas turning to blood and the skies black, fish dying on the shore and the trees dead in the soil, mountains torn from the earth in protest. In these modern times of the twentieth century, ancient prophecies of thousands of years ago were, finally, coming to pass.

Baillard knew he must find the Codex. Not only because it was the one thing that might serve their cause and change their present. But also because in it lay his only chance of salvation. If he found it and spoke the verses set down, not merely fragments of them, then the army would come. Alaïs might come. Baillard did not think he could carry on living without her.

'Every death remembered ...'

The minutes passed. The air became still. The land began to sing its usual song. Cicadas, the wind in the garrigue, the whistling of birds.

Little by little, Baillard returned to the present. No longer the soldier he once had been, but an old man again, standing in the fields beyond the Andrieu farm. The sun was sinking to earth now, setting the shadows chasing one another across the hills on the far side of the valley. He sighed, then turned his attention once more to the map in his hands. He didn't think Sandrine or Raoul had noticed there was a rudimentary signature on the bottom left-hand corner. Seven letters and an icon, some kind of mark, after the name. He peered closer. It was a cross with four equal arms, a symbol that had more in common with Roman images of the sun and the wheel than the Christian cross.

Proof, surely, that the Codex had been smuggled from the great library of Lugdunum. By someone who was part of the community. He looked at the signature again, holding it carefully to catch the light and managed to read the name written in the corner of the map.

Arinius.

‡

Codex XII

‡

GAUL
AQUIS CALIDIS
AUGUST AD 342

Arinius woke at dawn after a restless night. He knew he would soon have to leave his stone sanctuary. August was entering her final weeks, the temperature was growing less fierce. It was time for him to move on. He could not afford to stay any longer in these tranquil valleys.

For a week and more he had slept well. But last night the sweats had come once more and he had coughed and coughed until he thought his ribs might break. There were specks of blood on his clothes and a tight pressure in his chest. He was bone tired. A visit to the baths in Aquis Calidis, he hoped, might just keep the illness from taking hold.

The trail down the hillside was pleasant, following the river on its meandering path through the valley and deep and ancient woods. Arinius felt his spirits lift. There was a breeze, and white wisps of clouds were veiling the face of the sun. There was no one about. He'd seen no one since Couzanium. No sign of bandits or trouble of any kind.

The confluence of salt- and freshwater rivers made Aquis Calidis a natural place for the Roman conquerors of the region to build a bathhouse. Hot, warm and cold springs, bristling with minerals, flowing naturally out of the ferruginous rock. Once, so he had heard in Couiza, visitors from all over Septimania had travelled the Via Domitia to the settlement. Senators, generals, the descendants of the families of the Tenth Legion, who had settled the land when Gaul had been absorbed by Caesar into Rome's Empire. Times had changed. Now, most of those old spa towns were deserted, down on their luck, the once busy streets echoing with the footsteps of the past.

At the entrance to the town, Arinius stopped and looked at the buildings of the *thermae* with pleasure. Like the town itself, the buildings had seen better days, but there was nonetheless an elegance and a faded beauty in the Ionic columns and white marble caryatids and vaulted ceilings of the atrium. A row of arched windows and diamond-shaped openings, all perfectly in proportion. A classical building in the folds of the green hillside.

He peered into the gloom beyond. There was no attendant on duty and, not knowing the way things were run, he couldn't tell if that was because he had come too early or because the baths no longer regularly opened. He could detect no signs or smells of an *unctuarium* or gymnasium. The mosaic floors in the *tepidarium* were chipped and dull.

Arinius was disappointed, even though he had not expected much. The merchant had told him that few made the journey here any more and that local people – the grandchildren and great-grandchildren of the original inhabitants of the valley – had, little by little, turned away from the customs the Romans had imposed upon them and gone back to the ways of their ancestors.

Giving up on the idea of the bathhouse itself, he followed the signs to the hot springs, which were accessed via a narrow path leading down to the gorge cut by the flow of the water. He made his way along the riverbank on the far side, until he saw the hot spring at the side of the river. Arinius removed his leather sandals, left his cloak, tunic and undergarments folded on a rock, took off the bottle from around his neck. Then he climbed down into the hot, rust-coloured waters and settled himself comfortably.

With the water lapping pleasantly on his legs and feet, he looked up at the halo of green and wine-coloured leaves on the hillside that flanked the river gorge. He wondered what the archbishop of the community in Lugdunum would say if he could see him.

Arinius was aware that, in his months of solitude, he had travelled some distance from the strictures of the way of life in which he had been raised. He no longer saw privation as requisite, as essential for a greater understanding of God. Now he believed that God dwelt more in the natural world than in the confines of a building, a church, a shrine, anything made by men. He saw the hand of God in the stars at night, heard His breath in the birdsong and the music of the river. As he had become stronger, Arinius felt God moving in his blood, his bones, his muscles. This was the essence of his faith. Not in proselytising, not in the impulse that sought to subdue heresy, other faiths, but rather in a private and personal covenant. Arinius lay back in the water, a stone for his pillow, and closed his eyes.

He had no idea how long he had been lying there, only that the voice, when it came, was shockingly loud in the silence of the day.

'*Salve.*'

His eyes snapped open. He looked up to see a man of middle years, a shock of grizzled grey hair on his head and chest, with broad arms and shoulders.

'Mind if I join you?'

Arinius could not place the accent. He was immediately on his guard, but he gestured with his hand.

'Of course not, please.'

The newcomer lowered himself into the waters with a grunt and a sigh. To begin with, he seemed content to sit in silence. From the scars and marks on his torso, the crooked line of his nose, Arinius suspected he had once been a soldier.

'Where are you from, friend?' the man asked.

Arinius didn't believe the Abbot would still be hunting him after all these months, or so far south, but he blurred his answer all the same.

'Carcaso,' he replied. 'A castellum some forty miles north.'

The stranger nodded. 'I know it.'

'What of you, *amice*?'

'Tolosa,' he replied.

Arinius recognised the name. He knew there was a large Christian community there. He looked at the stranger with a keener interest, wondering if he was of the same faith.

'You are a long way from home,' he said lightly.

The man looked directly at him. 'As are you.'

Arinius nodded, but said nothing more. For a while longer they sat in awkward proximity, their feet nearly touching. Arinius glanced at the pile of clothes the man had placed on the riverbank, seeing the iron tip of a dagger in a leather sheath, resting on a heavy brown tunic. His sense of calm had left him and he was nervously aware that the Codex in its cedar tomb was in his bag. He had not felt he could leave it unguarded in his shelter, but the man had only to reach out a hand to find it. Arinius wanted to leave the pool, but he didn't wish to offend his companion. Or provoke trouble.

He sat, uneasy, uncomfortable, conscious of the man watching him, until he could bear it no longer. Then he smiled and excused himself. He got out of the hot waters, walked a little way along the bank to dry and to dress, then, as quickly as he could manage, and without making it obvious, he retraced his steps back up to the road.

Only when he had climbed up out of the gorge and was standing close to the *thermae* did he turn around. He was disquieted to see the man was now nowhere to be seen.

Chapter 80

Coustaussa
August 1942

Dawn. The first of the birds were beginning to sing. Light was giving shape back to the room. The heavy dresser, the objects collected over a lifetime.

Sandrine and Raoul were lying side by side in her father's bedroom at the back of the house. A mirror image of one another, his dark hair and hers, his suntanned face and arms and her shoulders, lying bone to bone, skin against skin.

'Are you frightened of what might happen?'

'Not any more.'

'No, I'm serious,' she said.

Raoul smiled. 'So am I.'

Sandrine sat up. They were lying on top of the sheet, almost dressed, a layer of innocent cotton and silk still between them. She looked towards the open window, the shutters left open to let the new day in, pinching herself. She was astonished that she didn't feel the slightest bit self-conscious or awkward. She glanced at him, then away. She didn't know if he had spent the night with a girl before; she assumed he had.

'Are you all right?' he said, sensing the shift in her. 'You don't want me to go?'

'No. Stay.'

A small voice in her head wondered what Marianne would say, what Marieta would say, but she didn't feel guilty. Nothing about it felt wrong.

'Are you sure you're all right?' he asked again.

Sandrine wrapped her bare arms around her knees. 'Just thinking.'

'That way madness lies.'

'Yes.'

For a little while, they were quiet again.

'Do you think Monsieur Baillard's plan will work?' she said eventually.

'We'll find out soon enough.'

'You can't be seen in Tarascon,' she said. 'The posters are everywhere now.'

'I'll be all right. I'm more worried about you,' he said quietly. 'You're the one taking the risk.'

'Monsieur Baillard will be there. And Geneviève and Eloise.'

'I'm not happy. I don't like the idea of Coursan – whatever his name actually is – being anywhere near you.'

'I'll be all right,' she said, echoing his words. 'Don't worry.'

'You can't blame me for wanting to look after you.'

'I don't, it's just . . .'

From below, the sounds of breakfast being prepared floated up the stairs, intruding into their private world.

'We'd better get up,' she said.

She dressed in a pair of shorts and a sleeveless shirt, then ran downstairs to the kitchen. Marieta was sitting in the armchair darning a tea towel. Liesl was reading a book on photography, which Sandrine recognised from her father's study. Monsieur Baillard sat at the table. If any of them realised that she and Raoul had spent the night together in the same room, nobody said anything.

Sandrine poured herself a cup of ersatz coffee from the pan on the stove, then joined Monsieur Baillard at the table. She looked at the sheet of paper, which had been transformed into a heavy yellow papyrus, the texture veined and covered with sharp black geometric letters.

'Are you making progress, Monsieur Baillard?'

'The age of the paper will not deceive an expert – it is many centuries too recent – but with what we have done, I believe it should be sufficient to fool an untrained eye. For a short time, at least.'

'What language is it?'

'Coptic. Many of the early Christian texts, although originally in Greek, were translated into local languages. In Egypt, in this time period, Coptic was the language of theology and thought.'

'Monsieur Baillard speaks and reads many ancient languages,' said Marieta. 'Hieroglyphics even, medieval Latin and Arabic, Hebrew ...'

'Now, Marieta,' he said softly, raising his hands in embarrassment.

Sandrine grinned at the pride on Marieta's face, relieved to see she was ever more like her old self. She heard footsteps, then Raoul appeared in the doorway. She felt Marieta's eyes on her and suddenly worried she might guess, as she always did, what was going on.

'Are you all right, Madomaisèla?' Marieta said under her breath.

Sandrine smiled at her, then nodded. 'I'm happy,' she said.

Marieta held her gaze a moment, then turned to Raoul. 'Sénher Pelletier, I hope you slept well. There is coffee on the stove.'

Chapter 81

Carcassonne

Lucie was waiting in the blue Peugeot 202 at the corner of the rue Mazagran. Marianne came out of the front door with her usual shopping basket. Suzanne went out of the back with the luggage. They didn't want to risk Madame Fournier seeing the suitcase and putting two and two together.

Marianne and Lucie were both dressed for the sun, in short-sleeved cotton dresses and straw hats. If they were stopped, they would look like any other girls going for a summer outing. Suzanne was wearing her customary slacks and shirt.

'How did you get the car?' Marianne said, putting her things in the boot.

'My father went back to the Café Edouard last evening. His drinking companions carried him home, out for the count. I waited until I could hear him snoring, then crept in through the workshop, took the key and the car. By the time he wakes up, we'll be south of Limoux.'

'How did you manage to get enough fuel?' Suzanne was peering at the three full cans of petrol on the floor in the back of the car.

'From the "official" pumps,' Lucie said. 'I said it was for him. Returning POW and all that . . .'

They drove out on the Route de Toulouse, heading for the Montréal road. A few kilometres out of town, they saw their first roadblock. Ahead of them, a car was pulled over, the doors and bonnet open, being searched by police.

'Shall we take another road?' suggested Marianne.

Lucie turned off and doubled back, then followed a smaller road heading south.

They arrived in Couiza a little after midday. Lucie turned off the engine, then slumped theatrically back in her seat.

'I know it's not much further, but she's got to cool down a little. I need to put fresh water in the radiator, otherwise she won't cope with the hill. It's steep, you said?'

Marianne nodded. She got out, then Suzanne climbed through from the back.

'Hot,' she said.

Lucie rolled her neck, to shake the drive out of her shoulders, then reached into the glove compartment, pulled out her powder compact and lipstick, tilted the rear-view mirror and started to do her face.

'I look a sight,' she said.

Suzanne lit a cigarette and walked away from the car.

'She always has tobacco, how come?'

'She claims her father's allowance, I think,' Marianne said, not adding the fact that it came more often from people Suzanne and she had helped. 'How long do you think we'll need? I'm keen to be there.'

'Once I've filled her up with water, it won't be long.'

The girls went to the Grand Café Guilhem on the bridge. One or two people recognised Marianne and nodded, but mostly people kept themselves to themselves. They took a table in the shade, close to the door, and ordered three glasses of wine.

Suzanne nodded to Marianne. 'You think we're safe here?'

Marianne shrugged.

'How are you holding up, Lucie?' she said quietly.

'Fine and dandy,' Lucie replied, though her eyes were anxious.

In the heat of the day, nothing was stirring. Few sounds were heard, just the occasional clatter of a plate or a glass from somewhere in the dark interior. They finished up, paid and walked back out into the blistering August sun.

Lucie fanned herself with her hat, Marianne looked around at the familiar landmarks, then her eyes widened.

'It can't be.'

'What?' Suzanne said.

'There, look.'

Coming towards them, on the far side of the concourse, was Sandrine, accompanied by an elderly man in a pale linen suit.

Chapter 82

At first Sandrine thought she was imagining it. She lifted her hand to shield her eyes and saw she wasn't mistaken. Lucie's corn-coloured hair and Suzanne's short crop were so distinctive. And her sister was wearing her favourite blue dress.

'Marianne!' she cried. She walked faster, then broke into a run. 'Marianne, I can't believe it.'

She flung her arms around her, then kissed Suzanne and Lucie.

'I can't believe it,' she said again. 'What are you doing here? More to the point, how did you even get here? We had such a storm, the line's still closed at Alet-les-Bains. There've been no trains for days.'

'Lucie "borrowed" one of her father's cars,' Marianne said, making inverted commas in the air with her hands. 'As for why, since you didn't call – and didn't answer the telegram I sent – Suzanne and I thought we had better come to see for ourselves everything was all right.'

'Telegram?' Sandrine shook her head. 'Didn't get anything, but never mind. Marieta will be so pleased to see you. *I'm* so pleased to see you.'

'It's nice to be out of Carcassonne,' said Marianne. 'How's it been? Everything all right?'

'A bit odd at first, without you and Papa,' Sandrine admitted, 'but then …' She paused, choosing her words carefully. 'But the thing is – and there's nothing to worry about now, because she's going to be fine – the thing is, Marieta was taken ill almost immediately we arrived.'

'What do you mean, ill?' Marianne said quickly.

'A heart attack,' Sandrine said, then, seeing Marianne's expression, rushed on. 'Very mild.'

Marianne put her hand to her mouth. 'Oh God.'

Sandrine hugged her. 'She's on the mend, really she is. It was more of a warning, but it was pretty frightening at the time. The doctor says there's no reason she shouldn't make a full recovery. She just has to keep off her legs and let us do the work.'

'How's she managing that?'

'Not awfully well. But Liesl's been wonderful. And without Monsieur Baillard, well . . . Let me introduce you.' He was standing a little apart, his hat held in his hands. 'He's the friend Marieta wrote to, remember? She used to work for him in Rennes-les-Bains when she was young and why she was so keen to come to Coustaussa in the first instance.' She smiled. 'Monsieur Baillard, may I present my sister Marianne.'

He held out his hand. 'Madomaisèla Vidal.'

'It's a pleasure to meet you, Monsieur Baillard.'

'The pleasure is mine,' he said formally. He turned to Sandrine. 'I will leave you to your reunions. You are certain, *filha*? There is still time for you to change your mind.'

Sandrine shook her head. 'No. I want to do it.'

He nodded. 'Very well. Until Wednesday, then. *Dimècres*.'

Sandrine dropped her voice. 'Promise me you'll look after Raoul, Monsieur Baillard. Don't let any harm come to him.'

'I will do my best,' he said.

He raised his hat again, then slowly walked across the concourse towards the Espéraza road. Sandrine watched him go with a catch in her throat, something about his unruffled presence reminding her of her father. She sighed.

'What's happening on Wednesday?' Marianne asked.

Sandrine turned to her sister. 'Antoine Déjean's funeral in Tarascon.'

'Yes, we saw in the newspaper he had been found,' she said quietly, 'though I'm not sure—'

'Antoine was working for Monsieur Baillard.'

Marianne looked doubtfully after the frail white figure, like a ghost on the far corner of the square.

'Working for him? In what capacity?'

'I'll explain when we're home,' said Sandrine, dropping her voice even lower. 'Raoul's stepped in to help now.'

Marianne's eyes narrowed. 'He's been in touch?'

A brief smiled played across her sister's lips. 'Better. He came in person.'

'How did he know you were here?' she said.

Sandrine shrugged. 'He took a chance. He was worried that now Antoine has been found, Coursan would make renewed efforts to track me down.' She shrugged again. 'I don't know if he's right.'

'Coursan . . .'

'Coursan, or whatever his name is. The man who set Raoul up.'

'Authié,' Marianne said. 'It's Authié.'

'It is? How do you know?'

'I had his description from several people, in the end,' Marianne said, going on to explain what had happened in Carcassonne. 'Attached to the Deuxième Bureau.'

'Well,' Sandrine said, keeping her voice steady. 'I'm sure everyone's worrying too much. If he – Authié, Coursan – wanted to find me, he could. Everyone knows we have a house here. And as Lucie said, it was me who handed my details to the police in the first place. It's not her fault.'

'All the same . . .' Marianne started, then decided to hold her tongue. 'Where's Raoul now? Still in Coustaussa?'

Sandrine shook her head. 'He left this morning with Geneviève. She's taking him to somewhere south of

Belcaire, where Eloise will meet him and take him on to Tarascon. He can't travel openly, there are posters everywhere.'

'Seen them,' Suzanne said. 'And I'm sorry to interrupt, but are you ready to get going? The waiter wants the table and Lucie needs to lie down.'

'Why? What's wrong with Lucie?' asked Sandrine.

Marianne sighed. 'We have a lot more to tell you too.'

Codex XIII

Gaul
Aquis Calidis
August AD 342

Arinius walked quickly up through the woods. He was breathless and his chest was tight, but he didn't slow his pace, despite the heat. He could see no one and heard nothing unusual, nothing more than the sounds of the land – rabbits in the undergrowth, the occasional bird on the wing, the stridulation of crickets in the dry grasslands. Common sounds that somehow now carried a sense of threat within them. There was no one around, the hillside was deserted, but he felt he was being watched.

In the deepest part of the wood, he paused. Faint but unmistakable, he heard it. The crack of a twig, the sound of footsteps in the bone-dry undergrowth, the indication that there was someone – or something – on the slopes below. An animal, a boar or stag? A person? Arinius stood still, straining to hear, but the wood echoed silent around him.

After a minute or two more, he set off again, walking even faster. Turning round, looking into the ancient evergreen shadows of the wood. Breaking into a run, his own fear snapping at his heels.

Without warning, he felt himself flying backwards. His cloak wrenched hard at his neck and he felt the clasp on his mother's brooch snap and fly off into the undergrowth as his feet went from under him. He started to fall, tumbling off the path into the thick undergrowth. Arinius threw out his hands to protect himself, trying to grasp at a root or the trunk of a tree to slow himself down, but he kept somersaulting down the slope.

Finally he came to a halt. For a moment he lay sprawled on the steep ground, looking up through the canopy of leaves to the blue sky, dazed and disorientated. Little by little the world came back into focus. He rolled on to his side, then got himself into a sitting position. He put his hand to his leg, and his fingers came back sticky with blood. His hands were scratched too.

He looked back up to where he'd slipped, and realised he hadn't lost his footing, but had rather walked into a rope tied between two trees. A trapper's net. At least, he hoped that was what it was. The alternative was more disquieting.

Then he heard the sound again. There was no doubt that someone was walking up the path, following the route he had taken, someone trying not to make any noise. A steady and careful placing of one foot after the other.

Arinius looked around in panic, then realised that in fact his fall might be the saving of him. Unless the person tracking him left the path and descended into the thicket of the slopes, they wouldn't see him. Struggling not to make any noise that would betray his hiding place, he slithered into the narrow gap between the thickest of the laurel bushes, and pulled his cloak around him. He had a clear view of the path and, above and to his left, the trapper's net itself.

The footsteps got closer, closer. Arinius held his breath, certain the frantic beating of his heart would give him away. He peered up through the veil of leaves. Feet, legs, a hand resting on the hilt of a hunting knife. Broad shoulders and back, a shock of grizzled grey hair. Even though he had been expecting it, it was a blow to find his suspicions confirmed. The man had followed him from Aquis Calidis.

Suddenly Arinius felt the familiar rasping in his throat. Desperate to prevent an attack, he swallowed hard, then again to stop himself coughing. He put his hand over his mouth, steadying his breathing as he had learnt to do, and gradually felt the irritation recede.

He crossed himself in silent thanks.

He watched the man bend down and touch the rope, as if he was hoping to see some indication that his quarry had passed this way. Then he straightened up, stepped over it and carried on up to where the path diverged. The left-hand spur led towards the shepherds' settlement. The right-hand route doubled back towards the villages to the east of Aquis Calidis.

Arinius pressed his bag close to his side, grateful that he had left little of value in the camp.

Time passed. Arinius lost track of how long he waited, but still he didn't move from the sanctuary of the deep evergreen. Still, he heard the occasional crack of arid leaves or a stone dislodged on the path. Finally, the footsteps grew more and more faint, until there was no sound at all.

He thought the man had gone in the opposite direction. He was certain of it, yet waited longer. The cut on his leg was stinging, but it didn't really hurt. The shadows lengthened as the sun moved round, turning the leaves from gold to green once more in the changing of the late-afternoon light.

Finally, when he was certain the threat had passed, Arinius came out of his hiding place. He stood up and stretched, flexing his muscles and bringing the life back into his fingers and his toes. There had been no sound at all for some time, but he was still careful.

He climbed back up to where he'd fallen and paddled his hands in the dry leaves, looking for his mother's brooch. He couldn't find it. Much as it pained him to leave it behind, he didn't feel he could delay any longer. He had put his own wishes before his mission. He should never have stayed in the valley for so long.

When he caught his first sight of his stone dwelling, he stopped and cast his eyes around. He saw no signs the camp had been discovered, and when he cautiously went inside, everything was exactly as he had left it.

Already nostalgic for the time he had spent in this patch of land, he packed his few belongings. He left anything that was not essential for his journey.

Arinius looked out over the garrigue, the grassland bleached white in the heat of the day, and wondered if he would return to watch the sun set over these hills again. He feared he would not. He put his hand on the stone, still retaining some heat from the day, imprinting the shape of it on the flesh of his palm. Then he took a look around at the curved entrance and the flat plot of land behind it where he might, in a different story, have planted chard or carrots. Created his own garden.

With a catch in his throat, Arinius set out on the last leg of his journey. Bearing the Codex to its final resting place in the mountains of Pyrène.

Chapter 83

BELCAIRE
AUGUST 1942

Raoul was sitting in the woods south of Belcaire. Knees drawn up, his jacket unbuttoned and the laces of his boots loosened at the top, he had his pistol in his pocket and his rucksack propped between his legs.

They had made good time. Geneviève Saint-Loup taking him across country through Quillan and Lavelanet, skirting around the road leading to Montségur, then on to Belcaire where he was due to meet her sister, Eloise, who'd guide him to the final destination.

'Smoke?' he asked.

The boy who'd come to tell him Eloise had been delayed had the same dark hair and dark skin of most of the people of the Tarascon valleys. He nodded, and Raoul passed him the cigarette. The boy took a couple of deep drags, then passed it back.

'Where are you from?'

'Hereabouts,' the boy replied. He'd obviously been told not to give any information away. 'You?'

'Carcassonne originally.'

'You're a long way from home.'

'It's not really home any more,' he said with a sudden flash of grief for Bruno. Grief, then guilt. He hadn't thought about his mother for some days. He had considered writing, but he was sure the house would be under surveillance. He sighed. His mother wouldn't read a letter anyway.

'Where were you stationed?' the boy asked.

Raoul brought his thoughts back to the present. 'On the Maginot Line to start with, the *secteur fortifié* in Faulquemont. What about you?' he added, despite the fact the boy didn't look old enough to have fought anywhere.

'Missed it,' he said. 'Making up for it now.' He cast a quick look at Raoul. 'You know?'

'More important now,' Raoul said, and saw the boy flush at the compliment. 'After the first few months, I got sent to the Ardennes. March 1940.'

'Did you see much fighting?'

'Not much. Spent most of my time being posted from one place to another.'

'What was the point of that?'

'You tell me.' Raoul shrugged. 'None of it makes sense to me. Didn't know what they were doing.'

The boy offered Raoul his canteen. Raoul took a swig, blinked as the rum hit the back of his throat, then wiped the neck before handing it back.

'You got someone?' he said. 'A girl?'

The boy rummaged inside his top jacket pocket. He produced a cheap holiday snapshot and held it out to Raoul between dirty, nicotine-stained fingers.

'Coralie,' he said proudly. 'We can't afford to get married yet, but as soon as I've got enough for a ring – silver, something classy, you know – I'm going to ask.'

Raoul looked at the photograph of a gentle, plump girl holding an unwilling kitten. She looked the spit of Geneviève.

'Pretty,' he said, handing the picture back. 'She's a lucky girl.'

'Thanks.' The boy put the photo away. 'What about you, are you married?'

Raoul shook his head. 'Not married, no.'

'Don't want to be tied down?'

The simple innocence of his attempt at a man-to-man conversation made Raoul smile. He passed the cigarette across again. 'No, it's not that,' he said. 'There is someone.'

'Got a picture?'

Raoul tapped the side of his head. 'Up here, you know?'

'Coralie and me have known each other since we were so high. Can't wait to be married, she can't. One of four sisters, all look just the same. It's her oldest sister, Eloise, who's coming later.'

Raoul smiled. 'I've met Geneviève.'

The boy put the snap away again. 'If you're happy with your girl,' he said, 'I'd hang on to her.'

'I intend to,' he said seriously. 'Maybe I should even take a leaf out of your book.'

'Then why wait? I'm telling you, it's all girls want. Marriage, a nice house to look after, a couple of kids.'

Raoul hid a smile, suspecting that Sandrine might want rather more than that. But the simple image caught at his heart all the same. The thought of her standing at the door, waving him goodbye as he went off to work in the morning, being there when he came home. A world that no longer existed.

He finished the cigarette, pinched the ash at the end, then put the stub in his pocket. He leant back against the tree, looking around at the deep green of the woods and the mountains beyond, and waited for night to come. It was going to be a long wait.

Chapter 84

COUSTAUSSA

Sandrine, Marianne, Suzanne and Lucie were sitting at the table in the kitchen. While the sisters talked, Suzanne had raided Monsieur Vidal's cellar. Geneviève had cycled up from Rennes-les-Bains to let Sandrine know Raoul had arrived safely in Belcaire, and stayed to help Liesl – under precise orders from Marieta – prepare a scratch meal.

Two hours later and the table was covered in empty plates and dishes, wine bottles. Suzanne sat by the cold fireplace, smoking. Lucie was curled up in an armchair like a cat, taking quick, sharp puffs of a cigarette and tapping the ash into the ashtray. Geneviève and Liesl were at the sink, washing up, and Marieta had gone to lie down.

The atmosphere had been convivial and sociable until Sandrine had told Marianne what Monsieur Baillard was planning. She hadn't shared with her all the information about the Codex, imagining what her reaction might be, but had confined her explanation to the plan itself.

Even so, the mood changed.

'It's ridiculous,' Marianne said again.

Sandrine glanced at the clock. 'If all goes according to plan, by this time tomorrow Raoul will have set the trap.' She frowned. 'Then we'll see.'

Marianne threw her hands in the air. 'Suppose it does all go "according to plan", as you put it. And they – who-ever they are – fall for this ruse of Monsieur Baillard's. Then what? If Authié is pursuing you and Raoul because of this, then he's going to come looking for you. Even if it's someone else, with German money behind them, you and Raoul are making yourselves sitting targets. You're playing with fire.'

Sandrine sighed. 'We've been through this. All we're doing is attempting to buy Monsieur Baillard more time to find the real Codex and also to deflect attention away from us. As soon as Monsieur Saurat in Toulouse confirms—'

'If they find the forgery, if it's taken to him,' Marianne interrupted. 'If.'

'All right, *if*,' Sandrine said, throwing a look at her sister. She wished Marianne would stop putting so many obstacles in the way. She was terrified enough as it was without her pointing out all the things that could go wrong.

'When they – Authié – do find out it's a fake, there's no reason for them to think I was involved in the deception,' Sandrine said firmly. 'I'll have passed on information in good faith, that's the point. Just women's chattering.' She paused. 'Can't you see, Marianne, it's the only way to get Authié to leave us alone. The problem's not going to solve itself of its own accord.'

'You are being naïve,' Marianne said, her voice hard with frustration. 'All of you.'

Geneviève turned around from the sink. 'Monsieur Baillard won't let anything happen to Sandrine,' she said.

'In the same way he didn't let anything happen to Antoine Déjean?' Marianne snapped.

Geneviève flushed.

'I'm sorry,' Marianne said quickly. 'That was uncalled for. I'm just on edge.'

'Antoine didn't follow Monsieur Baillard's instructions closely enough,' Geneviève said quietly. 'But Sandrine will. Raoul will.'

Marianne said nothing for a moment. She glanced at Suzanne, then started talking again.

'I know you all think I'm making too much fuss. But I think it's absurd that you're deliberately putting yourselves in danger for something like this … this fantasy. There's real work to be done, real people suffering every day.'

She stopped, the fight suddenly going out of her voice. Liesl too now turned around and looked at Marianne. An uncomfortable stalemate settled like a cloud over the kitchen. Suzanne reached across and squeezed Marianne's hand, then sat back. Geneviève was watching Sandrine. Only Lucie, having excused herself to go to the bathroom, seemed unaffected by the awkward atmosphere when she came back into the kitchen.

'I've been thinking,' she said.

'Yes?' said Sandrine quickly, grateful for a change of subject.

'About how to get a letter to Max. We're not so far from Le Vernet. Wouldn't it be possible to go there? To the village, at least. See if someone won't take a letter to him.'

Sandrine glanced at her sister, who was now staring in disbelief at Lucie.

'For crying out loud, what on earth's got into everyone? You can't just turn up at Le Vernet. It's madness. You'll be arrested.'

'But you read all the time of messages being smuggled in, smuggled out of prison camps. Raoul told you, Sandrine, didn't he, about how the women would stand outside the camp at Argelès and push letters through the wire to their husbands?'

'Yes,' she admitted, 'but that was before the war. Le Vernet's different.'

'Why's it different?'

'It's a prison camp,' Marianne snapped. 'Not a refugee camp.'

'But Suzanne told me it's still under French control,' Lucie replied. 'And you yourself told me, Marianne, that the Croix-Rouge are allowed to go in. They deliver food parcels, letters.'

'It's impossible.'

Lucie looked at her, then decided not to argue any more. Suzanne opened another bottle of wine and drew Marianne aside. Geneviève and Liesl finished drying up and started to put the dishes away in the cupboard. Lucie hesitated, then came and sat down beside Sandrine.

'How are you feeling?' Sandrine asked her.

Lucie pulled a face. 'So-so. Better in the evenings.'

'Are you excited about it?' she said, glancing at Lucie's flat stomach.

'It doesn't feel real yet.'

'I suppose it doesn't.'

They sat for a moment longer.

'It's not such a stupid idea,' Lucie said in a low voice. 'I can't just sit here doing nothing. Max not knowing. It's not right. I have to tell him. He has to know he will have a family waiting for him when he's released.'

Sandrine frowned. 'It's true, the camp isn't entirely sealed off. The village certainly isn't, at least it wasn't. Raoul knows people who were held there. But, again,' she sighed, 'who knows how much things have changed.'

Lucie looked at her. 'Will you come with me?'

'Me, why me?'

'Obviously Marianne won't,' she carried on. 'She'll try to stop me, and she's still cross with me anyway, whatever she says.' She dropped her voice even lower. 'I've been thinking about it all day. I'm going to have a go, whether you come or not. I'd just rather I wasn't on my own.'

Sandrine found Lucie's bravado strangely impressive. Liesl, who'd clearly been eavesdropping on the conversation, now joined them.

'If I write a letter too, would you take it, Lucie? I know

I can't go, but if I could let Max know I'm all right. That you're all being so kind.'

'Hold on,' Sandrine jumped in. 'Nothing's agreed.'

'Of course I will,' Lucie said to Liesl.

'Will you drive?'

'We're nearly out of petrol and it will be hard to get any all the way out there. Besides, the car might draw attention. By now, my father's probably reported it missing.'

'The train, then. What line serves Le Vernet?'

'It's on the Toulouse to Foix line,' Geneviève said, overhearing the conversation. 'The station after Pamiers. That section of track wasn't affected by the storm, though it's a very small line. Unreliable.'

'What's unreliable?' Marianne asked, catching the tail end of the conversation.

Sandrine didn't want the argument to blow up again. More than that, she saw how exhausted her sister looked and didn't want to make things worse.

'Nothing really,' she said. 'We're just talking things over.'

'The railway to Le Vernet,' Lucie said. 'I'm still thinking about how to take a letter to Max.'

'It's a hopeless idea,' Marianne said wearily. 'You'll be arrested long before you get anywhere near the camp.'

'I agree she can't just turn up at the gate,' Sandrine said. 'But if we go to the village, we could at least find out how other relatives manage to be in contact with their men inside.'

'There might be a way of paying someone to take the letter in. A guard, perhaps,' Geneviève said.

'Perfectly hopeless,' Marianne repeated.

'I'm prepared to give it a try,' Sandrine said, keeping her voice calm. 'At least go to the village, then see.'

'I don't mind going too, if that's helpful,' said Geneviève.

Marianne shook her head. 'Nobody's going anywhere. Don't you understand anything?'

To Sandrine's astonishment, she saw there were tears in her sister's eyes.

'Hey,' Suzanne said in her gruff way. 'It's all right.'

Without another word, Marianne got up, put her chair under the table, and walked out on to the terrace. The door rattled shut behind her. For a moment, none of the girls moved. The room itself seemed to be holding its breath. Suzanne was on the point of following Marianne, when Sandrine stood up.

'I'll go,' she said.

Chapter 85

Marianne was sitting on the wooden seat, looking out at the dusk. Long shadows stretched across the garrigue as the last vestiges of light slipped from the sky.

'We didn't mean to upset you,' Sandrine said, sitting down beside her. 'We're only thinking out loud, trying to find a way to help Lucie.'

She tailed off, seeing her sister wasn't listening. Marianne continued to sit motionless, her hands resting in her lap.

'I didn't mean to upset you,' Sandrine said again.

'I know,' Marianne said.

'Lucie's desperate, that's the thing. She'll try to get there on her own if one of us doesn't go with her.' She paused. 'And you and Suzanne, you do things to help other people – strangers – all the time. You take risks. Is this really so different?'

'We never deliberately put ourselves in harm's way,' she said. 'But it's not that.'

'Then what?'

Marianne shook her head, as if no words would be enough. Sandrine couldn't remember seeing her sister so beaten down before, so unsure. She was always so certain, so self-controlled.

'What is it, Marianne? Tell me?'

For a moment Marianne didn't react, then she gave a long, deep sigh.

'The thing is, I don't think I can do it any more,' she said. 'That's all. I'm too tired, I'm …' she shrugged. 'I'm worn out.'

'Of course you are …'

'I can't do it any more, Sandrine. Worry about everyone, keep everyone, be responsible for everyone. Make sure that the bills are paid, that we have enough to eat. I'm just worn out and I wish …' She broke off. Sandrine took her hand, but it felt like a dead thing, cold and lifeless. 'Sometimes I wish I could look away, like other people seem to be able to do. Not feel it's my job to put things right.'

'But you've always been the one to put everything right,' Sandrine said gently, 'even when we were little. Papa always said, didn't he? You always made everything right.'

'This situation with Lucie, like this business with Monsieur Baillard, I feel it's my job to say no. To try to keep you all safe, even though it makes you – Lucie – cross. I do understand why she wants to try to go to Le Vernet, of course I do, and why you want to go with her. But it's always me that has to tell everyone to be careful. To watch out for you all.'

'Well then,' Sandrine said affectionately.

'I'm frightened all the time, can't you see it?'

'Frightened, you?'

'Terrified. Terrified we'll be caught, terrified of the knock on the door in the middle of the night when the police come. Then what will happen to you? To Marieta? I can't do it. Not any more.'

Sandrine hesitated for a moment, then spoke. 'I can look after myself now,' she said in a steady voice. 'I can make my own decisions – mistakes, no doubt. You've done enough.' She paused. 'I'll go with Lucie, keep her from getting into trouble. I feel I owe her, you know? For not doing something when Max was arrested. I know you think I'm being silly, but it's what I feel.' She paused. 'We'll be back before you know it.'

For a moment, Sandrine didn't think Marianne had properly heard. She put her arm around her sister's shoulder and drew her close.

'You don't have to look after everyone any more.'

Marianne gave a hollow laugh. 'It's not as simple as that. I can't just stop worrying, turn it off like a tap. I've had a lifetime of it.'

Sandrine smiled. 'I know that. But from now on, you're no longer the big sister and me the baby. We'll just be sisters. Equals.'

'Just sisters.' Marianne looked at Sandrine, then held out her hand. 'All right, it's a deal.'

'Deal.' Sandrine hesitated. 'But you won't give up? You'll keep doing things, you and Suzanne?'

Marianne sighed. 'Of course. Someone's got to.'

The girls sat there a while longer, looking out over the landscape of their shared childhood, the house that had kept them safe for so long. Then, from inside, Suzanne's laugh and Liesl's lighter tones, Geneviève talking. Then the slap of cards on the tabletop, and Lucie's triumphant cry.

'There!'

Marianne smiled. 'She's a funny mixture, Lucie. Tough as old boots in some ways, but so naïve in others. Head in the sand.'

'Has she always been like that?'

'Always. She was never the slightest bit interested in the world around her. Before Max came along, it was all films and magazines, Hollywood, the latest releases. Endless discussions of fashion and movie stars. And now a baby on the way.' Marianne sighed.

'Do you think it's wrong?' Sandrine asked, genuinely interested in what she thought. 'Marieta does.'

'Because they're not married, do you mean?'

'Yes.'

'I think they should have been more careful. But wrong, no.'

'Lucie wanted to get married. It's not their fault they aren't.'

'I know,' Marianne said quietly. 'But even if by some miracle Max is released, that won't change. In the meantime, Lucie can't go home. She's got no money. How's she going to live?'

'She'll have to stay here, won't she?'

Marianne nodded. 'I can't see an alternative. She can't go back to Carcassonne, not now her father's there.' She was quiet for a moment, then she turned and looked at Sandrine. 'You are determined to go to Le Vernet?'

'Lucie is,' she replied, 'and I don't see how we can let her go alone.'

'Won't it interfere with what you've agreed with Monsieur Baillard?'

Sandrine hesitated. 'No. I'm not supposed to do anything until I go to Tarascon on Wednesday. I'd rather do something, instead of sitting around waiting and worrying about Raoul, or whether the plan will work. Five days. Plenty of time to get to Le Vernet and back.'

Marianne thought for a moment longer. 'If she's determined,' she said, in her more usual, practical voice, 'tell Lucie not to write explicitly about the baby in the letter. She has to find a way of telling Max without spelling it out, as it were. So the censor doesn't realise.'

'Would it matter so much if the censor knew?'

'This baby will have Jewish blood, Sandrine. If no one knows he – or she – exists, then there's a chance of the child being safe. Whatever happens to Max.'

Sandrine turned cold. She felt stupid not to have realised for herself.

'Of course, yes.'

'And only go to the village,' Marianne continued. 'Find

someone to take the letter up to the camp. I'll telephone Carcassonne and see if the Red Cross has been allowed into Le Vernet recently.'

'Lucie will be really grateful.'

'She should be,' Marianne said, with a flicker of her old impatience.

She stood up and smoothed down her skirt. Sandrine stood up too.

'Do you feel less wretched now?'

Marianne thought for a moment. 'Oddly, I do.' She smiled. 'Come on, let's join the others.'

Inside the kitchen, the air was thick with tobacco smoke and the gentle scent of a *citronelle* candle.

On the table, the new bottle of red wine stood half empty. The white china ashtray was patterned with grey ash and white filters with smudges of red lipstick. The game of cards immediately stopped. Everyone looked round.

'All right?' asked Suzanne.

Marianne nodded. 'Yes. Fine now.'

Suzanne held up the bottle. 'A glass?'

'Please.'

'Sandrine?'

'Just a little.'

Lucie immediately went over to Sandrine, another cigarette between her red-painted nails.

'Well?' she said in a whisper.

'It's all right. We'll go,' Sandrine replied. 'But to the village, not to the camp itself.'

Lucie sighed with relief. 'You talked her round, thank you.'

'No,' Sandrine said, feeling protective of her sister. 'No, not at all. Marianne understands how you feel, Lucie. She's just trying to keep us from getting into hot water.'

'Well, however you did it, thanks, kid,' she said, sounding like her old self. 'I intend to go, one way or the other, but I'd rather have Marianne's blessing.'

Sandrine put her hand on Lucie's shoulder. 'We'll try to find someone to deliver the letter for you. Whatever happens, there's no chance of you seeing Max. You accept that?'

'I know, I know.'

From the expression on Lucie's face, Sandrine could see she wasn't listening.

'Lucie, I'm serious.'

'I know,' she said. 'I understand.'

'Just so long as you do.'

Sandrine caught her sister smiling at her, a mixture of amusement and affection on her face. Something else too, regret perhaps. Sandrine smiled as well, then raised her glass to the room.

'Since we're all here for once,' she began.

'Wait!' Liesl said, seizing her camera. 'All right, I'm ready.'

'To us,' Sandrine gave the toast.

Geneviève, Suzanne and Lucie all raised their glasses. Marianne tilted hers towards Sandrine.

'To us all,' Sandrine repeated, as the flash went off. *'A notre santé!'*

Chapter 86

TARASCON

Baillard made good speed to Tarascon and went immediately to Pujol's house, where he explained what he was intending to do with Sandrine and Raoul's help.

'Do you trust Pelletier?' Pujol asked.

Baillard had considered the question seriously. Raoul reminded him of men he had known in the past, one man in particular. The same combination of bravery and certainty, lack of judgement on occasion, coupled with loyalty and courage. That man had proved himself to be a true *cavalier* of the Midi. They had been rivals. In the final hours of his life they had become, if not friends, then certainly allies.

'I do.'

Pujol stared at him. 'You don't look too sure about that, Audric.'

'An old man's memories, nothing more.'

Pujol grunted. 'Boy's got a murder charge hanging over him.'

'Yes.'

'Is he guilty?'

'No.'

'Framed?'

'It seems so.'

Pujol topped up his glass. 'Where's Pelletier now?'

'Went with Geneviève Saint-Loup as far as Belcaire, then her sister Eloise was to meet him and take him to the site.'

'Why didn't you travel together?'

'Safer alone. And people less likely to remark on the presence of a young man with a girl, *è*?'

'Where have you chosen to hide it?'

'On the Col de Pyrène. It is far enough away from the real site, but at the same time within the region where excavations have taken place. We cannot be sure how much information Antoine was forced to give them.'

'No,' Pujol said. 'I suppose it's worth going to all this trouble? You don't think it's a bit of a sideshow? Now you have the map, why not simply concentrate on retrieving the genuine Codex?'

'Smoke and mirrors, Achille. We need to give them something to stop them looking. If they believe they have the text they seek, that will give us a free hand without fear of interruption. It's also the only chance to persuade them to lose interest in Pelletier and Madomaisèla Sandrine.'

'Possibly,' Pujol said, then poured himself another glass of wine. 'Where did Antoine find the map? Did Rahn send it to him?'

Baillard shook his head. 'If it had come from Rahn, Antoine would have acted sooner. There is a gap of some two years between Rahn's death in March 1939 and Antoine being demobbed and beginning to search the mountains in earnest.'

'I dare say you're right.'

Baillard sighed. 'Have you had any luck with the names I gave you?'

Pujol pulled a piece of paper from his pocket. 'I asked around, but I'm afraid the news is all bad.' He put his spectacles on. 'César Sanchez was stabbed near the railway station in Carcassonne a day or two after the Bastille Day demonstration. It's been dismissed as a blood feud between Spanish workers. No one claimed the body, no family so far as the police can tell, but my contact said a woman had been asking after him.'

Baillard remembered something Sandrine had told him. 'In all likelihood that will be Suzanne Peyre. She and Sandrine's sister, Marianne, are active in Carcassonne. Sanchez was a friend of hers.'

'Did Pelletier know?'

'No, he saw César being arrested. Someone must have given an order for him to be released from custody.'

'I checked. There was no arresting officer listed.' Pujol went back to his notes. 'Gaston and Robert Bonnet were both arrested and released, in the end, without charge.' He peered at Baillard over the top of his glasses. 'You know there are nearly seven thousand men held in Le Vernet now. Communists, partisans, gypsies. They will need enormous camps if it goes on like that. Jewish prisoners, apparently, are being moved to other camps in the East. Even so, soon there won't be any room left at all in any of these places.'

'No one is coming back, Achille,' Baillard said quietly.

Pujol stared at him. 'What are you saying, Audric?'

'Tuez-les tous . . .'

'Kill them all,' Pujol muttered. Infamous words said to have been spoken in Béziers at the beginning of a genocide against the Cathars of the Languedoc, more than seven hundred years ago. They, too, had been forced to wear scraps of yellow cloth pinned to their cloaks, their robes.

'This is evil of a different order,' Baillard said. 'And why we must not fail.'

Pujol was silent for a few moments. 'Do you want me to come with you, Audric?'

Baillard's gentle face softened. 'At the risk of offending you, Achille, I think we might make quicker progress alone.'

Pujol laughed. 'When do you expect Pelletier?'

Baillard looked up at the dusk sky.

'Dins d'abòrd,' he said. Soon.

Belcaire

'There are no trout in the stream.'

Raoul stood up, immediately alert, and gave the response. 'My cousin says the fishing will improve when the melt waters begin.'

A pretty, dark-haired woman appeared in the opening between two trees and walked towards him. She was carrying a *panier* containing wild flowers and wore a pale blue summer dress with a pattern of tiny white blossoms on it. He thought how well it would suit Sandrine's colouring, then smiled that he was even thinking such things at such a moment.

'Monsieur Pelletier?'

'Raoul,' he said, shaking her outstretched hand.

'I'm Eloise. I'm sorry I'm late. I was held up.'

'Trouble?'

'None. You?'

'All quiet.'

Eloise nodded. 'That's how we like it.'

'I'm grateful for your help. How long will it take to get there?'

'Two hours, give or take. Monsieur Baillard arrived in Tarascon this afternoon. He's going to meet you at the cave.'

'OK.'

Raoul hauled his rucksack on to his shoulder. It was heavy now with tools borrowed from the outhouse in Coustaussa.

Eloise led him west along a network of lowland mountain paths, cross-country from Belcaire towards Tarascon. They didn't speak much. From time to time they heard a car and took cover, waiting until it had passed before continuing on through the dark land of the Ariège. Raoul wanted to ask her about Sandrine. He'd attempted to quiz Geneviève earlier, but her loyalty to her friend meant she deflected all his questions.

'Sandrine said your families have known each other all your lives,' he said, hoping to draw Eloise out.

'That's right.'

'She said she and Geneviève were particular friends, whereas you and Marianne were more the same age.'

'Yes. We're very distant cousins, in fact, on our mother's side.'

'Really?'

Raoul wanted to know what Sandrine had been like as a child, the sorts of things they'd done in the long summers in Coustaussa before the war. He wanted to know about Yves Rousset. When Sandrine had mentioned him, against all common sense he'd felt jealous.

'Sandrine said that—' he began.

'Best we don't talk, Monsieur Pelletier,' Eloise said quietly but firmly, though Raoul thought he heard a flicker of amusement in her voice.

‡

Codex XIV

‡

GAUL
PIC DE VICDESSOS
AUGUST AD 342

Arinius screamed.

Scrambling to his feet, still holding his arms in front of him to keep the demons away. Striking the air with his hands in an attempt to drive out the images of skull and bone. Empty sockets and unfleshed limbs, the tendrils of skin trailing like weed.

Blood and fire and glass.

He fell to his knees, his head bowed and his eyes open, fighting to survive the horrors embracing him. A rushing of air, spirits, creatures, brushing against him, skimming his head and his legs, flying and sweeping, physically present but transparent also. Invisible.

'Deliver us from evil …'

His heart was thudding, as if trying to force its way through the carapace of bone. His skin was slippery with sweat and the sour smell of fear. Lips automatically mouthing prayers, holy words of God to cast out the darkness of his thoughts.

'*Libera nos a malo*,' he repeated. 'Amen,' he cried, making the sign of the cross. 'Amen.'

He was in the presence of something powerful, malevolent, though he did not know what.

'Lord, save my soul.'

He continued to pray without ceasing until his throat was dry and his mind was exhausted. Using words as weapons to drive out the evil threatening to swallow him whole. Every prayer or incantation he had ever been taught, the word of God to ward off the temptations of the Devil.

Finally, just when his strength was extinguished and he could fight no more, Arinius felt the threat lift, like an animal slinking away to its lair. Gradually his pulse slowed. Gradually the sounds of the glade around him came back to his consciousness, birds and the light call of an owl, rather than the screaming and the agony of the voices inside his head.

Arinius sat back on his heels, felt the welcome support of the damp grass beneath his legs, the sweet texture of the earth under his hands. Then he laughed. A single shout. Like the great battles foretold in the books of Tobias and Enoch, the Armageddon promised by the Book of Revelation, Arinius knew he had been tested. Tested and not found wanting.

Exhausted, but with a lightness of spirit he had not felt for some days, he stood up. Carefully, he opened the cedarwood box and lifted the papyrus out. He stared at the seven verses, each of which told a story he could not read.

With the memory of the shadow of evil still upon him, he wondered. Had he been misguided? Was the Abbot right to order the destruction of such works? Did he know that the power contained within the Codex was simply too strong for men to bear? That these were words that would not save the world, but destroy it?

For the first time in many weeks, Arinius felt the need of the comfort of the Christian offices. He prayed for guidance, kneeling on the hard ground while he tried to decide what he should do. Listening for the word of God in the silence. A moment of gnosis, of illumination. All doubt banished.

He made the sign of the cross, then stood up. There were two patches of damp on his knees, circles of dew. He was resolved. Comforted by his thoughts.

It was not his decision to make. He was no more than a messenger, a courier. Such a judgement was not in his hands. The knowledge should not be destroyed.

Arinius returned the Codex to the box, and the box to the bag. He had faith that others could withstand such an onslaught, as he himself had done. In the full and certain promise of the resurrection and the life to come.

He coughed, but this time there was no blood. He took a deep breath, drawing the fresh dawn air into his lungs, then continued on his way. The sky turned from white to a pale blue. Couzanium was many miles behind him. The Pic de Vicdessos was within reach. A lodestar, guiding him to his final destination at the edge of his known world.

Chapter 87

LOMBRIVES
AUGUST 1942

The sky was turning from white to a pale blue in the hour before dawn when Raoul saw a solitary figure making his way up the hillside.

Baillard was no longer wearing his pale suit. Instead, he was dressed in the open smock shirt and blue canvas trousers worn by the older men of the Tarasconnais villages, though his shock of white hair and his bearing were unmistakable.

Although there was no one about, Raoul didn't reveal he was there, in case Baillard was being followed. He watched and waited in silence as Baillard made his way up the hillside with the steady pace of a man half his age.

'*Bonjorn*, Sénher Pelletier.'

'Monsieur Baillard.'

'We have two hours before it will be properly light.'

Raoul nodded. 'I'm ready.'

They were south of Tarascon, in the deep valleys that ran all the way down to Andorra. Raoul followed Baillard up through a gully on a gravel path, passing several small caves with irregular openings leading into dark tunnels beyond.

'Do you have somewhere particular in mind, Monsieur Baillard?'

'A place the locals call the Col de Pyrène.'

After ten minutes more, they reached a plateau. Baillard stopped. Raoul saw there was a distinctive ring of large boulders, natural protection, and a cluster of juniper bushes. Beyond that, woodland.

'This is it?' he said doubtfully.

Baillard gestured that he should follow. When they reached the summit, Raoul saw that there was in fact a narrow opening in the rock. Invisible from below, it looked as if it led nowhere. When he peered closer, he realised there was in fact a small gap between two spurs of rock.

'Easy to describe.'

'Exactly so. We have to rely on Sandrine to pass on the information without them realising she's doing so. She needs to pinpoint the place, but without coordinates or any map reference.'

Raoul bent down and looked into the darkness.

'It's distinctive, Monsieur Baillard, but isn't that a problem? It doesn't seem likely that anything hidden here would remain concealed for long, let alone thousands of years. Local people must know this stretch of the mountains.'

'You will see,' was all Baillard said.

He produced a battery torch from his pocket. Raoul did the same and followed him, threading his way through the limestone chicane into a tunnel shielded from the world outside. The ground sloped down. Raoul was forced to duck his head. The further they went, the lower the temperature dropped, but the air was fresh.

After a few minutes, the tunnel opened out into a wide clearing about four metres across, with a high domed roof and jagged fissures of rock that seemed to sparkle.

Raoul sent the beam of his torch all around to gauge the space. 'I've heard of the Tomb of Pyrène in Lombrives and the Salon Noir in Niaux, but nothing about this.'

'The *bons homes* took refuge in these mountains,' Baillard said. 'There are hundreds of hidden places that do not appear in the tourist guidebooks, though one day no doubt they will.' He walked to the centre of the cave, his torch sending elongated shadows dancing over the ground. 'But it is this that interests us.'

Raoul looked and saw that there was a long, cylindrical shaft in the centre of the ground, like a bore hole.

'Is it natural or man-made?'

'It's a sink hole, a fissure widened by water dissolving the limestone. But the land has shifted. This one has been dry for millennia. If I am not mistaken, the site chosen by Arinius will have many of the same properties. A number of the caves in this stretch from here to the foot of the Pic de Vicdessos have cracks in the earth like this.' Baillard angled the beam of light down into the spiralling darkness. 'This is why it is right for our purposes. There is a narrow ledge, do you see? If you could make it a little wider, enough to hold this, that would be ideal.'

Baillard produced a small box from his pocket.

'Is that a forgery too?' Raoul asked.

'Oh no,' he said lightly. 'It dates from the fourth century.'

Raoul wondered how Baillard could have acquired a Roman box in the space of twenty-four hours.

'This is walnut wood, which was widely used in the Ariège in the past. I do not yet know if Arinius himself placed the Codex in such a box – in a box at all – but again it is a story that will serve our purposes for the time being.'

'It's amazing it's survived all this time,' Raoul said.

'The temperature is constant and it is very dry. Many things do survive undisturbed, more than we realise.' Baillard nodded. 'Now, if you will, Sénher Pelletier, we must hurry.'

Raoul opened his rucksack and took out the tools Sandrine had given him from her father's garden store. A hammer, a chisel and a wrench. He peered down into the shaft, seeing that it was narrow enough for him to be able to hold himself up with braced legs. Then he took a stone and dropped it into the darkness, counting until he heard it land at the bottom.

'About ten metres,' he said.

He sat on the side, then put his legs out, bending at the knees, and lowered himself into the space. The rock pressed hard into his shoulders, but it was relatively flat. He took the strain of his own weight in his upper back and his thighs.

'OK,' he said, reaching up his right hand. Baillard passed him the hammer and the chisel. 'Thanks.'

Slowly, Raoul worked his way down the shaft, braced across the opening, until he was level with the ledge. He found a toehold for his left foot, then jammed his right leg and knee into the rock, leaving him enough space to manoeuvre. He started to chip away at the cavity above the ledge, enlarging the space little by little, until it was wide enough to hold the box.

'Here you are.'

He tossed the tools up to Baillard, who caught them easily and put them aside.

'Are you ready?' he asked Raoul.

'Yes.'

Baillard lay flat on the ground, holding out the box at full stretch into the hole. Raoul strained to reach up to take it.

'A little further,' he said. 'I've almost got it.'

Baillard worked his way further forward on his stomach, spreading his legs for balance until Raoul's fingers grasped it.

'Got it,' Raoul said.

He put the box inside the cavity, then scooped some of the dust and scree from the ledge and smeared it over the lid.

'Is it done?' Monsieur Baillard asked.

Raoul heard the urgency in his voice.

'All done,' he said.

He made it back to the surface more quickly than he had gone down. Raoul wiped his hands on his trousers, brushed the worst of the climb from his clothes, packed the tools back in the rucksack and stood up.

In silence, the two men made their way back along the tunnel, through the chicane of rock, towards the light. Raoul stopped in the entrance, half expecting to see a line of soldiers waiting for them, but the countryside was as still and quiet as before.

He sighed with relief. He struck a match and lit a cigarette.

'Do you want me to secure the cave?' he asked.

'No. When Madomaisèla Sandrine talks about Antoine having found the Codex, she will imply that this is a new hiding place, one chosen by Antoine, rather than the original place. In truth, I think little will happen until Antoine Déjean's funeral. Madomaisèla Eloise is already setting rumours running in Tarascon that something's been found.' He looked at Raoul. 'You are willing to remain here and keep watch? You might be waiting some time.'

'I'm as safe here as anywhere,' he said. 'How will I get a message to you when I need to?'

'Madomaisèla Eloise will arrange for food and drink to be brought to you. Each afternoon at three, a messenger will wait for you at the crossroads on the Alliat road.' He broke off and pointed to the crest above the plateau. 'The password will be: "Cazaintre's garden is overgrown." Your response will be: "Monsieur Riquet is tending to it."'

Raoul wondered if the choice of password was a coincidence or deliberate in some way. If not, how did Monsieur Baillard know he'd hidden from the police on Bastille Day in the Jardin du Calvaire, designed by Cazaintre, or that his home was on the Quai Riquet?

'All right.'

Baillard looked at the sky. 'My profound thanks, Sénher Pelletier. But now, if you will forgive me, I must leave you. I should be back before it gets much lighter and the town begins to wake.'

He turned to go.

Quickly, Raoul reached out and touched his arm. 'Don't let anything happen to her, Monsieur Baillard.'

Baillard stopped. 'She told me to do the same for you,' he said gently, 'though Sandrine is more than capable of looking after herself. It is one of the reasons you can let yourself love her.'

'Let myself?' he echoed.

Baillard gave a soft smile. 'There is always a choice,' he said quietly. 'You have chosen to try to live again, have you not?'

Raoul looked at him, trying to understand how the old man could see inside him so well.

'Just keep her safe,' he said. 'Please.'

'*Si es atal es atal*,' he said. '*A bientôt*, Sénher Pelletier.'

Raoul watched as Baillard walked away down the hillside, waiting until he was out of sight. Then, with a cold fist of dread in his chest, he turned and climbed up into the woods above the cave to find somewhere to keep watch. All the time, Monsieur Baillard's parting comment going round in his head like the half-remembered verse of a song.

The words gave him no comfort. He tried to reassure himself. At the moment, at least, Sandrine was with Marianne and Marieta and the others in Coustaussa. It was Saturday now, so four days until she was to go to Tarascon to put Monsieur Baillard's plan into action.

'What will be will be,' he repeated.

Chapter 88

Le Vernet

Lucie looked out of place, pretty in powder and paint. She was wearing a tailored blue and white dress and jacket, with high-heeled blue shoes and matching handbag. She looked as if she should be listening to the Terminus Band at Païchérou. Sandrine felt shabby by comparison, in a flowered summer dress and sandals, her hair held off her face with a white ribbon.

The journey was long and frustrating. They drove south from Couiza to Quillan, then cross-country to Foix – where they left the car in a lock-up garage belonging to an old friend of Marieta's – before boarding a train that stopped and started. There was no one checking papers, but there was no published timetable either, and they spent much of the morning travelling very short distances from branch line to branch line.

The closer they got to their destination, the more Sandrine perceived a heaviness, a brooding malevolence in the countryside around them, like a slumbering animal resting somewhere out of sight. Finally the train stopped. Sandrine saw the modest station house, a dull whitewash, and read the name LE VERNET on the side. Conifers and birch lined the road leading from the station into the village.

Lucie stood up. She looked purposeful, though Sandrine could see the strain in the lines around her eyes and the corners of her mouth.

'Here we are,' she said in a bright voice.

They disembarked into the flattening heat of midday. There was a pleasant breeze coming down from the mountains and the air was fragrant, fresh, which struck a false note. It seemed wrong, Sandrine thought, that the village should be beautiful and tranquil, given what she knew was hidden within the folds of the hills ahead.

A few other passengers got off too. Some were local, dressed in heavy mountain skirts with shawls knotted at the waist. An old man held a dead goose upside down, its glassy eyes seeming to fix on Sandrine. There were two men in black suits, lawyers Sandrine thought, or perhaps members of the military administration. They seemed to know where they were going.

Sandrine looked at the carriages that had been added at Foix. They were being uncoupled by the guard, but no one was getting out. Then she saw the blacked-out windows and realised there were prisoners inside. Remembering the bleeding faces and shackled hands of the men as they were forced into the carriages at Carcassonne, she glanced at Lucie. She looked anxious but hopeful, and the sight of her hardened Sandrine's resolve. Whatever they achieved today, at least they were doing something. Something had to be better than nothing.

On the outskirts of the village, the man with the goose disappeared towards a series of modest houses and cottage gardens. The two countrywomen took a road to the right, which appeared to lead to a park a little further along the banks of the river Ariège.

The girls followed the lawyers. Sandrine overheard fragments of conversation, like morsels of bread dropped on the path. Something about a fire that had broken out in the Galerie Nationale du Jeu de Paume in Paris, destroying works by Picasso and Dalí.

'All reappropriated,' one of the men said. 'Jewish art.'

Above the red roofs of the houses, the spire of a church

was visible. Sandrine assumed that was the centre of the village.

'We need to ask someone,' she said. 'No sense just wandering about.'

'What about there?' Lucie said, pointing at a café with a cheerful yellow and white awning.

It was gloomy inside the café. Three or four old men were standing at the bar, elbows propped on the zinc, drinking Pastis. There was a scattering of damp stubs of cigarettes already smoked on the bare earth floor at their feet. They looked up as Sandrine and Lucie walked in. One of them said something under his breath and the others laughed.

'How about here?' said Sandrine, choosing a table with a view of the street and as far away from the bar as possible. 'This should do us all right.'

They sat in silence, Lucie holding her handbag neatly on her lap. Her joie de vivre had deserted her. Sandrine put her parcel on the stool beside her.

The waitress, with a mass of black hair and eyes the colour of coal, came out from behind the bar.

'Señoritas, what can I get you?'

'Do you have any wine?' Sandrine asked.

'Red only.'

'That's fine. Lucie, is that all right for you?'

'Anything,' she said. She stood up. 'Is there a bathroom?'

The girl pointed to a door at the back of the café. 'Across the courtyard, second door on the right.'

Lucie stood up and left.

'Your friend got someone in there?' the waitress said sympathetically.

'In the camp?' Sandrine looked at her in surprise. 'How did you know?'

'I've never seen you here before and your friend is all dressed up. That's how they usually look.'

Sandrine glanced towards the door, checking Lucie was out of earshot, then back to the waitress.

'We were hoping to see him.'

The girl raised her eyebrows. 'You'll be lucky, unless you have friends in the administration there. Or you have a pass to visit.'

Sandrine shook her head. 'No.' She looked at the girl. 'You know how things work up there?'

She nodded. 'I've been here five years.'

'You've seen some changes.'

'My grandfather remembers the camp being built in the summer of 1918. It was just barracks for French colonial troops. Then it was used for German and Austrian prisoners of war. When they'd all gone, it was empty for a bit, then it became a reception camp for International Brigade prisoners fleeing Franco's forces. That's when I arrived, in 1938.'

'And stayed.'

'Family,' she said, then shrugged. 'They've been building new huts in all the sections over the past few months to house more and more prisoners. Even though they're shipping the Jewish prisoners out as fast as they bring them in.'

'Where are they being sent?'

'Camps in the East, they say. Poland, Germany. Vichy is cooperating with Hitler to hand over all foreign Jews captured in the region.'

'And if someone's French?'

'Technically, it's only foreigners,' said the girl, dropping her voice, 'but everyone knows that Vichy has quotas to fill. It's more of a transit camp.'

The girl stopped dead, clearly seeing the expression on Sandrine's face.

'Your friend is Jewish?'

'Yes.'

'I'm sorry, I should have thought before I rattled on.'

'Better we know what the situation is,' Sandrine said.

'After the Armistice, everyone expected the Germans to take over the camp, but they didn't. It's still run by "our" police, though conditions are appalling. At least, conditions are bad in Section A and Section B – where the ordinary criminals are held – but in C section . . .' She shrugged. 'Even if you could get inside, I'm not sure it would do your friend much good to see it.'

'Do you think there's any chance we'll be able to deliver a parcel in person?'

'No, not unless you've got the right piece of paper from the authorities.'

'Can we do that from here?'

'Not a chance. It takes months. The Préfecture in Toulouse say it's a matter for the Sûreté Nationale, the Sûreté claim it's a matter for the military authorities and they send you back to the Préfecture. Occasionally, someone fetches up at the Mairie here, hoping to try their luck.'

'Are they successful?'

The waitress pulled a face. 'Occasionally. The camp is under the jurisdiction of the Deuxième Bureau. Before the Armistice, it was at least possible to apply for a permit to visit. Now, it's closed to everyone except military personnel, occasionally though, someone from the Red Cross gets in to see a particular prisoner or another.'

'My friend has sent a letter but not heard anything back. She doesn't know if it's even been delivered.'

'Technically there's a delivery twice a week, parcels less frequently.' The waitress shrugged. 'It rather depends who's on duty. Some are decent enough. Others take what they fancy and don't pass mail on.'

Lucie emerged from the back of the café.

'Anyway, I'll get your order,' the waitress said.

Lucie still looked pale, but there was a glint of determination in her blue eyes.

'That's more like it, nothing like a little war paint.' She shrugged off her cropped jacket and sat down on the nearest stool, one leg crossed over the other.

Sandrine gave her an edited version of what the waitress had told her. Lucie sat jiggling her leg up and down. Sandrine felt the gaze of the men at the bar, disapproval visible in the stiff line of their shoulders.

'Not used to female company,' she said when the waitress returned.

'Take no notice,' the girl said. 'It's the closest any of them has been to a woman for quite some time, if you get my drift.'

She crooked her little finger. Sandrine laughed.

'What are we going to do?' asked Lucie, in a brittle voice. 'Will you help us?'

'Lucie,' Sandrine said quickly.

'It's all right,' the waitress replied, putting their drinks on the table. 'If you give it to one of the guards, it's possible the letter will get through.'

She rubbed her fingers together.

'We have money,' Lucie said, immediately rummaging in her bag.

'I don't know all of them, but there's a sous-lieutenant who's got a thing for blondes.'

'Do you think it's worth a try?' Sandrine said.

'Frankly?'

'Yes, be honest.'

'Not really. But you don't have much of a choice, do you? You'll not find anyone prepared to go up there.'

Lucie interrupted. 'How do we get there?'

'Walk,' she said. 'It's not far. They just might accept a letter at the guardhouse if the pair of you turn up.'

Lucie stubbed out her cigarette in the ashtray and stood up. 'I think it's worth a try. We've come all this way.'

Sandrine stood up too. She had promised Marianne not

to go further than the village, but she kept thinking of herself in the same position. If it had been Raoul in there and she was so close, she would do everything to get to see him.

The waitress stood in the doorway and pointed, giving them directions up a woodland track.

'Well, obviously you can't miss it.'

Lucie picked up the parcel from the stool, hooked her handbag over her shoulder, then looked down at her blue high heels.

'I should have thought there might be walking,' she said.

Sandrine laughed. The waitress grinned, plunged her hand into her apron pocket and fished out her order pad and pencil.

'This is our telephone number here,' she said, scribbling a note and handing the scrap of paper to Sandrine. 'If you're back this way, let me know.'

'Café de la Paix,' she read.

'I know, my father-in-law's idea. Renamed it in 1918, when he came home from the Front.'

Sandrine smiled. 'Thank you. How much do we owe you?'

'On the house.'

'I can't accept that.'

'Next time, then you can pay. Good luck, *compañeras*,' she said.

Chapter 89

It was lunchtime, so everything was quiet, no one about. From time to time, Sandrine picked up the sound of a car engine or lorry in the distance. The sound of the bells of the church in the square ringing one o'clock. For ten minutes or so they followed the track through the woods. Birdsong, robin and thrush, the occasional scurry of rabbits through the hard, dry undergrowth and a few fallen leaves.

Sandrine stopped. 'Did you hear that?'

A harsh shouting, someone giving orders. Sandrine walked to the end of the track where it joined the road.

'*Dépechez-vous, vite. Allez.*'

Some way ahead was a wide column of men, old and young, all carrying suitcases, blankets over their shoulders, brown cardboard boxes and old leather briefcases.

'*Poussez-vous*,' shouted one of the armed guards bringing up the rear.

'The prisoners from the train,' Sandrine said.

Lucie came up and stood beside her. As they watched, Sandrine saw an elderly, stooped man, near the back of the line, drop his luggage. He stopped, clearly struggling. The guard shouted. The old man raised his hand, asking for patience, for a few seconds of rest. The guard shouted again. Sandrine watched in disbelief as he drew back his arm and struck the old man across the face with a leather crop.

The *vieux* cried out, fell to his knees and began to sob. The desperate sound of it cut through Sandrine. She started forward.

'There's nothing you can do, kid,' Lucie said quietly. 'Don't get involved.'

The guard raised his crop again. This time, a young man with black hair and a pale, drawn face stepped forward. Putting himself between the guard and his victim, he took the force of the blow on his own shoulders. Sandrine saw him flinch as pain reverberated through him, but he stayed on his feet. Then, without a word, he helped the old man up, picked up the battered suitcase and encouraged him to carry on along the dusty road.

Sandrine had a lump in her throat, at the pointless and deliberate humiliation of an old, defenceless man.

'So that's how it is,' said Lucie.

From the look on her face, Sandrine knew she was thinking of Max and wondering what he'd endured.

The girls stepped out on to the road and slowly continued their approach to the camp. Sandrine started to hope they wouldn't get past the gatehouse. Not better maybe, but certainly easier for Lucie. Max had only been at Le Vernet for a few weeks, but he was a gentle man, a musician. How would he have fared?

The sound of running feet broke into Sandrine's reflections. She instinctively stepped out of sight again, pulling Lucie with her, into the silver shadow of a copse of birch trees.

'Un-deux, un-deux.'

The guards' coarse orders kept the troop in step, about thirty men in all. Each had his head shaved. Each carried a spade. All of them were in rags, clothes encrusted with dirt or grown tatty through constant wear. Some had slippers on their feet, others shoes with their toes sticking out of the end, some rubber galoshes over bare feet. The expression on their grey, filthy faces was of apathy and defeat. They looked like convicts.

'One-two, one-two.'

The steady rhythm of the men's feet echoed away up the hill, overtaking the column of prisoners.

'What if,' Lucie said in a quiet voice, 'just by turning up we make it worse for Max?'

'I don't know.' Sandrine wanted more than anything to turn back, but knew Lucie would never forgive herself if they did. Neither would she. 'It can't be much further.'

They walked for a few minutes more, then rounded a final bend in the road. Ahead of them was the camp. A wide central gate and a barrier with a guardhouse and sentry box to the side. Acres of barbed-wire fencing surrounded the enclosure, punctuated only by high search towers. Above the gate was a wooden sign: CAMP DU VERNET. Visible behind the chicane of barriers, three separate rows of wire separated the camp from the outside world, and the different sections from one another.

And behind the wires, wretched huddles of men, skin and bone, all with the same shaved heads and dull expressions as the chain gang that had passed them on the road.

Row after row of wooden huts with shallow pitched roofs, stretching endlessly into the distance like a hall of mirrors in a fairground. The huts were long and narrow, like animal shelters, and seemed to be built from plank, with some kind of waterproof covering in place of a roof. No windows that Sandrine could see, only rectangular spaces cut out of the planks to serve as crude shutters.

With every step closer they took, Sandrine expected a shot to ring out. She had to force herself not to pull her white handkerchief from her sleeve and wave it.

'Here goes nothing,' said Lucie.

Sandrine was astonished at how Lucie adopted a role. Patting her hair, exaggerating the sway of her hips as they covered the last few metres under the full glare of the soldiers and guards. One wolf-whistled, another called out to Lucie to blow him a kiss. She winked, encouraging a volley of catcalls and lewd suggestions as they walked up to the sentry box.

'Are you lost, ladies?' the guard said with a leer.

Lucie gave her dazzling smile. 'Actually, we're in the right place, Lieutenant. We've walked all the way from the village.'

His eyes ran over Sandrine, then back to Lucie.

'And why's that, mademoiselle?'

'I have a parcel to deliver.'

The guard looked at her in disbelief, then at his colleague, and the two men laughed.

'You can't just walk up and deliver a package.'

Lucie's blue eyes flared wide. 'Well, isn't that the ticket. We were on the train with two lawyers, Parisians. They said if I brought it in person, you would be sure to take it in. That you were in a position to make a decision like that.'

The compliments dropped like pearls from Lucie's lips.

'I'm sure you do have the authority, Lieutenant,' she said, tilting her head to one side. 'It's only a parcel and a letter. You can open it if you like, I wouldn't mind. There's nothing of a … personal nature, if you know what I mean.'

She winked again, and, despite the nerves in her stomach, Sandrine had to force herself not to smile as the soldier turned pink.

'I wish I could help, mademoiselle. I would. But we've a new consignment of prisoners just arriving. Everyone's busy. And visitors from Carcassonne expected any minute now.'

In the camp behind them, another guard shouted out. Sandrine didn't hear what he said, but the young lieutenant turned from pink to red. Lucie, however, had heard. Sandrine saw embarrassment flicker in her eyes, quickly hidden.

'Tell your friend that if he wants to come down here and put things to the test, I'm sure we can oblige.' She leant forward and whispered to the lieutenant, 'Though between you and me, kid, I don't think he's got it in him.'

For a moment, the boy behind the uniform was revealed. He laughed, embarrassed yet delighted. Then, as quickly as the moment had come, the smile fell from his face. He stood to attention.

Sandrine noticed that everyone was suddenly alert. She turned to see a black Citroën slowly picking its way through the potholes in the road.

'The visitors from Carcassonne,' she said under her breath.

The guard saluted as the car stopped at the gatehouse. The driver wound down his window. A pass was handed over for inspection. There was a single passenger in the back seat.

'The Commandant is expecting us,' the driver said.

The lieutenant nodded, and signalled to his colleague inside the sentry box to open the barrier, clapping his hands to hurry him up. Lucie and Sandrine stood back as the car purred forward. Then, abruptly, it braked. The guard ran after it and leant in through the driver's window. A few words were exchanged, then he turned to look at the two women. The Citroën reversed back to them.

'What's going on?' Lucie whispered.

'I don't know.'

The rear door opened and a man in a grey suit got out. Sandrine had no idea who it was, but she heard Lucie catch her breath.

'Captain Authié,' Lucie said, stepping forward. 'This is a coincidence.'

Sandrine's heart started to hammer in her chest. The man who'd promised to help Lucie, who'd been hunting her. The man who, if Marianne's suspicions were right, was responsible for everything that had happened to Raoul. A very dangerous man.

'Mademoiselle Ménard, it is something of a surprise to see you here.'

'I am here to deliver a letter to my fiancé,' Lucie said firmly.

'I see.' He turned to Sandrine. 'And this is?'

She held out her hand, not seeing that she could do anything else.

'Sandrine Vidal,' she said, meeting his gaze.

He barely reacted, though she saw sharp interest in his eyes. 'That is rather more of a coincidence.'

Sandrine did her best to smile. 'It is?'

He raised his eyebrows. 'I'm sure Mademoiselle Ménard and your sister have told you what efforts I've made to talk to you in Carcassonne. Now here you are.'

'You promised to help,' Lucie said.

'I am here, Mademoiselle Ménard.'

'So you hadn't forgotten?' she said, relief and hope flooding her voice. 'Well, since we are here, is it at all possible you could arrange for me to see him? I would be so grateful, Captain Authié.'

'Or at least ensure that Mademoiselle Ménard's parcel reaches Monsieur Blum?' Sandrine put in.

She felt his cool grey eyes slide over her. 'I'll see what I can do,' he said. 'If you ladies would care to accompany me.'

Lucie didn't hesitate, climbing into the back seat of the car. Sandrine didn't move, not sure what to do. Warning bells were ringing in her head, but she couldn't see she had a choice.

'Mademoiselle Vidal,' said Authié, holding open the door for her.

It sounded like an order. Sandrine felt her insides turn to water. She didn't know how to avoid getting in the car without provoking Authié's suspicions. She paused, then climbed in beside Lucie.

Authié slammed the door, got into the front and the driver started the car. They drove forward into Le Vernet. The metal gates clattered shut behind them.

Chapter 90

In the centre of the camp was a large open space where hundreds of men with shaven heads were working the dust-dry ground, each with a pickaxe or a shovel. Most were stripped to the waist, shoulders red in the fierce sun. All around the periphery, the same sullen *gardes mobiles* and police flicking at their boots with their leather crops. The prisoners worked in silence.

Lucie was chattering to Captain Authié, expending her energy on being charming. She wasn't talking about Max, but rather asking Authié about himself. What was his position, what had he done before the war? Authié listened and responded pleasantly enough. Sandrine didn't know if it was an act or if Lucie did trust him, despite everything, but she felt her nails digging into her palms. She was terrified Lucie might let out where they had come from, even though she had stressed and stressed again the importance of being discreet. She prayed she wouldn't get carried away and say too much.

'It sounds quite a journey,' Authié was saying. 'I hope this fiancé of yours appreciates the effort you have gone to on his behalf.'

'He will,' said Lucie. 'And he'll be grateful for your help.'

They stopped at a tidy brick structure with two windows either side of the door, clearly an administrative building. The two guards stood to attention. The driver opened the door for Authié and followed him into the building, leaving Lucie and Sandrine sitting in the back of the car.

'What an extraordinary piece of luck,' Lucie said.

'It might be,' Sandrine said in a low voice, 'but be

careful. I don't believe for a moment that Max is the reason Captain Authié is here.'

'Neither do I,' Lucie said, 'but it's the best piece of luck all the same.'

They continued to wait. The door of the office remained closed. The air rang with the sound of pickaxes striking the stony and parched land, the oppressive huts stretching out as far as she could see, and everywhere the endless barbed wire, three layers thick, with trenches in between, furrows of dried brown dirt. Hell on earth was how Raoul had described the camps at Rivesaltes and Argelès. Until now, Sandrine had thought he was exaggerating.

'I need some air,' she said, opening the door and getting out of the car.

She stood beside the Citroën, looking around. Behind the administrative block stood a patient, silent line of men with luggage, blankets and coats, the prisoners from the train, she realised. Despite the ferocious sun, Sandrine wrapped her arms around herself, to protect herself from the chill seeping into her bones.

Lucie also got out of the car. She was very pale again and Sandrine hoped she wasn't going to be sick. Finally, when Sandrine had started to give up on anything happening, the door opened and a soldier beckoned them inside.

'This is it,' Lucie whispered. Sandrine squeezed her hand, but didn't answer.

They followed him up the steps and into a bare office with a wooden desk, two metal filing cabinets and three chairs. Authié was sitting in one, though he got up as the girls entered. On the far side of the desk, a heavy-set man in uniform remained in his seat. On the wall behind him was a large paper map of the camp, the various sections marked in different-coloured ink.

'I've been explaining your situation to the Commandant,' Authié said, 'and although it is irregular – you shouldn't be here at all – he has kindly agreed to make an exception on this occasion. He will allow you, Mademoiselle Ménard, to see Blum for five minutes. They are going to fetch him now.'

Lucie's blue eyes shone with gratitude. 'Captain Authié, I can't tell you how much I appreciate this.'

'It is not me you should be thanking,' Authié said, smiling at the Commandant. 'It is under the condition that I sit in on the interview. I hope that will not be too uncomfortable for you.'

'If the Commandant thinks it necessary,' Lucie replied, 'then of course you must.'

'Standard practice,' the Commandant said. 'In these "exceptional" circumstances Captain Authié has mentioned.'

The telephone rang. The Commandant stretched forward. 'Yes?' He nodded. 'Yes, good.' He dropped the receiver back in its cradle. 'Blum is here. Next door.'

'Thank you,' Authié said, standing up. 'Mademoiselle Vidal, if you might be so good as to wait in the car. We don't wish to cause the Commandant any more inconvenience than is strictly necessary.'

There was a knock on the door and a police officer came into the room and saluted.

The Commandant pushed himself out of his chair. 'Over to you, Authié. Five minutes, no more.'

'Mademoiselle Ménard?' Authié said, opening the door for Lucie to go through.

Lucie looked vulnerable. Sandrine smiled at her, trying to give her courage, watching until she was out of sight. Then she went back outside, as she'd been asked to do.

Certain she would go mad if she had to wait in the confined atmosphere of the car – there was something claustrophobic about the smell of the overheated leather and the lingering scent of old tobacco – she stood beside the open door.

The driver was half leaning, half sitting on the bonnet. He pulled a cigarette from a packet in his pocket. Sandrine heard the scratch of the match, then a sigh as he exhaled. A white trail of smoke drifted in her direction.

Although she was worried about how Lucie might be holding up, Sandrine was grateful for time to marshal her thoughts. Monsieur Baillard's plan was to set a rumour running, then for her to talk about the forged Codex at Antoine's funeral. His reasoning was that if Antoine's murderers weren't in Tarascon already, they were likely to turn up for the funeral. Authié certainly – the man Raoul knew as Leo Coursan – as well as others. If there were others. Monsieur Baillard clearly believed that at least two rival groups were seeking the Codex.

Now here, at Le Vernet, was an unexpected opportunity to set her part of the plan in motion four days early. Sandrine frowned. If Raoul and Monsieur Baillard had hidden the forgery already, as planned – and she could get a message to them to let them know to be on their guard immediately – then all would be well.

But if there had been a hitch? She knew, via Geneviève, that Eloise had delivered Raoul safely to the rendezvous. But what if Monsieur Baillard hadn't arrived? Or if the site they'd chosen turned out not to be suitable after all?

Sandrine glanced towards the gatehouse. Did she really have a choice, though? Authié was going to ask her questions, she couldn't avoid that. If she appeared to be ignorant of the Codex now, yet full of information by Wednesday, the whole plan would look suspicious and start to fall to pieces.

Wishing Marianne was here to advise her, Sandrine stood by the car, trying to work out what she should do. She also wondered why Authié had really come to Le

Vernet in the first place. And what, exactly, was his job?

The driver lit a second cigarette, this time offering the packet to her. Sandrine shook her head. The echo of metal striking the unforgiving earth continued to reverberate around the camp. The sun continued blasting down upon the bare heads of the prisoners. Suddenly the door flew open and a young officer she'd not seen before appeared on the steps of the gatehouse.

'Captain Authié wants you, Mademoiselle Vidal,' he called. 'There's been an incident. Come quickly.'

Chapter 91

Sandrine's stomach lurched. 'What's happened? Where's Mademoiselle Ménard, is she all right?'

She blinked, accustoming her eyes to the gloom after the brightness of the day outside, then followed the guard down a corridor to a small interview room. Lucie was sitting on a chair in the centre of the room, holding a handkerchief to her face. Her blue and white dress was stained down the front with splashes of blood.

'Oh God,' said Sandrine, crouching beside her. 'What happened?'

'It's nothing. I'm all right.'

Sandrine turned on the guard. 'What happened?' she demanded. 'Where's Captain Authié? Where's Max?'

The young officer looked embarrassed, but didn't answer. Sandrine turned back to Lucie.

'Tell me what happened,' she repeated, dropping her voice. 'Did you see Max?'

Lucie nodded. 'They've taken him back.'

'Is he all right?'

A wail came from behind the handkerchief. 'I hardly recognised him, he's so thin, and his glasses – they won't let him have his glasses – and I, well I just lost my head.'

Sandrine put her hand on Lucie's leg. 'I don't understand. Where is Captain Authié?'

'He's so thin, so pale. His eyes are hollow.' She stopped. 'He couldn't believe it, though, Sandrine. He couldn't believe I'd come. His face, when he saw it was me, I ...' She broke off. 'I know you don't like him, Sandrine, but Captain Authié was pretty decent. He was called away, or pretended to be, and left us on our own for a while.'

'So did you tell him?' Sandrine said quietly. 'Did you manage to tell him your news?'

For a moment a smile lit Lucie's face. 'You should have seen him, Sandrine, when he understood. He was so happy.' The smile began to fade. 'Happy at first, then . . .'

'How did this happen?' asked Sandrine, pointing at the handkerchief.

'Stupid. I was stupid,' said Lucie. 'When the guard came back to take Max away, I'm afraid I flew at him. Tried to stop them.'

'The guard hit you?' said Sandrine in disbelief.

'No, he pushed me, I lost my footing. Banged into the door.'

'Oh Lucie.' Sandrine looked towards the open door. 'And where's Captain Authié now?'

'Trying to smooth things over with the Commandant.' Lucie shook her head. A single drop of blood dripped from her nose on to her lap, a starburst on the skirt of her dress. Sandrine saw her shoulders slump a little more. 'I've made things worse for Max, haven't I?'

She squeezed Lucie's arm. 'I'm sure you haven't.'

'What do you think will happen now?'

The sound of a siren suddenly split the air, making both girls jump.

'What's that?' Sandrine said, glancing at the guard.

'Roll call. Four times a day. Make sure everyone's where they're supposed to be.'

'Where else are they likely to be?' Sandrine muttered, then broke off at the sound of Authié's voice.

'Mademoiselle Vidal, if I may have a moment of your time.'

To her surprise, he took her elbow and steered her into the corridor.

'Your friend's behaviour was remarkably ill judged …' he said.

'I appreciate that,' Sandrine began.

He kept talking over her. '… and it certainly won't help Monsieur Blum. The Commandant has absolute power here, do you understand? He only allowed Mademoiselle Ménard to see her fiancé – although I gather there is some doubt about her status – as a personal favour to me. He had no obligation to do so.'

'Lucie is aware of that,' Sandrine said. 'She was upset, but deeply regrets causing you personal embarrassment.'

'Does she?'

For a moment, they held one another's gaze. Sandrine forced herself not to look away. He was dangerous, she knew that. But, for whatever reason, he had helped. Sandrine felt the full force of his character, realising how Raoul had once been prepared to follow him and why Lucie had wanted to put her trust in him.

'What can we do to alleviate the situation, Captain Authié?'

'I have dealt with it,' he replied.

'Will it make things worse for Monsieur Blum?'

'I regret that is not something over which I have any influence.'

Again, for a moment, Sandrine thought she saw the mask slip. Something in his voice suggested that he felt the injustice of what was happening here in the camp. An awareness of the barbarity of the place.

'Most of these men here,' she said, 'have they even done anything wrong?'

Authié's expression altered. Sandrine willed him to say something, to speak beyond his position or responsibilities or the chill air of the corridor, but he did not.

'Shall we?' he said.

Sandrine helped Lucie to her feet, then walked

along the corridor and out down the steps.

In silence, they got into the car. Authié sat with his driver in the front, a different man in a lieutenant's uniform. Sandrine and Lucie sat close together in the back.

As they drove through the camp to the gate, Sandrine saw rows of prisoners gathering under the burning sun, men as thin as sticks, standing and looking straight ahead. The guards' voices were harsh as they shouted the roll call.

She couldn't help herself twisting round as they pulled out of the gate and on to the road to the village, watching the camp get smaller and smaller behind her. Then they turned the bend, and Le Vernet disappeared from view.

Chapter 92

Lucie looked utterly dazed. Sandrine sat back on the bench seat and squeezed her hand.

'Are you all right?' she mouthed.

'Not so bad,' Lucie said.

'I regret I am not returning to Carcassonne,' Authié said, turning round from the front. 'Assuming that's where you have come from?'

Sandrine felt relief wash through her. 'We'll be fine,' she said, ducking the question. 'If you could drop us in the village, we'll make our own way from there.'

Lucie had finished her running repairs to her face, lipstick and a dab of powder, and was now smoking.

'You came to Le Vernet by train?'

Sandrine met his eye. 'We did, yes.'

'From Carcassonne?'

'I told Captain Authié you had been staying out of town,' Lucie said quickly.

'Surely not here in Le Vernet?'

'No, of course not,' she said, desperately trying to decide what to say for the best.

In the mirror, she saw he was staring at her.

'Where have you been, Mademoiselle Vidal? I have called on you at home in Carcassonne several times in the past week without finding you at home.'

'I've been in Tarascon,' she said, unable to think of anything better.

His eyebrows went up. 'A charming place, but not somewhere I would imagine could hold many attractions. The sort of place which attracts partisans and those determined to cause trouble.'

'Really, I didn't know that,' she said. 'It seems pleasant.'

'However, now I have found you,' he continued, 'I might take the opportunity of asking a few questions. You don't object, I assume?'

'No, no of course I don't,' she said.

Her eyes slid to Authié's driver, who was clearly following every word. She frowned. There was something familiar about him, though she couldn't think where they might have met.

'... in your own words, Mademoiselle Vidal, if you would,' Authié was saying.

Sandrine forced her attention back to him. 'I beg your pardon?'

'Monday the thirteenth of July,' he said in a level voice. 'You were attacked at the river in Carcassonne. Near Païchérou.'

Sandrine's mouth was dry. She glanced at Lucie. Hoping her friend hadn't given Authié more information than she'd owned up to.

'That's right,' she said. 'I went to the police station. Someone took my statement.'

'It's always better to hear it in your own words, Mademoiselle Vidal,' he said.

For the next few minutes, the questions went back and forwards. Polite and courteous, there was nonetheless an undercurrent to everything Authié asked, and Sandrine was exhausted by the effort of saying enough, but not too much. By the effort of working out how to slip into the conversation the information Monsieur Baillard wanted shared.

'He said nothing to you, the man you helped?'

'Nothing that made any sense,' she said, keeping her voice as casual as possible. 'I mean, he rambled on and on, but it was all nonsense. I didn't pay much attention.'

'Try to recollect, Mademoiselle Vidal,' said Authié. 'What kind of things?'

Authié turned round in his seat. He pulled out a packet of cigarettes from his pocket and offered one first to Lucie, who accepted, then to Sandrine. She shook her head. The moment had come.

'Something about a book, I think it was – though that wasn't the word he used.' She pretended to think. 'Codex, that was it. Yes, something about finding it and how it was valuable, very valuable.'

'Did this man say he had seen this Codex?'

Authié's voice was still calm, controlled, but Sandrine could hear the keen interrogation behind the words.

'I think so, yes. He said it was hidden and it was safe, but I didn't take much notice. I was more concerned about finding help. I was rather scared, to tell you the truth.'

'Did he mention a key?'

'A key?' she blurted the word out. 'No.'

'Or a particular place?'

'Something to do with Pyrène,' she said slowly. 'The Col de Pyrène, I think it was?'

'Do you know the place, Mademoiselle Vidal?'

'No.'

Authié narrowed his eyes. 'Yet you remember the name?'

'Only because he said it so many times,' she said quickly. 'He kept describing it. A place with a rock that looked as if it was covered with glass, or something like that. But maybe I misunderstood.' She gave another shrug. 'He was in such a state, Captain Authié, I'm afraid I wasn't really paying attention. He'd had some kind of accident, you see. As I said, it all sounded like nonsense.'

Authié fixed her with a long, hard look. Sandrine worried she'd overdone it, made herself seem too gullible or naïve, too incurious. A frisson of fear went down her spine. Her fingers gripped the side of her seat.

'But then,' she rushed on, 'I slipped on the rocks and, like an idiot, banged my head. And in fact the man can't have been so badly hurt as I thought, because when I came round, he was gone.'

'You are quite sure – quite sure – you saw no one else at the river?'

Sandrine met his gaze. 'Quite sure.'

'You don't remember someone helping you?'

'Well, yes. Lucie and Max,' she said. The nerves were thudding louder and harder in her chest. 'It was awfully lucky they were there, otherwise I don't know what would have happened.'

'Before that,' he said with a touch of steel in his voice.

'No,' she lied.

Lucie took her lead from Sandrine. 'We looked, but there was nobody there.' She pulled a face. 'I'm afraid we thought you were making it up, you know.'

'I know,' Sandrine said, throwing a grateful smile at Lucie. 'I must have sounded quite mad.' She turned back to Authié. 'I'm sorry not to be of more help.'

He didn't reply. In the mirror, Sandrine saw him exchange a glance with the driver. The car slowed for a moment. Sandrine's heart skipped a beat, suddenly anxious that they were going to be left in the middle of nowhere at the side of the road. Then, she realised, that might be better. Now she'd done what she had to do, she was desperate to be out of Authié's company. She also had to get a message to Monsieur Baillard to let him know the plan was already in motion.

The car idled for a moment at the junction. Authié leant over and talked in an undertone to the driver. Then, instead of turning towards Le Vernet, they instead pulled out on to the main road that led towards Tarascon. A flash of alarm went through her.

'You were going to drop us at the railway station,' she said quickly. 'There is a train due at the end of the afternoon.'

'It's such an unreliable line, Mademoiselle Vidal. I am more than happy to take you back to Tarascon.'

'Tarascon?'

'You said you were staying there,' he said.

'I don't want to put you to any trouble,' she said, immediately trying to work out how they would be able to get back to Foix where the car was hidden.

'It's no trouble. We are going that way anyway,' he said. A few more seconds of silence fell between them. 'I wonder, is your presence in Tarascon related in any way to this matter, Mademoiselle Vidal?'

Sandrine muddled her expression. 'Is there a connection? I am simply accompanying our housekeeper to visit old friends. She's rather unwell and can't travel on her own.'

'Most people don't choose to travel these days unless necessary.'

'Marieta isn't most people,' she replied, forcing another smile.

Authié's face was inscrutable. 'I shall need an address where you're staying,' he said.

'Of course,' Sandrine said brightly, wondering what the hell she was going to do when they arrived in Tarascon in an hour's time.

Chapter 93

TARASCON

'We're here,' Sandrine whispered. Her stomach was a knot of nerves. 'Wake up.'

Lucie's halo of blonde hair bobbed away from the glass. She jumped at the sound of Sandrine's voice, then quickly sat up straight.

'Where are you staying, Mademoiselle Vidal?'

Sandrine stared at him, then, at the last moment, remembered the name of a hotel in the town.

'We're staying at the Grand Hôtel de la Poste,' she said, 'but actually I promised I would meet a friend in the Café Bernadac at the end of the afternoon. Thanks to you, Captain Authié, we've made good time. If you could let us out here, we can walk to the centre of town.'

'You are staying there too, Mademoiselle Ménard?'

Sandrine glanced at her friend, worried that she might give the game away. Lucie gathered her thoughts and said the right thing.

'I am. Just for tonight.'

'You are both returning to Carcassonne tomorrow?'

'I am,' Lucie lied. 'I can't answer for Sandrine.'

The girls exchanged glances when the car didn't stop. Sandrine leant forward and touched Authié on the shoulder.

'Really, we can walk from here.'

'I wouldn't dream of leaving you in this heat.'

'If you're sure,' she said, struggling to keep the growing anxiety from her voice. 'It's in the Place de la Samaritaine.'

'Do you know it, Laval?'

Sandrine turned cold. Sylvère Laval was the man who'd planted the bomb, who'd set Raoul up. Her eyes shot up and met his in the driving mirror. With a stab of fear, she knew he'd noticed her reaction to his name.

'You've been so kind, Captain Authié,' she said, struggling to keep her voice steady. Her heart was thumping in her chest. Sandrine told herself to calm down. Everything had gone to plan, if ahead of time. She had to hold her nerve, not give herself away now.

Laval negotiated the narrow streets, then drove into the main square and pulled up outside the shadowed colonnades of Les Halles. Sandrine's fingers were on the door handle and she was out of the car looking across to the awning of the café on the far side of the square. Behind the buildings, the boucherie and the tabac on the corner, the rise and fall of the Vicdessos and the Pic de Sédour were visible. Castles floating in the sky, she thought.

Authié also got out and looked at the tables outside the café.

'Do you see your friend, Mademoiselle Vidal?'

Sandrine pretended to look. She shook her head. 'Not yet, but, as I said, I'm awfully early. You don't need to wait with us. We'll be quite all right.'

She saw him hesitate. 'When will you and your housekeeper be returning to Carcassonne, Mademoiselle Vidal? You didn't say.'

'After the weekend,' she replied. 'On Monday or Tuesday. It depends on the trains, of course.' She held out her hand. 'You've been more than kind, Captain Authié.'

He did not take it, but instead turned to Lucie. 'And you, Mademoiselle Ménard?'

'I told you,' she said in a tired voice. 'Tomorrow.'

'So you did.'

Sandrine glanced at her. Under her powder, she looked

grey and drawn, as if she might faint. There were beads of sweat on her forehead.

'Come on, Lucie,' she said softly. 'Let's find a seat.'

Still Authié didn't go. Sandrine could do nothing but sit down at the nearest table and pray that he wouldn't join them. He stood in front of her, blocking the sun. Then, to her relief, she saw Eloise Saint-Loup on the far side of the square.

'There she is,' she said, raising her hand to attract Eloise's attention. 'Eloise, over here.'

She saw Eloise take in the little group and immediately change direction and walk towards them. Sandrine leapt up and ran to meet her, talking in a loud, excited voice.

'Thanks to Captain Authié, we are early to meet you here. I said you wouldn't expect us yet.' She turned to him. 'Again, thank you for driving us back.'

Authié ran his eyes over Eloise. 'And you are?'

'Eloise Saint-Loup,' she replied, meeting his gaze.

Authié glanced at his watch, then nodded to Laval.

'If I need to talk to you again, Mademoiselle Vidal, I'll call on you in Carcassonne.'

'If you think it necessary,' she said.

Authié gave a cursory bow, then got back into the car. Laval shut the door, then climbed in himself and they left.

Sandrine stood until they'd disappeared around the corner of the square, then she whistled and slumped down on the chair. Her legs were shaking.

'That was the longest few hours of my life,' she said.

'What was that all about?' Eloise asked. 'I wasn't expecting you until Wednesday.'

Sandrine explained what had happened.

'Which is why it was so lucky you came along when you did,' she finished. 'I was dreading Captain Authié would insist on escorting me to the hotel and ask to see the register.' She sighed. 'And his driver, Sylvère Laval, do you know him?'

'I don't think so, why?'

Sandrine shrugged. 'I don't know, he seemed to be looking at you. It's probably nothing.' She glanced at Lucie, who was looking more wrung out than ever. 'Are you all right?'

'I've felt better, kid.'

'It's not surprising, it really is dreadfully hot,' Sandrine heard herself saying. 'You could do with a rest.' She stopped, then smiled at the realisation she was sounding more like Marianne every day.

'Our car is in Foix,' she said to Eloise. 'But before I think about how to get it back, I have to find Monsieur Baillard and tell him what's happened. It's terribly important. It's all so much earlier than we'd planned.'

'He's staying with Inspector Pujol,' Eloise said. 'I'll take you, if you like.'

'Is anyone else with him?' Sandrine said, the words slipping out before she could stop them.

Eloise smiled. 'No,' she said sympathetically. 'Raoul stayed up at the site to keep watch. He's fine. Everything went like clockwork. My husband's acting as the messenger between him and Monsieur Baillard.'

Only now did Sandrine know for certain that Raoul had made it to Tarascon without being caught. That he was safe.

'Thank you,' she said quietly.

'He seems nice,' Eloise said. 'Mind you, he asked an awful lot of questions.'

Sandrine looked at her. 'Questions about what?'

Eloise laughed. 'What do you think? About you, of course.'

‡

Codex XV

‡

GAUL
PIC DE VICDESSOS
AUGUST AD 342

Arinius felt he had reached the edge of the world, the heart of the mountains dividing Gaul from Hispania. For three days he had walked. He had no particular destination in mind, only that he had to find somewhere distinctive and sheltered, somewhere where the pattern of the ridges and crests might retain their shape for centuries to come. He had rejected a hiding place in the woods lower down the slopes. Forests might be cut down or burnt or drowned when a river burst its banks. Fire and sword and flood. Only the mountains stood firm.

He stopped to catch his breath before continuing. The last rays of the sun were slipping from the rock and sinking down behind the peaks. Arinius wondered if he should stop and continue in the morning, but he did not want to rest. It was the third day since he had been tested – his vision, as he had come to think of it – but he was still full of vigour. He was so close now.

The path was dry and slippery with dust, and the foothills were steeper than he had hoped. It was hard going, but he had coughed little in the past days and there was a welcome breeze. He was weary of his mission, the responsibility, but he knew he was almost there. So very close now.

Finally, up ahead, he saw a sequence of caves, each facing west across the valley and set within the pines and oak, the deep ancient green of the forest. He climbed higher until he found what he needed. A single cave, set within a low range of rock and crevice. He smiled as he looked up at the natural sequence of dolmen and stelae, the way the light fell upon the mountain, casting the sign of the cross on the rock face.

'*In hoc signo vinces*,' he said.

He did not know if the Emperor Constantine had indeed uttered such words, as it was said, only that the symbol – the cross – that once had indicated persecution and exile had now come to symbolise strength. Even before the burning of ancient texts had begun, Arinius had feared the way in which the Church was changing. From persecuted sect to persecutor. He did not wish to see the restrictions and indignities once suffered by Christians – by good men and women, like his mother Servilia – turned instead on others. He did not wish to witness Jewish friends abused, wise men from the old tribes. His God preached peace and acceptance and love to all men, but yet he saw already how the plain and gentle words of scripture were being turned into weapons. Manipulated to suit the desires of those seeking power, rather than grace.

Arinius continued to climb. Now he was closer, he could see that the shadow cast by the scattered pink light was not merely a cross, but rather a double crucifix. A horizontal and a vertical line, with a second shorter horizontal arm beneath the first. He wondered how often was this phenomenon to be seen? At dusk only? In August only, or all summer long? Or was the configuration of land and wood and light so constant that, regardless of the season, the sun cast such a shadow on the mountains?

He passed a clump of juniper bushes at the edge of the path, then made his way through an avenue of oak trees. Through the thicket and heavy undergrowth, until at last he stood on the plateau in front of the crucifix cave, as he had come to think of it. Arinius took a few moments to catch his breath. His fingers stole to the plain knot pin at his neck, a replacement for his mother's brooch, lost when he had fallen on his way back from Aquis Calidis.

This close, the light fell differently, so the outline of the cross was no longer so clear. Instead, a slanted pattern of dark lines intersected as if painted by the hair of a brush. The sky was slashed through with shards of pink and orange now, lilac behind it. The white wisps of cloud were melting into the grey rock face on the opposite side of the valley, gold in the setting sun.

Arinius looked back at the avenue of oak trees, at the ash and the beech, then up at the ring of stones seeming to frame the entrance to the cave, and knew it was perfect. It was a place that would serve.

'A place of refuge,' he said.

His weariness left him. He crouched on the ground and removed the bearing block, spindle and fireboard from his leather sack, all carried with him from Carcaso. He'd inherited his quick fingers from his mother, who, in the nine years he had walked beside her, had taught him a great deal. He pulled out his tinder bundle, a mixture of grass and dried hazel bark, and placed it in position ready to catch the embers created by the friction. Placing the tip of the spindle into the hole in the block, he wrapped the string around it, taut, so as to make sure it didn't slip. He put his right knee on the ground, with his left foot on the board to keep it in place, then, pushing down with the handhold, began to turn the spindle. Twisting, faster, feeling the heat begin to warm his hands. Arinius still felt the strain of the muscles in his thighs, across his shoulders, but the pain did not hinder him. He kept going, building a steady and regular rhythm, needing to create a constant friction between the fireboard and the spindle. In the indentation in the fireboard, the dust was collecting.

Finally, a glow, then a spark, and the smallest of flames.

Arinius blew upon it, the heat catching the dry tinder. It flared up. He began to cough, ash and dust sticking in his throat, but the light mountain wind helped him. Moments later, he was rewarded by the red glow leaping and starting to spread.

He sat back on his heels to rest his aching limbs for a moment, then he went back to work. He took the small torch from his sack, an old rag soaked in pitch, and wrapped it around a short wooden stick like a fist. He held it towards the fire. The material spluttered, then the rag began to smoke, then spark. The fire took hold.

He stood up. He took a last look at the beauty of the sky, here at the top of the world then, with the cedarwood box containing the Codex safe in the bag on his back, he turned and stepped into the darkness of the cave.

Holding the burning torch before him in his right hand, his left touching the wall of the cave to guide him, Arinius walked slowly forward. The ground sloped down and the passage grew narrower and narrower until he was forced to duck his head. He felt the chill of earth and the temperature dropped with each step he took, but the air was fresh. He knew that he was in no danger.

Presently, the passage opened into a small cavern. The flame sent shapes scattering over the uneven surface of the walls and ceiling, shadow dancers in the subterranean world. He stood still for a moment, then noticed an opening ahead of him in the ground. He went carefully forward and saw that it was a natural well, a tunnel down into the centre of the earth, no wider than the reach of his arm. He dropped a stone into the darkness, listening as it fell. Moments later, an echo reverberated around the cavern. A dry well, not water. This would serve his purpose.

In order to free his hands, Arinius collected a few larger

rocks, stacked them in a small pyramid shape and wedged the wooden shaft of the torch into the gap. Once he was certain it was secure, he went back to the opening in the earth and knelt down beside it. He reached down into the hole, his fingers looking for somewhere to secure the box. There was nothing wide enough, so he lay on his chest and stretched further into the black. Now he found what he needed – a cleft in the stone large enough to hold the box on its side.

He pulled himself up, then took the box from his bag and rested it in his lap. The temptation to look upon the Codex one last time was overwhelming. But he was mindful of what had happened, the test he had barely survived, so instead he raised the box to his mouth and kissed it, then wrapped the cedarwood in his handkerchief. He did not know if a layer of cotton would make any difference, but he wanted to do all he could to protect the Codex from the passing of time.

Lying on his belly, Arinius reached down into the chasm until his searching fingers found the cleft. Slowly, taking care not to make any mistakes, he pushed the box into the fissure as far back as he could manage, checking several times that it was secure, that it could not dislodge or fall.

When he'd finished, he sat up. Rather than feeling pride or satisfaction in the fact that he had achieved what he had set out to do, Arinius felt bereft. As if he was leaving the truest part of himself behind in the cave. A limb, a piece of his soul never to be regained on this earth. He felt utterly and completely alone. The same absolute solitude he had felt as a boy when his mother was taken from him and he had been handed into the care of the community.

He sat back on his heels and bowed his head. He pressed his empty hands together in prayer. This time, not the words of the Lord's Prayer that had sustained him for so long, but instead words from the Revelation of St John the Divine. The only Gnostic text that had not provoked Athanasius' disfavour.

'A new heaven and a new earth,' he said.

Here, in the heart of the mountain, Arinius believed such prophecies might be so. After the fear engendered in him by his terrifying vision, now a sense of peace went through him. The calm after the storm.

Unlearned as he believed himself to be, he understood now what the scripture meant. He understood the basis of faith. The promise of the covenant and judgement.

'I am He that liveth,' he murmured, 'and was dead. Behold, I am alive for evermore. Amen.'

Chapter 94

Col de Pyrène
August 1942

Leo Authié and Sylvère Laval drove past the Grand Café Oliverot, along the Route de Foix.

'We cannot afford to waste time, Laval,' Authié said angrily.

'I'm sorry, sir. I hadn't allowed for the detour to Tarascon.'

'Where is the nearest garage?'

'About an hour's drive north, sir. This side of Foix.'

Authié slammed his hand down on the dashboard in frustration, though he accepted there was no choice. They had to have petrol. There were few official suppliers in Ariège and none between Limoux and Carcassonne. But to have the Codex in his sights, and be forced to wait, was intolerable. His hand went to the crucifix on his lapel. His desire to see the heretical text with his own eyes was overwhelming. To hold it in his hands, to see if the rumours about its power were true.

Then, to be the man to destroy it.

For a moment, they drove on in silence.

'How do you know where the Col de Pyrène is, Laval, if it's not in any guides?'

'It's well known locally,' Laval replied in the same neutral voice.

'If that's the case, why the hell haven't we investigated the site before?'

'It was excavated before the war, sir. Nothing was found there.'

'By whom?' he said sharply.

'By Herr Bauer's predecessor, I believe. And by a French team.'

Authié turned in his seat to face Laval. 'Is Bauer aware of this?'

'I don't know, sir.'

'It makes no sense.'

'Could it be Déjean found the Codex elsewhere, then chose to hide it in the Col de Pyrène for safe keeping, rather than keep it with him, precisely because he knew the site had been excavated before and dismissed?'

Authié didn't reply, though he could see Laval's theory made sense.

'Drive faster,' he ordered.

Tarascon

'There's no one here,' Sandrine said, gazing up at Pujol's house.

Lucie looked quite desperate. 'I must sit down before I fall down,' she said.

'There's a terrace along the back,' Eloise said. 'You can rest there.'

Sandrine and Lucie followed Eloise around the side of the building, then up a flight of narrow stone steps on to a small stone terrace. An old metal table and two chairs, at right angles to one another, were orientated towards the evening sun.

'You take the weight off your feet,' Sandrine said. 'I'll see if I can find you something to drink, at least.'

In normal circumstances Sandrine would have cavilled at the thought of breaking into someone's house – especially a policeman's – but Lucie was tired and needed a glass of water. She was slumped on the seat. All the life seemed to have gone out of her. The adrenalin of having succeeded in getting into the camp, then seeing Max, had gone. The reality of the horror of his situation had hit her.

'This window's open,' Eloise called.

'I'll see if I can get in that way,' Sandrine said.

Eloise grasped the thin arms of the chair, holding it steady. Sandrine put her hand through the tiny gap at the top of the window. Careful not to push too hard, she eased it open with her shoulder, then stretched down as far as she could until she reached the clasp. Pressing her face against the glass, she worked at the fastening until, finally, it opened. After that, it was easy enough to climb up on to the ledge, jump down to the kitchen floor and unlock the door.

'I hope Inspector Pujol doesn't mind too much,' Sandrine said, handing a glass of water to Lucie.

Lucie drank it all, then said in a defeated voice, 'What are we going to do now?'

'You're going to do nothing. Just sit quietly,' Sandrine said.

'I'll go and see if I can find Guillaume,' Eloise said. 'He might know where Monsieur Baillard and Inspector Pujol are. I must warn them about Authié and Laval.'

'I'll come with you,' Sandrine said. 'We'll cover more ground if we both look.' She put her hand on Lucie's arm. 'Will you be all right on your own?'

Lucie nodded. 'I'll manage.'

'You sit tight. I'll be back as soon as I can.'

She and Eloise walked back towards the town, Sandrine still wondering if it would be more sensible to stay put. On the other hand, they could be waiting for hours.

'I'm going this way,' Eloise said, pointing at a narrow flight of steps winding up into the oldest quartier of the town. 'If I were you, I'd start with the Grand Café Oliverot, on the Foix road. Inspector Pujol's often there.'

Sandrine remembered seeing it on the corner as they drove into Tarascon.

'If not,' Eloise continued, 'there's another café he likes, close to the railway station.' She sighed. 'And, if that fails, there's a bar below the Tour Castella, on the opposite riverbank. A real old-timers' place.'

'All right.' Sandrine nodded.

'Let's meet back at Pujol's in an hour? See if we've had any luck.'

Sandrine walked quickly towards the Oliverot, all the time hoping to see a glimpse of Monsieur Baillard's distinctive pale suit and panama hat. On the far side of the Pont Vieux, she noticed a heavy-set man with an old-fashioned hat. Was it Inspector Pujol?

'May we have a word?'

Her heart skipped a beat. She'd been concentrating so much on the road ahead, she hadn't noticed the man standing in the shadow of the doorway of the épicerie. She glanced at him, trying to place his accent. She was certain she didn't know him.

'I'm sorry, I'm in an awful rush. If you'll excuse me.'

Sandrine tried to walk on, but he stepped in front of her and blocked her way.

'Excuse me,' she said again, trying not to sound scared.

'It won't take long, Fräulein.'

This time the voice came from behind her. Sandrine spun round to see a second man standing there, also blocking her way. Fear jabbed her in the chest.

'Just a question we need to ask,' he said.

His accent was far stronger. German, but was he a civilian or something more? And why did they want to talk to her?

'All right,' she said, attempting to sound calm.

'We were overhearing your conversation earlier. You are mentioning a friend of ours.'

'Was I?' she said, furiously trying to remember what she'd told Eloise and, at the same time, work out what the men wanted.

'Sylvère Laval,' he said. 'You know him?'

Her relief that it wasn't Raoul they were after was short-lived. Sandrine felt a battering of nerves in her stomach. Monsieur Baillard had said he thought there might be more than one group looking for the Codex, German as well as French.

'We are anxious to speak to him, Fräulein,' the second man said.

'I'm afraid I don't really know him awfully well,' she said, wondering if they had seen her with Laval and Authié or just heard her talking to Eloise.

'Do you know where he is?'

Sandrine's heart was thumping, but she forced herself to pass on the same information as she had given to Authié earlier. Setting the same trap, or so she hoped.

'It was just something I'd heard. Apparently, he – Sylvère – was going to somewhere called the Col de Pyrène. I don't know any more than that, messieurs.'

The Germans exchanged a glance, then the man standing in front of Sandrine stepped to the side and waved her through.

'*Danke schön*,' he said.

Sandrine waited until they had gone then, on shaking legs, ran the rest of the way across the bridge. The man with the hat had gone, so she turned and ran back to the Café Oliverot. It was now even more urgent she find Monsieur Baillard.

And what about Raoul? She had to warn him too.

Col de Pyrène

'Hurry,' said Authié.

Laval put his foot on the pedal, pushing the car as fast as he could towards the mountains. Authié was going over his conversation with Sandrine Vidal in his head once again. In the past couple of hours he had become more suspicious. There was something about the guileless way she had told him what Déjean had said at the river that didn't sit right with her self-possession. He couldn't decide if she had let the information about the cave slip out by accident. If she genuinely didn't realise the significance of it or was not interested in it. Given her sister's record, was it possible she was such an innocent?

'As soon as we have secured the site, Laval, we'll return to Tarascon,' he said. 'I want to talk to Sandrine Vidal again.'

'Very good, sir. And there was another thing I was going to mention. The girl who came to meet Vidal gave a false name. Or, strictly speaking, Saint-Loup is her maiden name. She's Eloise Breillac now.'

Authié glanced at him. 'Why would she lie?'

'She's married to Guillaume Breillac, another established local family, like the Saint-Loups. He's a partisan sympathiser, though we haven't got anything against him yet. Not enough to bring him in.'

'Then I shall talk to Madame Breillac too,' Authié said.

Laval pulled off the road, then drove as fast as he could along the increasingly rutted track until they reached the site. Ahead of them was a field-brown Opel Blitz truck, just visible beneath the trees. It was clear that the branches had been pulled back to allow the vehicle in, then pulled over it again as camouflage.

'What the hell's going on?' Authié demanded.

Laval immediately went to investigate. Authié got out and waited, watching as his lieutenant looked in the window of the cab, then examined the open cargo bed and licence plates before coming back.

'Civilian plates, sir,' he said. 'This was on the front seat.'

It was a copy of *Der Stürmer*, the most notoriously anti-Semitic, anti-Catholic of the tabloid Nazi newspapers. Many top-level party officials condemned it as pornographic propaganda, but others – such as Himmler – endorsed it and appeared often in its pages. Authié frowned. He'd always known Bauer was an enemy of the Church.

Authié thrust it back at Laval. 'When you talked to Bauer's men in Le Vernet, did they say anything?'

'No.'

'Would they have been able to keep the information to themselves? In the circumstances.'

Laval held his gaze. 'I was thorough, sir. I believe that if they had known anything, they would have chosen to tell me.'

Authié nodded. He had seen the results of Laval's 'thorough' interrogations in the past. 'In which case, how the hell is Bauer here before us?'

'Given how freely the Vidal girl talked to you, she's probably gossiped to other people. Tarascon's small. Things get around.'

'You believe she was telling the truth?'

'I don't think she realised what she was saying.'

Authié pulled his revolver from his pocket. 'Bring what we need.'

Laval took a cumbersome canvas holdall from the boot. 'Shall I conceal the car?'

'We have every right to be here,' Authié said drily, 'whereas Bauer does not.' He paused. 'Let them do the hard work.'

'You are not going to approach Bauer?'

Something in Laval's tone of voice caught Authié's attention.

'No,' he said slowly, watching his lieutenant's face. 'Bauer chose not to communicate the information about the Col de Pyrène to me. So I don't intend to give him the chance to explain. At least, not yet.'

Authié followed Laval up the path, his weapon drawn and alert to any sounds of life. Once they'd climbed through the woods, the land was open and with little shade or cover, but there was no one around. Presently, he saw a cluster of juniper bushes and what appeared to be an unbroken rock face.

'The entrance isn't obvious from here, but that's it,' said Laval.

'Is this the only entrance?'

'To my knowledge, yes.' Laval paused. 'Are we going in, sir?'

Authié thought for a moment. 'No, I don't want to lose our advantage. We'll wait and see what they do.'

They took cover behind a small outcrop of rock, shielded from the entrance. Laval took two Mauser K98 rifles from the bag, standard Wehrmacht issue. Authié had decided against using weapons that could be traced back to French operations. He wanted everything to look like a German undertaking. He waited while Laval loaded five rounds into each magazine and secured the bolt.

Authié had not yet decided whether he was going to kill Bauer or not, but he was ready. A holy warrior. His hand went once more to his lapel, then he flexed his fingers, feeling the weight of his gun in his hand.

Raoul lay flat on his stomach, watching Sylvère Laval and Leo Coursan as they took cover behind the outcrop. He steadied his breathing, his anger. His finger itched to pull the trigger. The temptation to shoot was overwhelming, but he couldn't give away his position. Yet to have Coursan in his sights and be unable to shoot him was almost too much to bear.

The Nazis had been in the cave for two hours. Raoul had heard the catarrhal chug of the truck engine some time after four o'clock, then the sounds of equipment being unloaded and fragments of German. Eloise had told him it was common knowledge in Tarascon that there were Wehrmacht and SS in the area, though everyone pretended otherwise. Some, because they benefited from their presence. Others, because they weren't sure if they had the right to be in the *zone nono* or not. Even so, it was a shock to hear German spoken so freely and so openly.

There were five of them. One wore a suit and hat, struggling in the heat even though the sun was still low. The other four were in working clothes and carrying equipment, including hurricane lamps, a winch and hoist, pickaxes and shovels. Raoul had managed to get to the rendezvous point to meet Guillaume Breillac, so Baillard should by now be aware of the German presence. He didn't understand how it had happened so quickly – Sandrine wasn't due in Tarascon until Wednesday – though rumours were clearly spreading. But he couldn't see a way to inform Baillard about the latest development without leaving his observation point, and he didn't want to do that.

He glanced at his wristwatch. It was six o'clock now. Breillac wasn't due back until nine. Raoul put his hand on his revolver, and kept his eyes trained on Coursan.

Chapter 95

'Sir,' murmured Laval.

Authié nodded. Four men had appeared in the mouth of the cave. They stretched their arms and squinted into the early-evening sun after the gloom inside. Their shirts, open at the neck, bore signs of hard work, streaks of machine oil and subterranean grime. Their faces and lower arms were tanned by the weeks of Midi sun, but the skin beneath their collars was pale.

The largest of them pulled a pack of cigarettes from his pocket and offered them around. The group had the satisfied air of men who'd achieved what they'd set out to do.

'*Morgen?*' Tomorrow?

The big man shook his head, and looked over his shoulder towards the cave.

'He says tonight. We head for Pau and cross into the *zone occupée* there. Then up the Atlantic coast.'

'*Wieder nach Hause?*'

'Home, yes.'

'Out of this heat.'

'Proper beer.'

'And the rest of it,' a third leered, his mime leaving no doubt what he had in mind.

'What about your wife, Hans?'

'She can wait a day or two longer,' he said.

The men all laughed.

Authié calculated. If Bauer was preparing to leave tonight, it was confirmation that he had found something worth taking to his masters in Berlin. So he could approach Bauer and attempt to negotiate with him. Or he could take it by force. Not leave any loose ends. He had briefed Laval for both eventualities. He had prepared himself for both eventualities.

For a moment, the decision hung in the balance. Authié closed his eyes, praying for guidance. His fingers touched the metal on his lapel. The cold physicality of the crucifix gave him the determination he needed. There were four of them against two. If the negotiations turned sour, the odds were not in his favour. The only advantage they had was surprise. To strike first.

He turned to Laval, and nodded. Laval got into position. Authié lifted the Mauser K98. He wedged the stock tight against his right collarbone, braced his left elbow hard against the stone, adjusting his grip several times until it was secure.

His focus narrowed. The noise of the men talking, the sound of their feet on the gravel and rock of the path, the whisper of the cicadas in the long grass below, everything faded away. He lowered his head to the sight, feeling the muscles strain in his neck. He lined up his target through the notch sight then, slowly and gently, he pressed down on the trigger, keeping his aim true, giving life to the bullet in the chamber. The propellant gases expanded, exerting pressure on the bolt, then there was a deafening crack and a starburst flash as the bullet left the rifle.

On the path below, an explosion of red as the shot hit, taking away half of the man's head. Blood, brains, bone.

For an instant, the other three froze. Then their training kicked in. Soldiers, not civilians.

'Get down!' the leader shouted. '*Volle Deckung!*'

One threw himself behind a boulder, another rolled into the juniper bushes at the edge of the path to take cover. The third, hesitating a moment too long, resting his hand on his dead friend's shoulder, gave Laval a perfect shot. Laval struck the target straight in the chest, a clean hit. His body slammed back against the trunk of a beech tree.

Authié lowered his rifle, pulled back the bolt, reloaded and locked into position, then fired again. This time his shot went wide. The survivors returned fire, but their pistols – Authié guessed standard German army-issue Lugers or Walther P38s – were no match for the range and power of his weapon.

The man behind the boulder loosed off several rounds, splintering wood and branches some five metres below Laval's position, but posing no real threat. The German paused to reload, breaking cover momentarily. It was just long enough to give Authié a clear shot. He pushed down on the trigger again. Another blast, another flash of burnt propellant. More blood. Three of the four men were down.

The final target ran for the woods. He kept low, zigzagging to left, to right. Laval couldn't get a clear shot. The man disappeared into the trees.

Gesturing to Laval to cover him, Authié withdrew from his hiding place and made his way up towards the cave itself. Suddenly, he was terrified Bauer wasn't there. That he had already gone.

He had to go in and see.

Behind him another shot rang out and struck the ground, shattering the wood of the trees. Authié ran through the undergrowth to the entrance of the cave. He glanced at the bodies. Their weapons were 9mm Lugers, new models. He picked one up and, seeing the magazine was full, took it.

He pressed himself against the cave wall. 'Bauer?' he shouted.

Only the echo of his own voice came back at him. Laval fired another shot. Authié put down the rifle, too heavy for close combat, and stepped into the darkness of the cave.

The silence was deafening. Adrenalin surged through him. It had been years since he'd been involved in active operations. For too long he'd been directing matters from behind his desk, rather than leading men out in the field. It felt good to be a soldier again, a Christian knight.

'Bauer, are you in here? Come out and we'll talk.'

Nothing. He listened, but could hear nothing. No sound of digging or breathing or footsteps, nothing. His heart sped up. If Bauer was here, why hadn't he shown himself? Was he hiding? Or was he so far underground he hadn't heard the shooting?

Authié hesitated, in the end the silence persuading him that Bauer didn't have other men inside. Laval had reported that the German's team was comprised of six men. Two were in Le Vernet. The other four were neutralised outside.

Laval joined him. He, too, had abandoned the rifle in favour of a Luger.

'All down?'

'Yes,' Laval replied. 'Any sign of Bauer?'

Authié shook his head, motioning for Laval to go in front as they made their way into the tunnel. The ground sloped down and the temperature was dropping, but hurricane lamps had been set at regular intervals along the passage so they could see where they were going.

He reached out his hand to get Laval to stop. In the stillness, Authié heard the sound of metal banging against rock. He tightened his fingers around the Luger, then ordered Laval forward once more, until he saw a glow ahead. The tunnel opened out into a chamber, floodlit by lamps on high metal tripods. And there was Erik Bauer. He was standing beside a wooden structure that had been erected over a hole in the ground. A rough frame with a crankshaft handle, a metal pail hanging from a rope.

Authié watched Bauer for a moment, realising he had sent his men away so they didn't witness what he'd found. He cast his eyes around, double-checking there was no one else with him. He could see no sign that Bauer was armed. There were only digging tools within reach.

'Bauer,' he said, coming out from behind the rock.

The German spun round. Authié saw the look of shock on his face immediately turn to horror. Bauer's hand went to his pocket.

'What have you found?'

But before the German had the chance to answer, the sound of a shot rang out, a sharp crack echoing off the stone walls of the chamber, hitting Bauer in the chest.

'Hold fire!' Authié shouted.

The order was lost in the sound of a second shot, this one striking Bauer in the shoulder. He swayed on his feet, then crumpled sideways to the ground.

Authié covered the distance with a few long strides. Bauer was lying in a pool of blood, a splinter of white shoulder bone showing through his skin and cotton shirt. He pushed the body with his foot. A gush of blood spurted from the wound in Bauer's chest, though his pale eyes were still open. Authié reached down and took a small wooden box from the German's hand.

'Were you going to tell me about this? Were you?'

'Go to hell,' the German managed to say.

Authié crouched down and pressed the muzzle of the gun to Bauer's temple.

'Who told you to look here?'

A bubble of blood foamed in the corner of Bauer's mouth. *'Meine Ehre heißt Treue.'*

Honour and loyalty, the motto of the SS. Even if Laval hadn't fired, Authié was certain Bauer wouldn't have told him anything. He pulled the trigger. Bauer's body jerked violently once, then slumped motionless on the rough earth.

'I thought he was pulling a gun,' Laval said.

Authié held out the box. 'No, he was going for this.'

'Is it the Codex?' Laval asked.

Authié ignored him. He hesitated, then lifted the lid

of the box. A wave of triumph went through him at the sight of the papyrus inside. He lifted it out and unrolled it. Yellow, brittle to the touch, the surface covered in jagged brown symbols, letters. Seven short verses – a work of heresy, despite the sign of the cross. He was caught between awe at the power the proscribed text was said to possess and revulsion at the heresy it represented.

'*Hostem repellas longius, pacemque dones protinus* … so shall we not, with Thee for guide, turn from the path of life aside.'

The battle cry of the Catholic crusaders as they defeated the Cathar heresy – in Béziers, in Carcassonne, at Montségur. They were not the right words for the occasion, but Authié felt in need of protection. He returned the scroll to the box and closed the lid.

'Sir?'

'Bring the rest of the bodies inside, then secure the cave,' he ordered.

Authié bent down and searched Bauer's pockets, but found nothing of significance. For a moment, he looked down at the indistinguishable pulp of matted hair, blood and brain, then he slipped the Totenkopfring from Bauer's finger and put it in his own pocket. Finally, picking up the precious box, he made his way back to the surface.

Laval was dragging the last of the bodies into the mouth of the cave.

'Are the charges ready?' asked Authié.

'In a couple of minutes they will be, sir.'

Removing himself out of range of the blast, Authié watched Laval take two small mines from his rucksack. He placed one at each end of the entrance, then took cover and pressed the handle. The two explosions, seconds apart, were muffled. Clouds of grey smoke and dust billowed out into the green countryside, the sound of rock and stone collapsing on itself. It was the way the Germans secured each of the sites they'd excavated. By sealing the cave, Authié hoped to avoid any problems. Despite his contacts, five murdered men would be difficult to conceal and he did not want to be caught up in lengthy enquiries.

Laval collected the spent cartridges and the two rifles.

'What do you want to do about the truck, sir?'

Authié thought for a moment. 'We'll have to leave it. It's well camouflaged. Let's hope no one finds it in the next day or so. Or if they do, that they steer well clear.'

Laval held the door open for Authié, then got into the front seat and started the car.

'Back to Tarascon, sir? You wanted to talk to Sandrine Vidal again.'

Authié sat back in the seat, holding the box on his lap. A long sigh escaped from between his lips.

'She can wait,' he said. 'Head for Toulouse.'

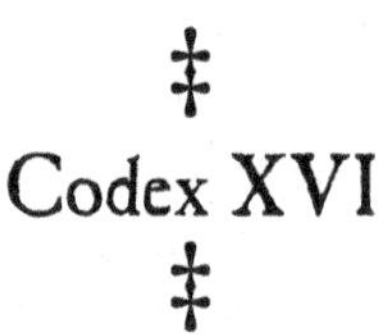

Codex XVI

GAUL
PIC DE VICDESSOS
AUGUST AD 342

Arinius emerged from the cave to a world of a luminous purple and pink sky. Green and silver leaves dancing in the breeze, a golden sun beating down upon the earth. He felt unburdened, but also bereft. He wondered if this was how women felt after giving birth, having carried a child within them for so long. A sense of emptiness. Of being alone.

He looked out over the ancient forest. He felt closer to his God than he had ever felt within the stone walls of the community. The memory of the *liturgia horarum* was faint in his memory now. It had been Passiontide when he last celebrated God's presence in each of the hours of the day.

Here at the top of the world, in the ancient borderlands in the sky, Arinius knew he was as near to a state of grace as he would ever be. More than in his home city of Lugdunum, following the arc of the river Saone, standing on the quayside in Massilia, waving farewell to his friends. More completely at peace than he had been when travelling the Via Domitia or praying in the simple chapel in the fortified town of Carcaso. Even during this last voyage south through the vines on the plains of Septimania.

He wondered if he might stay here to keep watch over the Codex. Live as a hermit, like Paul of Thebes. Make his home in the caves of Gaul and Hispania, waiting until the times had changed and the true word of God could be heard. An ancient, like Moses or Abraham or Enoch. A Christian patriarch spending his life in meditation and silence and reflection.

Arinius shook his head. His mission was not yet completed. He could not renounce civilisation until he had ensured that those coming after him might have the means to retrieve the Codex in the future.

He was tired after his exertions and the labours of the day, but he knew he couldn't afford to rest. His bones were aching and he felt the threatening pressure in his chest that often presaged a full-blown attack. He had no time to waste.

Feeling the stiffness in his shoulders and arms, Arinius bent down and picked up the bearing block, spindle and fireboard, cool now, and put them back in his sack. He tipped the grey ash on to the ground, and the few sticks in the tinder bundle that had not caught he scattered behind the rocks framing the entrance to the cave. He had left the torch shining inside the chamber.

Settling himself on the plateau below the cave, he looked around, judging the distance between the juniper glade and the cruciform entrance to the cave, studying the avenue of oak trees and the way the light patterned the face of the rock. Arinius coughed and pressed the heel of his hand against his ribs, trying to steady his breathing and not let an attack take hold. He unpacked his materials from the bag: the squares of milk-coloured wool, an earthenware bowl, oil and the ink he had made.

He coughed again, feeling the ache in his ribs. This time, the attack lasted a little longer. Struggling to catch his breath, Arinius poured a little oil from the bottle and mixed it with the ink. With the tip of a blackbird's feather, he experimented with a few strokes until he had the pressure and daub just right. To his relief, he found the wool held an image perfectly well and did not smudge.

Another bout of coughing, but he drank some barley beer and it soothed his throat. He had little appetite these days, but the beer always helped. Then he took a new square of wool and, dabbing the tip of the blackbird's wing in the ink, began to paint a map of the valley.

Arinius worked quickly, glancing up from time to time, then back to the work of art taking shape in his hands. Finally, it was finished. He signed his name and, beside it, put the sign of the cross. Then he laid the map out to dry, holding it in place with a stone at each corner.

He was very breathless now and he felt the familiar irritation in his throat that often came before a bad attack. He tried to stop it, but he couldn't help himself. He felt as if his lungs were turning inside out as he gasped for air. There was a metallic taste in his mouth and, when he looked down, he saw starbursts of bright blood all down the front of his tunic. Then it took him again and he became light-headed, dizzy from the repeated coughing. He wrapped his arms around his ribs, trying to stop the pain, but nothing made any difference. He was losing his strength. He tried to catch his breath, tried to stay on his feet, but he couldn't hold himself up any longer. His legs buckled and he fell to the soft ground. In desperation, he stretched out towards the map, but it was out of reach.

'God spare me,' he tried to say. 'Lord, deliver me.'

The words died on his lips.

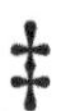

Chapter 96

Toulouse
August 1942

Leo Authié walked through the labyrinth of small streets in the oldest part of the city, heading towards the Place du Capitole. In the 1930s, the area had been bohemian, full of jazz bars and poetry cellars and eccentric pavement cafés. Now it was more like a slum, whole families living in single rooms, men with no work on every street corner, children with bare feet begging and holding out their hands.

He walked down rue de la Tour until he found the street he was looking for, and turned into it. Halfway along the rue des Pénitents Gris was an antiquarian bookseller. There was no name, no number, but the display of books in the window – Bertolt Brecht, Walter Benjamin, Einstein, Freud and Engels, Gide, Zola, Stefan Zweig, Heinrich Heine, Arthur Koestler, all authors banned by the Vichy government in accordance with Berlin's wishes – told Authié he was in the right place. The proprietor of the bookshop was known to the police in Toulouse as a leading socialist and a distributor of radical newspapers. He had been arrested several times.

Authié pushed down on the old-fashioned handle and stepped inside on to a coarse rush mat. The silence thronged around him, the air long undisturbed. He strode across the wooden floor, taking off his hat and gloves, then put them down and tapped the bell on the counter.

'*Service*,' he said. '*S'il vous plaît*.'

A man in his sixties, dressed in black and with a shock of white hair, appeared from the back of the shop. His face was smooth, but his skin hung loose around his neck, his hands, as if he'd been a bigger man once.

'Monsieur Saurat?'

The man nodded, his eyes wary. He didn't look like the medieval scholar Authié had been led to expect.

'You are Saurat?' he said again.

This time, the man answered. 'I am.'

Authié produced the box from the inside pocket of his jacket, making no attempt to conceal the revolver in its holster as he did so.

'I have a job for you,' he said.

He opened the lid, revealing the scroll of papyrus. Saurat's eyes widened.

'Monsieur,' he said, his voice high-pitched. 'The oil in the tips of your fingers, in your skin, could cause irreparable damage.'

Authié was still in two minds. The man was unsound, he knew that from his police file, but he was said to be an authority.

'May I?' said Saurat.

Authié nodded. Saurat put on a pair of half-moon spectacles, then took a pair of white linen gloves from under the counter.

'I want to know how old this document is,' Authié said.

Saurat picked up the box first, turning it over in his hands to examine it from every angle.

'Walnut wood. Commonly used in the third and fourth centuries, in particular. In good condition. I assume it has been in a museum?'

'I am not interested in the box, Saurat. What can you tell me about the text?'

Without a word, Saurat placed the box on the counter and turned his attention to the papyrus.

'Have you unrolled it?'

'Yes.'

Saurat's hand beneath the counter again, this time bringing out a large magnifying glass. He leant even closer and slowly read each line.

'I was told you were the expert,' Authié said impatiently.

'*An* expert.'

'In what particular field?'

'In medieval texts – Latin, Greek, Old French, Occitan. This is written in Coptic, outside my usual period.' Behind his glasses, his eyes lit up. 'Is it for sale?'

Authié stared at him. 'How old is it?'

Saurat looked back to the document. 'I cannot be certain, although it is not unlikely it also dates from the fourth century. May I ask where you acquired this, monsieur?'

'All I need to know is if it is genuine.'

Saurat laid the glass back on the counter. 'Without running proper tests on the papyrus, it is impossible to be certain. You would do better to take this to the university.'

Authié stared coldly at him. 'It is a simple yes or no, Saurat. I'm not asking you to translate it or do anything other than give your considered opinion as to whether this appears to be authentic.'

Saurat took off his spectacles. 'I still recommend you have it analysed properly. But, having said that, within my knowledge of documents of this era from Egypt, primarily, perhaps also Syria and Persia, I would be confident saying that this one could be dated to the third or fourth century.'

'Thank you,' said Authié. 'Put it back in the box.'

Saurat picked up the papyrus, replaced it and closed the lid, then pushed the box across the counter.

'Is it for sale, monsieur? I would give you a good price for it.'

Authié laughed. 'Do you people think of nothing but money?'

'Business doesn't stop,' Saurat replied, meeting his gaze.

Authié put the box back in his pocket. He was aware of the man's eyes jealously following his every move.

'It is not for sale, Saurat. It never will be.'

'A pity,' he said mildly. 'I would very much like to own it.'

Authié took up his hat and gloves and walked quickly to the door.

'It would be in your best interests not to mention this conversation to anyone. Do I make myself clear? Not least, the selection of books in your window could get you into a great deal of trouble.'

The bell jangled as the door shut.

Saurat stood in the silence for a few moments. Security, secret police, Deuxième Bureau, he didn't know, only that the man wasn't to be trusted. When he was sure Authié wasn't coming back, he locked and bolted the front door and pulled down the blind. Then he went to the telephone. It took a couple of minutes for the operator to place the call.

'It's in play,' Saurat said, without identifying himself. He listened, then answered the question. 'Oh yes, he believed me. What? Yes, he was French.'

He hung up and poured himself a generous measure of brandy. He hoped the information would get to its final destination.

Three hours later, a telephone rang in a small house in the Ariège. A heavy man levered himself up out of his chair on the terrace and went inside to answer.

'Pujol,' he said.

He listened, then nodded.

'I'll tell him.'

‡

Codex XVII

‡

GAUL
PIC DE VICDESSOS
AUGUST AD 342

'I thought you were dead.'

The words were spoken in a dialect Arinius did not know, so he struggled to make sense of them. He opened his eyes to see a girl of fifteen or sixteen looking down at him in the half-light of the dusk.

'Or ill,' she added.

He realised he must have been unconscious for hours. The light had fled from the mountain and the woods around him were now black. Arinius stared up at the pretty, round face. She was wearing a blue tunic with wide sleeves, though her hair was loose rather than braided. He could see from her colouring that she was a descendant of the Volcae or the Tertelli who lived in the valleys before the Romans came.

He sat up. 'I'm not dead,' he said, though for a moment he thought he might be. Perhaps she was an angel?

'I can see that now.'

He smiled. 'Of course.'

'Are you ill?'

Arinius looked down and remembered the attack, the panic as he lost consciousness. Quickly, he glanced over at the rock and saw that the map was still there, undisturbed.

He sighed. 'I am tired. I've been travelling for some time.'

'Where have you come from?'

'Where have *you* come from?' he said back at her, enjoying her spirited way of talking and meeting his eye.

'I asked you first.'

Arinius laughed. 'Aren't you afraid to be out here on your own?'

'Why should I be?'

'It's nearly night,' he said, though, even as he was speaking, he could see there was no trace of fear in the girl's face. Only wide-eyed interest and confidence. He laughed again, and, this time, was rewarded with a smile.

'What were you doing?' she asked, looking at the writing materials spread all around him, his bag and the squares of wool. 'It's too dark to see anything out here.'

'It is now,' he agreed. 'It wasn't when I started.'

She looked at him curiously. 'Why would you come here to paint?' she asked. 'Or whatever you're doing.'

'Well,' he began, then realised he couldn't think of a plausible answer. 'It's as good a place as any.'

'It isn't! It's a stupid place to come!' she said crossly. 'There are wild animals out here, didn't you think? Down there, we have houses and tables where it might be easier to work.' She shrugged. 'But if you are all right in the woods, then ...'

With a flick of her long brown hair, she picked up her basket and turned away from him.

'Don't go!' he called, desperate not to lose her company. 'I was unaware there was a settlement so close. I would, of course, much prefer that. Could you show me the way?'

She looked at him for a moment, then nodded. 'If you like.'

Arinius gathered his belongings and, aware of the girl's sharp eyes on him, returned everything to his bag. He retrieved the map, rolled it and put it inside the bottle.

'What were you painting?' she asked.

He smiled. 'Nothing that matters.'

'Most people don't come here,' she said, changing the subject again. 'That's why I was surprised to see someone. You.'

'Why don't they come here?'

'There are legends about this valley. The Vallée des Trois Loups, it's called.'

'What kind of legends?'

She stared cautiously at him. 'You have heard of Hercules?'

Arinius hid a smile. 'I have,' he said seriously.

'It is said that when he abandoned his lover, Pyrène, the daughter of King Berbyx, she tried to follow him and was torn to pieces by wild animals. Here. Wolves, obviously.'

'Obviously.'

She looked suspiciously at him, thinking he was making fun of her, but Arinius smiled, and after a moment, she continued.

'When Hercules found her remains, he was turned half mad with grief. He ripped the land apart with his bare hands and that's how the mountains were formed.' Her face creased in a frown. 'I don't think it's a true story.'

'Maybe not,' he agreed.

'But it's where I got my name,' she added.

'What is your name, will you tell me?'

For a moment, he thought she would refuse.

'Lupa,' she said.

Arinius smiled, thinking there was perhaps something of the wolf about her. The way she walked with purpose, her long hair lying flat against her back.

'What's your name?' she asked.

'Arinius,' he said.

'Where do you come from?'

'I've travelled long distances,' he said. 'But I suppose I might call Carcaso home.'

Her eyes widened with interest, but then she shrugged,

as if to say that such far-off places were of no interest to her. Taking him by surprise, she suddenly set off back down the wooded path and he was forced to hurry to keep up with her.

Arinius was aware of her glancing at him out of the corner of her eye, though, as if to check he was real.

'Are you ill?' she asked again in a serious voice. 'There's blood on your clothes.'

Arinius thought of the gasping for air and the pain. He'd thought he was going to die, but, for whatever reason, God had spared him.

'I am ill,' he said. 'But I feel better at the moment.'

Lupa stared at him for a while. 'Good,' she said abruptly, then continued even faster down the hill.

It was almost dark by the time they reached a small circle of houses, buildings, huts on the far side of a wide-open plain. Tiny splashes of colour, blue and pink and yellow. Tall poppies, the colour of blood, punctuating the green with red.

'There it is,' she said.

'What's it called?'

'It doesn't have a proper name.'

'All right,' he smiled. 'What do you call it?'

'Tarasco,' she said.

Chapter 97

Tarascon
August 1942

'Your plan's worked,' Pujol said, coming back out to the terrace. 'Authié took it to Saurat, like you predicted, Audric. Saurat authenticated it.'

Raoul whistled.

'*Ben.*' Baillard nodded. 'Good. My thanks to you all, especially you, madomaisèla. Because of your courage and quick thinking, we are further ahead than I could have dared to hope.'

'I was glad to help,' Sandrine said, squeezing Raoul's hand.

'My thanks to you too, Madomaisèla Lucie.'

Lucie nodded, but didn't say anything. She continued to stare out over the cottage gardens, almost invisible now in the fading light. Sandrine and Raoul exchanged a look. Sandrine touched her arm. Lucie jumped, then caught her breath. Sandrine wanted to tell her that everything would work out all right, but she couldn't bring herself to give her false hope.

Baillard, Pujol and Raoul had all arrived at the house at the same time, to find the girls waiting for them. Baillard and Pujol had been on their way back to the Col de Pyrène, Breillac having passed on Raoul's earlier message that a German team was at the cave. They had met Raoul coming down from the mountain to tell them about the gunfight, the mining of the cave and the fact that Coursan – Authié, as he was learning to call him – had the forgery.

Sandrine was delighted to see Raoul, although furious that he'd taken the risk of coming into town. For his part, he'd been horrified to learn about her trip to Le Vernet and that she had been in such close proximity to Authié and Laval. Quickly though, his anger had given way to pride at how she had held her nerve and set the trap.

'Was there a real Leo Coursan?' Sandrine said.

'I think there must have been,' Raoul answered. 'That's what alerted César in the first place.' He sighed. 'If only he'd confided in me, then.'

He looked at Baillard. 'Do you think Authié was responsible for César's murder?'

'Yes, although I imagine Laval actually killed him.'

'And Antoine.' Raoul's face hardened. 'And I was that close to him. I could have shot him. Both of them.'

'There was nothing you could have done,' Sandrine said quietly. 'You had to let him go for the plan to work.'

'Not next time,' he said. 'Next time, I will kill him.'

She looked at him for a moment, then turned to Monsieur Baillard.

'What do you think will happen now?'

'I will watch to see what Captain Authié does with the forgery now Sénher Saurat has authenticated it. Even though Bauer is dead – thanks to you, Pujol, we know the identity of those men – it doesn't mean that there isn't Nazi money behind Authié.'

'What do you think he will do with it?'

'He might do many different things. He might offer it to the Ahnenerbe in Berlin, or even to the Weltliche Schatzkammer Museum in Vienna. He might have his own experts in Paris.'

'Or keep it?' she asked.

'Or, indeed, keep it,' Baillard agreed.

'What are we going to do about the bodies?' Raoul asked.

'Leave them to rot up there,' Pujol said.

'Achille . . .' Baillard reproved him.

Pujol held up his hands. 'I know, I know. You want them safely in the earth, don't you, Audric? But we can't. If we open the cave, word will get back to Authié.'

Baillard sighed. 'I understand. And it is better if he thinks he has got away with this unnoticed, yes.'

'Are you going to stay in Tarascon, Monsieur Baillard?' Sandrine asked.

'I cannot. I am expected in Ax-les-Thermes to help a new group of refugees. It is an old promise and I must keep it. After that, in September – and once things have quietened in Tarascon – I shall begin the business of searching for the real Codex.' He inclined his head to Raoul. 'A business that, thanks to you, Sénher Pelletier, will now be easier.'

'Let me know if I can help,' Raoul said. 'Perhaps I could come back in a few weeks, if you want me to.'

'I will.'

For a moment, nobody spoke. Lucie was asleep in her chair. Pujol was tapping the ash of his cigarette on to the flagstones of the terrace.

'Is Sandrine still in danger, Monsieur Baillard?' Raoul asked quietly.

'We're all in danger, one way or another,' Sandrine said, not wanting to think about it.

Raoul put his hand on her arm. 'Sandrine, please.' He looked back to Baillard.

'Is she?'

Baillard paused. 'I believe Madomaisèla Sandrine is in less danger than before. Captain Authié has no need of her. He believes he now knows all she has to tell. Not only that, he has the Codex itself – or so he believes.'

'I hope you're right,' Raoul said, pulling Sandrine even closer to him.

'Your part in this story is done, madomaisèla,' Baillard said. 'You should return to Coustaussa tomorrow, then decide what to do for the best.'

'I've already decided, Monsieur Baillard. Liesl will stay there with Marieta, as we'd always planned. Geneviève's close at hand. They all know each other now.' She paused and looked at the old policeman. 'And Eloise and Inspector Pujol are here, if there's any trouble.'

Pujol nodded. 'I'll keep an eye on things.'

'I don't know what Lucie will want to do, but I'll return to Carcassonne with Marianne and Suzanne. There's no need to wait.' She met Baillard's eye. 'I'm going to help them. Work with them.'

'I don't think that's a good idea,' Raoul started to say. 'I'd be happier if you stayed in Coustaussa.'

Monsieur Baillard gave a slight smile. 'No, Madomaisèla Sandrine is right. It is the wisest thing to return home. If you carry on as usual, Captain Authié has no reason to be suspicious. If you disappear from view, you run every risk of making him wonder what else you have to hide.' He held her gaze. 'But be careful, all three of you. Be very careful and circumspect in what you choose to do.'

His words sent another shiver down her spine. 'I will.'

Lucie suddenly stretched, then sat up in her chair. Sandrine wondered how long she'd been awake.

'There's nothing that can be done for Max other than to keep writing, keep hoping we can get him out,' Lucie said. 'He said that there are trains taking the Jewish prisoners to the East. Frenchmen, not foreigners.' She stopped, clearly struggling to keep her fear under control. 'If they send him away, I'll never see him again.' She put her hand on her stomach. 'We will never see him.'

Sandrine got up and put her arm around Lucie. She felt rigid, tense, unyielding. Sandrine didn't say anything, couldn't think of anything to say.

'Is it true?' Lucie said, looking at Monsieur Baillard. 'There are special trains?'

'It is what they say.'

Lucie looked at him for a moment longer, then nodded, as if she had come to a decision. She turned to Sandrine.

'If it's all right with you, I'll stay in Coustaussa. If it's possible. At least until the baby is born.'

'Of course.'

She stood up. 'Now, I'm sorry to be a bother, but is there somewhere I might lie down for an hour or so? We'll have to set off for Foix to pick up the motor, if you want to get back to Coustaussa in the morning.'

'Only if you're up to driving,' Sandrine said.

'I will be. A couple of hours' sleep will see me right.'

Pujol hauled himself out of his chair. 'It might take a moment,' he said gruffly. 'I've been using the bedroom as something of a store.'

Lucie rested her hand on Sandrine's shoulder as she passed. 'Thanks, kid,' she said, 'for all of it. For coming with me, for putting up with the fuss. You and Marianne, you've been wonderful. Real pals.'

For a moment after she'd gone, they sat in silence.

'What about you?' Sandrine said in a soft voice to Raoul.

'My only hope is to keep moving. Despite what we've done today, nothing's changed for me.'

'I suppose I thought ...'

'The warrant against him is for murder, *filha*, as well as insurgency,' Baillard said quietly. 'He cannot go back to Carcassonne.'

'No.' Sandrine felt a lump in her throat. She looked at Baillard, then at Raoul.

'I just hoped that ...'

'I'll send a message whenever I can,' Raoul said swiftly. 'If there's a chance to meet, I'll take it.'

Sandrine squeezed his hand. She knew as well as he did that it was a promise he'd struggle to keep.

'I'll find a way,' he whispered.

'I know.'

From inside the house, the sound of Pujol preparing a bed for Lucie. Low voices, a door shutting.

'You should rest too, madomaisèla,' said Baillard. 'And you, Sénher Pelletier.'

Sandrine shook her head. 'I couldn't possibly sleep. I've got too many things going round in my head.' She looked out towards the Pic de Vicdessos, shrouded now in the blackness of the night. 'You believe the Codex is still there?' she asked.

'I do.'

'And . . . you believe it can raise the ghost army?'

Baillard smiled. 'Can you not hear them?' he said in a quiet voice. 'The shadows in the mountains?'

Sandrine stared at him for a moment, then she closed her eyes. She took a deep breath, trying to float free of the real world around her, what she could see and feel and touch. Instead, she tried to listen to the older echoes and sounds held in the memory of the land.

For a single, dazzling moment she saw their faces clearly. Not shadows or echoes, but instead a girl with long copper curls pinned high on her head. Another, more radiant still, in a long green dress and with dark hair loose on her shoulders. Shimmering and bright against the night sky, spirit and a transluscence of colour.

'Can't you hear them?' Baillard said again. 'They are waiting to be summoned.'

Chapter 98

COUSTAUSSA

On Wednesday 19 August, the day of Antoine Déjean's funeral, Sandrine boarded the northbound train at Couiza to return to Carcassonne. This time, Suzanne and Marianne sat in the carriage with her and there was no one to see them off. They had said their goodbyes to Liesl, Lucie and Marieta at the house. Geneviève and Eloise were in Tarascon with Inspector Pujol to pay their respects. Monsieur Baillard had left for Ax-les-Thermes.

Raoul had spent two days with her in Coustaussa, then left on Tuesday for Banyuls-sur-Mer. In his rucksack were false papers and a roll of francs bound up with an elastic band to pay the *passeur* for the next group of refugees and Allied soldiers to be guided through the mountains to Spain, then Portugal. Sandrine was proud of him. It was important work.

'Soon,' he whispered as he left. 'I'll come back to you as soon as I can.'

Sandrine had nodded and pretended she believed him.

The train pulled out of the station. Every jerk and jolt of the old rolling stock put more and more space between them.

'It's for the best,' Marianne said, misinterpreting the expression on her face. 'Marieta will look after them.'

Sandrine dragged her thoughts back to the present. 'I think Lucie will be all right. Having told Max their news, all her attention is on the baby now.'

'She's always been like that,' Marianne said. 'Single-minded to a fault.'

'She's worried that you haven't forgiven her for talking to Authié in the first place.'

Sandrine saw Marianne's expression change, but she kept going.

'We talked about it a fair bit. She panicked. She didn't mean to do the wrong thing – she genuinely didn't think it could hurt – and she doesn't want it to be something that gets between you.'

'I have forgiven her, as you put it, but I can't forget it. We all have to make choices – how best to protect the people we love – and it is hard.'

'She just didn't think. And I don't want to be the cause of bad feeling between you. You've been friends for so long.'

Marianne sighed. 'Everyone compromises. There's no black and no white, just shades of grey. Everybody's trying to get by. Everyone tells themselves it's all right to inform on a neighbour or give the police a tip-off, because it will go better for their family. Or thinks that what they do can't really make a difference.' She sighed. 'But the small betrayals lead to bigger ones, morality is eroded. Whatever the inducements, whatever the threats, it's simple. You do not betray your friends.'

'Marianne, come on. She didn't betray me. That's too strong.'

Her sister met her gaze. 'She traded information for a favour, so she thought,' she said in a level voice. 'The fact that they already had the information is neither here nor there. So, although I'm still very fond of her, I can't pretend it didn't happen. I will do everything I can to make sure she is all right. But I won't forget.'

'I didn't realise you felt so strongly.'

'Yes you did.' She paused. 'And she knows you feel

you should have done something to help Max in the first place, although you couldn't. I think she plays on that.'

'No, she's never said anything like that. I just feel awful, I can't help it. I know it's silly.'

'It is.' Marianne glanced at Suzanne, and, for a moment, her expression relaxed. Then the smile slipped from her face once more. 'We have so much to do in Carcassonne. So many men are in prison, we are going to have to work twice as hard. And there's Authié to contend with. All we can do is carry on as normal. Hope he leaves you – leaves *us* – alone. Be particularly careful.'

Sandrine realised how nervous she was at the thought of being back in the Bastide. Knowing Madame Fournier would be watching from next door. Accepting that she would have to be constantly on her guard.

'So you see,' Marianne was saying, 'Lucie is the furthest thing from my mind.'

'Yes, I see,' Sandrine said, wishing she hadn't brought it up.

She leant her head against the wooden frame of the carriage window and tilted her face to the hot August afternoon. The train hummed its lullaby song along the metal tracks parallel to the river. She wondered where Raoul would sleep tonight. She wondered how long it would be before she saw him again. Two weeks, two months? Longer?

What if the war never ended? Was that possible?

She closed her eyes, willing there to be some truth in the legend. That just as Dame Carcas had defeated the armies of Charlemagne, the ghost army might once more be summoned and drive out the new invaders from France. Only when they were free from occupation once more could she and Raoul hope to be together. She glanced at her sister and at Suzanne, and smiled.

Until such time as Monsieur Baillard found the Codex, they would do everything they could. They would play their part.

Chapter 99

The Haute Vallée

At first sight, everything appeared the same as always. The wide *drailles* were empty and it didn't look as if anyone had passed that way for some time. All the same, Baillard was anxious. To start with, the group was larger than he liked – it was safer to take people in twos and threes over Roc Blanc – and larger than he had been expecting. Three of the men were quiet and on edge, in the usual sort of way. One English airman who spoke no French, a Dutchman and a Jewish dissident, a scholar. All bore the marks of hardship and experience on their faces. The fourth, a Frenchman, was nervous too, like the others, but he kept glancing over his shoulder and looking at his watch.

'Just wondering how much longer to the summit,' he said, when he noticed Baillard looking at him.

'Some time yet.'

'Where are we now?'

'Do you need to know, sénher?' Baillard said mildly.

'No,' he said quickly, 'just interested.'

Keeping the water to their left, Baillard led the group on towards the pine forest that lay between Étang de Baxouillade and the plains before the Étang du Laurenti. At least in the woods they would be less exposed. He glanced behind him and saw the man was lagging behind.

'Sénher, you must hurry,' he said.

'I had to stop. Something in my shoe.'

Baillard peered ahead. One of the most hard-working

passeurs had been caught last week, which was why he had agreed to take the group higher up into the mountains than he usually did. He was expecting to see the Spanish guide hired to take them over the border, but there was no sign of him.

The Frenchman caught up and walked in step. Baillard's misgivings grew. He glanced at the Dutchman and could see he was suspicious too. Baillard's hand went to his pocket and found his pistol. He slipped the safety catch off and positioned his finger on the trigger, ready to act if need be.

'Put your hands up.'

The shouted order came from the woods. A line of police, armed with semi-automatic rifles, were stepping out of the cover of the trees. Baillard immediately dropped to the ground.

Another shout. 'Drop your weapons!'

The Englishman tried to run. The police opened fire. Blood and guts exploded from his chest as a hail of machine-gun fire hammered into him. The other two immediately put their hands on their heads. The informer leant close to him.

'You've got no chance, old man,' he said.

Baillard pulled the gun from his pocket and let off a shot, but it went wide. He saw the informer's hand come up, then felt a blinding flash of pain on the side of his head. As he lost consciousness, he was aware of his hands being dragged up behind his back.

When Baillard came round, he was in the back of a police van. The Dutchman and the dissident were also there, along with several other men. Some had been roughed up, others looked as if they'd been arrested at work or in their homes.

It was hot and airless and there was a stench of blood

and dirt, the sour smell of fear. The van wasn't moving.

'How long have we been here?'

'Two hours, maybe three,' the Dutchman said.

Baillard could feel dried blood on his ear and neck. The force of the blow still seemed to be reverberating in his head. He tried to move, but the handcuffs tightened on his wrists and pinched his skin.

'What are they waiting for?' the scholar asked.

'For the last lot to come in. Five raids today, all tip-offs,' the Dutchman said. 'That's what they were saying.'

The door of the van was suddenly thrown wide and the faces of two guards appeared in the opening. They peered through the metal grille.

'Audric Baillard?'

No one spoke.

'We're looking for him, an old man. Arrested today.'

Without appearing to move, the Dutchman and the Jewish dissident both slightly shifted position in the van, so that Baillard was blocked from the policeman's view.

'No?'

'This lot were arrested in the mountains,' the younger officer said. 'If he's as old as they say, he'd hardly be all the way up there.'

The door was slammed shut again. For a moment, no one spoke. Then Baillard gave a long sigh of relief.

'Gentlemen, I am in your debt,' he said quietly.

'It's the least I can do to repay the compliment,' the Dutchman said. 'I've been shown nothing but kindness.'

'And I know your work, Monsieur Baillard,' said the dissident. 'It is an honour to meet you, even in these circumstances. I wish I had realised earlier.'

'Better that you did not.'

There was a bang on the side of the van. The driver fired the engine, and they moved off. Baillard closed his eyes, thinking of the trials of the past. Of a young man murdered in the dungeon of the Château Comtal many centuries ago. Of those tortured in the cloisters of Saint-Etienne and Saint-Sernin in the name of religion. Of those being sent to camps in the East. An endless cycle of persecution and death, or so it sometimes seemed. Perhaps it would never end.

If he died now, then everything he had suffered would have been in vain. The wars he had fought, the disappointments he had endured, the endless task of bearing witness to the worst of human nature for the sake of the downtrodden and the defeated. Baillard thought of those he had failed to save in the past and those he was trying to help now. He didn't know where they were taking him, or how they knew his name, only that his life could not end here. He had to find a way to escape, to survive until the end.

The story was not over yet.

'*A la perfin*,' he murmured.

PART III

The Last Battle
July 1944

TWO YEARS LATER

‡

Codex XVIII

‡

GAUL
TARASCO
JULY AD 344

'Please, Lupa,' Arinius pleaded. 'When the time comes, you must promise me you will take the boy and go to the mountains with the others.'

His wife folded her arms and fixed him with a stony look. 'I'm not leaving you.'

Lupa was a woman now, a mother, someone others looked up to in their growing community of Christians. Arinius still saw in her the strong-minded girl who had found him unconscious on the plains below the Pic de Vicdessos and taken him to her father's house. The girl who had nursed him back to health – with the burden of carrying the Codex lifted – looked after him and, to his great and everlasting gratitude, loved him. A few of his brothers in the community in Lugdunum had refused to take wives, believing they should dedicate their bodies as well as their souls to God alone. But it was rare. Arinius knew that the love he felt for Lupa was a reflection of all that was good in the world, a sign of God's grace for his creation.

The past two years had been the happiest of his life, the most tranquil. But no longer. The fragile peace that held in the borderlands between Hispania and Gaul, while the rest of the Empire disintegrated into warring factions, had finally broken. Tarasco was no longer safe.

'They say there are soldiers lower down the valley,'

Arinius said. 'Everyone is leaving to seek refuge in the caves. I beg you, take Marcellus and go.'

'There are always rumours,' Lupa said stubbornly. '*Bagaudes*, bandits. They've said such things for as long as I can remember, and nothing happens.' She folded her arms. 'I won't leave you.'

'It need not be for long.'

'I shan't go.'

Arinius turned to look at their son, lying on his back in the shade of a silver birch tree. Brown arms, brown legs against the pale blanket, kicking and stretching up into the air as if reaching to heaven. He smiled with pride. Marcellus was a joyful child, a happy baby. They barely ever heard him cry.

'They say more than a hundred men are heading south,' he said quietly. 'An army.'

He picked up his son and Marcellus' face lit up with pleasure. Although little more than a year old, he had, Arinius was certain, inherited his own gentle temperament. There was nothing fierce about the boy. Arinius had no doubt that if they had daughters, they would inherit their mother's fighting spirit.

'These men are not bandits,' he said. 'They come from beyond Lugdunum – perhaps even from beyond the great eastern river. Couzanium has been put to the torch, Aquis Calidis has been sacked. The people massacred where they stood.'

'Do we know that to be true?' Lupa said, tossing her long plait over her shoulder.

Arinius remembered the exhausted, bloodied messenger who had run for days through the forests, without resting, to carry the dreadful news, half crazed with the horror of what he had witnessed.

'Yes,' he said quietly.

Lupa faltered, but then continued. 'Well, even if it is,

Couzanium is many miles away. Two days' walk, at least. There's no reason why they should come this far.'

Despite his frustration, Arinius felt proud of her courage.

'Lupa, you would be a great comfort to the others if you were with them,' he said. 'You know the mountains better than anyone. You know the safest places to hide until the soldiers leave. Help to keep the children safe.' He paused. 'You could stand in my stead. Pray for our deliverance.'

He saw her now reconsider. Lupa's faith was, in some ways, stronger than his. In the valleys surrounding Tarasco, where Christianity had never previously shown its face, there was something in the people that accepted the presence of a single God in everything they saw in the world about them. In the rocks and the sky, the melody of the water as it came down from the mountains, in the crops growing on the southern slopes.

'There are always rumours,' she said, though her voice was less certain. 'Why would they come so far? What could they hope to find here?'

Arinius laid Marcellus back down on his cloth.

'The Empire is crumbling, Lupa. Divided. From the East, a new enemy has already taken much of the territory once claimed by Rome. They live by different laws. Have no respect for the lands they conquer.'

'But you told me they are Christians, like us,' Lupa threw back at him. 'They believe what we believe. Why would they harm us?'

'This is a battle for territory,' he said. 'It is not about faith, but power.'

Lupa stared at him. 'But you told me that those who take up the sword in the name of God are not true Christians.'

Arinius sighed. 'It is what I believe.'

'It is against the Word,' she said. 'What you tell me scripture says. How can this be so?'

Arinius turned his head and looked up towards the Pic de Vicdessos and the cave where the Codex remained undisturbed. The texts that preached peace and tolerance had been destroyed. The spirit in which they had been written had been driven out of the Church. What he feared had come to pass. That those who lived in a state of grace were silenced and those who pursued faith through the sword had triumphed.

'It is not for us to question the way God works in the world,' he said.

Lupa raised her chin. 'I cannot accept that. Why can I not think for myself?'

Arinius knew she was trying to deflect him. 'When the time comes—'

'*If* the time comes,' she interrupted.

'When the time comes, Lupa, you must promise you will take Marcellus and go with the other women and children.' He took the bottle from around his neck and placed the leather strap over his wife's slim, dark shoulders. 'And when you do, you must take this.'

She looked at the iridescent glass. In two years, she knew he had never let it out of his sight. Knew that it was the most important thing he possessed, the reason he had come to Tarasco in the first place.

Now, she understood how serious he believed the situation to be. How he believed it might be the end of things.

'No,' she whispered, her eyes filling with tears. For several seconds, minutes, they stood locked in a gaze that shut out the rest of the world. Then she turned and looked out over the valley.

'I cannot believe God will let anything happen to us. Not in so fine a world as this, a place like this. He will protect us.'

'I pray that you are right,' he said.

Arinius looked at his wife and saw a different expression on her face.

'You will go, then?' he said.

Lupa wrapped her fingers around the green glass and he saw she had changed her mind. 'When do you think they will come?'

He sighed with relief, though with grief too at the thought of losing her company. At being parted from his son. 'I don't know.'

'No.' She nodded. 'Well, when the time does come, I will go.'

Arinius leant forward and kissed her on the forehead, felt her arms go around his waist. For a moment they stood there, clinging to one another for comfort. Then Marcellus let out a wail.

'He's hungry,' Arinius said, releasing her.

Lupa nodded. 'He is always hungry,' she said with a smile. 'Much like his father.'

Chapter 100

CARCASSONNE
JULY 1944

Sandrine raised her Walther P38 and took aim. She steadied her hand, squeezed the trigger and felt the pistol jump as the bullet left the chamber. A fraction of a second later, she heard the glass of the lamp marking the entrance to the Berriac tunnel shatter, and the railway was plunged into darkness.

She darted back into the undergrowth at the bottom of the steep slope that fell away from the railway track. Silence. If anyone had heard the shot, they weren't coming to investigate. Still, she stayed in position for a moment longer. From her hiding place she could just make out the faint outline of the village houses a kilometre or so to the north. To the west, a little further away, the brighter lights of the cafés on the Canal du Midi in Trèbes, favoured by junior Nazi officers.

The Berriac tunnel was of great strategic importance. The line linked Carcassonne with Narbonne, forming part of the key west–east German supply lines. Food and ammunition were transported from the stores in the old hat factory in Montazels to the Wehrmacht and SS troops stationed on the coast. All the old beach resorts were garrisons now. There had been two attempts at sabotage in the past month, one closing the tunnel for twenty-four hours. But this was an unscheduled train and Sandrine was determined to stop it. So far, she had seen no French or German guards on the line.

She looked across the waiting land to the window of the tiny chapel where the candles would be lit as her sign to act when the convoy was approaching. She tucked the weapon back into her belt. She hoped she wouldn't have to use the stolen gun again tonight.

Sandrine hated this dog-end time before an operation, the counting down to zero hour. It was the moment she ceased to be Sandrine Vidal, sister of Marianne, daughter of the late François Vidal, and became instead Sophie – *résistante*, saboteur, one of many still fighting the German occupation of the Aude.

Ever since the Nazis had crossed the demarcation line on 11 November 1942 and taken control of the rest of France, Sandrine had lived this double life. She, Marianne and Suzanne in Carcassonne, helped by Robert and Gaston Bonnet and – on the few occasions he'd risked coming into town – by Raoul. Geneviève, Liesl and Yves Rousset were in Coustaussa, with Eloise and Guillaume Breillac fighting in Tarascon. Together they made up the network known as 'Citadel', with the men who supported them, although no one but them used the name. So far, they had not been caught.

Sandrine glanced at her watch. Ten forty-five.

There was always a first time.

This last half-hour was always the worst. The time when dread took hold and the fear that, this time, their luck would run out. Her fingers, toes, bones, roots of her hair, her whole body itched with anticipation.

She hoped Marianne was bearing up. She was in the chapel, more a shrine really, outside the village, her hair covered by a country headscarf and her figure hidden beneath a drab coat. When Marianne heard the train coming, she would light four candles and exit by the main door, leaving a *panier* packed with explosives and fuses by the wooden chancel door for Suzanne to collect and deliver to the small electricity substation next to the track some five metres before the entrance to the tunnel. Suzanne would prime the device, then double back to where Robert Bonnet would be waiting on the Villedubert road. From that moment, Sandrine had to wait until the optimum moment to light the fuse, then get out of the way before the bomb went off.

Sandrine's plan was to knock out the power and block the entrance to the tunnel at the same time. There was a key Wehrmacht munitions store at Lézignan, halfway to Narbonne, where German troops were also billeted. If she succeeded, Nazi operations would be seriously compromised, for a day or two at least. But it was the sort of operation she hated most. So many things could go wrong: Robert might fail to get to the rendezvous on time to pick Marianne and Suzanne up; any one of the three of them might be seen; the device might not work or go off too soon. Sandrine took several deep breaths, settling the butterflies in her stomach. Suzanne was as good as they came, but several partisans had been injured – even killed – by their own home-made devices in the past few weeks.

It will go off all right, she told herself.

She rolled her shoulders, feeling the tightness in her muscles as she flexed and unflexed her hands.

Ten fifty-five.

Suddenly Sandrine saw a flicker of light through the plain glass window of the chapel. Twenty minutes early. She watched to make sure it was the signal, waiting as the pale flames grew stronger, then stronger again as Marianne lit each of the candles in turn. There was no mistake.

The instant she saw the fourth flame, Sandrine was on her feet. Nerves gone, her senses on high alert, adrenalin propelling her up the bank and towards the substation. Keeping as low as she could, she ran across the open ground. The main grid was in the upper storey of the squat, rectangular tower, three metres or so above ground level. The porcelain shields protecting the connectors shone an eerie white in the dark of the night.

The *panier* was in place. Sandrine crouched down and lifted the red and white chequered napkin from the top of the basket. A jumble of wires and pipe. As she located the fuse without touching anything, she could hear the hum of the tracks and the rattle of metal sliding over metal. She held her breath, listening and counting to gauge the speed of the train, then took a box of matches from her pocket. The flame guttered and flared, but went out. Sandrine slipped the match into her pocket, so as not to leave any evidence, then took another and scraped it along the strip. This time, the flame held steady.

With a practised hand, she leant forward and lit the fuse, hearing the cord hiss. She gave it two seconds, to check it had taken, then blew out the match, shoved the box back into her pocket, and ran.

The railway lines were humming louder now. Soon the buzz would be overtaken by the sound of the engine as the train thundered closer. Sandrine drove herself on, heading for the only available cover in the thicket. There wasn't enough time to get back to her hiding place. As she threw herself down the bank, she heard a small crump, not much louder than a shotgun in fields in August. Then a massive explosion rent the air. Sandrine felt the force of it like a hand in her back, as she half flew, half rolled down the slope.

She took a second to gather her thoughts, then looked up, desperate to see, the blast ringing in her ears. She heard the shriek of the brakes, then the sound of metal connecting with rubble and concrete, the noise of the collision and derailment echoing through the silent countryside. She raised her head, feeling the heat on her face, watching as a golden cloud of flame, red, blue, leapt into the air. White light sparking as the electricity cables popped and fizzed like the Catherine wheels and Roman candles that used to engulf the walls of the Cité in Carcassonne on Bastille Day before the war. Before the occupation.

Before this life.

Sandrine let her breath out, all feeling suspended for a moment. Then, as always, self-preservation kicked in. She inhaled again, and, forcing the power into her tired legs, she turned and fled. This time she didn't stop until she reached the cover of the wood. The bag with her change of clothes was waiting where she'd left it. A nondescript summer dress in place of shirt and trousers, a working woman's headscarf instead of the black beret. Only her rubber-soled shoes might look incongruous. She rolled the clothes into a bundle, unfolded a mesh shopping bag from her pocket, and put them in beneath two damp cloths and a duster. So long as she wasn't stopped and her bag searched, there was no reason for anyone to think she wasn't a cleaner on her way home after her Monday-night shift.

It wasn't until she saw the towers of the Cité in the distance that Sandrine heard the first of the sirens. She looked down from the Aire de la Pépinière as a fire truck, followed by a Feldgendarmerie truck and a black Citroën Traction Avant, the car favoured by the Gestapo, shrieked along the route de Narbonne towards Berriac.

She took a moment to catch her breath, then quickly carried on towards home. Going through residential areas, where patrols were less likely, she avoided the Wehrmacht checkpoints on the Pont Neuf and arrived back in the Bastide as the bells were striking one. She turned into the rue de Lorraine, rather than the rue du Palais, so that she could get in through the back. Her fingers were crossed – as they always were at the end of an operation – that the others had made it safely home, too.

Carefully, Sandrine opened the gate and glanced up

at the Fournier house next door, to check that no midnight watcher was there. The windows were dark, shutters closed. She crossed the garden and ran up the steps, stopping to listen at the door before going in.

She felt a rush of relief at the sound of voices inside, then a moment of caution. She could hear Marianne and Suzanne, but a man was talking too. Sandrine frowned. Robert Bonnet never came to the house. She hesitated a moment longer, then opened the screen door a fraction to look, to see who it could possibly be at this time of night.

She caught her breath. It had been eight weeks. Eight long weeks. She hadn't been expecting him. With a smile and a slight stumble of her heart, she pulled off the headscarf, shook out her hair and went into the kitchen.

'Hello,' she said lightly.

Raoul stood up. '*Ma belle.*'

Chapter 101

CHARTRES

'This way, monsieur,' said the housekeeper.

Leo Authié followed her through the mahogany-panelled entrance hall, past the tapestries and the dimly lit glass display cases. A flight of grand wooden stairs led up to the private rooms on the first floor. Beneath them, a small door led to the extensive wine cellar, which was, Authié knew from his personal experience, as good now as before the war.

In the past two years, Authié had been invited to the rue du Cheval Blanc on several occasions. The courtesies were always the same. Outside, the consequences of months of bombing. Rubble in the streets, the airport destroyed and the threat of Allied forces advancing through western France from Normandy. Here, in the shadow of the great Gothic cathedral, nothing had changed.

'Monsieur de l'Oradore will be with you shortly,' said the housekeeper, showing him into the library.

'Thank you,' he said, taking off his hat. Authié did not wear the uniform of the Milice, preferring to remain in civilian clothing as in his days of attachment to the Deuxième Bureau.

The library was more like a gentlemen's club than a room in a private house, the atmosphere one of cigar smoke and old money. A large three-seat leather sofa stood beneath the window, and armchairs either side of the fire-place. The shutters were closed, with the blackout curtains drawn. A single lamp pooled yellow light on a side table.

Bookshelves ran from floor to ceiling along three sides of the room, with sliding book ladders set on metal rails in the oak floorboards.

'Ah, Authié.' François Cecil-Baptiste de l'Oradore walked into the room, his hand outstretched in greeting. 'Forgive me for getting you out of bed at such an unconscionable hour.'

'I was still up, monsieur,' Authié replied. However cordial his host appeared to be, there was never any question of them being friends.

The two men were of a similar age, both in their mid-thirties. But where Authié was of medium height and broadly built, de l'Oradore was very tall and thin. His black hair, touched with grey, was swept back from a high forehead and prominent cheekbones. He was, as always, immaculately dressed and had clearly come from dinner. A white dress shirt, bow tie, silver cufflinks just visible beneath the sleeves of his jacket, and a purple cummerbund. Like Authié, he wore a crucifix pin on his lapel.

'Good of you to come all the same,' de l'Oradore said, waving his hand to indicate that Authié should sit down. 'Please.'

Whatever the matter was, it had to be serious for de l'Oradore to summon him at one o'clock in the morning.

'Smoke?' He offered a box of Cuban cigars.

Authié shook his head. 'No thank you,' he said. 'What can I do for you, Monsieur de l'Oradore?'

His host sat on the sofa and rested his arm along the back. 'The situation in Chartres is, how shall I put it, precarious.'

'But Montgomery and his troops have failed to advance,' Authié said.

De l'Oradore waved his hand dismissively. 'I'm sure the Panzer divisions are more than capable of containing them, yes,' he said. 'However, my most pressing concern is the question of safeguarding my collection. A great many of the pieces – in particular the thirteenth-century books and manuscripts – are irreplaceable.'

As well as the wine cellar, Authié was aware there were other extensive chambers beneath the house. In May, there had been an attempted burglary. Two Waffen-SS officers who had been dining with de l'Oradore that night in the rue du Cheval Blanc had shot the intruders. Authié had been summoned to dispose of the bodies.

He had never seen the extent of the underground space, but he knew de l'Oradore was one of the most successful private collectors in France. Jewellery, tapestries, medieval manuscripts. At the centre of his collection were objects acquired from Napoleon's Egyptian expeditions at the end of the eighteenth century. Recently, these had been supplemented by pieces from the Galerie Nationale du Jeu de Paume in Paris, among other galleries. Works stolen from Jewish deportees and artists.

'Do you not consider your storage facilities here to be adequate?' Authié asked carefully.

'They will be of little use should Allied troops reach the city.'

Authié paused. He had not thought things so serious. Thanks to his position, his information about the truth of matters between the Axis and Allied forces was good. But de l'Oradore's intelligence was better.

'Are there reasons to think that is an imminent possibility?' he asked.

Now it was de l'Oradore's turn to pause. 'There are rumours that more American troops will disembark on the northern coast,' he said eventually. There was no suggestion of alarm or fear in his voice, only the thoughtful concern of a businessman for his investments. 'I am sure the threat is exaggerated, but, as a precaution, there are certain objects I intend to remove from Chartres until the situation is clear.'

'To Berlin?'

He shook his head. 'America.'

'I see.'

'My intention is to close up the house.' He fixed Authié with a sharp look. 'I would like you, therefore, to return to Carcassonne. To resume the investigations for which I engaged you in the first instance.'

Authié was surprised, though he kept his expression impassive. He wondered what had changed. De l'Oradore had suspended his search for the Cathar treasure, after the Nazis had invaded the *zone libre*, without explanation. For nearly two years he had not mentioned it. His interests appeared to have shifted.

'I thought you were of the opinion that there was no value in continuing to excavate the area around Montségur or Lombrives?'

'There is a suggestion,' de l'Oradore said, 'that a Languedocien scholar, one of the significant authorities on the history of the region, might have information. It could influence where we look next. I want you to find him, Authié. See if there is any substance to this rumour.'

'How has this new information come to us?'

'That bookseller of yours. Saurat.'

Authié narrowed his eyes, remembering the strange man with his high-pitched voice and his dark bookshop in Toulouse.

'Saurat?' he said. 'Is it possible I could talk to him myself?'

'I regret he is no longer with us. He was arrested in Lyon. Helping the partisans, it seems. He was very helpful, however. The information he shared seems credible.'

Authié was not convinced, but he kept his expression neutral. He was aware of the reputation of Hauptsturmführer Barbie, head of the Gestapo in Lyon. Many suspects would say anything, true or false, to bring their interrogation to an end.

'There is a transcript of the conversation,' de l'Oradore added, perhaps sensing Authié's scepticism. 'If that would be useful.'

'It would, thank you.' There was nothing to be gained by voicing his true opinion or going against de l'Oradore's orders.

'This scholar Saurat mentioned, is he attached to the university in Toulouse?'

'An author rather than an academic, I gather.'

'I see,' Authié said again. 'Do you have a name? An address?'

De l'Oradore pulled an envelope from his pocket. 'He's called Audric S. Baillard. I've heard of him, in fact. Quite an expert on Ancient Egypt. Wrote a biography of Champollion, the man who first deciphered hieroglyphic text.' He paused. 'Baillard lives in some tiny village in the Pyrenees. Los Seres.' He handed the envelope to Authié. 'It's all here. I can't imagine he'll be hard to find; he's an old man, judging by the date of publication of most of his books. He might also know something about a book I am most interested in acquiring. Extremely interested. To complete part of my collection here, you understand. Medieval. Perhaps with the symbol of a labyrinth on the cover, distinctive. I have had these notes prepared for you. To help the process.' He fixed Authié with a look. 'I would be most appreciative of any information. However you see fit to acquire it. Do you understand me, Authié?'

Authié took the heavy cream envelope and put it in his breast pocket. 'I do.'

De l'Oradore held his gaze for a moment longer, then glanced away. 'I have spoken to your superior officer, who is prepared to release you immediately. I have arranged transport south for Friday. Bastille Day, rather appropriate, I thought. The announcement has already been given to the radio stations.'

'Announcement?'

'That you are taking over the battle against the Resistance. Who better than a local man? Take Laval with you.' He gave a slight smile, then stood up. 'Congratulations on your promotion, Major Authié.'

Authié also got to his feet, impressed by the extent of de l'Oradore's influence.

'I hope to live up to your faith in me,' he said.

'I hope so too.' De l'Oradore paused. 'I know you have made several visits to the south in recent weeks, Authié.'

'I have.'

'Satisfactory?'

'Effective, certainly.'

'Will you be pleased to return for good, I wonder?'

Authié met his cool, appraising gaze. They both knew he had no choice. It would have made no difference if he hadn't wanted to return to the Midi. But he took care over his answer all the same.

'I have very much enjoyed my time in Chartres, but of course I am happy to do whatever best serves our cause.'

'Quite right,' said de l'Oradore. From the slight smile on his face, Authié knew he had said the right thing.

Perhaps to underline Authié's new position, de l'Oradore showed him through the dimly lit hall to the front door himself, rather than ringing for the housekeeper.

'Keep me informed, Authié. Send any communications via the normal route. I shall be travelling, of course, but any message will get to me, even if it takes longer than usual.'

‘Of course.’ Authié put on his hat. ‘I am grateful for your support, monsieur.’

De l’Oradore opened the front door on to the dark street. No street lamps; the blackout was rigorously observed after months of night-time bombardments on Luftwaffe aircraft at Champhol airfield to the north-east of Chartres. In the moonlight, the twin spires of the magnificent cathedral stood tall against the sky.

‘By the way,’ de l’Oradore said, ‘Saurat said something else of interest before he died.’

‘He did?’

‘About that alleged fourth-century text you brought me. The Codex.’

Authié became still. ‘Alleged?’

‘It appears it was a forgery,’ de l’Oradore continued casually. ‘Saurat admitted he’d known, even though he authenticated it. The Ahnenerbe have confirmed it. A very high-quality forgery, but fake all the same.’ He paused. ‘Goodnight, Major Authié. I shall expect to hear from you when you have settled in on Friday.’

The door was closed before Authié had the chance to react. He stared at the painted door, the polished handles and letter box. He realised that de l’Oradore’s timing of the information about the Codex was deliberate. He had been set the challenge to find Audric Baillard to compensate, in part, for his mistake with Saurat.

For two years, Authié had regretted handing the Codex to de l’Oradore. He’d assumed he would destroy it as a heretical text, although perhaps not before analysing it to test the truth of the power it was said to contain. Instead, he had given it immediately into the custody of the Ahnenerbe, where it had remained ever since.

Now, it seemed, there might still be a need to find the true Codex. For himself. To do what he should have done in the first place: put his loyalty to the Church above his loyalty to de l'Oradore.

Authié turned and walked quickly along the rue du Cheval Blanc, a cold anger growing inside him. Saurat was beyond his reach, but Raoul Pelletier was not. Sandrine Vidal was not. Someone must have hidden the forgery in the cave within the Col de Pyrène. Pelletier? And Vidal had told him of the discovery, in innocence or put up to it, it didn't matter. He would find out soon enough.

At the front of the great Gothic cathedral, he stopped and looked up at the three stone arches of the Royal Portal. A book in stone, Authié had heard it called. Not only New Testament images of redemption and faith, but also older stories of judgement and vengeance from the Old Testament.

He hesitated a moment, turning over in his mind what de l'Oradore had said about the medieval book. If this Baillard knew about that, as well as having information about the Codex, Authié did not think it would be difficult to persuade him to talk.

He knew God was on his side. He was doing God's will.

Authié looked up at the west Rose Window, depicting Christ's Second Coming as judge. To condemn all those who had turned away from the true faith. To save only those who had adhered to the precepts of the Church. In the faint light of the moon, the blood red and death blue of the glass was just visible.

He lingered a moment longer, then gathered himself. There were few *résistants* left operational in the centre of Chartres, after another successful raid last week, but his face was known. It only needed one lone marksman. Authié walked fast until he reached the cover of the rue des Changes.

The time was right to return to the Midi. He would find Audric Baillard for de l'Oradore. Then he would hunt down Pelletier and Vidal for himself.

Chapter 102

CARCASSONNE

'We should get going,' Sandrine said.

'All right, little man,' said Lucie, leaning over the pram. 'Off to get the bread. You like to fetch the bread with Mama, don't you, J-J?'

Jean-Jacques looked up at her with sleepy eyes, surprised to be out in the morning so early, but he smiled all the same. Perhaps it was too early to say, but he didn't appear to be short-sighted like his father.

While Lucie continued to fuss and tuck in his blankets tightly again, making sure the sheets of blank paper hidden underneath the mattress could not be seen, Sandrine glanced up at her bedroom window. Inside, Raoul was sleeping. He was even thinner than when she'd last seen him in May and, like they all were, exhausted. There had been several Allied parachute drops recently that had missed their target and much-needed weapons hadn't got through. There had been many arrests too. Raoul looked worn out, and it had taken all her self-control to leave him and carry on as planned. But it was essential to get the news out of the attack on the Berriac tunnel before the Nazi and Milice propaganda machine got going. Besides, Raoul needed to sleep. They would have time to talk as soon as she got back.

Lucie was still fussing. She seemed full of jitters this morning, Sandrine thought. She bent forward and kissed her godson on the top of his head. Jean-Jacques wrinkled his nose, his podgy hand flapping at the air.

'No!'

In her *panier*, Sandrine had a piece of rotting fish wrapped in newspaper – designed to put off even the most zealous of Wehrmacht patrols. Beneath the fish was a roll of film from Liesl that Raoul had brought, and her copy about the sabotage of the Berriac tunnel.

'I know,' Sandrine whispered to the boy, 'it's an awful stink.' She pinched her nose. 'But it will keep the nasty soldiers from talking to us, J-J, so we don't mind, do we?'

Jean-Jacques giggled. 'Gun, gun,' he said. 'Gun, bang.'

Lucie raised her eyebrows. 'I can't imagine what his father would say.'

Sandrine smiled. Lucie always talked as if Max was with them. She'd not seen him since that day in Le Vernet in August 1942, though she wrote every week. The waitress in the Café de la Paix in Le Vernet village sent news of the camp when she could. It pained Lucie not to be able to tell Max anything about their son, the things he did or the words he was starting to speak. But she was keeping a diary, so Max would be able to read about J-J's first few years when he came home. She behaved as if it was never in doubt that Max would come back.

Sandrine wasn't sure if Lucie believed it, or was putting on a good face. Ever since the invasion of the *zone nono* and the arrival of German soldiers on the streets of the Bastide, the deportations of Jewish prisoners from camps in the Ariège had accelerated. For whatever reason – perhaps his skill with languages, or the constant enquiries by Marianne's Croix-Rouge colleagues – Max had been lucky. Lucie, she suspected, was still inclined to put it down to Authié's intervention, though she never said as much and Sandrine didn't ask.

In the last few weeks, though, things had changed. The Allied landings in the north of France in June proved the tide was turning against the Axis forces, whatever the newspapers claimed. As a reaction, the number of Jewish prisoners being deported from Le Vernet was being stepped up. To a place called Dachau, in Bavaria, a camp on the site of an old munitions factory, so she'd heard. Sandrine knew of no one who had ever been released from that camp. She didn't know how Lucie would manage if Max's name was finally put on the list.

Lucie had stayed in Coustaussa with Liesl and Marieta until Jean-Jacques was born, but country living didn't suit her at all, and in the summer of 1943, she had come back to Carcassonne. A *fille-mère*, an unmarried mother as the result of a one-night stand with a soldier, was the story put about. Her position was difficult, but by keeping Jean-Jacques' paternity a secret, she kept her son safe. Since Suzanne lived mostly at the rue du Palais, Lucie lodged with Suzanne's mother and worked in a haberdasher's shop near the station owned by one of Madame Peyre's friends. Her distinctive blonde hair had gone, returned to its natural sparrow brown, and she was thin. She dressed in plain dresses designed not to attract attention, rather than the trim two-pieces she'd worn before the war. Once, she had run into her father in the Bastide. He had frowned slightly, as if trying to recall where he knew her from, but had not recognised her.

'Ready for the off?' Sandrine asked.

'As I'll ever be, kid.'

Sandrine smiled. Lucie gave the same response every time. She wasn't really involved, though from time to time – like this morning – she was prepared to run an errand. She felt the best way to help keep Max safe was to do nothing to draw attention. To follow the rules. She had no idea Sandrine, Suzanne and Marianne did anything more than produce an underground newspaper.

'Kid, kid, kid,' sang Jean-Jacques. At seventeen months,

he was already talkative, keen to try words and sounds out loud.

Lucie's expression softened for a moment, then she handed him a crust of stale bread and put her finger to her lips.

'Nice and quiet, *mon brave*. Quiet.'

Jean-Jacques' eyes grew wide. Sandrine, too, put her finger to her lips and puffed them out, as if blowing out the candles on a birthday cake. The little boy copied.

'Ssshh,' he whispered loudly. 'J-J quiet.'

They walked towards boulevard Antoine Marty, the front wheel of the perambulator squeaking horribly loudly in the quiet of the morning. Their shoes, too, were noisy. Like everyone else, they were having to make do with wooden soles when the leather wore through.

'Who's there to meet us?' Lucie asked.

'Gaston. Suzanne will come later when the sheets are ready to be distributed.'

The idea for a weekly newspaper had been Sandrine's. Inspired by the underground press in northern France, after the Germans had invaded the South she had produced the first copy of *Libertat* – the Occitan word for freedom. She wrote the editorials, articles on atrocities carried out by the Milice, naming collaborationists, passing on information about successful Resistance raids. From time to time they published photographs. Geneviève or Eloise smuggled films from Liesl – of munitions depots, troop movements, leading Gestapo or SS officers, the layout of prisons – to Carcassonne. Suzanne was in charge of the printing, Marianne arranged the distribution, Robert and Gaston Bonnet delivered the newspapers to their couriers. Lucie kept the machines in working order. A childhood spent in her father's garage had given her a useful knowledge of all things mechanical.

Sandrine's aim was to highlight the continuing,

worsening crimes of Vichy and to expose '*la barbarie nazie*'. *Libertat* was only one of several partisan newspapers – *Combat*, *Libération*, *Humanité*, *Le Courrier du Témoignage Chrétien*, *Libérer* and *La Vie ouvrière* – each attempting to counteract the increasingly hysterical collaborationist and Nazi propaganda. Every week, tracts were discovered in a suitcase under a bench at the railway station in Lézignan, or pushed under the doors of cafés in the centre of Limoux during the night, or left in the bus depot in Narbonne.

Sandrine reserved her harshest criticism for the Milice, the Frenchmen who collaborated and did the occupiers' work for them. Formed at the beginning of 1943, the Milice was an amalgamation of the various Rightist groups. In Carcassonne, it had been under the control of Albert Kromer until February, when the Resistance finally succeeded in assassinating him. Their next-door neighbour, Monsieur Fournier, had been killed in the same attack. Lucie's father was a member, like most of the former LVF members who met at the Café Edouard.

Carcassonne was now a city at war with itself. After two years of living a double life, Sandrine divided the Bastide into places she could go and places she should not. The Feldgendarmerie, under Chef Shröbel, occupied the white stucco building on the corner of boulevard Maréchal Pétain, overlooking the Palais de Justice, where the Deuxième Bureau had been based. The counter-espionage bureau, Abwehr, had established itself in Boulevard Barbès. The Laperrine barracks, where once the mothers of Carcassonne had waved their husbands and sons off to war in 1914, was now the headquarters of the SS, and the Gestapo headquarters was on the route de Toulouse. Of all the commanders of the Aude, Chef Eckfelner and Sous-chef Schiffner, who led the hunt against partisans, were the most vicious.

It was not just their future and their present that was

being taken away from them, but their past too. The *vert-de-gris* had occupied the medieval Cité. A landmark of local pride and international significance, it was now closed to civilians. No ordinary citizens were allowed past the Porte Narbonnaise without a work permit. Sometimes, when Sandrine looked across the water to the majestic towers and turrets, she was almost relieved that her father hadn't lived to suffer the sight of the 'green-and-grey' walking through the cobbled streets, drinking cognac in the lounge of the Hôtel de la Cité. Standing on the battlements where once Viscount Trencavel had commanded his men to stand firm against the northern crusaders. Where Dame Carcas had deceived Charlemagne.

Almost relieved.

For some time, Sandrine felt they were working alone. Then, on 27 January 1943 – the same day Lucie had given birth to Jean-Jacques – the disparate partisan groups were brought together as the Mouvements Unis de Résistance, under the leadership of Jean Moulin. The southern zone had been carved into six divisions. The Aude was R3 and the Ariège R4. Ranks and passes, a structure of order and command and control was established. Sandrine heard the code names whispered – 'Myriel', 'Bels', 'Frank', 'Le Rouquin' (because of his red hair), 'Robespierre' and 'Danton'. She would not have recognised any of them if she'd passed them in the street. Nor they her.

As well as Sandrine's code name, 'Sophie', Suzanne was 'André' and Marianne was 'Catherine'. Christian names only, unlike their male counterparts. Raoul and Robert Bonnet knew them, but no one else. It wasn't a question of not trusting Liesl or Geneviève, or Eloise and Guillaume Breillac, but common sense. The less one knew, the less one could be forced to tell. Jean Moulin had been murdered only six months after forming the MUR – caught by, or betrayed to, the Gestapo – but after a month of torture in the notorious Lyon prison, he died without revealing anything. Without giving anyone's name away.

'Are you all right?' Lucie said, her voice cutting into Sandrine's reflections. 'You seem tired.'

Sandrine blushed. 'I didn't sleep much,' she said.

'Ssshh,' said the little boy, holding his finger again to his lips. 'J-J *dodo*.'

Sandrine and Lucie smiled. 'That's right, Jean-Jacques. Everyone's sleeping,' Sandrine whispered. 'We mustn't wake them up.'

'*Dodo*,' he said loudly.

'*Bubi*,' Lucie said quickly. 'Hush now, that's my little man.' He looked at her with his wide brown eyes, but immediately became quiet. 'He looks so like Max when he does that, doesn't he?'

'Yes,' Sandrine nodded, though in truth she could hardly remember what Max looked like.

Even after everything that had happened, Sandrine still felt a residual sense of guilt when she thought about Max. Remembering the morning with the Croix-Rouge at the railway station in Carcassonne and wondering if there was anything she could have done to stop him being taken. She knew it was pointless to think that way, but she did. Somehow it made keeping secrets from Lucie seem even worse.

They walked on, the wheels of the pram rattling on the pavement, a little further into the heart of the Bastide. The sound of the carts delivering milk and the bakers transporting bread to the German garrison in the Hôtel Terminus.

'Did you hear they blew up the line at Berriac last evening?'

Sandrine hesitated, tempted for a moment to confide in her. But then common sense prevailed. It was better that Lucie didn't know. Safer for them all.

'They?'

'Resistance, I suppose. And it makes sense,' Lucie said, stumbling over the words, 'that's to say, of what I heard on the wireless.'

Sandrine glanced at her. 'What did they say on the wireless?'

'I don't know if it's true, of course. They so often get these things wrong, don't they?'

'I don't know what you're talking about, Lucie,' Sandrine said. 'What makes sense?'

'There was an item on the wireless. I wasn't listening properly, so I might have misunderstood. They were talking about how, since the head of the Milice in Carcassonne was killed . . . I can't remember his name.'

'Albert Kromer,' Sandrine said.

'Yes, they said that since he was killed in January, the number of attacks on the Milice has gone up.'

'That's true enough,' Sandrine agreed.

Both the Maquis and the Resistance units – 'Citadel' among them – had become bolder after having claimed the scalp of such a high-profile target as Kromer. Two weeks ago, with Suzanne's help, Sandrine had broken into the Milice offices in Place Carnot and burnt a stack of recruitment posters. As soon as any new poster was put up in the street, partisans defaced them with the Cross of Lorraine, symbol of the Resistance, using penknives or white ink. But better to destroy them at source. In retaliation, the Milice had raided a café on the rue de l'Aigle d'Or.

'So,' Lucie continued, 'the bulletin also said that although the Milice and the Germans were winning the battle against the insurgents—'

'Rot!'

'That's what they said,' Lucie said defensively.

'It's what they always say.'

'Also that although the Germans were winning,' Lucie

continued, 'increasing numbers of local men and women were supporting the partisans.'

Sandrine nodded. The number of maquisards had been growing and growing, ever since the STO had been introduced in February 1943. A draft to send men to munitions factories or farms in Germany to support the Nazi war effort, the Service de Travail Obligatoire had been voluntary, but soon became compulsory. Food, shelter, messages. A car left with fuel and the keys in the ignition. All ways that ordinary men and women could help. In recent weeks, even Wehrmacht soldiers were deserting and joining the Maquis.

But the cost was high and the reprisals were becoming increasingly vicious. Two days ago, a German unit, supported by local Milice, had launched an attack on the Villebazy Maquis in their forest hideout to the east of Limoux. A warning had got through and the maquisards had fled, so the troops had turned on the villagers instead. Several men were arrested, hostages taken and houses ransacked. One man was dead.

'The point is …' Lucie took a deep breath. 'The point is, they said that because of all this, a high-ranking commander from the north is being brought in to lead the offensive against the insurgents in the Aude.'

Sandrine thought about the latest rumours. Entire villages being rounded up. In June, nearly a hundred people murdered at Tulle and nearly seven hundred at Oradour-sur-Glane near Limoges. Closer to home, stories of hostages being taken and summary executions, most recently in Chalabre, to the west of Limoux. The authorities denied any such atrocity had taken place.

'Sandrine?' Lucie said anxiously.

'I'm sorry,' Sandrine said, forcing herself to stop thinking about things she couldn't do anything about. 'Sorry, I am listening.'

'They said his name, you see, that's what got my attention.'

Without warning, Sandrine's mild impatience with Lucie transformed into a sick, sharp fear. Immediately, she realised. Realised what Lucie was struggling to say and why she was finding it so hard to get the words out.

'Did they say who it was?' she asked, although she already knew the answer. 'Did they give a name?'

Lucie raised her head and looked her in the eye. 'Leo Authié.'

Chapter 103

'Captain Authié.'

'*Major* now,' Lucie said in a rush. 'I thought you'd want to know.'

Sandrine stared blindly, then pulled herself together. 'Yes, of course I do.' She paused. 'Did the bulletin say when he was taking up the position?'

'No.'

'Or if he was to be based in the Milice headquarters in Place Carnot? In Carcassonne?'

'I don't think so. I'm sorry.'

Sandrine fell silent. Authié was a malignant presence in the corner of her mind, always there even though the fear he inspired in her had become weaker as the months – years – had passed without anything happening.

When she'd come back to Carcassonne in August 1942, Sandrine had expected to see Authié or his deputy, Sylvère Laval, on every street corner. She'd anticipated the knock at the door. Then in October, Raoul managed to confirm that, having consulted Monsieur Saurat in Toulouse, Authié had gone on to Chartres and remained there. There was no record of him returning to the Midi at all.

Nonetheless, that autumn and winter, Sandrine still avoided walking past the headquarters of the Deuxième Bureau on boulevard Maréchal Pétain and kept her ear to the ground for any gossip. She even listened to the hated Radio Paris, but heard nothing. Not a whisper.

Then in November the Germans crossed the demarcation line and everything changed. The headquarters of the Deuxième Bureau were occupied by the Feldgendarmerie.

The enemy was now everywhere, in possession of the streets of the Bastide and the Cité. There was more to contend with than Leo Authié.

Since then, Sandrine had come across Authié's name only twice. The first time was in a pro-Nazi newspaper, in November 1943. A class at the lycée where Marianne worked had staged a protest on the first anniversary of the invasion of the Midi, marching around the courtyard with placards and singing 'La Marseillaise', banned since the occupation. The girls, children all of them, had been suspended for fifteen days, but their point was made. Walking through Square Gambetta later that afternoon, Sandrine had seen a copy of *Le Matin* lying on a bench. She'd picked it up and been taken by surprise by a photograph of Leo Authié with two SS-Obergruppenführer officers. She had thrust the newspaper into the nearest rubbish bin, feeling contaminated by having even touched it.

The second time was eight weeks ago. Marianne had shown her an article in *L'Echo*, commending the joint efforts of the Chartres Milice and their 'German guests' in preventing an attack on a private museum in the city. Authié hadn't changed. A little broader perhaps, but the same hateful expression of condescension and arrogance. He was being honoured by Nazi High Command for having masterminded a series of raids against – as the editorial put it – 'agitators, saboteurs and terrorists'. Sandrine still remembered the exact words, though her abiding memory was one of swooping relief at knowing Authié was still in the North.

In Chartres, not Carcassonne.

'The thing is,' Lucie was saying, 'I was giving Jean-Jacques his breakfast, so I wasn't really paying attention. It was just his name. Because I wasn't expecting it, it jumped out at me.'

'I know,' Sandrine said, not really listening.

On impulse, Sandrine suddenly turned round and looked back in the direction they had come. At the empty street stretching out behind them in the early-morning sunshine. What if Authié was already back in Carcassonne? All she wanted to do now was run back to the house, where Raoul was sleeping, and tell him to get out while he had the chance. Before Authié came looking for him.

'Do you remember the drive that day from Le Vernet?' Lucie said quietly. 'That lieutenant of his, staring at us all the time. He gave me the creeps.'

'Yes,' Sandrine said.

'Sandrine, you don't think . . .' Lucie stopped again. 'You don't think, if Authié finds out about Jean-Jacques, he'll put two and two together?'

'What? No, of course not,' she said quickly, guilty she'd been thinking only about herself and Raoul. She focused her attention on Lucie. 'There's no reason why you should run into him at all. Anyway, it was a long time ago. You didn't even show then.' She put her hand over Lucie's on the handle of the pram. 'Don't worry.'

'Because if they try to take him, I—'

'No one's going to take Jean-Jacques from you,' said Sandrine firmly. 'It'll be fine.'

They continued along rue Antoine Marty with the rising sun at their heels and the squeak of the pram filling the quiet morning air. Jean-Jacques chatted quietly to himself, forming sweet, meaningless sounds.

They turned right, then left into the narrow alley that ran parallel with the route de Minervois. The baby let out a sudden shriek of delight at the rare sight of a pigeon sitting on a windowsill in the shadows. Most of the city's birds had been caught and eaten.

'Bird!'

'Jean-Jacques, quiet!' Sandrine snapped sharply.

The little boy stared at her, shocked she had raised her

voice to him. Sandrine was immediately contrite, but also angry she'd let Authié get under her skin already. She bent over the pram.

'Sorry, J-J, but it's important we are quiet, do you see? We mustn't disturb the bird. The bird is sleeping. Sshh.'

He nodded, but his eyes were wary.

'I'm sorry,' she said, to Lucie this time.

They walked the rest of the way to the print shop in silence. For some time after César's murder, the darkroom beneath the Café des Deux Gares had sat empty. Suzanne had discovered it was still operational, and between them they had got it up and running.

Sandrine knocked on the side door that gave into the alley. Three sharp taps, pause; three sharp taps, pause; then another three sharp taps. She heard footsteps, then the welcome rattle of the chain and the key being turned in the lock. Gaston Bonnet's face appeared in the doorway.

She didn't like Gaston much – he drank and he was abrasive – but Robert vouched for him and Marianne said he was always reliable in helping to distribute *Libertat* to their couriers, so Sandrine put up with him.

'Got it?' he said.

'Yes.'

Sandrine folded back the pram blanket, Lucie held up the mattress, and they started to unpack the paper and hand the sheets to Gaston.

'Not much,' he said.

'All I could find at such short notice,' Sandrine said.

He shrugged. 'Have to do, then.'

It was difficult to get hold of enough ink and paper these days. Robert's lady friend, Yvette, was a cleaner at Gestapo headquarters and, smuggling it out beneath her dusters and mop, she stole paper for them, one or two sheets at a time. But she had been laid low this week with a stomach bug and had not gone to work, so their stocks were running low.

'That's the last of it,' said Lucie. She flipped the blanket back over J-J's feet. 'Shall we go and look at the boats, little man?' she said. 'Say hello to the lock keeper?'

'Thank you, Lucie,' Sandrine said quietly. 'And remember what I said. Everything will be fine.'

Lucie gave a salute, and continued on down the alley towards the Canal du Midi. Sandrine watched her go, then followed Gaston inside. She locked and bolted the door.

'What's the stink?' he said.

Sandrine prodded the fish. 'There's a film I need developing. Didn't want anyone tempted to take a closer look.'

Gaston grunted.

'She's in the darkroom,' he said, picking up the pile of paper. 'I'll take this down and get the machine ready to print.'

Sandrine smiled her thanks, then went down the steps to the basement and knocked to let Suzanne know she had arrived.

'It's all right to come in,' she called from inside.

The darkroom was lit by a dim red lamp in the ceiling. Supplies were running low and the long slatted shelves were mostly empty. A single bottle of developing fluid, an enlarger and a dryer for prints. Suzanne had left the house before it was light, evading the curfew in order to get things ready.

She glanced at Sandrine. 'Everything all right? You look tired.'

'I'm fine,' Sandrine said, then lowered her voice. 'Lucie heard something on the wireless about Leo Authié being posted back to Carcassonne.'

Suzanne grew still. 'When?'

'She didn't know.'

'What are you going to do?'

Sandrine shook her head. For the first time in a long while, she thought of Monsieur Baillard and how much she would value his advice. Nothing had been seen or heard of him since that night two years ago in Tarascon after they had hidden the forgery in the caves of Col de Pyrène. She couldn't bring herself to accept he might be dead.

'After we've finished here, I'll see if I can speak to Jeanne Giraud,' Suzanne said. 'Her husband often hears things before anyone else. Some of the *résistants* talk under anaesthetic.'

Sandrine nodded her thanks. 'It would be good to know how much time we've got, at least.'

Suzanne stared at her, then carried on. 'Right,' she said in her normal voice. 'Have you written the copy for printing?'

Trying to push thoughts of Authié from her mind, Sandrine took the film from her *panier*.

'Yes,' she said, 'but will you develop this first? Raoul brought it from Liesl last night.'

In the dim red glow, Sandrine watched as Suzanne got the temperature of the tank just right, then agitated the fluid so that the film would develop evenly. She took the film out of the casing and put it in the solution to give it time to develop. Sandrine washed her hands in the sink, trying to get rid of the smell of fish.

As soon as the negatives were ready, Suzanne pinned them on the wire above the wooden counter and waited for them to dry. They watched as the hateful images revealed themselves. Ten photographs in all, each of partisans in the course of being executed. In one, five men lay face down on the ground, four clearly dead already, a *milicien* standing with his foot on the back of the fifth as he delivered the *coup de grâce*. In another photograph, the suspended bodies of two *résistants*, hands bound and hooded, left hanging low beneath a bridge so that every vehicle that passed hit their feet. Sandrine could see their swollen toes, feet broken, the ankle bones jutting out through blistered skin.

Her jaw tightened.

'Where did Liesl get these shots?' Suzanne asked quietly.

'I think it's Chalabre,' Sandrine said, struggling to contain her anger. 'The authorities deny anything happened. Here's the proof we need.' She looked at Suzanne. 'Can you give me fifteen minutes to write something?'

'What about the Berriac report?'

'It'll have to share the page,' she said. 'This is just as important. More so.'

Sandrine sat at the counter. She thought for a moment, then wrote her headline: *POUR ARRÊTER LES CRIMES DE LA GESTAPO ET MILICE.*

She looked up at the images once more, seeing now the clear imprint of a soldier's boot on the back of a dead woman's leg. Suzanne was putting the negatives through the enlarger to make the prints.

'Sandrine,' she said in a low voice. 'You'd better take a look at this.' She adjusted the focus. 'There, can you see?'

'What am I looking for?'

'Look. In the top right-hand corner of the shot. The man in charge?'

Sandrine leant forward. The officer was turning away from the camera, his face partly obscured by his hat, but there was no doubt about it.

'It is him, isn't it?' said Suzanne.

Sandrine nodded. She felt cold. Not fear, she realised, but anger.

'Yes,' she said. 'That's Authié.'

Chapter 104

Banyuls-sur-Mer

Audric Baillard fell against the prisoner next to him as the van jerked to a halt. His shoulder jutted into the man's side. A skeleton, no flesh on his bones, his life all but beaten out of him. Baillard nodded an apology, but the brutalised eyes saw nothing.

Baillard recognised the look of surrender. The moment when, having survived years of mistreatment and privation, a man gave up the fight.

'It will not be much longer,' Audric whispered, though he suspected his words were unheard.

They had been travelling for two days, though not covering much ground. The heat, the stench of despair and sickness. In the very early hours of Saturday morning, when it was still dark, they had been woken and told that the entire camp, a satellite to the main internment camp at Rivesaltes, was being evacuated. All prisoners were being sent elsewhere. To other camps or factories in Germany.

Baillard had been among the last to leave – in a convoy of eight cattle trucks with slatted wooden sides rather than military transport. They were all old men, weakened by months – in some cases years – of starvation and hard labour, too old to be considered a high risk. They were handcuffed, but not shackled, and when they stopped en route, the guards allowed them out. In any case, it was pointless to argue with the barrel of a gun.

Baillard was surprised when the convoy headed south, rather than north. Along the coast, not away from it. From

Rivesaltes to Argelès, from Argelès to Collioure, where they spent the night. Finally, at dawn this morning, from Collioure to Port-Vendres, close to the Spanish border. They were given a little water, no food. Their first escort had been Milice, then yesterday they were handed over to the Germans. Now Baillard could hear French being spoken again. It made little sense.

The prisoner beside him had closed his eyes. A blue vein pulsed faintly in his neck. Baillard could see the skull beneath the skin and knew the man was dying.

'*Peyre sant*,' he murmured, praying for the safe delivery of his soul. The man gave no reaction.

Baillard put his cuffed hands to his cracked lips. For a moment rage burned in his amber eyes as he remembered others who had died. Friends incarcerated within the walls of a prison. In the stone dungeons of the Cité in Carcassonne or Saint-Etienne in Toulouse many years ago. In Montluc. The trains leaving from Gurs and Le Vernet, going to the death camps in the East: Drancy and Auschwitz, Belsen, Buchenwald and Dachau. Names of places he had heard, but never seen.

He let out a long exhalation of breath, as if expelling the poison from his lungs, then shook his head. He could not afford to think of the past. He could not allow anger to cloud his judgement. This moment was all that mattered. His life could not end here, not with so much left undone. The vow he had taken in his youth and the promises he had attempted to keep – so much remained to be accomplished.

Outside, he heard voices, the strike of a match. The sun was starting to rise in the sky, sending ladders of light to break up the foul, fetid air. Bracing his legs and pushing back against the side of the truck, Baillard managed to get to his feet. He put his eye to the gap and saw two guards standing in the shade of a tree about two metres away. He pressed his ear to the timber, catching the frequency of their conversation until the muttered indistinguishable sounds became individual words.

'Where next?'

'Banyuls-sur-Mer.'

'Why there?'

'It's secluded.'

The soldiers' voices became indistinct again. Baillard looked and saw they had turned their backs on the truck. He watched them grind their spent cigarettes into the dry earth, then walk back towards the vehicle. The slam of the doors, and seconds later, the heavy vibration of the engine started up.

He sat down again, so as not to be thrown off balance by the uneven jolting of the truck. Now he understood. No one wanted to take responsibility for them. In Argelès they had taken a roll call, but not in Collioure. He should have realised what was going to happen then. There were to be no records. If they were not going to have to account for the prisoners they were transporting, why bother? They were of no use. Too old to fill the Nazis' forward labour quotas, but in the absence of orders about where to send them, there was another solution. To kill them all.

Baillard leant back and started to formulate a plan. There was always a moment when they arrived at a new destination when the guards were less attentive. Except for the roll call being dropped, the routine had been more or less the same. The convoy stopped. The latches were lifted, the doors were opened and the prisoners allowed out. The guards took it in turns to go into the bushes to relieve themselves, to stretch their legs, to smoke. The drivers talked to one another, confident that the rifles cradled in their hands were enough to discourage any attempt at resistance.

If Baillard was going to escape, it would have to be in those first few minutes.

He looked around at his fellow prisoners, working out

who might be thinking the same. The regime in the camp had been harsh. Anyone who disobeyed orders was brutally punished. Solitary confinement, three days without food or water, hard labour. Some were brave, but most were too defeated to act. They had lost the will to save themselves. Even so, Baillard knew he had to try.

'When we stop,' he whispered, 'we must take our chance. It might be our last.'

He looked around, but there was no reaction to his words. A wave of pity washed through him, anger at how these men had been reduced to valuing their lives at so little.

'We must act,' he repeated, though hopes anyone would listen were fading. 'We outnumber them. It is better to try.'

'They're armed, we're not, what can we do?' came a voice from the furthest corner. 'Better not to cause trouble. The next camp might not be so bad.'

'There will not be another camp. They do not intend to let us live,' Baillard said.

'You can't know that. It might be better, who knows?'

Baillard realised there was nothing he could do. He could not save them if they were not able to save themselves. But it grieved him. He turned and pressed his eye to the letter-box gap. He could see they were following the main coastal route south. It was a stretch of road he knew well. In the distance, in the early dawn light, the soaring grey of the foothills of the Pyrenees. On the slopes, the green vineyards and the streaks of blue copper sulphate between the rows of vines. In other circumstances, one of the most beautiful views on the Vermilion Coast.

He made a calculation. The distance from Port-Vendres to Banyuls-sur-Mer was about four or five kilometres. Provided there were no roadblocks or delays – anti-tank blockades had been erected at many of the junctions – Baillard estimated it would take little more than a quarter of an hour. He did not have long to decide.

Baillard took a deep breath. The Spaniard on the opposite side of the truck was now watching him. García, he thought he was called. A former member of the International Brigade, a man who'd dedicated his life to fighting the fascists, Baillard knew him to be brave and principled. Their eyes met, then the slightest nod and Baillard knew he had one ally at least. Perhaps, when the time came, the others would find their courage.

The convoy stopped twice, although the engines kept running – perhaps to let other traffic past – but soon the swoop and curve of the bay came into view. A few houses, the grey rock a sharp contrast with the blue of the Mediterranean.

They continued through the town, then the driver swung to the right, heading away from the sea towards the uninhabited hinterland of the Puig del Mas. Tarmac gave way to stones, potholes on an unmade track. Baillard felt his heart lurch against his ribs. A shot of adrenalin through his veins, hope too. He knew this part of the land. In the distant past, he had travelled this way, heading for Portbou on the Spanish side of the border. The odds against them getting away were high, but they were better than they might have been.

'Can you not see what they are going to do?' he said urgently.

He and the Spaniard exchanged another glance, García acknowledging with a grimace how Baillard's fears were justified. Not one of the others reacted, just continued to sway with the motion of the truck in defeated silence.

They continued to drive for ten minutes, a little less. Then, without any warning, the driver slammed on the brakes. Everyone slid, or fell, forwards, then struggled back to a sitting position. All except the man beside Baillard, who remained lying on his side on the floor of the truck.

The driver killed the engine. Seven pairs of eyes turned towards the doors. Seven sets of ears listening as the chain was released and knocked against the wood, then the metal bolt was slid back. Fresh air and pale sunlight flooded in.

'Out,' ordered the guard, jabbing the first prisoner with his rifle. A Mauser Karabiner K98, supplied by the Germans. More proof, Baillard thought – though it was hardly needed – of what the local Milice and Waffen-SS had agreed between them.

Everyone did what they were told. Baillard bowed his head, feigning a stiffness in his legs and arms. He felt García move up to stand beside him, shuffling forwards to join the other prisoners. Eight trucks, more than fifty wretched men.

Baillard gave silent thanks at their luck. They were in a clearing he recognised. On three sides, low scrub and woodland. There was an old smuggler's path through the woods, he knew it well. Of the eight trucks in the convoy, they were closest to the wood.

'À la izquierda,' he whispered.

The Spaniard glanced to the left, saw the narrow path, and nodded. It was a risk, but it was the only chance they had.

'I said, everyone out,' the guard shouted into the back of their truck.

Baillard watched him climb up inside, kick the collapsed prisoner with his boot, then he turned and shouted.

'Hey! Give us a hand.'

While two other guards went towards the truck, Baillard and the Spaniard seized their chance. Taking small steps, Baillard began to edge backwards towards the trees. He had no way of knowing if his fellow prisoners would realise what they were doing, if others were planning the same thing or might even try to stop them.

The *miliciens* heaved the body from the truck.

'One more we don't have to worry about,' one guard said, letting the corpse drop to the ground.

Baillard kept his eyes pinned on the truck and the ragged huddle of prisoners. Still no one reacted. No one shouted a warning to the guards. Baillard and García reached the edge of the wood. Immediately, they turned and walked quickly into the deep shade. Baillard knew that if they could make it unobserved to the first fork in the path, they had a good chance of staying free. The left-hand spur went sharply down to what looked like a dead end. The wider, right-hand side led towards the higher pastures. If soldiers did come after them, he thought they would head up the hillside. It was the logical decision.

An explosion of gunfire stopped him in his tracks. Both men froze. Baillard forced himself not to turn around and to keep moving, faster along the path to the dividing of the ways. Another burst from the rifles, the shots chasing on one another's tail, but none aimed in the direction of the woods. His foot slipped, he flung out his hand to steady himself. More gunfire.

How many dead? Twenty? Thirty?

Baillard gestured to a flat ledge, a narrow gap in the underhang of the cliff. The Spaniard dropped to his stomach and slithered inside. The guns had fallen silent. Baillard hesitated, then followed him in. Then, violent in the peace of the mountains, they heard an explosion, followed by another. Minutes later, black plumes of smoke, pushed by the Tramontana, blew across the sky in front of where they were hiding.

'*Los despósitos de combustible*,' said Baillard. The fuel tanks.

The Spaniard crossed himself. Baillard closed his eyes, praying now that none of the prisoners had been left alive to burn. He had seen death by fire too many times – in Toulouse, in Carcassonne, at Montségur – and the sounds and smells and sights had never left him. The screaming and choking, the sweet stench of burnt flesh, bones slipping from the carcasses.

He bowed his head, regretful at how he had failed to persuade them. How he had not been able to save them. So many lives lost. Then he felt a tap on his arm. He opened his eyes to see the Spaniard holding out his hand.

'*Gracias, amigo*,' said García.

Chapter 105

CARCASSONNE

By the time Sandrine came away from the Café des Deux Gares, leaving Gaston to pack up the copies of *Libertat* for distribution, it was nearly ten o'clock. The Bastide was going about its daily business. An ordinary Monday morning. Suzanne went back separately to the rue du Palais to tell Raoul and Marianne that Sandrine was on her way.

Sandrine had one more job to do before she could go home, but every minute seemed endless. She hoped Robert would be on time. She walked past the Brasserie Terminus, feeling exhausted and jittery. The combination of little sleep and Liesl's photographs of the atrocities perpetrated at Chalabre had set her nerves on edge. Even so, she realised it wasn't just her. There was a high level of tension in the air. Everyone was more watchful than usual, anticipating trouble.

She crossed the boulevard Omer Sarraut, thinking about what might be the cause of it. Because people were already talking about the sabotage of the Berriac tunnel? Or the wireless broadcast about Authié? Her hands gripped the wooden handle of her *panier* tighter. Even those who didn't know his name would understand that the arrival of a senior commander, dispatched from the north, signalled a new phase in the battle.

Without breaking stride, Sandrine looked in through the window of the Café Continental to see if Robert Bonnet was already there. He wasn't, so she kept walking down rue Georges Clemenceau. She'd go as far as the junction with rue de Verdun, then come back again.

Just outside Artozouls, a group of men were coming towards her. Filling the width of the street, forcing other pedestrians to step out of their way, their voices loud and belligerent. Several different conversations seemed to be going on at once. Sandrine spotted Lucie's father. She didn't think Monsieur Ménard would recognise her, but she turned her face away all the same.

'It was the Amazone,' one of the veterans said as they drew level. 'That's what I heard.'

Quickly Sandrine stepped into the doorway of the nearest shop and pretended to be looking at the limited display of household goods.

'Some tart? Bloody figment of your imagination, that's all. Partisan propaganda to undermine us. Make the Milice out to be weak. Whipped by some female.' A coarse burst of laughter. 'It's communists behind Berriac. It'll come out soon enough.'

Sandrine waited until the men had gone into the Café Edouard, then stepped back into the street. She knew 'Sophie' had several nicknames – 'Amazone' being one of the most polite. Others were less complimentary: whore, lesbian, gypsy. She reached the junction, then turned round and started to walk back. Much as she hated to admit it, the truth was the sentiments expressed by the LVF were shared by many on their side too. There were plenty of partisans who resented even the idea of an all-female *réseau*. They believed that war was a man's business and it offended their sense of honour. Flag, faith, family, they still clung to a Pétainist view of the world. Men like Raoul, Yves Rousset, Guillaume Breillac – even Robert and Gaston Bonnet, though they were of an older generation – were in the minority.

'Amazone,' she muttered, allowing herself a brief smile. As long as people refused to believe that a women's network could exist, they were safer. A few insults was a small price to pay for that.

She looked back up the street and saw Robert Bonnet hurrying towards their rendezvous. She gave him a few moments to go inside, then slowly walked back towards the café.

Robert was standing at the counter nursing a glass of something that passed for beer. She walked up and stood at the far end.

'*Bonjour*,' she said to the proprietor. '*Un café, s'il vous plaît*.'

He nodded. Before the war, an unaccompanied young woman at the counter in a café by herself might have attracted attention, but not now. Everyone was busy trying not to notice anyone else. Sandrine stood in silence until he came back with the small white china cup and saucer.

'*Merci*,' she said, pushing a folded note across the counter. Inside it was a list of the places Robert would need to take the copies of *Libertat*, once Gaston had packed the supplies and Marianne had notified the couriers.

The proprietor took the note, rang up the amount in the till, then walked to the other end of the counter and gave the change, and the list, to Robert. Then he returned to the centre, took a glass and began to polish it with his tea towel.

'Anything else I can get you, mademoiselle?'

Sandrine drank the foul chicory mixture down in one. 'No, that's just what I needed. A pick-me-up.'

He nodded. '*Á demain?*'

Sandrine gave a sigh of relief. Perhaps things were going to be all right after all.

'Yes,' she said, raising her voice so Robert could hear too.

'Tuesday it is,' said the proprietor. 'Market day.'

Chapter 106

There was no one about when Sandrine got back to the rue du Palais. She left her basket outside the back door, to get rid of the smell of the fish, washed her hands again with washing powder Marianne had exchanged for some matches, then went upstairs and quietly opened the door to her bedroom.

The morning light filtered grey through the gaps in the shutters. As her eyes became accustomed to the gloom, she picked out the bureau of bleached mahogany against the wall between the two windows. To the right of her bed, the high-backed couch covered with washed green Chinese silk and the bamboo plant stand. Opposite, beside the door, the shelves of the low bookcase were almost empty now. They had hidden some of the books, now banned, in the cellar, not wanting to let them go. Others, of less sentimental value, they'd been forced to use for the fire in the salon during the bitter winters.

Raoul was still asleep in her child's single bed. One arm above his head, the other flung wide, claiming ownership of the space. His hair, set free from oil or wax, was tousled on the pillow and the sheet was drawn up no higher than his waist, revealing his strong, though now thin, body. In the gathering light, Sandrine could see the shadow of rough growth on his chin.

She knew she had to wake him up. But, just for a moment, she let him sleep in peace. Before the Germans had invaded all of France, the murder charge hanging over him had kept him out of Carcassonne. Two years later, so very many men were criminals or in hiding that Raoul no longer stood out. It had made it possible for him to come in and out of Carcassonne from time to time.

Sandrine sat on the bed beside him and ran her fingers down his smooth tanned arms, so brown next to the white of his chest. She could feel the life moving beneath his skin, the hardship and strength of his hilltop existence. And when she remembered how they had spent the hours between dusk and dawn, she blushed, even though there was no one there to see.

Even after two years, Sandrine was still overwhelmed by the strength of her feelings. The way her heart leapt when she caught unexpected sight of him, the way the ground shifted beneath her feet when he smiled at her. In all that time, they had never spent more than a few days at a time together. She occasionally wondered whether, if they lived together week in, week out like any normal husband and wife, this sense of the miracle of emotion and need would fade. Grow tired, habitual? Was it only because they saw one another rarely and for such short periods of time that there was this intensity, this sense of being sick and weak with desire when they did meet? There was no way of knowing.

They all lived in the present. Even so, Sandrine sometimes allowed herself to dream of a time when she and Raoul might have the chance to grow weary of one another's company. When the war was over and they no longer had to live in the shadows. The chance to become a dull, old married couple like any other, rejoicing in the mundane and the everyday.

'Sandrine Pelletier,' she muttered, trying out the name in her head. 'Monsieur et Madame Pelletier.'

She sighed. Somehow, it didn't suit her. Didn't suit either of them, truth be told. It made them sound too grown up, too staid. Sandrine hugged her arms around herself, disliking the imprint of her ribs under her own fingers. She had grown thin, they all had. It suited Lucie's prettiness and Marianne's fine features, but she herself felt merely ungainly, all long arms and legs. A *garçon manqué* once more, as Marieta had called her when she was little.

In the bed, Raoul stirred and shifted position, though he did not wake. Sandrine looked down at him, astonished to see how open and trusting his face was in sleep, despite everything he had done and seen. The way he lived in the mountains.

'*Mon còr*,' she whispered.

Even those quietest of words were enough to wake him. Straight away, Raoul was alert. Eyes open, twisting round, his hand reaching for the gun he'd placed on the floor beneath the bed.

'I'm sorry, I didn't mean to wake you.'

His eyes focused on her, then immediately his expression changed and he smiled.

'You're back,' he said, pushing himself into a sitting position and leaning against the headboard. 'What time is it?'

'Just after ten.'

He looked at her outdoor shoes. 'You've been out already?'

'Café des Deux Gares.'

'Of course,' he said, running his hands over his hair to flatten it down. 'Was Liesl's film any good? Anything you could use?'

Sandrine nodded. 'Dreadful, but what we need.'

'Did you get the edition finished?'

Sandrine nodded. 'Printed and ready to distribute tonight.'

He put his hand on her waist. 'So you have done your work for the day?'

He smiled, the same crooked-eyed smile that still made her heart skip a beat.

Sandrine laughed. 'If only,' she said, then the lightness faded from her face. 'There's something I need to tell you, something I just heard.'

'Let it wait,' he said, undoing the top button of her dress.

'It's important,' she said, though she didn't want him to stop.

'So's this,' he said, undoing the next button, then the next, to reveal her plain white chemise underneath.

'At least let me shut the door,' she laughed, slipping out of his hands.

The latch snicked loudly. Sandrine stepped out of her dress, which fell like a pool of water at her feet, and walked back towards him. Slowly she raised her arms and pulled her chemise over her head, then removed her slip and knickers. Raoul lifted the corner of the sheet to let her under.

'Welcome back,' he said.

Sandrine lay in the corner of his arm, on pillows that still held the memory of him. She heard him exhale, a sigh half of relief, half of expectation, and she smiled. For a moment, they lay arm to arm, side to side, her feet a little cold against the heat of his just-woken skin. Then Raoul bent over her. Now Sandrine could feel his breath, whispering over the surface of her skin like a summer breeze. His lips dancing, his tongue slipping, sliding over her breasts. She gasped as he took her nipple into his mouth, licking, teasing.

Raoul raised himself on his elbow and reached out to the pocket of his trousers, lying on the chair beside the bed.

'Wait a moment, I have something,' he whispered.

Sandrine stopped him. 'No,' she said. 'It's all right.'

Raoul looked at her in surprise, with gratitude. 'Are you sure?'

'Yes.'

He lowered himself beside her and stroked the length of her arm with the back of his fingers, then moved his hand across her stomach, down to the space between her legs.

'*Mon còr*,' he said, echoing her words.

Gently he moved until he was covering her body with his, looking down at her. Sandrine met his gaze, then, without warning, threw her arms around his back and rolled him over, so that now she was sitting astride him.

'That's better,' she teased. 'I prefer the view from here.'

Raoul laughed and put his hands on her slim waist. She leant forward, letting her breasts skim against his chest, then gently eased him inside her, little by little, until she had taken the whole of him. For a moment he lay still, contained with her, as if resting.

She leant forward again and, this time, kissed him on the lips, then the hollow of his throat. She felt strong, powerful, as if at this moment she could do anything. A hypnotic, heavy heat seeped through her limbs, and her head was filled with the sound of her blood beating. She had no sense of time or space. There was only Raoul and the sunlight slipping through the gaps in the shutters.

Slowly, she began to move.

'Sandrine.'

The word slipped from between his lips. She took his hands and held them against hers, palm to palm, fingers entwined. She could feel the force of him, the power in his tanned arms and firm thighs, a mirror of her own strong arms and legs. She kissed him again, and, this time, felt his tongue dart between her lips, hot and wet and hungry.

He was breathing harder, driven on by desire. An echo of her own feelings, emotions, need. They were moving faster now, Sandrine rocking against him, pushing his hands back against the headboard, the roaring in her head fiercer, separate from thought. She wanted to imprint the memory of his face on her eyes, the memory of muscle and bone and heat. The urgency of what she felt kept her moving on and on, until suddenly she felt the blood rush to her head, and held on to him as he cried out her name. He shuddered, then was still.

Gradually, the roaring in her head faded away too, until nothing remained but the hushed silence of the room. Sandrine leant forward, her head on his chest for a moment, hearing the rhythm of his heart slowing down, returning to its normal beat. Then, she moved and lay back down beside him.

Without intending to, they drifted to sleep. Outside, the sun grew stronger, climbing higher in the Midi sky. Safe in one another's arms, they were unaware of the hours passing or the life of the house going on downstairs. For now, only for now, their universe was bounded by the four walls of the bedroom, the closed door, the wooden shutters keeping the world at bay.

Chapter 107

Coustaussa

Liesl glanced back over her shoulder. Early in the morning, she had taken food up to the Maquis in the garrigue, then come down into Couiza. The man was still standing in the doorway, smoking a cigarette. No reason to think he was watching her. To think he was watching anyone. But there was something about him that set alarm bells ringing. Liesl didn't think she'd seen him before. Or had she? Dark suit, a little too smart for this small, out-of-the-way town. He wasn't local, certainly.

She lifted the blue and white check cloth in her basket to make sure she had nothing incriminating. There was a handkerchief full of cherries, a late crop. Yves Rousset had given them to her, half for Marieta and half for his mother. Liesl had promised to deliver them herself. She was out of film, so hadn't brought her camera with her. She had her *carte d'identité* and her ration book.

Feigning indifference, she looked again. The man was still there, still smoking. Out of place in his dark suit and hat, staring in her direction. Straight away she adopted the usual procedures when they thought they were being followed. She went into the épicerie, though she had no coupons, then came out and went into the tabac. It was under new management now, the previous owner, a notorious local informer, having been found dead in the river six weeks before. A reprisal killing. Liesl didn't know who'd done it. Not 'Citadel', nor anyone from the Couiza Maquis either. That wasn't how they operated.

She chatted for a while and bought a sheet of one-franc stamps. When she emerged into the sunshine, she crossed the square and went into the post office. Its wide double door wasn't visible from across the road. If the man was following her, he'd have to move.

She spent ten minutes queuing inside, pretended to have left the letter she wished to post at home and came out again. The Tramontana was starting to blow, sending the dust swirling up and around. She glanced again towards the doorway and, this time, saw nothing.

The man had gone.

Liesl let out her breath, hoping it was just a false alarm. She, Geneviève and Eloise saw shadows everywhere. It was hard to distinguish real threat from their overheated imaginations.

She paused a moment, allowing her heart to steady, then headed to the Grand Café Guilhem, where she was due to meet Geneviève. Liesl knew she was late, but she was still within their agreed time frame. As she walked, with her long, elegant strides, someone wolf-whistled. She turned and a rather sweet-looking man grinned at her. Liesl didn't acknowledge him, but she did smile slightly as she walked past. No sense in making a fuss.

In two years, Liesl had grown from a solemn, quiet girl into a tall, graceful and self-possessed young woman. She was very slim, but it enhanced her beauty rather than diminishing it and she was much admired. She could have had her pick of the few young men left in Couiza, if she'd wanted. Only a few close friends knew how much time she and Yves Rousset spent in one another's company. It was harder now, but they contrived to meet when they could. Like this morning. She smiled at the memory.

Liesl sat at their usual table on the terrace, the one with the best view of both the bridge and the road. She caught sight of her reflection in the window and wondered, as she often did, if Max would even recognise her now. It had been so long since they'd seen one another.

No one in Coustaussa or Couiza had ever challenged the story that Liesl was a cousin of the Vidals from Paris. So many of the old mountain families were distantly related – Sandrine and Marianne were cousins of the Saint-Loup girls, several times removed. Liesl had rarely been asked to produce her papers and, when she had, there'd been no trouble. The false documents Suzanne had obtained for her continued to pass muster. But the need to keep her true background secret meant Liesl rarely got news about her brother. What few scraps of information they did receive came from the waitress in the Café de la Paix in Le Vernet village, who telephoned Sandrine in Carcassonne, who then relayed the news back to Coustaussa via Raoul. As for her nephew, little Jean-Jacques, Liesl hadn't seen him for over a year.

The waiter came to take her order. '*S'il vous plaît?*'

Liesl looked in her purse and discovered it was all but empty.

'Actually, I'm expecting a friend,' she said. 'We'll order when she gets here.'

'*Un café* . . .'

'No, really, I'm happy to wait.'

'. . . on the house,' he said.

'Oh.' Liesl looked up at him. 'That's very kind,' she said quietly. 'Then, yes please.'

She checked the road, wondering where Geneviève had got to, then glanced at her watch. It was unlike her to be late, despite the difficulties in getting from one place to another. She had gone to Limoux yesterday to hand over a film to Raoul for Sandrine, but Liesl had expected her back before now.

The waiter brought the ersatz coffee and she sipped it as slowly as she could, making it last for as long as possible. She looked at her watch again, tapping the glass in case it was losing time. The hands continued to move steadily round. Liesl felt a flurry of nerves in her stomach. The meeting place might have been discovered, someone might have talked. The rule was that if a contact was more than half an hour late, you left. You took no risks. The fact that the contact was Geneviève – her closest friend – made no difference.

Time was up.

Liesl smoothed down her dress, picked up her basket and walked quickly down the steps to the road. She looked towards Limoux, the direction she'd expect Geneviève to be coming from, willing her to be there. The road was empty.

She collected her bicycle, put her basket on the front, then began to cycle towards home. It was only as she passed the boulangerie on the corner that she saw him again. The same man. She pedalled faster, not wanting to run the risk of him stepping out in front of her. He did nothing, though he made no attempt to hide the fact that he was looking at her. And as she cycled east on the road towards Coustaussa, Liesl felt his eyes drilling into her back.

Liesl took a roundabout route, doubling back in case the man had somehow managed to follow her in a car or by motorbike. By the time she walked into the kitchen in Coustaussa, she was hot and worn out.

She handed the cherries to Marieta. 'The rest are for Madame Rousset,' she said. 'I'll take them over to her as soon as I've got my strength back.'

'What happened?' said Marieta, looking at her flushed face.

'I was followed,' Liesl said, pouring herself a glass of water and sitting down at the kitchen table. 'At least, I think so. Didn't want to take the risk.'

Marieta's eyes sharpened, though her voice didn't change.

'Followed, you say,' she said, putting the cherries into a colander. 'Where?'

'In Couiza. Not before.'

'When?'

'About an hour ago. I was due to meet Geneviève in the café, but she didn't arrive. I was late, so it's possible I missed her. In the end I decided it was better to come home.' She met Marieta's gaze. 'Just in case.'

Marieta nodded. 'Perhaps Madomaisèla Geneviève went straight down to Tarascon?'

Liesl looked up. 'Why would she change her plans when we'd arranged to meet?'

Marieta frowned. 'An old friend of Na Saint-Loup passed away at the weekend. It was a natural death and Pierre was old, but even so. Geneviève would wish to be there to comfort her mother, I'm sure of it.'

The explanation gave Liesl some comfort. It made sense and Geneviève was usually so reliable.

'Yes, I can see she would want to be there.'

'No reason to think anything else,' Marieta said sternly. 'No sense worrying yourself to a thread.'

Liesl sighed. 'No.'

Marieta held Liesl's glance for a moment, then pointed to the empty glass bottle on the draining board. 'Could you pass me that?'

Liesl got up and handed it to her, then sat down again. She watched as Marieta ladled the cherries into the narrow neck, pushing them down with the handle of a wooden spoon.

'What are you doing?'

'What I can,' Marieta said quietly. She took a small bottle of cognac from the table in front of her and started to drizzle the brandy on top of the cherries. 'Making a kind of Guignolet. It is Monsieur Baillard's particular favourite drink.'

'But . . .' Liesl began, then stopped. She had been about to ask what the point was in making Monsieur Baillard's favourite drink, but knew better than to say the thought out loud. 'Where did you get the brandy?' she asked instead.

'Madomaisèla Geneviève was given it.'

Liesl smiled. 'They all adore her.'

'She has a good nature,' Marieta said.

Liesl hid her smile, perfectly certain that it wasn't Geneviève's good nature the maquisards appreciated so much as her face and her figure. Unlike everyone else, she had kept her perfect hourglass curves and looked as healthy and pretty as ever.

Marieta drained the half-litre of cognac. 'When Monsieur Baillard comes back,' she said, with a slight tremor in her voice, 'I want to welcome him home properly.'

'Yes,' Liesl said. Her heart went out to the old woman. She knew Marieta missed Sandrine and Marianne. Little Jean-Jacques too; the house had seemed so quiet when he'd gone. But she forgot that Marieta missed her old friend most of all. 'Yes, of course you do. He'll be so delighted.'

For a moment, silence fell between them. The only sound was the knocking of the spoon against the glass. Liesl watched as Marieta put the flat blue metal cap on the bottle, twisted it shut and turned the bottle over and back several times, like an egg-timer. Then she walked slowly to the larder and put the Guignolet inside on the shelf.

'There,' Marieta said, 'perfect in a week or two. At least, good enough.'

She lowered herself on to a chair with a sigh, poking wisps of grey hair back into the bun at the nape of her neck. 'So, you said you were followed. Is there any particular reason, madomaisèla, why such a thing should have happened today?'

'What do you mean?'

Marieta fixed her with a look. 'You know quite well what I mean.'

Liesl met her gaze. Marieta was perfectly aware that the girls delivered food and weapons to the men. But she also knew that they carried out small acts of sabotage or disruption, and that Liesl took great risks to photograph the atrocities committed by the Milice and the occupying forces, when she could get the film.

'No. I paid a visit to the hills, that's all.'

'There is nothing particular being planned?'

Liesl wasn't sure what Geneviève would want her to say. The fact was, there was something being planned, but as the guerrilla war between the maquisards and the Gestapo grew more vicious, no one was safe. They told Marieta what was happening only in general terms, therefore, hoping it might keep her safer.

'No,' she replied, though she couldn't meet Marieta's gaze. '*Si es atal es atal*,' she rushed on, quoting one of the housekeeper's well-worn phrases back at her. She found a smile, trying to persuade herself that everything would be all right. 'What will be will be,' she said. 'Isn't that what you're always telling me?'

Marieta didn't return the smile. 'Even if there is nothing planned,' she said in a sombre tone, 'it would be wise not to go down into the town for the time being. Your friends can manage for a day or two without you, do you hear me?'

Liesl stared. Marieta never made a fuss, never over-reacted. That she was taking this seriously upset her more than any scolding would have done.

'Wait until Geneviève and Eloise come back,' Marieta said, 'then we'll see, *è*?'

Chapter 108

CARCASSONNE

'Sandrine?'

There was a sharp tapping on the door. Sandrine blinked, stretched and half woke, without identifying what had disturbed her. The knocking started again.

'Sandrine, are you in there?'

She opened her eyes, surprised to hear Lucie's voice. She glanced at the clock, and was horrified to see that it was early afternoon. They'd slept for hours.

Slipping out from beneath Raoul's arm, she took her cotton dressing gown from its hook, pulled the belt tight around her waist, then opened the door and stepped out into the corridor.

'Sorry to barge in and all that,' Lucie said in a whisper, 'but Marianne wants you to come.'

'Why? What's happened?'

'We're in the kitchen,' said Lucie. 'I'll tell her you're on your way.'

Sandrine nodded. Quickly she gathered the items of clothing that lay strewn across the bedroom floor. She took a last glance at Raoul, pleased that he was so peaceful. A month's worth of sleep in a real bed to catch up on.

'*A bientôt*,' she murmured, then, resisting the temptation to kiss him again, she crept out of the room and downstairs.

Marianne, Lucie and Suzanne were sitting at the kitchen table. The windows were tilted open to let in a little fresh air, but the door to the garden was closed and the room was hot.

'I'm sorry, I'd no idea it was so late.'

'But you're all right?' Marianne was saying. She looked harried, exhausted, the lines around her eyes dark as if drawn on with ink.

'Fine,' said Suzanne gruffly. 'Don't fuss.'

Lucie was sitting in her chair, frowning.

'They had to release me,' Suzanne continued. 'They had no grounds to hold me. No evidence.'

'Evidence!' Marianne said. 'Did they tell you why you'd been arrested?'

'I wasn't arrested.'

'You know what I mean.'

Sandrine sat down at the table with a thump. 'When?' she said.

'After I left the Café des Deux Gares,' Suzanne said.

'What happened?'

'Two plain-clothes—'

'Gestapo?' Sandrine interrupted.

Suzanne shook her head. 'Police. Not local. I didn't recognise them.'

'Had they been following you?' Sandrine asked.

Suzanne shook her head. 'I don't think so. They took me to the Commissariat. Must have been about ten thirty.' She glanced at the clock on the wall. 'I got back fifteen minutes ago.'

'I'd been trying to find her all morning,' Marianne said to Sandrine. 'Lucie came to tell me what had happened.'

Sandrine threw a glance at Lucie, then back to her sister. 'How did Lucie know?'

Lucie answered for herself. 'Gaston Bonnet saw them. J-J and I had spent the morning by the canal, looking at the boats, and in the Jardin des Plantes. He noticed I was still there and asked me to let Marianne know.'

Sandrine met her eye. 'Thank you.' Although Lucie was prepared to run errands for them from time to time, mostly she kept her distance for the sake of Jean-Jacques.

Lucie flushed. 'My pleasure, kid.'

Marianne looked distressed. 'They didn't—'

'No,' Suzanne said firmly. 'No one laid a finger on me. They just asked questions.'

'About *Libertat*?' Sandrine asked.

'Not to start with. They were fishing. Who my friends were. Tossed a lot of names about, all *résistants* who've been arrested recently – Léri, Bonfils, Lespinasse – but nothing that could stick.' She looked briefly at Marianne. 'They asked about the protest your students staged last November. If I knew anything about it.'

'What did you say?'

'I admitted we were friends, there's no secret in that. Said that Marianne was engaged to my cousin.'

A sudden wail from Jean-Jacques in the salon stopped the conversation for a moment.

'He's teething,' Lucie said, getting up. 'I'll be back in a moment.'

'Go on,' said Sandrine quickly, as soon as Lucie had gone.

'They asked if I was aware Marianne had been suspended for refusing to take books by Jewish writers off the classroom shelves.'

'That was eighteen months ago,' Sandrine said.

'I know. I said I didn't know anything about it.' She looked at Marianne. 'I told them you were a bookworm. That it had been an oversight, nothing political.'

Marianne smiled, but didn't say anything.

'Did they believe you?' Sandrine asked.

'Possibly, but what could they say?'

Sandrine was frowning. 'It's odd for the police to ask about that. That sort of thing's not their responsibility.' She paused. 'Who conducted the interview?'

Suzanne gave a wry smile. 'They didn't formally introduce themselves.'

Realising Suzanne was now deliberately playing it down so as not to worry Marianne, Sandrine mustered a smile.

'No, sorry. Stupid of me to ask.' She thought for a moment. 'But you were at the Commissariat de Police all the time?'

Suzanne nodded. 'It was all courteous and formal, but I'm sure someone outside the room was listening. There was a mirror. Could have been two-way.'

'Did you hear any German?'

'In the corridor outside.' She took another hard drag of her cigarette. 'After an hour or so they got on to *Libertat*. But even then all they asked was if I read it.'

Sandrine glanced towards the corridor, listening for signs of Lucie coming back.

'I said I'd seen it, but I didn't read it.'

'They didn't ask about anything else?'

'No.'

'Nothing about last night?'

Suzanne shook her head. 'No.'

Sandrine let out a long sigh of relief. 'That's something, at least.' She paused. 'What were they really after, do you think?'

'I honestly don't know. They switched topics so quickly, everything in the same tone. I said I'd seen the newspaper around Carcassonne, but I was too busy to spend time on the regular dailies, let alone underground newspapers, et cetera, et cetera. I thought they'd press me more than they did, but they suddenly jumped to asking about the Croix-Rouge. They even asked if I was a member of the Communist Party. They must know I'm not.'

'And they asked about Marianne, but not me?'

'That's right.'

'No one else?'

'No one.'

'Not the Bonnets? Not Coustaussa?'

'No.'

Sandrine traced a pattern on the table with her finger, thinking hard. 'All we can hope is that this is nothing to do with "Citadel", then. That it simply comes from next door, no real information. Just tittle-tattle from Madame Fournier.'

Marianne sat forward in her chair. 'She did stop me on the doorstep yesterday and asked how many people actually lived here.'

'Perhaps it's all right,' Sandrine said, aware that she was trying to convince herself. 'They have your description on file, Suzanne. A couple of officers saw you, decided to bring you in. A fishing expedition, nothing more.'

Suzanne was nodding. 'You and I are more often together,' she said to Marianne. 'And although we do everything not to duplicate the arrangements, or use the same distribution routes for *Libertat* too often, there are plenty of other people like Madame Fournier looking out of their windows.' She rubbed her fingers together. 'Hoping to make a little extra.'

'What do you think we should do?' Marianne said quietly. 'Just sit tight?'

'Everything's in train for getting this edition out tonight,' Sandrine said. 'It's more of a risk to try to stop it than to let the arrangements go ahead as planned.'

'I agree,' said Suzanne.

'But it's probably a good idea not to do anything else for a week or two. Let the dust settle.'

Suzanne met her gaze. 'You don't think it's connected to Authié?'

Immediately the cold feeling in the pit of her stomach came back. Sandrine had managed to put Authié out of her mind and concentrate on the matter in hand. Then, of course, she'd come home to Raoul and everything had been forgotten. She hadn't even told Raoul about the news report and, judging from the look on Marianne's face, Suzanne hadn't had the chance to tell her either.

'What about Authié?' Marianne said. 'What have you heard?'

Sandrine put her hand over Marianne's. 'There was a bulletin this morning on the wireless. Lucie heard it.'

There was a sound in the corridor, and everyone stopped talking and looked towards the kitchen door. Sandrine turned round, expecting it to be Lucie. It was Raoul. Despite the tightness in her chest, she felt a smile come to her lips.

'Am I intruding?'

Sandrine reached out her hand to him. 'No, not in the slightest. Come in.'

Raoul nodded to Suzanne and Marianne, then dropped a kiss on Sandrine's head before sitting down.

'I haven't slept so long for . . . well, I can't even remember.'

'No,' Sandrine said softly.

'Authié,' Marianne said again.

Immediately, Raoul's expression changed. 'What have you heard?'

Briefly, Sandrine told them both what she knew. From the look on his face, she realised he'd already heard something. 'You knew?'

'Not for sure,' he said. 'Rumours.' He ran his hand over his hair. 'I'd hoped it wasn't true.'

'He was in one of the photographs on the film Liesl sent,' Sandrine said. 'It looked like Chalabre.' She glanced at Raoul. 'Did she take the pictures herself, do you know?'

'I don't. She just asked me to bring the film to you. I met Geneviève in Limoux, and she handed the package over.'

'Authié's here already?' Marianne said, her voice rising. 'He could be in Carcassonne.'

For a few days now, Sandrine had known her sister was close to the end of her tether. She feared that this final piece of bad news, coming hard on the heels of Suzanne's arrest, might be too much.

'I don't think so,' she said firmly. 'What happened in Chalabre was several weeks ago. If he'd been in the Midi all this time, we would have heard about it.' She paused. 'In any case, the fact that they announced it on the wireless means they want people to know about his presence. It's a statement of intent, they've got no reason to keep it secret.'

'I was going to ask Jeanne Giraud if her husband had heard anything,' said Suzanne, 'but then I was picked up.'

Sandrine frowned. 'How recent are the rumours you've been hearing?'

'Last couple of days, nothing before that.' Raoul paused. 'What about Bonnet's lady friend? Yvonne, is it?'

'Yvette,' Sandrine said.

'That's it. She works at Gestapo headquarters on the route de Toulouse, doesn't she? If there's anything to hear, she might know something.'

'I agree. She's been unwell over the weekend, so hasn't been able to go to work.'

'She's better now, according to Gaston,' Suzanne said with a wry smile. 'Think he's got a bit of a thing for Yvette himself.'

'What if they arrest you again?' Marianne said.

Suzanne gave her hand a quick squeeze. 'They won't.'

'They might.'

'I'll be all right.'

For a moment, no one spoke. Everyone locked in their own thoughts. Then Sandrine got up and closed the door. This was one part of the conversation she absolutely didn't want Lucie to hear.

'What we need is reliable information,' she said, looking round the table. 'About when Authié's due to arrive, where he is now, where he's going to be based once he gets to Carcassonne. Until we know the facts of the situation, we can't plan anything.'

'Agreed,' Raoul said.

'So, Suzanne, find Jeanne and see if she knows anything more than they've given out on the wireless.' She turned to her sister. 'Marianne, can you talk to Robert? Find out if Gaston's right that Yvette is going to work tonight. If she is, set up a meeting for her to talk to Raoul later. Can you do that?'

Marianne looked exhausted, but she nodded. 'Where?'

'Usual bar on the Canal du Midi, off rue Antoine Marty,' Raoul said. 'Bonnet knows the one. The password is: "Monsieur Riquet is unwell." The response is: "His friend, Monsieur Belin, has the medicine." Is that all right?'

Most of the passwords Sandrine came up with were inspired by local Carcassonnais men and women of note – architects and engineers, artists, industrialists. All the local history her father had taught her, coming to practical use now.

Marianne nodded again. 'Yes.'

'Good.'

'But we can't stay here,' Marianne said, her voice cracking. 'We'll have to clear out. This is the first place he'll look.'

'It hasn't come to that yet,' Sandrine said, still thinking. 'We must also make contact with Liesl and Geneviève. Find out if they've heard anything, especially work out how Liesl got the photographs.' She smiled at her sister. 'We can't rely on anyone calling – there's no reason why they would – so I think the best thing would be for you and Suzanne to go in person, once you've finished here. Go to Coustaussa. Get out from under Madame Fournier's nose, if nothing else.'

A look of such relief swept over Marianne's face that

Sandrine knew she'd made the right decision. If her sister was picked up now, she could see she hadn't the fight left in her to stand up to them.

'But what about you?' Marianne was saying. 'You're in more danger than anyone if Authié comes back.'

Sandrine saw Suzanne and Raoul exchange a glance. They knew what she was thinking. That they had to strike first, before Authié had the chance to do anything.

Marianne saw the look. 'What is it? What are you going to do?' she said in a low voice. 'Sandrine?'

Sandrine hesitated, then took a deep breath. 'The only thing we can do,' she said. 'We have to kill him.'

Chapter 109

The next few hours passed quickly.

Suzanne headed to the rue de la Gaffe, in the shadow of the medieval Cité on the far side of the Aude, where Jeanne Giraud lived with her husband and father-in-law. Her papers were checked as she crossed the Pont Vieux, but the *vert-de-gris* paid her no more attention than usual.

It was an abortive mission. Jeanne knew no more than they did, namely that Major Leo Authié was being sent back to Carcassonne to lead the ongoing campaign against the Resistance. Her husband, Jean-Marc, was in Roullens, treating two survivors from Maquis de Mas Saintes-Puelles, but was expected back at any moment.

Jeanne's father-in-law was inclined to talk. 'I remember Authié,' old Giraud said, turning and spitting his contempt on the ground. 'He's the one who questioned me in the hospital. After the bomb on Bastille Day that damaged the cathédrale Saint-Michel. He threatened us. Remember, Jeanne?'

'I remember,' Jeanne said.

'Bastille Day,' he said, his voice rich with age and nostalgia. 'We used to have such fireworks. The fourteenth of July, the whole sky lit up white and red. The stones of the Cité themselves looked like they were on fire.' For a moment, his face was bright with happier memories. Then the light faded from his eyes. 'Back in the day, back in the day.'

'And we'll have fireworks again, you'll see, when all this is over.'

The old man simply shook his head and went back inside.

Jeanne dropped her voice. 'He's losing heart,' she said to Suzanne. 'It's gone on too long.'

Suzanne nodded. 'Yes.'

Jeanne sighed. 'When my husband gets back, I'll find out if he's heard anything about Authié. If he has, I'll get a message to Sandrine or Marianne. Are they still in rue du Palais?'

'For the time being,' Suzanne said.

Jeanne's eyes narrowed. 'Has something changed?'

'I don't know. Maybe.'

Suzanne strode back along rue de la Gaffe, aware of eyes behind every shuttered window, and out on to rue Barbacane. She stood in line in the hot sun, waiting to be allowed to cross the bridge. Once more she produced her papers for the Wehrmacht patrol at the checkpoint. Once more, she was waved through.

Two Waffen-SS soldiers were posing for photographs with the backdrop of the fortified city behind them. She was tempted to walk in front of the camera, but knew it would be stupid to draw attention to herself for no gain.

Marianne was in the Bastide looking for Robert Bonnet. She tried the Café Continental first, with no luck. She went past the apartment where Max and Liesl had once lived, looking up at the first-floor window. Another family had it now, all traces of the previous occupants eradicated. She passed the rue de l'Aigle d'Or, unable to prevent herself glancing to the back door of the café. It had been raided the previous week, it was presumed as some kind of retaliation for Sandrine and Suzanne's sabotage of the Milice recruiting office.

She had to stop herself breaking into a run as she felt the familiar twist of fear in her stomach. These days she was rattled almost all of the time. Her nerve had gone. She found it hard to sleep or to eat, but couldn't seem to do anything about it. There was a ticking clock in her head, like a stopwatch counting down, telling her that their luck was about to run out.

Marianne eventually found Robert in the Café Saillan, near the covered market. There was a queue of men in the tabac opposite and the usual lines of women outside the boulangeries and the épicerie. The café was dark and smoky, and she was conscious of being the only woman. All the same, she was so desperate to do what she had to do, then get ready to leave for Coustaussa, that she simply walked up to the table without any kind of precaution.

'Robert, I have a message for you.'

He looked up with surprise, glanced anxiously around, then stood up and steered her by the elbow back into the street.

'What are you doing here? Did they let Suzanne go?'

She nodded, then explained what Sandrine wanted. 'If Yvette can do that?'

Robert nodded. 'She'll be there.'

She began to give the password, but Robert held up his hand. 'Don't worry about that, I'll be there too. I'll point Raoul out to her.'

'I'll tell him,' she said, turning to go.

Robert put a hand out and touched her arm. 'Are you all right, Marianne?' he said, concern written across his face.

Marianne caught her breath, tempted to answer honestly for once. Then she shrugged. 'I'm just tired, Robert. Very, very tired.'

'Be careful.'

Raoul smiled. 'I will.'

Sandrine straightened his tie and smoothed the shoulders of her father's lightweight linen jacket. It had hung unworn in François' wardrobe for four years, gathering dust. Raoul looked older in it. It was a good disguise. But the sight of him in her father's favourite summer suit twisted at her heart strings. She thought they would have liked one another if they'd ever had the chance to meet.

'Hey,' he said tenderly. 'It'll be all right. I'll be there and back before you know it, don't worry.'

Sandrine picked a piece of fluff from his lapel. 'Be very careful,' she said again, not wanting to explain. 'I'll check you're clear to go.'

She crept into the salon. Lucie had fallen asleep on the sofa, with Jean-Jacques cradled in the crook of her arm. Sandrine peered out of the window at the house next door. She could just make out the familiar silhouette behind the glass. She let the net drop, then went quickly back to the kitchen where Raoul was waiting.

'Madame Fournier's at the front. Go.'

He kissed her and turned away in his borrowed clothes. Sandrine felt a tug of déjà vu. At least this time she knew he'd be coming back.

As she stood at the kitchen door and watched Raoul cross the garden and go out of the gate, she wondered when it would stop. The sense of the ground going from under her feet when she suddenly thought, against all common sense and knowledge, that she'd seen her father. In the street or at the turn of the stairs or sitting at the old desk in his study, his head bowed over some pamphlet or lecture he was writing. That he was still alive. She had not expected, after nearly four years, that grief would still cut so deep, so easily.

She wandered back into the kitchen and poured herself a glass of water. She glanced up at the clock. Two hours since Marianne and Suzanne had gone. Only two minutes since Raoul had left, but already she was restless. She felt out of sorts, partly because she had slept so long during the day. Although it was her decision they should never all be away from the house at the same time, Sandrine hated being cooped up inside.

She sat down at the kitchen table, then got up again. She took the glass from the draining board and, this time, went to the cupboard and poured herself a finger of red wine. They tried to make it last, and it was early in the day to start drinking, but she needed something to steady her nerves.

Sandrine took a deep breath and then, slowly, exhaled. She had learnt how to be confident on the outside, to be tougher than the men. To keep her nerve. She knew how important it was for the others that she gave no hint of doubt or indecision. But things were different when she was on her own. She didn't have to put a brave face on it. The truth was, the thought of planning to murder in cold blood – even Authié – made her feel sick to her stomach. Every act of sabotage 'Citadel' had undertaken had been against property, buildings, supply chains. They had gone out of their way to make sure no one was killed – not Gestapo agents, and not Milice. Some casualties were unavoidable. There was little chance, for example, that the driver of the Berriac train had survived the blast. But planning an execution seemed different. Was different.

The *résistants* thought it was because they were women that they baulked at killing. Sandrine didn't agree. The evidence was that direct assassinations usually led to extreme reprisals – hostages, executions, mass arrests – and ended up the worse for their side.

Fifteen months ago, one of their first direct actions as 'Citadel' was to hit a café used by the Gestapo. They'd timed it deliberately so there'd be no one there. It was intended more to cause disruption, to be a warning. It was three in the morning and the premises should have been empty. They weren't. A senior SS officer – a second lieutenant – had been killed. However much she told herself he deserved it, Sandrine was horrified that she had taken another human life. When it came out that the man was notorious among the working girls of the Bastide for his violent tastes, she'd managed to persuade herself she had done a good thing. Untersturmführer Zundel – it had seemed important to know her victim's name – was the first man she'd killed. There had been others since. But still she had never before sat down and worked out how to murder someone in the way she was intending to assassinate Authié.

Sandrine drained the wine and poured herself another small glass, then walked to the door and stood leaning against the jamb, looking out over the empty garden. Barely any figs on the tree this year. A shame. She hated figs now, having eaten too many of them – they all had – but they were better than nothing.

She swilled the wine round in her glass, wondering what Monsieur Baillard would think of the woman she'd become. Would he be proud of her? Disappointed at how easily she had crossed the line between compassion and retaliation? Sandrine often thought about him, measuring her decisions against what she imagined he might have done in the same situation. It seemed extraordinary to believe that, in fact, they had only met on a few occasions. Even more impossible to believe that he was dead.

Sandrine tipped her head back and drained the glass in one. It was possible, of course, that Authié would leave them alone. But they couldn't risk sitting on their hands and waiting to find out. There was no reason to think that his presence was anything to do with the Codex. The public explanation for his return to Carcassonne made sense enough. He had been successful against the Resistance in the North. Now he was to repeat the trick in Carcassonne.

She shook her head. When she looked back on that first

summer, at the fairy-tale promise of deliverance Monsieur Baillard told her the Codex could offer, she was astonished at how easily she'd believed such an impossible story. Two years of fighting and resistance, she knew the truth now. No *chevaliers* were riding to save them, like the tales of old, no Jeanne d'Arc.

No ghost army.

It was down to them, a small band of women and men, like all the other groups in the hills and the hidden alleyways. Just them against the Milice and the Gestapo and the might of the occupation. And with Monsieur Baillard gone, even though the Nazis still sent teams to excavate the mountains around Tarascon and Foix, there was no one to tell her about the ancient spirit of the Midi rising up to lead them to victory.

Sandrine sighed. There was so much to do, so many decisions on her shoulders. She didn't even dream any more. The shimmering figures on the periphery of her mind, the sense of something beyond the world she could see, had gone. Silenced by fear and the relentless hardship of the lives they were forced to live.

No one was coming to help them. Everything was down to them. To her.

Chapter 110

In the very early hours of Tuesday morning, Yvette was waiting for the doors to be unlocked by the Gestapo officer on duty. A complicated system of passes, checks, going from one locked room to the next. Finally, she was out into the yard. Then the outer gate, and back on to the route de Toulouse.

'*Bon soir*,' she said.

The two guards ignored her, looked through her as if she didn't exist. She wasn't surprised. She didn't know them – this wasn't her usual shift; she'd needed to make up the money she'd lost by being ill last week – but they seemed the type to look down their noses, think it was beneath their dignity to be civil to the cleaning staff.

Yvette walked down towards the station. She was due to meet Robert in an unofficial late-night bar on the Canal du Midi, but she was much later than she'd expected. The problem was they were short-staffed, so she'd had to do a double shift back to back in order to get the job done. Fingers crossed he hadn't given up and gone home. She could do with a drink and a bit of fun. He was a good man.

She walked quickly, quietly, through the labyrinth of streets behind the station. The shabby front door – no sign, no advertising – gave no indication that it was anything other than a private house. From the outside it was all quiet, but she rang the bell anyway.

A small hatch in the door was shot back. A black eye peered out into the unlit street, recognised her and let her in.

'You're late tonight,' the doorman said.

She slipped him a coin. 'You know how it is. A girl's got to work.'

Yvette was forty if she was a day, but it was the sort of bar that made allowances. She untied her headscarf, put it in the pocket of her coat, then hung the coat up on the row of hooks that lined the left-hand wall.

'Got many in tonight?'

'A few,' he said, climbing back on to his stool beside the door. 'Go on down.'

She went along the dimly lit passageway, her shoes pinching her tired feet, pushed open the door and walked into a large open-plan room. The heat rushed out to meet her, the smell of booze and cigarettes and too many men in a confined space.

There were three bulbs hanging in a line from the ceiling, one red, one white, one almost blue, though the paint was peeling off. Along the width of the room, the large single window was blacked out. The bounce of light off the obscured glass, the attempt at patriotic colours and the haze of smoke gave everything a blurred, smudged air, as if looking at a scene with the wrong pair of glasses.

Yvette glanced around hopefully. There were six tables, with assorted unmatched chairs, and two baize card tables in the far corner. A selection of working men, all different ages, talking, playing bezique, two old-timers playing dominoes. Only one other woman so far as she could see, no better than she ought to be. Cheap white earrings and a blouse that was several sizes too small.

She couldn't immediately see Robert. Resigned to buying her first drink herself, Yvette went to the bar, a short wooden counter with bottles set in front of a mirror and glasses over the top of it. Robert told her once it had been 'liberated' from the Café Industriel when the military requisitioned all the buildings round the back of the Caserne d'Iéna. It looked temporary, but she knew it had been in the same spot for three years at least.

'What can I get you?' the barman asked.

'The usual,' Yvette said, pushing a note across the counter. 'Robert been in?'

He put a glass of beer on the counter. 'Talking to some young chap in the far corner, last I saw.'

She looked again, and this time saw him, sitting with his back to the room. She walked over, but he was so deep in conversation he didn't notice her until she was standing right in front of him.

'That's a fine welcome, I'm sure.'

Robert broke off, pulling awkwardly at his moustache until he saw who it was. Then a smile broke out on his face.

'All right, love?' he said, levering himself to his feet. 'I'll get you a chair.'

She looked at the young man with him. 'If I'm not interrupting . . .'

'Not at all,' Robert said. 'Just passing the time until you came.'

She held out her hand to the stranger. 'Charmed, I'm sure.'

'Pleased to meet you . . .?'

'Yvette.'

'Yvette,' the man repeated, offering her a cigarette.

'Don't mind if I do,' she said, letting him light it for her. She waited for him to introduce himself, or for Robert to do it, but neither of them took the trouble.

'Hard night?' Robert said.

'Long,' she admitted. 'Did a double shift.'

She glanced at Robert's friend. He looked quite a serious young man, but lovely eyes. Funny kind of smile, a bit lopsided, but nice all the same.

'You two old friends?' she fished. 'Relatives, maybe?'

The young man smiled at her. 'Robert's been telling me

how they always rely on you to step in when they need an extra pair of hands. All top secret.'

'He's making it sound more important than it is,' she said, blushing at the compliment. 'Of course, I'd rather not work for them. You know. But what's a girl to do?' She glanced at Robert. 'Can be useful, when all's said and done.'

Robert put his heavy hand on her arm. 'Very self-sufficient, Yvette. Knows how to look after herself. She's a fine woman,' he said, his words a little slurred. 'I'm a lucky man.'

'Get away with you!' she laughed.

'A lot going on at the moment?' the young man asked. 'Robert says it's been busy, cars going and coming.'

'Last week, all go,' she said, her face falling. 'After that business in Montolieu, they brought a few of them in. A raid in Limoux too, poor sods.' She took another mouthful of beer. 'But not in the last few days. All quietened down again, for the time being.'

'You don't get the idea anything's planned, then?'

She glanced at Robert to see if she should answer. He nodded.

'When there's something big, there are officers there round the clock. Lots of places I'm not allowed to get into to clean. Means it takes longer next time.' She tapped her cigarette over the full glass ashtray in the middle of the table. 'I have to hand it to them, they mostly keep things in order. Tidy, the Germans. Credit where credit's due.'

'So, busy tonight then, was it?' the young man asked again.

'Not at all. Quiet as the grave.' She noticed his eyes narrow, as if what she'd said was of enormous significance, and sat a little straighter in her chair. He really was a most attentive young man.

'No,' she said. 'Apart from the night guards on duty,

miserable sods. They're expecting someone, though. A lot of fuss about that. Some bigwig from Paris.' She paused. 'No, not Paris, Chartres.'

'Really,' he said. He smiled at her. She liked that. 'How do you know, do they tell you things? I bet you don't miss a trick!'

Yvette gave a trilling laugh, thoroughly gratified by the young man's interest.

'Don't be daft,' she said, tapping him playfully on the arm. 'But they never pay any attention to us working people, hardly notice we're there.'

She felt Robert's possessive hand go round her waist. 'Everyone notices you,' he said, giving her a squeeze. 'Good-looking girl like you.'

She pecked him on the cheek. 'Isn't he a one?' she said to the young man, delighted at how the evening was going. She'd forgotten about her aching feet and her sore back from lugging the bucket up and down the stairs, the way the guards looked right through her. 'Such a charmer,' she giggled.

'They were talking about someone coming, then?' the young man said. 'I don't suppose you caught his name?'

Yvette frowned. 'Well, I'm not sure they mentioned a name as such,' she said. 'He's from the north, that much I do know, and he's due to arrive some time on Friday. Sous-chef Schiffner was talking to that miserable toad of a lieutenant, Inspector Janeke, about some big dinner they're holding in his honour. I didn't get the impression Schiffner was best pleased about it, if truth be told.'

'This is so interesting, Yvette. And where's this swanky dinner to take place, did they let that out?'

'In the Hôtel de la Cité,' she said triumphantly. 'They were complaining about having to get all the special passes made up for the staff.'

He smiled encouragingly. 'And this is on Friday night?'

'That's what I gathered.' She nodded. '*Freitag*,' she said. 'At least, I think that's right. My German's not perfect, just enough to get by.'

'She's a clever girl,' Robert put in. 'Speaks German and a bit of English too.'

'Put the rest of us to shame, Yvette,' the stranger said, getting to his feet. 'You've been very helpful.'

She was disappointed. 'You're not off already, are you?'

'Need my beauty sleep,' he said. 'Unlike some!'

'Get away,' said Yvette, tapping him with her hand. 'But don't go on my account, not if you boys have got business to discuss. I'm discretion itself. Not a thing passes my lips.'

The young man smiled. 'I only stayed this long because Robert wanted to introduce me to you, Yvette,' he said. He put a couple of coins on the table. 'Get yourself another on me.'

He dropped his voice. 'Usual place, Bonnet?'

Robert nodded, not a trace of inebriation in his eyes. Then he held up his glass and said in the same loud, slurred voice, 'Next time, it's on me.'

The young man gave the slightest of bows. 'It's been a pleasure to meet you, mademoiselle.'

'Mademoiselle indeed,' she giggled. '*A bientôt*.' But he was already halfway to the door.

Yvette sat back in her chair. 'Seems a nice boy,' she said. 'Bit serious, but then they're like that, those boys, aren't they?'

'What boys?' Robert said sharply.

'Oh, you know, boys,' she said, looking wistfully after him.

Robert let his hand drop heavily on to her thigh. 'One more for the road, then home? What do you say?'

She kissed him again. 'Don't mind if I do.'

‡

Codex XIX

‡

Gaul
Tarasco
July AD 344

The wooden carts stood ready to leave. Possessions piled high, cooking utensils, flagons of *posca* and barley beer, blankets for the nights, which even at this time of year could be cool.

'We've discussed this so many times, Lupa,' Arinius said wearily. 'You said you would go. You promised.'

'I said I would go when the time came. Not a moment before.'

Arinius put his hand on her shoulder. 'The time has come,' he said quietly. 'The army is on the far side of the river. In three days, four at most, they will be here.'

Lupa turned and saw her sisters beckoning. She ignored them. Lifting the baby higher on her hip, a look of extreme stubbornness on her face, she turned back to face him. Despite himself, Arinius smiled. Already their son's expression was a reflection of hers.

'You only have to say the word,' she said. 'I told you I would obey you.'

He put his hand on her arm. 'I will not command you, you know that.'

For a moment, her face softened, then she renewed her objections.

'We have seen invaders off before.'

'These are opponents of a different kind, Lupa. They come to kill, not to conquer.'

For a moment, a lightning flash of fear appeared in her eyes, but it was quickly doused.

'God will protect us,' she said. *'Deus suos agnoscet,'* she recited, a touch of pride in her voice that she had remembered the Latin he'd taught her. 'God will know his own, that's what you told me.' She glanced back at the friends, neighbours, waiting to leave. 'It is what you told us all. They have faith in you, Arinius. So do I.'

'And so He will,' Arinius said. 'But He would not want you to take unnecessary risks.' He lowered his voice. 'Please, I am looking to you to set an example. As my wife, you must take care of them. Lead them to safety.'

For a moment, still he thought she would refuse. But then, in one of the mercurial changes of temperament he so much loved, quicksilver like a fish in the river, she took him by surprise by standing on her tiptoes, leaning forward and kissing him on the lips.

'Very well,' she said.

'Lupa?' he said suspiciously, sensing some sleight of hand, some trick.

'I will lead them to safety.'

Still he stared, but she was already walking away to join the others. She handed Marcellus to her grandmother, in one of the carts, then stood beside her two older sisters.

'Come to fetch us soon,' she called, her head held high. 'I do not wish to spend the winter in the mountains without you.'

Grief suddenly overwhelmed him. Having been so intent on persuading her to go, he had forgotten how he would feel if she did what he asked. It was thanks to Lupa that he had learnt to love and to live in the world. She gave his life meaning, she and Marcellus. Arinius rushed forward and put his arms around her, held her tight, breathing the deep musk scent of her hair and her skin.

'Arinius,' she chided him softly.

He let her go, realising he was making it worse for them both. He kissed his little son on the top of his head, gave Lupa a last, private smile, then stepped away. He raised his right hand to bless their journey.

'*Dominus vobiscum*,' he said. Some of the young women made the sign of the cross, under the open gaze of their mothers and grandmothers and aunts. Then, under his breath, he told Lupa one last time that he loved her.

She smiled. '*Te amo*.'

The cart moved off, joining the chain of wooden wheels and rattling nails winding up the path through the box and the silver birch trees, the mules and the goats pulling the smaller traps.

Only once did Lupa turn round to look at him. Arinius watched as the cart rumbled into the shadow of the hill, then let his hand drop back to his side.

When they were out of sight, he put his hands together and prayed, with an open heart and with open eyes, for God to spare them all.

To spare her.

Arinius stood there a while longer, hoping for a sign that his orisons had been heard, but there was nothing. The sweet empty air settled around him. Then he heard his father-in-law calling his name.

With a final glance at the empty track, the forest now silent once more, he drew his sword and quickly walked down to join the men in the valley.

Chapter 111

Carcassonne
July 1944

'We have to try,' Sandrine said again.

She and Raoul were in the kitchen in the rue du Palais. It was late on Tuesday afternoon and they were at loggerheads. Had been ever since Sandrine had laid out her plan for getting to Authié. Neither of them wanted to fight, but they were unable to stop the row developing. Marianne and Suzanne had crept away and left them to it.

'You'll never get anywhere near him,' Raoul said for the third time.

'We – they – got Kromer,' Sandrine said. 'And Fournier with him.'

'That was outside his house, in a public street,' Raoul threw back. 'The Cité is a garrison. It's crawling with soldiers. Every one of the postern gates is either boarded up or manned twenty-four hours a day. The Porte de l'Aude has been bricked up, and there are blockhouses on the Pont Vieux and all the approach roads. Even if you get in, you'll never get out in one piece.'

Sandrine put her hand on his arm. 'Raoul, I know all of this.'

He shrugged her off. 'You won't get anywhere near, surely you can see that. It's too much of a risk. You could go with the others tonight. Go to Coustaussa with Marianne and Suzanne. Leave now before Authié gets back.'

Sandrine forced him to meet her eye. 'You're saying you think I should run away?'

'It's not running away, it's common sense!' he said, unable to stop his voice rising in frustration.

'Don't shout at me,' she shouted.

'Sandrine, please.' He sighed. 'Just for once listen to someone else's advice. Listen to me. Please.'

She saw the desperation in his eyes, but knew she couldn't let it affect her.

'I have thought it all through, Raoul. If you'd listen to me, you'd see that I – we – can pull this off. We have people inside the Hôtel de la Cité and—'

'That won't do any good!' he said, throwing his hands in the air.

'Germans as well as local supporters,' she continued.

'I know that.' Suddenly the fight went out of him. 'Why does it have to be you?' he said quietly.

'Because it does,' Sandrine said.

Raoul pulled a hand-rolled cigarette from his breast pocket and lit it. The match grated loud, rough, in the quiet room.

'I'm serious,' he said. 'Let me go in your place.'

Sandrine stared at him. 'Don't you think I'm capable of it?'

'That's not the point.'

'Then what *is* the point, tell me?' she demanded.

Raoul sighed, pushed his fingers through his hair, paced up and down, the floorboards creaking under his anxious feet.

'There are some things you shouldn't be doing,' he said in the end. 'That's all.'

'Because I'm a woman?'

'No, that's not what I mean. I don't think like that, you know I don't.'

Sandrine took a deep breath. She knew they were arguing because they were frightened about what might happen, both of them.

'Look,' she said quietly. 'I know you're trying to protect me, but there's no need. There's much less chance of success if you go. You are more likely to be stopped than I am.' She took his hands in hers. 'We have to try, you know we do. The moment Authié gets to Carcassonne, whatever the real reason for him coming back, we've lost the advantage. We have to strike. If it wasn't me, you'd agree to it like a shot.'

Raoul was about to argue, then stopped.

'You see,' she said, 'you know I'm right.'

He didn't answer, so she carried on. 'Of course there will be extra security around the Cité, but I've taken that into account. Marianne knows someone who works in the kitchens of the Hôtel de la Cité. Suzanne's copying her pass to make one for me.'

Despite himself, Raoul was drawn in. 'Will it be good enough?'

'Suzanne's good. We'll see. I think so.'

Sandrine looked at him for a moment, then went to the row of glass jars above the stove. Once, Marieta had filled them with rice and salt and flour. She reached up and took out the stock from one, the magazine from another, and started to assemble the gun. Usually she kept it loaded, but the mechanism tended to jam. After Monday's expedition to Berriac, she'd taken it apart to clean it.

'Surely you're not going to attempt to shoot him?' Raoul said. 'There's no way you'll get close enough. At least, not close enough to have a clear shot and get away without being caught.'

'I know,' Sandrine said, locking the magazine into place.

'What then? A bomb?'

She nodded. 'Not in the hotel itself, of course. Too many people.'

'Where?'

Sandrine was relieved Raoul was finally treating it like

any other operation. He seemed to have put his objections to one side, for the time being at least.

'Schiffner and Authié are scheduled to take a tour of the *lices* before they go into dinner. Only Gestapo and Milice will accompany them, no civilians. Our people inside the hotel will make sure everyone stays well out of range during the time that matters.'

'Suzanne's making the device, I suppose?'

'Yes.' Sandrine nodded. 'Her record's better than most. You know they call her "*le fabricant*". They assume she's a man, of course.'

'It's true,' Raoul said wryly. For an instant, a flash of humour came into his black eyes. 'Not a single *résistant* has been injured on her watch, that's what they say.'

'And they're right.'

'It's some record,' Raoul said. Many of the smaller injuries suffered by partisans were the result of improvised devices going off too early, blowing up in people's hands before they'd been properly primed.

Sandrine pushed her black curls back behind her ears and looked him in the eye. 'So? What's it to be?'

Raoul met her gaze and held it for a few long seconds. 'What do I think?' he said. 'I think it could work, but ...'

'Good,' she interrupted.

'But it's a long shot. And ...' He paused, framing the words carefully. 'And I want to help. You have to have back-up, Sandrine.'

'No, I don't want you ...'

She stopped. She resented him trying to protect her, yet here she was considering doing the same thing to him. Usually she had Suzanne and Marianne as back-up. If they went to Coustaussa tonight, as planned, they wouldn't be available, and she didn't want them to delay their departure.

'What is it?' he asked, puzzled by her expression.

Sandrine smiled. 'I accept your offer,' she said. 'It

will make everything better if you're with me.'

Raoul stared at her, then let out a long sigh of relief. 'Well, that's something.' He smiled, then his expression changed. 'Right. When do you plan to do this?'

'Suzanne's out in the Bastide getting hold of what she needs to construct the device. All being well, I'll put the bomb in place tomorrow night, before Authié arrives and security is stepped up.'

'How's it going to be detonated?'

'I'll go back and do it,' she said. 'I can't see any other option. They will be searching all bags on Friday, of course, even more than usual, but since I won't have anything incriminating with me, that should be fine. Then all I've got to do is get to the device in time.'

'But if . . .' He stopped.

Sandrine guessed he'd been about to object again, but this time he thought better of it. Instead he cupped her face with his hands and kissed her on the forehead.

'You are too brave for your own good, *ma belle*.'

'Brave?' she said, looking down at the gun in her hands. She didn't feel brave, only scared.

Sandrine suddenly remembered a conversation she'd had with Marianne in this very kitchen, the morning after the demonstration. Two years ago, she hadn't understood what Marianne was trying to tell her about the chasm between what she did and how she felt about it. To Sandrine, then, everything had sounded exciting and courageous.

Now she understood. She shook her head.

'No,' she said, echoing her sister's words. 'I'm not brave. I hate it, I hate it all. But there's no choice.'

Chapter 112

TARASCON

At ten o'clock on Wednesday morning, the funeral procession left the église de la Daurade and made its way slowly towards the yew-lined avenue that led to the cemetery. At the head of the line, behind her husband's coffin, Célestine Déjean walked slowly and with dignity on the arm of Eloise Breillac. Geneviève and her mother were a few steps behind.

Achille Pujol stood apart from the others. He was there as a family friend, one of Pierre's only surviving comrades-in-arms, but his darting eyes betrayed the fact he was watching the blue berets of the *miliciens*, rifles cradled in their arms. A little behind them, four Gestapo soldiers.

Audric Baillard fell in beside him. He was very thin, his wrists, neck and shoulders jutting through his collar and cuffs. His lined face was gaunt and his once thick white hair was little more than down on his head, but his eyes were the same amber colour. Autumn leaves turning to gold.

'Achille,' he said quietly.

At first Pujol frowned at the intrusion, then his expression changed. First to horror at the sight of his friend, then to joy.

'Audric, how the hell . . .?' He shook his head. 'Damn you, I thought you were dead. We all did.' He broke off and peered. 'It is you?'

Baillard smiled. 'Yes, *amic*.'

'You look dreadful.'

'I am well aware of that,' Baillard said lightly.

'Where in the name of God have you been?' said Pujol, under his breath.

'Not here.' Baillard looked at the cortège. 'What happened?'

Pujol sighed. 'Fact is, Pierre never recovered from Antoine's death. Célestine is strong, but Pierre … Kept going as long as he could, I suppose, but in the end he gave up.'

Baillard nodded, then his eyes drifted to the soldiers. 'Why so many?'

'There are teams of Nazi archaeologists and engineers everywhere down here,' Pujol said heavily. 'Worst at Montségur, but also Montferrier, Ussat-les-Bains, Quéribus. Lombrives and Niaux, you can imagine.'

'Soularac?'

'Soularac?' Pujol said, narrowing his eyes. 'Not so far as I've heard.'

'Good.'

Pujol waited for a moment, in case Baillard had something to add, then continued.

'Added to which, they suspect Tarasconnais are smuggling food and supplies to the Maquis at Salvezines and the Roc Blanc. Our own lads.'

'Are they right?'

'Of course they're right,' Pujol growled. 'I'm surprised you even need to ask.'

Baillard held up his hand. 'Forgive me, my friend. I have been gone some time. Things change.'

'Not here they don't,' said Pujol fiercely. He jerked his head towards the phalanx of soldiers. 'They're hoping some of the maquisards will come to pay their respects.'

'They would not be so ill advised, surely?'

Pujol shrugged. 'You know what these boys are. Living

like outlaws in the hills. Put a gun in their hand, think they're invincible.'

Baillard gave a thoughtful smile. 'We used to call them *faydits*,' he said. 'Dispossessed. Now they are maquisards. But it is the same spirit, whatever the name.'

'*Faydits*? You're about seven hundred years out of date, Audric,' Pujol said. 'Anyway, Célestine put them right. Told them she'd tan their hides if any of them set foot in the town.' He gave a brief smile. 'Oh yes, none of them would get very far without Célestine.' He stopped, the smile slipping from his face and the strain painfully evident. 'It's been two years, Audric,' he said softly. 'I thought you were dead.'

Baillard sighed. 'I know, my friend. I know.'

The two old men looked at each other for a moment, then Baillard glanced again at the blue berets of the Milice.

'If you do not mind, I shall excuse myself for now.' He dropped his voice. 'But you do still have the map? It is safe?'

Pujol nodded. 'It's just where you left it.'

Baillard let out a long exhalation of release. 'Then there is still hope,' he said.

'Even when we couldn't find you, Audric, I could never bring myself to believe you were gone. That you wouldn't be back,' Pujol said in a rush, then stopped and turned red.

Baillard put his hand on the other man's arm. 'I am here now, Achille.'

'Yes, yes, of course you are,' he said gruffly, embarrassed by his show of emotion. He stepped back into the line. 'I'll meet you at my house later, as soon as I can get away. There's a wake at the Oliverot. I ought to show my face.'

'Thank you.'

'The key's where it always was,' Pujol said. 'And help yourself to something to eat. God knows, you look like you could do with it.'

*

When Pujol arrived, it was past two o'clock. Baillard was sitting at the kitchen table holding the antique glass bottle in his hand.

'You found it, then?'

'It is more of a relief to find this kept safe than you can know, Achille.'

Pujol shambled to the cupboard, got out two glasses, filled them with Guignolet. He handed one to Baillard, then sat down opposite him.

'Did you find something to eat?'

'What I needed, yes.'

Pujol nodded. 'What happened, Audric? Where've you been? I thought they'd got you. We all did.'

Baillard closed his eyes. Memories of his long, debilitating, violent incarceration came rushing back. The smell and the heat. Later, the cold. The endless sounds of suffering and the stench of the ditches filled with corpses and excrement when dysentery spread through the camp. In the past, in his youth, Baillard had seen epidemics like it – siege sickness, they used to call it – but nothing as bad as what he had witnessed in the past two years.

'Audric?' Pujol prompted.

He opened his eyes. 'Before I tell you, what of you, *amic*? What of here? How many have we lost?'

'Too many,' Pujol said in a quiet voice. 'From Tarascon, Espéraza, Couiza, Coustaussa, Limoux, all over the valleys.' He trailed off. 'Too many.'

'Each life lost is one too many,' Baillard said. 'The things I have seen, the stories I have heard about the camps in the East. This is a war like no other I have known, Achille.' He shook his head, as if trying to shake away the memories. 'Forgive me. Tell me of life here.'

'Very well,' Pujol sighed, accepting that Baillard would

not tell his story until he was ready. 'Pierre and old Breillac are gone,' he said. 'Gestapo. Breillac went down fighting. Young Guillaume is still fighting. Formed the Couiza Maquis with Yves Rousset. Do you know him?'

'I know Madame Rousset.'

'Guillaume's wife Eloise is still hereabouts. Geneviève and Liesl stayed in Coustaussa with Marieta.'

A slow smile spread across Baillard's face. 'That is the best news yet, my friend. She was so ill, I feared she might not have survived another winter.'

'I knew you'd be pleased,' Pujol said with a satisfied smile. 'Marieta's still going strong. Will see the rest of us out, I don't doubt. Looks after those girls like a mother hen.'

'Good, *ben*.' Baillard smiled, nodding his head. He paused for a moment to gather his thoughts. 'And Madomaisèla Sandrine and her sister?'

'They both returned to Carcassonne shortly after you left. They do a great deal to help the *résistants* there. Taking messages, keeping lookout, what have you. Mademoiselle Ménard and her son stayed in Coustaussa for a time, but went back to Carcassonne last summer.'

'Her son, you say?'

Pujol smiled. 'Jean-Jacques. Bright as a button, must be eighteen months old by now.'

'*Tèn perdu, jhamâi se recobro*,' murmured Baillard, thinking of all he had missed and all that was yet to come. The joy as well as the sorrow.

'What's that you're saying?'

'Time lost can never be regained,' Baillard translated. 'An old Occitan proverb my grandmother, Esclarmonde, was rather fond of.' He smiled. 'And Sénher Pelletier?'

'He, too, has proved to be a courageous man. With Guillaume and Yves some of the time, but travels to Carcassonne to help there too.'

Baillard raised his eyebrows. 'And to see Madomaisèla Sandrine?'

'That too,' Pujol said impatiently. 'But now, for pity's sake, tell me where you've been.'

Baillard looked into the honest, anxious face of his friend. He raised his arms and then let them fall again, a gesture of resignation.

'I was caught, Achille. That very day after I left you. A collaborator, pretending to be a partisan. Walked straight into a trap some two hours out of Ax-les-Thermes.'

Pujol drained his glass and poured himself another measure. The air in the kitchen was infused with the sweet smell of cherries.

'Where did they take you?'

'I was arrested, one of five or six raids that day.' Baillard sighed. 'They asked for me by name.'

'Why?'

He shrugged. 'I had done that route many times. Too many times, perhaps. Someone talked.' He paused as he took himself back to that day. 'Two of those I was helping knew who I was – a Jewish scholar, quite brilliant, and a Dutch *résistant* – but did not give me away. I was able to give false information and so was charged under that name instead.'

'That explains why "Baillard" didn't show up on any lists,' Pujol said. 'I checked everywhere.'

Baillard smiled. 'Thank you, my friend.'

Pujol flushed. 'You'd have done the same for me,' he said gruffly, then waved his hand for him to continue.

'During those first weeks after I was arrested, I was moved from place to place. It was only after the Germans crossed the line and occupied the Midi as well that I was finally sent to a satellite camp close to Rivesaltes.'

'So near,' Pujol said, shaking his head. 'If only I'd known you were there, Audric, I swear I would—'

'I know, my friend. Don't reproach yourself. We were the unwanted prisoners. Too old to fill the STO quotas, most of us veterans of other wars.'

'Left to rot.'

'That saved us,' Baillard said simply. 'We were not considered dangerous. They assumed that age and the bitter weather would do their work for them.' He paused. 'The worst of it was knowing how much needed to be done, but being trapped, unable to act.'

He fell silent, remembering his sense of frustration and rage. The endless tiny humiliations of the camp, the relentless grinding down of men's spirits. The waste of life.

'Audric,' Pujol said gently, misinterpreting his silence, 'you don't have to go on if it's too much.'

'No,' he said quickly. 'If I do not, you will imagine things to be worse than they were.'

Baillard recounted the story of his incarceration and his escape, then gave a long sigh. He took a sip of Guignolet, letting the sugar and alcohol ease his bones, before continuing. 'We waited until it was dark, then the Spaniard and I went our separate ways. García headed for the border. I came here.'

'I still can't quite believe it,' Pujol said gruffly, digging in his pocket for a scrap of tobacco. He rolled himself a thin cigarette. 'You made good time, I'll give you that. It must be a hundred and fifty kilometres, give or take.'

'People were kind. I walked to Collioure, then found a lift almost all of the way to Belcaire. From there, cross-country to here.'

Pujol put out his hand and touched Baillard's arm. 'You can stay here as long as you want. You need to rest. Recover your strength.'

Baillard reached out and took the antique glass bottle from the table. 'I have rested long enough, *amic*. This task I must now finish.'

Pujol's expression changed. 'Not that, Audric. Surely not now, after all this time. Why stir it all up again? Let sleeping dogs lie.'

For a moment, Baillard didn't speak. He turned the bottle over in his hand, thinking about the precious information contained in the map.

'Why, Audric?'

He sighed. 'Because it was announced this morning on the wireless – I heard it at the Café de la Gare as I waited to see you – that Leo Authié is being sent back to the Midi. Although it is said he is to lead the fight against the Resistance, I do not believe that is the true reason.'

Pujol's expression froze. 'He's just one man,' he said eventually. 'There are many like him. Leave it be, Baillard. The tide is turning in our favour. Don't draw attention to yourself.'

Baillard met his gaze. 'It is true that Führer Hitler is losing the war. And after the Allied success in northern France, it is likely he will pull back troops from the south to defend Paris and the eastern territories.'

'Well then.'

Baillard shook his head. 'Do you not understand, Achille? This will make Authié more dangerous, not less. More desperate. He is a clever man. He knows there is little time left. When the Wehrmacht leave the Midi, he is aware of what his fate will be. If he is to find the Codex, he needs to act now and be ready to leave when the Nazis withdraw.'

'There's not been a whisper they ever found out the document was a forgery,' Pujol said. 'Not a hint of it.'

'Saurat is dead. He has family near Collioure, that's why I went there first. His cousin told me he died in Montluc at the hands of Hauptsturmführer Barbie.' He sighed. 'He will have talked, Achille. For all his qualities, he was not a strong man.'

'Poor devil,' muttered Pujol.

Baillard looked out of the window towards the Pic de Vicdessos in the distance. The fierce afternoon sun blasted down upon the exposed peaks, casting long shadows across the land.

'Authié has spent the past two years in Chartres, if the wireless report is to be believed. So I am certain, now, for whom he works and what other prize that man is seeking.' His voice hardened. 'I intend to make sure he does not get it.'

'If you say so, Audric.'

'The story is coming to its end, *amic*,' he said. 'This story, at least.'

'So long as it's a happy ending,' Pujol muttered.

Baillard did not answer.

Chapter 113

CARCASSONNE

Sandrine stood by the sink, feeling the cold edge of the porcelain in the small of her back. Marianne was at the stove. Raoul was sitting at the table, his hands in his pockets, watching Suzanne work.

Suzanne placed her ingredients on the table. Forty centimetres of cast-iron pipe, a section of a drainpipe taken from one of the derelict houses near the abattoir in the Aire de la Pépinière. The pipe was already packed with explosive. Sandrine watched as she bolted a stopper into each end, drilled a small hole about halfway down, and pushed into it a fuse that went down into the explosive.

'It's a simple, reliable, basic device,' Suzanne said. 'A child could do it. There's two centimetres of fuse here, which will take about two minutes to burn, give or take.'

Sandrine glanced at Raoul's face.

'Not much time to get out of the way,' he said.

'Long enough,' Sandrine replied.

'What's the rest of it?' Raoul asked, pointing at the duplicate parts.

'A decoy,' Sandrine explained. 'We've done it before, placing two identical devices in locations close to one another – one in the Tour du Grand Burlas and the other in the Tour de la Justice – except one is live and the other one's a dummy. It means that if anyone talks, the soldiers have a fifty-fifty chance of finding the wrong device rather than the real one.'

Raoul nodded. 'Good idea. Who's responsible for the dummy?'

'Gaston has a friend who works in a restaurant by the Porte de l'Aude, a kitchen porter. He's going to set it in the Tour de la Justice tonight. It's the closest we can get to the Hôtel de la Cité, where the dinner's being held.'

Suzanne turned to Marianne. 'Is that ready yet?'

Marianne came over from the stove holding the tin saucepan at arm's length in front of her. Raoul wafted his hand in front of his nose.

'Goose fat,' Suzanne said, seeing the expression on his face. 'Vile smell, I grant you, but the best way to keep the pipe airtight. More efficient than wax. Less volatile.'

They watched as Suzanne greased the pipe, then put the last few components in place.

'Right, that's done.'

She stood up, gathered everything up in a tea towel and gently carried the device to the sideboard beside the kitchen door. Marianne handed her a cloth for her hands.

'I'll show you what to do before we go,' Suzanne said to Sandrine. 'You're sure you don't want me to stay? Just until it's in place, at least.'

Sandrine glanced at her sister and saw the look of resignation in her eyes, then shook her head.

'No, it's all right. Better you should go. Take the package to Gaston, then catch tonight's train. Who knows when there'll be another.' She smiled. 'Raoul and I will manage.'

'Isn't Lucie going with you two?' Raoul asked.

Marianne shook her head. 'Not at the moment. She doesn't want to uproot Jean-Jacques.' She paused. 'Suzanne's mother is very fond of him. She helps out with him a great deal.'

'Lucie should be all right,' Sandrine said, seeing the look of concern on Raoul's face. 'She's so changed since

Authié last saw her. And even if he did go looking for her, he'd never think to try Madame Peyre's address.'

Raoul nodded, but Sandrine could see he wasn't convinced.

'The most important thing at this moment is for Suzanne and Marianne to leave,' she said.

'Are you ready?' Marianne asked Suzanne.

'I need to pack this lot up, then change.'

'The train isn't until six thirty, is it?' Sandrine said.

'Yes, but the checks are bound to take some time,' Marianne said. 'Why don't I do this for you,' she offered, gesturing at the components for the decoy, 'and you go and get ready?'

'Give me five minutes,' Suzanne said, walking out of the kitchen. Seconds later, Sandrine heard the heavy tread of her boots on the stairs.

For a moment, no one said anything.

'Could you do me a favour and check the wireless, Raoul?' Sandrine said. 'Just in case something's happened we should be aware of. There should be a bulletin any minute now.'

Realising that she wanted time to say goodbye to Marianne in private, he got up quickly and went out of the room.

The two sisters were left alone. Marianne found a canvas bag and carefully put the parts into it, then sat down at the table again. Overhead, they could hear Suzanne moving about.

'This is it, then,' Marianne said.

'For a day or two, that's all,' Sandrine said. 'We'll do what we have to do, then we'll join you. By Sunday we'll all be together in Coustaussa.' She smiled. 'Like old times.'

Marianne nodded. 'Now the time's come, I can't wait to see Marieta. I've tried not to miss her too much.'

'Me too,' Sandrine said. 'Though I bet she won't have changed a bit.'

Marianne smiled. 'I wonder what Liesl will be like? Two years is a long time between sixteen and eighteen.'

'Raoul says she's very beautiful.'

Marianne threw a glance at her. 'Is that a touch of jealousy?'

Sandrine blushed. 'No, not at all. I'm just saying.'

Marianne laughed, then the smile slid from her face. 'You will be careful, won't you?'

'You know I will,' she said softly. 'And Raoul will be with me. He'll make sure I'm all right.'

Marianne nodded. 'I'm sorry I've been going to pieces in the last few weeks. You keep going and keep going then, suddenly, you lose your nerve. No reason, or rather ... I suppose Suzanne being picked up, that did for me.'

Sandrine nodded. 'I know. I understand.'

She hesitated, then decided to ask outright what she had known for a long time.

'You love her,' she said.

Marianne met her gaze. She hesitated, on the point of framing the conventional response, then stopped. It was clear in her face that she, too, was conscious of the fact that however much care Sandrine, or Marianne herself, took – however matter-of-fact their conversation – this might be the last time they spoke to each other.

'I do.'

'Did Thierry realise?' Sandrine asked, genuinely curious. 'Or is it a more recent thing?'

'Certainly Thierry knew.' Marianne smiled. 'It suited him just as well, you see. Harder for him, of course.'

Sandrine frowned, then realised what Marianne was saying. 'Oh. I see. You were a cover for him.'

'It's the only good thing that's come out of any of this,'

she said quietly. 'In some ways, it's been easier than it would have been in peacetime.'

The sound of Suzanne coming back down the stairs brought the conversation to a close.

'I'm glad for you,' Sandrine said quickly.

Marianne nodded. 'Me too.' She turned and smiled as Suzanne walked in. 'Are you ready to go?'

Suzanne nodded. 'All set,' she said.

The three women walked back into the hall, where two suitcases were sitting at the bottom of the stairs. Raoul came out of the salon to say goodbye.

'We'll join you as soon as we can,' he said. 'Sunday, Monday at the latest.'

'Look after her,' Marianne said, as Raoul hugged her.

'I will.'

Raoul shook hands with Suzanne, then went back into the salon to act as lookout at the window.

'You're clear on what to do?' Suzanne said to Sandrine.

'Lord, you two are as bad as each other,' she said with a smile. 'I will be careful, as I always am. I will go through the exact same procedures as I always do.' She smiled. 'And it will be fine, as it always is. Don't worry.'

'All clear,' Raoul called from the salon.

'All the copies of *Libertat* were collected by the couriers,' Suzanne said, 'so nothing to worry about there.'

'Good.'

Suzanne turned to Marianne. 'I'll see you on the platform at half past five. If for any reason I'm not there, you go on. I'll catch you up.'

'Why wouldn't you be there?' Marianne said quickly. 'I'm not going without you.'

'Come on, don't get rattled. It's just the usual precautions, you know how it is. I will be there. But if there's a problem, it will be better if I know you're on your way. Safe. You see?'

Marianne pulled herself together. 'Yes. Yes, of course.'

Sandrine opened the door. Suzanne picked up her suitcase, then, without a backward glance, walked down the steps and away to the right, out of sight.

A few minutes later, Marianne did the same, though headed in the opposite direction, away from the station.

Sandrine stood listening to her sister's footsteps echoing down the rue du Palais, blinking away the tears. Neither of them had said it, but both sisters knew it was possible they were saying goodbye to their childhood home for ever.

'Just us now,' she said, as Raoul came to stand beside her.

'Just us,' he said, putting his arms around her.

Finally, and for the first time in longer than she could remember, Sandrine gave in. She broke down and cried. Raoul held her, stroking her hair and saying nothing.

Chapter 114

Tarascon

'*Pour arrêter les crimes de la Gestapo et Milice*,' Baillard said, reading the headline on the tract lying on Pujol's kitchen table. 'Where did this come from?'

'The railway station,' Pujol said with a smile. 'The guard said there was a suitcase under the seat in the last carriage. Nobody claimed it, so he opened it up and found about fifty of these inside. He called the Milice, but of course they were all otherwise occupied keeping guard at Pierre Déjean's funeral, so the perpetrator – whoever he was – was long gone.'

'Of course,' Baillard said. 'What happened to the rest of them?'

'As the guard explained to the *milicien* who came to collect the suitcase, there was an unfortunate gust of wind at about the moment he opened the lid, so strong he was unable to prevent some of the tracts from being blown out of the station and into the street.'

A smile lit Baillard's gaunt face. '*Es vertat*. It is true that the Tramontana can be particularly fierce at this time of year.'

The two old men looked at one another. Pujol read the headline again.

'Sure you didn't write this yourself, Baillard?' he chuckled. 'The fact that it's called *Libertat* rather than *Libération* or *Liberté*? And that final sentence – "the world belongs to the brave" – sounds like something you'd come out with.' He gave a snort of amusement. 'It's my guess this is what you've been doing. Your story about being in a prison camp is all just a cover, isn't it?'

Baillard held up both hands in mock surrender. Pujol gave a bark of laughter, then sat down in the chair opposite, expelling air from his lungs as the cushion expelled dust.

'It is a good piece of work,' Baillard said. 'Honourable.'

Baillard wondered. In Coustaussa he had talked to Sandrine Vidal about how important it was to bear witness to the truth. Had he used the word *libertat* to her? If so, was it possible that she had taken the suggestion?

'Honourable?' Pujol said, picking up the newspaper. 'Yes, I suppose it is. I haven't come across this one before.' He shook his head. 'These photographs, it must have taken a great deal of courage to get them.'

'So you do not know who might be responsible?'

'Not a clue,' said Pujol. 'There are so many, they come and go. Most of them get shut down in the end,' he added, the smile fading from his eyes. 'You know how it is.'

Baillard nodded. There had been several well-publicised arrests by Gestapo of *résistants* working for the underground press. The men had all been executed, the women deported to Ravensbrück, a camp just north of Berlin.

Pujol shambled to the cupboard, took out two glasses and a bottle of red wine, then sat back down at the table.

'Have a little something, go on,' he said. 'Present from the mother of one of the lads up the hill, you know. Help keep your spirits up.'

Baillard smiled properly this time. 'Your answer to everything, Achille!'

'Have you got a better suggestion?'

As Baillard took the glass, there was a tap at the front door and the atmosphere shifted. Pujol gestured for him to go into the bedroom, out of sight. Baillard nodded and left, taking his glass with him.

Pujol put his own down on the table and shambled into the corridor.

'All right, all right, I'm on my way.'

'It's me, Inspector Pujol.'

Pujol stopped and called back to Baillard. 'It's all right, it's Geneviève Saint-Loup.'

Baillard emerged from his hiding place and went back into the kitchen as Geneviève and Eloise came rushing down the corridor.

'It is you!' said Geneviève with delight. 'Eloise, I was right. It was Monsieur Baillard.'

She rushed up to him, then stopped. Baillard saw her battling not to let her shock at his emaciated appearance show. Eloise had no such qualms.

'You look terrible!' she said.

'Eloise!' Geneviève said, elbowing her in the ribs.

Baillard smiled. 'Already I begin to improve at the sight of you all.'

'Marieta will be so happy to see you, Monsieur Baillard,' said Geneviève. 'She always said you would come back.'

Baillard sighed. 'We have experienced many things over the years, she and I,' he said quietly. 'Death and loss. Yes, I believe she would have known.'

'That's odd,' Eloise said, pointing at the iridescent bottle on the table.

Baillard's eyes narrowed. 'How so?'

'Our father had one just like it, didn't he, Geneviève?' She picked it up. 'Do you know, in fact, I think it's the same one. Look at the hole at the top.'

'What happened to it, Madomaisèla?'

'I'm not altogether sure, pawned probably, or sold. It was a family heirloom, passed down from generation to generation, but it wouldn't have mattered. He was always in debt.'

'Can you remember when you last saw it?'

Eloise shook her head. 'It was the first time – though not the last – that we had no money and everything was sold. I seem to remember he sold boxes of stuff to some German chap who was setting up a guest house near Montségur. Don't think it lasted long.'

Pujol's eyes widened. 'Could it be Rahn, Baillard?'

'Possibly,' Baillard said.

'But if Rahn had it, surely he would have looked inside?'

'Not if, as Madomaisèla Eloise says, it was in a box with many other objects.'

Pujol frowned. 'You think Rahn had it all shipped back to Germany, then found it just before he died and sent it to Antoine Déjean?'

'I think that might very well be the case,' Baillard said thoughtfully. 'I do not suppose you remember when this happened?'

Eloise shook her head. 'Not precisely. I was little, no more than nine or ten, which makes it about fifteen years ago.' She turned to her sister. 'You were even younger, so I don't suppose you recall anything about it.'

But Geneviève was staring at the newspaper. Baillard saw the look of surprise in her eyes, then alarm, and his earlier suspicions were confirmed. He put the bottle to one side.

'The wind has done the work,' he said innocently. 'It seems a suitcase was left at the railway station and the contents were blown about.'

'How unfortunate,' said Eloise.

Baillard looked at them both, then slowly a smile broke across his face.

'I wonder, Madomaisèla Geneviève, do you know something about this publication, *Libertat*?'

'It is difficult to say . . .' she replied, throwing a glance at her sister.

Baillard's smile grew even wider. 'I do not think she

would object to you telling me, Madomaisèla Geneviève,' he said quietly. 'But, of course, you must be guided by your conscience.'

Pujol stared at Baillard, then at the two girls. 'Do you have the first idea what he's talking about?'

'The thing is . . .' Geneviève began to say.

Baillard suddenly let out a bellow of laughter. It was so out of character, and so unexpected, that Pujol jumped in surprise.

'What the devil's got into you, Audric?' he said irritably.

'Monsieur Baillard knows anyway, I think,' Eloise said, sitting down at the table.

'Perhaps you could humour an old man, madomaisèla,' he said. 'You forget, I have been gone for some time.'

'Of course, Monsieur Baillard.' Genevieve smiled. 'Liesl took the photographs. I took the film and left it at the *boîte aux lettres* in Limoux on Sunday, for Raoul to collect and take to Carcassonne.' She glanced at the images. 'All went to plan, clearly.'

'Suzanne's in charge of the printing,' Eloise said. 'Marianne sees to the distribution, with the help of two brothers. I don't know their names, but they're local. Originally contacts of Raoul, I think.'

Baillard nodded. 'And this?' he said, pointing to the small paragraph about the sabotage of the Berriac tunnel.

For a split second, Geneviève hesitated. But knowing that, of all people, Monsieur Baillard could be trusted, she explained how 'Citadel' had come into being.

As the Saint-Loup sisters talked, the story passing backwards and forwards between them, Baillard watched his friend's craggy face. Pujol's astonishment was obvious, for although he knew that the girls ran errands for the Resistance and helped to carry food and messages to the maquisards in the hills, it was clear he'd never dreamt of anything more.

'I'd heard a story or two about a network with women in it, but I mean to say . . .' He shrugged. 'Never thought for a moment it was true.'

'It is because others think the same as you do, *amic*, that they have remained undiscovered for this long.'

'And who's running the show?' asked Pujol.

Eloise and Geneviève didn't say anything. Baillard allowed a brief smile to touch his lips.

'Well?' Pujol said. 'Pelletier?'

'No, not Sénher Pelletier,' Baillard replied.

'Who, then?' Pujol demanded, sounding irritated.

Baillard took a moment before he answered. 'Two years ago,' he said slowly, 'Madomaisèla Sandrine and I discussed what might be done. Unless I am much mistaken, she is behind both the newspaper and the *réseau* "Citadel".'

He looked at Geneviève. 'I am right, madomaisèla?'

She smiled, then she nodded. 'Yes.'

'Sandrine Vidal,' Pujol objected. 'But she's only a child!'

Baillard sighed. 'I know. But this is a war like no other, my friend. It is no respecter of age or experience. In this war, everyone is involved. Men, women, the very old and the very young.' He picked up the newspaper and looked at the block-letter headline again. 'A war like no other.'

Chapter 115

CARCASSONNE

At seven o'clock on Thursday 13 July, Leo Authié drove along the boulevard Maréchal Pétain. As the car glided past the building where his office had been, he saw a white banner with the word FELDKOMMANDANTUR 743 on it. Though it was dusk, he could see that two swastikas had been pinned to the balustrade above the main entrance. It was an odd sensation.

Carcassonne seemed small after two years in Chartres. Which made it even more shameful that the insurgents continued successfully to operate in the narrow streets of the Bastide. There was little excuse for the fact that the Gestapo and the Milice had failed to eradicate all opposition entirely.

'*Canaille*,' he muttered. Vermin.

Laval was driving. He said nothing. Authié wouldn't expect him to speak. Laval obeyed orders now. He did not question or challenge. The abrupt news they were to return to the south, then Authié's announcement that they were to schedule their arrival a day earlier than de l'Oradore had suggested, had been met with a lack of curiosity. Two years in the north, being subordinate to the Gestapo and Wehrmacht personnel with whom Authié fraternised, had cured Laval of his tendency to query his superior.

De l'Oradore had ensured that the murder of Erik Bauer and his men in August 1942 had not come to the attention of Nazi High Command in Paris. It had given de l'Oradore a hold over Authié, but since it did not interfere with or limit his ambitions, it was a situation he was prepared to tolerate. In turn, Authié had created a paper trail implicating Laval in the massacre. Should at any stage his deputy step out of line, this evidence would prove Laval had acted on his own initiative. That he had, in fact, been working as a double agent. It was true, of course. A simple conversation with the two German prisoners in Le Vernet had confirmed Laval had been selling information to Bauer. Authié had never had to make the threat explicit.

He smiled. 'Do you know, I believe I shall enjoy Carcassonne, Laval,' he said.

Laval didn't respond.

'Lieutenant,' Authié said sharply.

Their eyes locked. 'Yes, sir,' Laval said.

The car turned left and drove past the Hôtel Terminus, heading out of town towards the route de Toulouse. The Gestapo had set up their headquarters in a rather ordinary suburban villa, although the majority of its number were garrisoned at the Caserne Laperrine.

Authié had no doubt Schiffner and his men resented his arrival – it was a clear criticism of their inability to suppress the insurgents in Carcassonne – but they were not in a position to object. Schiffner could not fail to be aware of the support Authié had in Chartres and Paris. His recent contributions to the strikes against Resistance and Maquis targets in the south had been widely acknowledged. In Montolieu in May, in Conques and Chalabre. Schiffner would know that Nazi High Command thought highly of Authié.

'What time did you inform them we would be arriving, Laval?'

'I said between eight and nine o'clock this evening, sir. I thought it better not to be too specific.'

Authié nodded. 'How did they react?'

'They were unhappy, suspected you were trying to catch

them out, sir. But they attempted to conceal it.'

'Good.'

As they drove past the Jardin des Plantes, Authié went over his plans in his mind. The first twenty-four hours would be critical. Tomorrow was Bastille Day. Any kind of celebration was now illegal, which of course meant it was an obvious date for a partisan attack or protest.

He would spend an hour or so with Schiffner, both of them going through the motions of pretending they were equal and willing allies. He needed to know how many men he might have at his disposal. His erstwhile informant, Fournier, had been murdered in the same attack that had killed the leader of the Carcassonnais Milice, Albert Kromer. But there was no reason to assume Fournier's sister would have moved from the rue du Palais. While he was with Schiffner, he intended to send Laval to find out if the Vidal house was still occupied.

So far as the forgery was concerned, Authié had made a convincing enough case against Sandrine Vidal in his mind. It was now only a matter of finding her and ascertaining the extent to which she was involved. But now there was more.

Authié leant back in his seat. When they had stopped at Milice headquarters in Toulouse to make the telephone call to Schiffner, Authié had seen a report about a women's network operating in Carcassonne. He had no idea if there was truth in the story, but he remembered the way Marianne Vidal and her friend had closed ranks when he visited the house in the rue du Palais in search of Sandrine Vidal. And he had started to wonder.

Two birds with one stone, a net gradually tightening.

Laval killed the engine. 'We're here, sir.'

Authié waited for Laval to open his door, then got out. From the outside, it looked like an ordinary suburban house. Inside – beyond the mundane offices and 'grey mice', as they were known, typing and sending telegrams and receiving messages – Authié knew it would be a different matter. Here, regardless of intention, most men and women were persuaded, in the end, to talk.

Authié gave Laval his orders, instructing him to return in an hour, then turned and walked towards the entrance. After the usual security checks, he was taken to a large office at the back of the building and announced. Schiffner, with a fixed smile on his face, came out from behind his desk and offered Authié his hand. He spoke in German.

'A pleasure to see you again, Major Authié.'

'*Je vous en prie*,' Authié replied.

Schiffner switched to French. He gestured to the two officers in the room with him. 'You know Inspector Janeke and Inspector Zimmerman?'

Authié nodded at Schiffner's deputies. Between them, these three men were in charge of pursuing the war against the Resistance in the Aude. In his eyes, therefore, they were responsible for the failure to suppress the insurgency.

'You catch us somewhat by surprise,' Schiffner said. 'Our arrangements were for tomorrow.'

Authié met his eye. 'We made better time than we had anticipated,' he said. 'I hope I have not inconvenienced you.'

Schiffner waved his hand. 'Not in the slightest, not in the slightest. But the formal dinner to welcome you to Carcassonne is arranged for tomorrow night.'

'*Back* to Carcassonne,' he said lightly. 'This is my home town.'

'Of course, I forget.'

'A dinner was not necessary though it is, of course, most kind.'

'It is an honour,' Schiffner said, with a smile that did not reach his eyes.

'I shall look forward to it,' Authié said, equally formally.

As second in command only to Chef Eckfelner himself, the seniority belonged with Schiffner. But Authié's position was without parallel. He was French, yet had powerful supporters. He had authority over the operations of the Milice in Carcassonne, though the chain of command was blurred. It was not clear to whom he answered, Chartres or Paris or even Berlin. As a result, Schiffner was wary. Authié could see the caution in the German's eyes. He let the silence stretch.

'Can I offer you something to drink, Herr Authié?' Schiffner said in the end. 'Whisky? Brandy?'

'Thank you, brandy.'

Schiffner gestured to Janeke, who went to a drinks cabinet in the corner of the office and poured two measures of cognac.

'I confess I am not entirely clear what your instructions might be, Herr Authié.'

Authié allowed himself a slight smile at Schiffner's unwillingness to use his military rank. It was the second time, so deliberate rather than a slip of the tongue.

'Tell me, Herr Schiffner, do you consider you are winning the war against the insurgents?'

The Nazi flushed. 'There is still work to do, but I would say so. Our figures compare favourably with other regions.'

'How many terrorists have you deported?'

Schiffner glanced at Inspector Janeke as he handed him the brandy. The lieutenant said nothing.

'I cannot say without checking our records,' Schiffner said. 'All the details are in our files.'

'One hundred, one hundred and fifty, more?'

'In excess of two hundred, I should say.'

'The majority of those in June and July,' Authié continued.

'Herr Authié, forgive me,' Schiffner said, trying to mask his impatience. 'Is there something *specific* you would like to know? Please, do ask. It will save us both time.'

Authié leant forward and put his untouched drink on the desk. 'Very well. It seems to me that, with the intelligence provided to you, your attempts to clean the vermin from the Bastide are less successful than they might be. The majority of the insurgents seem to have been left at liberty to join other groups.'

'The Maquis are not our prime concern in Carcassonne, as you well know,' Schiffner said stiffly. 'Having said that, I believe our actions against the guerrilla forces in the countryside are successful in the main.'

Authié sat back in his chair. He pulled his cigarette case from the inside breast pocket of his jacket and offered it to Schiffner, who shook his head. He shrugged, took out a cigarette and tapped it on the silver lid to settle the tobacco, then got out his lighter.

'Perhaps if you dismiss your officers,' he said, 'we could talk more frankly.'

'I would prefer them to remain.'

Authié snapped the lid shut, killing the flame.

'In which case,' he said, pleasantly, 'I regret we have nothing to say to one another at this stage.'

He stood up.

'Wait,' Schiffner said quickly. 'Very well.'

Authié stared at him, then slowly sat down again. Schiffner could not afford either to alienate Authié – not until he had ascertained the true extent of his authority – or to jeopardise the Gestapo operation in Carcassonne. Both men were aware of it. Schiffner turned to his lieutenants.

'Draußen Warten.'

The door closed behind them.

'A wise decision,' Authié said. 'So, you asked me what *specifically* I wanted to know.'

Schiffner nodded. 'I did.'

Authié sat forward in his chair. 'You have heard of the

agent code-named "Sophie"? Or the *réseau* she is said to command in Carcassonne?'

Schiffner gave a bark of laughter. 'It is common knowledge that such a network does not exist. It's a fairy tale, *ein Märchen*, something out of the brothers Grimm. A unit of women, it is propaganda only.'

'Do you think so?' Authié said. 'Yet most of the heroines of your fairy tales are girls, are they not? There are women who support the insurgents, as you are well aware. Now more than ever.'

Schiffner waved his hand. 'Running errands, maybe, but setting explosives, sabotage, destroying power lines, this I do not believe.' He gave another hollow laugh. 'What is more, this *réseau* is everywhere. In the countryside, in Carcassonne itself, on the coast, any attack that cannot be attributed to someone else is laid at their door.'

Authié met his gaze. 'If you wish to improve your standing, shall we say, then I suggest you listen very carefully. For reasons I do not propose to elaborate, I am interested in "Sophie". If you are prepared to help me, I will be prepared to share with you intelligence that will enable you to bring into custody the leaders of the R3 network.'

'Excuse me?'

Ever since the various Resistance networks had been brought together in January 1943 – and France divided into different zones – there had been a game of cat-and-mouse as the Gestapo attempted to hunt down the leaders of the various factions.

'You need to find "Myriel", do you not?' Authié said. 'His real name is Jean Bringer. He is the leader of the FFI, working with Aimé Ramond – a serving police officer here in Carcassonne – as well as Maurice Sevajols and others.'

'How do you know this?' said Schiffner.

Authié held his gaze. 'If you give me your full support for the next three days, perhaps more, then I will give you all the information you need to move against R3.' He paused. 'Since you claim not even to believe in this women's *réseau*, it seems a more than fair bargain.'

He watched Schiffner wrestling with the decision. His anger at finding terms being dictated to him was in conflict with his self-interest.

'Well?'

Finally, the Nazi nodded. 'I accept your terms.'

Authié gave a sharp nod.

Schiffner frowned. 'You talk as if you know the identity of this "Sophie". Is that the case?'

Authié gave a cold smile. 'A suspicion, only. But one I intend to prove. If I am right, I suspect some kind of action will be planned for tomorrow night. It is widely known, no doubt, that you have a dinner arranged.'

Schiffner flushed. 'It is impossible to organise such a thing without it becoming common knowledge. The staff alone ...'

'You took no special precautions?'

'Of course we did. There is increased security. All personnel going in and out of the Cité will be searched. Everyone has been issued with special passes for tomorrow night. Of course, if you had given us prior warning, we would have brought arrangements forward.'

Authié gave a cold smile. 'Where is this dinner to be held?'

'The Hôtel de la Cité.'

'Good.' A slow smile spread across his face. 'Telephone your men in the Cité and tell them to be alert. To report anything unusual, particularly in the vicinity of the hotel itself. Anything at all.'

Chapter 116

CARCASSONNE

Sandrine waited until it was dark before crossing the Pont Neuf. To her right, the distinctive arches of the Pont Vieux were blockaded at each end by Nazi anti-tank installations. She wore a dark pullover, black canvas trousers over her dress and rubber-soled shoes on her feet. Her hair was tucked up in a black beret.

To her right, she could see the turrets and towers of the medieval Cité, now occupied by the Wehrmacht. The Porte de l'Aude had been closed up and the inhabitants of the Cité, like their ancestors in the summer of 1209, expelled from their own streets. When they were children, she and Marianne had played in the ramparts, climbed the old stone walls, darting in and out of the postern gates that led to the moat and the roads surrounding the citadel. Always a *garçon manqué*, a tomboy, Sandrine had played the *chevalier*. Marianne preferred to be the châtelaine.

Sandrine quickly left the main road and ducked down to the path running along the right bank close to Maingaud's distillery. Walking fast, head down, she passed the night fishermen casting their lines out into the drifting current of the Aude.

There was a bright and cloudless sky, not ideal for this kind of operation. Sandrine remembered sitting in Coustaussa listening to Monsieur Baillard's stories of taking 'cargo' to the Spanish border. How the moon was an enemy. Praying for misty nights, for overcast nights, to conceal them from the French border patrols. Then, she had no idea that she would learn to feel the same.

Raoul was waiting for her in the shadow of the walls below the Lafarge factory. When he smiled, quickly, in the dark, Sandrine let her fingers touch his, briefly. He too was dressed in black, with a dark handkerchief around his neck. He was carrying a holdall over his left shoulder.

'You have everything?' she whispered, even though she'd packed the bag herself.

'Yes.'

Her despair of a few hours ago utterly forgotten, Sandrine now felt calm and focused on the job in hand. They made their way down rue Barbacane, past the église Saint-Gimer and a handful of small shops, an old-fashioned mercerie with a dwindled display of thread and buttons, and the boulangerie, shuttered for the night. In the days of austerity in the twenties and thirties, the quartier had fallen on hard times. It became a rough neighbourhood. Before the war it was home to refugees from Spain and North Africa, gypsies from Romania and Hungary, and impoverished Carcassonnais. The police regularly raided the area, looking for communists and Spanish émigrés, anyone without papers or whose name was on a list. Now, many of the houses were officially unoccupied, though dark eyes looked out through the cracks in the shutters. Even the Wehrmacht patrols were reluctant to come here.

Raoul turned left into a narrow dead-end road, rue Petite Côte de la Cité. The houses, two and three storeys high, showed the signs of many families crammed in together. Boarded windows and cracked wooden shutters, crumbling brickwork and peeling paint. The street sloped steeply, leading to a flight of worn stone steps with high flint walls on either side. It led up to the Cité through densely cultivated market gardens. Branches of fig trees, bare of fruit, hung low over the steps and pinpricks of green light from glow-worms illuminated the dark cracks between the stones.

Raoul took the steps two at a time, barely pausing for breath. Sandrine kept pace. Up, up they climbed, following the winding steps round, until suddenly they were out in the open space below the Porte d'Aude, the western entrance into the Cité. Straight ahead were the sheer western walls of the Château Comtal, the Tour Pinte, like a finger pointing to heaven.

For a fleeting instant, Monsieur Baillard came into her mind. Remembering his voice, rich with age and knowledge, telling of how the Tour Pinte bowed down to Charlemagne on Dame Carcas' orders. The last time, or so he told her, that the powers of the Codex had been called upon. Sandrine shook her head, surprised that she should think such a thing at such a moment. She had no time for fairy tales now. But even so, as she cleared the last of the steps, she couldn't help casting her eyes, briefly, to the dark sky.

Was Monsieur Baillard up there? Looking down on their endeavours, keeping them safe? Sandrine couldn't believe in such superstition, in a God that let such things happen, but sometimes she envied Marieta's simple faith. And she wondered why Monsieur Baillard was so vivid in her memory tonight.

'Which way?' Raoul whispered.

Her reflections scattered. 'Right. Follow the path all the way along, then come back at the Tour du Grand Burlas from the gardens to the south.'

Raoul nodded.

'Keep as low as you can.'

Sandrine was aware of the patrols on the walls, the great white beams of the searchlights as they swept over the grass and slopes. There was a patch of exposed land between the top of the stone steps and the market gardens.

Even today, the south-western corner of the Cité was still rural. Orchards and wooded gardens, pens that once held rabbits and chickens. There was little meat to be had now, except in the dining room of the Hôtel de la Cité or the garrison mess in the Hôtel Terminus, where a portrait of Adolf Hitler looked down from the fireplace in the *salle à manger* where once the jazz band played.

Raoul covered the distance first, clutching the bag to his chest like a child held close. Waiting for the sign it was safe to follow, Sandrine looked back out over the Bastide. In her mind's eye she saw the glittering outline of the town in the days before the war, the bars and restaurants and houses all lit up, garlanded about like a string of pearls.

Then, through the silence, the low chug-chug-chug call of an owl. Sandrine smiled, picturing Raoul with his hands cupped round his mouth, breathing the sounds into the darkness, and immediately she set out to join him.

Together they followed the line of the outer ring of fortifications. Here, in the old days, Marieta had told her, the Spanish textile workers laid out their swathes of cloth on the grass to dry, like the huge sails of seafaring boats. The distinctive outline of the Tour du Grand Burlas loomed into view, lit suddenly a ghostly white as the cloud cleared the face of the moon.

This was the most dangerous part of the operation. The Cité was highly guarded, patrolled day and night, but there was a moment at midnight when the watch swapped over. There had been no trouble in this part of Carcassonne for weeks, and after several days of observation, Suzanne had reported that the four Wehrmacht soldiers tended to share a cigarette and pass a few minutes together before the new patrol relieved the old. That was their chance to get in through the postern gate and leave the device in the store at the base of the tower, then get away before the lights were manned once more.

Raoul lowered his bag to the ground, reached inside for a pair of pliers.

'Can you get to work on that?' he said, indicating the padlock on the wooden door of the tower.

She gave a mock salute.

'Very funny,' he said drily, but his voice cracked with tension.

'It'll be all right,' she said.

'Let's just get on with it and get away as soon as we can.'

Sandrine manoeuvred the pliers backwards and forwards, twisting the chain until the metal gave and the padlock fell to the ground.

'Surely they'll search everywhere before Authié arrives?' Raoul whispered.

'Yes, but I'm gambling on them concentrating their efforts close to the hotel. They'll expect something when he arrives and leaves. If they do find it, then we'll have to think of something else. Try again.'

Dread suddenly took hold of her, the thought of success and the thought of failure both equally repellent.

'Are you all right?'

Sandrine pulled herself together. This was how it had to be. Men like Authié forced them to live like this. There was no room for sentiment.

'Fine,' she said quickly. 'Do you have the torch?'

Raoul held the weak beam steady. Sandrine took out the primer and the roll of coarse twine rolled in gunpowder. Next, the detonating cord, treated with a fabric waterproof covering, though it was hardly necessary. It had been dry for weeks. Filled with PETN, it would detonate at about six thousand metres per second. Lastly she took a thin copper tube from the bag, about six centimetres long. One of the ends was open.

'I haven't seen one like this before,' Raoul whispered.

'It's a non-electric blasting cap,' she explained. 'No idea

how Suzanne got hold of it. It goes in the end, here. Then all I have to do is crimp it into place to ensure the main charge blows.'

With deft fingers, Sandrine finished what had to be done. Then she checked and double-checked everything was in place, and stood up.

'*C'est fait.*' All done.

Raoul turned off the torch. Sandrine carefully carried the device into the tower. When she came out, Raoul pulled the door to and reattached the padlock so that it wouldn't be obvious, from a distance at least, that anyone had been in there.

Another cloud passed across the moon. Raoul suddenly put his hand around Sandrine's waist and pulled her to him. He kissed her hard on the mouth, seconds before the silver beam of the searchlight lit the grass around the base of the tower.

'Let me come back and finish it,' he said, releasing her. 'You've done enough.'

Sandrine shook her head and touched his cheek with her hand. 'Come on,' she said.

The soldier on duty in the Tour Grand Canissou was flicking through an American magazine, pin-up girls in bathing suits, pretty in polka dots and bright lipstick. He noticed nothing. Everyone was on duty tomorrow, extra security, but tonight was like any other night. They'd been told to keep an eye out for any unusual activity, but it was as quiet as the grave. He lit a cigarette and looked across at the other towers, thinking about his girl in Michelstadt, wondering how she'd look in a swimming suit like Jinx Falkenburg. He glanced at his wristwatch, seeing that he still had a full four hours before his shift ended.

But the zealous guard in the Tour de l'Inquisition was

looking north out of the ramparts and thought he saw a figure in the shadows beneath the outer walls, just under the Tour de la Justice. He watched it disappear into the long grasses below the stone barbican that led down towards église Saint-Gimer in the quartier du Barbacane. When the shape was out of sight, he radioed his commander.

'One person sighted,' he said down the uneven line. 'Western sector of La Cité, below the Château Comtal.'

'Man, woman?'

'I couldn't tell.'

'Very well,' his commander replied. 'The order is to investigate anything unusual and report back. If you find something, don't disturb it. Leave everything in place. We don't want them to know they've been seen.'

To the south-west of the Cité, Raoul and Sandrine followed the narrow footpath leading down to the Domaine de Fontgrande.

'My uncle worked those vines,' he said softly. 'Autumn after autumn, carrying a high wicker basket on his back filled with purple grapes, white grapes. He had a stubby, thick-bladed knife for cutting the vines. Bruno and I loved it, argued all the time about whose turn it was to use it.' He wriggled his fingers. 'I still remember that tingling atmosphere waiting for the perfect moment for the *vendanges*, everyone watching the sky for the harvest to begin, chasing the clouds.' He paused. 'Even his dog used to sit and watch the sky.'

Sandrine was struck by the contrast between what they were doing and this unchanging rhythm of the South. Generations of families of the Aude valley living out their lives in the same steady way. Having a place in the world, being part of something bigger than themselves.

This, in the end, was what they were fighting for. To not have this way of life stolen from them. She felt suddenly weak with nostalgia. If everything went according to plan, when she left Carcassonne tomorrow she might never be able to return. Certainly not until the war was over. Whatever the outcome.

As she thought about all the places she would miss, she felt her heart coming unstitched a little, like tiny tears in a piece of cloth. All the lost opportunities, the small dreams that hadn't had time to come true. In the darkness, she clutched for Raoul's hand. Found it.

He squeezed, then she let go and they continued to thread their way down the narrow path in the silent darkness. Down past the Moulin du Roi and on to the island that lay between the Aude and one of its smaller tributaries. There was no bridge, but the river was low below the weir and, provided they waited until the moon was obscured, it was a good place to cross back to the Bastide. It was common practice not to retrace one's steps. It cut down the chance, in the event that someone reported them to the authorities, of their being able to give an accurate description.

Raoul crossed first. Sandrine crouched in the reeds and the shelter of the trees that went right down to the water's edge, alert all the time to any sound, praying not to hear anything. No shouted orders, no report of a gun ringing out, nothing to indicate they'd been spotted. She noticed they weren't far from where she and Raoul had first met. The place where she had pulled Antoine Déjean from the water and everything had been set in motion. For the third time that night, her thoughts went to Monsieur Baillard. Had he genuinely believed in a ghost army that would march to save the Midi? She supposed that now she would never know.

'And the number was ten thousand times ten thousand.'

For the first time in many months, Antoine's words came echoing back into her head, ringing as clear as a bell.

And, for a moment, Sandrine thought she heard something, like she had before. A sense of voices calling out to her, somehow just beyond the limits of her hearing, but there all the same in the shimmering silence.

'A sea of glass …'

Then she realised that what she was hearing was the absence of sound. No longer the lap, the ripple, of water, the noise of the river folding in and over upon itself as Raoul made his way across. She focused her eyes into the darkness, looked for his outline on the far bank.

He was safely across. Her turn now. Carefully, her muscles vibrating with anticipation, Sandrine stepped out into the water. The further she went into the current, the faster the water swirled about her legs, harder and fiercer against her calves, her knees, the backs of her thighs. Deeper, colder, and she struggled not to be knocked off her feet, but she was stronger now, and easily made it to the other side.

Raoul held out his hand and helped her up on to the bank. Together, they traced their way through the woods below the cimetière Saint-Michel, where they removed their night clothes. Sandrine took off her slacks, untucked her dress and tried to smooth out the creases, then from Raoul's bag took her cherry-red shoes. Raoul changed his trousers, took off his pullover and put on a jacket. His felt hat was squashed, but Sandrine pushed it back into shape.

'There,' she whispered, as he shoved their damp clothes into the bag and concealed it in the crooked hollow beneath the gnarled roots of a tree. 'So very smart.'

The curfew was still in place. It was observed rigorously in areas which were considered to be important or sensitive – in Place Carnot near the Milice or Waffen-SS offices, anywhere in the vicinity of any of the German military headquarters – but in quiet residential streets, mostly the patrols allowed the Carcassonnais to go about their business.

'You look beautiful,' Raoul whispered.

Sandrine looked at him in surprise. He wasn't given to paying compliments, even to noticing. Sometimes she felt guilty, silly, for minding about something so unimportant.

'Come on,' he said, taking her hand.

'Where are we going?'

'You'll see.'

He led her towards the café at Païchérou. It was dark inside, with all the chairs tilted forward against the spindly white metal tables. The gates were shut, but they were not locked. He pushed them open a fraction, then pulled her inside.

'What are you doing?' she hissed. 'We don't want to push our luck.'

'There's no one here,' he said, turning her round to face him and sweeping her into his arms.

'Someone will see us!'

He paid no attention. 'Didn't you tell me your father promised to take you dancing at Païchérou on your twenty-first birthday?'

'Well, yes,' she said.

'In his place, I feel it's my duty to step in. A little ahead of time, I grant you. But it's our anniversary, after all.'

She made a half-hearted effort to pull away. 'Our anniversary?'

'It's the thirteenth of July, *ma belle*. Our two-year anniversary's today.'

She became still in his arms. 'I suppose it is,' she said, a smile touching her lips. 'Of course, you're right. It is.'

'And here we are by the same river. Except it's not the Aude any more, but the river Seine.'

'It is?'

'Why not?' he said eagerly, bringing the dream to life. 'This is Paris. Can't you hear the band? The trumpet, the accordion player with his fingers skating over the buttons? Can't you hear Piaf? And here we are, dancing in a down-and-out nightclub on the Left Bank, me in my best suit, you – well, beautiful as always, for our second anniversary, with so many more to come. Listen to the band playing a song for us.'

Raoul began to sing under his breath in the darkness. His voice wasn't strong, but he could hold a tune and the song came from the heart.

'J'ai dansé avec l'amour, j'ai fait des tours et des tours . . .'

Sandrine followed his lead, moving gently in his arms, hearing in her mind the squashed blue notes of the saxophone, the rattle of champagne glasses and the rustle of silk dresses and beads.

'. . . elle et moi, que c'était bon, l'amour avait dans ses yeux tant d'amour, tant d'amour.'

For a moment, the memory of the notes hung in the air. Then, he stepped back and pretended to clap.

'And a round of applause, *mesdames et messieurs*. Another round of applause for *la Môme Piaf* and the band.'

For a moment they stood still, safe in their imaginations. The clouds cleared from the face of the moon and they were lit, uniquely, by silver light filtering through the canopy of the lime trees. Sandrine put her hand on the back of Raoul's neck and drew his face close to hers, kissed him on the lips, then stepped back.

'Thank you,' she whispered, appalled to find her eyes filling with tears.

Sensing the shift in her mood, Raoul twirled her round. 'It was my pleasure, Mademoiselle Vidal.' He nodded. 'Same time, same place next week, perhaps?'

Sandrine could not answer.

Then his mood changed too. Common sense pushed

romance and dreaming back into the shadows again. Carcassonne once more, not the intoxicating perfume of champagne and the melody of Paris.

'We should go,' she said in her everyday voice. Not a voice hoarse with singing or the smoke of an imagined nightclub. She turned towards the gate that they had left ajar.

'Sandrine,' he said quickly, catching at her hand. 'I love you. You know that?'

She stopped. 'I know.'

'And when this is over, all of this, I'll take you dancing every weekend. Every night, if you want to.'

Sandrine smiled. 'Would my feet even stand it?' she whispered.

'Better times round the corner,' he said. 'Like in all those ghastly English songs they're always playing.'

They stood together for a last moment, cheek to cheek, then Sandrine stepped back.

'We must go,' she said quietly. 'We've been here too long.'

Raoul gripped her hand even more tightly. 'I mean it, when it's over, I'm going to show you such a time . . .'

'We'll be all right,' she said, her voice suddenly fierce. 'We'll get through, if we can just hold out for a little bit longer. We'll be fine, you and me. All of us.'

'Yes?'

She heard the doubt in his voice and her heart cracked a little.

'Yes,' she said firmly. 'Yes. Now, come on. You can walk me home, Monsieur Pelletier. And if you're good, I might even let you come in for a cup of cocoa!'

'Cocoa!' he laughed. 'Now that's too English for me! In any case, I should go to the bar and see if Bonnet and Yvette are there. Just in case she's heard anything.'

The smile faded from Sandrine's face. 'Yes,' she said

quietly. 'That's sensible. We should make sure nothing's changed.'

Together, with thoughts of the day ahead in their minds, they walked quietly, quickly through the sleeping streets of Carcassonne. The unreliable moon lighting their way home.

‡

Codex XX

‡

GAUL
TARASCO
JULY AD 344

Arinius stood with his brother-in-law, watching another sunrise over the Vallée des Trois Loups. Each day the soldiers did not come was a reprieve, though he knew the waiting was making the others careless. They were starting to take the threat less seriously.

The Tarascae had taken it in turns to keep watch through the short summer nights. Only a few hours of darkness between dusk and dawn. Each was armed. Those who had fought, either in the service of the Roman army, or to defend their land, held swords or javelins, slings. Many were armed with clubs, knives, their weapons the spoils of war, skirmishes and ambushes, rather than campaigns or battles. Most of the villagers were guerrilla fighters, using the woods and the forests, untrained in the art of fighting but with a raw belligerence suited well to these lawless border lands.

Arinius had a heavy rectangular shield. His old hunting knife was in his right hand, though he prayed he would not be called upon to use it. He was prepared to fight to the death to protect his friends, their community, but he did not wish to take the life of another.

He knew he was being naïve – and that Lupa, had she been there, would have laughed at his moral distinction. She, more than him, was able to reconcile God's commandments with the cruelties of the world in which they lived. For him, though, the gentleness of the gospels, the words of John and Luke sang more truly. His God was a God of light and redemption, not of vengeance and judgement.

He did not wish to kill another human being. Only God, he believed, had that right. And he had seen too much death in his youth, saw how it corrupted and despoiled all that was best in human nature, left a scar on the soul.

'A false alarm, do you think, *peyre*?' one of the young men asked him.

He had tried so many times to make them address him by his name, feeling dishonest and humbled to be singled out and ranked above his station. And '*peyre*' was a strange, local word, a hybrid, neither Latin nor any other language Arinius had come across. But they insisted and he had given up trying to stop them.

'Could it be a false alarm?'

Arinius wanted to give them hope. 'No,' he said. 'I do not think so.'

He could feel the twist and shift of evil in the air, a malignancy like a physical presence stalking them, coming closer.

'No, they are coming,' he said. 'Maybe not tonight, maybe not tomorrow, but they are close at hand. Soon they will be here.' He caught his breath. 'May God deliver us.'

‡

Chapter 117

Carcassonne
July 1944

'But with respect, sir,' Laval said, 'why not arrest them now? Marianne and Sandrine Vidal still live there. Another woman is always there, tall with cropped hair.'

'What did Fournier's sister actually tell you?' Authié demanded.

'That they are discreet, careful to observe the blackout. Sometimes they are out late. Past the curfew.'

Authié had drunk more than he'd intended with Schiffner, then spent the rest of the night going through the surveillance files. It was now five o'clock and he had a headache, but he wasn't ready to call it a night. Laval had spent the past two hours gathering information about interrogations and arrests – firstly, in the past week, then, the past fortnight – going backwards and forwards between the Commissariat and the Feldgendarmerie. Much of it was classified and, although Laval had requested the records, they would not be made available until the morning. But Authié had read enough to have a clear picture of the state of affairs in Carcassonne.

There was a great deal of circumstantial evidence, though no proof, that all three women were involved in partisan activity. Suzanne Peyre, whom Authié remembered, had been taken in on Monday, but released without charge. Authié intended to institute several such raids today. It didn't matter who they arrested or why, only that the population should be aware that there was a new regime in place.

'What about Pelletier? Did she mention seeing him at all?'

'Madame Fournier said she hadn't seen a man answering Pelletier's description,' Laval admitted. 'It doesn't mean he's not there.'

'Have you tried the Quai Riquet?'

'Not yet, sir.'

'Well do it,' he snapped. He rubbed his hand across his forehead. The headache was getting worse.

'Sir,' Laval said cautiously, 'I think we should act now. Raid the house. Arrest everyone there.'

Authié opened his eyes and stared at his lieutenant. For a moment, he wondered if he was right. If it would be better to strike while everyone was asleep. It was only instinct telling him that Sandrine Vidal had anything to do with the device the guards had discovered in the Tour de la Justice – it could have been put there by any partisan group – but since reading the police reports in Toulouse, he had been unable to shake the idea that Sandrine Vidal and 'Sophie' were the same person. And nothing he had read in the surveillance files in the past few hours had caused him to change his mind. If he was right, then even more reason to bide his time.

De l'Oradore had ordered him to find and interrogate Audric Baillard. Sandrine Vidal might be his best chance of tracking down the historian.

'Two birds with one stone,' he repeated to himself.

Authié met Laval's gaze, his moment of indecision over. 'No, we are going to wait. Wait to see what happens in the Cité tonight. See if they – anyone – act. Otherwise, we shall be waiting for them tomorrow.'

He could see from his expression that Laval thought he was wrong.

'But surely . . .'

'I don't want to run the risk of the terrorists calling off their attempt in the Cité.'

'Why would they?' asked Laval.

'Rumours will be spreading that something is planned. Both our side and theirs will be aware of the dinner. I want to give the insurgents something else to think about. Draw their attention to the Bastide and away from the Cité.'

'Very good, sir,' Laval said, though it was clear he didn't understand what Authié was trying to do.

Authié waved his hand. 'Get some sleep, Laval. Check on Madame Pelletier first thing, go back to the Vidal house, then report back. I have set in train a series of raids for tomorrow afternoon. I want the insurgents to believe that those arrests are our main priority.'

Laval saluted, then walked quickly across the room and out into the corridor. The sound of the door slamming ricocheted through Authié's head. He opened his desk drawer and hunted around for an aspirin. It was his own desk, and he had already hung his maps back on the wall. Schiffner had provided space for him in the Feldgendarmerie, rather than on Gestapo premises. It was an odd sensation to be back in the same white building, one floor higher up. As if nothing had changed.

He closed the drawer. There were no aspirin.

Raoul came out of the club and stood on the street. The light was just beginning to turn from a deep blue to the pale white of early morning. His euphoria at their successful operation last night, in setting the bomb and getting away unobserved, had drained away. Now he was left with a vague, anxious feeling in his stomach. He pushed his hands deep into his pockets, breathing in the warm night air. He didn't know what time it was, but it felt nearer to morning than to night.

He wished he hadn't drunk so much. But Robert had kept filling his glass while they waited for Yvette to arrive. Raoul needed to think but his brain was sluggish. All he wanted was to get back to Sandrine and sleep. Sleep and never wake up. He was too tired to think. But something Yvette had said had set off a ripple of alarm in his head. What was it? Why couldn't he think straight?

He headed towards the Canal du Midi, down the shabby side street and on to the towpath. For an instant, he looked across the still water towards the Quai Riquet to see if there was a light burning in his mother's window. He had visited once or twice, but his presence so frightened her – she seemed to think he was a ghost – that he'd given up. Kinder to stay away, though he felt shabby about it.

The window was dark.

He made himself run through yet again what Yvette had said. A telephone call had been received at Gestapo headquarters as she came on shift. Plans for the dinner tomorrow night. Schiffner and his deputies were angry. Someone was coming from Toulouse, but arrived earlier than expected. She hadn't been able to work out if the visitor was German or French, but arrangements were disrupted because of it.

Then what?

Raoul felt his chest tighten. Something was eating away at him, something that struck a wrong note. He kicked a stone into the water. It fell into the canal with a dead splash. He hesitated, a glimmer of a thought piercing his consciousness, but he couldn't get hold of it.

He tried to imagine the scene. The visitor arrives and goes into Schiffner's office. Yvette hears raised voices, but then the telephone rings again and the mood changes. She hears laughing and a trail of cigar smoke comes from under the door. The door opens and the visitor's talking about his girlfriend, or his wife, Yvette can't tell. Pretty name, though. All disjointed, fragments overheard as the door closes again.

Raoul frowned. Yvette said so much, it was hard to work out what mattered and what didn't. He stopped, took his cigarette packet from his pocket and saw he was down to his last two.

Laughing in Schiffner's office, talking about tomorrow. No one much about. Raoul stopped dead, a trickle of realisation finally penetrating his sleep-starved mind. Was that all that was niggling at him? That there *should* have been more going on? That the Gestapo should be on full alert for Authié's arrival? Why wasn't Schiffner in the Cité himself, ensuring the finishing touches were in place? It was an obvious target for an assassination attempt.

Raoul struck a match. Was it possible the visitor from Toulouse was actually Authié? That he had arrived a day early? And that second telephone call, when, as Yvette put it, the mood changed? From the garrison in the Cité? No reason to think so, but yet, now the thought was in his mind, Raoul couldn't shake it. Because if the bomb had been found, then of course Schiffner didn't need to be in the Cité. He already knew what was planned. He just had to sit tight and wait for them to put their plan into action. Schiffner and Authié, laughing and smoking and drinking. Sociable, she'd said.

Finally, he realised. Remembered the one word that had stuck like a splinter under his skin and had been festering there all this time. Yvette's cheerful voice in his head, rattling on and on.

'Such a pretty name. If I'd had a daughter, I'd have called her that. Too late now, I suppose.'

'Sophie,' said Raoul.

Yvette had said the visitor's girlfriend was called Sophie. Except he wasn't talking about his girlfriend.

Raoul began to run, away from the Quai Riquet, across the boulevard Antoine Marty, doubling back towards the rue du Palais just as the birds began to sing.

Chapter 118

Sandrine heard the sound of footsteps on the stairs. She had dozed on and off since she'd got back, running over the events of the night in her mind, but was too full of adrenalin to go to sleep properly. She hated the fact that Raoul hadn't stayed, though she knew it was the right thing to make contact with Robert to see if Yvette had heard anything more. It felt as if they had pushed their luck far enough, and she wished he wasn't out on the streets as the day was dawning.

'Sandrine?' he called.

A rainbow of scattered light from the landing window slipped into the room with him. Sandrine felt relief flood through her. He was back, safe. Now he would come to bed and lie beside her. Kiss her. And, for a moment at least, there would be nothing else.

'Sandrine, wake up.'

She heard the urgency in his voice and sat up, instantly wide awake.

'Raoul? What is it?'

'I think he's already here,' he said, the words tumbling out.

'He? Who, Authié?'

'At Gestapo headquarters with Schiffner. Yvette said there was a visitor from Toulouse.'

'Toulouse? Raoul, slow down. Start again.'

Raoul forced himself to draw breath. 'Yes.' He sat down on the edge of the bed. 'Sorry. Yvette didn't come in until four. She said a visitor arrived unexpectedly. At first it was difficult, but then there was a telephone call and the atmosphere changed. The visitor was talking about his girlfriend, Yvette said, but I think she misunderstood.' He hesitated. 'She heard him say the word "Sophie".'

Sandrine froze. 'They were talking about me?'

'I think so. She also heard them talking about the Cité. She assumed it was to do with the dinner tonight, but again ...'

Sandrine swung her legs out of bed and started to get dressed. Raoul watched her for a moment, then stood up too.

'Is there any proof it was Authié?' she asked, stepping into her slip and dress, her fingers hurrying with the buttons. 'From what she said, I mean?'

'No, but it's logical to assume it was.' He ran his fingers through his hair. 'You didn't notice anything after I left you here last night?'

'No, I did the usual checks before coming in. Madame Fournier was in her position at the window, as always, but there was no one watching the house so far as I could see.'

'You've not heard anything from Marianne and Suzanne? You don't know if they arrived in Coustaussa all right?'

'No, but I told them not to call.'

Sandrine laced her shoes, then they both went quickly out of the bedroom and down the stairs.

'If you're right – if Yvette has passed on what she heard accurately – are you saying you think Authié's come back because of "Citadel"? That his presence is nothing to do with the Codex?'

'I don't know. There's no reason to think anything's changed on that front. Monsieur Baillard is ... well, we don't know where he is. We've both kept our ears to the ground and heard nothing about the Codex.' He sighed. 'In any case, I'm not sure it even matters. Either way, he's searching for you. It makes no difference why. The end result is the same.'

'How would he know I'm "Sophie"?' she said. 'We're jumping to conclusions based on a conversation overheard by Yvette. She could have got the wrong end of things entirely.'

'True.'

Sandrine stopped at the bottom of the stairs, her thoughts racing ahead of themselves. 'There's no reason to think Authié knows about Coustaussa,' she said slowly. 'No one's ever come looking for me there.'

Raoul frowned. 'Are you sure? It must have been common knowledge you used to go out of town for the summer. Madame Fournier must have known.'

'Yes, but my father never liked Monsieur Fournier, or trusted him. He was always courteous, of course, but careful about what he said. Even before the war.'

They walked down the corridor to the kitchen.

'How many people know the house is called CITADELLE?' Raoul asked.

'Not many, actually. The name was a joke of my father's, a bit of fun. He put up the sign, made it himself during the last summer we were there all together.' She broke off, remembering her father's face smiling with pride at his handiwork. 'It only lasted for about two weeks. Papa wasn't awfully practical and the sign wasn't strong. It came down in the first storm.'

'So it's not officially registered under that name?'

Sandrine shook her head. 'No, and what's more, it's actually registered in my mother's maiden name. Saint-Loup.' She saw the look of surprise on Raoul's face. 'It's a huge family, cousins all over the place. It's a very commonplace name.'

'The first time I met her, Eloise Breillac told me you were distantly related. I'd forgotten until now.'

Sandrine smiled. 'It was my mother's family house, not his. Papa always meant to get the deeds changed into his name after she died, but he couldn't bring himself to do it.' She paused. 'Authié would have to dig deep into the records to find the connection. At least, that's what I hope.'

Raoul was frowning. 'But everyone knows Marieta is there, and her connection with you and Marianne. It only takes a neighbour here, or in Coustaussa, to say something in front of the wrong person. It's hardly a secret.'

'I know that,' Sandrine said quietly. 'But there's nothing we can do about it.'

'If Authié's determined to find you, he will.'

'I know that too.' She looked at him, his eyes wild with worry and lack of sleep. 'Let's think it through. Not rush into anything.'

Sandrine filled the kettle with water and put it on the stove to boil. She put a spoonful of tea into the china pot, then took two cups from the dresser and set them ready on the side with the remains of the honey.

'I don't think we can risk going through with the attack on Authié,' Raoul said. 'Even if it wasn't him with Schiffner last night, he'll arrive today. From what Yvette said, they've found the device. If that is the case, Authié won't go anywhere near the Cité tonight. They'll be waiting for us.'

Sandrine poured the hot water on to the leaves.

'They'll flood the Cité with men,' he continued. 'Milice, Gestapo, the Wehrmacht troops garrisoned there as back-up.'

She stirred the pot, then got the strainer and poured the tea into the cups. A half-spoonful of honey each for flavour. Then she joined him at the table.

'I agree,' she said.

Raoul stared. 'You do?'

'I agree that they might very well have found the device,

and plan to simply lie in wait for us to return to detonate it.' She took a deep breath, knowing that Raoul wasn't going to like what she was about to say. 'But I'll still have to go back tonight.'

'Why?' he demanded.

'It's dangerous, Raoul. We can't just leave the device there. Even if the Gestapo are watching the tower every minute of the day, who's to say someone won't find it – a child – and set it off by accident?'

Raoul threw his hands in the air. 'You can't seriously be considering going back to disable it? If I'm right and they have found it – and put guards in the tower itself – you'll be caught.'

'Innocent people could be killed,' she said firmly. 'We can't leave it.'

'If they've found it, you'll never get into the Cité and out again without being seen. It's impossible.'

'Difficult, not impossible,' she said.

'Almost impossible then,' he said sharply.

'Look, they aren't aware that we know they have – might have – discovered the bomb is there.'

'You'll be caught,' he said again.

'I don't think so,' Sandrine continued. 'They will be expecting us to act at the moment Authié's scheduled to arrive in the *lices.* Yes? When they see we're not coming, they'll either remove the device themselves or, more likely, put out that he will be there on another occasion, trying to encourage us to make a move the following day.'

'Or, more likely,' Raoul said, 'they will simply sit it out. Wait for you for as long as it takes. Then arrest you,' Raoul said.

Sandrine raised her hands, then let them drop. 'I know it's a risk, but I can't see any other option.'

'The logical option is to leave it. Hope it doesn't get accidentally detonated. That's the only sensible thing to do.'

'I'm not prepared to do that,' Sandrine said. 'If we kill innocent people, then we're just as bad. We sink to their level.'

Raoul paused. 'OK, if you insist. I'll go.'

Sandrine smiled. 'You can't possibly try to get into the Cité. You'll be stopped straight away. They're less suspicious of women.'

'Not if they're looking for "Sophie",' he said.

Sandrine didn't answer. She knew he was right. For a moment, they both fell silent.

'If you're determined to go through with this,' Raoul said eventually, 'isn't there someone who could go in your place? Authié will recognise you.'

Sandrine sighed. 'We haven't the time to find anyone and besides, I know the device, how it works. It's got to be me.'

There was a knock at the back door. Sandrine glanced at the clock – it was just shy of six o'clock, very early for anyone to be calling. She stood up, immediately on her guard, as Raoul slipped behind the door to the cellar, out of sight. She heard the click as he released the safety catch on his revolver.

'Who is it?' Sandrine said.

'Me,' Lucie whispered through the wire mesh of the fly screen. 'I'm on my own.'

Sandrine let out a long breath. Raoul stepped from his hiding place, putting his gun back in his pocket.

She put her hand to his cheek. 'Before I let her in, are we agreed?'

'I don't like it.'

Sandrine nodded. 'Neither do I,' she said softly.

'Authié has this address. He could be here at any moment.'

'We'll see the plan through tonight, then we'll leave, I promise. Go to Coustaussa. There's nothing more to worry about than there was before, it's just going to take longer to get to Authié than we'd hoped.'

'Sandrine,' Lucie said, a little louder.

'Ask Lucie to go with you,' Raoul said suddenly. 'You can't go alone. Take her.'

Sandrine was about to say no, but then stopped. She could see the sense in his suggestion.

'Actually, that's not a bad idea.'

'Authié won't recognise her, she's changed so much. And she's not known to the Milice or the Gestapo, is she?'

'No.'

'Sandrine!' Lucie repeated. 'Let me in.'

'But I won't pressure her,' Sandrine said, turning the key, 'not if she doesn't want to help. She's got Jean-Jacques to think of.'

She opened the door. 'You took your time,' Lucie said.

There was a pause as she looked at Sandrine, then at Raoul. The colour slipped from her face.

'What's going on?'

'We need your help,' Sandrine said.

Chapter 119

'Are you sure?' Sandrine said for the third time.

Lucie tapped the cigarette Raoul had given her on the side of the glass ashtray. She was pale and her eyes kept darting to and fro.

'I've said so, haven't I?'

'I know, but I want you to be clear about what we're asking of you. It will be dangerous.'

'It's dangerous, I understand. I get it.'

Sandrine exchanged a glance with Raoul, who shrugged.

'No, I mean it, Lucie,' Sandrine persisted. 'This isn't simply delivering a message or smuggling a little paper from one place to another.'

'The consequences are the same, aren't they?' Lucie said. 'I'd have been in trouble if we'd been stopped on Monday morning on our way to the Café des Deux Gares.'

'Yes, but . . .'

Lucie shrugged. 'Well then.'

Sandrine frowned. 'But we've always agreed I'd say you didn't know anything about it if we were stopped and searched.'

'No one would have believed that for a moment,' she said wryly. 'You know as well as I do, I'd have been for it. Same as you, kid.'

Sandrine stared at her.

'Sandrine,' Raoul said gently, 'if Lucie says she's willing to help, then it's her decision.'

Sandrine shook her head. She understood why Raoul wanted Lucie to go with her – it was the only thing he felt he could do to keep her safe – but it felt wrong. She was still not convinced Lucie was aware of what she was agreeing to.

'Maybe it's best if I go alone,' she started to say.

'No,' Raoul said, his voice loud in the quiet of the early morning.

Lucie ground the stub out in the ashtray. 'You want me to help create a diversion,' she said.

'Well, yes,' Sandrine said carefully. 'But if I'm caught, Lucie, and they realise you were helping me, then it will go badly for us both. Do you see?'

'So it's the same story,' Lucie said. 'I'll say I didn't know anything about it.'

'They won't believe you.'

'I'll persuade them,' Lucie said firmly. 'Look, I understand.'

'What about Jean-Jacques?'

'Tonsils,' she said. 'That's what I came to tell you. I thought he was teething, but his temperature kept going up and up. Dr Giraud diagnosed it straight away.'

'Well then, you can't possibly leave him,' Sandrine said in a rush. 'In fact, shouldn't you be with him now?'

'Dr Giraud's taken him into the Clinique du Bastion. He's promised to operate as soon as he can, though it probably won't be until tomorrow morning.' The light faded from her face, revealing how worried she really was. 'It's too risky to smuggle me in too – and if Authié is back, I can't risk my name being on any list – so, well, I had to leave him with Jeanne.' She lowered her voice. 'I'll go out of my mind if I have to sit around doing nothing.'

Now Sandrine was even more worried about Lucie's involvement. The fact that she seemed to see this as a good way to keep her mind off her little boy in hospital proved absolutely that she didn't understand the seriousness of the situation.

'Dr Giraud's excellent,' she said quickly. 'J-J will be in

safe hands. But, really, I think you should go home. Wait for news.'

'I want to help,' Lucie said firmly. 'I can't sit around worrying myself to a thread.'

Raoul stepped in. 'Thank you,' he said firmly. 'I appreciate this. Sandrine does too.'

'I don't think it's a good idea,' Sandrine said, but neither of them paid any attention.

'What time will we leave to go to the Cité?' Lucie said, turning to Sandrine. 'You have a pass, you said? Will I need one too?'

Sandrine glanced up at the time, then gave in. Raoul was right. She had to have someone on lookout, and Lucie was willing to do it.

'Yes, everyone's been issued with an additional special pass for today,' she said. She went to the kitchen table and got two cards from the drawer. 'Suzanne made one for me and left the original too.'

Lucie stared at the blurred photograph. 'It's not a bad likeness. And if I do my hair in the same style, I think I can pass for . . .' she peered at the name, 'Marthe Perard.'

Raoul nodded. 'Authié and Schiffner are supposed to tour the *lices* before dinner, which is scheduled for eight o'clock. Sandrine will need to be in place well before that.'

'You're not going through with it?' Lucie asked. 'Even if Authié does actually make an appearance?'

'No,' Sandrine answered, throwing a glance at Raoul. 'No, in the circumstances, we decided it was too much of a risk. I'm just going to disable the device, so that nobody else gets injured, and get out.' She paused. 'There will be other opportunities with Authié.'

Lucie nodded, but didn't ask anything more.

'You won't be able to come back here,' Raoul said. 'It's likely—'

'Possible,' Sandrine interrupted.

'Likely,' Raoul reiterated, 'Authié will come here as soon as he realises the mission's been aborted. He has this address.'

Lucie blushed. And Sandrine realised that in the same way she still felt she should have done more to stop Max being taken, Lucie still felt guilty for talking to Leo Authié.

'Oh, Lucie,' she said in a rush, 'it was such a long time ago. There's nothing to make up for, not now.'

'I know, kid,' Lucie said. 'But even so …'

'It's all forgotten.'

'Forgotten, no.' Lucie met her gaze. 'Two years ago, you came with me to Le Vernet. Despite what I'd done, talking to Authié. It was stupid to go and I shouldn't have let you take the risk. But I was an idiot and you came all the same.' She caught her breath. 'You did it for me. For Max, though you didn't know him. And even before we knew Max wasn't going to be coming back, you and Marianne took Liesl in too.' She looked at Sandrine. 'Do you see now, kid?'

For a moment, they just looked at one another.

'Yes,' Sandrine said. And for the first time since they had put the plan to Lucie, she thought it might be all right. She'd underestimated Lucie. Assumed she was walking into this without thinking, when in fact she knew precisely what she was doing. And why. 'Yes, I see.'

'Good,' Lucie said briskly. 'That's settled then.' She pulled a handkerchief from her sleeve, blew her nose, then nodded, to confirm the decision taken.

Sandrine glanced at Raoul and saw the relief in his face.

'Happy now?' she murmured, taking his hand.

He laughed. 'Less unhappy.'

'What are you going to do?' she asked. 'I don't think Authié will come here before tonight, but he might. You shouldn't stay here.'

'I agree.'

'Where will you go? Can Robert Bonnet help?'

'Home,' he said quietly. He gave a long, weary sigh.

'Do you mean the Quai Riquet?' Sandrine said with surprise. She knew he felt bad about how infrequently he visited his mother, but he thought it kept her safer. 'Has something happened? Has her neighbour been in touch with you?'

Raoul shook his head. 'No. But when we leave tonight, we're not likely to be back. Are we? Not now Authié's here.' He sighed. 'I owe it to her to say goodbye.'

'She didn't know you last time, did she?' Sandrine said quietly. 'Are you sure it's not better to leave her be?'

'Other people have looked after her, when it should have been me,' he said. 'I've stayed away. For the right reasons, but I feel I owe it to her.'

'Authié might have put the apartment under surveillance, have you considered that?'

'I doubt it. I've barely been there in two years, anyone would say the same. There's no reason for him to think I'd be there.'

Sandrine didn't want him to go, though she accepted he had to spend the next twelve hours somewhere. But every time he went into the Bastide, she was terrified he'd be spotted and picked up. It hadn't happened yet, but that didn't mean anything. It only meant their luck had held.

'I don't think ...' she began, then stopped herself. 'Be careful,' she whispered.

'Aren't I always?' He smiled. 'Where shall we meet? You shouldn't come back here either.'

'No.'

Raoul rested his hand against her cheek. 'What about *chez* Cazaintre?' he said. 'I'll make sure the side gate's open.'

Sandrine nodded. 'All right.'

Lucie frowned. 'Where's that? Is it a bar? Would I have heard of it?'

Sandrine shook her head. 'Cazaintre was the architect of the Jardin du Calvaire in the 1820s. It's one of the places we use as a drop-off and collection point for *Libertat*.'

'One of them?'

'That's right. "The Naiads" is the fountain in Place Carnot, "Monsieur Riquet's bathing house" is the steps on the north side of the Canal du Midi and "Monsieur Courtejaire is asleep" means that the pick-up is Courtejaire's grave in the cimetière Saint-Michel.'

Lucie smiled. 'Smart.'

'It's worked so far,' Sandrine said.

Raoul took her hand. 'I'll wait there until you come.'

She smiled, masking the way the nerves were already hammering in her chest.

'Don't worry,' she said. 'It's going to be all right. You'll see. This time tomorrow, we'll be in Coustaussa.'

Chapter 120

TARASCON

A silver mist skimmed the tops of the trees on the slopes below the Pic de Vicdessos, as dawn began to give colour back to the world.

Audric Baillard had come alone, leaving the house before first light while Pujol was still sleeping off the effects of the previous evening's wine. He thought Pujol would have tried to stop him or else insisted on accompanying him. Neither suited Baillard's purposes. He knew these old Cathar routes like the back of his hand. Despite his weakened state, he was certain he could evade any Nazi patrols operating in the mountains. More, he didn't want to put his old friend at risk.

He looked down at the milk-white scrap of cloth in his hand, Arinius' map of where the Codex had been hidden some sixteen hundred years before. Safe, there, for all that time. For a moment, in the shimmering dawn, Baillard suddenly saw his younger self reflected back at him. A boy still, being entrusted with another map by his grandmother, a map leading him and those for whom he was responsible to the village of Los Seres.

'La Vallée des Trois Loups,' he said aloud. Eloise and Geneviève had told him the valley had such a name, though it appeared on no map. Even with his extensive knowledge of the myths and legends of the hills, he had never heard it called that.

He closed his eyes. As the timelessness of the ancient forests and mountains seeped into his tired bones, another memory. Himself as a young man – no older than Raoul Pelletier was now, no older than Viscount Trencavel when he gave his life to save the people of Carcassonne – travelling through these lands during another occupation. Remembering how the Inquisitors went from village to village, accusing and denouncing and condemning. Spies everywhere, neighbour denouncing neighbour, until no one knew who to trust. Corpses exhumed to be burnt as heretics. The Cathars and freedom fighters of the Midi being pushed back and back into the mountains. The raid in Limoux just days ago, reminding him of another raid in the peaceful mountain town where friends of his had been seized. The inquisitional courts, mirrored now by the trials conducted by the Gestapo. And those few who survived the interrogation to be released, forced to wear a scrap of yellow cloth stitched to their garments.

A cross then, a star now.

Baillard shook his head. The time had come. While he was imprisoned in Rivesaltes, he had not been able to act. The decision had been taken from him. Now he could avoid it no longer. As he looked up at the ridges and crests ahead and compared them to Arinius' map, he knew he was in the right place. Although the forest had been cut back over the centuries, the essential landscape remained unchanged.

Now, as then.

In his youth, Baillard had taken a vow to bear witness. To speak out so that the truth should not die. He had given his word. He had known great joy in his life, but also great sorrow. His destiny was to watch those he loved live and grow old. In time, to die. Generation unto generation.

He allowed his thoughts to fly north to Chartres. It was a city that had been part of his life for so long, even though he had never been there. Several times he had tried, several times he had failed. He had never seen the labyrinth in the nave of the great Gothic cathedral. He had never met the descendants of those he had fought so long ago and fought against still. But he knew the jackals were coming. Once more, from Chartres to Carcassonne. The names were different – Leo Authié and François Cecil-Baptiste de l'Oradore – but their intentions were the same. Coming, as Baillard's enemies had done before, in search of the secrets of the Languedoc.

As he stood in solitude, the soft morning air on his face, Baillard knew he was not yet strong enough to begin the climb into the mountains. But he needed to be here, in the peace and silence, to make his decision. To listen to the voices and to hope they would guide him.

'*Per lo Miègjorn*,' he murmured.

In his head, he heard the battle cry. Trencavel's brave *chevalier*s attempting to defend the Cité against the northern crusaders. The clash of steel and the sweet, hot smell of blood. In a matter of days, the Jewish quarter had been destroyed, the suburbs of Sant-Vincens and Sant-Miquel put to the flame, the women and men of Carcassonne expelled like refugees from their homes.

Then, as now.

There was no doubt in his mind. He would return, as soon as he had gathered his strength. He would gather to him those who would help him. Sandrine Vidal and Raoul Pelletier, Achille Pujol and Eloise and Guillaume Breillac. With their help, he would retrieve the Codex and bring it down from the mountain.

Most of all, Sandrine Vidal.

He did not know why he was certain that she was so important in this story, only that she was. Two years ago she had told him of the dreams she sometimes had at night. Of the sensation of slipping out of time, falling from one dimension into another through white space. Of the indistinct figures hunting her down – white and red and black and green – their faces hidden beneath hoods and shadow and flame. The glint of metal where should have been skin. Baillard did not know yet what the Codex contained, but he recognised echoes of the Book of Revelation in her nightmares and wondered at it.

Was she linked in some way to the Codex and its history? Was it chance, or was there a design behind the fact that Sandrine had come upon Antoine Déjean at the river that day and heard the words he spoke? Happenstance or destiny?

Baillard sighed. Once more, he was being called upon to drive the invaders from the green lands of the Languedoc. Once more, to fight to liberate the Midi. To protect the ancient secrets buried in the mountains. He turned to the west, where the labyrinth cave lay hidden within the folds of the Sabarthès mountains. Then returned his eyes to the images on the milk-white scrap of cloth.

Baillard feared the power of the Codex. He feared he would not be equal to the task and would fail to control the forces that might be unleashed. But he was resolved to act. He had no other choice, whatever the consequences might be.

'Come forth the spirits of the air.' He spoke the words that had lain in the dusty recesses of his mind through his long captivity. 'Come forth the armies of the air.'

He paused. He listened. And, carried on the air, he heard the land begin to answer.

'*Benlèu*,' he whispered. Soon.

Chapter 121

CARCASSONNE

Raoul didn't want to leave, but Sandrine sent him away as soon as the curfew was lifted. She and Lucie needed to get ready and he shouldn't be out on the streets for any longer than absolutely necessary.

'And you can't stay here,' she said.

Raoul put his arms around her waist and drew her to him. 'Be careful, *ma belle*.'

She smiled. 'You too.'

'*Chez* Cazaintre.'

Sandrine nodded. 'And don't be late!' She leant forward and kissed him.

Raoul left the rue du Palais by the garden gate, into the rue du Strasbourg, down to the riverbank and along. He took an even more circuitous route than usual, to make sure he wasn't being followed. His eyes darted left and right, watching for patrols or Milice informers. Every journey he was obliged to make during daylight hours was undertaken with a knot in his chest, hands balled into fists, his heart bumping one beat into the next.

No one paid him any attention.

He went out of town towards the Aire de la Pépinière, then doubled back to approach the Quai Riquet from the route de Minervois. There was a blind corner underneath the railway bridge by the station. Coming at it from the eastern side of the Bastide, he could see the whole sweep of the road clearly.

There were no police, no military vehicles, no sounds.

Nothing to see but the ripple of the Canal du Midi, and no noise but the water lapping against the wooden hulls of the barges moored on the riverbank.

Raoul walked quickly along the narrow pavement in the light of the rising sun and into the building. Careful not to hurry, careful not to idle. The street door to the building where his mother lived stood open, as it always had done. The familiar smell in the hallway, polish and the chill of the floor tiles, caught at his heart. Taking him back to a time when he and Bruno had been rough-and-tumble brothers, eager every morning to be allowed out to play. Watching the barges transporting food and grain along the Canal du Midi, the coopers with barrels of beer and wine from Toulouse, the stevedores with their wide-brimmed hats and faces tanned dark by the sun. Sometimes a *sou* for holding a horse's harness while the men went to the down-and-out bar to drink after the sun had gone down.

He took a deep breath, banishing the ghosts of the past, then mounted the stairs two by two to the first floor. It seemed strange to do it, but he didn't want to scare his mother, so he knocked at the door. Nothing happened. He heard no footsteps, no sound from the wireless or voices talking. He hesitated, then fished the latch key out of his pocket. He put it into the lock and turned.

'*Maman, c'est moi*,' he said, stepping into the apartment.

The silence surged around him like a living thing, curious and intrusive. It seemed cold in the flat, though Raoul couldn't have said why.

'*Maman?*'

A sense of foreboding swept through him.

'It's me, Raoul.'

There was a strange noise he couldn't identify. High-pitched, angry, like a thousand flies trapped in a boy's jar. The buzzing and humming, and the smell. A putrefying stench that seemed to seep from under the door, sticking to his skin and his hair and his clothes. He looked down and saw that he was standing in water.

'*Maman*,' he said, fear catching in his throat. Or was it grief?

Raoul put out his hand and pushed open the door into the kitchen. Time stopped. He seemed to be looking down on the scene from outside. His hand on the wooden panel of the door – eyes open, heart thudding, the pulse of blood in his head – and seeing, but being unable to take in what he saw. And the sound. The drone of the buzzing and the humming of the black cloud around his mother's face.

She was sitting in a chair facing the kitchen window. Her body was swollen, purple turning to black, plump in death as she had not been in life. Raoul swallowed hard, snatching his handkerchief from his pocket and clamping it over his nose and mouth. Struggling to keep his emotions in check, he forced himself to think.

Think, not feel.

He had seen men die. Seen their bodies decay when they couldn't be reached to bring them back to base, in France's six weeks of fighting in May 1940. So he knew that the death chill that set in immediately was followed, within two to six hours, by rigor mortis. From cold to warm again, it was only days later that the body started to putrefy. Bloating, swelling, turning in upon itself.

The arrangement had been that their neighbour came in every other day. But what if she had forgotten? What if she'd been arrested? What if she stopped bothering, knowing no one else would come?

Was this his fault?

Raoul stood still, his emotions suspended, aware of the lap of water around his shoes, yet unable to process the information. When had his mother died? Two days ago? Three? Where had he been when she'd taken her last breath? In Limoux, in Carcassonne?

Feeling as if everything was happening to someone else – a man who looked like him, stood like him, grieved like him – Raoul looked around the room. He realised the tap was running into the overflowing sink. He crossed the room in a couple of strides and turned it off, then took the plug out. A gurgle and a gulp and the sink began to drain. He leant forward and opened the window as high as it would go, then rushed through the flat opening every other window to let the foul smell seep out. He couldn't bring himself to go closer to the chair where his mother sat.

There were no obvious signs that anyone had been here, but he had to be sure. People didn't just die. They didn't just sit in a chair and stop breathing. Did they?

What had happened?

Raoul shook his head, numb with disbelief. He should do something. Call the undertaker, ensure that the dignity that had been taken from her in the hour of her passing was restored to her. Be a good son in this, at least. But he couldn't, not yet.

He searched the flat. In each room, the same story. His distress grew, his sense of failure at having let her become so ill. Having left her alone. Everywhere were the scribbled notes, the same words written over and over again. On scraps of newspaper, on the cover of a paperback book, on the brown-paper packaging of a loaf of bread delivered and not eaten.

'*Les fantômes*,' he muttered. Ghosts.

He screwed up the scrap of newspaper and threw it to the floor. The cheap paper swelled in the centimetre of water, then opened up like a flower.

A shiver went down his spine. He remembered how she stood at the kitchen window, looking out. Waiting for Bruno to come. How much it had frustrated him and upset him and made him angry, because he could do nothing to assuage her grief. All the time talking about how the ghosts would come, that the spirits were waking.

Ghosts?

He had dismissed all of it as delusion. The result of grief and heartbreak too much to bear, and the loss of her favourite son. But that was then. Before he met Sandrine, before he sat in Coustaussa and listened to Monsieur Baillard tell stories of the Codex and a ghost army that might save the Midi.

Raoul ran back into his mother's bedroom, throwing everything to one side, searching for something he'd seen on her nightstand. He took a deep breath and looked down at the desperate message. An empty pill bottle, was that it? But everywhere, words printed in block capitals in pencil on a sheet of cheap blue writing paper: FANTÔMES, ARMÉE, MONTAGNES. Then, on the lines beneath, single words written over and over again like an embroidered pattern: VERRE VERRE VERRE, FEU FEU FEU.

'Glass and fire,' he murmured.

He rushed back into the sitting room, thinking he must tell Sandrine. See what she thought. Then he remembered. She and Lucie were on their way to the Cité.

Finally, the horror hit him.

He turned round and saw his mother, for the first time saw her as she was. He doubled over, sorrow and pity ripping his insides open, and emptied his guts. Raoul realised, now, of course. His mother had been dead for two days. The anniversary of Bruno's birthday. How had she done it? Those pills? Or had her heart simply stopped beating? She had kept going, but where was the sense in it? The loss did not get easier to bear and the war did not end. Bruno was dead and he – the son she did not miss – never came.

Raoul gathered his mother's last testament – the ghosts that only she had been able to see – and left the apartment where he had spent the first eighteen years of his life.

He slipped a note under the door of their neighbour on the ground floor, hoping no harm had come to her, then stepped out into the street.

The peaceful sunlight on the canal mocked the horror of the scene in the room he had left. Raoul hesitated for a moment, then turned and walked to the underground bar. He didn't know if it would be open or if they would let him in without a password, but he couldn't think of anywhere else to go.

Was it his fault?

The hatch slid back. He sensed a pair of eyes looking at him, then the grating sound of the bolt being shot, and the door opened a fraction.

'I need a drink.'

A hand pulled him inside. Raoul heard the door shut behind him. He turned to thank the man and found, for some reason, he couldn't see him properly. He raised his hand to his eyes and realised that his cheeks were wet.

'Sandrine,' he whispered, wanting only for her to be with him. For her to be safe.

'Come on,' the man said. His voice was gruff, but kind. 'There's one or two others in already.'

Chapter 122

The *milicien* stood to attention when Laval came into the room. Laval took no notice of him, merely strode to the side window and looked out, then moved to the front window which gave on to the rue du Palais itself. The street was empty in both directions.

'No one's approached the house?'

'No, sir.'

'So as far as we know, the subjects are still inside?'

'Yes, sir.'

'Anyone else?'

'Not that I've seen.'

The police officer was too scared to admit he had fallen asleep at his post. He'd come on duty at six, after a late shift at the railway yard – every night there were attempts on the rolling stock, thefts of metal and wood – his second in a row. The combination of the stuffiness of the house and the shot of brandy Madame Fournier had given him to perk him up had sent him off for ten minutes, possibly more. He thought he might have heard something, voices perhaps, but he wasn't sure if they'd come from the house next door or the street. He decided to say nothing.

Madame Fournier, her hands clasped in front of her, appeared in the doorway.

'Is there anything I can get you, *monsieur lieutenant*?' she asked. 'Anything you need? Or your men need?'

'No,' Laval said abruptly.

He found her presence irritating – he always hated undertaking surveillance in civilian houses – and her need to be useful repelled him. Madame Fournier's face hardened for a moment, then settled back into its habitual obsequious expression.

'Well, if you do, let me know,' she said, and went away.

The *milicien* glanced at her disapproving back. Laval ignored her. In his opinion, she had been of limited help. In addition to Marianne and Sandrine Vidal, and Suzanne Peyre, she'd said there was another woman with a little boy who visited occasionally. When pressed, she said that 'foreign-looking' men did sometimes call. Laval knew her type. Trying to make herself important.

Laval glanced at the clock, then back to the road. In the absence of hard evidence, he did not share Authié's conviction it was Sandrine Vidal – with or without Raoul Pelletier's assistance – who'd set the device in the Tour de la Justice. Apart from the sentry confirming something was there, they had not gone into the tower on Authié's orders. He didn't want the insurgents to know that it had been spotted.

Laval still thought Authié had made a mistake in not raiding the Vidal house the previous night, even though it suited his purposes to be able to be in the rue du Palais at this point.

After more than two years at Authié's side, he had learnt to read his commanding officer well. He was aware that Authié had evidence to implicate him in the murder of Bauer and his men in August 1942. He also knew Authié had been shocked when de l'Oradore, a devout Catholic, had not destroyed the Codex. The words had been condemned by the Church in the fourth century. Authié assumed that instruction still held good in the twentieth.

Now it appeared the document was a forgery. This time Laval knew Authié would not hand the Codex over. He would deal with the matter himself, believing he'd been given a second chance. He had told Laval as much.

Which was why Laval had to make sure he found the Codex before Authié did. And he agreed that the surest way was to find Sandrine Vidal. He, too, had a second chance.

Laval glanced again at the clock. His visitor should be here at any moment. A middle-ranking officer and senior archaeologist working for the Ahnenerbe, he reported directly to Reichsführer Himmler. In return for handing over the Codex, Laval would be given a guarantee of safe passage to Berlin if – when – the Wehrmacht pulled out of the Aude.

Laval heard footsteps on the stairs, then another *milicien* came into the room.

'A man approaching the house, sir.'

Immediately the atmosphere changed. Laval turned to face him.

'Front or back?'

'Front.' He paused. 'German, sir. Not one of ours.'

Laval moved to the window and saw a tall man, black cap, black tunic and breeches, black dress boots, on his arm the distinctive insignia – the double sig rune – of the Ahnenerbe.

'You,' he ordered, pointing at the first *milicien*, 'keep Madame Fournier out of the way.' He turned to his colleague. 'You, let our visitor in. No one is to do anything – anything at all – except on my orders. Is that clear?'

Raoul was sitting with Robert Bonnet. The bar was tawdry and down at heel in the harsh light of day. It smelt of yesterday's sweat and spilled beer and stale tobacco. The owner didn't want trouble. Having let Raoul in, he'd taken one look at him, at the state he was in, and sent someone to fetch Bonnet.

'You did what you could, Pelletier,' Robert said again.

Raoul ran his finger round the top of his glass. He felt

crushed by guilt, by the horror of what he'd witnessed. Bonnet had taken charge and sent Yvette to the undertaker with an unsigned note asking him to call at the Quai Riquet – none of them could risk giving their names. The undertaker would publish details in the newspaper of the funeral arrangements.

'I didn't do enough. I handed over my responsibility to someone else. I should have made sure she—'

'Pelletier,' Bonnet said sharply, putting his hand on Raoul's arm, 'she'd had enough. You told me that almost the first time we met. When was that? Three years ago, give or take? You said then she had never got over your brother's death. If anything, you should be pleased with yourself that you kept her alive for so long.'

'Why wasn't the neighbour there?' Raoul put his head in his hands. 'When did she leave? My mother …' He paused, then began again. 'She must have felt abandoned, no one coming to see if she was all right. What if she wanted help?'

'You found the bottle empty,' Robert said quietly.

Raoul felt numb, dead through shock.

'If she wanted to go,' Bonnet continued, 'there's not a thing you – or anyone else – could have done to stop her. If it's any consolation, she won't have suffered. Pills, all very peaceful. Just gone to sleep and not woken up. It's what she chose.'

'But the state of the place, Bonnet,' Raoul said, picturing the scraps of paper, the words written on every surface, over and again. 'She wasn't in her right mind. She can't have been.'

'The doctor will record it as a heart attack,' Bonnet said. 'You needn't worry about that.'

Raoul looked up at him. He hadn't even been thinking about what would happen if her death was registered as a suicide.

'It was no one's fault,' Bonnet continued. 'One of those things you couldn't do anything about.'

Raoul knew Bonnet was doing his best to help. 'If you'd known her before, before Bruno died, before she got ill. A wonderful woman. One of those rare people, popular with everyone. Our friends, neighbours. No one had a bad word to say about her.'

Robert nodded, letting him talk.

'Never the same after my brother died,' he continued, knowing he was repeating things he'd already said. 'She never got over it.'

Bonnet got up and went back to the bar, returning with another couple of glasses of what passed for beer.

'What are we doing, Bonnet?' Raoul gestured at the empty bar. 'Look at us, cowering underground. Everything we do, all of this? Does it even make any difference?'

'You know it does.'

Raoul suddenly stopped. He shouldn't drink any more, he knew that, but he was caught between grief and fear. And guilt. His mother dead in the apartment. Sandrine somewhere in the Bastide. Making her way towards the Cité. Perhaps she was inside already?

Caught?

He rubbed his eyes. The not knowing was the worst of it. Sitting on his hands, unable to do anything. He had a flash of insight into what it must have been like for Sandrine over these past months when he'd been in the mountains. Never knowing if he was alive or dead.

'I let her down.'

Robert lit a cigarette, handed it to Raoul, then took one for himself. 'No sense thinking like that,' he said.

He shook his head. 'If you'd seen the mess, Bonnet. Water everywhere. Paper everywhere . . . Awful.'

Raoul slumped forward, elbows on the table, going over in his mind the arguments Sandrine had put forward about why it should be her who went back to the Tour du Grand Burlas, not him. Her reasons had made sense at the time, but not any more.

What kind of man was he that he'd let her go?

'I should have stopped her,' he muttered.

'I'm telling you, Pelletier, there was nothing you could have done. Your mother knew what she was doing.'

Raoul shook his head. 'Not my mother,' he said. 'Sandrine.'

For a moment, Robert sat very still, then he dropped his voice. 'She'll be all right,' he said. 'She's special, that girl of yours. She knows what she's doing.'

Raoul looked at him, remembering a similar conversation he'd had with a young boy in the hills outside Belcaire. Fiercely in love, carrying a photograph of his girl, Coralie Saint-Loup. They were still out there, so far as he knew, doing their best. Trying to live normal lives in the middle of all the madness.

'When all this is over, you should make an honest woman of her,' Bonnet continued.

Raoul nodded. 'Will you stand as my best man, Bonnet?'

'It'd be an honour.' He drained his glass and stood up. 'But you're no use to her like this, Pelletier. Let's get you sobered up. Sandrine will be back soon. You need to be ready. Yes?'

Raoul met his gaze. He knew Bonnet was right. His mother was beyond his help. Yesterday, he had held Sandrine in his arms and comforted her. He had looked after her. He needed to be ready to look after her again, if she'd let him. Pushing his three-quarters-full glass away, he stood up.

'Thanks, Bonnet,' he said quietly.

'You'd do the same for me.'

'I would.'

Raoul felt his heart return to its regular beat, his resolve strengthen. The knot of fear in his chest loosened just a little. Life went on. Maybe it shouldn't, but it did, all the same. They had to hold their nerve a little longer. Then it would be over. Everyone said it would be over soon.

'Ready?'

Raoul nodded. Bonnet raised his hand to the barman, then the two men walked to the narrow stairs that led up to the pavement.

'I'll stand for you, Pelletier, and you can do the same for me and Yvette,' Bonnet said. 'What about that?'

'Have you asked her?'

Bonnet patted his pocket. 'Not yet. Waiting for the right time.'

As he waited for the door to be unbolted, Raoul tried the name out in his head. Madame Raoul Pelletier. He smiled. No, Madame Sandrine Pelletier. He thought it suited her. A strong name.

The doorman shot the bolt. Raoul took a deep breath. 'I'll go first,' he said. 'And thanks again.'

The doorman checked the street was empty. He gave a brief nod, and without a backward glance Raoul stepped out into the sunshine and headed back towards the Aire de la Pépinière to wait out the afternoon.

'The library was evacuated to Ulm,' the Nazi said. 'For a year now since the Allied bombing of Hamburg.'

'That's where you want me to deliver the Codex?' Laval asked.

The Nazi narrowed his eyes. 'If it should take longer than you anticipate – and I am therefore unable to take the document with me personally – then you will make arrangements.'

'But you are based in Swabia?' Laval persisted.

'I am not. While the library was taken to Ulm, the Ahnenerbe staff were located to Waischenfeld in Bavaria.

It is a small village, but at the centre of operations all the same.'

Bavaria was the heartland of Nazi support, even now as the tide was turning against the Axis forces.

'You'll provide appropriate papers?' Laval asked. 'A guarantee of safe passage?'

'If you deliver what you promise, Herr Laval, you will be coming to Germany as our guest. There will be no difficulties.'

Laval nodded. 'How long do you intend to remain in Carcassonne, Unterscharführer Heinkel?'

'A day or two at most.'

Laval held out his hand. 'Then we shall see what might be achieved in the next forty-eight hours.'

The two men shook hands. Laval showed him out. Madame Fournier was lurking behind the half-open kitchen door. He affected not to see her. She wouldn't say anything that would lead Authié – anyone – to think that the meeting was out of the ordinary. However, it was important neither of the *miliciens* said anything out of turn. Laval didn't think they'd identified Heinkel's SS rank or realised he was not from the unit involved in the surveillance operation, but he needed to be sure.

He shouted for the pair and they came running, one from the back of the house and one down from the first floor.

'According to the liaison officer, everything is as planned,' Laval said sharply. 'All personnel are in position in the Cité. I have reported that there has been no activity around the Tour de la Justice this morning, but I have given assurances that you will both remain at your posts here and radio immediately should anything change.' He looked at the two men in turn, fixing them each with a cold, appraising eye. 'Clear?'

'Yes, sir.'

'Sir.'

Laval nodded. He looked at the clock. The meeting with Heinkel had lasted longer than he'd expected, which didn't give him much time before he was due to report to Authié at two and then to go to the Cité himself. He needed something to demonstrate he had been active during the morning. Information on the French scholar that de l'Oradore had asked Authié to obtain. He would return to the police archives and see what – if any – information they were holding on Audric Baillard.

'I will return at five,' he said. 'When does your shift finish?'

'At six, sir.'

'Good.' Laval nodded. 'In the meantime, if anyone goes in or out, inform headquarters.'

Chapter 123

Sandrine and Lucie sat on a bench in Square Gambetta. Both wore headscarves, plain summer dresses and flat lace-up shoes. They looked like any other Carcassonnais women ground down by the daily struggle of trying to get by.

Sandrine hadn't wanted to risk staying in the house, so she and Lucie had spent the time moving from place to place in the Bastide. They avoided their usual haunts, in case they were being followed, staying instead in public places where there were more people coming and going.

Her plan was that they should change their clothes once they were on the Cité side of the river. Although security was always tight – and it would be tighter than ever today – there were usually girls in the garrison, *collabos horizontales*. The soldiers turned a blind eye.

The heat had driven most people indoors, but four little girls were playing *un, deux, trois loup* on the steps of the bandstand. A podgy child with pigtails and a checked dress spun around and roared, and her friends scattered squealing.

'You notice the wolf always wins,' Lucie said.

Sandrine smiled. 'The odds are stacked in her favour.'

She looked over at the statue. For a split second, with the shimmering heat haze and the deep contrast between the light and the shade, she could have sworn she saw the angel's stone wings move. Her white hands grasp the sword tighter. She frowned and blinked, then looked again. This time the folds of wing and feather were lifeless and fixed firmly in place.

Sandrine caught her breath.

'Are you all right?' Lucie asked.

'Yes.' She gave a sharp shake of her head, bringing herself back to the present. 'What about you? Not worrying too much about Jean-Jacques?'

Lucie shrugged. 'You can't help yourself, you worry all the time anyway.' She glanced at Sandrine, then back to the still waters of the lake in the centre of the gardens. 'You'll have a son of your own one day, then you'll know.'

A son, Sandrine thought. A son or a daughter. Actually, she'd prefer a daughter first. Maybe two girls, like her and Marianne. For a moment, she allowed her thoughts to float free, thinking of ribbons and smocked dresses and Marieta drawing a bath with soap bubbles on a Sunday evening in readiness for school the next day.

Then the sound of the bells of Saint-Michel floated across the Bastide in the hot afternoon air and the smile faded from Sandrine's face. She felt Lucie turn to look at her.

'Time to move on again?' she asked.

Sandrine nodded and got up. 'We're going to cross the river now.'

'Whatever you say, kid.'

They crossed Square Gambetta and went past the hospital, then joined the queue of people waiting to be allowed across the Pont Vieux. Sandrine was nervous and her heart was beating nineteen to the dozen. From Lucie's quick, small steps, Sandrine knew she was on pins too.

'*Ausweis*,' the guard said.

In silence, Sandrine handed over the false identity card. The soldier scanned it and thrust it back at her without a word. Then he took Lucie's, looked at it closely and glanced up at her face. Sandrine held her breath, but Lucie kept her nerve. She didn't look nervous or smile or do anything to suggest she was worried. After a few tense seconds, the soldier gave it back and waved them both past the checkpoint and on to the bridge.

'Danke schön,' Sandrine said.

They went through the same procedure with the Wehrmacht soldiers manning the concrete fortifications on the far side of the bridge. Again, the time dragged as their cards were checked, but then they were through and walking into rue Trivalle.

Sandrine forced herself not to hurry, not to give them away by rushing or looking wary. During the course of the day, she'd revised the plan. Rather than go in through the Porte Narbonnaise, putting the false cards to the test, she'd decided it might be better to see if the route into the Cité she and Raoul had used last night was still a possibility. Unless a local had pointed it out, the soldiers might not be aware of the secondary gate – it wasn't visible from the inner fortifications. And even if the Wehrmacht or Gestapo had brought in Milice to sweep the area, in the south-west quadrant of the Cité, too, there was still cover from trees and bushes.

If they had found the gate, or if there were soldiers outside the walls, not only posted in the *lices*, then Sandrine intended to continue round to the Porte Narbonnaise and revert to her original plan.

'This way,' she said.

She guided Lucie to the right and along rue de la Barbacane. To her credit, Lucie didn't miss a step, just followed Sandrine. They walked past the rue de la Gaffe, where the Giraud family lived, then crossed in front of the église Saint-Gimer, left into rue Petite Côte de la Cité and right into rue Longue. She stopped at the fourth house along, knocked three times on the wooden shutter. She paused, then knocked again.

The door was opened, though Sandrine saw no one. They found themselves in a dark hallway, with a door standing open to the right. Without a word, Sandrine and Lucie removed their scarves, sensible shoes and dresses, and put on the cheap, gaudy dresses laid out on the chairs. Lucie clipped on white plastic earrings and a matching necklace. Sandrine tightened a wide patent belt with a gold buckle around the waist of her shiny green dress and slipped her feet into the high heels set beside the hearth.

Lucie produced a tube of red lipstick. She leant forward, looking at her reflection in the mirror above the mantelpiece, then handed it to Sandrine.

'Powder?' she offered.

Sandrine shook her head. 'This'll do,' she said. 'And you're quite sure you want to go through with this? It's not too late to back out.'

'I'm sure, kid.'

Leaving their old clothes in the room, together with a bottle of rosé as payment, the girls let themselves out. Moving more slowly now, in their heels, they walked to the end of rue Longue, through a switchback of alleyways, then on to the chemin des Anglais. All the time, Sandrine was watching for patrols, for soldiers, for police. They got almost all the way to the top of the road before their luck ran out.

A jeep carrying four Wehrmacht soldiers was coming towards them. Sandrine hoped they would be too busy to stop, but since they were on the edge of a restricted area, she knew the odds were against them.

One of the soldiers gave a wolf whistle, but was immediately silenced by a look from the commanding officer, who jumped down, his lieutenant beside him, and walked over.

'Captain,' said Lucie brightly.

He didn't smile. '*Ausweis*,' he demanded, holding out his hand.

Both women again got out the false cards and passed

them over in silence. He returned Sandrine's card, but stared more carefully at the image on Lucie's.

'This is you?' he said, holding the photograph close to Lucie. 'Marthe Perard?'

'It is,' she said, putting on a blowsy voice. 'It's an old photograph and there's a little less of me than there was.' She shrugged. 'Not so good for the looks. Ever so difficult to find what a girl needs.'

In the truck, one of the soldiers sniggered.

'*Ruhe!*' the captain shouted.

'It's a restricted zone,' he said in stilted but accurate French.

'Even for ladies with an invitation?' Lucie said.

The captain flushed. For a long moment, Sandrine thought he might insist on accompanying them. But he returned her card.

'Present your papers at the Porte Narbonnaise,' he said coldly. 'If your names are on the list, you will of course be permitted to enter.'

'Thanks ever so,' Lucie giggled. '*Danke*.'

The captain and lieutenant got back into the truck and continued down the chemin des Anglais. Lucie gave a little wave to the soldiers looking longingly back at her as they drove round the corner and vanished from view.

Sandrine gave a long sigh of relief. 'Well done,' she said. 'That was . . .'

Lucie pulled a face. 'You're going to have to make a bit more effort than that, if you want to persuade them you're a working girl.'

Sandrine blushed. 'I'm just no good at that kind of thing.'

'It doesn't come naturally to me either,' Lucie said wryly.

Sandrine shook her head. 'I know, of course it doesn't. But you're very good. A born actress.' She sighed. 'Come on, we need to keep moving.'

The small hairs on the back of Sandrine's neck were standing on end. She'd concentrated so much on the practicalities of getting to the Tour du Grand Burlas unobserved that she'd hardly thought about what she had to do. Suzanne was good, one of the best. Her devices rarely malfunctioned, rarely blew up before they were designed to. But it happened, Sandrine knew it could happen. One false move, one touch of the wrong wire.

'If anything goes wrong,' she said to Lucie, 'save yourself. Get away as quickly as you can.'

'Nothing's going to go wrong,' Lucie said. 'I have every faith in you.' She smiled. 'Always have, kid.'

Chapter 124

'Why am I here?' the old man said.

Giraud was in an airless interrogation room in the Commissariat. A table, two chairs, no window. He was hiding his fear as best he could, but his watery eyes skittered from the table to the door to the two blue berets keeping guard.

'On whose orders have I been brought here?'

It was the end of the afternoon. Giraud had been arrested in boulevard Barbès. Since midday he had been sitting in the shade of the lime trees, keeping watch on the door of the Clinique du Bastion. His son had been forced to change his plans. Rather than a day of performing operations, he'd been called to help two injured maquisards, hiding at a house in Trèbes. His daughter-in-law Jeanne had spent the morning telling patients about the delay and had then taken a little boy, due to have his tonsils out, back home. Giraud had offered to sit guard outside the clinic to stop anyone Jeanne hadn't been able to tell about the change of plan from trying to go in.

Then the Milice had come. A hand on his arm, a hand in his back, no need to draw their weapons. His only consolation was that he was not the only one, but his fears for his son and daughter-in-law were growing.

'Why am I here?' Giraud asked again.

Neither of the *miliciens* even looked at him. He stood for a moment longer, then sat down again. A few minutes went by in the same heavy silence. No one speaking, Giraud aware of his own nervous intakes of breath, fear growing all the time. If only he knew what they wanted, he could be prepared.

Finally, the door opened. The *miliciens* sprang to attention and a man walked in. Wearing a light grey suit, he was broader than when Giraud had last seen him, but he recognised him immediately.

'Wait outside,' Authié said, dismissing the police.

The *miliciens* left immediately, closing the door behind them. Giraud watched Authié leaf through his papers. The old man felt tired. Felt his age.

'Giraud, is it?' Authié looked up, then his eyes narrowed. 'Have we met before?'

'Bastille Day, July 1942,' he said. 'You came to talk to me when I was in hospital.'

Authié stared, clearly trying to remember. 'That's right.' He looked back at the list in his hand. 'Félix Giraud. Residing in rue de la Gaffe, quartier Trivalle? Is that still correct?'

'It is, Captain Authié.'

'Major.'

Giraud raised his hand in apology. 'Major Authié.'

'And your son is Jean-Marc Giraud?'

'He is.'

'Did they force you to help, Monsieur Giraud? If that is the case, the courts have it in their discretion to give a lighter sentence. Two or three years, at most.'

The old man's eyes flashed with shock at the abruptness of the threat, but he kept his head.

'I don't know what you're talking about, Major Authié.'

Authié gave a thin smile. 'Did they really think they'd get away with it?'

'They?'

'Your son and his colleagues.'

'There's obviously been some mistake. My son is a doctor.'

‘A mistake? No, I don’t think so,’ Authié said, tapping the paper. ‘It’s all here. All the comings and goings, odd times of the night. It disturbs the neighbours, you see. They don’t like it.’

‘I don’t know what you’re talking about,’ Giraud repeated. ‘He is a doctor. A good man.’

‘A doctor who helps the insurgents, patches up the terrorists so they can continue to maim and kill innocent people.’

Giraud managed not to react. ‘I can’t tell you anything. I don’t know anything.’

Authié stared. ‘Believe me, Monsieur Giraud, I can assure you that you will discover you have plenty to say.’ He smiled. ‘Although I hope it will not come to that.’

‘I’m a veteran. I live quietly.’

‘Yet you are a supporter of Général de Gaulle?’

‘I am a patriot.’

‘De Gaulle is a traitor. Whereas Maréchal Pétain has worked tirelessly for men like you.’

The old man’s face clouded in confusion. ‘I don’t . . .’

‘To bring home our prisoners of war, Monsieur Giraud. French prisoners of war. Your son among them. He’d still be in a POW camp were it not for the Maréchal. The “hero of Verdun”, I’m sure you called him that yourself once upon a time.’

The old man’s expression hardened. ‘That was then.’

Authié let his words hang in the air for a moment.

‘Tell me, Giraud, what do you think about the bombing of the tunnel at Berriac?’

Giraud blinked, struggling to cope with the sudden change of subject.

‘I don’t think anything about it. I don’t know anything.’

‘You didn’t hear about it on the wireless?’

‘I may have done. There’s no crime in listening to the wireless.’

'What about your daughter-in-law?' Authié made a show of looking at the papers, although he clearly didn't need to. 'Does Jeanne listen to the wireless?'

For the first time, concern flickered in the old man's eyes. He said nothing. Confident that the threat had been heard and received, Authié moved on.

'A veteran, yes. Highly decorated. France is – *was* – in your debt.' He made another show of glancing at his papers. 'You don't belong to the LVF?'

Giraud met his gaze. 'I do not care for organisations. I keep myself to myself. Live quietly, as I said.'

'The driver of the Berriac train is in hospital, Monsieur Giraud, two broken arms, broken back. Even if he survives, he will never walk again. Lost the use of his eyes. That's the reality of being a "patriot".'

'I have nothing to say.'

Authié leant forward. 'Witnesses talk of seeing a young woman in the vicinity of the village of Berriac itself. That wasn't your daughter-in-law, Monsieur Giraud?'

The alarm in his eyes intensified. 'Jeanne was at home with me on Sunday night. She's a good girl.'

'Sunday night, monsieur?' he said smoothly. 'So you do know something about the incident?'

Giraud's throat was dry. Authié's questions were muddling him up. He didn't know what he wanted, so was terrified about, somehow, saying the wrong thing.

'It was on the wireless. Everyone knows when it happened.'

Authié sat back on his chair. Giraud was one of a dozen older men and women he'd ordered to be rounded up and brought in. None of them had done anything in particular. It was a random selection designed to scare Carcassonne and make it clear that things would be different now he was back.

The *résistants* and maquisards were skilled at avoiding

patrols. Those who were captured mostly refused to talk. Authié considered the Milice – Schiffner's men too – had failed to pursue tactics that would have delivered information more quickly to the intelligence services. The old Carcassonnais men and women had courage and they were steadfast, but they feared for their children as much as any young mother.

Authié got up and walked around the desk, to perch on the edge immediately in front of Giraud.

'I don't know anything about it.'

Authié's eyes narrowed. 'Nothing about all the visitors who come to the rue de la Gaffe?'

'I'm an old man. I don't get involved.'

Authié saw the old man's gaze slip to the cross pinned on his lapel.

'Do you believe in God, Monsieur Giraud?' Authié said, jabbing him in the chest.

The unexpected physical contact caused Giraud to flinch, but he held Authié's gaze.

'My beliefs are my own business.'

'Do you fear God?' Authié continued. 'Do you think God will save you?'

'I believe men are responsible for their own fate,' Giraud said with dignity. 'Our lives are in our own hands.'

'Do you now?' Authié murmured. 'A pity …'

'What do you mean?'

Authié put his hand to his pocket. Giraud flinched, half expecting him to pull out a gun. It was only a photograph.

'Do you recognise this man?' Authié asked.

Giraud looked at the black and white image and relief flooded through him. It was not his son – nor any of the men or women who came regularly to the house – though there was something familiar about the face.

'I may do,' he said. 'Who is he?'

'A man called Raoul Pelletier,' said Authié. 'Do you

remember, Giraud? That demonstration outside Saint-Michel. You were there. Your daughter-in-law was there.'

Giraud remained silent.

'A boy died that day,' he said. 'Murdered by this man. I interviewed you then.'

'It was two years ago.'

'Perhaps you saw Pelletier detonate the bomb?'

'You asked me then, the answer is the same. I saw nothing.'

'Are you refusing to help the police, Monsieur Giraud?'

Giraud could feel fear churning in his stomach, but he held his head high and looked Authié in the eye.

'I cannot testify to something I know to be untrue.'

Authié glanced at him for a moment longer. Then, without emotion, he drove his fist into Giraud's face. The old man cried out with shock and pain, blood splattering down his shirt. As he put out his thin and frail wrists to break his fall, he heard Authié shout an order.

'Bring in Jeanne Giraud. Perhaps she will be able to help us.'

'No,' Giraud tried to say, but the door slammed shut on his protest.

Chapter 125

Sandrine took off the high-heeled shoes and hid them in the bushes.

'Good luck,' Lucie said. 'If anyone comes, I'll whistle "Lili Marlene". Appropriate, don't you think? The girl under the lantern?'

'Lucie, be serious,' Sandrine warned.

'I am serious,' Lucie said, the lightness gone from her voice. 'If you hear me whistle, stay out of sight.'

Sandrine looked up at the outer walls of the Cité. The huge searchlights, blind in the flattening heat of the late afternoon, were set at intervals along the outer walls. She could see Wehrmacht soldiers in pairs patrolling the battlements, but there were no signs of additional troops on this section.

From her hiding place, she counted the time it took for the sentries to walk from one tower to the next before turning back again. The question was how many extra men had been drafted in. Most of the Gestapo wore plain clothes, so Sandrine couldn't be sure. She hadn't caught sight of any *miliciens*, but it didn't mean they weren't there.

She wished she could talk her changed tactics over with Raoul. It just seemed obvious, now she was here, that she should act straight away rather than waiting for night to fall. It wasn't that they weren't watching now – there had to be some increase in security already – but the Gestapo would expect them to wait until it was dark, until close to the time Authié had been scheduled to arrive.

Motionless, Sandrine could hear nothing more than the usual sounds from the Cité. The soldiers' boots on the rough stone surface of the battlements marching up and down, occasional orders shouted. It was calm. There was no sense of expectation, no sense that everyone was poised, waiting for something to happen.

Not yet.

For a fleeting moment, a snapshot of herself sitting in Coustaussa with Monsieur Baillard on the evening they had met came into her mind.

'Evil has not yet won,' that was what he'd said.

For two years she had fought to make that true. She and Raoul, Marianne and Suzanne, all of them. And, for all the hardship and the fear, they had succeeded in part. They had never given in, they had never allowed themselves to become people they would be ashamed to know. They had held true to their principles and a sense of right and wrong. No collusion, no compromise.

'Now or never,' she murmured to herself.

The next time the patrol turned, Sandrine ran. She covered the open ground and threw herself against the grey shadow of the outer wall. She stopped, held her breath, anticipating the wail of an alarm or Lucie's warning whistle. But nothing happened. The only sound she could hear was her own heart beating, strong in her chest, and the roar of blood in her ears.

She made her way to the low door set in the thick stone walls at the foot of the Tour du Grand Burlas. She studied the padlock. It didn't look as if it had been tampered with. Trying not to make a sound, she reached out, unhooked the lock and removed the chain, then went inside.

Everything was as they had left it. The device was still propped in the corner, the fuse sticking out like the tail of a mouse, waiting only for the flame to bring it to life. Sandrine gave a sigh of relief. Carefully, she removed the fuse and took the pipe packed full with explosives, as

Suzanne had told her to do. It was a waste to leave the rest, but she couldn't hope to conceal it.

The whole business lasted less than two minutes. She said a silent prayer to a God she didn't believe in, then started to make her way down towards where Lucie was waiting. She almost tripped on the gravel path, keeping her balance with a gasp and holding the explosive tight against her chest. Just as she thought she was safe, she heard a man's voice. Immediately she pushed herself back into the shadow of the walls.

'You after a bit of company?'

'No, thanks ever so much, I'm waiting for my friend,' she heard Lucie reply in the same blowsy voice she'd used earlier. She didn't sound frightened or alarmed.

'You sure about that?'

'Quite sure.'

'That's a shame ...' he said. 'I could do with some company.'

Sandrine sighed with relief. He sounded drunk. Not a soldier, not Milice. She edged closer until she could just see them. He reached out an unsteady hand.

'Come on, love.'

'No,' Lucie said sharply, taking a step back. 'Thanks.'

'I'll show you a good time,' he was promising. 'The best. I know where a girl can get a drink.'

He dropped two heavy hands on Lucie's shoulders.

'Get your hands off me!'

'Give us a kiss then.'

Lucie tried to pull away. 'That's enough.'

'Keep it down out there!' someone shouted out of a window.

'Sshh,' the drunk slurred, putting his finger to his lips. 'Sshh.'

The man's voice was getting louder and louder. Then he started to sing. Desperately Sandrine leant out and gestured at Lucie to go. Lucie's eyes widened when she saw her and she shook her head, but Sandrine insisted. Lucie hesitated for a second or two more, then slipped away down the path towards the chemin des Anglais.

'Hey, come back here! *Salope!*'

The drunk started to hurl abuse. Sandrine kept glancing up to the walls, praying the soldiers would not turn and see the man, hear him. She realised she was holding her breath, counting the seconds.

She pressed herself further back against the wall, the rough edges of the stone sticking into her back, until the noise died away. Finally, when she thought it was safe, she ventured out. She ran to the bushes to retrieve her shoes, then across the open ground, with the heels in her hands, into the cover of the trees.

Now all she had to do was return to rue Longue, change back into her other clothes, leave the pipe and fuse and get to the Jardin du Calvaire to meet Raoul.

In her anxiety to get away, Sandrine didn't notice the red glow of the tip of a cigarette in the shadows beneath the stone steps until a hand shot out and grabbed her arm.

'My lucky day,' said the same voice, though now it was stiff with anger. Before Sandrine could stop him, the drunk had shoved her forward into the wall and twisted her arm up behind her back. She forced herself not to cry out. He gave a savage jerk upwards.

'That *salope*, all the chat. All I wanted was a kiss, but no.' His voice was ugly with frustration now. He pushed her hard in the small of her back. 'But now here you are.'

He was half leaning against her, he was so unstable, but the drink hadn't robbed him of his strength. Sandrine didn't dare cry out. She was more terrified of the soldiers hearing. The patrols on the wall, going backwards and forwards, it would only take one man to look down and see them. Come to investigate.

Then below, at the bottom of the slope, she saw a black Citroën slowing down and pulling in beside the church. A Gestapo car. Any moment, they would look up and see the two of them locked in this grotesque dance. Sandrine started to struggle, trying to pull herself free. The man hit her hard, on the side of the head.

'Keep still,' he threatened. 'I'm warning you.'

Desperate now, Sandrine knew it was her last chance. It was a gamble, but she couldn't see what else to do. She screamed. As she'd hoped, the man clamped his hand over her mouth and she bit down on his filthy fingers as hard as she could.

'Bitch,' he yelled.

He grabbed for her hair, but Sandrine was too quick for him. She ducked out of his grasp and ran, away down the steps and on to the path.

Behind her, she heard a whistle blow. Then the sound of boots on the cobbled stones and the beginnings of an argument. In the street below, windows were opened, a door.

The Gestapo shouted at the man to put his hands up. She heard the confused response, his bravado collapsing into self-pity.

'*Fumiste! Idiot!*' the drunk protested. 'I've not done anything.'

Sandrine didn't turn around, just kept running. Her bare feet were being cut on the stones and the dry grass, her breath burnt in her chest, but she didn't let up. Through the fields and heading down to the river. She heard the screech of tyres.

Had they seen her? Were they following her?

From her summer of helping with the *vendanges*, Sandrine knew the farms to the south of the Cité walls. There was a way out along the road. She ran until she reached the wooden gate into the first of the fields of vines. She stumbled over, then through the rows of grapes, crouched down and struggling to keep her footing on the uneven earth. At the bottom of the field, the gate had rolls of barbed wire over the top, to keep thieves out. At her back, she thought the siren was getting closer.

She pushed herself on, her muscles as taut as piano wire, the blood pumping in her ears. Ahead on the Pont Vieux, she saw the *vert-de-gris* of the Wehrmacht patrol, but there was no sign of the black Citroën. She couldn't possibly wade across the Aude in broad daylight. She dropped the explosive into the water and decided she'd have to brazen it out. Hope that the pass would still be good.

She straightened her skirts, pushed her dirty feet back into the high heels, and walked on to the bridge towards the checkpoint. She held her breath, expecting them to notice her high colour or that she was carrying no basket or bag, but they didn't. They waved her through like before.

Weak with relief, Sandrine walked over the Pont Vieux, forcing herself not to break into a run. Only a few steps further, a few steps further, one more checkpoint, and she would be back in the Bastide. Then, behind her, she heard the siren, followed by shouting.

'Halten Sie!'

Sandrine blocked out the voices. Then again, in French this time. 'Stop or we'll shoot!'

She didn't turn round, praying they weren't speaking to her. Why would they be? But, seconds later, she heard the rattle of a semi-automatic, fired into the air as a warning, then the same order shouted once again.

'Stop!'

Sandrine started to run. It was bright and the soldiers had a clear view of her, but she was banking on the fact that she knew the town better than they did. She ran past the tiny chapel, sharp right past the hospital, then swerved right again into the rue des Calquières, through the dark arched tunnel beneath the Pont Neuf and down on to the riverbank.

She could hear them on the bridge, shouting instructions in German to one another, as she continued to run. She knew her legs wouldn't hold her for much longer. Here, on this forgotten stretch of river opposite the Andrieu distillery, there were several gaps where a person might hide, fashioned by the passing of time where the river had worked away the stones. Unless they struck lucky, she didn't believe they would find her.

Sandrine pushed back the nettles and crawled inside backwards, feeling the sharp sting on her skin. Once inside, she forced herself to rearrange the weeds that had grown high around the opening, so it didn't look like they'd been disturbed. Her hands roared in complaint.

The hollow stank of urine and rubbish, blown in by the prevailing wind. The space was barely big enough for her to sit down, but it gave her a good view of the Pont Vieux. Two soldiers were still standing on the bridge. And she could see an officer pointing and shouting. In the street above the riverbank, already she could hear the hammering on doors and the demands to be let in.

Had Lucie been caught?

Sandrine closed her eyes, regretting that she had brought trouble down on other people's heads. She waited and watched, her heart thumping. Sweat pooled between her breasts and at the back of her knees and in the hollow of her throat, and she understood, in a single moment, how Marianne could have reached the end of her strength.

Sandrine wasn't sure how much longer she would be able to carry on either. If she got out of this, did she have what was required to go on fighting?

Chapter 126

'What do you mean?' Lucie said, holding her son tightly to her. Jean-Jacques' eyes were wide because of the urgent whispered conversation of the two women, but he sat quietly in his mother's arms.

Lucie had quickly made her way back to Madame Peyre's house from the Cité. At first she'd felt exhilarated that they'd pulled it off. She understood why Sandrine and the others had been prepared to take such risks. But the closer she got to home, the more her nerves started to play up. Her stomach was now in knots. What if she'd been seen? What if Milice were on their way here now? What if Sandrine had been caught?

Then she'd found Jeanne waiting for her on the doorstep.

'What do you mean?' Lucie repeated.

'He was arrested early this afternoon.'

'Your husband?' Lucie said, still muddled by what Jeanne was trying to tell her.

'No, not Jean-Marc. My father-in-law. A neighbour was in boulevard Barbès and saw it happen. Came to tell me.'

'Monsieur Giraud? But why would they arrest him?'

'I don't know. He was keeping an eye on the clinic. My husband had to cancel all his operations to go . . .' she hesitated, 'out of town.' She shook her head, trying to get her fears under control. 'It might be that he was in the wrong place at the wrong time. Either way, I've got to see if I can find him. His heart's not strong, he's . . .'

Lucie put her hand on Jeanne's arm. 'I'm sure they won't mistreat him. He's an old man.'

'That means nothing now,' Jeanne said bitterly. She

ruffled Jean-Jacques' hair. 'He's been very good. His throat doesn't seem to be hurting too much, but …' She met Lucie's eye. 'I don't think my husband will be able to do the operation at the moment. Not now.'

Lucie met her gaze. 'I understand. Thank you for bringing him all the way across town.'

Jeanne turned to go, then stopped. 'We don't know each other very well. To tell you the truth, I was surprised that you …' She broke off. 'I don't know what you were doing today, but you're a friend of Sandrine and Marianne's, so I can imagine. Something's happening today in Carcassonne. My father-in-law's arrest is just part of it. If I were you, I'd get out while you still can. Take Jean-Jacques and go as far away as possible.'

Lucie stared at the young woman, her face taut with fear and distress, and she nodded.

'I intend to, don't worry.'

'Good. And good luck.'

'To you too. Thank you again, Jeanne. I'm sure your father-in-law will be all right. Jean-Marc too.'

Jeanne didn't answer, just turned and left. For a moment Lucie stood, her son in her arms, watching her go. She allowed her thoughts to go to Max. There were rumours circulating in the town that the very last prisoners were being transported from Le Vernet. She couldn't bear to think of it being true. That Max might have survived all this time, only to be deported now. She felt the familiar tightening of her throat. When she got to Coustaussa, at least she could see if Eloise or Geneviève had heard anything.

Lucie gave an impatient shake of her head, knowing she couldn't afford to waste any time thinking. Sandrine and Raoul had wanted her to go with them to Coustaussa. She had been in two minds, but today she'd realised she wanted to be with the others. And although she felt bad about leaving Madame Peyre, the thought of seeing Marieta and Liesl again made her smile. J-J's other adopted gran'mère and his aunt. It would be lovely for him.

Quickly, Lucie unlocked the door and went inside.

'You play with this, J-J,' she said, putting the little boy in the playpen in the centre of the room and handing him a wooden truck. 'Be good for Mama.'

Lucie rushed into the bedroom and changed her clothes, rolling the dress she'd worn to go to and from rue Longue into a ball and pushing it to the back of the wardrobe. She dressed in a plain shirt and skirt, comfortable shoes, then packed a change of clothes for her son. She couldn't look as if she was going away. The only thing she took of her own was the brooch Max had given her the first time they went dancing at the Terminus. For a moment she allowed herself to remember, the look on his face as he produced the paper-and-ribbon package, his smile as he pinned the brooch to her coat. She went back to the wardrobe. The blue twill was far too heavy for the season, but suddenly she couldn't bring herself to leave it behind. She fastened the brooch on the left lapel, shrugged her arms into the sleeves, then went back into the main room.

She wished she could leave a note for Madame Peyre, telling her what she was doing, but she knew it would be safer for them both not to give any indication of where she'd gone. Even that they had gone.

'Not for long,' she murmured, wondering if that was true.

The pram was in the hallway. Lucie deliberated for a moment. It would be easier not to carry Jean-Jacques all the way through the Bastide to the Jardin du Calvaire, but it would be a nuisance after that. And a pram left abandoned in the street would be sure to attract attention.

'Come on, my little man, up we come,' Lucie said, picking up her son. 'Shall we go on an adventure?'

*

Sandrine heard the bells of Saint-Gimer strike six, followed moments later by the bells of the Minimes convent in rue Trivalle. The beating of her heart marked the passing time, the stillness punctured by the occasional splash of a fish in the shallows, a rare survivor in the plundered river, a distant Wehrmacht truck or the engine of a Milice vehicle prowling through the streets of the Bastide.

She couldn't hear the soldiers any more, though she knew they wouldn't give up. She had a restricted view of the bridge, but none of them seemed to have come back.

Sandrine tried to imagine where Raoul might be now. Because she had dismantled the device earlier than they'd agreed, he wouldn't be worried yet. He wouldn't expect her until after it was dark. He'd be holed up somewhere, waiting for dusk. Safe.

But she wished she knew if Lucie had made it back all right. That was often the worst part of it, not fear for oneself but for those one loved. In the early days, Sandrine had thought she'd always know if something bad had happened. That she would feel if any one of them – Marianne, Suzanne or Lucie, Liesl, Geneviève or Eloise – was in trouble. She'd learnt from experience that it wasn't the case. Sometimes she assumed the worst, felt the violent tug in the gut, the twist in the chest. Sometimes it was justified, sometimes it was not. In the case of Monsieur Baillard, for example, she could not accept he was gone. After two years with no news, Sandrine knew it was stupid to cling to the slim hope that he was alive. And yet she felt his presence. Faint, but there all the same.

She tried to change position, to stretch out the stiffness in her cramped arms and legs, as the minutes ticked slowly on. The light of the end of the afternoon gradually gave way to the white of early evening. Just after the bells had struck seven, she heard – then saw – a convoy of military vehicles drive on to the bridge. Orders were shouted in German first, then repeated in French, as three trucks of Gestapo and Milice travelled from the Bastide to the Cité. A little later, just after the quarter-hour had struck, a black armoured Waffen-SS staff car went by with its hood closed.

Was Authié in it? Was the dinner genuine after all? Perhaps it wasn't a trap and they'd made a dreadful mistake in not going through with the attack tonight. Missed the best opportunity they would have.

The vehicles cleared the bridge and the barriers came down again. Silence returned to the river. Sandrine stayed hidden, watching the guard patrol the section between the two checkpoints.

The light turned from white to the purple of dusk then, gradually, to black. The bells of Saint-Gimer were striking nine now. Sandrine's sharp ears picked up another sound. This time, the sweet sound of a woman's voice, singing an old Occitan lullaby.

Bona nuèit, bona nuèit …
Braves amics, pica mièja-nuèit
Cal finir velhada …

It was a song Marieta used to sing to her when she was a baby, always restless, always hard to get off to sleep. Sandrine felt tears prick in her eyes. She didn't brush them away, but mouthed along with the words, the familiar words of childhood, as the lilting melody floated out over the river.

Cantem pas mai …
Anem tots al leìt

An old song, a song of the mountains to give comfort to all

those who could not sleep, for those who were weary and wakeful.

Raoul stared at Lucie.

'It's been six hours since you came down from the Cité. Something's gone wrong. Something must have happened.'

Night had fallen over the Jardin du Calvaire. The stone apostles were sleeping in the Garden of Gethsemane, their shapes providing cover for Raoul, Lucie and Robert Bonnet. Lucie was rocking Jean-Jacques in her arms to keep him from waking.

'Something must have gone wrong,' he said.

'Nothing went wrong,' Lucie repeated. 'I saw her. She came out of the tower. There was no alarm sounded. Just a drunk. Sandrine waved at me to go, so I did.'

'We don't even know if she made it back to rue Longue,' Raoul said, running his hands through his hair.

'No, we don't,' Lucie said patiently. 'But there's no reason to assume she didn't.'

'Then why's she not here?'

'She'll be here,' Lucie said, though the strain was starting to show in her voice too.

'We can't wait very much longer,' Bonnet said. 'We'll be stopped.'

'I'm not leaving without her,' Raoul said.

Bonnet shook his head. 'You know the system, Pelletier.'

The 'Citadel' network followed the same rules as every other group. If someone was more than half an hour late, the assumption was either the location had been discovered or it wasn't safe enough to keep the rendezvous, or that the contact had been arrested. At that point, their responsibility became to save themselves and to warn the others.

'This is different,' Raoul said.

'Sandrine won't expect us to wait,' Bonnet insisted. 'She'll rely on us to do the right thing. Expect you to have faith enough in her to know she's capable of looking after herself.'

'What if Authié found her?'

'Everything went well, Raoul,' Lucie repeated. 'There was no sign of Major Authié at all.'

'I'm not leaving Carcassonne without her. Bonnet, will you take Lucie to the handover instead of us, then come back in the morning? I know it's a lot to ask, but you must see I can't go. I can't leave her.'

'I don't know,' Bonnet said, shaking his head again.

They both knew the odds on them being caught were much higher if Bonnet left and then came back to the same rendezvous.

'Please,' Raoul pleaded. 'This is no place for Jean-Jacques, but I can't go. It's only right. After all she's done.'

Robert held his gaze for a moment longer, then he nodded. 'All right. But stay here. If you're not here when I come back, I'll not be able to do anything.'

Raoul's shoulders slumped with relief. 'Thanks, Bonnet.'

Lucie put her hand on his arm. 'We'll see you in Coustaussa. Don't be too long, do you hear?'

Time had changed its shape. The past and the future both seemed to coexist with the strange and fragile present. Sandrine felt the presence of spirits all around her now, friendly ghosts who held out their hands and whispered of their lives, and shared their secrets. They connected her to all those who had walked the streets of Carcassonne before and all those who would come after her.

Sandrine could see a cloud of midges hovering over the surface of the water. Trapped in the confined space, with nothing to drink or eat, she had lost track of how long she had been hiding. She had stopped counting the tolling of the bells.

The great sweeping spotlights from the Cité sent their

beams shining out of the quartier Trivalle and the quartier Barbacane, but all was quiet. The occasional slamming of a car door, or an engine, but nothing more. Sandrine prayed Raoul would have gone. That he would do the right thing and leave without her, though the thought choked her.

Finally, night fell. The sound of trucks coming back over the bridge, the heavy thrumming of the engine of a large car. Sandrine felt a strange peace come over her. An image slipped softly into her head, indistinct, an impression, almost a memory. A girl in a long red cape, the hem embroidered with an intricate green and blue pattern of squares and diamonds, interspersed with tiny yellow flowers. No, not flowers, but stars. Seven stars. A girl with a gentle yet forceful expression.

And between the two Carcassonnes, as it always had, lay the dark and silent river. A sea of glass.

Chapter 127

Laval stared impassively at Authié, carefully hiding his satisfaction at being proved right. He wasn't sure how Authié would react at having made the wrong decision. Schiffner had already made his displeasure clear at the waste of resources.

'Still no sign of her?' Authié demanded.

'We don't know who it was,' Laval said. 'The report was only that a woman and a man were seen on the slopes above rue Petite Côte de la Cité. When the Gestapo ordered them to stop, the girl ran off.'

'The man?'

'Not Pelletier,' Laval said. 'A drunk, wandered into the restricted area accidentally – so he claims. He's in custody, but he doesn't know anything.'

Authié looked down at the Wehrmacht report. 'It says here she crossed the Pont Vieux. Why the hell did they let her through?'

'The sentries weren't aware there was a problem at that stage, sir,' Laval said. 'By the time they were, she'd got away. The Wehrmacht did a house-to-house in the vicinity but didn't find her. Nobody claimed to have seen her.'

Authié tapped the paper again. 'It says here that two women were seen in the vicinity of the chemin des Anglais at four thirty. A good hour before this other incident. Why were we not immediately told?'

'They were working girls. It was only when the captain arrived in the Cité that he realised we were looking out for women – a woman – and decided to radio the information through.'

'That was eight hours ago, Laval,' Authié said.

Laval said nothing. The report had come to him and he had decided not to put it immediately in front of Authié. He didn't share his superior's complete conviction that either the device – or the decoy – had necessarily been set by Sandrine Vidal. But he agreed with Authié that questioning her about the Codex was the obvious place to start. By keeping the Wehrmacht report from him for a few hours, he had hoped to get a head start on his commanding officer. But by the time Laval arrived in the Cité, there was no sign of the girls matching the description given by the Wehrmacht soldiers. The dinner had gone ahead, but for the guards, the evening had been spent in dull inactivity: watching both the Tour de la Justice and the Tour de Grand Burlas, waiting for an attack on the hotel that neither Laval nor, increasingly, Authié believed would take place.

Laval met his gaze. 'I think we should go to the house in the rue du Palais now,' he said.

Authié's face grew white. 'Where's Schiffner?' he demanded, ignoring Laval's comment.

'He returned to headquarters. To file his report.'

Authié frowned. 'Do you have the men you need?'

Laval nodded. 'Yes, sir. There have been two *miliciens* on duty in the Fournier house for the past twenty-four hours, round the clock.'

'Has anyone gone in or out?'

'No.' He paused, then decided to push Authié a little further. 'I think it's likely the women have already left.'

'Do you?' snapped Authié. 'Based on what information?'

Laval didn't say anything.

'Precisely,' Authié said. 'We don't know one way or the other.' He scribbled a note, then thrust it at Laval. 'This is what you need.'

Laval looked down at the requisition slip. 'Five o'clock? With respect, sir, why wait?'

Authié stood up and leant forward on his desk. 'Because if – as you have pointed out, Laval – there's no one there, two hours won't make any difference. Out of courtesy I need to inform Schiffner personally what I am going to do. Give him due warning.' He pointed his finger at Laval. 'And it gives you the time to fetch the information about Audric Baillard.' He glanced at his deputy. 'I assume you have it?'

Laval had not found the time to return to the Commissariat and he doubted there would be anyone in the archives now to help him get the files out, but he knew better than to admit it.

'I'll bring it as soon as I can, sir.'

Authié met his gaze. 'I'll be waiting.'

Raoul worked his way from bar to bar. The Bastide was crawling with police and soldiers. Gestapo in the centre, the Milice a little further out, guards on every corner, but he avoided being stopped.

No one had heard anything about a woman being arrested in the Cité, although there had been two round-ups earlier in the day. Old men mostly, no one was sure what was going on. There was talk about houses being raided in the quartier Trivalle late afternoon and door-to-door searches in the area around the hospital, but nothing seemed to have been found. Reports of Wehrmacht trucks going in and out of the Cité, but again no suggestion that anyone had been arrested during the night.

In the Café Saillan, Raoul overheard two men talking about a woman who'd been found decomposed in her apartment. It had taken him a moment to realise that they were talking about his mother. The rush of relief that the message had got through to the undertaker was followed by a sharp stab of grief. Then, guilt.

Raoul returned to the Jardin du Calvaire to find Robert Bonnet waiting for him. Lucie and Jean-Jacques had been safely handed over in Roullens. Most of the Faïta Maquis had gone south, but Ramón – who'd given Raoul a place to hide when he fled Carcassonne after the Bastille Day demonstration in July 1942 – was still there and was prepared to help. He was to get them to Cépie, just north of Limoux. Provided Suzanne and Marianne had arrived in Coustaussa as planned and set things up all right, someone else would be waiting in Limoux to take Lucie and her son on the last part of the journey.

'Ran into trouble coming back,' Robert said. 'A boulangerie van was "borrowed" to intercept a convoy of ammunition being transported from the Wehrmacht depot to the Domaine de Baudrigues. The Germans are storing all their heavy ammunition there, rather than waiting for supplies from Montazels.'

'I'd heard that.'

Bonnet sighed. 'Someone had talked. The Gestapo were waiting for them.'

'Any connection with us?' Raoul said. 'With Citadel, I mean?'

'No, but two dead and four arrested,' Bonnet said.

Raoul shook his head. 'Do we know how they were tipped off?'

'Not yet,' Bonnet said. He paused, then added: 'Any word about Sandrine?'

'No.'

'You've tried all the usual places?'

'Yes.'

'What do you want to do?'

Raoul took a deep breath. 'Will Yvette be at work tonight? I tried the bar in Quai Riquet earlier, but she wasn't there.'

'Doesn't finish until later on Saturday mornings,' Bonnet said. 'Midnight until six.'

'Can you get a message to her to come to the bar when she gets off shift? In case she's heard anything.'

'I'm sure there's nothing to hear,' Bonnet said, 'but I'll do my best.' He met Raoul's gaze. 'Don't go back to the rue du Palais, Pelletier. Sandrine will find us or get a message to us.'

'I can't rest until I know,' Raoul said.

'I know, but trust her. She's a clever girl.'

Raoul nodded, but he could see from the look in Bonnet's eyes that he was worried too.

Chapter 128

Sandrine waited until it was completely dark before emerging from her hiding place beneath the bridge. She was stiff and her calves and ankles were covered in red marks from the stinging nettles, but she was too numb to be aware of any pain. She couldn't bear to think of how Raoul might be feeling. She remembered, now, he had been intending to try to see his mother. She hoped it hadn't been upsetting. She prayed that he was safe, not worrying about her too much, and she felt even more guilty than before about involving Lucie.

She had to decide what to do next. The drunk was the worst piece of luck she could have had, drawing the Gestapo's attention. She was so tired she couldn't think straight. Sandrine looked down at the cheap green dress, now smeared with dust and debris from the riverbank. It was gaudy and distinctive, and she'd no doubt her description had been circulated by now. She needed a change of clothes at the very least, otherwise her chances of getting away from Carcassonne were even slighter.

She thought of where she might go. She wasn't far from the Giraud house in the rue de la Gaffe, but it would be madness to go back over to the quartier Trivalle. She couldn't go to Madame Peyre's for fear of putting Lucie in danger. Was there anywhere else?

In the end, she couldn't think of anything other than to go home. Her feet seemed to be taking her there of their own volition. It was stupid, so she reasoned the Gestapo, or Milice – whoever Authié was working for – would never think she'd go back to the rue du Palais. Sandrine felt incapable of coming up with an alternative plan. She felt dizzy with exhaustion, defeated by the long days and nights that had led up to this moment. And she was so close now. She could go there, fetch fresh clothes, then be gone before it got light. She wouldn't be putting anyone else in danger. After that, all she had to do was work out how to get safely to Coustaussa to join the others.

Ten minutes later, she was walking quickly up the rue de Strasbourg and through the gate into their back garden. The house was dark, she could see nothing unusual, no signs that anyone had been there. She rested her hand for an instant against the trunk of the fig tree as if, by touching something solid, she would anchor herself. But she felt only sadness at the loss of her old life. The ground was sticky with windfalls. Sandrine was pleased Marieta couldn't see how she and Marianne had let the garden run wild.

For a moment, she pictured herself sitting peacefully on the old white wrought-iron furniture. Reading a book or sipping a glass of Marieta's home-made lemonade. She shook her head. Such nostalgic thoughts were no use to her now.

Keeping close to the periphery of the courtyard, Sandrine made her way to the stone steps. Taking the key from beneath the glass jar on the window ledge, she opened the back door and slowly walked in, locking it again after her. She held her breath, listening to the silence, trying to distinguish sounds of other people in the house. Intruders.

She let out a long sigh. The house was empty, she could feel it. Just her and friendly ghosts, the memories of all of them held in the waiting air. In the gloomy kitchen, she could see nothing had been touched since she and Lucie had left. Their crockery washed and draining by the sink. The remains of a loaf on the wooden board beneath the cloth.

Using her hands to guide herself in the dark house, Sandrine walked into the corridor, remembering all the people who had passed through in the early years of the war. The Dutch *résistants* and German anti-fascists.

On she went through the silent house. Her father's study, where the four Belgian soldiers, fighting with the Secret Army, had camped out for a week, waiting to be taken to the house of Abbé Gau prior to the long journey south and out of France, via the Roc Blanc escape route. Then Belcaire or Rouze – or Ax-les-Thermes, where Monsieur Baillard had last been seen – over the Pyrenees to Andorra and Spain.

Her fingers found a box of John Bull safety matches on the desk, left behind, she presumed, by the one British airman who had found his way to the rue du Palais. They regularly cleared the house of any potentially incriminating objects and she was amazed it had survived for so long. She picked it up and slipped it into her pocket, recalling the Englishman's open expression and his inability to speak even the most basic French. They had communicated in sign language, but his gratitude for the risks they were taking on his behalf, he had taken great pains to make clear. When he'd left, he had kissed her hand and put his own to his chest. Sandrine had never forgotten it. She hoped the courteous young man had survived.

At the foot of the stairs, she stopped. The moon was shining through the window, illuminating the photographs on the wall. Sandrine now realised what had been niggling in her mind. Lucie had helped her destroy the few things that could give a clue as to where they'd gone. All the official documents had been taken to safety a long time ago – deeds and bills of sale – but there were a handful of letters with the Coustaussa address on them. They'd got rid of everything except the pictures of the *capitelles* and the ruined castle. It would take no time at all to identify the village.

Sandrine hesitated. The photos were precious. Her mother had taken them and she didn't want to destroy them. It felt as if she was doing Authié's work for him. She hesitated a moment more, then, with quick, sad fingers, she took them down from the wall and carried them to the sink in the kitchen. She eased each black and white photograph out and, with a silent apology to her mother, put the match to them.

She watched the paper curl and scorch, then flare and burn black, the orange glow too bright in the dark kitchen. The pipes thumped as she turned on the taps to damp the heat. Then she wrapped the soggy ash in a tea towel and carried it down to the cellar for the mice to find. The frames she hid behind the empty wine racks.

Aware of the time passing, Sandrine went upstairs again. Passed the empty spaces on the wall, dust marking their silhouette, telling herself she should hurry. She ran her hand over the warm wood of the unpolished banister, remembering the girl she had been. An innocent time, better times.

She glanced up at the window on the landing. The silver rays of the moon sent the diamonds of coloured light sparkling on to the stairs. She was taking too long, she was too slow, she knew it, but the nostalgia for her lost life was too strong to resist.

She went past Marianne's room, past her father's room – where first Liesl, then Suzanne had slept – and pushed open her own bedroom door. She ran her hand along the high back of the Chinese chaise, remembering all the times Marianne had sat herself down there to dispense advice, twilight tête-à-têtes and midnight confidences. Her sheets still rumpled from where she and Raoul had lain side by side.

Sandrine took a plain skirt from the wardrobe and an unremarkable shirt, nothing too fancy. She hesitated, then pulled on her old tartan woollen socks to cover the red bites and nettle stings on her legs. She sat down on the bed to put on her shoes, a pair of Marianne's old teaching shoes. The soles were worn through and she had lined them with cardboard. They'd do all right for now.

She realised that her mood was in part because of the lack of sleep, the endless disabling isolation of fear. But also because it was finally hitting her that this really was the last time she would be in the house, perhaps ever. She and Marianne had said as much, but she hadn't really taken it in. And when Raoul was here, then she and Lucie were rushing to clear everything, activity had stopped her from thinking.

Now, in this silent and private moment, she felt overwhelmed with grief. She looked up at the familiar damp patch on the ceiling above her bed, a legacy of that bitter winter of 1942, when the pipes all froze and the guttering cracked. Then, with the thaw in the spring, the rain had come dripping through.

She smiled ruefully. Suzanne had promised to fix it. Raoul had offered to fix it, but no one had. Sandrine felt so utterly exhausted. She knew it was a mistake to sit down at all, but she couldn't drag her eyes away from the tear-shaped stain. She smiled. Likely as not, the patch would still need fixing by the time Jean-Jacques was grown up and old enough to do it. Or even a child of her own. She put her hand on her stomach, thinking of how they had made love when Raoul arrived on Sunday night, how it had felt different. She didn't feel anything had changed, but all the same, she couldn't help herself wondering.

The words of the lullaby came back to her. A mother singing to her baby? *Bona nuèit, bona nuèit.* A child of their own, a son or a daughter, Sandrine realised she didn't care.

Would Raoul prefer a son first? She didn't think so.

For a few stolen moments more, she sat quietly in her childhood room. Forgetting who she was, what she was supposed to be doing, dreaming in the darkness instead of what might have been.

Then, abrupt and violent, the sound she'd imagined so many times. The hammering on the door, the rough voices, the shouting.

'Police. *Polizei!*'

Sandrine jolted awake. Bolt upright, her eyes wide open, her right hand stretched out as if she was trying to grasp something. For a moment she was neither asleep nor awake, as if some part of her had been left behind in the dream.

The noise she'd expected every waking minute of every day, every night, for the past two years. She was amazed at how calm she felt, how she seemed to go into action without thinking about it. Muscle memory, anticipation, her arms and limbs moving seemingly independent of her.

In the hall below, now, the sound of wood splintering as jackboots kicked in the front door. An idiot to have let herself drift to sleep, an idiot to have come here at all. Men's voices in the hall, French and German. The remembered familiar voice of Laval, heard only in snatches, but embedded in her memory like a splinter of glass.

Instinct kicked in. No reason why Raoul would come looking for her here, why anyone would come. She had promised not to come back to the house, why would he disbelieve her? But even so, she quickly scribbled a note, stuffed it into the matchbox and dropped it from the window of the *salle de bains*, praying the soldiers would not search the garden properly and it might lie undiscovered.

Then she headed upstairs for the attic, hoping she could hide herself. That they might pass by. But a flash of grey, of green. Now the *vert-de-gris* were storming up the stairs, the blue berets of the Milice trailing behind. Glass smashing, drawers, the tearing of fabric as the search began.

Then, a Gestapo agent grabbing her by the hair, feeling the skin tear on her scalp, being pulled down from the ladder, a second pair of hands around her waist, holding her legs, dragging her to the ground.

Laval's voice in her ear. '*C'est fini, maintenant.*'

Sandrine felt her arms being dragged up behind her back, handcuffs pinching the skin around her wrists, and she was half carried, half pushed down the stairs to where the car was waiting in the street.

Laval threw her into the back.

'Where are you taking me?' she managed to say, struggling to sit upright.

He struck her hard on the side of her head. Stunned, Sandrine fell sideways on the seat, then struggled to right herself.

'You've caused a lot of trouble,' he said in a low voice. 'Don't make it worse for yourself.'

Chapter 129

Raoul knew it was a risk, but it was the only place left to go. Bonnet had told him to stay away – and he and Sandrine had agreed they wouldn't return to the house – but he didn't know where else to try.

Sandrine had to be here. Because if she wasn't, then it meant … Raoul couldn't let himself think about the alternative. By five thirty, he was standing at the corner of the rue de Strasbourg and the rue de Lorraine, trying to see if he could get into the garden without being spotted. Madame Fournier wouldn't be up this early, but he couldn't see any sign of Milice or Gestapo watching the house either.

He looked out of place in this quartier. Because of the Feldgendarmerie and the Deuxième Bureau offices in rue Mazagran, many senior Gestapo and Wehrmacht officers had lodgings in these elegant nineteenth-century streets near the Palais de Justice. Sandrine had always felt it kept them secure. This wasn't the sort of area where safe houses were usually to be found. The Gestapo raids happened in the poorer quarters.

Raoul walked quickly and slipped in through the garden gate, surprised to find it unlocked. The ground beneath his feet was sticky with rotten figs and there were weeds everywhere. He crept up the stone steps and, cupping his hands, peered in through the glass. It was dark inside and he couldn't see anything at all, though he detected a slight smell of burning. He tried the handle, but the door was locked. He looked for the key under the usual glass jar, but it wasn't there.

He frowned. Then he noticed that the bathroom window on the first floor was open. Not just open, but wide open.

Glancing at Madame Fournier's windows, and seeing no movement, Raoul scaled the railings and stepped across on to the wide window ledge on the ground floor. He still couldn't see in. He jumped back down, landing in a pile of twigs and dried leaves, blown into the corner of the courtyard last autumn and never swept up. He bent down. In among the browns and greens was a red and black matchbox. English brand. It was clean and dry. It certainly hadn't been there all winter.

His heart beating fast, Raoul slid open the box. Inside, three unspent matches and a small piece of paper. He unfolded the paper and recognised Sandrine's handwriting: SD – 5 A.M.

'No, no, no, no.'

Raoul felt as if he'd been punched in the chest. His heart hammered against his ribs, his breath caught in his throat. SD stood for Sicherheitdienst, the Gestapo. The note told him they'd come for her at five o'clock.

He wanted to scream, to rip the sky in two or tear down the house with his bare hands. He screwed the paper in his fist, tighter, forcing all the fury, the terror out through his fingers, into his nails, into the palm of his hand until he drew blood.

Little by little, he controlled the rage thundering through his brain. He looked at his watch. Nearly six. Sandrine was writing a note for him an hour ago. She was alive an hour ago.

Raoul shook his head, he couldn't think like that. Of course she was alive. He took a match from the box and burnt the note. He had to think. Concentrate. The Gestapo would have taken her either to the villa on the route de Toulouse or to the Caserne Laperrine.

One hour ago. If he'd come earlier, he could have stopped them.

Raoul forced himself not to think about what might be happening. Many partisans had been detained in the route de Toulouse and had suffered at the hands of the Gestapo interrogators. It was impossible to get in, impossible to get anyone out. There had been attempts in the past, none successful.

It didn't matter. It was Sandrine. Wherever she was, he would find her and get her out. Or die trying, a voice in his head whispered.

Raoul ignored it. He ran back through the courtyard and into the street, heading once again for the Quai Riquet.

Chapter 130

'Where is it?' Laval said again.

Sandrine was no longer aware of the boundaries of her own body, only that everything was singing with pain. Her muscles were stretched to their limits and her head was throbbing.

She knew she hadn't been here long. She wasn't quite sure where she was either. Not far. One of the soldiers had put a hood over her head before they dragged her out of the car, then across a hard surface and into a building. But before she went inside, she thought she heard the shriek of a train on the tracks and a whistle, so she guessed she had been brought to the Gestapo headquarters on the route de Toulouse, which backed on to the railway.

She had been left alone for a while, hooded and strapped to the chair. It was hard to breathe beneath the heavy fabric and the air in the room was fetid. She'd felt she was suffocating.

Then Laval came back and started to question her. And with each question unanswered came pain. His hand across her face, once his fist into her stomach, a boot hard against her shin bone, she never knew where the next assault would come. And, always, the threat of something much worse.

'Where is the Codex hidden? Who has it?'

'I don't know.'

She tried to twist away, but her arms were tied behind her back. Instinctively she kicked out at him and he hit her, hard, on the side of her ankle with something. A rod, a stick. For the first time, she screamed.

'You will tell me what I want to know in the end,' he said. 'Why not save us all a lot of trouble?'

'I don't know where the Codex is,' she said again, bracing herself for another blow. 'I don't know why you're asking me about it.'

'Because you sent us on a wild goose chase, didn't you?' he said, his mouth close to her ear. 'So I know you are involved, you see.'

Sandrine tried to stay inside her head, a quiet and still place where she was safe and Laval couldn't reach her. So far she had said nothing, nothing at all. She couldn't think of anything but how to survive the next blow, then the next. She thought of Jean Moulin, tortured to death by Hauptsturmführer Barbie in Lyon and the countless others who never talked, never betrayed their comrades. She didn't know how much she could stand, but she would do her best to be as strong as them. Survive the next blow, then the next.

'Tell me,' he shouted with frustration.

Although she knew it would be worse for her in the long run, his anger gave her a little spark of courage. Her moment of triumph was short-lived. An iron grip pulling her to her feet, being marched, pushed, driven across the room. She felt even more vulnerable away from the chair. She didn't know how big the room was or where she was being taken, and she tried to struggle free.

Then a hand – Laval's hand – on the back of her neck, pushing her to her knees. A shudder of horror went through her, and then her face was plunged forward into ice-cold water. She felt the cloth sodden around her mouth, her nostrils, blocking the water and trapping the air, and she began to struggle. Her blood was roaring in her head, pounding as if her vessels would burst, her lungs shouting against the lack of oxygen.

She kicked harder, again, thought she heard someone

laughing as her bare feet skeetered and slipped and thrashed on the wet floor. Then, just as she thought she would pass out, they pulled her up.

'Where is it?'

'I don't know,' she gasped.

This time she was ready for it. As she was pitched headfirst into the stinking water, Sandrine held her breath. She told herself she was swimming in the Aude at Rennes-les-Bains, diving down to the bottom of the muddy water to fish for stones, for jewels hidden in the riverbed. She and Geneviève had spent hours each summer when they were children playing games in the water. Weighting themselves down, trying to stay beneath the surface for as long as possible.

When the lack of oxygen started thundering in her head, her lungs screaming for air, Sandrine made herself imagine she was floating slowly up through the beautiful green. The bright Midi sky, blue, high above. Told herself she didn't want to wake up. That she could seal her silence by dying.

He left her under longer this time. When they eventually pulled her out, she slipped from their wet hands and smashed her head on the tiles. For an instant, Sandrine lay there and wondered if she might go to sleep. She felt pain reverberating all down her side, where bruises and wounds were in contact with the floor, but she hadn't the strength to shift position.

How long had she been here?

They had come for her at five o'clock, not quite light. Was it day now? Night? It felt endless but might have been only minutes. She wondered if anyone else was being held here. She tried to push the names from her head, unremember them so that they were buried too deep to be excavated. Tried not to think about Raoul or Robert, Lucie or Monsieur Baillard.

Then she was being dragged to her feet and someone – Laval again – seized her wet blouse and pulled hard, causing her to stagger forward into him. Someone laughed. She felt the material rip and the sound of the buttons bouncing lightly on the floor. He dropped her back on to the chair.

'Who helped you with the forgery?' Laval was saying. 'Very good, by the way, you had us all convinced.' He put his hand around her neck, resting it gently at first, then beginning to tighten his grip.

'All I'm asking is where the Codex is now. You tell me, then this stops. You see? This will stop.'

'I don't know anything,' she managed to say.

Suddenly there was a shuffling of feet and the sound of the door being flung back against its frame. Laval's hand dropped from her throat and she felt him step away. Felt other hands dragging her to her feet. Even in her disorientated state, Sandrine realised the atmosphere in the room had changed. An angry voice through the ringing in her ears. Then, the hood being untied and taken from her head.

For a moment, Sandrine felt only pleasure at the touch of air on her skin. She closed her eyes and turned her head away from the bare bulb, bright after the darkness of her confinement.

'*Asseyez-vous.*' Sit down.

Although she tried not to give him the satisfaction of reacting, Sandrine flinched at the sound of Authié's voice. She stood, swaying slightly, held up by the hands of the Gestapo officers standing either side of her, then she was being pushed down on to the chair, her arms dragged behind her again and secured.

The swelling above her right eye was pushing her lid closed, making it hard to see properly.

'Mademoiselle Vidal,' he said.

Sandrine forced herself to raise her head, determined to look him in the eye, but the motion made her feel sick.

Despite everything she had endured at Laval's hands, she feared Authié more, though he had never laid a finger on her. Sweat pooled in the small of her bruised back, between her breasts; she could smell it coming off her skin, sour, feral.

'Major Authié,' she said. 'Lieutenant Laval has been asking me questions. I don't know why. I don't know what he wants to know.' She realised she was rambling, but hoped she might be able to persuade him of her ignorance despite having failed to convince Laval. 'I don't know what he wants,' she said again.

Authié walked round behind her, standing so close that she could smell aftershave, soap and tobacco, in sharp contrast to the smell of blood and wet material. Sandrine felt her body shrink into itself, as if there were thousands of tiny wires pulling at her skin. Furious that she was allowing him to affect her so utterly, she forced her chin up, ignoring the pain thudding in her neck and her jaw.

He dropped his hands on to her shoulders. Sandrine recoiled from his touch. He dug his fingers deeper into the skin and muscle, increasing the pressure, then let his right hand slide lower, hooking under the thin cotton of her blouse, and lower still.

'No,' she said quickly.

'You flatter yourself,' he said. 'Lieutenant Laval informs me you have been less than helpful.'

'He cannot accept I don't have the answers he wants.'

He leant forward. Sandrine thought he was going to touch her again, but instead he jerked the chair so she was teetering backwards towards the floor. She swallowed a cry, determined not to show any fear in front of him.

'Come, you can do better than that,' he said.

'Please,' she said, despising the pleading tone in her voice. 'I don't know anything.'

'Please,' he mimicked. He set the chair roughly back on

its legs, sending a jolt of pain snaking the length of her spine. She bit her lip to stop herself crying out.

'You see, I think you're lying when you say you don't know anything, Mademoiselle Vidal – "Sophie", as I believe you're known now.'

Sandrine forced herself not to react.

'I think you knew exactly what you were doing when you told me about the forgery. And that you know where the actual Codex is.' He leant forward. 'Do you have it?' he said, whispering like a lover into her ear. 'It's true, isn't it? You know where it is?'

'I don't know about any forgery,' she said. Every part of her was smarting, battered, damaged, but her mind felt suddenly sharp. 'And my name is Sandrine.'

'A birth certificate is an easy thing to find,' Authié laughed. 'I would have thought you'd be more inventive. But Sophie, Sandrine, it doesn't matter at the moment. I have all the time in the world,' he said. 'I am quite happy to stay here until I get what I want.'

'You're talking to the wrong person,' Sandrine insisted. 'I don't know anything.'

She raised her head and forced herself to look into his eyes. They were dark, devoid of any emotion. All she could see was her own fear reflected back at her. Then her eyes slid sideways, a glint of light, to the silver crucifix on his lapel.

'We seem to have reached an impasse,' he said. 'In which case, I had better find a way to help you remember what you do know.'

Authié drew his gun from his belt. Sandrine felt the atmosphere in the room change. Laval half stepped forward.

'I have nothing of value to tell you,' she said, with as much courage as she could muster. At the same time, she knew that if he killed her, at least it would be over.

She would die without giving anyone away.

Authié suddenly pulled her skirt up above her knees, then pushed the muzzle of the gun between her legs, slowly pressing the cold metal against her skin.

'Where is the Codex?' he said. 'Let's start with this.'

'I don't know.'

Authié moved the weapon higher up the inside of her thigh. 'Come now, you can do better than that.'

Sandrine felt the muzzle of the gun jabbing against her pubic bone now and realised what he intended to do. She closed her eyes.

'I don't know,' she said again, bracing herself for the pain.

Then she heard it, the same whispered word. The same voice, just for a moment.

'*Coratge.*'

And then another memory. The warrior stone angel in Square Gambetta. Her determined stare, her hands wrapped around the hilt of her sword, her wings broken but her fighting spirit undimmed. And the thought of her gave Sandrine the courage to hold out. For a little longer.

'I don't know anything,' she said again.

Chapter 131

Raoul had been in the bar since six fifteen. Bonnet and Yvette arrived about half an hour after that.

'They came in at five fifteen, you say,' Raoul said desperately.

Yvette nodded. The bar was noisy, even at this time in the morning, and she had to raise her voice to be heard. 'Milice and Gestapo. Six of them for one prisoner.'

'You saw her?'

Yvette shook her head. 'I can't say that I did. There were so many of them shielding her.'

'But how do you know it was a woman?'

'She was wearing a skirt,' she replied, 'and had a funny pair of socks on. Those Scottish tartan things that were all the rage a couple of years back.'

'Anything else you noticed?' Robert prompted.

'I didn't see anything else. They took her to one of the rooms at the back.'

'Did you hear anything?'

Yvette shook her head. 'Not allowed in that part of the building.'

'What part?' Raoul said quickly.

'The interrogation rooms,' she said quietly. 'I'm sorry.'

Raoul blanched, but didn't let himself think about anything other than how to get her away.

'As I was leaving, Major Authié arrived. He looked angry. I think he'd been with Schiffner already, but I'm not sure. I overheard him saying they would move the prisoner this morning, then he went striding down the corridor and into the room, and I didn't hear anything else.'

She glanced at Robert, then back to Raoul. 'Robert was waiting for me. Asked me to come to meet you.' She frowned. 'I don't know if it's your girl,' she said quietly. 'I'm sorry.'

'You've been a great help, love,' Robert said, putting his large hand over hers. 'Thanks to you, at least we know she's there.'

'Someone's there,' Yvette corrected.

Bonnet turned to Raoul. 'From what Yvette says, there might be a chance of getting to her.'

'How?' Raoul lit a cigarette, jiggling his leg up and down. He couldn't trust himself to speak.

'Apparently they don't keep suspects in the cells for long. If Authié wants to move her, more than likely it will be to the detention centre in the Caserne Laperrine. That's the usual pattern once an interrogation's completed: the Gestapo transfer prisoners either to the hospital—'

Raoul interrupted, unable to bear thinking about that. 'You say she was alone?'

'Yes.'

'That's what I was coming to,' Bonnet said. 'A single prisoner, a woman, they're likely to transfer her in a *panier à salade* rather than use a prison van. Should make it easier. Is she likely to be able to help herself?'

'You know Sandrine,' he said. 'She's brave. She won't talk.'

'You think she'll need help?'

Raoul met his gaze. 'She'll have held out for as long as she can.'

For a moment, no one spoke. Then Robert turned to Yvette. 'Can you go to the Clinique Bastion and warn Dr Giraud that we might have a patient for him?' He paused. 'On second thoughts, he won't be at the clinic. There was a round-up in boulevard Barbès and Trivalle, so he's more likely to be in the cabin he uses out at Cavayère. Can you find out if he's there? Warn him to expect us?'

Yvette nodded and stood up, tying her headscarf beneath her chin.

'We need to be in position, ready for when they move her.'

'If they move her,' Raoul muttered.

'You go now. I'll fetch a car, a little extra help, then meet you there. Brown Peugeot, corner of boulevard Omer Sarraut.'

Raoul nodded.

Sandrine didn't think she could take any more. Her body was broken, racked with pain. The blood had dried between her legs, but she felt as if her insides had been ripped out. She had told Authié nothing, but each time it became more difficult not to give in. All she wanted after these hours, minutes – could it be days, she didn't know – was for it to stop. The questions, the barrage of questions and blows.

'If you'll let me continue, sir.'

'I don't want her dead, Laval,' Authié snapped, but then he clicked his fingers.

She'd forgotten Laval was still in the room. She registered that they were arguing. Then she was being dragged to her feet. She felt the slightest touch of fingers against her back, Authié or Laval, she didn't know, then her shirt being torn from her back.

Before, she would have reacted, but she couldn't see it mattered now. There was no humiliation she hadn't been subjected to already, no pain they hadn't inflicted on her. But then she smelt something new – the smell of heat and of metal, a hiss of iron – and discovered that she still had the capacity to experience fear.

'Hold her down.'

Sandrine felt herself being pushed forward, her face

hitting the hard surface of a table or a counter top, she didn't know. Then, the most excruciating agony she'd ever felt as he pressed the poker into her shoulder, branding her. The spit and hiss of skin, the sickly smell of burnt flesh. It was seconds before her body and her mind caught up with one another. She tried to turn herself to stone, like the warrior statue. Impervious to pain.

Y penser toujours. Never forget.

It was too much to ask. Finally, Sandrine submitted. She screamed and screamed, letting out everything she had kept inside her for the past hours.

Witnessing her being branded, even after everything he had seen, was too much for one of the *vert-de-gris* in the room. She heard him vomit and the angry response from Authié at the running feet. The murmured orders as someone was sent to clear up the mess. Even in her half-conscious state, Sandrine experienced a moment of triumph. One last, tiny triumph.

But now all she wanted was to sleep. The dark pull of oblivion. A few words, that was all it would take, to put an end to this.

The door opened again. The sound of shoes striding across the tiles, then stopping dead.

'Vous avez obtenu les renseignements desirés, Herr Authié?'

A German voice speaking accented, formal French.

'The prisoner continues to withhold information,' he replied. 'But we will make her talk.'

Sandrine was dimly aware of this new person leaning over her. She could feel the fire spreading through every part of her body, pain coming in waves from the place where the poker had met her skin.

Then disgust in the German's voice. 'What have you done to her, Authié?'

Another tiny moment of triumph.

'*Y penser toujours*,' she muttered before she passed out.

*

Raoul raced through the labyrinth of small streets running parallel to the route de Toulouse. When he was certain he was not being followed, he crossed to the far side of the road, then into the network of suburban cul-de-sacs lying between the railway sidings and the main road, until he was in position at the back of Gestapo headquarters.

There was no corner of the ancient city, north or south, west or east, left untouched by the war. Mostly, the Gestapo and the Wehrmacht had requisitioned the grandest of the buildings. This nondescript villa was the exception, a provincial house rather than a military installation, despite the fact that Chef Eckfelner, Sous-chef Schiffner and Inspectors Janeke and Zimmerman were key Resistance targets. Several attempts had been made on the building and had failed.

Armed guards patrolled the perimeter, cradling standard-issue sub-machine guns and with pistols at their belts. Raoul scanned the roof and windows on the first floor, seeing no signs of snipers or additional guards. Square, heavy floodlights were trained on the yard and, over the walls, out into the street.

Raoul glanced at his watch. From what Yvette had overheard, they would transfer her this morning. Always assuming it was Sandrine. That she was still alive. He shook his head, telling himself he could not allow himself to doubt. He wanted a cigarette, but knew the smoke would give him away.

Fixing his eyes on the metal grille, he emptied his mind and listened for the mechanism of the gate getting ready to open. Ten minutes passed before, as Robert had explained, a red warning light began to flash by the vehicle exit. There was a clunk of heavy machinery, then the gate itself began to slide open. Moments later, a green police car shot out of the compound into the small street and rounded the corner, heading towards the main road. It had been so quick, he wasn't sure of what he'd seen, but it looked like a driver and a guard in the front, then two people in the back. A glimpse of black hair.

Raoul broke cover, along the track that led beside the railway sidings, to the corner of the boulevard. Robert's brother Gaston was waiting with a Luger ·38 special tucked into the waistband of his trousers, half shielded beneath his jacket.

Raoul held up three fingers, to confirm what he'd seen. Gaston nodded and set off quickly through the Jardin des Plantes, watching out for the green Citroën.

Raoul stayed on the far side of the road, drawing his pistol but holding it pointed down to the ground by his side. Keeping Gaston in his sights, his attention was caught by the flapping of the Nazi flag on the building opposite. Most public buildings now carried the hated Croix Gammée, the swastika, in place of the Tricolore of the French Republic.

He located the brown Peugeot and darted across the boulevard. Robert was waiting at the top of the rue du Port. There was no other traffic of any kind.

'A driver and guard in the front, two people in the back,' he said.

'Was it her?'

Raoul hesitated. 'I think so.'

Bonnet nodded and pushed the starter. The engine spluttered into life. Raoul looked back up the road, seeing the green Citroën turn the corner and drive towards them.

'Here they come.'

He stepped away from the car, looking for Gaston in the shade of the trees. Located him, raised his hand.

Then everything happened at once. Robert stamped down on the accelerator pedal. The Peugeot shot forward, forcing the police car to swerve. He put the car immediately into reverse, slamming into the side of the *panier à salade*, driving it back into the kerb. The police car juddered, jerked, its back wheels skidding, steam billowing from the buckled bonnet.

Robert kept his engine running.

Gaston came alongside the nearside window, raised his pistol and emptied the clip. Glass shattered everywhere. The driver was thrown back, then slumped forward on the dashboard, the guard collapsed sideways on top of him. Blood, glass, scattered, shimmering on the road.

Raoul ran to the car. He could see Sandrine and a man in plain clothes lying across the back seat. He pulled at the handle, but it was jammed. He hesitated, then smashed the window with his pistol, trying not to send too much glass in. He reached in and released the lock, and dragged the door open. The street was filling up, customers from the Café Continental and Café Edouard coming out to see what was happening. German soldiers rushing out of the Hôtel Terminus, weapons raised.

'Unconscious in the back,' he said to Gaston. 'Cover me.'

Raoul put his arms beneath Sandrine. She cried out in pain. It was the sweetest sound he'd ever heard, though a violent torrent of rage and desire for revenge swept through him at the sight of her. Her eyes were swollen shut, her clothes torn. Blood was dried on her face, her arms, her legs. On her shoulder, an open weeping burn. Desperate not to inflict any more pain on her battered body, he placed her on the back seat of the Peugeot and got in beside her. As he shut the door, Robert was already accelerating, leaving Gaston to make his getaway through the shaded, overgrown alleyways of the botanical gardens.

The car swung round as Robert doubled back to avoid a roadblock. Outside the Terminus, soldiers raised their machine guns and opened fire. Bullets ricocheted off the bumper and Raoul felt one tyre blow, but Robert kept control of the car. Cradling Sandrine in his arms, Raoul looked back at the scene of devastation behind him. A man staggered out of the back of the *panier à salade*, then straightened up with his hand on the roof of the car. Soldiers and police rushed to help him. Raoul felt his chest tighten another notch. He had barely looked at the man in the car. His only aim was to get Sandrine out and away. But now he could see it was Leo Authié.

He had had him there, and hadn't realised. He should have killed him. Shot him while he was unconscious. He'd had another chance at him, but had let it slip through his fingers.

Robert turned the corner, driving dangerously fast, then up towards the cimetière Saint-Vincent. The motion of the car disturbed Sandrine.

'I don't know anything . . .' she murmured.

Raoul felt her shift in his arms and cry out again in pain, and he forgot everything.

'I've got you, I'm here,' he whispered. 'You're safe now.'

He thought he saw a smile flicker across her bruised lips.

'I didn't tell them anything . . .'

'*Ma belle*,' he muttered, trying to keep the distress from his voice. 'I'm here. It's going to be all right. Everything's going to be all right.'

But as he looked down at her bruised and battered body lying beside him, the blistered skin and the blood on her legs and skirt, he didn't know how it could ever be all right. The car screeched around another corner, then started to struggle up the hill.

'Hurry.'

Robert glanced at him in the rear-view mirror, then slammed his foot hard on the accelerator. The old engine stuttered and whined, but the car leapt forward again as they climbed into the hills around Cavayère.

'Hurry,' Raoul said again.

Chapter 132

COUSTAUSSA

'Thank you,' said Lucie, getting out of the back of the van. One of the men handed Jean-Jacques down to her.

'You'll be all right with the little one?'

She nodded. 'There's bound to be someone who can give me a ride to Coustaussa.' The man looked doubtful. She wondered if she was wrong. She'd been gone for eighteen months. She had no idea how much Couiza might have changed.

When the van had driven off, Lucie walked through the woods and down to the river's edge, her son's chubby little hand in hers. It was such a pleasure to be away from the watchful streets of the Bastide that she felt in no hurry. The dappled sun through the canopy of leaves, the sweet sound of the Aude flowing over the rocky riverbed.

'Careful now, J-J,' she said. 'Watch where you're going.'

The little boy put his arms up. 'Mama, carry. Carry, carry, carry.'

'Come on, my little man, you can do it on your own. Just a few more steps.'

Jean-Jacques started to frown, then changed his mind and stumbled the last few paces to the water's edge on his own. Lucie knelt forward and splashed water on her cheeks, then used her handkerchief to wipe her son's face.

'Swim?' he sang hopefully. 'Swim, swim, swim.'

Lucie laughed. 'Not now,' she said, scooping him up.

'Too early to go swimming. We need to find everyone and have breakfast, then we'll see.'

Jean-Jacques frowned.

'We're going to see Marieta and Tante Liesl.'

The little boy smiled. 'Liesl.'

'Good boy.'

Lucie began to walk along the river towards the town. Now he was away from the city, Jean-Jacques no longer had a sore throat. He was playing with the buttons on the collar of her shirt. He couldn't have any memory of either Marieta or Liesl, but she hadn't wanted them to be disappointed, so she had talked to him about them all the time.

'And Tante Marianne and Tante Suzanne will be there too,' she added.

The little boy's eyes brightened. 'Suzu,' he said. 'Plane.'

Lucie smiled. His favourite toy was a cardboard aeroplane Suzanne had made him and repaired a hundred times.

'That's right,' she said. 'Plane. If you're a very good boy, perhaps Suzu will make you a new plane? What about that?'

'Plane, plane, plane . . .'

As Lucie came into town, she immediately knew the place had changed. Raoul had warned her, but she hadn't expected it to be so obvious. There was a major Wehrmacht arms depot and food store on the hill at Montazels, which meant there were military vehicles on the roads a lot of the time. He'd also told her there was a small Maquis unit hiding out in the garrigue between Alet-les-Bains and Coustaussa, on the opposite side of the valley. The Milice had made several attempts to destroy the group, but had so far only succeeded in driving them higher into the hills.

Lucie hugged Jean-Jacques closer to her. She walked towards the Grand Café Guilhem. There were a few women sitting at the tables on the terrace. She didn't recognise any of them. No men at all.

'Faim, faim,' Jean-Jacques suddenly said, trying to wriggle down from her arms.

'You're hungry, little man?'

Jean-Jacques pointed at the bread one of the women was dipping in a cup of black barley and chicory coffee.

'Tartine.'

'No, we're going to the boulangerie to choose something nice. Shall we do that? J-J help me choose?'

To her relief, Jean-Jacques vigorously nodded his head. 'Choose. J-J choose.'

Lucie walked briskly across the square, her bag swinging from her arm, heading for the patisserie run by the station master's wife, Mathilde. She stepped through the fly curtain in the doorway, grabbing at J-J's hand to stop him pulling the beads, then into the cool interior.

Mathilde looked up with a neutral expression. She frowned, faltered, then recognised Lucie and a smile broke out on her face.

'Madomaisèla!' she said. She leant across the counter and pinched Jean-Jacques' cheek. 'And look at your little chap, hasn't he grown? I hardly recognised either of you. Where's all that lovely blonde hair of yours gone?'

'Couldn't get the peroxide,' Lucie replied. 'Aren't I a sight? But what can a girl do but go natural?' She smiled. 'You don't look any different at all, Mathilde. How's Ernest?'

Mathilde's face clouded over. 'He's no longer with us,' she said.

'Oh, no.'

'Got caught up in the Gestapo attack on Villerouge-Termenès,' she said. 'He killed three of them before they got him. His bravery allowed his comrades to get away, so they told me.'

'I'm so sorry, Mathilde,' Lucie said quietly.

'It's how he would have wanted to go,' the older woman said simply. She gave a brief nod, to indicate the conversation was over, then put her broad hands on the counter. 'So. What can I do for you, madomaisèla?'

Lucie looked at the empty shelves. There were no baguettes, just two loaves of black bread wrapped in a twist of paper with a name written on it. It was clear that everyone else had come in much earlier in the morning.

'A little something for J-J to keep him going until I get to the house,' she said, fishing in her bag and producing a strip of coupons.

Mathilde waved them away. 'No need to worry about that,' she said. 'Let's see if I can find something special.'

She vanished into the back, reappearing a moment later with a madeleine sponge cake. 'My own recipe,' she said. 'I have to make do with powdered egg and saccharine, but they seem to go down quite well all the same.'

'That's very kind,' Lucie said warmly.

'Here you are, little chap.' Mathilde handed it to Jean-Jacques. 'A special cake for a special boy.'

He reached out and took it.

'What do you say, J-J?' Lucie said sharply.

He paused. '*Très bon*.'

The women both laughed.

'I don't suppose the Saturday market bus still runs?' Lucie asked.

'No, but someone's sure to be going that way. If you give me a minute, I'll arrange something.' She reached under the counter and produced a package wrapped in newspaper. 'And if you could take this for Marieta, that would save the boy a journey later.'

'How are things in Couiza generally?' Lucie said, dropping her voice.

'As well as can be expected,' Mathilde said, putting the

bread in Lucie's bag. 'A few work for the other side. And there's plenty of *miliciens* about because of the Wehrmacht depot. One or two parachute drops have missed their targets recently. Brings the Gestapo into the town.' She shook her head. 'Nothing to do with me,' she said firmly, meeting Lucie's eye.

'No. Of course not.'

'Are you back for good?' Mathilde asked. 'You and Jean-Jacques?'

Lucie hesitated, then she smiled. 'I hope so.'

It took no time for Mathilde to organise a ride to Coustaussa on the back of Ernestine Cassou's dog trap. An hour later, Lucie was sitting in the kitchen at CITADELLE with Marieta and Liesl, Marianne and Suzanne and Geneviève. There had been tears and embraces, a rapid-fire exchange of day-to-day news – nothing serious – as she was brought up to date with everything Marianne and Suzanne had already been told. She felt as if she had never been away.

She exchanged a look with Liesl, who smiled. Lucie had expected Liesl to have changed a great deal. She was tall and beautiful, a woman, not the nervous child Lucie remembered. Sandrine and Raoul spoke of her as very resourceful and brave. Lucie found she was a little intimidated by her.

They had gone outside on their own to show J-J the garden and talked for a few minutes about Max. They had cried a little, then discussed the rumours that the camp was being evacuated. There had been no news from their friend in the Café de la Paix for more than a week, so Liesl was intending to try to go to the village herself, if at all possible, to find out the truth. As Lucie looked at her now, so self-contained and still, she hoped that she and Liesl would have a chance to get to know one another again.

Also that the sense of feeling a little at a disadvantage in the younger woman's company would pass.

'Ernestine Cassou wasn't as awful as I remembered,' Lucie said. 'She didn't say much, but she seemed happy enough to bring me here.'

'She and her father aren't unusual,' Geneviève said. 'They went along with Pétain to start with. They turned a blind eye because they thought it was for the best. Then they realised what collaboration actually meant – no food, forced labour, being second-class citizens in their own country. They don't know what to do.'

'But they're not doing anything to help bring the occupation to an end,' Suzanne said.

'No,' Geneviève admitted.

Marianne nodded. 'You didn't say anything in front of her?'

'Lord, no.'

After only two days in Coustaussa, Marianne was already looking less haggard and gaunt, though there was still that underlying nervousness. Lucie smiled at her son, hoping the country air would do him good too.

'Mathilde told me about Ernest,' she said.

'Dreadful,' Marieta said, without looking up. 'A dreadful loss.'

'But to know Monsieur Baillard is all right,' Lucie continued, 'that's the most wonderful news.'

Marieta stopped what she was doing, a smile breaking across her tired, worn face.

'I never doubted it,' she said.

'Have you seen him yet, Marieta?' Lucie asked. 'How is he?'

'Not yet. He's in Tarascon with Monsieur l'Inspecteur,' she said. 'He has business there. He will come when he can. For now, it's enough to know he is well.'

'Eloise and Guillaume are helping him,' Geneviève

said, 'although …' She paused, casting her mind back to the conversation they'd had on the day of Pierre Déjean's funeral. 'Though I get the feeling that it's Sandrine he's really waiting for. Eloise says he is planning to go into the mountains to search for the Codex, even though the entire area is now off limits. There are SS patrols everywhere. Anyone caught in a prohibited zone is arrested.'

'Or shot,' Liesl said.

Straight away, Lucie's contented frame of mind vanished. She knew Suzanne had told the others about Authié's return to Carcassonne, so at least she didn't have to be the bearer of bad news. But as she looked at Marianne, she saw her thoughts had returned to her sister.

'I'm sure Sandrine's all right,' Lucie said. 'Raoul stayed behind so they could travel together. Sandrine will be all right. She always is.'

Chapter 133

CARCASSONNE

Raoul cradled Sandrine's head in his lap, doing his best to insulate her from the jolts and potholes on the track. Her breathing had grown shallow and her skin was drained of colour.

'How much further, Bonnet?' Raoul said. 'I'm not sure she can last any longer.'

They had pulled off the road some time back and were slowly making their way along a forestry path between the pine trees in the woods around Cavayère, the chassis of the car bumping over the uneven surface of the *draille*.

'We're nearly there.'

He made one final switchback turn, following a winding path that led steeply up, then parked beneath the branches of a *pin parasol*.

'This is it.'

Raoul looked up at the log cabin. An idyllic location in the hills, perfect for hunting. A warm oil lamp glowed in the window.

'He's here,' Bonnet said, quickly getting out of the car. He knocked on the door of the cabin, then came round to Raoul's side to help him lift Sandrine out. She had lost consciousness and there was a slick of blood on the back seat.

Jeanne Giraud appeared in the doorway. Raoul saw distress flood her face at her first sight of Sandrine, but she kept her head.

'Bring her through,' she said.

'Is Giraud here?' Raoul asked desperately.

'My husband's washing his hands,' she said.

Carefully, so as not to open any of Sandrine's wounds, Raoul and Robert carried her into the cabin. A sturdy table had been covered with a rough woollen blanket in the centre of the single room.

'Is there nowhere else? A bed?' Raoul said.

'This is what Jean-Marc needs,' she replied calmly. 'We'll make her comfortable afterwards.'

Between them, Raoul and Robert laid Sandrine down on the makeshift operating table, on her side so the burn wasn't in contact with the blanket.

Bonnet stood back. 'I'm going to leave you, Pelletier. Get back to the Bastide and make sure Yvette and Gaston are all right.' He glanced at Jeanne. 'Someone will let me know? If you need me to come back later.'

'She'll be here for a few days,' Jeanne said in the same calm and steady voice.

Raoul nodded his thanks. Moments later, he heard the engine start up and the car begin its careful descent down the rough track through the forest.

He looked around the cabin. There was one small window and a bookshelf on the far wall. In the corner there was a small table with a typewriter on it. Madame Giraud noticed him looking and covered up the papers lying on the desk.

'I can't tell you how grateful I am that—'

'They are monsters,' she said in a low voice. 'They arrested my father-in-law yesterday.'

'I'm so sorry, I didn't realise.'

Jeanne met his gaze. 'They released him, but not before giving him a broken nose and a black eye. Sixty-five years old. He knows nothing.' She poured him a large measure of brandy. 'Anyway, drink this. You look like you need it.'

Raoul knocked the measure back in one go, then moved

to stand closer to Sandrine's head. She was very pale and her breathing was shallow, snatched, as if every gasp cost her more than she could spare. Raoul wanted to hold her hand or stroke her hair or rest his head on her shoulder, but everything about her was battered and torn.

The back door opened and a dark-haired, wiry man in his mid-twenties came in, drying his hands on a towel. He didn't waste time with niceties, but went straight to his patient. Raoul saw him blanch as he saw the extent of her injuries.

'Will she be all right, Giraud?'

'Did my wife say your name was Pelletier?'

'That's right.'

He looked at his patient. 'And she is?'

'Sandrine.'

'Marianne Vidal's sister?'

'That's right.'

'She was a pupil of mine,' Jeanne said. 'She was the girl who helped on Bastille Day when the bomb went off at Saint-Michel, remember? Papa thought a lot of her.'

Giraud met Raoul's eye. 'Might I know her by another name?'

Raoul held his gaze. 'You might.'

He said nothing more, but Raoul realised Giraud knew her reputation and hoped it would make him even more determined to save her.

He took an ophthalmoscope from his bag, lifted the less swollen of her eyelids and shone the light in her eye.

'Mademoiselle Vidal? Sandrine? Can you hear me?'

There was no reaction. Giraud looked up at Raoul. 'How long's she been unconscious?'

'She talked a little in the car at first, but not for half an hour or so.'

'What happened?'

'Gestapo. We managed to rescue her as they were

transferring her from the route de Toulouse to the Caserne Laperrine.'

Giraud didn't look up, but continued to examine Sandrine's injuries. 'How long was she with them before that?'

'She was arrested at five o'clock this morning,' he said quietly.

Giraud stopped. 'She was there for six hours.'

'Yes.' Raoul hesitated. 'Will she make it?'

Giraud paused and looked up for a moment. 'So long as no infection sets in, she'll make it. Physically, at least, though she's going to be pretty uncomfortable.' He pointed at the suppurating burn on her shoulder. 'But mentally? I don't know. They did a job on her, Pelletier.'

Raoul forced himself to look at the burn properly, realising that it wasn't a random shape at all, but rather something specific.

'It's some kind of crucifix, by the look of it,' Giraud was saying.

Raoul felt the bile rising in his throat and took several deep breaths. 'It's the Cross of Lorraine,' he said quietly. They had branded her with the symbol adopted by the Resistance.

Giraud peered. 'Gestapo, did you say?'

Raoul thought about Authié staggering out of the car. 'I'm not certain.'

'I've never seen anything like this before,' Giraud said. His gaze moved down to the blood on Sandrine's skirt and thighs. 'If you want to wait outside, Pelletier,' he said quickly, 'Jeanne will assist me. No need for you to watch.'

'I'm staying.'

Giraud held his gaze, then nodded. 'Very well. I need to disinfect the burns, to prevent infection – that's the challenge.' He paused. 'It will hurt.'

Raoul noticed that Jeanne was holding a jug of vinegar.

'We haven't got any antiseptic,' she said. 'This will have to do.'

'Take this,' Giraud said, thrusting a cloth into Raoul's hand. 'Fold it over. Make a wad.'

'What do I . . .?'

'Put it between Sandrine's teeth when she screams,' Jeanne said.

Raoul felt his stomach clench as Jeanne, gently, helped her husband roll Sandrine further on to her side. As Giraud dabbed the disinfectant on to the livid red weals, Sandrine let out a deep, wild howl, shocked back into consciousness. For a moment, Raoul was so relieved to hear her voice, to see she was awake, that he just stared down at her.

'For God's sake, man. The cloth!'

Jolted into action, he put the wad into her mouth, and Sandrine, despite the madness of the pain, understood what was required and bit down hard as Giraud cleaned, then dressed the wound.

'That's it, Sandrine,' Jeanne murmured. 'It will be over in a moment.'

Raoul saw the agony in her half-open eyes, but she didn't cry out again. He felt her fingers reaching for his. Her grip was strong and he struggled to keep the tears from his eyes.

'You're so brave,' he whispered to her. 'No one more so.'

It took nearly an hour for Giraud to clean and dress every wound, sending Raoul out of the room to fetch water as he moved to the injuries further down. Raoul felt a coward for not wanting to know. When he came back with a pail from the stream, Sandrine was covered with a sheet from the waist down.

'That's the best I can do,' Giraud said, as he wiped the blood from his hands.

'Thank you.'

'She shouldn't be moved, but you need to think of where you can take her to recuperate. It's going to be a good few weeks before she's up on her feet again. And they'll be looking for her. For you both.'

Raoul nodded. 'There's somewhere we can go, yes.'

'Good. We'll leave her to sleep a while. You could do with it too, by the looks of things. Let the painkillers take effect. I've given her an injection of morphine to take the edge off things, but it will wear off. The wounds are all clean, but it's possible infection will set in. Internally, well, have to see. Tricky.' He broke off. 'The burn on her back, that's the one you have to keep an eye on. She needs to be kept as still and as quiet as possible.'

Despite everything, Raoul smiled. 'Try keeping her still.' Then he looked at Sandrine and his face clouded over once more.

Giraud's professional expression faltered for a moment.

'You can both stay here for the rest of today and tonight,' he said quietly. 'It's safe up here, so far as anywhere's safe. Tomorrow too, if she's not well enough to be moved.'

'There aren't any other cabins nearby?'

'One or two on the far side of the hill,' he said. His expression grew grim. 'And they've not found us yet.'

Raoul gave a long sigh. 'I can't thank you enough, Giraud. You too, madame.'

'It's an honour.'

'She's a brave woman,' Jeanne said, putting a cushion under Sandrine's head.

'Sandrine would be thanking you herself,' he said, glancing at her, 'if she could.'

'She can thank me when she wakes up,' Giraud said briskly.

Raoul frowned. 'Aren't you going to move her somewhere more comfortable?'

'Later,' Giraud said. 'Best to leave her be for now. Jeanne

will sit with her, if you want to get a bit of rest yourself.'

Raoul shook his head. 'I'm not leaving,' he said.

Giraud and his wife exchanged a look, then Jeanne nodded.

'I'll fetch you a chair,' she said.

Chapter 134

TARASCON

There was another burst of gunfire in the hills. Were they anti-aircraft guns? Audric Baillard could not tell at this distance. In the mountains, the sound was distorted.

Achille Pujol and Guillaume Breillac stopped alongside him. They had crossed into the restricted zone some half an hour ago. The Wehrmacht patrols were known to shoot on sight.

'Do you wish to go on, sénher?'

In the distance, Baillard heard the faint sound of a plane. All three men looked up at the sky. A parachute drop for the Picaussel Maquis was due tonight but, in recent weeks, many of the Allied attempts to get weapons and provisions to the Resistance and Maquis had gone wrong. They either missed their target or, worse, maquisards arrived to find the Gestapo waiting.

Baillard nodded. 'We should go on,' he said quietly. 'The disturbance sounds some way off.'

Breillac accepted the decision without argument. He knew the easiest route up towards the Pic de Vicdessos for his elderly companions. Baillard had not yet regained his full strength but, even so, he was finding the going easier than Pujol. His old friend had been determined to come with them, but he was breathing heavily and there was a sheen of sweat on his forehead.

'There's no reason why Authié should be able to find you, Audric,' Pujol panted, 'any more than I could. They'll try Los Seres, I dare say, but you've not been there for so long, what can they find?'

'That is true, my friend,' Baillard said.

Pujol's magpie network of police officers, working undercover with the Resistance, had done their job well. In the past twenty-four hours, news had come from a sympathiser in the Carcassonne Commissariat that Authié's deputy, Sylvère Laval, had requested the police file on Baillard.

Pujol had taken the news badly. Since then, he had barely left Baillard's side. But it was only what Baillard had expected. Saurat would have given the Gestapo his name. The SS in Lyon would have passed it on to de l'Oradore. It wasn't important. It only meant that he had to act sooner than he would have chosen. He would have preferred to wait for Sandrine Vidal and Raoul Pelletier before going in search of the Codex. There was something about the young couple that made them central to his plans.

'They don't know you're here, Baillard,' Pujol said again.

Baillard put his hand on his friend's arm. 'Save your breath, *amic.*' He gestured up the slope. 'There is still some way to go.'

They walked on in silence for a while, Baillard listening for signs that they had company on the hillside, but hearing nothing to cause alarm. No more gunfire, no evidence that they were getting closer to a patrol, no sound of an engine.

'Eloise tells me it is called the Vallée des Trois Loups,' he said to Guillaume as the path levelled out. 'The Valley of the Three Wolves. Do you know where the name came from?'

Guillaume took the bottle, slaked his thirst, then handed it on to Pujol.

'Her family is descended from the early inhabitants of the area. Most of the oldest Tarasconnais families claim descent from the same three sisters who lived here in the fourth century. One of them was called Lupa – I don't know what the others were called – which is where their surname, Saint-Loup, supposedly comes from. I don't know why. She was never made a saint, to my knowledge. Perhaps they were named after the place, rather than the other way round.'

'Names are important,' Baillard said lightly.

Breillac continued. 'Marianne and Sandrine Vidal are related to them too, through their mother's side of the family.'

Baillard stopped. 'Is that so?' he said quietly.

Pujol stared at the changing expression on his face. 'Is that important, Audric?'

'I do not know,' he said softly. 'It may be. We will see, we will see.'

They went on in silence. The path was dry and slippery with dust, and although Guillaume kept a steady pace, both Baillard and Pujol took each step carefully. Soon Baillard saw a sequence of caves, facing west across the valley, cradled within the ancient pines and oak, the timeless green woodland. He could also make out a pattern, cast by the rays of the sun, on the face of one sheer wall of limestone.

He smiled. The air might be less clear, pylons and buildings might scar the landscape, but the sun rose in the east as it ever had, and sank back to earth in the west. He put his hand to his pocket, where Arinius' map lay folded, but he did not need to get it out. He could see it in his mind's eye. In sixteen hundred years, the essential character of the land had not changed. And on the flat surface above the entrance to one of the caves, the mountain still cast a shadow much like the shape of a cross.

'A place of safety,' he said.

'Is this it?' Guillaume asked.

Baillard nodded. 'I know the way now.'

Now Baillard led, fixing his gaze on the shadow cast by the scattered pink light. As they drew closer, the pattern changed. There appeared to be a second arm beneath the first, a double cross, much like the Cross of Lorraine. An ancient symbol, adopted now by the Resistance.

A cloud crossed the face of the sun and, for a moment, Baillard felt a jolt of horror, a fierce premonition of something dreadful. The shadow symbol transformed from a sign of strength to an image of burnt and scarred flesh. He could smell it, familiar from mass burnings he had witnessed at Montségur in days past. He could feel the victim's agony.

Then the cloud moved on. The sun reappeared and the air was calm once more. He put his hand to his chest and felt how his heart was racing.

'Are you all right, Baillard?' Pujol asked. 'Do you want to rest a while?'

Baillard shook his head. 'No,' he said quickly. 'No.'

They passed a clump of juniper bushes at the edge of the path, went through an avenue of oak, up the hillside through the thicket and heavy undergrowth to the plateau in front of the opening in the mountainside. This close, the light fell differently so the outline of the cross was no longer so clear. Instead, a slanted pattern of dark lines intersected. The sky was slashed through with wisps of white cloud. Everything was as he had visualised it from the woollen map.

Baillard looked back at the avenue of oak trees, at the juniper, then forward to the ring of stones seeming to frame the entrance to the cave. He suddenly remembered the brooch Sandrine Vidal had told him about two summers before. Found in the ruins of the castle outside Coustaussa and given as a present to her father. He let out a long sigh. Sandrine was linked to this place.

'A place of sanctuary,' he murmured.

Like Baillard, the monk Arinius had been a witness to truth, dedicated to the preservation of knowledge, not its destruction. In his long life, Baillard had found other allies. And in this single moment of understanding, he allowed himself to remember one in particular. Not Sandrine, not Léonie, though he admired them both. But the only woman he had ever loved. Loved still. The reason he had to keep de l'Oradore at bay.

'Alaïs,' he said.

He wondered if it was now too late to hope she might ever come back to him. If too much time had passed.

'Is this the place, Sénher Baillard?' Guillaume asked.

'It is.'

Baillard held out his hand. Pujol passed him the torch.

'Do you want me to come in with you, Audric?'

Baillard looked at his friend's anxious expression, then at Breillac's careful, thoughtful face. He wondered what the sisters after whom the valley was named could have done to be remembered with such respect and affection.

'I shall go in alone,' he said. 'You keep watch. Should I need you, I will call.'

He depressed the button on the torch, then, in the beam of the pale yellow light, he stepped into the cave the map maker had found so many centuries before. To bring the Codex back out at last into the light.

‡
Codex XXI
‡

Gaul
Tarasco
August AD 344

July gave way to August. And although the stories of atrocities in the settlements in the valleys continued to be carried on the wind to Tarasco, still the soldiers never arrived. Arinius waited as the days tipped over, one into the next. The men grew less vigilant, more resentful of the lives they were being asked to live.

By the third week, they were restless. Some wanted to bring the women and children back down to the village, believing the threat had gone. Others wanted to muster as many troops as possible and head north to attack their enemy first. Only Arinius and a few stalwart allies held firm. He could feel evil stalking the valley like a living creature. He knew the time was coming and he was torn. He, too, made journeys up into the mountains to visit his family from time to time. His son, Marcellus, was growing stronger by the day. But Arinius always came back at night, to keep watch.

Finally, after the moon had waxed and waned once more, the moment they had feared so long, that had ruled their lives for so long, arrived. A fine August day, when the birds were flying and the sky was clear. The sort of day to give thanks for the world, Arinius thought, not one for bloodshed or death or ruin.

At first, an awareness of a disturbance. A hint of time suspended, waiting, like a whisper through the trees. All but imperceptible at first, then louder and louder again, the sound of men moving through the oak and pine of the lower slopes, the juniper disrupted and the rustle of fallen leaves underfoot, dry and brittle like kindling. A little closer, and the unmistakable sound of metal on leather, swords unsheathed and the rattle of shield and knife.

Arinius looked for his brother-in-law. He, too, never missed his watch.

'It is time,' he said. 'We must summon the others. We have too few men. We must bring everyone back.'

He called his nephew, a boy of eight, but strong and fearless, and instructed him to gather what support he could.

'Quick, now,' he said. 'There is little time.'

The truth was, as Arinius knew, that it would be a matter of numbers and the nature of the forces marching against them. If they were trained soldiers, soldiers deserting their commissions, then Tarasco would have little chance. But if they were only bandits, dispossessed and ramshackle themselves, worthy more of pity than resistance, Arinius prayed there might be hope of winning the battle.

He organised a line of defence, checking that the ditches surrounding the settlement were filled with dried leaves and twigs to burn. Then he ordered everyone to the higher ground, where javelins or spears would be most effective and they had an uninterrupted view of the path as it climbed towards them. The noise grew louder, a tramping of feet on the lower paths, the murmuring of voices as the attackers came closer. Arinius looked back up the mountain, desperate for the sight of his nephew returning with reinforcements, but saw nothing.

Below, he saw someone emerge from the distant tree line. A scout? He was a huge bear of a man with arms broader than Arinius' legs. He looked around, then darted back into the safety of the trees. How many were there? How many would come?

Arinius tried to pray, but he found he could not. Fear had driven every word of intercession from his head. Then, behind him, he sensed movement. He turned, and, as his eyes focused, he saw a host of men coming down the hill. Not just those from their own village, but men from neighbouring communities, some Christian, some not, but each armed and walking down the path.

And at the head of the line were Lupa and her two sisters, Calista and Anona. Arinius was unable to trust the evidence of his own eyes. He simply stood, staring at his wife as she grew bigger, drew closer, until she was standing in front of him. He found he did not know what to say.

Lupa looked at him, a little shyly at first, then stretched up and kissed him on the lips.

'You sent me away. I did as you asked. I went.'

'But …' He indicated the mass of people standing behind her.

'I asked for help,' she said simply, 'and God heard.'

Arinius shook his head. 'No, what I mean is, where have all these people come from?'

Lupa smiled. 'They are all who remain of the villages that have already been put to the sword, the men of the woods. While you have kept guard, I have travelled from settlement to settlement to ask them to stand beside us to fight.' She waved her hand. 'And they have come.'

Arinius looked round at the army his wife had mustered, men with different faces and different tongues, yet standing ready to fight shoulder to shoulder with them. Then he let his gaze return to his extraordinary wife.

'Lupa,' he said with admiration.

She smiled, then stepped back into line. Arinius held her gaze for a moment longer, then he climbed up on to a rock and stretched his arms wide.

'*Salvete*,' he said. 'Friends, you are most welcome. You know the ill that has been done by the men in the valley below. My wife – Lupa – tells me that many of you have already suffered at their hands. I thank you for your courage in coming to our aid. Whatever happens today, you will have God's blessing.'

Some of the men bowed their heads and made the sign of the cross. Others watched with open-eyed curiosity. A few shuffled awkwardly.

'May God be with us,' he said, raising his voice. 'Amen.'

A small chorus repeated the word after him, Lupa's voice the clearest and strongest of them all.

Arinius stepped down from the rock. 'If we survive what is to come, it will be in no small part because of you.'

He drew his sword from his belt and handed it to his wife.

'You're not going to send me away?'

'How could I?' Arinius said. 'This is your army, Lupa. These are your men to command, not mine.'

She smiled. 'They will follow you, Arinius,' she said proudly. 'But I shall stand at your side. We will show these barbarians what it is to fight.' She looked around. 'Are the defences complete?'

'Yes.'

'Then we are ready for them.'

Only then did Arinius notice that Lupa was no longer wearing the iridescent bottle on the leather thong around her neck.

'Don't worry,' she said. 'I gave it into the safe keeping of my grandmother. She will keep it – and our beloved Marcellus – safe until we return.'

‡

Chapter 135

Coustaussa
August 1944

Baillard looked up at the sky. It was a perfect black tonight, unbroken by clouds and scattered with stars.

And they shall sleep once more.

He had studied the verses over the past three weeks, translating them from the Coptic. His understanding of the transcendent promise concealed within the Codex had grown with each reading.

Intimation, incantation, prophecy.

Those of fair heart and true, from the blood of the land where once they fell, come forth in the final hour.

The words ran through his mind, spoken only inside his head. An incomplete song without a tune. He had not said the words out loud. Not yet. He knew that, once spoken, there would be no turning back, though he feared that time was nearly upon them.

Come forth in the final hour.

He stood a moment longer in the silver starlight, then heard the door open and sensed someone making their way across the garden.

He turned.

'Are you ready, Monsieur Baillard?'

'Yes, *filha*.'

Sandrine had cut her hair, so it was as short as Suzanne's, while the clumps pulled out by Laval grew back. She was very thin, though her skin was tanned from the sun so it wasn't so obvious. She had taken to wearing slacks to hide the scars on her legs and loose shirts so as not to aggravate the burn scars on her shoulder.

'Raoul is saying goodbye to the others,' she said. 'He won't be long.'

Three weeks had passed since the events at the villa on the route de Toulouse and most of Sandrine's injuries had healed. The mark of the cross on her back and a small scar above her right eye, a little finger that hadn't properly healed, were the outward evidence of what she had endured. But the worst of the damage was inside, body and spirit. She was in pain much of the time. Her hand often went to her stomach when she thought no one was looking, grieving for the children she would no longer be able to carry.

Sandrine hadn't told anyone else what had happened in the cell on the route de Toulouse, and no one had pressed her. She felt the details of the assault would be more than Raoul or Marianne or Lucie could bear, and Baillard knew she was right. They saw only what she wanted them to see. She had suffered and she had survived, but the experience had changed her. And she told no one but Monsieur Baillard about the voice she had heard. About the warrior angel in stone who seemed to give her courage.

Over the same three weeks, the violence in Languedoc had got worse and worse. There were rumours that the Allies were about to invade from the Mediterranean. That the Germans would withdraw. In the Haute Vallée, Resistance activity continued – at the Port d'Alzau, in Alet-les-Bains, in Limoux. But Allied advances in the North led to increased conflict in the South. German attacks on partisans had intensified, growing ever more brutal. The Maquis in Villezby, Faïta and Picaussel were routed and there were spies and informers everywhere. In Carcassonne, Leo Authié's iron grip tightened. Every day, more men were taken, friends and comrades fell. Robert and Gaston Bonnet and Jean-Marc Giraud were arrested in the same Gestapo raid that claimed the FFI departmental leader, Jean Bringer – 'Myriel' – as well as Aimé Ramond, Maurice Sevajols and Docteur Delteil, Giraud's colleague at the Clinique du Bastion. Two attempts to rescue them from the prison on the route de Narbonne had been unsuccessful.

Throughout all of this, Raoul refused to leave Sandrine's side. Baillard's heart went out to the young man. He did not yet understand there was nothing he could do. Sandrine would recover in her own time, or she would not, but his constant presence – his desperation to see her condition improve – was not helping.

Then, the previous evening, they'd received word that the airdrop of weapons for a proposed attack on the local Nazi arms depot had missed its target, jeopardising the operation. It was common for the Allies to be a few kilometres out, but help was urgently needed to transport the equipment to the partisans' temporary base in the hills above Alet-les-Bains. Sandrine had enlisted Baillard's help to persuade Raoul to go. She had spent hours reassuring him she would be all right without him, for a few days at most. In the end, Raoul had agreed.

Baillard knew Sandrine had an ulterior motive. It wasn't just that Raoul's concern for her well-being was overwhelming. With him constantly at her side, she was unable to put her own plan into action. She knew Raoul would try to stop her, and that for all his courage and experience, he didn't understand that there was only one way left to end things.

Though it grieved him, Baillard agreed. He was appalled by what they intended to do – what they had to do – but the final hour was approaching.

'You are resolved to go through with this, *filha*?'

'I can't see we have a choice. Do you, Monsieur Baillard?'

He hesitated, then slowly he shook his head. 'I do not.'

'How will I know when you've arrived?' she asked.

'I will try to get a message to you, madomaisèla. If I cannot, we shall trust that we are each able to fulfil our side of the arrangement. And at the appropriate time it will be done.'

'Is a week enough?'

'I believe it is.'

Sandrine sighed. 'So soon,' she whispered.

For the first time since they had begun to make their plans, Baillard heard fear in her voice. He felt a glimmer of hope. If Sandrine was starting to experience normal emotions again, that was a good sign – an encouraging sign – that she might recover.

'You are sure you have to go back to the Pic de Vicdessos, Monsieur Baillard?' she said. 'Isn't there a way you could stay in Coustaussa?'

He gave a long, weary sigh. 'I am not sure of anything about this matter,' he said quietly. 'Instinct draws me back to the Vallée des Trois Loups. Perhaps to speak the words there, where the Codex lay hidden for so long, will give our endeavours a greater chance of success.' He went to put his hand on her shoulder, then thought better of it. 'That is what we want, is it not?'

'Perhaps,' she said.

Baillard looked at her, holding her safe in his gaze for a while longer. She sounded so very lost.

'You stand in a long line of women of the Midi, Madomaisèla Sandrine. Courageous, brave women, warriors all, who fought for what they believed to be right.' He paused. 'What we attempt to do is not without danger. What we attempt to do may not succeed. But it is right and it is just. We act for the good of all.'

'Yes,' she said more forcefully.

He smiled at her. 'And we shall triumph, I feel sure of it.'

The sound of someone coming down the wooden steps drew their attention. They both turned and saw it was Raoul. The time had come.

'Good luck,' Baillard said quickly. 'And be careful.' He raised his voice. 'Now I will allow you to take your leave of your young man. Tell Sénher Pelletier I will be waiting for him at the crossroads.'

Before she could say anything else, Baillard was walking across the garden and out into the garrigue.

Sandrine watched him go, then felt Raoul take her hand in the dark. She turned.

'Monsieur Baillard says he will meet you at the crossroads.'

'I don't want to leave you,' he said.

'Raoul,' she said gently, 'we've been through this. I'll be fine for a day or two. Everyone's here. They'll look after me.'

'It's not the same.'

'Of course it's not,' she said, quickly kissing him on the lips, then stepping away again. 'But it's important you go. You're needed. You can't stop fighting because of me, I couldn't bear that.'

Raoul sighed. He reached forward and put his arms around her. Sandrine flinched, then quickly tried to cover her reaction.

'What? I didn't hurt you, did I . . .?'

'No, it's all right. It's nothing.'

She couldn't bear him to touch her. However gentle he was, however careful, she couldn't keep the ugly memories out of her head. Laval's hands around her neck, Authié forcing her legs apart, the thrust of hard metal, the stench of burning flesh as he pressed the poker against her back. Raoul was patient and he was understanding. But even when they lay down to sleep, the slightest movement of his skin against hers had Sandrine shaking with fear. Awake in the dark, reliving each black second she had suffered in that airless room.

She put her arms around him and held him tight. And, for a moment, she was able to make herself forget. Only for a moment.

'Monsieur Baillard's waiting,' she said softly, stepping away.

'He won't mind,' he said.

'No.'

Carefully, he reached down and took her hand. 'How many times have we done this, do you think?'

'Done what?'

'Said goodbye. Not knowing when we're going to see each other again.'

'It's different this time,' she said, trying to raise a smile. 'I know where you're going and you'll only be gone a few days.'

'I have a bad feeling. I don't want to leave you.'

Sandrine smiled. 'You always say that,' she said. 'You always think something's going to go wrong, but it never does.'

Raoul didn't answer.

'Look, they desperately need the weapons, Raoul,' she said firmly. 'The longer the consignment's left where it came down, the more likely the Gestapo will hear about it.'

'I suppose so.'

'Well, then.'

He stared at her for a moment longer, as if trying to commit every tiny feature to memory. Then he leant forward and kissed her on the forehead.

'I love you, you know.'

Sandrine smiled. 'I know.'

She felt his fingers loosen their hold, then the connection between them was broken.

'Be careful,' she said.

'I will. I always am.'

'Go, then.'

This time, he did what she asked. Raoul was walking away from her, as he had done many times before. Grief suddenly overwhelmed her. Having been so desperate for him to go, Sandrine had underestimated how broken she would feel if he did.

'Raoul!' she called after him into the darkness.

She saw him turn and start to run, back towards her, gathering her into his arms. She hung on tight, holding him as if she would never let him go. Her skin touching his without fear, his hair against her cheek, like the very first kiss they had shared on the corner of the rue Mazagran. And now, at last, everything was forgotten but the smell of him and the feel of him and how they fitted so perfectly with one another.

'I love you, you know,' she said, echoing his words.

'I know,' he said.

Chapter 136

It had been an hour since Raoul and Monsieur Baillard had left. Sandrine leant back against the dresser, her hands in the pockets of her trousers.

'Do you need anything?' Marieta asked again.

'I'm all right.'

'Are you sure?' Since Raoul had gone, Marieta seemed determined to take over as her guard dog.

'Yes. I'm fine.'

'Fine, fine,' sang Jean-Jacques, sitting on Lucie's lap at the table and banging a wooden spoon.

'That's right, J-J,' Sandrine smiled. 'Everybody's fine.'

Lucie kissed the top of his head. 'Though it is a long way past your bedtime, little man,' she said fondly. 'Time to go *dodo*.'

He immediately started wailing and tried to wriggle out of his mother's arms.

Marieta struggled to her feet and took him from Lucie. 'Now, none of that. Why don't you come along like a good little boy and you can choose a story.'

Jean-Jacques immediately stopped crying. 'Two stories?'

'We'll see,' Marieta said firmly. 'A kiss goodnight for Mama.'

Lucie ruffled her son's hair. 'Thank you, Marieta,' she said.

'Night, night, night.'

Marieta took Jean-Jacques' hand to stop him waving, and led him out into the corridor. 'Now what story shall we have, *è*?'

'Two stories,' came the same response from the stairs.

Everyone laughed.

'A born negotiator,' Sandrine said.

For a moment, the room was quiet. They all went back to what they'd been doing. Lucie lit a cigarette. Liesl was cleaning the inside of her camera. There was no film to be had now, not even on the *marché noir*, but she kept it in good working order just in case. Marianne was at the stove with Geneviève, preparing a meal.

Suzanne stood up. 'I'm just going to check on the *capitelles*,' she said. 'The maquisards are using the larger ones to store weapons. Is there time before supper?'

Marianne nodded.

'Do you need a hand?' asked Eloise.

'Thanks.'

Eloise got up too.

'We'll be back in ten minutes,' Suzanne said.

Marianne went back to stirring the pan. Lucie was tapping the ash from her cigarette into a saucer and throwing increasingly anxious glances in Sandrine's direction. She was the only one who had noticed how distressed she was when she came back inside. Sandrine avoided her gaze. What Lucie didn't understand was how relieved she felt that Raoul was gone. Now that the initial sadness was over, it was a comfort not to have to put a brave face on things.

'All I wanted,' Lucie said, 'when I was growing up, I mean, was a husband and a family. Keeping house, seeing the children off to school.' She pulled a rueful face. 'Saving the fact that Max isn't here, you could nevertheless say that, out of all of us, I've got closest to fulfilling my ambitions.' She looked around at her friends. 'What about the rest of you? What did you want to be?'

Sandrine smiled at her. Over the past three weeks, she had come to admire even more than ever the way Lucie kept her spirits up. The camp at Le Vernet was almost empty. Raoul, Suzanne and Liesl had all tried to find out where Max had been sent or if he was still in the Ariège, but his name didn't appear to be on any list. In all likelihood, because his arrest in 1942 had been unlawful. Now, of course, such distinctions were forgotten. Did Lucie still honestly believe he would come back? Sandrine didn't know.

'Come on,' Lucie said, trying to get the conversation going. 'Marianne? What about you, you must have thought about it? Headmistress of the Lycée?'

Marianne turned round and put her hand on her hip. 'Well, yes. Though I always rather fancied teaching in a university. In Toulouse, perhaps.'

'What would you teach?' Sandrine asked. 'Literature?'

Marianne shook her head. 'Not now. I'd teach history. The truth of things.'

Sandrine nodded. 'I think you'll do it and be quite wonderful.'

'Good,' said Lucie, pleased they were joining in. 'What about you, Liesl? You could be a pin-up, if you were minded to. Or an actress. You've got the looks for it.'

Geneviève laughed. The idea of Liesl, the most reserved of them all, posing for a camera in a bathing suit was ridiculous, and was meant to be. 'No, I've got it,' she said. 'Liesl will be another Martha Gellhorn. Going all over the world, a war photographer.'

'My father was a reporter,' Liesl said. 'I'd like to follow in his footsteps.'

'You could start your own magazine,' Lucie said, warming to her theme. 'Then when J-J's old enough, there'll be a job waiting for him! How's that for a plan? BLUM ET FILS, I can see it now!'

'Blum and Son,' Liesl said. 'Keep it in the family, why not?'

'As for you,' Lucie said, pointing her cigarette at Sandrine, 'you should be a politician. One of the first women to sit in de Gaulle's provisional government. What do you say?'

Sandrine shrugged. 'Maybe.'

'I'd certainly vote for you, kid. I can tell you that for nothing.'

'So would I,' said Marianne.

Lucie nodded. 'That's that sorted, then.' She turned to Geneviève. 'Your turn. What about you?'

Geneviève pretended to think. 'Eloise and I could start a chain of shops,' she said. 'A general store selling clothes and food, anything anyone wants. SAINT-LOUP AND SISTER, I can picture the sign.'

'Sisters,' said Eloise, coming back into the kitchen with Suzanne. 'We've got Coralie and Aurélie to think about too.'

Suzanne washed her hands at the sink, then shook the water off before sitting down.

'What's all this?'

'Lucie's organising our lives for us,' Marianne said. 'What we're going to do when the war is over.'

'So we do have rather a problem with you, Suzanne,' Liesl laughed. 'Not much call for lady bomb-makers in peacetime.'

'Even though I am the best,' Suzanne said, putting on a silly voice. 'The acknowledged master.'

'Or should that be "mistress"?' Geneviève suggested.

Lucie raised her eyebrows. 'No, that's altogether something else.'

Everyone burst into gales of laughter, until Marieta banged angrily on the floor from upstairs and they all had to be quiet again for fear of waking Jean-Jacques.

Chapter 137

'Supper's nearly ready,' Marianne said. 'Do you want me to wait until Marieta comes down or serve up now?'

Sandrine took a deep breath. She had been working out how to say what she needed to say.

'In fact, while Marieta's upstairs, I want to talk to everyone.'

Immediately, the atmosphere sharpened. Liesl put the camera down. Marianne took the pan of ratatouille off the stove and covered it with a cloth, then she and Geneviève joined the others at the table. Lucie turned round in her chair and looked enquiringly at Sandrine.

'We made a mistake in not going through with our attack on Authié in the Cité,' she said.

Lucie frowned. 'It wouldn't have worked, kid. They knew all about it.'

Sandrine carried on. 'Then Raoul didn't realise it was him – Authié – in the car. With me. If he had, he would have shot him then. It was another missed opportunity.'

'His job was to get you away,' Suzanne said firmly, 'and he did. Neither of you have anything to reproach yourselves for.' She shrugged. 'It's how it goes.'

'Other people have borne the burden of our failure,' Sandrine continued. 'And now ...' She stopped, looked down at the little finger on her left hand, crooked from where Laval had broken it. 'Authié is looking for Monsieur Baillard and the Codex. We have to try again.'

Liesl frowned. 'I have a great regard for Monsieur Baillard, but surely we should concentrate our strength on things that matter. That are real. Like trying to find Max.'

'I agree,' said Lucie.

'And you can't possibly be contemplating going back to Carcassonne,' Marianne added. 'You'd never get anywhere near him.'

Sandrine glanced at Eloise and Geneviève and knew they would support her. For all their modern clothes and habits, they were as rooted to the timeless ways of the mountains as Marieta or Monsieur Baillard himself. Myths and realities, they saw no contradiction.

'Not Carcassonne,' she said. She hesitated, then continued. 'I appreciate that this will sound absurd, after all the trouble we've taken to stay hidden, but . . .' she paused again, 'we need to entice Authié here.'

Marianne, Suzanne and Liesl all immediately started to argue. Sandrine raised her voice.

'Listen. We have the advantage here. We know the terrain. We can choose the time and place of attack. We will evacuate the village, it will be us against him.'

Marianne was shaking her head. 'But he could bring hundreds of men with him. It's absurd. The odds are completely against us.'

Not if Monsieur Baillard is right, Sandrine thought, but she knew better than to say so.

'What does Raoul think of your idea?' Lucie asked.

Sandrine hesitated. 'He doesn't know about it,' she admitted. 'He doesn't think I should do anything.'

'And he's right,' Marianne said. 'You're not strong enough.'

For a moment, no one spoke.

'You know,' Suzanne said, 'it might work. If we make sure we clear everyone out, then lure him here, it might just work. If the rumours are true, if some of the German units are pulling out, then he's hardly going to be able to muster much support.'

Marianne turned on her. 'How can you say that? You

saw what that monster did to her. When Raoul brought her here I didn't think she'd survive. But she's strong, she refused to give in. We kept her safe.' She stopped, her voice cracking. 'For three weeks we've hidden her from Authié, from Laval – for two years before that. Everyone says the Allies will come. That the Germans are getting ready to withdraw. We should wait.'

'It's because of what he did to her that we have to do this,' Suzanne said softly. 'Can't you see?'

Marianne looked at Sandrine. 'Is Suzanne right? Is that what this is about? Revenge?'

Sandrine thought for a moment before she spoke. 'No, it's about justice,' she said. 'It's about not looking away, about standing up against tyranny. About not spending the rest of our lives in hiding.' She paused, then added softly, 'And it's about making sure that Authié will never again be able to do to someone else what he did to me.'

Marianne stared, now with tears in her eyes, then sat back in her chair. She looked defeated.

Suzanne reached over and covered her hand with her own. 'Come on,' she murmured.

Lucie and Liesl exchanged glances. Geneviève and Eloise both looked at Sandrine and waited.

'What's your plan?' Lucie asked.

Sandrine glanced at Marianne, then explained. 'We attack the electricity substation in Couiza. Tomorrow, or the day after. It's not guarded, and it's far enough away from both the Maquis camp and any houses not to cause difficulties for anyone else. It's an ideal target. We deliver a letter to the Milice in Limoux denouncing it as the work of "Citadel" – that should make it certain the news will get back to Carcassonne.'

'I can take it,' Eloise said.

'If you, Geneviève, could spread the same story in Couiza?'

Geneviève nodded. 'Nothing easier.'

Liesl was still unconvinced. 'I agree with Marianne. I don't think we can be sure Authié will come in person, or when. And what if he brings a huge force with him? We'll be heavily outnumbered.'

Sandrine met her gaze. 'He thinks I have the Codex,' she said. 'He will come.'

For a moment, the word hung in the air like a challenge. Sandrine knew that Marianne, in particular, hated her talking about the Codex.

'If we allow a day for the information to get from Limoux to Carcassonne,' Sandrine said quickly, 'then for Authié to react, my estimate is the earliest he would get to Coustaussa would be the twentieth of August.'

'Sounds about right,' Suzanne said.

'You've no way of knowing for sure,' Marianne said.

'No,' Sandrine conceded. 'But if Eloise stays in Limoux, unless Authié takes a very indirect route, she'll hear when they pass through. We'll have advance warning. That will give us enough time to evacuate Coustaussa and get everyone out of harm's way.'

'It will be a ghost village,' Lucie said. 'Just them and us.'

Sandrine glanced at her. She couldn't know, but it was almost as if Lucie guessed what she and Monsieur Baillard were planning. She held Lucie's gaze for a moment, then looked round the room.

'So, what do you say?'

One by one, each woman nodded. Only her sister did not answer.

'Marianne?'

'There's so much that could go wrong. You're gambling on your guesses – about the date, about the numbers Authié brings with him – being accurate. You could be right, you could be utterly wrong, but … I understand.'

She stopped again and sighed. 'So, yes. I don't like it, but of course I'll help.'

Sandrine smiled. 'Thank you,' she said softly.

Marianne pushed her chair back from the table and walked over to the stove. 'Now, we should eat. The food will spoil.'

After the tension of the conversation, the atmosphere became light-hearted as they brought everything to the table. Geneviève helped Marianne carry the two large serving dishes – one a casserole, one of ratatouille – and glasses were clattered out of the cupboard. Liesl and Suzanne cleared the papers.

Sandrine had no appetite and she was exhausted. Unobtrusively, she slipped out of the kitchen and on to the terrace. She could still hear the others laughing and joking, but she had no energy left.

'Ladies, please,' Geneviève was saying, 'you shouldn't mock. My *milicien* is a good catch, or so my mother's always telling me. A widower, his own teeth! Most of them, at any rate …'

Sandrine let her thoughts drift away. The girls' voices became fainter until she could no longer make out word from word. She let the scent of the sweet wild lavender and rosemary in the garrigue, the sound of the cicadas and the singing of the birds of the night, nightingales and owls, wash over her.

She thought of her father and was surprised to feel tears pricking her eyes. It had been so long. Since her interrogation, she had not been able to cry. She feared that if she gave way, even for a moment, she would shatter into a thousand pieces and never stop. So she kept her emotions wrapped tightly inside.

'To "Citadel",' said Lucie in the kitchen.

'To the chef,' said Suzanne firmly. 'To Marianne.'

Sandrine heard the clink of glasses and the thump of

the *pinard* on the table, then Liesl's voice floating out on to the terrace.

'Where did Sandrine go? Did she turn in already?'

Sandrine closed her eyes and let the darkness hide her.

Chapter 138

Alet-les-Bains

'Is that it?' Raoul asked.

He had worked all night with the men from the Salvezines Maquis, moving the heavy cylindrical drums containing weapons parts, maps and ammunition, the twelve kilometres from where they'd been dropped in error to the makeshift camp above the Gorges de Cascabel near Alet-les-Bains.

'That's the lot, yes.'

Raoul wiped his forehead and neck with his handkerchief, then jumped down from the cart and patted the donkey's neck. 'He's worked as hard as any of us,' he said. 'Where did you get him?'

The maquisard shrugged. 'Who knows?' he said, then held out his hand. 'Thanks for your help, comrade.'

Raoul shook the man's hand. From fragments overheard, he'd worked out that a strike was intended in the next couple of days. He wondered if Sandrine had heard anything about it.

Straight away, Raoul felt the same tightening of the chest he now always had when thinking about Sandrine. If he'd been able, he would have put her on a plane and taken her across the world. To America or England, somewhere away from the war-torn, divided Midi. Then he shook his head. Even if he had all the money in the world, Sandrine wouldn't leave. She'd never run away. She'd stay and fight to the bitter end. His expression hardened. Whatever else Authié had done, he hadn't crushed her spirit. She was still as stubborn and determined as ever.

The light was just coming up. Raoul felt an unaccustomed sense of peace as he looked around the glade, recognising some of the men with whom he'd worked. They'd been in pairs, carrying and loading, never all together until now. Most of them looked like he felt. A little dazed from lack of sleep, tired, sharing a bottle of beer or a pouch of tobacco. Relieved that it had all gone off all right. No raid, no shooting, no sirens.

No one dead.

One of the maquisards had set a charcoal fire to burn in the centre of the clearing. Two rabbits were roasting on a spit, breakfast for the men before everyone went their separate ways. On the far side of the fire, Raoul noticed Coralie Saint-Loup's fiancé sitting on a log rolling a cigarette.

'Got any going spare?' Raoul asked, sitting down beside him, struggling to remember what he was called. Some old-fashioned village name.

'Sure.' The young man handed over the pouch. 'Help yourself.'

'How's Coralie? I heard you got married.'

'Expecting our first,' he said. 'I don't know, it doesn't seem right, bringing a kid into all this mess, but life goes on, I suppose. It's what she wanted.'

Raoul nodded.

'If it's a boy, we'll call him Alphonse.'

Raoul sighed. 'After you,' he said, remembering.

'And my father and his father before him. Family tradition. If it's a girl, Coralie wants to call her Vivien. After that film actress.' He shrugged. 'Can't say I like it much, funny sort of name. What about you? Still with the same girl?'

'I am.'

'Married?'

'We haven't got round to it yet,' he said, 'but we will. As soon as all this is over.'

'They say the Germans are pulling out. Do you think it's true?'

'I don't know,' Raoul said.

For a moment, they sat in silence in the still dawn air, both smoking, passing a tin cup of coarse red mountain wine between them, the smell of the game roasting on the fire curling up into the air.

'Are you going with the others?' Alphonse asked, dropping his voice.

'Going where?'

The boy looked alarmed that he'd spoken out of turn, then decided Raoul could be trusted.

'There's a few going to try and catch up with the ghost train,' he said, lowering his voice even more. 'See if they can hold it up until the Allies get here.'

Raoul turned to look at him. Like everyone, he had heard rumours about the *train fantôme*. The last remaining Jewish prisoners in Le Vernet were alleged to have been loaded on to a train bound for Dachau. Lucie's fiancé should have been one of them, but his name wasn't on the list. And because Raoul had been caring for Sandrine, he realised he didn't know if Liesl or Lucie had ever found out where Max actually was. The train had passed through Toulouse on the thirtieth of July, going towards Bordeaux, then north. Thanks to the Allied advance, though, it had been turned back again.

'Where is it now?' Raoul asked.

Alphonse shook his head. 'Heading towards the south-east, so I've heard. Provence, maybe. That could be the best chance of getting them free. They say the Allies are going to attack from the Mediterranean.'

Raoul swallowed another mouthful of wine, thinking hard. He wanted to go back to Coustaussa immediately.

He'd hated leaving Sandrine, even though he knew she was in safe hands. But he remembered what she'd said to him last night – that she wouldn't be able to bear it if he stopped fighting because of her. More than that, what would she think of him if he'd had a chance to save Max – assuming Max was even on the train – and hadn't taken it? Raoul knew she still blamed herself for not intervening when Max was arrested in Carcassonne. It weighed on her mind. This might be a practical way of paying that debt for her. It was one way he could make things easier for her.

'Are you going?' he asked Alphonse.

The boy shook his head. 'I'd like to, but not with the baby due any day now. Wouldn't be fair on Coralie.'

Raoul patted his pockets, trousers and jacket, until he found a pencil.

'Got anything to write on?' he said quickly. 'Anything at all?'

Alphonse looked in his own pockets and came up with a notification for a doctor's appointment. He glanced at the date, saw it had already passed and handed it over.

Raoul quickly scribbled a note for Sandrine, telling her what he was going to do and promising to be back within the week. He hesitated, still in two minds, then folded it and gave it to Alphonse.

'Can you pass this to Coralie,' he said urgently, 'and tell her to get it to Geneviève or Eloise? It's very important she delivers it. Very important indeed. Just to let them know where I am.'

The boy nodded and put it in his pocket.

'Do you know who's in charge?' Raoul asked.

'He's the one I heard talking about it,' Alphonse said, pointing out a tall, lanky man with sandy-coloured hair.

Raoul stood up and held out his hand. 'Good luck with the baby,' he said.

'Come to the christening, if you like,' Alphonse said.

'I might just do that,' Raoul replied.

Then he crossed the wood and went to introduce himself, still thinking of how pleased Sandrine would be if he could come back with good news about Max after all this time.

Twenty minutes later, he was in a truck heading north on the unpatrolled back roads towards Carcassonne.

Alphonse walked slowly along the stony bank of the Aude back towards Couiza. The river was silver in the early-morning light and the foam of the current tumbled and eddied white over the low rocks.

He reached a point where the bank disappeared and the water was deeper. He hesitated a moment, then decided to climb up to the road. He was sure he could avoid any Wehrmacht trucks or SS cars. There was so little traffic on the road, he'd hear anything coming from several kilometres away. He was pleased to be carrying a note to Coralie. She said she didn't mind, but Alphonse thought she was too often in the shadow of her older sisters, who always knew everything first. It would be nice for Coralie to be the one with information for a change.

Alphonse tripped over a log and bashed his shin. He fell forward on to the road and cried out in pain before he could stop himself. He gave a deep sigh, then heard the sound of a safety catch.

'Levez les mains.'

As he started to put his hands up, he saw the flash of a blue Milice beret and panicked. The woods were dense behind him. He hesitated a moment. Wouldn't it be better to make a run for it?

He turned and charged back down the slope towards the cover of the beech trees. He heard a bullet fly over his head and embed itself in a tree. Then another shot. He kept running, back down towards the river.

It took him an instant before he realised he'd been hit. He pulled up, suddenly short of breath, then a second bullet hit him in the back and he fell, face forward, into the water.

'Vivien, what a name ...' he muttered to himself.

He started to choke. Blood spurted out of his mouth, turning the silver waters of the Aude red. Raoul's note fell into the river and was carried away unread.

Chapter 139

Couiza

Sandrine rubbed her temples. She had her usual pre-operation headache, the period of counting down to zero hour. She rolled her shoulders, wincing as the skin around her burns stretched sore. She took several deep breaths, trying to calm herself down. The plan was almost identical to Berriac. The same signs, the same systems. When she'd come down to it, Sandrine had found herself unable to think of anything new.

In two days, there had been no word from Raoul. No word from Monsieur Baillard. She told herself it wasn't any different from any other mission they'd done, but it was her first since coming back to Coustaussa.

Her first since she knew what it was like to be caught.

'Blow the whistle twice if you see anyone coming. Three short blasts if you hear a vehicle – car, motorcycle, *petrolette*, anything.'

Liesl nodded.

'Twice for a person,' Sandrine repeated, 'three for any kind of vehicle.'

'I know,' Liesl said quietly.

Sandrine looked at her watch. Seven forty-five.

Lucie and Marieta were at home with Jean-Jacques. Marianne was on lookout, watching the road from the south. Suzanne was covering the bridge and Geneviève was making her way towards the electricity substation with a basket packed with explosives. It had worked in Berriac, so why wouldn't it work again?

She looked at her watch again. Seven fifty.

'I'm going now,' she whispered to Liesl. 'Don't forget, if anyone comes, whistle. We don't want anyone hurt. If all goes to plan, when you hear the blast, leave straight away.'

'I know,' Liesl said patiently.

Sandrine came out of the shadow of the empty chicken coops. She felt as if she couldn't breathe. There was no one about. At the war memorial, a black and white dog, scruffy, thin, sat as if guarding the dead.

'Good boy,' she whispered. It was rare to see an animal nowadays and the last thing she wanted was for the mongrel to bark, alerting the village to her presence.

Sandrine reached the small, colourful house in the far corner. Suzanne had identified the porch as a good spot to wait, not least because the owners were away. Or detained.

She checked the time again.

'Three minutes,' she murmured to herself. 'Three minutes.'

At eight o'clock, the bells began to ring. Perfectly on time, Geneviève came into view. She walked towards the substation, put the basket against the door and carried on up the track without breaking her stride.

Sandrine waited until she was out of sight, then stepped forward. She lifted the red and white tablecloth, located the fuse in the jumble of wires and pipe, then tried to strike the match. Her hand was shaking so badly that it guttered, flared, and went out. Sandrine took another, scraped it along the strip, and, holding her right hand in her left, this time the flame held steady. Tonight she felt no satisfaction at the hiss of the cord, only relief.

She gave it two seconds, to check it had taken, then made it out to the track behind the vegetable gardens before the bomb went off. She experienced a vivid flashback to Berriac, remembering how exhilarated she had felt that night. Now she felt nothing but fear and loathing for the things she had to do.

She started to run, but a sharp, jagged pain in her lower abdomen forced her to stop. She doubled over, feeling the heavy, dull drag, and knew she was bleeding again. She waited as long as she dared, then carried on. The hope that Raoul might have returned was what got her up the hill.

Liesl and Marianne were waiting for her, both safe, as was Geneviève. There had been no word from Eloise, but no reason to think anything had gone wrong there either.

'And Raoul?'

'Nothing so far,' Marianne said quietly.

'He'll be back,' Lucie said.

Marieta made her a glass of lime tea with plenty of saccharine, then helped her with her bloodied clothes. Lucie sat with her until she went to sleep.

Chapter 140

CARCASSONNE

Carcassonne was in darkness as Raoul made his way along the Canal du Midi.

He'd got out of the truck on the Villegly road. From there, it had been a short tramp over the hill to come down into the Bastide via the cimetière Saint-Vincent. He had not thought to be back in Carcassonne so soon and, now that Sandrine was no longer here, he was shocked at how alien the city seemed to him.

Below him, boulevard Omer Sarraut – where he had lifted Sandrine's broken body from the *panier à salade* – was silent. Even now, Raoul could hardly bear to look at it. All he saw was her bruised face and her branded skin and the blood dripping from the leather of the seats on to the floor of Robert Bonnet's car.

He stopped to catch his breath for a moment. Was Robert still alive? Gaston? Or Dr Giraud, who had saved Sandrine's life? What about Aimé Ramond and Jean Bringer? He had not even had time to grieve for his mother. Raoul shook his head. Trying to clear his mind. There would be time to mourn for those taken or lost, but not now.

The blackness made it easy for him to make his way unobserved towards the offices of the railway transportation department. Although it was being called the ghost train, the truth was that there were records. Every stretch of the line, every day the prisoners spent confined to the cattle trucks, was written down. All Raoul needed to do was find the information and let his comrades know. Then, at least, they would have a chance of delaying the transport.

He climbed the embankment and crawled out over the line. There was no hum of metal. The gravel between the tracks cracked and crunched, but no one seemed to hear. Raoul stepped over one sleeper, then the next, like a child playing a game in the schoolyard. He was surprised there was no patrol, but assumed perhaps that the Gestapo – that Authié – were concentrating their attention closer to the station buildings.

Without too much difficulty, Raoul located the station master's office at the far end of the westbound platform. Even in the dark, the plaque seemed to gleam: CHEF DE GARE.

The door was solid oak. There was no way of breaking it without making enough noise to get the guards running all the way from the Caserne Laperrine. Instead, Raoul climbed on to the metal bench beneath a small window and reached his hand up. The catch had been left *à l'espagnolette*, to allow a shaving of cool air in, so it wasn't difficult to lever the fastening up with his hunting knife.

He slithered through, head first, then lowered himself carefully down to the tiled floor. As his eyes adjusted to the gloom, he could make out the metal filing cabinets in the corner of the room and the huge leather-bound diary in pride of place on the station master's desk.

He struck a match and turned the pages, looking for today's date. There was nothing recorded. He frowned, then turned the pages back, looking for something that might tell him where the train had been, at least, if not where it was going.

After a few minutes, he found it. A list of names, Max Blum among them, and an hour-by-hour record of how the prisoners from Le Vernet were to be transported up the eastern border. Through Provence to Bourgogne, then into Lorraine and on to Bavaria in southern Germany. Heading for Dachau.

Raoul leant forward and traced the route with his finger. This was all he needed. If they moved quickly, they could position themselves to block the line and stop the train moving forward. If the rumours were true and the Allies were launching a second attack from the sea, then all they had to do was delay the train.

He put the spent match in his pocket, imagining Sandrine's face when he told her – and her pleasure at being able to explain to Lucie and to Liesl what had happened. He moved a chair beneath the window and had put his hands on the sill, ready to pull himself up, when without warning the door was flung open. Raoul went for his gun as the electric light was switched on.

'Stehen bleiben!'

His heart hammering in his chest, he turned slowly around. Four against one, Gestapo. He put his hands above his head.

'Come down.'

Raoul had no choice but to do as he was told.

'Name?' one of the Germans barked.

Raoul didn't answer.

'Your name?' he said again, shouting this time.

Raoul met his gaze.

The Nazi stared at him, then so quickly that Raoul didn't even see it coming, he raised his rifle and swung it into the side of Raoul's head.

Chapter 141

TARASCON

Audric Baillard sat at the table with the Codex before him. The shutters were open and the light of the moon came in through the window and lit the beautiful letters of the ancient Coptic script. He let his thin white hand hover over the papyrus, his skin mottled with age, then withdrew it again.

The story of its long journey was finally clear in his mind. Arinius had smuggled the Codex from the community in Lyon to the mountains. Baillard suspected it was not the only version of the text. There were rumours about excavations in Egypt close to the Jabal al-Tarif cliffs, not far from the settlement of Nag Hammadi. He thought of his old friend Harif, dead many years now. It was Harif who'd taught him to understand the ancient languages of Egypt – Coptic and Demotic, hieroglyphs – and had told him of the network of some hundred and fifty caves on the west bank of the Nile two days' ride north of Luxor, used as graves. A hiding place too? A secret library entombed in the rocks?

Baillard wished he knew what had happened to Arinius himself. Had he lived to make old bones? Had he remained close by, keeping watch over the Codex? Had it lain here undisturbed for hundreds of years until called upon by Dame Carcas to drive the invaders from the walls of the Cité?

He knew that the border regions in the fourth century had been violent, lawless places. Whole tribes decimated and villages put to the sword. But had Arinius' settlement survived? Part of it, at least? Eloise and Geneviève Saint-Loup – Sandrine and Marianne Vidal too – were descended from those early Tarasconnais Christian families. The iridescent glass bottle containing the map that had been passed down from hand to hand to hand was proof of that. And even though Baillard now knew that the map had been bought by Otto Rahn from Monsieur Saint-Loup – when he'd been forced to sell the family possessions – Rahn, in turn, had sent it to Antoine Déjean in 1939, thereby returning the map to the land from whence it had come.

Baillard closed his ears to the noise of the world and lifted his eyes to the mountains, picturing in his mind's eye the dark path he would take up to the Pic de Vicdessos. He believed that the power of the words would be strongest spoken there, where they had lain safe for so long.

There was a tap on the door. He stood up. Leaving the cedarwood box on the table, he placed the Codex in one pocket and his revolver in the other, then stepped out to join Guillaume Breillac.

'Any word from Eloise?' Baillard asked. He knew the young man was worried about his wife.

'Not yet, sénher,' Guillaume replied.

'It is only a matter of time, I am sure.'

Guillaume didn't answer.

‡

Codex XXII

‡

Gaul
Tarasco
August AD 344

The invading army attacked at dawn. From the cover of the trees, they began to beat their swords against their shields. They shouted strange and foreign battle cries. The ground started to shudder beneath their stamping feet as grey smoke twisted up into the blue sky and across the face of the rising August sun.

'There are so many, *peyre*,' said one of the youngest men nervously.

'They are making noise to make you think they are more numerous than they really are,' Arinius replied, although he didn't know if it was true. 'They want to scare us.'

'I'm not frightened,' the boy said immediately.

'Nor should you be,' said Lupa. 'Not when God is on our side.'

The boy nodded and tightened his grip around the club in his right hand, though Arinius saw his left steal into Lupa's. She smiled down at the child and he saw how her courage and calm strengthened him.

'Why don't they advance?' she said.

'They hope to weaken our spirit by delaying.'

'Can you see anything?'

'Not yet.'

The shouting and the beating of the shields continued. Arinius looked along the line, seeing the boy's fear reflected in the faces, young and old, of the men of Tarasco. But his wife's expression was steadfast. She saw him smiling.

'What was it that you hid within the mountains?' she said quietly. 'So important that it all but cost you your life?'

Arinius stared at her. In the two years he had loved her, she had never asked what had brought him to Tarasco. She had never asked what he had been doing in the Vallée des Trois Loups. Never asked why he wore the green bottle like a talisman round his neck, nor what he had placed inside it.

'Did you think I did not know?' she said gently. 'Why else do you think there are stories of the mountains being haunted except to keep those with sharp eyes and quick fingers away from the box?'

'You have seen it?'

Lupa had the grace to blush. 'At the very beginning, before I knew you. I was curious.'

Arinius looked at her fierce, intelligent face, then he smiled.

'It contains a precious text, a codex, stolen away from the library in Lugdunum. It is considered a heresy by the Abbot, but I believe future generations will see it differently.'

'You have not read it yourself?'

'It is a language I do not understand,' he said, 'though there are some phrases I have heard spoken.'

'What do they promise?'

'That when the words are spoken aloud, in a place that is sacred – and by one prepared to give his life so that others might live – death is conquered. That the quick and the dead will stand side by side. An army of spirits.'

Lupa frowned. 'Must he who speaks the words die? Or only be prepared to give his life for others?'

Arinius shook his head. 'I don't know.'

Lupa thought for a moment longer. 'And only the good may see this?'

Arinius paused. 'We each see what we deserve to see. So you, my brave, courageous Lupa, would see spirits, angels. Men with dark hearts will be brought face to face with the worst of their fears.'

'I think God is with us all the same, Arinius.'

'As do I.'

'Will you teach me the words you know?'

Arinius looked at her. 'Why?'

'I would like to know them,' she said simply.

He looked at her a moment longer, then whispered softly the few phrases he had heard spoken by his brother monk. Lupa listened, her face lit up with the beauty of what she was hearing. When he had finished, she put her hand upon his arm and smiled.

For an instant they stood together, forgetting everything but one another.

Then a roar went up from the woods below and, suddenly, the invaders broke out from the cover of the trees. At his side, he heard Lupa catch her breath. They were outnumbered seven to one, perhaps more.

'May God protect us,' he said.

Arinius drew his sword and let out an answering shout of his own. At his side, he felt Lupa steel herself. She drew her knife from her belt, looked at him one last time. Then, together, they ran forward into the fray.

Chapter 142

CARCASSONNE
AUGUST 1944

'Forgive me, Father, for I have sinned.'

It was Friday the eighteenth of August and the cathédrale Saint-Michel was empty so early in the morning. Except for him and the priest, there was no one. Authié had insisted upon it. He did not wish there to be any possibility of someone overhearing his confession.

He had chosen to kneel rather than sit. He could feel the chill of the stone seeping through the knees of his trousers, comfortingly austere. His hands were loose by his sides and he felt a deep peace and power in the rightness of his cause. He believed it was how the crusaders of old might have felt. Holy warriors pursuing a just and holy war.

In a matter of days, it would be over. Sandrine Vidal had made a fool of him twice. She had defeated him twice: the first time through her lies, the second time through her silence. He knew the Gestapo officers, even Laval, admired how she had withstood the interrogation and still not talked. Few men lasted so long.

Authié did not admire her. Like the Inquisitors of old who felt no pity for those who chose to defy the teachings of the Church, he knew there was no honour in disobedience. By her actions, Vidal defied scripture and allowed heresy to flourish. The fact that she might not possess the Codex was no longer of relevance to him. She had collaborated with the enemies of the Church, had helped them. That was enough.

She might have escaped, but she would not stay at liberty for long.

'I have dissembled and lied for the purpose of bringing the enemies of the Church into plain view,' he said. 'I have consorted with those who deny God. I have neglected my spiritual salvation.' He paused. 'I am sorry for these and all the sins of my past life.'

As Authié catalogued his sins of commission and of omission, he felt the wordless horror of the priest from behind the grille. Could smell the man's fear, rank on his skin and his breath.

'In the name of the Father and of the Son and of the Holy Spirit,' the priest said, stumbling over the words of absolution.

'Amen.'

Authié made the sign of the cross, then stood up.

He took his gun from his belt and fired through the mesh. The world turned red, blood staining the metal and the curtains and the worn, old wood. Authié came out, genuflected to the high altar, then walked back down the nave.

The secrets of the confessional. Everyone talked in the end.

Sylvère Laval looked up and then down rue Voltaire, into the cross streets and over the garden in front of the cathedral. For Authié's security, he had put a police block on the road at both ends; even so it was possible a car might come out of nowhere. But, after the latest raids, which had finally caught the leadership of the Resistance in Carcassonne, the streets had been quieter.

Laval glanced at the west door, wondering how much more time his commanding officer was going to waste. He couldn't complain. Authié's obsession had served Laval well and he had become rich on the back of Authié's links with the Church in Chartres. But now things were coming to an end. Laval intended to tell Authié what he had discovered about Citadel, but keep from him the fact that he had found Audric Baillard. Although Baillard had not been seen since the late summer of 1942, one of their informers in Tarascon had reported that a retired police inspector had an old man staying with him. Since it was common knowledge Pujol and Baillard had been friends, Laval had put two and two together.

The Allies had landed in Provence. The Germans were preparing to withdraw from the Midi. If Laval was to go with them, he had to get the Codex in the next twenty-four hours.

Laval heard footsteps on the pavement and turned, the list in his hand. As Authié got closer, Laval saw he had blood on his face.

'We've found Vidal, sir,' he said.

Authié stopped dead. 'Where is she?'

'Coustaussa,' Laval replied. 'Seven or eight of them, all women. It's all here. The *réseau* "Citadel".'

Authié snatched the paper and ran his eyes down the names. 'Vidal, Peyre, Ménard ...' He broke off. 'Who's Liesl Vidal? Have we come across her?'

'It seems she's been living in Coustaussa with the housekeeper, Marieta Barthès. They put it about she's a cousin from Paris, but I think she might be Blum's sister.'

'The Jew Ménard visited in Le Vernet?'

'Yes. He had a sister who vanished, about the right sort of age.'

Authié looked back at the list. 'Who's this Eloise Breillac?'

'She's the sister of Geneviève Saint-Loup, who's also part of the network. Breillac was arrested in the Hôtel Moderne et Pigeon in Limoux.'

Authié was nodding. 'This is good work, Laval. Where did you get this information?'

'It seems Liesl Vidal – Blum – has taken up with a local boy, Yves Rousset. Another chap felt edged out, wanted to get back at them. Talked to one of his friends in the Milice in Couiza. The links between them started to show up on various lists. Rousset's with the Couiza Maquis. It all fell into place from there.'

'Is Pelletier with them?'

'Not so far as I've been able to find out, sir.'

'What about Baillard? Have you managed to track him down?'

'Baillard's file is incomplete. I haven't been able to locate him.'

Authié stared, then shrugged. 'Keep trying. I would like to have something to tell Monsieur de l'Oradore.' He paused. 'You've done well, Laval.'

'Thank you, sir,' he said, opening the car door.

Chapter 143

COUSTAUSSA

Sandrine rubbed her forehead. Her headache was bad again. 'I don't like it. We should have heard something by now.'

'I'm sure he'll be all right,' Lucie said quickly.

'Not Raoul,' Sandrine said sharply. She was sick with worry about where he was, but was pretending not to be. She hated the way Lucie and the others kept looking anxiously at her all the time. A mixture of concern and pity.

'Sorry,' she said. 'I meant Eloise, not Raoul. It's been three days.'

'But he's—'

'I expected a message from Limoux,' Sandrine pressed on.

'There was an attack on a convoy in the Gorges de Cascabel the day before yesterday,' Suzanne said. 'They're probably dealing with that.'

'Any casualties?'

'An American died. Don't know about anyone else.'

'Does it make it less or more likely that Authié will come?' Lucie said.

Suzanne shrugged. 'Impossible to say.'

'What do you want to do?' Liesl asked. 'Should we evacuate the village just in case? Or wait?'

The nineteenth of August, Sandrine thought. Nearly a week since Raoul had left, and she'd heard nothing. Nothing, either, from Monsieur Baillard, to let her know he was in position in the Pic de Vicdessos.

'Sandrine?' said Marianne with concern.

'What do you want us to do?' Liesl repeated.

Sandrine took a deep breath and forced herself to concentrate. She had to wait for Monsieur Baillard.

'Wait, for one more day at least. If we evacuate everyone now, and nothing happens, they'll be less likely to leave their homes a second time.'

Liesl nodded, then looked round. 'Where's Geneviève?'

'Couiza,' Sandrine said.

'Didn't we agree we'd steer clear of Couiza for the time being?'

'Yes, but do you remember, her younger sister Coralie is expecting a baby? Since Eloise hasn't come back yet, she felt she ought to look in.'

Sandrine turned to Lucie. 'But perhaps you should go with Marieta and Jean-Jacques this morning? Out of harm's way.'

'J-J will be happy with Marieta in Rennes-les-Bains,' she said quietly. 'I'm staying. I want to do my bit.' Lucie was pale and she was clearly rattled, but her eyes glinted with determination.

'Are you sure?' Sandrine asked.

'Quite sure.'

Sandrine and Suzanne exchanged a glance. Then Suzanne stood up.

'If you want to help, you'd better come with me.'

'Go with you where?'

'Do you know how to handle a gun?'

Lucie turned even whiter. 'No.'

'Well then. Time to learn.'

'Are you sure we're doing the right thing bringing Authié here?' Marianne said softly.

Sandrine shook her head. 'No. But it's too late to stop it now.'

Geneviève rushed to the sink to fetch a glass of water, then back to the table. Coralie and Alphonse's flat was tiny and airless. Every window was closed and the shutters were latched shut.

'What's wrong?' she said nervously. 'Have you started, do you think? Is that it?'

Coralie was red-faced and gasping for air. She seemed to be in shock. Her stomach was rising and falling at a rapid rate and Geneviève was terrified she would go into labour before the midwife arrived.

'Come on,' she said, pressing the glass into Coralie's hand. 'It can't be good for the baby for you to get so worked up.'

Gradually Coralie's breathing steadied, but she was still in a dreadful state. Geneviève wasn't sure if she was frightened about the thought of the baby coming or something else. She didn't know how long her sister had been like this.

'That's better,' she said, taking the empty glass. 'Good girl.' She felt Coralie's pulse. It was rattling along. 'Now, what set this off?'

Coralie stared blankly at her, as if she hadn't even heard.

'Coralie,' Geneviève said sharply, waving her hand in front of her sister's face. There was no reaction. 'Where's Alphonse?' she said.

Coralie suddenly let out a single wail. A high-pitched keening, a sound barely human.

'Coralie, stop. You'll make yourself ill. Tell me where to find Alphonse and I'll fetch him.'

Her sister clamped her hand over her mouth. Geneviève looked at her, at a loss to understand what was going on.

'Good girl,' she said cautiously. 'That's better.'

Coralie took a deep breath. 'Dead.'

Geneviève stared at her sister, then quickly placed her hand on Coralie's stomach and held it there until she felt movement. She let out a sigh of relief.

'No, the baby's fine. They go quiet just before they come. Remember when Aurélie was born?'

'Not the baby,' Coralie said in a flat voice. 'Alphonse.'

'What?' she said in disbelief. 'No, he can't be dead.'

'On the Alet road. Found his body in the river.'

Geneviève shook her head, struggling to make sense of what her sister was saying. Was it true?

'The plane dropped the weapons in the wrong place. He went to help.'

Geneviève turned cold. She couldn't be sure, but she thought that was where Raoul had gone too. Was that why he hadn't come back? Had they all been caught or killed?

She put her arm around her sister's shoulders and felt her begin to cry.

'Hush,' she murmured. 'Hush now.'

'They came to tell me. Four of them.'

'Who?'

'Gestapo.'

Geneviève caught her breath. 'When?'

Coralie didn't answer. 'They asked about you and Eloise. Wanted to know about Sandrine. Asked if it was true she lived in a house called "Citadelle".'

'What did you say?'

'That I didn't know,' she said. She looked up. 'That was right, wasn't it? They were going to arrest me, but they saw how far gone I was. Let me be.' She started to cry again. 'What am I going to do? I'm going to be on my own.'

Geneviève didn't know what to do. It meant their plan had worked, though she didn't understand why Eloise hadn't been in contact to tell them Authié was coming. Was it good news or bad? She wasn't sure.

'What am I going to do?' Coralie wailed again.

Geneviève didn't want to leave her sister, but she had to tell Sandrine as soon as she could.

'I'm going to fetch Mathilde from the boulangerie,' she said, trying to keep her voice steady. 'She'll sit with you.'

'No!' Coralie's hand shot out and grasped Geneviève's arm. 'Don't go.'

'I'll be as quick as I can.'

Shutting her ears to the sounds of her sister's sobbing, Geneviève let herself out of the house and rushed towards the boulangerie, not thinking about what she would do if Mathilde wasn't there.

She rounded the corner and stopped dead. There were soldiers in the square, rounding people up. Quickly Geneviève turned and walked in the opposite direction. Grey uniforms everywhere, four men being herded towards the bridge, their hands above their heads, the proprietor of the Grand Café Guilhem among them. The other end of the road was blocked by soldiers too. Geneviève turned again and barrelled into a man coming out of the tabac.

'What's going on?' she said.

'Someone tried to blow up the bridge at Alet,' he said. 'Stop a German convoy getting through. Americans opened fire. Commander's been killed, apparently.'

'What about the others, did they get away?'

'The maquisards?'

'Yes,' she said quickly.

The man gave a slow smile. 'Dead, most of them.'

Too late, Geneviève realised what she'd said. She turned. A *milicien* was stepping out of the interior of the shop.

'You're under arrest,' he said.

She put her hands up. The *milicien* turned towards another man in a grey suit.

'What do you want us to do with her, Major Authié?'

Geneviève froze. How was he here so soon? They

weren't ready. Why hadn't Eloise warned them? Then, the ground seemed to go from under her. If 'Citadel' had been discovered – not through the plan they'd put into action, but betrayed – then the drop-off at the Hôtel Moderne et Pigeon wasn't secure any more, either. Had Eloise been arrested? Or killed?

Geneviève felt her legs start to shake. More than ever, she had to get a message to Sandrine. To warn her that Eloise might have been caught, that Alphonse was dead, that Raoul might have been taken. She caught her breath, trying to calm herself. She glanced around, trying to see if there was any possibility she could get away.

Too many soldiers, too many police.

She looked back to Authié. For a moment, his eyes locked on to hers. Cold, devoid of emotion.

'Your name?' he said.

Geneviève said nothing. Without warning, Authié drew back his arm and hit her. Her head snapped back. The force of it, the shock of it, sent her staggering.

'Your name,' he repeated.

Slowly, she shook her head. Authié stared, then turned to the *milicien*.

'Where's Laval? He'll persuade her to talk.'

'I haven't seen him, sir.'

Geneviève wiped the specks of blood from her mouth. Authié lifted his hand again and she flinched, anticipating another blow. But instead he adjusted the silver brooch on the lapel of his jacket.

'Put her in the van with the others,' he said.

Chapter 144

'Where the hell is Laval?' Authié demanded, looking round the concourse in front of the railway station. Everywhere was a mass of black shirts and brown, the blue berets of the Milice, and he couldn't see him.

'We can't find him, Major.'

Authié had last seen Laval in Limoux three hours ago. While he was interrogating Eloise Breillac, news had come through that Raoul Pelletier had been arrested four days previously. Authié had sent Laval to telephone the warden of Carcassonne prison to instruct him to hold Pelletier there. Events seemed to be spiralling out of his control. He felt a desperate urge to act.

Then, after holding out for several hours, Eloise Breillac had begun to talk, so Authié didn't notice Laval hadn't come back. She admitted that the plan was to lure Authié into an ambush scheduled for Sunday the twentieth of August. Seeing a perfect opportunity to turn the attack against 'Citadel' by surprising them a day early, Authié had immediately left Limoux to drive to Couiza.

He'd assumed Laval was following in a separate vehicle.

'Well find him,' he shouted. 'I want to see him immediately. Immediately, is that clear?'

The *milicien* saluted and disappeared back around the corner of the building. The concourse looked like a military encampment. Four Feldgendarmerie trucks and a black Citroën Avant belonging to SS-Sturmbannführer Schmidt, his opposite number. A joint operation, he and Schmidt had ordered everyone to be fully armed. Grenades, bandoliers slung over shoulders, glinting in the sun like chain mail. Some with M40 sub-machine guns, the majority with Kar-98 semi-automatic rifles.

'Any sign of the targets?'

They had taken the usual step of rounding up the local population as hostages and bringing them to the square. Even so, Authié assumed that somebody would manage to get a message to the insurgents. Someone always did.

In any case, he wanted Coustaussa to know he was coming. By arriving twenty-four hours ahead of time and by posting patrols on the surrounding roads, he would make sure that 'Citadel' would be unable to evacuate the village. Authié knew that his reputation preceded him. The more intimidated Coustaussa was, the more likely it was they would negotiate and hand Vidal over.

Authié took a deep breath. This was the moment he had been waiting for. In a matter of hours, he would have Vidal and the others in custody. And he would have the Codex.

'What can you tell me?'

The radio operator removed his headphones.

'Reports of two women – one of them matching the description of the agent "Catherine" – sighted in the garrigue to the north of the village. Another two – again, one identified as fitting the description of "André" – have been seen in the vicinity of the castle ruins.'

'Marianne Vidal and Suzanne Peyre,' he said. 'No sign of "Sophie"?'

'Not yet, sir.'

Authié nodded. 'Has anyone else attempted to leave Coustaussa?'

'An old woman and a child in a dog cart,' he replied. 'Heading towards Rennes-les-Bains. As per your orders, they let them go. Also, a man and a woman trying to get out on the Cassaignes road.'

'And?'

'The report is that they resisted arrest,' he said.

Authié nodded. 'Good.' His orders had been brutal and clear. Except for the very old and the very young, anyone offering any kind of resistance should be shot on sight. It served as a warning. 'Radio all units and tell them to advance on the village.'

The man nodded, put his headphones back on and started to broadcast Authié's orders back up the hill.

'What would you like done with the hostages?' Sturmbannführer Schmidt asked, gesturing to the several hundred old men, women and children standing in the fierce August sun. A heavily pregnant young woman was struggling to stay on her feet in the heat. A mother was trying to shade her baby with a newspaper.

'They will remain here until the operation is successfully concluded. This town has supported maquisards and aided partisans. This is the consequence.'

Schmidt nodded and waved his men forward. Six Unterscharführer immediately took up position. Authié gave orders to the Milice, Schmidt repeated the same orders in German, then they got into the car. The Citroën pulled away, past the damaged substation and on to the dirt track that led through the garrigue. Two of the trucks followed, sending up stones in a cloud of dust. The other two vehicles were to approach from the lower road. They would begin rounding everyone up, as they had done in Couiza, and searching every house.

Authié and Schmidt did not speak as they rolled slowly up the hill towards the village. Authié was aware that the insurgents might try to attack the car before he reached Coustaussa. He looked up over the garrigue, then down towards the village. The road was empty as far as the eye could see.

They rounded a bend. He could see a collection of small flint buildings, and then the first of the houses on the outskirts of Coustaussa. Small dwellings and a large whitewashed farm building next to a field of vines. Finally, the first indications that the battle had already begun. The bodies of a man and a woman were hanging from the branch of a holm oak. Their faces hooded and their hands tied behind their backs, twisting slowly round in the heat.

'A warning to the rest,' Authié said. Schmidt said nothing.

On the outskirts of the village, Authié saw a starburst of blood on the white wall of the farm building. Lying between the vines, the body of a teenage boy. He got out to examine the body, then walked back to speak to the officer in charge of the truck behind them.

'He's not dead yet. Take him to the square with the others.'

Two soldiers jumped down from the truck. Shocked back into consciousness, the boy started to struggle, his feet thrashing on the ground. The soldiers dragged him down towards the village, leaving a trail of blood in the dust.

Authié nodded with satisfaction when he reached the Place de la Mairie. So far, no attack. No ambush. Most of the inhabitants were already in the square. One of the other Feldgendarmerie trucks was parked across the rue de la Mairie, and Schmidt told their driver to park across the rue de l'Empereur, blocking the other escape route.

Authié got out.

'Women and children that side,' he ordered, pointing to the war memorial. 'Men over there.'

The soldiers immediately started to push and shove the prisoners, making no allowances, no exceptions. Old and young, physically able or frail, jabbing and threatening as they had done in Couiza.

'You expect the attack to come from below the village, not above it?' Schmidt asked.

'If they had intended to attack from the north, they

would have made an attempt on us already,' he said.

'So what do we do? My men are asking.' Schmidt paused. 'They have heard stories.'

Authié glanced around at the faces of the German soldiers. The usual belligerence and bloodlust on some, but also confusion and fear on others. The *miliciens* were the same.

'What stories?' he demanded.

'That the village is haunted,' he said. 'That these women are …' He broke off, clearly embarrassed.

'That the women are what, Sturmbannführer Schmidt?' Authié said coldly.

'That they are in league with … That they are ghosts, some say.'

Authié felt a wild rage sweep through him. Who else but Laval knew about the Codex? Had he talked?

'Do you believe such stories?' he managed to say.

The Nazi flushed. 'Of course not.'

'Well then,' Authié said, making no attempt to hide his contempt. 'They are your men. They will follow your orders.'

'But what, precisely, *are* your orders, Major Authié?' Schmidt said.

'To wait,' he replied. 'To wait until she comes.'

Chapter 145

Coustaussa

Sandrine felt nothing, heard nothing.

The beating silence hung heavy over the waiting land. The air seemed to vibrate and shimmer and pulse. The heat, the cicadas, the sway of the wild lavender and shock-yellow genet among the thistles, the whispering wind of the Tramontana in the garrigue.

It was all her fault. Authié had come, but too soon. Before they were ready. All she had intended was to kill Authié and, with Monsieur Baillard's help, drive the invaders once and for all from the Midi.

But she could see the bodies of a man and a woman hanging dead from the branch of the old holm oak and she'd heard gunfire on the outskirts of the village by the Andrieu farm.

It was her fault. She had gambled Coustaussa and everyone in it, so sure was she that her plan would work. She had lost. Every death was her responsibility. All she could do now was to try and save as many people as she could.

She peered out from the cover of the *capitelle*. Marianne and Lucie had taken up their position in the Camp Grand, while Suzanne and Liesl were in the ruins of the castle.

There was no sign of anyone else. Sandrine no longer thought Raoul would come. She no longer believed Monsieur Baillard would be able to help. In the end, the Codex was no more than a dream. A beautiful, but useless, myth.

It meant nothing in the end.

In these last moments of stillness, she tried not to think about Eloise or Geneviève. Where were they? Coralie's husband was missing, too. And Raoul? She dropped her head on her arms, so tired of it all.

No one was coming. The land was silent and still. And although she feared what was to come, more than anything she wanted it to be over.

Forcing herself to act, Sandrine half crawled behind the low, long wall that ran alongside the track down towards the village. There was a gap of fifteen feet, maybe twenty, between the end of the wall and the first outbuildings of the old Andrieu farm. No cover, no shade. If Authié was waiting for her, watching from the blackened windows of the house beside the abandoned cemetery, this exposed patch of land was where the bullet would find her.

She assumed everyone had been taken to the Place de la Mairie while the soldiers searched the farms and houses. There was a sudden burst of machine-gun fire from the hills and the answering staccato chatter of an automatic weapon closer to hand. Sandrine's thoughts shattered, like fragments of bright glass. She pulled her Walther P38 from her belt, the familiar weight of it reassuring in her hand.

Breaking cover, she ran, low and fast, until she reached the edge of the Sauzède property. She vaulted the low wall, then on to the next garden, zigzagging from one square of land to the next and coming into the village from the east.

She crossed the rue de la Condamine and into the tiny alleyway beside the round tower, giving her a clear view of the square.

Authié was there, she could feel it. Then she saw a ribbon of red blood and the body of a young boy lying on his back on the dusty ground. His right hand twitched and jerked, then fell still back to his side.

Still she couldn't see him behind the ranks of grey jackets and black. The rattle of a machine gun from the ruins of the castle rent the air. Taken by surprise, a soldier jerked round and returned fire. A woman screamed and pulled her children to her, trying to shield them.

Jacques Cassou broke away from the group, trying to run to the safety of the rue de la Condamine. He was an easy target. Sandrine could only watch in horror as the Schmeissers ripped into him. His daughter Ernestine tried to catch him. But she was too slow, he was too heavy. Jacques staggered, dropped to his knees. The soldiers kept firing, this second hail of bullets bringing them both down.

Hearing the gunfire, Lucie and Marianne launched the first of the smoke canisters from the Camp Grand. It soared over the houses and landed at the edge of the square by the truck. Then a second canister, and another, releasing plumes of blue and pink and orange and yellow smoke into the stifling air. The soldiers were disorientated, cross-firing into one another's positions. Sandrine realised they were nervous too. Whatever Authié had told them about the operation, they realised there was more to it than just another raid on a partisan stronghold.

'Halten! Halten!'

The Sturmbannführer shouted the order to hold fire, repeating it in French. Discipline was immediately restored. But the hiatus had been long enough for the hostages to scatter. Some headed for refuge in the church or in the shaded undergrowth below the chemin de la Fontaine, others to the cellars of the presbytery. Marianne would do her best to smuggle everyone away.

As soon as the square was clear of civilians, Suzanne and Liesl launched the main assault from the castle. Their bullets raked the ground. A grenade exploded on impact with the war memorial. In response, the mixed German and French unit divided into two, some firing into the hills, others indiscriminately after the fleeing hostages. Through the coloured smoke and the dust, Sandrine glimpsed the blue berets of the *miliciens* vanishing into the rue de la Peur and realised they intended to leave no witnesses.

Because of her plan, a plan that had failed, the whole village would die. She couldn't let that happen. There was no choice but to give herself up in exchange for the hostages. Besides, she could see Authié now, standing with his right hand resting on the black bonnet of the car and his Mauser hanging loose in his left. He looked calm, disengaged, as the firefight raged around him.

Sandrine dropped the hammer on her pistol and stepped out into the light.

'It's me you want, not them. Let them go.'

It wasn't possible that he should hear her and yet, despite the noise and the shouting, he did. He turned and looked straight at her. Those eyes, she thought. Was he smiling, she wondered, or did it pain him that it should end like this?

He said her name. Her real name. The soft music of it hung suspended in the air. Threat or entreaty, she didn't know, but she felt her resolve weaken. He said it again. And this time, it sounded bitter, false in his mouth. A betrayal. The spell was broken.

Sandrine lifted her arm. And fired.

Chapter 146

Pic de Vicdessos

The sun was full in the sky when Audric Baillard and Guillaume Breillac cleared the crest of the hill. It had taken them three days to make their way south from Tarascon, evading the Nazi patrols. Baillard had seen the beginnings, and the ends, of many wars in his long life and knew that the last days were often the most dangerous. He knew that Dame Carcas had spoken the words in Carcaso to save her stronghold and still the ghost army had come. Even so, he believed his chance of success would be greater in the Vallée des Trois Loups.

'This last part of the journey is my responsibility,' he said. 'I cannot ask you to go further.'

Guillaume nodded. 'I'll wait here. Keep watch.'

Baillard continued alone. After reading the words and allowing the text to take root in his mind, he had finally understood that the verses could be spoken only on behalf of another. That to offer one's life willingly and freely, so that others might live, was what gave the words power.

That the greatest act of war was love.

Baillard now understood how, if the words were spoken, each person would see their own heart reflected back at them. The good would see the good they had done, the bad would see their own ill deeds. But, as he looked up at the pattern of the cross reflected on the face of the rock, the way the light danced and swayed between the branches of the oak trees, he prayed that he was not mistaken.

He hoped Raoul was back standing at Sandrine's side. That each – Marianne and Suzanne, Liesl and Lucie, Geneviève and Eloise – would understand what she had to do and why. And still Baillard did not know whether the act of reading the words out loud would kill him. Whether he must die so that others might live, or whether merely to be prepared to sacrifice his own life was sufficient.

He waited a few moments more, until finally he was ready. Then he took the Codex from the pocket of his pale suit and began to read the seven verses out loud.

Come forth the spirits of the air. Come forth the armies of the air.

From the blood of the land where once they fell, come forth in the final hour. Travel over the sea of glass. Travel over the sea of fire. The sea shall engulf you and fire shall cleanse you and you shall arrive at a place that you know and do not know. There, the bones of the fallen, the warriors, await you and time will be time no longer.

Every death remembered.

Then the broken tower will fall. The sepulchre will be rent asunder. The mountain stronghold will release those summoned by the courage of he who speaks: 'Come forth the spirits of the air. Come forth the armies of the air.'

And though their number be ten thousand times ten thousand, they will heed you and they will answer. Those who died so others might live, those who gave their lives and now live, will hear your call. They will return to the land from which they came.

And the ghost army shall carry with them the tools of their lives – sword and javelin and quill and plough – and they shall save those who shall come after. The land will rise and defend those who are pure of heart.

Then, when the battle is over, they shall sleep once more.

The air closed around the verses spoken. His words echoed away into silence.

Slowly, Baillard let his arm drop. For a moment, he stood in the green embrace of the glade. At first, nothing but a faint rumbling of thunder in the sky.

Then, he began to hear them. A movement in the trees, the earth breaking open. The shadows of those he had loved and had prayed to see again.

He let out a long and gentle sigh. No apocalypse, no destroying of all that was good, along with all that was bad, but the words made flesh. An army of ghosts, the spirits of the fallen, was coming to stand upon the land where once they fell.

'*A la perfin*,' he murmured. At last.

He smiled. And might he see her now? Would she come in the army of ghosts?

Baillard heard a crack, sharp in the silence of the valley. He looked down and saw blood. He stared at the stain spreading on his jacket, red against white. A hole where a bullet had hit him in the side.

His body met his mind. Pain suddenly hit and his legs buckled. Then he was falling. He held the Codex to him. The vow he had taken in the labyrinth cave so many years ago had kept him living beyond his allotted time, but could it be that he was dying now?

A stranger broke out of the cover of the trees, striding towards him, a gun in his right hand. Short black hair, dark skin, cold eyes. Baillard did not know him, though he had met his kind many times before. There was blood on his clothes. Baillard prayed it did not belong to Guillaume Breillac.

'Where is it?'

'Who are you?'

'It doesn't matter.'

Many times during his long and lonely life, Baillard had found the burden he carried too much to bear. Now he discovered in himself a desperate desire to live.

'Alaïs,' he said under his breath.

He had been waiting so long for her to come back to him. He would not be robbed of the chance to see her again. Baillard saw the man lift his arm and aim his weapon.

'Where's the Codex, old man?'

'It is not intended for you,' he said.

Through the thin material of his jacket, Baillard found the cold metal of his gun and pulled the trigger.

The man's eyes flared open with surprise as the bullet hit him in the heart. He stared, swaying on his feet, then blood jetted from his mouth and he dropped to his knees, his gun still grasped in his hand.

'You shall not take it,' Baillard managed to say.

He was no longer in any pain. Rather, he was aware of a dreadful longing. He could hear them now. He could hear the land itself beginning to move, the graveyards opening as life was breathed back into the bones of those who dwelt in the earth. His words had summoned them. The ghost army had awoken and was beginning to walk.

The ancient words lay beneath him, the papyrus slippery now with his blood. Drowning.

Those who died so others might live, those who gave their lives and now live.

Was that to be his fate?

As consciousness slipped away, Baillard saw Guillaume Breillac staggering up the hillside. His left arm hung limp by his side and there was blood on his face, but he was on his feet. It seemed to take him an eternity to cover the ground from the edge of the path. He stopped briefly beside the man Baillard had shot, then bent down and put his hand to Baillard's neck to check for a pulse.

'Who was he?' Baillard managed to ask.

'Sylvère Laval,' Guillaume replied. 'Authié's man.'

'Is he dead?'

'Yes.'

Baillard closed his eyes. He felt Breillac struggle to pick him up. He tried to speak, to tell him to save his strength, but his voice was too weak. He knew he was not mortally wounded – Guillaume Breillac neither – though he thought they would be forced to rest in the Vallée des Trois Loups awhile.

Baillard realised he was smiling. Because now, so clearly, he could hear the voices in the mountains. The whisperings of the ghost army reclaiming the land that was rightly theirs.

He hoped – prayed – it would be enough. That it was not too late.

Chapter 147

COUSTAUSSA

Sandrine knew the bullet had gone wide. The sound of Authié's voice had sent a memory of pain, of humiliation, sharp through her, making her hand shake.

She raised her gun again, but sensing someone behind, she swung round. This time she hit her target. A grey uniform went down, blood spurting from his right thigh. He managed to drag himself to cover and lifted his Mauser K98 rifle.

Sandrine threw herself sideways. She saw the flash of unburnt propellant and heard a distinctive sharp crack as the bullet nicked the wall, then ricocheted into the ground.

'I want her alive!' Authié shouted.

She located his position through the smoke. He had taken cover behind the black Citroën at the corner of rue de l'Empereur. Trying not to look at the corpses of Jacques and Ernestine Cassou, Sandrine emerged from the alleyway. Keeping low, and with her left shoulder hard against the wall, she crouched down, looked along the sight, lining up the notch and the front blade post. She fired. The front nearside tyre exploded.

Another grenade landed in the Place de la Mairie, striking the south-west corner of the square this time, blowing out all the windows of the Cassou house on the corner. From every window, the explosion of glass shattering, glinting, spiralling silver like a child's kaleidoscope. Smoke clouds of blue and pink and yellow, like the air around the old aluminium factory in Tarascon, blotted out the blue

Midi sky. The corner of the Sauzède house crumbled, its sharp right angles giving way to a disordered jigsaw of jagged, wrecked stone.

Out of the corner of her eye, Sandrine saw Liesl. They had moved the weapons cache from the *capitelles*. Now Liesl was leading the old men and women back into the streets holding antique Saint-Etienne revolvers, World War I .32-calibre Webleys. Even a couple of Labelle carbine bolt-action cavalry rifles.

A Gestapo officer dropped to one knee. He pressed the butt of his SMG hard into his shoulder, then pulled the trigger. Sandrine heard the sickening whump as rounds smashed into an old man at the front of the group. The hot lead burning through bone and muscle, ripping through liver and heart and stomach. Another explosion, to Sandrine's left, near the cemetery.

Then she glimpsed Suzanne's trademark cropped hair. And, behind her, a glint of metal. A beam of sunlight glancing, fleetingly, on the metal tip of a rifle. Sandrine narrowed her eyes. Not a K98, so far as she could make out, but a British Lee Enfield. The tip of the rifle jolted as the soldier got into position. Ready for the shot.

'Suzanne!' she shouted. 'To your right.'

Everything seemed to happen at once. A single shot rang out. Sandrine watched the rifle drop to the ground, then the soldier – not Suzanne – fell. Marianne stepped out from the cover of the building. Briefly, Sandrine saw them kiss, then Suzanne continued down the rue de la Condamine and Marianne ran back towards the church.

As Sandrine gave a sigh of relief, she felt the cold, hard barrel of a gun pressed against her temple and a hand reaching out to take her P38 from her hand. Watching the battle unfold, she had forgotten to guard her own position.

'It's over,' he said.

Sandrine began to shake. Authié's voice, the pressure of

his body against hers, taking her back to the villa on the route de Toulouse.

'Where is it?' he whispered in her ear.

'I don't have it,' she forced herself to say.

He jabbed the barrel against her skin. 'I don't believe you.'

Sandrine tried to kick back at him, but Authié smashed her forward into the wall and she felt her top lip split. A gentle trickle of blood seeped, warm, into her mouth. Then he was dragging her back by her hair towards the square.

'Where are you taking me?'

He punched her. 'Tell me where it is,' he said, his voice rising.

Winded, Sandrine couldn't speak. She felt a dull ache, a tug, in her abdomen and knew she was bleeding.

'Where is it?' he repeated.

'I don't have it,' she managed to say again.

As Authié held the gun against her head, his finger poised on the trigger, they heard a noise. A sound, a rumbling like thunder in the mountain. His hand wavered and he looked up.

'What was that?'

Chapter 148

Sandrine glanced up at the sky, but it was completely clear. An endless blue, no clouds. Then she heard it again, a deep reverberation that seemed to come from the centre of the earth. She felt a spark of hope. Had Raoul come back? Was he here with men from Tarascon, from Salvezines, to help?

She looked around. The soldiers were also gazing up. The men and women of Coustaussa too, all staring, confusion on everyone's faces. The guns had fallen silent.

Without hesitation, Sandrine drove her heel back into Authié's shin, throwing him momentarily off balance. He recovered straight away and let off a shot, but she managed to throw herself under the car and roll to the other side, then stagger across the road into the alleyway between two buildings. The pain in her abdomen intensified. She felt something tear, rip.

Authié fired, two more bullets into the wall. He couldn't see where she'd gone. He looked mad, his eyes darting wildly from left to right in his desperation to find her.

Some of the *miliciens* were starting to retreat. Sandrine couldn't see what they were looking at, only that their faces had gone from confusion to fear. Then the ground started to shake. She wondered if it might be a tank, though the idea was absurd. Now even the sky seemed to be shaking too but, although the noise was getting louder, it wasn't the sound of a plane.

'Come forth the spirits of the air.'

Sandrine heard herself utter the words, though they didn't seem to leave her mouth. Then she began to hear other voices. More like the sound of the wind in the trees than words, yet she thought she could make out what they were saying. Voices, and the sound of a multitude of marching feet.

'Come forth the spirits of the air.'

She watched the MP40 slip from a young soldier's grasp. The man behind him was gripping his weapon so hard, his fist was white with the strain of it. He jolted, then turned and ran.

Terror took hold. Some were transfixed, petrified, as they stumbled back, held in thrall by whatever they thought they saw. She caught fragments, muttered imprecations of the Devil and the dead, prayers she didn't understand. She watched as the body of a young soldier turned black, his tongue protruded and his eyes brimmed with blood.

'*Teufel.*'

Terrified by something more than the guns and the bombs and the mortars destroying the square, the soldiers were scattering.

'*Geister.*'

This, a word she did understand. Ghosts.

'Monsieur Baillard,' she whispered. He had done it. He had summoned them, as he had promised he would. And they had come.

Now all the soldiers were turning, starting to run, making no attempt to take cover. They were brought down by a storm of bullets. Friendly fire or hit by Suzanne and Lucie, Sandrine didn't know. In the corner of the square she saw Liesl leading the villagers away to safety. Marianne was shooing a gaggle of children out of the church and towards the woods. The Gestapo and Milice forces trampled each other in their desperation to get away. They fell as they staggered over fallen comrades, the bullets seeming to come from all sides. Some had wounds as if they'd been shot, others as if they'd been attacked with a spear or javelin. Stabbed with the blade of a knife.

Sandrine was struggling to comprehend what she was witnessing. The girl she had been and the woman she was now, brought face to face at this single moment in her life.

Was this it? Was this the promised salvation? Or was it a different sort of justice the Codex promised?

Then, in the centre of the killing field, Sandrine saw Authié again. He wore a look of mute terror. His grey eyes were wild with horror, fixed on the graveyard on the corner of the rue de la Condamine. Finally, this was her chance. She ran back to the square and snatched a weapon abandoned on the ground. Not her gun, but one that would do.

'Authié,' she shouted. 'This was what you were seeking. This is what the Codex brings to you. To men like you.'

He swung round to look at her. For a split second, she saw a flash of the old Authié. The man who had hunted her down, who had brutalised her and stolen her future from her.

'Men like you,' she repeated.

Before he had a chance to respond, Sandrine raised the gun and fired. This time, she did not miss. Two shots. One to stop, one to kill.

For an endless moment, Authié stood swaying on his feet. Then he fell forward, his body hitting the corner of the car, then sliding to the ground. A ribbon of blood was smeared on the bonnet, red against the black. Straight away, like the others, the bullet hole in his forehead began to blacken and his tongue to swell. White eyes filling with blood started to rot in their sockets.

Sandrine dropped the gun. Her legs went out from under her. She clamped her hand over her mouth in horror. Authié was dead. She had killed him. But at what cost?

'Coratge, sòrre.'

A shiver went down her spine. The same voice, but this

time as clear as if someone had been standing beside her. Sandrine raised her head. She didn't want to look. She was frightened to look.

She struggled to her feet. If Monsieur Baillard was right, then she would not see what Authié had seen. What the treacherous and murderous men who had come with him to Coustaussa to murder them all had seen.

Slowly, Sandrine turned around.

At first she thought the smoke had floated back to the square. Then she realised it was a haze, like a summer mist.

Come forth the spirits of the air.

To start with, she could see nothing distinct. But then the impression of movement, a shimmering in the atmosphere. Slowly, they emerged. Row after row after row of people, beyond a glass sea. Not people, but outlines. Indistinct shadows of white and red and black, pale green robes, faces hidden beneath hoods and shadow and flame.

And the number was ten thousand times ten thousand.

Steadily, Sandrine walked towards the army of light. Thousands of women and men standing side by side. One face grew clearer. A girl – like her, perhaps – smiling. Sandrine felt a sensation of peace, of recognition. A whole life perceived in an instant. A woman, known in life as Alaïs Pelletier du Mas. She wore a long green dress, drawn tight at the waist, with a red cloak around her shoulders and her dagger strapped to her belt. Her long dark hair fell unfettered down her back. Her expression was gentle yet resolute, peaceful with the knowledge of one who had died once and would die again. Her eyes were clear and bright and alive with the wisdom of all she had seen, all she had suffered. All she had tried to teach those who came after her.

Even though they were strangers, now other lives emerged from the ranks of the ghost army. Beside Alaïs stood Rixende, a woman who had died to save her mistress and for her faith. In death, now, a friend as she could not be in life. Standing, too, in the vanguard of the army of the air, a girl with long copper hair. Parisian by birth, but in courage and spirit and honour a daughter of the Languedoc. Léonie Vernier. And, more recent still, their spirits not yet at rest in the cold earth, those who had died in the last days and weeks, in the company of those long departed.

Alaïs looked to her husband, Guilhem, in whose sleeping arms she had lain. Sandrine saw their memories, hidden in the caves of the Sabarthès. She saw his lips shaping the words imprinted on her own heart. In this world and the next, echoing down the centuries.

Mon còr.

Sandrine felt the pattern of the syllables, the vowels, the consonants, though the words were not spoken aloud. Did not need to be spoken out loud. Here, in the army of the dead, time and space and the temporal order of things meant nothing. Were nothing. Here was only light and air and the memory written in blood, and that did not fade. Here, the cares of the world were set to flight.

Spirit only. Courage only. Love.

My love, yes.

Guilhem had died in the arms of the woman he loved and lay unburied at her side. One of the unknown dead destined to lie there for decades more. It was not yet their time to be found, to be mourned, to be buried. But soon. Soon, someone would come and their names would join the ranks of those who had lived and died for their country.

Guilhem stood, as he had stood many times before, at the right hand of his liege lord, Raymond-Roger Trencavel. Trencavel's skin was pale from the sleep of ages, but his eyes were battle bright. His right hand gripped the sword that had served him so well in life, insubstantial skin touching familiar iron. Fingers that were not there, blood that did not move or slip, skin that could not be pierced or burnt or cut any longer.

In this August of 1944, his restless spirit remained the same as it had been in 1209 as he waited within the walls of Carcassonne. Then, Guilhem had set out through the Porte Narbonnaise at his seigneur's side to beat back the crusaders massed at the gates. On that day, the battle had been lost, though he had never given up. His life had been dedicated to driving the invader, the occupier, the collaborators from the land he loved.

Every death remembered.

Viscount Trencavel had not lived to see his son grow up, as so many others would not see their children grow up, but he watched him from another realm and was proud of the man his son became. Raymond had fought, as he himself had fought, been defeated as he had been defeated. Reunited now, the son at the father's side, his place assured in the ranks of the fallen dead.

And on the far side of his son, Trencavel's friend and steward, Bertrand Pelletier.

Thousands upon tens of thousands massed, or so it seemed. The ancient lords of the Sabarthès and the Corbières and Termenès, Pierre-Roger de Mirepoix, Amaury de Montréal, Pierre-Roger de Cabaret and Amiel de Coursan. And lower *chevaliers* also, Thierry de Massabrac and Alzeu de Preixan, dubbed the same Passiontide as Guilhem du Mas. Simeon the Bookbinder with his long black beard, returned now to the side of his old ally, Pelletier. Esclarmonde de Servian, the bravest of women, and Guiraude, the Lady of Lavaur, under whose protection the *bons homes* had lived. And Dame Carcas, her hair hidden beneath her veil, also in the ranks of the army of spirits which had once come to her aid.

Those who died so others might live, those who gave their lives and now live, will hear your call.

Pascal Barthès, all those whose lives were taken by fire or flood or iron. White bones on the battlefield, picked clean by time. Grey bones in the arms of the earth, fallen in the mountains of the Sabarthès, scorched in the pyres of Montségur or the Domaine de la Cade, on the fields of Flanders and France.

Now they were moving, murmuring. The ghost army had been summoned to this one place and it had come. In the shadow of Rennes-les-Bains and Rennes-le-Château, the ruins of the castle, the ancient green forest of Arques and Tarascon and the grey wall of the mountains beyond, they walked to Coustaussa. Gathered here to fight once more. Once more, a call to arms. To rid their lands of occupation, of the oppressor, of the shame of the yellow cross and the yellow star. A drift of autumn leaves, the marks of oppression fluttering free now. This, the final battle for the soul of the Languedoc.

They had each heard the call and they had answered. Those sleeping in the cimetière Saint-Michel, in the cimetière Saint-Vincent, in the country graveyards of the Haute Vallée. A shifting, a murmuring through the cities of the dead, words carried on the wind.

Were they here in Coustaussa only, or everywhere throughout the Languedoc? She didn't know.

Sandrine felt tears come to her eyes. She could not see Raoul. Surely, if he was dead, she would see him? There was still hope, then. If he was not here, he had not died. Quickly, she sent her eyes flying over the thousands of faces and heads and folds of cloth. She could not see Lucie or Marianne, Suzanne or Liesl either. She could not see Monsieur Baillard.

But then she turned her head and saw the stone wings of the statue, the sword clasped in her hands. Beside her, a little apart from the group, she found the smiling, pretty face of Geneviève Saint-Loup. And on the other side, Eloise Breillac. Alphonse, who had never held his child in his arms, and Yvette and Robert Bonnet, brave and stoical. And a man so like Raoul that the sight of him caught at Sandrine's heart. His brother Bruno, she realised. The tears fell down her cheeks.

Next, Sandrine saw a man with a calm expression. A long grey woollen robe, like a monk's habit.

'Arinius, the map maker,' she murmured.

Beside him, with her hair braided over one shoulder, a bright-eyed girl with quick, searching eyes. Lupa, one of the unsung Christian saints, who had died at her husband's side to protect the people they loved. For a timeless instant, Sandrine met her gaze and saw something of herself reflected in Lupa's silver eyes.

Finally, in the white centre, her father – François Vidal – with the same gentle, loving smile on his face as he had worn in life. She reached out to him, wishing more than anything that she could feel his hand in hers again, but she knew she couldn't cross the distance between them.

Sandrine understood it was almost over. Time had run its course. The ghost army had done what it had been summoned to do. It had sent the invaders from the land, driving their enemies to death or to flight. Suzanne, Marianne, Liesl and Lucie had led the people – and, God willing, themselves – to safety. Only she remained to gaze upon the faces of the spirits who had risen to fight for the Midi once more.

Sandrine watched as each turned towards Viscount Trencavel. They seemed to wish him to speak. As he did so, his voice carried on the wind. Metal drew against metal, against leather. An intake of breath, ghosts yet, but the sense of purpose remained.

Per lo Miègjorn.

Words not spoken, but heard. Words beyond words, imprinted in the soul and the spirit of those who had given their lives so others might live. And would again.

Then, when the battle is over, they shall sleep once more.

Chapter 149

BAUDRIGUES

Sandrine opened her eyes. At first she didn't know where she was. She could remember little, except that she had killed Authié and the act had brought her peace. And then something had happened and ... She tried to sit up, but pain shot down her leg and she remembered. She put her hand to her abdomen and knew, this time, the bleeding would not stop.

Marianne and Suzanne had got everyone away, hadn't they? And Liesl and Lucie? Everyone safe. She sighed with relief, then remembered. That wasn't quite right. Lucie had come back to find her lying unconscious in the Place de la Mairie among rotting corpses.

Together, they had made it halfway down the hill, but then they had run into a Milice patrol. Those soldiers who'd fled before the ghosts looked into their souls had staggered back to Couiza with stories so wild, so horrifying, their commanders had ordered a four-man patrol back to Coustaussa to investigate.

Lucie had tried to stop the soldiers arresting them. A gun had been fired, but who had fired it, Sandrine wasn't sure. She remembered Lucie falling to the ground, her kneecap blown and bloodied. Shattered bone and cartilage, screaming with pain.

Then, the rattling wheels of the trucks heading east. For a while, peace, when Sandrine realised they had done it. They had won. They had saved Coustaussa. The Gestapo and Wehrmacht were withdrawing.

Every unit and battalion leaving the South.

Sandrine was finding it hard to think now, but she wished she understood why they had been brought here rather than been killed. They had no more need for hostages, did they? She realised they were in the munitions store at the Château of Baudrigues outside Roullens. She knew the place from the outside. They'd tried to attack it, more than once. Suzanne, Marianne and her. They had never succeeded.

Sandrine turned her head and saw that Lucie was there. Of course she was there. Brave, brave Lucie to have come back to rescue her.

She felt a wave of affection wash through her battered body. For that first day when they were all together – Bastille Day, Tuesday 14 July 1942, in the boulevard Barbès. Her, Suzanne and Marianne and Lucie, Max and Liesl. And Raoul.

'Raoul …'

Sandrine's cracked lips broke into a smile as she remembered the sense of promise that day. The blue sky, the sweet summer air. A perfectly captured memory set in a gilt frame. Their voices raised in song.

'*Vive le Midi*,' she whispered, remembering the hope in their voices. '*Vive Carcassonne*.'

Geneviève and Eloise, brave women who had died for their friends. All the others too, known to her and unknown, she had admired. César Sanchez and Antoine Déjean, Yvette and Robert Bonnet. Gaston, too, in the end.

She wished she knew for sure that Liesl and Marianne and Suzanne were all right. Yves Rousset. God willing, Max. Little Jean-Jacques and Marieta.

'Raoul,' she murmured again.

Where was he? Why hadn't he come?

Sandrine thought of Audric Baillard, of his wise face. If

France was free again, it would be in part thanks to him. She didn't understand what had happened, or why he had not been there with them. Only that he was a guardian of the land, the conscience of the Midi. That he linked what had been, and what was, and what was to come.

Sandrine shifted position, the cord seeming to cut deeper into her wrists. She knew she was dying. The internal injuries inflicted by Authié were too severe to allow her to survive. She thought how disappointed Raoul would be.

The minutes slipped by. The air was so still and so hot. Sandrine drifted in and out of consciousness, or sleep, she wasn't sure. Elsewhere, outside in the park, noises filtered into the dirty room in which they were being held. She knew there were other prisoners here too – Jean Bringer, Aimé Ramond, Maurice Sevajols – she could hear voices from surrounding rooms.

The sound of footsteps, rough orders given in German and in French, the sound of the heavy doors of a Feldgendarmerie truck being slammed shut.

A scream of pain, a single shout splitting the air, then nothing.

The minutes ticked on, ticked on. The sun climbed higher in the sky and the shadows came round. Sandrine felt something on her leg. She opened her eyes and saw that a black spider was crawling across her ankle, the lightest of touches. She thought she should move, shake it off, but she lacked the strength even to do that now. The hours of sitting still, hands behind her back, legs bound, had robbed her of strength.

'It's supposed to be good luck, kid,' murmured Lucie. 'Maybe you're going to come into money.'

Sandrine turned her head, pleased to hear the sound of Lucie's voice.

'I think it depends on what kind of spider it is,' she replied.

'A black widow?'

Sandrine gave a half-laugh. 'Could be.'

'I like your socks,' Lucie said softly. 'Unusual.'

'My father brought them back from Scotland.' She said the familiar words. 'A gift.'

'Ah … I remember, yes. They're really something. Thought that the first time we met.'

The silence of the hot afternoon lapped over them again. Sandrine dozed, slipping in and out of consciousness. Strange to be so weightless, so cut adrift from sensation. Everything was blurred now, body and mind and emotion, all run together.

When she next came to her senses, Lucie was talking again.

'We got everyone else away. We did that much.'

'Yes,' she murmured.

'What happened to them?' Lucie asked quietly. 'The soldiers. Their bodies were black, Sandrine. Blood in their eyes …'

'Yes.'

'What did they see that terrified them so much? That could do that? Like they'd been burnt, all black and scorched.'

Sandrine thought of Alaïs and Léonie and Lupa, Dame Carcas and Viscount Trencavel.

'I don't know,' she said. 'Not really.'

Lucie fell silent. Sandrine couldn't make sense of it either.

'Just us, kid.'

Sandrine felt a lump in her throat. 'Just us.'

Outside, the grunt of a lorry being started. More shouting, a sense of panic and fear, perhaps. Nothing ordered about the withdrawal.

'The last ones are leaving,' Lucie said, trying to prop herself up.

Sandrine bit back tears as she saw Lucie struggle, her disobedient and broken limbs no longer doing what she commanded.

'How about that? We sent them packing after all.'

Sandrine looked at the ceiling. The patches of damp in the corner and the stains on the wall where a pipe had burst and water had seeped through. The smears of blood, brown and ridged in the gaps between the tiles. They were not the first prisoners to be held in this room.

'I've been thinking,' Lucie said. 'Next year, you'll be twenty-one. We should have a grand party. Invite everyone, everyone we know. What do you say? May the eighth 1945. Make it a red-letter day. We'll have cake for Jean-Jacques, and beer for Raoul.'

'And Suzanne. She never really did much like wine either.'

'We should invite everyone we know,' Lucie continued. 'Coming of age, and all that.'

'Raoul will find us,' Sandrine said, wanting to give Lucie something to cling on to.

''Course he will.'

'We have to be patient. Hold on for just a little bit longer.'

Lucie was smiling as her eyes flickered shut. 'Raoul will find you. Like Hercules and his Pyrène, he'll tear the Aude apart to get to you. Nothing will stand in his way.'

Sandrine smiled. 'Yes,' she whispered. 'He will.'

Chapter 150

CARCASSONNE

Raoul could feel nothing, see nothing. The days were darkness and nights without sleep. He had lost all sense of time since he was arrested in the station master's office. Had lost all sense of self. Everything was as if it was happening to someone else, as if he was watching. Between the beatings and the pain, the blissful punctuation of black rest, he had separated himself from the reality.

He hadn't talked. He hadn't named names.

Raoul hoped the others had halted the *train fantôme* and rescued the prisoners. Max among them. Imagined how happy Lucie and Liesl would be. How pleased Sandrine would be.

He felt a tear slip from his eye. He couldn't bear the thought of Sandrine worrying, waiting for him to come back. Her face had haunted him every second since he'd been captured. All he could think about was how to get a message to her to let her know he loved her. That he was thinking of her.

Raoul didn't think the alarm bell had rung, yet he knew all the prisoners were awake. Everyone knew when one of their own was about to be executed. The knowledge swept through the prison like wildfire. He thought how odd it was that beyond the prison walls were the river Aude and the sky and the Montagne Noire. The turrets and towers of the Cité, and Païchérou where he had first set eyes on Sandrine. Where he had taken her dancing only weeks ago.

The backdrop to the beginning of his life. Now, it seemed, the backdrop to the ending of it.

They came for him. Raoul felt a rough hand, the butt of a rifle in the small of his back, pushing him out of the cell and into the corridor. He lost his footing and stumbled, was pulled to his feet before he had the chance to fall. The idea of lying face down on the cool stone was appealing. Raoul thought he could lie and lie and sleep for ever, skin against the damp flagstones.

'Keep moving,' said the guard, harsh.

Most of the Nazis had gone. Senior officers of the Milice were travelling with the Kommandant in the midst of the German convoy. Those left behind, Raoul knew, would be hunted down and killed. They knew it too. Retaliation would be quick and brutal and summary. No one would protect the collaborators once the Gestapo was gone.

Raoul staggered forward, hearing the murmuring of voices, like the tide coming to shore, growing and getting louder. Cells filled with Spaniards, French and Belgians and Dutch partisans, occasionally a German voice – deserters who had joined the Resistance – once, a Polish voice. The sound gave him the strength to lift his battered head.

The murmur became a chorus, rising loud and strong. The song of the partisans, 'La Butte Rouge', hanging in the air, other songs that each prisoner knew, all sung in their own languages. He remembered what Monsieur Baillard had said once about how words were more powerful than anything else, that they did not lose their power or fade or grow weaker over time.

La Butte Rouge, c'est son nom, l'baptême s'fit un matin
Où tous ceux qui grimpèrent, roulèrent dans le ravin
Aujourd'hui y a . . .

Raoul felt his mouth forming itself into a smile. The cut

on his lip was infected and most of the teeth in his lower jaw were gone, but his muscles remembered what it was to smile. He wished he could raise a hand to acknowledge the men's voices, to wave as he walked by, but he could do no more than nod and turn his head from side to side as he passed. He hoped they understood that their voices made the difference.

It was not how one lived, but how one chose to die. One of Sandrine's headlines in *Libertat.* Such a long time ago now, such a very long time ago.

The men started to bang on the bars, a drum tattoo walking him to his final judgement. He wished Sandrine could know he was not alone in these last minutes. He imagined her searching for him, searching every prison, every cell, until she'd found him and set him free. Such courage, such refusal to give up.

She would grieve for him, he knew, but he hoped she would build a new life with someone else. Learn to laugh again. When the war was won.

But he would have liked a child, a daughter. A little girl with Sandrine's black curly hair, her spirit. They could call her Sophie, perhaps, to remind them of how once they had lived.

Raoul sighed. Not Sophie. Something new, for the future. He would leave it to Sandrine, she'd know.

'This way.' Again the jab in the back.

Raoul knew he wasn't the first to be taken out today. He'd heard them, from four in the morning. In the early days of the occupation, at any execution there was a rabbi or a priest. As the years passed and there were too many souls to be shriven, too many in need of absolution, the practice ceased. The rabbis were all dead or deported and the good Christians could not collude with such unchristian acts. A last cigarette, the condemned man's last supper, that too had gone.

He turned his head from the light as he was pushed into a room, too bright after the darkness of the cell. Disorientated, not certain what was happening, he stood between the two warders. He smiled then, realising that even now, even today, the pretence of fairness and the rule of law was being played out. A court martial, though there was no lawyer and no debate.

For a moment, letting his thoughts drift free, Raoul imagined what Sandrine might say. He heard himself laugh, so missed the pronouncement of the summary sentence, though it was only going to end one way.

Death by firing squad. To be carried out immediately.

The executioners were waiting as Raoul walked out of the courtroom and into the open air. Sand at his feet, the sun too bright. He thought how odd it was that he was to die on so beautiful a day. There was a single wooden stake in the centre of the yard. Even with his eyes narrowed against the light, Raoul saw blood on the stake from the last man who had stood there. Red, not yet brown in the sun.

'Pelletier, Raoul.'

For a moment, the handcuffs were removed, but only so his hands could be tied around the stake with rope.

'This?' one of the guards was saying, waving a black hood in front of his face.

'No,' he said.

Raoul was pleased at how clear his voice sounded. Sandrine would be proud of him, he thought. Then the memory of her took the strength from him, and he felt his knees buckle.

'No,' he said again.

He looked at the twelve men ranged against him. Then he stood up straight and looked his killers in the eye. His countrymen.

'*Mon còr*,' he said. The only words that mattered any more.

He watched as the rifles were raised. He let his eyes slip, fleetingly, up to the Midi sky. So blue and clear. How strange, he thought again, that there should still be such beauty in the world. And he hoped she was safe beneath it.

'Sandrine,' he whispered.

Raoul heard the sound before he felt the bullets slamming into his chest, his legs, his arms, his head.

Chapter 151

'Raoul!' Sandrine cried out, her heart suddenly racing. 'Raoul?'

For a moment she was neither asleep nor awake, as if some part of her had been left behind in the dream. She was floating, looking down at herself from a great height, like the stone gargoyles, dragons, lions that leered at passers-by from the cathédrale Saint-Michel. A sensation of slipping out of time, falling from one dimension into another through white, endless space.

'Has he come for us?' Lucie murmured.

Sandrine smiled at the sound of Lucie's voice. She had been quiet for so long.

'Not yet,' she replied. 'Soon.'

The flies were worse now. The room was airless, the sun ferocious, and the heat and the smell of blood caught in Sandrine's throat. She turned her head to the right and could see, through the high windows, a patch of sky so blue and clear and endless. It seemed wrong, she thought, that there should be such beauty in the world on a day like this.

She rolled her head to the other side. Lucie was very pale, barely breathing. Sandrine could see her thin chest, beneath her broderie anglaise blouse, rising and falling faintly. Sandrine smiled a little. Lucie had always said she'd get married in that shirt. Smart, she said, but not too much.

A sudden memory of Lucie waltzing around the salon in Coustaussa, holding Jean-Jacques in her arms. Liesl was there, taking photographs as always. Marieta was grumbling the baby would get overexcited and never go down. Marianne was smiling and clapping her hands, Suzanne, with a wry expression, watching Marianne more than the baby. Had Monsieur Baillard been there? Sandrine frowned, she couldn't remember. Had Raoul?

The gentle past faded once more. The pain was constant now, as if her insides were being turned inside out. She could feel the infection moving under her skin, hot and angry and swollen. As for her hands, she couldn't feel them at all any longer.

But now she was aware of a weight on her chest that she couldn't identify, a despair. As if the air had all been sucked out of her lungs.

She would have liked a child, a daughter. She and Raoul, a little girl, with her father's lopsided smile and his passion. They could have called her Sophie, perhaps, to remind them of how life once had been. Sandrine shook her head. No, she would have a name for the future, not for the past.

'Vida,' she whispered to herself. The Occitan word for life. She thought Raoul would like it.

'Are you still there?' Lucie whispered.

Even though her voice was faint, Sandrine jumped at the sound.

'I'm here.'

'What time is it?'

'I don't know.'

'It's not night?'

'No, it's daytime. The sun is still high.'

Overhead, Sandrine heard the sound of an aeroplane. Why could she hear a plane? Hadn't they all gone now? Hadn't they?

'I don't think anyone's coming,' Lucie said, a heartbeat later.

'Raoul will have found out where we've been taken,'

Sandrine said quickly. 'Marianne, too. They'll work it out and they'll come. You'll see.'

'If we're patient …' Lucie spoke so softly now that, despite the silence of the room, Sandrine could barely hear her.

'That's right.'

'But it's not night?'

'No.'

'The thing is, kid, I can't see anything. Everything's dark.'

Sandrine felt tears spring to her eyes. 'It must be the shadows of the trees.'

'Ah … that's good then,' Lucie said. 'I think I can hear the wind blowing through the trees, it must be that.'

'That's right,' Sandrine said, trying not to cry.

Motes of dust danced in the slatted sunlight coming in through the windows high up in the tiny room. Like dancers, Sandrine thought, spinning silver in the white haze.

'Thanks, kid,' Lucie said softly, too softly now.

Sandrine heard Lucie's breathing falter and knew she was dying. Knew there was nothing she could do. The bullet shifting beneath Lucie's skin in the cartilage and bone of her shattered knee, the muscles and skin screaming around the entry wound. The infection setting in.

Sandrine knew her pain would pass soon too. Feared it would pass. And she was wondering now – after everything that had happened, the blackness that had engulfed them – if France could ever recover. If there could be forgiveness. If all those thousands, millions who had died would all be honoured and remembered. If their deaths would count for something, mean something. Their names on a wall, on a street sign, in the history books. Sandrine tried to bring each face to mind, one by one, like the names on the marble wall in the Place de l'Armistice.

She smiled and felt her mind drifting free. She didn't

believe in God – could not believe in a God that allowed such things to happen – but, at the same time, the seductive thought that her father might be somewhere, waiting for her, brought a smile to her parched lips. He would have liked Raoul, if ever they had met. Would have been proud to have him as a son-in-law.

She knew Liesl would care for Jean-Jacques like her own son until Max came back. With Marieta's help, of course. Suzanne and Marianne would be there, too. She wondered what Max would tell J-J about his mother. The diaries that Lucie had painstakingly kept would help. About how brave Lucie was, how she fought every moment of her life to keep him safe.

And Raoul, would he talk about her?

Sandrine looked down at her ripped clothes, at the tartan socks rescued from the house on the rue du Palais, threadbare and through at the heel now.

'Really something,' she murmured, remembering Lucie's words on the day they'd first met.

She wanted more than anything to reach out and hold Lucie's hand, though she didn't seem frightened. All Sandrine could do was turn her head and watch. Lucie's features seemed to be changing, shifting. She looked suddenly young, all the worry lines falling away from her eyes, the corners of her mouth. A girl with the world at her feet.

'They'll be here soon,' Sandrine said.

Lucie didn't answer. Sandrine wasn't sure she was breathing any more.

Sandrine was floating in and out of consciousness, not tethered any more to the tattered, beautiful world. Not any more. She hoped it would be quick. And that, when it was all over, they would come to Baudrigues and find them. Know who they were. Remember their names.

'Not much longer now,' she whispered, finally allowing the tears to come. 'Raoul will be here soon.'

She heard the sound of boots in the corridor outside, leather heels on the black and white tiles, then a key turning in the lock. A German soldier in a grey uniform, or was it green, coming towards them. Something in his hands, two hand grenades, and Sandrine realised they meant to leave no evidence. Nothing at all.

He leant forward to force one into Lucie's mouth.

'Leave her,' she said quickly. 'She's gone. There's no need.'

The soldier hesitated.

'Please,' Sandrine repeated, in a whisper this time.

The young man took a step back, then another, towards the open door. She thought she saw pity in his eyes, shame even. He paused on the threshold and put one of the grenades carefully down on the floor, then he shut the door and ran. The sound of his boots echoing in the distance.

The room seemed to be vibrating beneath her. Outside in the park there was a wave of explosions, glass shattering, wood ripping through the gardens. Fireworks, firecrackers, a sequence of snapping, cracking, bursting. Then, a single, all-encompassing blast and Sandrine realised they were blowing up the entire munitions store.

'Raoul,' she whispered. 'Raoul.'

The grenade came to rest against her leg. Now, she saw that the soldier had pulled the pin after all. There was to be no reprieve.

'*Mon còr*,' she said. The only words that mattered any more.

EPILOGUE

August 2009

Château de Baudrigues
19 August 2009

On Wednesday morning at 9.20, people are gathering in the clearing at the Château de Baudrigues. Flags and a band, official colours and decorations and a sense of purpose.

The president of the delegation and the Mayor of Roullens are laying wreaths at the three gravestones: one for Jean Bringer – 'Myriel'; one for Aimé Ramond; the last inscribed to the 'Martyrs of Baudrigues'.

Men and women in their official sashes and chains remembering, on the sixty-fifth anniversary of their murders on 19 August 1944, those who gave their lives so that others might live. Also, representatives of the civilians massacred as the Germans left Carcassonne the following day.

The warrior stone angel – *Y Penser Toujours* – stolen away from Square Gambetta under cover of night so that it would not be destroyed. The statue stands, now, in the cimetière Saint-Michel, keeping watch over the military graves.

White crosses and white crescents.

The Martyrs of Baudrigues never got to see, only a few days later, the men and women of the Resistance come down from the hills and take possession of their town once more.

The Mayor steps back and everyone bows their head for the minute's silence. A man in his sixties turns and puts his hand on his father's shoulder. They are so alike, Max Blum and his son Jean-Jacques, people always remark upon it. Blum is well respected and well liked in Carcassonne. One of the last to be deported from Le Vernet on the ghost train to Dachau and one of the few to survive. Jean-Jacques' three daughters all resemble their grandmother, Lucie Ménard. They never met her, though they have grown up their entire lives with stories of the sort of woman she was. They think their father and Tante Liesl exaggerate a little, but they play along all the same.

Jean-Jacques smiles at Liesl, Liesl Rousset, a celebrated war photographer. Even though his aunt is in her eighties, she is nonetheless the most beautiful woman he knows. Her children live overseas, as does she, but she has come home today for this modest ceremony and to visit her oldest friends, Marianne Vidal and Suzanne Peyre, who still live in the rue du Palais.

The sixty seconds of silence comes to an end and the band strikes up 'La Marseillaise'.

At the back of the crowd, a young woman, named Alice, turns to her husband.

'Can you take her, Will? I think she's had enough.'

Will smiles and hoists their little girl on to his shoulders. So as not to disturb proceedings, he walks away into the deep green woods surrounding the park.

Alice moves closer to the front, singing the last few verses of the anthem in her undeniably English accent.

Amour sacré de la Patrie
Conduis, soutiens nos bras vengeurs
Liberté, Liberté chérie
Combats avec tes défenseurs!

She is not sure why she has come, other than because she believes Audric Baillard would have wanted her to. Or perhaps it is because, like many others, she has heard stories of a women's resistance unit said to have single-handedly saved an entire village from being massacred in the dying days of the occupation. Their names don't appear in any of the history books, but there's something that makes Alice certain the stories are true.

Sous nos drapeaux, que la victoire
Accoure à tes mâles accents
Que tes ennemis expirants
Voient ton triomphe et notre gloire!

She wishes she had asked Monsieur Baillard about it, but they were caught up in a different story, in a different time. And the time they had together was so short.

There is a polite, awkward smattering of applause. The dignitaries start to leave – there is another event to be held in Carcassonne later in the day – and the small crowd of onlookers starts to break up.

Alice finds herself left alone with two women. One is elegant in blue, her white hair braided at the nape of her neck. The other is tall, with tightly cropped hair and a tanned face.

'Are you a relative?' she asks, peering at the names on the tombstone.

Marianne Vidal turns and looks at her, then smiles.

'Our friend,' she says, with a quiet dignity. 'And my sister.'

'What was she called?' Alice asks quickly, wondering why their names are not on the memorial. There are only men's names.

For a moment, she thinks the woman will not answer. Then a smile lights up her eyes.

'Sandrine Vidal.'

At that moment, Alice's daughter runs back into the clearing and into her mother's arms. She scoops Sajhësse up and then turns to make the introductions.

But the two women, arm in arm, are already walking away.

Author's Note

Seventy years after the end of the Second World War, estimates vary as to how many people were involved in the Resistance and the Maquis. By its clandestine nature, people could not admit to involvement at the time for fear of reprisal. Subsequently, a veil of secrecy fell over the *années noires*, which has only begun to lift in recent years. What is clear is that, following the invasion and occupation of the *zone libre* by German forces in November 1942 – and the introduction of forced labour laws, the hated *service du travail obligatoire* (STO) in February 1943 – there was a significant increase in Resistance activity in the South. This continued until the liberation of the Aude in August 1944.

It is also clear that, as the history of the Resistance in France was written, the 'book of myths' – to use Adrienne Rich's phrase – women's roles were underplayed. In part this is because many women themselves wished to forget and return to their ordinary lives, and in part because some historians overlooked the particular, and different, nature of women's contributions. More than fifty thousand Médailles de la Résistance were awarded, both to those still alive and posthumously, though proportionately few were awarded to women. And of the 1,061 Croix de la Libération – presented by Général de Gaulle for exceptional acts of resistance and bravery – only six were given to women. Anecdotal evidence, not least talking to parents and grandparents of Carcassonnais friends, suggests there were many women involved in active roles in the Aude and the Ariège. I am indebted to contemporary accounts of female Resistance activity, in particular those of Lisa Fittko and Lucie Aubrac, as well as Margaret L. Rossiter's excellent *Women in the Resistance*, H. R. Kedward's *In Search of the Maquis* and Julien Allaux's comprehensive *La 2ème Guerre Mondiale dans l'Aude.*

There was never – to my knowledge – an all-female network such as my imaginary *réseau* 'Citadel', nor is there any record of a Coustaussa Maquis. But there certainly were women involved in active roles in networks in the South. It is also important to note that the Resistance and Maquis in the Midi was far from being an exclusively French affair – German, Belgian, Polish, Czech, Austrian, Dutch and Spanish anti-fascists all fought alongside their French neighbours.

Finally, although the story is based around real events between 1942 and 1944 in the Aude, this is a novel, not an attempt to fictionalise what happened. My principal characters are wholly imagined and I have taken one or two historical liberties for the sake of the story. So although there was a demonstration in Carcassonne against Maréchal Pétain's collaborationist Vichy government on 14 July 1942, there was no bomb attack and no one was killed. I have deliberately blurred exactly which organisation Leo Authié works for, to ensure he won't be mistakenly identified with any real person in the Milice, Deuxième Bureau or Carcassonne Commissariat in those years. It is extremely unlikely that anyone would have been allowed into Le Vernet in August 1942, even with a senior-ranking French officer. There was no Couiza Maquis, no massacre of prisoners in Banyuls-sur-Mer or executions in Chalabre in July 1944, and no Gestapo/Milice attack on Coustaussa in August 1944. The stone *capitelles* do not date back to Roman times and finally, even though a cache of ancient codices was indeed found in caves outside the village of Nag Hammadi in December 1945 – twelve codices, plus eight leaves, containing fifty-two texts – the Codex of Arinius was not among them. That Codex is, I regret to say, entirely imaginary.

Kate Mosse
Carcassonne/Sussex
2012 (revised 2014)

Acknowledgements

There are many people who have given help and support over the course of the researching, planning and writing of *Citadel*.

At Orion, I'm lucky to be looked after by so many enthusiastic, hard-working and professional people – sales, marketing, production, publicity, digital, audio, editorial and the lovely ladies on reception. Particular thanks go to Gaby Young, Anthony Keates, Mark Rusher, Mark Streatfeild, Juliet Ewers, Laura Gerrard, Jade Chandler, Jane Selley, Malcolm Edwards and the legendary Susan Lamb. My publisher Jon Wood and my editor Genevieve Pegg – helped by Eleanor Dryden in the closing stages of the project – have been extraordinary, even by their standards. Their support, speedy work and enthusiasm for *Citadel* have made all the difference.

Grateful thanks to all at LAW, in particular Alice Saunders and the incomparable Mark Lucas, who has not only been a great support and a wonderful friend, but also a terrier-like editor (despite the digital notes!). Also everyone at ILA, in particular Nicki Kennedy and Sam Edenborough; and all at Inkwell, especially George Lucas (and for the bike . . .).

In Languedoc, I would like to thank the following friends and colleagues: James & Catherine Kinglake; Kate & Bob Hingston, Le Centre Culturel et de la Mémoire des Combattante, Carcassonne; Chantal & Pierre Sanchez; the Musée Départemental de la Résistance et de la Déportation, Toulouse; the staff at the Hôtel de la Cité, in particular Nathalie Sauvestre and Jane Barnard;

everyone at the Jardin de la Tour and at Bar Félix; Patricia Corbett and Jean Dodelin of the Centres des Monuments Nationaux; Miriam Filaquier of the Aude Tourist Board; everyone at Cultura Carcassonne and the Librairie Papeterie Breithaupt; at the Mairie in Carcassonne, Jean-Claude Perez, Maire, and Chef de Cabinet, Christophe Perez; André Viola, Président du Conseil général de l'Aude and Jean Brunel, Chef de Cabinet; René Ortega, Maire de Lagrasse.

At the Defence Academy of the UK, Lt Col. John Starling, Martyn Arthur and Phil. Thanks, too, to Chris Hunter for arranging the best-ever research day out in Shrivenham.

Finally, as all authors know, it's friends and family who bear the brunt of deadlines and pre-publication jitters. There are so many people who've given practical help, encouragement and friendship during the course of writing *Citadel* that I can't list everyone – and of course, all errors are mine – but special thanks go to Jonathan Evans (not least for all the photos), Rachel Holmes, Robert Dye (for Coustaussa), Lucinda Montefiore (for the rosé); Peter Clayton (for Amélie and the Mums); the Dancing Queens, Julie Pembery and Cath O'Hanlon (and Tom P. and Sam O'H. for Chapter 5!); Patrick O'Hanlon; Jack Penny (for Granny R's G&T and bikes); Suzie Wilde (for *The Blue Guide*), Harriet Hastings, Amanda Ross, Tessa Ross, Maria Rejt, Sandi Toksvig (for the slippers), Lydia Conway, Paul Arnott, Jane Gregory, Diane Goodman, Alan Finch, Dale Rooks, Tim Bouquet, Sarah Mansell, Janet Sandys-Renton, Mike Harrington, Bob Pearson, Bob & Maria Pulley and Jenny Ramsay (for the Latin!). Also neighbours Jon and Ann Shapiro, Linda and Roger Heald, Sue and Phil Baker.

My family have been a tremendous support during the writing of *Citadel* and without such practical help and encouragement a big writing project is nigh on impossible. So love and thanks to my sisters Caroline Grainge and Beth Huxley and their husbands Chris Grainge and Mark Huxley. My love to my fabulous mother, Barbara Mosse, to my much-loved, much-missed late father, Richard Mosse, and to my brilliant mother-in-law, Rosie Turner (for all the coffee and dog-walking!).

Finally, as always, my largest thanks, love and gratitude go to my wonderful children Martha and Felix – who are always so enthusiastic and proud – and to my amazing husband, Greg, for his tireless hard work and editorial support, love and incredible patience. Without these three, nothing would matter at all.

Bibliography

Allaux, Julien, *La 2eme Guerre Mondiale dans l'Aude*, Editions Sapin d'Or, 1986

Andrieu, Martial, *Mémoire en Images Carcassonne Tome II*, Editions Alan Sutton, 2008

Aubrac, Lucie, *Outwitting the Gestapo*, translated by Konrad Bieber, with assistance of Betsy Wing, University of Nebraska Press, 1993 (originally published as *Ils partiront dans l'ivresse*, Editions du Seuil, 1983)

Bailey, Rosemary, *Love and War in the Pyrenees: A Story of Courage, Fear and Hope 1939–1944*, Weidenfeld & Nicholson, 2008

Fittko, Lisa, *Escape Through the Pyrenees*, translated by David Koblick, Northwestern University Press, 1991 (originally published as *Mein Weg über die Pyrenäen*, Carl Hanser Verlag, 1985)

Goodrick-Clarke, Nicholas, *The Occult Roots of Nazism: Secret Aryan Cults and their Influence on Nazi Ideology*, I. B. Tauris & Co. Ltd, 2009

Kedward, H. R., *In Search of the Maquis: Rural Resistance in Southern France 1942–1944*, Clarendon Press, Oxford, 1993

Levy, Marc, *The Children of Freedom*, translated by Sue Dyson, Harper, 2008 (originally published as *Les Enfants de la Liberté*, Laffont, 2007)

Ouvrage Collectif, *Mémoire en Images Carcassonne*, Editions Alan Sutton, 2000

Pagels, Elaine, *The Gnostic Gospels*, Weidenfeld & Nicholson Ltd, 1980

Panouillé, Jean-Pierre, *Carcassonne: History and Architecture*, Editions Ouest-France, 1999

Rahn, Otto, *Crusade Against the Grail: The Struggle Between the Cathars, The Templars and the Church of Rome*, translated by Christopher Jones, Inner Traditions International, 2006 (originally published as *Kreuzzug gegen den Grail*, Urban Verlag, 1933)

Rahn, Otto, *Lucifer's Court: A Heretic's Journey in Search of the Light Bringers*, translated by Christopher Jones, Inner Traditions International 2008 (originally published as *Luzifers Hofgesind*, Schwarzhaupterverlag, 1937)

Rossiter, Margaret L., *Women in the Resistance*, Praeger Publishers, 1986

Synnestvedt, Alice Resch, *Over the Highest Mountains: A Memoir of Unexpected Heroism in France During World War II*, International Productions, California, 2005

Teissier du Cros, Janet, *Divided Loyalties: A Scotswoman in Occupied France*, Hamish Hamilton, 1962; Canongate Classics, 1992

Weitz, Margaret Collins, *Sisters in the Resistance: How Women Fought to Free France 1940–1945*, John Wiley & Sons, 1995

CITADEL
Reading Group Notes

Q&A with Kate Mosse

Why do you write about Carcassonne and the landscape of the Pyrenees?

We bought a tiny house in the shadow of the medieval city walls of Carcassonne in 1989, knowing almost nothing about the place. On Bastille Day 1990, our first summer, fireworks engulfed the medieval Cité. My husband and I, with our six-month-old daughter, watched in amazement as the 52 towers of the fortified citadel were shrouded in gold, red, white and spent casings showered down, in a flurry of sparks and flame, into our garden. It was, for me, the beginning of a love affair that has inspired a whole trilogy of novels – *Labyrinth*, *Sepulchre* and *Citadel* – as well as a standalone novella, *The Winter Ghosts*, and a few short stories. Each tells the story of a particular key moment in the history of the south-west through the eyes of the women and men who lived, loved and died there.

Carcassonne is, in fact, two cities in one. Can you describe its two parts?

Carcassonne is a town divided by the river Aude. On the left bank is the Bastide Saint-Louis, founded in the 14th century. Today it is an impressive grid of 19th-century streets, built on the profits from cloth and linen. It is the home of Claude Marti, the Occitan poet, and historian René Nelli, the composer Paul Lacombe, the poet Joë Bousquet and the Béziers-born 17th-century engineer of the Canal du Midi,

Pierre-Paul Riquet. In the cimetière Saint-Michel, the great and the good of Carcassonne's history are there. Poets, composers, scientists, historians, philosophers, their names remembered on the street names alongside those who gave their lives for others – Jean Bringer, Aimé Ramond, Maurice Sevajols. On the right bank of the Aude, the medieval Cité – a crown of stone on the green slopes of the hills – for years abandoned and falling into ruin, but then saved; a testament to the tenacity, the determination of Cros-Mayreveille and Viollet-le-Duc. It is a city that celebrates individuals, eccentrics, non-conformists. The walls – two mighty stone rings – are punctuated with 52 towers. From the top, on a clear day one can see the snow–capped tips of the Pyrenees to the south, the Montagne Noire to the north, Minervois and the Corbières to the east, and the plains of Lauragais to the west.

In what way is Carcassonne special?

I fell in love with Carcassonne the moment I stepped off the train in that wet November in 1989. It was new to me, but immediately and mysteriously it felt like home. Perhaps you know how, out of season in the Midi, at one minute past seven the shops shut and everyone vanishes. That's like my home town in Sussex. And there was a cathedral and a theatre and a canal and an army barracks – like Chichester, too. And in the quiet, there were flickers of light behind shutters, the occasional car. We walked through the empty streets, over the Pont Vieux, heading for our lodgings in the quartier Trivalle. And there was the medieval Cité – extraordinary and special, not yet designated a World Heritage site, so a little down-at-heel. But you could read history in the stones – Roman tiles at the base of the walls, modern shops lodged in ancient rubble walls, the imposition of Christian stories on older myths …

So the way you write your books – with a time-slip between two exciting stories from different moments in history – that's how Carcassonne feels to you?

Yes, it does. And over the years I learned a little more, read a little more, discovered the real stories that lay behind the myths. Some of those stories took me out of Carcassonne and into the mountains and gorges of the Hautes Vallées – that's the upper reaches of the Aude and the Ariège, where the rivers are born in the melting snows – in particular in *Sepulchre* and *The Winter Ghosts*. But *Citadel* is different. It is a love letter to the Bastide and the grid of streets in which my lead character Sandrine lives her life.

For *Citadel*, you had to do a lot of new research, in particular into how World War II came to Carcassonne?

Yes. That was something quite new for me. Actually, the story of the 4th-century monk Arinius felt less foreign to me than the awful dilemmas of Collaboration or Résistance. I've been thinking about the evolution of faith in south-west France for many years, so I was already interested in the idea of a monk wanting to save the so-called heretical stories rejected by the Christians who put the Bible together. Coming from a country that hasn't been invaded in many lifetimes – not since the Dutch in the late 17th century – it was something quite new. But I read lots of books and visited all kinds of interesting blogs and websites that brought the era to life. For example, the beautiful Hôtel Terminus, opened in 1909, was used during the Nazi Occupation as the officers garrison. A portrait of Adolf Hitler hung over the fireplace.

You have said that you found the city studded with memorials.

I did. The little garden outside the cathédrale Saint-Michel commemorates the Nazi capitulation. There is a marble wall listing the names of those who died in WWI, WWII and the Algerian War. In Place Davilla, where an important early anti-German demonstration took place, there is a memorial to the Résistance and, in particular, to Jean Bringer – code name, Myriel – one of those murdered by the Nazis at the Château de Baudrigues, outside Carcassonne, on 19th August 1944. If you look up at the signs in the Bastide, many of the streets have – rightly – been renamed for those who gave their lives.

Graveyards are historical records too. Did you find inspiration there?

As a novelist, I spend a fair bit of time researching in graveyards – it's a good way to discover local names, to discover the ways in which families and stories fit together. The cimetière Saint-Michel is particularly inspiring. As well as the tombs of many distinguished Carcassonnais, it is also the site of the military graveyard, sobering rows of tombstones engraved with crosses, stars and crescents for soldiers who died in the service of France. There's also the extraordinary statue *Y Penser Toujours*, a winged stone angel holding a sword, which stood in the Square Gambetta in the centre of the Bastide until it was stolen away in the night in August 1944 to ensure it could not be destroyed by withdrawing German forces.

I believe you discovered a brand-new Carcassonne location too.

I did. It was quite extraordinary. Several times I had peered through a gate into a sombre garden, unsure of what was inside the walled enclosure. It seemed to be owned by the feral cats who lived there. Then, in April 2011, the place was reopened after many years of neglect. It's the Jardin du Calvaire – the Calvary Garden, designed by Cazaintre in 1825. Built within the old city walls of the Bastide, 14 sculptures depict the Passion of Christ as he moved through the Stations of the Cross. They lead to a shockingly realistic crucifixion at the top of the hill within the garden. Most interesting for me, given the sorts of places I like to explore in my imagination, is that there is also a sepulchre, with a tomb-chilled atmosphere and unrestored stone statues kneeling in the grey dust.

Finally, are you pleased with *Citadel*?

I am pleased, yes. It was very nerve-wracking. I didn't want to let my readers down. I know that many of them – rightly – feel that they too own the lives they have helped to create by reading my books with such generosity and interest. So I wrote it three times to try and get it as close as I possibly could to the book that was in my head. In the end, that's all a writer can do – to try and give the novel that they have dreamt about life in the imaginations of its readers.

Questions for Reading Groups

1. Kate likes to write about young people – especially young women – because 'they are brave, they feel they are invincible'. In *Citadel*, why does bravery lead to tragedy?

2. *Citadel* is a novel about how people react to calamity – the calamity of war and invasion. Under pressure, some people continue to 'do the right thing' and some don't. Can you still sympathise with people who 'do the wrong thing'?

3. Many of the inhabitants of Carcassonne – and throughout all of France – collaborated with the Nazis in good faith, because they thought it was the best option available to them. What would you have done?

4. Is it important to know about things like the Spanish Civil War – it took place just a few years before *Citadel* begins – in order to get the most out of Sandrine's story?

5. Is it important to have read *Labyrinth* and *Sepulchre* – and even *The Winter Ghosts* – in order to get the most out of *Citadel*?

6. Arinius the monk abandons his order and travels into the mountains with a vague idea that he must keep the Codex safe from harm. What makes the Codex so dangerous and so helpful?

7 Sandrine's sister Marianne becomes overwhelmed by the responsibility of caring for others. Sandrine takes her place at the head of the Resistance group Citadelle. Was Marianne wrong to let her do so?

8 Some people – good people – get written out of history. Audric Baillard's long life is dedicated to giving those people a voice. Is Kate right to use a novel to try and do the same?

9 When Sandrine and Raoul part for what turns out to be the last time, did you imagine that they might never meet again? Why is it so poignant that each believed the other safe?

10 Do you wish that Kate had crafted a happier ending to the story of *Citadel*?

Suggested Reading

Lucie Aubrac's *Outwitting the Gestapo* is non-fiction and was wonderfully helpful in furnishing all kinds of unexpected detail of daily life under occupation. Aubrac was a history teacher married to a Jewish engineer when World War II broke out. It is a harrowing read.

The Children of Freedom by Marc Levy is a wonderful novel – clearly deeply heartfelt – about life under occupation and the work of the French Resistance in Toulouse and elsewhere in the south-west of France. He is brilliant on the enormous contribution made by Spanish and eastern and southern European immigrant workers.

Suite Française by Irène Némirovsky is a quieter but still very affecting novel. Unfinished at the time of her death in Auschwitz, the book is in two parts, contrasting the German occupation of Paris with different pressures in a smaller rural community.

Rosemary Bailey, the author of *Love and War in the Pyrenees*, has lived in south-west France for more than 15 years. She has pulled together a brilliant collection of authentic individual stories of wartime hardship and heroism, weaving them seamlessly together.

Lisa Fittko's *Escape through the Pyrenees* is a fascinating non-fiction work. She and her husband fled Germany in 1933 and came to France. Then they had to flee once more, becoming

Pyrenean *passeurs*. They worked tirelessly to help others out of the Nazis' reach.

I am a great fan of Antony Beevor's writing. For *Citadel*, I often referred to his *The Second World War*. It is a proper big-canvas history but also pays attention to individual lives and experiences.

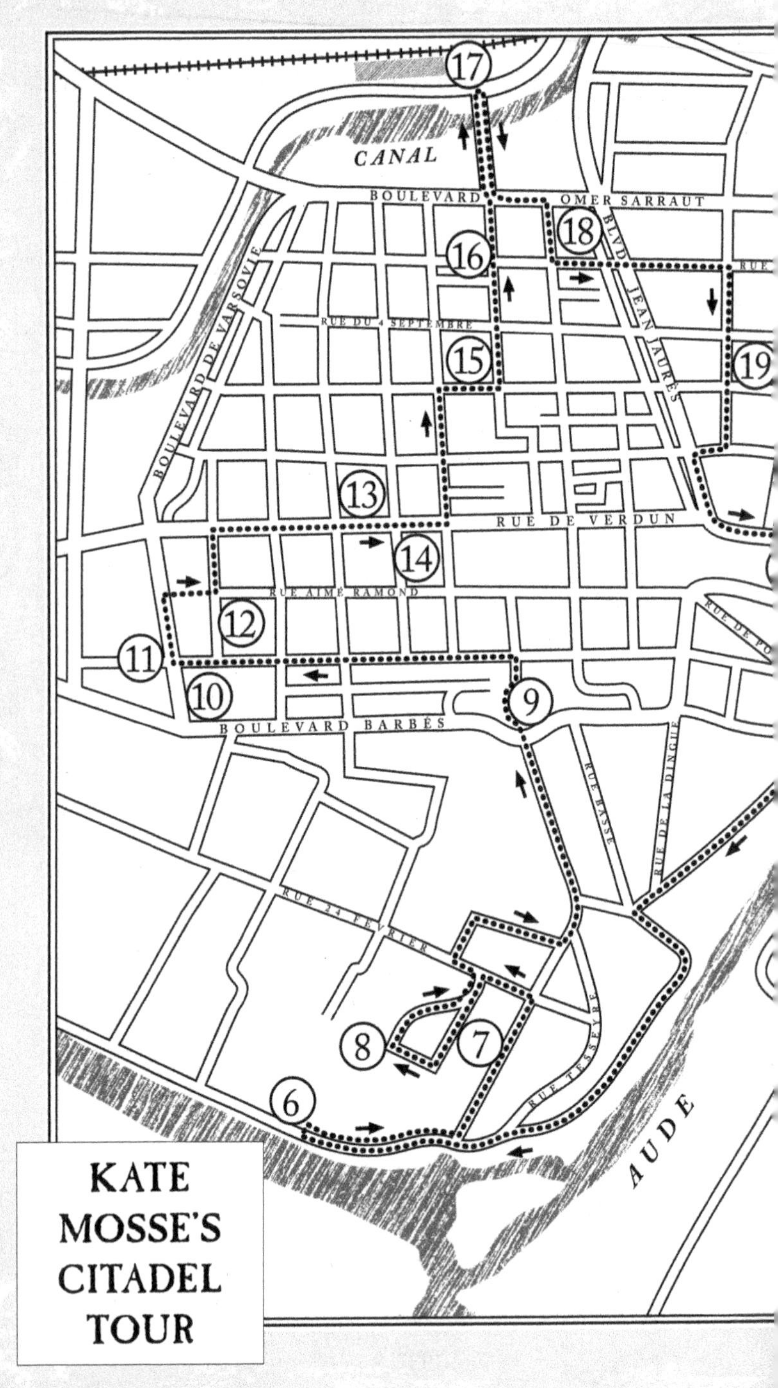
CANAL
BOULEVARD OMER SARRAUT
BLVD JEAN JAURÈS
BOULEVARD DE VARSOVIE
RUE DU 4 SEPTEMBRE
RUE DE VERDUN
RUE AIMÉ RAMOND
BOULEVARD BARBÈS
RUE BASSE
RUE DE LA DINGUE
RUE 24 FÉVRIER
RUE TESSEYRE
AUDE
6
7
8
9
10
11
12
13
14
15
16
17
18
19
KATE MOSSE'S CITADEL TOUR

1 Château Comtal
2 Porte de l'Aude
3 Lices
4 Saint-Gimer
5 Pont-Vieux
6 Païchérou
7 Saint-Michel Cemetery
8 Stone Angel
9 Saint-Michel Cathedral
10 Calvary Garden
11 Boulevard Marcou
12 Rue Aimé Ramon
13 Café Saillan
14 Boulangerie
15 Rue de l'Aigle d'Or
16 Precinct
17 Gare
18 Rue Jean Bringer
19 Rue du Palais
20 Square Gambetta

Part One – Carcassonne Cité and Bastide

We begin at the impressive front gate of the Château Comtal. In *Labyrinth*, this is where Alaïs lived, before the Crusaders came. From here, the best way to follow in

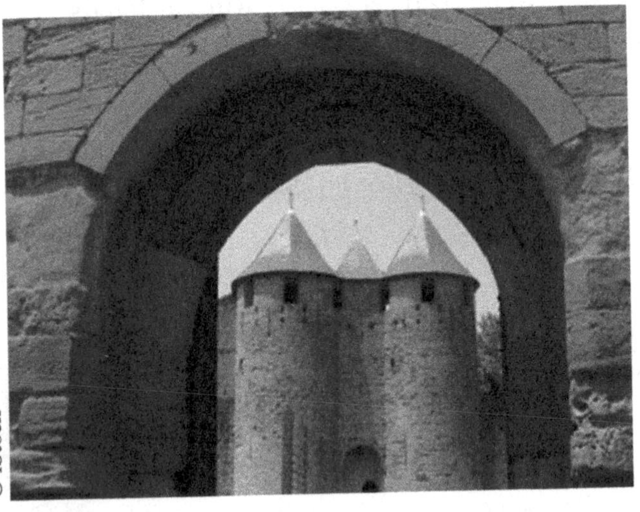

© iStock

Sandrine's footsteps is to head down past the Hotel du Donjon and the Jardin de la Tour restaurant – they have a lovely garden with shady trees for summer – and out through the Porte de l'Aude.

The Aude is the river – it curves from left to right as you look out over the battlements. Downstream of where you stand, there's a lovely old bridge with stone arches called the Pont Vieux. In *Sepulchre*, it was from the Pont Vieux that Léonie first saw the Cité of Carcassonne and disobeyed her

brother's advice. On the other side of the bridge is the grid of lovely 19th-century shops and restaurants and houses that make up the Bastide Saint-Louis. That's where we are heading.

We zigzag down through the *lices* – two rings of thick medieval stonework. At sunset, the orange sun through the murder slots will cast bright orange bars on the inner walls. We could creep along and find the tower where, in *Citadel*, Sandrine and Lucie tried desperately to defuse Suzanne's bomb. But for now, we emerge on to the western slopes and follow a long cobbled ramp downhill to the church of Saint-Gimer. (Gimer was bishop of

Carcassonne nearly 200 years before Alaïs was born. They say he stole his mother's bread dough and multiplied it miraculously for the poor.)

The church is by Viollet-le-Duc, the man who restored the Cité from its ruins. The location is probably where the majority of skirmishes between Trencavel's allies and

the Crusaders took place. It's all built up, now. We bought a house in this modest neighbourhood in 1989 – that was where it all started.

So, walk to the end of rue Barbacane and up on to the Pont Vieux. Look down to your left to the far riverbank. Beyond the formal gardens and playground, on the high stone wall, there used to be graffiti – *Sandrine, je t'aime.* It was there for years and it was how I knew what my lead

© Shutterstock

character in *Citadel* should be called. Look down to the right and you can see the niche in which she hid all through a long, stuffy night.

It's a lovely walk south along the river. There are some smart houses, an impressive weir and then the Païchérou, where Sandrine and Raoul went dancing in the moonlight, without any band playing, and dreamt of a future that events would conspire to deny them.

© Mark Rusher

From the Païchérou, we retrace our steps a little, then take a left fork steeply uphill on montée Saint-Michel – it will take us to the cemetery, of course. The wall is on the left. Inside, there are dozens and dozens of family tombs, some owned 'in perpetuity', some not. (What will eventually happen to those remains? I don't know.) Towards the southern end is a very orderly section of war graves – tidy monuments engraved with crosses, stars and crescents.

And there is a statue of a warlike guardian angel. It once belonged in Place Gambetta but somebody moved it, just before the Nazi withdrawal, perhaps to keep it safe. I'm glad they did.

We come back out on to rue du cimetière Saint-Michel and head north towards the Bastide. On the left we see the barracks of the paratroop regiment, then carefully cross busy boulevard Barbès towards the city walls. Saint-Michel Cathedral is just the other side – where the fanatic Leo Authié came to pray and Sylvère Laval set the treacherous explosives that meant

© Fotolia

that Raoul became a hunted man. The little courtyard where the bomb went off is now a memorial to the Nazi capitulation.

Raoul needed somewhere to hide. He couldn't go to Sandrine – they barely knew one another at that point. He eventually hid in the Jardin du Calvaire, the Calvary Garden at the top of rue Voltaire – a sombre, walled sculpture park containing fourteen representations of the Stations of the Cross. After many years of dereliction, it reopened in April 2011.

© Shutterstock

Leaving the Calvary Garden, it's only a step to boulevard Marcou where several interior scenes were filmed for *Labyrinth* in a wonderful old-fashioned town house. By coincidence, there's a white stone monument to the French Resistance close by in Place Davilla and a magnificent bronze statue, commemorating the dead of 1870. This corner of town is a tapestry of grief.

From Place Davilla, we could walk back down into the Bastide on rue Aimé Ramon. He is an unsung hero in *Citadel*, a real-life *résistant* who died on 19th August 1944, like some of my fictional characters, a victim of the defeated Nazis' spite. Further

down Aimé Ramon, we would see the police station where Sandrine unwisely – and against her sister's advice – gave her name and address. Luckily for her, the officer – could it have been Ramon? – threw it away.

© Mark Rusher

But, instead, we'll take the next street, rue de Verdun. About halfway down, we will come across Café Saillan on the corner of what was once rue du Marché. (Now rue du Dr Albert Tomey – many street names in the Bastide were changed after the War.) Raoul met poor César here. Much later, desperately worried about Suzanne being arrested, Marianne took a chance and spoke publicly to Robert Bonnet.

Still on Verdun, we pass the covered market where, in an early draft, Sandrine bought cheese from a Madame Bonnefous. I believe there is still a *fromager* of that name, though no relation to my fictional character. At the corner of Chartran and Verdun, there's a lovely baker's shop that looks like it hasn't changed since Sandrine cycled past.

© Mark Rusher

We continue on Chartran, along the west side of Place Carnot, the heart of the town. We pass buildings that Sandrine would have known as the Grands Magasin de Nouveautés and the Grand Hôtel Moderne et du Commerce – an imposing, five-storey terrace. Just beyond the square, we turn right into the beautifully named rue de l'Aigle d'Or – the road of the Golden Eagle. There is no sign of Raoul or the traitor Coursan. The password is '*Per lo Miègjorn.*'

At the bottom of Aigle d'Or, we join the pedestrian precinct and follow it north to the top of the town. We will pass the building where Max and Liesl Blum lived. At the junction with boulevard Omer Sarraut, we are surrounded by cafés: 'To their right was the Café Continental, traditionally a leftist meeting place. On the opposite side of the road, the Café Edouard where the LVF and the Jeunes Doriotistes

met. Sandrine realised she was already starting to divide the Bastide into them and us.' On the far side is the delightful *art nouveau* Hôtel Terminus. Perhaps we should stop here for lunch?

The Terminus was the Nazi officer garrison in 1944. The garage owned by Lucie's violent father was on boulevard Omer Sarraut. There was once a petrol station there, but it's gone now. Just across the canal lock is the railway station, where Sandrine failed to recognise Max, bloodied and without his glasses, on his way to the concentration camp at Le Vernet. Round the back of the station, out of sight of the street, is where Sylvère Laval murdered César – who kept his

© Alamy

suspicions too much to himself. César worked in a printer's attached to the Café des Deux Gares – now the Café Bristol.

The canal is a World Heritage site – a triumph of industrial engineering. If we're tired of walking, we could take a boat trip – west towards Bram and the Lauragais or east to Trèbes and the Minervois. When we return, we must once more explore the streets of the Bastide because we haven't yet found Sandrine's house. We disembark, turn left on to Omer Sarraut, past the old Colisée cinema, and right into rue Jean Bringer. Known by his Resistance code name of 'Myriel', he too was murdered on 19th August 1944.

We take the first left on to rue de la Liberté, carefully cross boulevard Jean-Jaurès into rue d'Alsace and come to the junction with rue du Palais. This is where Sandrine and her family lived in Carcassonne. The road is named for the Palais de Justice, the huge law courts where Authié and the collaborators of the Deuxième Bureau set up shop. Beyond the Palais de Justice is a tall white-stuccoed townhouse used by the Nazis as their Feldgendarmerie headquarters.

So the journey is almost done. It's just a step to Square Gambetta, today a rather barren paved area hiding an underground car park. There used to be fountains and ponds here. Our children once fed a turtle in the dark green water. Such an everyday place: 'Sandrine and Lucie sat on a bench in Square Gambetta. Both wore headscarves, plain summer dresses and flat lace-up shoes. They looked like any other Carcassonnais women ground down by the daily struggle of trying to get by.' And from here, we can walk down to the river and see the panorama of the Cité on the opposite bank once more . . .

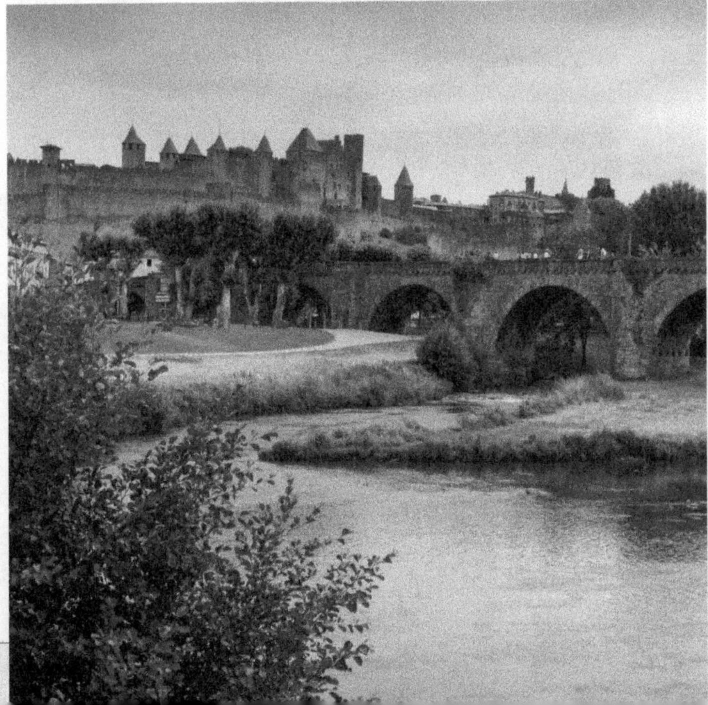

Part Two – Coustaussa and Tarascon

Throughout the summers of her childhood, Sandrine lived in Coustaussa. To get there, we take the road south, towards Limoux, towards the mountains. It will bring us close to the heart of the action in *Sepulchre*. Léonie came this way by train. Many years later, Sandrine and Marieta brought Liesl to hide here in the hills.

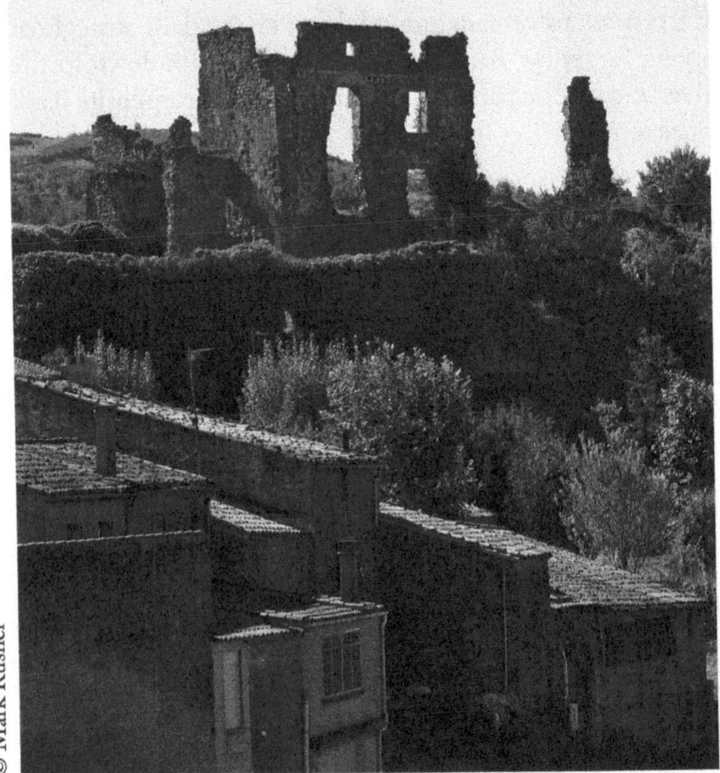

By the time Sandrine's War is approaching its sad end, Coustaussa has become a place of horrors: '19th August 1944 – She sees the bodies first. On the outskirts of the village, a pair of man's boots and a woman's bare feet, the toes pointing down to the ground like a dancer. The corpses twist slowly round and around in the fierce August sun.' But the strange, isolated village on the hillside opposite Rennes-le-Château was a joyful place when she was young.

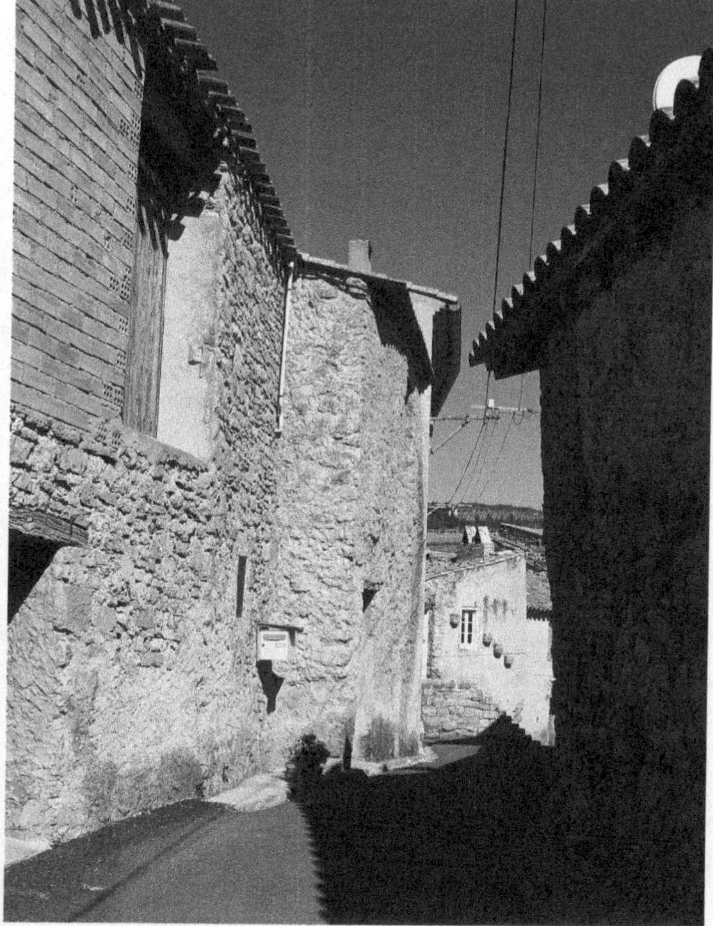

And out by the *capitelles*, the stone shelters in the lonely fields, it briefly became a happy place again. Raoul taught her to fire a gun: 'Raoul leant forward, aligning his arm with the length of hers. Now he was folding his hand over hers, helping her to raise the gun, her exact shadow. Heat flooded through her, making her aware of every inch of her skin, of his skin, of his breath on the back of her neck.'

© Mark Rusher

Then Raoul was gone – to Tarascon to join Audric Baillard in an audacious plot to mislead Authié with a decoy Codex. Later on, Sandrine would make the same journey through the mountains with Lucie in an attempt to reach Max at the concentration camp.

© Mark Rusher

My Languedoc Trilogy is complete. *Labyrinth*, *Sepulchre* and *Citadel* all grew out of this landscape – the city of Carcassonne and the villages, rivers and forests of the Pyrenees. I had no idea when I first started mapping the land – for days out, for picnics, for places to swim, for visits to vertiginous castles on scarred slopes – that it would lead me so far. I am very lucky to have found readers willing to follow me in my exploration of this part-real, part-imaginary land.

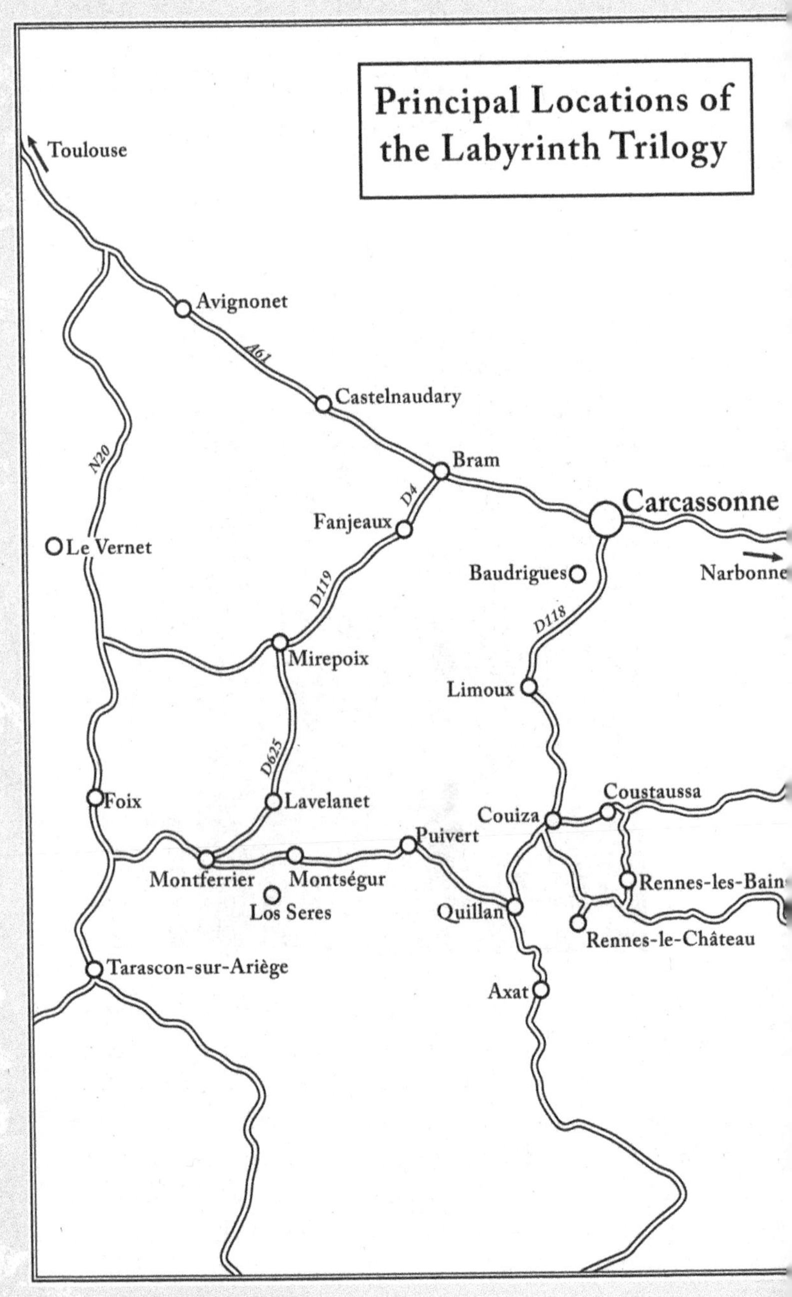
Principal Locations of the Labyrinth Trilogy
Toulouse
Avignonet
A61
Castelnaudary
Bram
D4
Carcassonne
Fanjeaux
N20
Le Vernet
Narbonne
Baudrigues
D119
D118
Mirepoix
Limoux
D625
Foix
Lavelanet
Coustaussa
Couiza
Puivert
Montferrier
Montségur
Rennes-les-Bains
Los Seres
Quillan
Rennes-le-Château
Tarascon-sur-Ariège
Axat